DISGUISES

DISGUISES

JAMES BROWN

Matador
9 Priory Business Park
Kibworth Beauchamp
Leicestershire LE8 0RX, UK
Tel: (+44) 116 279 2299
Fax: (+44) 116 279 2277
Email: books@troubador.co.uk
Web: www.troubador.co.uk/matador

ISBN 978 1783065 370

British Library Cataloguing in Publication Data.
A catalogue record for this book is available from the British Library.

Typeset by Troubador Publishing Ltd, Leicester, UK
Printed and bound in the UK by TJ International, Padstow, Cornwall

Matador is an imprint of Troubador Publishing Ltd

For Sam and Daniel

CHAPTER 1

The man who was hanging by his arms looked around him. His eyes darted quickly, impulsed by fear as they searched for any sign of escape. Instead he saw dark brown stains on a wall. They were about head height, dark enough and thick enough to tell of multiple horrors and many men who had gone before him. He looked underneath him and saw a thick plastic blanket. He could see himself enveloped in it. He looked above him and saw a dirty white ceiling with many holes in it, signs of where many men had hung like he did now.

The black cloth around his mouth tasted of something foul and distant, like the first strong stench of spilled petrol. He could feel it seep up his nose and into his head. He knew, however, that the cloth was not poisoned and it was not the cloth that would kill him. It was just the first rag that they could find when they bundled him out the car. That brought tears which he choked back. My life is worth a dirty rag. His eyes darted again to the three men standing below him. They behaved as though he wasn't there, talking to each other about football, politics, girlfriends, anything except the man dangling a few feet above them in the air. He thought about moving, twisting and contorting his body to attract their attention, trying to regain some lost sense of self-importance. It seemed futile.

He realised he was going to die and he knew why he was going to die but he didn't know how and that puzzled him. Was he going to be left to hang here forever? Surely the men would have just left him. Maybe he was to be tortured – just for fun, because he knew nothing – and then thrown away? His mind filled with images of films he had seen and of the horrors they espoused: of chainsaws, of drills, of axes, of sadistic sexual horror and he felt his body convulse in hellish anticipation. As the pain pulled at his arms and he felt them begin to be dragged away from his body he tried to see some way of killing himself but as he looked up and around all he saw was an empty powerlessness.

Then there was a noise and the man he knew only as The Capo walked in. The man's eyes watched The Capo as he walked up to the three men standing below him but never once did The Capo's eyes look up to the man dangling above his head. He spoke in quick hurried tones

1

with the men on the ground and one of the men went out and brought back with him a table and two chairs. The man who was hanging by his arms allowed himself a quizzical look: were they going to play cards underneath him until he fell on top of them, until his body left his arms? Without looking up at the man, The Capo signalled to his accomplices to take the man down and sit him opposite at the table and then to take the rag out of his mouth. The Capo then rolled a small bottle of water across the table to the man now breathing very heavily opposite him.

The Capo looked at the man and started to talk, slowly and deliberately. He looked the man straight in the eyes as he did so. His voice was never raised and his tone never varied, as if he was reciting a shopping list. "Maybe you have looked around this place of redemption and wondered what you are doing in here. This is the place where I deliver justice. It is quite dark if you look at the stains, the reminders that once there was life here, but I find it warm and comfortable. A bit like home. I like to come here, it makes me feel as though I am making things right again. Because sometimes they get out of control. Sometimes I find that I can't trust people that I thought I could. And that needs to be made right. You asked me to help you, to protect your business from the… I think you called them thieves and vagabonds… that make up the world. I helped you and treated you as one of my own. And yet for some reason you decided to make plans with my enemies and I don't understand why."

The man tried to talk and The Capo held up his hand: "Don't talk, don't say anything. I don't want answers from you. I have the answers I need. I have people in places that you simply would not believe. How do you think a man in my position gets to be a man in my position? Only through the people who are loyal to me. I know you got tired of paying the 12% I asked to ensure your security and you made acquaintance with a man who said he could free you from this enslavement. I know you were going to try to do this by telling me your business wasn't profitable and showing me false records. I know how much you were going to pay the man who you contrived to do this with. I also know how much business you did in cash which you never told me about, money which was 12% mine. I know about the deals you did with companies which went straight into your pocket. Almost from the day you started to get my protection, you started to betray me by not giving me what was – what is – rightfully mine. I know more about you than you would ever guess. I know where you get your shirts made, I know what you like to eat for lunch, I can tell you the colour of socks you're wearing today, I know about the bruise you got on your leg when you fell over drunk in the toilet of the casino last week. And I know about that little waitress you've been screwing when your wife goes to her fitness classes. And the stewardess you see when you tell your wife you have meetings and functions to attend… and how you want to 'Make love to her until there was no more morning to disturb you'."

The man looked at The Capo, shocked into silence. He wanted to talk and ask questions, to make some attempt to find out how his life had been lived so publically. The Capo drank slowly from his bottle of water and continued. "Your greatest sin was becoming a partner of mine but knowing nothing about me. How could you be so stupid to let a man take 12% of your earnings without knowing anything about him? You never asked any questions about me to anyone, you were simply told about a man who could protect you for a little payment now and then and you jumped at it. What sort of a man are you who would do such a thing?"

The Capo held up his hand. "Don't try to answer, it's a rhetorical question." He paused. "Now you are just a messy account. I have two options with a messy account – I can continue with it in the hope that it will become tidy or I can cut my losses. With you, I'm going to do the latter."

He pulled out a gun and the man held his hands up in front of his face and began pleading and shrieking. Sounds came out but no clear words. The Capo pointed the gun at the man. "Shut up. This is your choice. But I want you to know, with your last breath, with your last thought that since you made any sort of deal with me I controlled you. You had choices about what you did and who you did it with but only because I allowed you to have those choices. You won't be the first man who dealt with me who now regretted what he wished for. Know this and think on it now – I own you." And with that he despatched four bullets into the man's head and death came to him instantly.

The Capo rose from the table, motioned to the dead body on the floor with a slight movement of his head and the three men rolled the body into the thick plastic and carried it away. When the men re-entered the room The Capo was standing stationary, lost in thought as he tended to be at times like this about the ripples: the effect of the loss of this man's life on others, on his wife, his child, the two lovers, the people at work, his extended family, his friends. What changes were now effected in their lives because this man was gone from it? What sadness would ensue, how many tears would be wept over this man? How long might he be remembered? It wasn't that The Capo felt sadness or guilt. He blamed the man and people who had been in his position before for getting involved with someone they didn't know very much about. They weren't men. And the thoughts that The Capo had about their families and friends showed he thought more about them than these beings who were less than men.

He turned as his acquaintances came back into the room: "Anything else that needs to be dealt with today?" He was passed a thick brown folder which he left unopened on the desk.

Davide stepped forward: "These updates, routine stuff. And there are many requests for your help, Capo. There is one from Julietta, she's having problems with an unwanted suitor and 'No' doesn't seem to be working… I also heard from Giorgio who is desperate to win a contract for a fleet of company cars… Francine told me that she needs your influence to help her win a government construction contract… and then there is Paul, who was blinded recently in one eye by a guy who he says has been his enemy for years…"

The Capo raised his hand: "Paul? Paul? The guy in Monte Carlo? Married to Elaine? The one who likes his bit on the side to be young?"

Everyone in The Capo's organisation went by assumed names, code names. It made things easier, everything considered.

"Yes, that's the guy. There are more requests though…" Davide reached inside his pocket for a piece of paper but The Capo raised his hand to stop him.

"I think I am maybe owe Paul a favour. He entertained me well the last time I was there, he went above and beyond…" He paused, remembering opening the door of the suite to his hotel room and three women standing smiling at him, their arms round each other. One blond, one brown, one red. Lingerie attacked him as he took his first step into the room and he was lost in a fusion of colour and indulgence. He remembered most of all the smell, the beautiful haunting mixture of three women that still danced around his nostrils. He licked his lips – "So, yes, maybe…maybe I am owe Paul a favour. Julietta knows how to refuse a man, Giorgio can do some work for himself for a change and Francine deserves everything she doesn't get. Tell me about Paul."

"Well," Davide said, looking around at his friends as if for confirmation, "from what we can tell he was at a dinner in Monte Carlo. Some posh corporate thing. And this guy…well, he got into an argument with him over something" …he looked around at his friends… "maybe something to do with Elaine? I don't know, I'm not sure. Anyway, they ended up away from the dinner, having an argument that got more and more heated. Paul is not one to try to stay calm for long, especially where Elaine's concerned, and a fight broke out. From what Paul says, the guy grabbed a knife from a table and shoved the blunt end into Paul's right eye. He says he's blinded now, he's lost sight in the eye…"

The Capo held up his hand. "The blunt end? Why would he use the blunt end? Why not just try to stab him? And why did Paul let himself be got like that? He's not too bright, is he?"

Davide didn't answer. In truth, it wasn't really a question anyway. He continued: "He also says this guy has been responsible for putting Paul's business in danger. He says the guy has taken a few important clients and contracts away from him, there are rumours of money laundering, of him being attached to or working for your enemies…"

The Capo looked at Davide. "And this guy who's doing all these things uses the blunt end of a knife to attack someone? Odd. Still, like I said, I'm maybe owe him one….ok, what do we know about the guy?"

"We are fairly sure he's called Oliver. We are pretty sure he's still in France. He's certainly not crossed the border into Italy, he's not in Switzerland and he hasn't gone back to the UK. He's definitely British. Scottish. Married. But we are not exactly sure where he is now. There has been no word about him for the last two to three days. We have a photo and have sent it to all the usual contacts. We can activate them to look for this guy with a bit more purpose if you give the go-ahead. He won't get far."

The Capo looked thoughtful. "Who is this guy? What does he do? If he's British, what's he doing down here? And how did he get involved with Paul… with Elaine… Something isn't quite right here, I'm not sure what it is."

Davide looked around at his friends, who shrugged their shoulders. "We don't know much about him. I guess he must be in the business of internet provision if he's a threat to Paul's business. As for Elaine…what we do know is that Elaine is beginning to get suspicious about Paul. She's sensing there's someone else, there have been a couple of phone calls he's had that she asked him about. Unknown numbers. He brushed her off but not completely. She's been checking his mobile too though I'm not sure what she's seen. But where this Oliver fits in, we don't know. I'm sorry."

The Capo looked at Davide. "It's ok. Maybe he's never been on our radar because we've never needed to know anything about him. Alternatively, maybe he's remained undetected. Not anymore. Ok, find this guy. Find his wife, wherever she is – in Scotland I suppose. Watch her. Let everyone know I need a favour here, activate everyone you have to activate. But I want to talk to him. Understood?"

The three men nodded their consent. "Understood," Davide said as he led the other two men away and left The Capo alone. The Capo opened the folder in front of him and looked at the secret pictures and narratives on the men and women whose activities he was monitoring. The folder got bigger and bigger every week. This was reassuring and comforting to him and he smiled to himself. He stopped at a picture of the man he had just shot, making love with the air stewardess for the last time in a hotel. The expression on his face was one of utter ecstasy, with the stewardess' face partly hidden by the mass of her golden hair. He spoke quietly to himself: "Mr Oliver, whoever you are, wherever you are – I wonder what we are going to find out about you…."

Oliver's wife, Helen, paced slowly up and down the front room of her house. She put her hands to her head and ran her fingers, with some force, through her hair. It made her feel as though she was putting her head back together again. For the first two days Oliver had not been in touch, she had put it down to something that she had said. As people do. Perhaps she had offended him. Had she forgotten his birthday? Had she admonished him? She thought again, going over the same conversation as she began to press her fists against her head. Whichever way she looked at it, this was the third day that Oliver had not phoned. Every attempt to phone him on his mobile was met with an answering machine message, every attempt to phone the flat in Nice where his work had put him was met with no answer. She had sent numerous text messages: "Fine, if you're angry with me, it's ok. But is everything alright? Please let me know." No response.

This was not like Oliver. Oliver clung to home instinctively, in the way a baby will always know the smell and the taste of its mother. He hated going away and he phoned and sent messages every day. Helen appreciated and understood – and accepted – that this was as much to find out about their four year old son Terrence as it was about her but nevertheless his reliance on her being there provided reassurance to her and, so it seemed, some sense of order to him.

But this was getting towards the end of the third day that she had not heard from him. Already today she had scoured the internet for any reports of accidents in the south of France, had got one of her friends to help her translate some local newspaper stories from the Nice area and had phoned his boss in Edinburgh. They were as concerned as she was and had heard nothing for three days. They had got the local police involved. He wouldn't take off, would he, could he, she thought as she began to retrace her paces up and down the floor. How could he? Just leave both of us? For someone else? She couldn't see Oliver doing this. Then suddenly she saw herself confronted by police officers, telling her how often things like this happened and how no one would ever have thought the person involved could ever have done something like that. Is his life with me so bad that he has to run away? What did I do? What didn't I do? Is he fed up with me?

She began, very gently and almost imperceptibly, to shake and as she did so the darkness in her mind began to avalanche and she thought about how she had shouted at Terrence earlier, slapped him on the hand, screamed at him to behave, about how she was a bad mother, a bad wife, how it must be her that was the cause of Oliver's disappearance. She sobbed quietly and cursed herself for sobbing. If he's gone then he's gone and I have to accept that. But I must know. And the darkness came again as she raised her eyes skywards and said: "Why me? What have I done to have a husband walk away from me? And Terrence… How….? Why me," she outwardly pleaded again. What did I do wrong, so wrong, that I would be punished in this way, that he would desert us?"

She sat down and put her head in her hands. As she stopped moving, a clearer idea focused in her mind, one which made the fear in her stomach rise through her body. Just because she had seen nothing in the papers, it didn't mean he wasn't dead. Maybe hit by a car somewhere, not near the centre of town, perhaps a heart attack in the flat where no one would go for another day or two, maybe he'd seen the wrong thing in the wrong place at the wrong time and was lying dead in a backstreet or half dead in a hospital. She had to do something. She had to go and find him. She wouldn't come back until she had found him or at least knew that he was safe. And if he was with someone else…well, she rationalised, then at least I'll know.

As soon as she rose the reality of her situation struck. What about Terrence? He would go to his gran and granddad's for the occasional night – and she was grateful for this – but she couldn't leave him there for days. They couldn't look after him for days. Age had made them doting grandparents but had not left them without infirmity. Terrence had friends, and Helen had friends too, but none that she could leave him with for an indefinite time. And she simply could not take him with her. She started to pace again, but quicker now, with more purpose as she began to think of how she could get there.

Then she thought of Euan. Euan was her brother and one of Oliver's best friends since school days. It had been through Euan that Oliver had originally met Helen. She decided in that instant that she would not only ask him but that she would make him go. By fair means or foul, or by any sort of emotional blackmail, she would make him find Oliver. Euan was the answer.

Helen picked up the phone and stood by the window as she often did when she spoke on the phone in the living room. Perhaps it had been the years of disinterested conversations with her parents, not really listening to what they were saying, that left her looking out of the window for something to occupy her time. The house was on a relatively quiet street, the peace disturbed usually only by the bus that stopped directly outside the house, by children playing, cars and the odd drunken shout in the early hours of the morning at weekends. There was really not that much to see. But it was a habit and as she began to dial Euan's number she moved nearer to the window. She also flicked the switch to put the light on: it was not truly dark but it was at that dusky point where some cars have their lights on and some don't, where some house lights are on and some aren't, where some people would turn the light on to read and others would hold the book a little closer to their face. Helen's living room light was on and she was standing by the window when she dialled the last digit of Euan's number.

Anthony watched Helen from the car that was parked diagonally opposite her house. The car was not so close that Helen could see him looking at her from inside the car with his binoculars but it was close enough for Anthony to be where he wanted to be. He delighted as Helen put the light on and swayed towards the window. He liked to think she was doing this for him.

Anthony had watched Helen for about three weeks. She had helped him in the Library, she had helped him find a book. He had known where to find the book but it was easy for Anthony to pretend he did not know how to do things. His straight black hair, thick black glasses and stubbled slightly twisted face always made people feel uncomfortable and he had grown used to the stares and disturbed looks. He had seen people lead their children onto the other side of the street when he walked. Perhaps he had played on that when he saw Helen. He didn't know if she worked there or not but he would ask her. And she didn't work there but she still helped him.

He had chosen a book on the bottom shelf and as she bent down her soft blue jersey didn't cling as tightly to her body and he could see into a place of beauty and hope and desire that had always been denied him. In that instant he decided to become obsessed with her. The moment lasted for a thousand years as he slowly and deliberately drew in her smell.

He followed her home that day. Not so she would see him, for he had become very good at remaining hidden. He knew how to follow from two streets away, when to stay out of view, when to bend down to tie a shoelace and when to ask a stranger in the street for the time to make it look as though he was a normal person having a normal conversation the way people do. But now he knew where she stayed and sometimes he would walk by with his camera, taking pictures of the area in general as though he were selling a house or flat though all the time it would be to get pictures of her. He worked out that you could see into the front room downstairs and what seemed to be the bedroom upstairs from the street and from various angles too, because the windows were large and not those little squared partitioned windows that meant you couldn't really see anything from some positions. The back of the house had big windows too but it was hard to access: another garden backed onto Helen's garden and it meant you had to be in that garden to see properly. Except at night, that posed obvious problems.

Anthony knew Helen had Oliver and had seen Oliver but it mattered little to him. He also knew Oliver had not been home for a few days and he felt that things would be easier for him with Oliver not there. He looked at Helen again as she spoke on the phone, half-sitting on the sill as she usually did, twirling her hair round the index finger of her left hand as she always did. He thought she looked a bit more animated then normal: sometimes she would take her hand away from her hair and gesture with it, as though the person she was talking to was in front of her. It didn't make Anthony curious, however, and over the last three weeks, as his plan began to ferment, he thought less and less of Helen's humanity and more and more about how she would be when she was with him and how he would be when he was with her.

It was Anthony's plan to capture Helen and to keep her in his flat. He had made a special room for her and when he went home that night he looked at the walls in her room, covered from ceiling to floor with pictures of her. Some large, some small. Smiling in some, frowning in others. Some taken from behind, some at diagonals. He had none when she was directly in front, face on. He would have to wait until she was here to take those.

Anthony knew about Terrence. He had seen Helen with him and he knew the nights when he went to stay with his grandparents. But he didn't care about the little boy and he knew Helen wouldn't care about him when she was here. She would be overwhelmed, so much that she would forget about her life before she met him. She would be a princess when she was here and how could a princess think of anything before she became a princess?

It was obvious to Anthony from the first couple of days watching Helen what he would do to capture her. It was simple. On the days when she went to work she got a bus back that stopped a street away. She could be taken at any point between then and her house. Sometimes the boy was with her, sometimes not but what happened to him didn't matter. Anthony would simply grab her with a cloth around her mouth and bundle her into the car. Dazed, she wouldn't fully recover until she reached his house but she wouldn't know where she was or how long it had taken to get there.

Anthony looked at the photos on his wall. He drew his finger gently over one where she was standing in a t-shirt which clung to her body. He rested on her abdomen, at the part where her t-shirt met with her jeans. His finger went over and back, back and over, several times. He got his camera and looked at a photo he had taken earlier that night, when she had been sitting on the window sill. He enlarged the section around her abdomen where her shirt met with her jeans. He enlarged it further and slid his hand across it. He looked back at the photo. "You've lost a bit of weight, pretty one. Maybe only a pound or two. I hope nothing is worrying you." He looked again at the photo on the wall, Helen's face turned at an angle as she reacted to something he had shouted. "When you are here you shall worry about nothing. I will forbid it."

Unlike Anthony, Ambrose had met Helen before in a more social environment. One of her colleagues had a leaving party and had invited various friends and acquaintances as well as those with whom she had worked and Ambrose ended up sitting next to Helen at the meal. She had seemed interested in him, she had asked questions about what he did, what he did in his spare time, where he had travelled to. For Helen, these were the mundane type of questions you asked of someone you happened to have the misfortune to sit next to at a function such as this. But Ambrose had made Helen feel uncomfortable. He let his eyes rest on her for too long and seemed quite pleased when she saw him doing it. Almost, almost as if he wanted her to know.

You should know right away that Helen was beautiful. She could take your breath away. Those high cheek bones, wide open mouth and soft full red lips, piercing clear blue eyes and wispy blond hair which hung around her neck made her beauty a paradox: at times it consumed all who feasted upon her, relentless and awe-inspiring. At times the imagination could not envisage any more wondrous beauty anywhere in the world. At others it remained understated as though the woman herself had no idea of the gold that her face might hold. And the way she moved… whatever Helen wore clung tightly to her and hugged her. Trousers, skirt, jeans, t-shirt, blouse, jersey…any garment in any fabric hugged her as though she were the prototype upon which they had been created. She moved in a way that was neither graceful nor elegant but which encapsulated a sensuality that was more than primal. Her whole body pivoted on her hips, her legs swaying one way as, almost imperceptibly, her abdomen gently moved in the other. Her hair bobbed softly on and around her white, long neck and in the sunlight it looked like thin, fragile stands of gold had been placed around her head. Her figure was full in the sense that she had hips which curved outside the top part of her body and a chest which was one size bigger than it should have been. She was size 8 or 10 but you wouldn't – you couldn't – call her thin. She had a figure which exploded into her clothes and everything she wore screamed at the promise of what lay beneath. Helen never had to try to look as inviting or as beauteous as she did. It happened without her willing, without her knowing, at times without her even wanting.

It wasn't unnatural, then, that Ambrose fell in love with Helen almost as soon as he saw her. It wasn't unnatural that he thought she was interested in him because she asked him the dull questions which we ask of people we would never wish to see again. But Ambrose wasn't a particularly natural or ordinary type of person.

Helen's beauty dominated him, possessed him and controlled him and if there was one thing Ambrose could not live with it was being in the control of someone else. He needed the security of domination like a singer needs a song. He didn't like the consequences of violence but it was absolutely necessary. His ex-wife had taken years of threats, beatings and his over bearing mental presence until she managed to feel strong enough to escape. What finally forced her was that when he said "Sorry" she realised that he wasn't sorry because he had hit her, he was only sorry that she was crying and upset. Ambrose did not like to hurt someone because he could nor because he particularly liked it: he hurt because it was the easiest way to get what he wanted.

Ambrose did not understand why more people were not like him. He didn't understand why others felt they had to talk and negotiate to get what they wanted. It was easier to take it. He remembered being nineteen and his first real girlfriend telling him that she was going to go out with friends instead of seeing him. He couldn't understand why she would want to do something he didn't want her to do, why she would do something in preference to being with him and he felt frightened, almost as if she was trying to destroy him. She wants to prove she can control me, she can tell me what she will do and will tell me how I must feel about it. It was the first time he'd hit and raped a woman but he knew that she knew that it was the right thing to do.

Ambrose and his wife split up a few months ago and he had lived in rented accommodation since then. However, in the last month he had been forced to move and by chance, luck, coincidence or surreptitious observation he had managed to rent a flat that was opposite Helen's house. Not directly opposite, but close enough that he could watch her. The flat had been easy to get: it was quite a popular area with students and professional people and there was always somewhere available.

Ambrose did not look like an outsider in the more obvious way that Anthony did. He had sandy coloured thinning hair, a quite round jolly red face, a small dumpy nose and rather welcoming brown eyes. He was well built and beginning to get fat. To most people he was friendly, polite and someone who was fun to be around, most of the time. A couple of people at work had seen him lose his temper but in truth it never really raised more than an eyebrow – who doesn't occasionally lose their temper at work? He had confided to one or two of his close friends that he sometimes had urges he found difficult to control but it gave them no inkling of the violence of which he was capable. To most people, he seemed like a good sort.

As Ambrose looked out and across from his window he saw Helen half sitting on her window sill and he felt the desire for her take control of him. Immediately he imagined raping her and he replayed his favoured scenario of introducing himself as a neighbour who needed a phone. With no landline yet installed and a broken mobile, he had seen her and thought: "Oh yes, I know you, we met at a leaving night out, remember." And he'd have her as soon as she turned her back to lead him into the house. He wanted to feel her underneath him and his hands tightened as he imagined them tearing at her clothes, ripping the jersey, pulling her bra down. He could hear her pleads and they were reassuringly desperate. His hands would grab at her trousers and he would threaten her because tight trousers could be so difficult to get off. Then her underwear would just be ripped or maybe he would make her take that off herself. All the time he would be looking at her face, into her eyes as she realised she could not escape, could not move, that she could only do whatever he allowed her to do. Then he would raise himself as he had done many times before, slowly take off his own trousers, by this time hardened by the thought of being inside her and her underneath him, and push, harder and harder, watching her face as she winced and cried and pleaded. Then soon she would truly feel him inside her and he would look down or her. His hands would grab at her; her face, her breasts, her hair and she would feel him all over her. She would be consumed by him in every sense and any thought or action or reaction would be dictated by him. He would, in that instant, as he moved faster and harder, have consumed her. He would own her. As he climaxed he would hit her, hard, because he knew in that instant she would feel this was over. But he wanted her to know that it was only over when he decided it was over. And as he stood up she would be lying on the floor, for all the world like someone who had been shot. He would resent her for feeling injured, hate her for her crying, despise her for not wanting to cover herself up and return to exactly how she was before he came in. As he saw himself shut the door he wondered if he would do it again or if once would be enough. As he watched, however, and thought these thoughts, he felt himself harden and realised that, whereas he may be unsure as to whether he would do it to her more than once, he was absolutely certain that it must be done once.

As Helen spoke with Euan she realised very quickly that he understood her desperation and felt as worried as she did. There was no need to blackmail him or ask for a favour.

"It's odd," Euan said, "I sent him an email three days ago about getting together next weekend and I haven't got a reply. He always replies quickly. I was going to phone. Not like him. So what do you think's happened?"

"I have no idea! That's the thing. He could be lying dead somewhere, he could have run away. Another woman maybe? I don't know."

"Another woman?" Euan sounded incredulous. "I don't think so. Why would you think that? No, listen, this is what we'll do. I can take a few days….there is stuff to do but the restaurants can run themselves for a few days …and I'll go over there and won't come back till I've found him. But I think I want to ask the others too, is that ok with you?"

"The others?" Helen looked puzzled. "What others?"

"Ali, Aidan, Ellis……maybe another one or two. I'll ask them, if it's ok with you. More heads the better. If they're able to go great, if not, I'll go myself." He paused. "We will find out, Helen. I'm sure you're right in that the answer's in Nice somewhere. We'll find it. And I'm sure there will be some explanation….that doesn't involve another woman."

"Ok, sure, take who you want to, it would be good if they could help." She paused. "You know Euan I would even accept that now. At least I'd know."

"He's not in any trouble, is he?"

"Trouble? Trouble with who? What sort of trouble? Not that I know of. What sort of trouble could he be in?"

"Gambling debt?" He heard Helen snort. "Ok, anything with business?"

"He works for a company that makes metal war figures for children of all ages to play stupid war games. What sort of trouble could he get into – even if he wanted to?"

"Yeah, I know, I know. Ok, let me try and get the guys. We'll find out what's happened."

Somehow, even though she had no basis for being comforted by what Euan said, she believed him and briefly smiled as she put the phone down. She looked out the window, across the street, at the cars parked. She wasn't looking at anything or for anything except something in her mind which would give her a clue as to where Oliver might be. And she certainly wasn't looking at the three pair of eyes that focused on her as she left the window and went upstairs to check on Terrence.

Euan put the phone down and looked at it as though it may reveal something to him. He ran a hand through his mop of blond hair. "Shit," he announced. Despite what he had said to Helen, he felt no more able to whisk himself overseas and find Oliver that he did to win the lottery. Sounded to him as though he had about as much chance of success of finding Oliver too as he did of winning the lottery. What on earth am I supposed to do? Go over to Nice and say "Hey, everybody, gather round. I'm looking for thus guy called Oliver. Have you seen him? Ah, thought not" then fly home.

Euan was a restaurateur. He was a good one, owning two restaurants in Edinburgh that were in the upper echelons of taste, class and price. It was hard to get a table at either of them and celebrities ate there regularly. But a successful restaurateur had different essential key skills to a detective and Euan felt his own inadequacy to undertake what he had promised Helen he would do quite keenly. And what if Oliver was in trouble? A bumbling six foot pacifist, with his shock of blond hair and "It's going to be all right" philosophy might not be the best person to help him.

As he sat down, however, he knew that he had to go. It wasn't just because he and Oliver had been best friends since school, nor that he'd introduced – if you could use such a word for how one teenager meets another one – Oliver to Helen, nor that Oliver truly made him believe his restaurant business could be a great success. It wasn't even just for the times they had "been there for each other" – from teenage angsts to pre-wedding nerves, from marital disharmony and full blown relationship crises. No, the real reason he knew he had to go was because he knew how much he owed to Oliver for that one thing he had done a few years ago and for that he would almost have lain down his life.

Euan's girlfriend at the time was Suzie, a beautiful if flimsy girl who hung over Euan as though he were the source of life itself. Euan loved her, as he did with many girls, for a while. Euan really loved the idea of being in love more than he loved being in love. Being in love tended to mean the same body, the same routine, saying the same things to each other. Euan was constantly looking for the girl who would convince him that monogamy was the way things should be. It could take Euan up to a year to get bored, but get bored he usually did. Even then, in that year, there would have been quite a few one night things which "didn't mean anything". Well, nothing except that Euan was bored again. He always felt that the allure of a new woman, a new body to discover with its different sensations and pleasure spots, would never diminish. How

15

could you ever meet someone who would stop you wanting to make love with someone else? He loved the idea that he would meet someone who made him feel this, that she was out there somewhere. Someone who would take away this primordial urge… to do that, Euan thought, she must be just everything. Maybe he was searching for her much of the time yet he also took pleasure from the surrender of those who tempted him. He didn't find a purely sexual relationship "empty" or "vacuous" as many people may have done. He found them life-fulfilling, life–affirming, to be pursued and welcomed. Women brought pleasures to him that he needed and hoped he would never tire of.

Suzie was a little different in that she had had a child with a previous boyfriend. This didn't bother Euan and he loved the three year old boy, Luke, as if he was his own. In the last few months of their relationship, he probably only saw Suzie because he would get to see Luke and he still keeps in touch with Suzie really only to ask about Luke. One day, he'd have kids of his own.

On this particular occasion, he was in a large shopping centre with Suzie, Luke and Oliver on a bustling Saturday afternoon. It was an odd grouping at a strange place at an unusual time and Euan couldn't readily recall how they had managed to find themselves together, in this place, at that time. But the rest was very clear and his heart quickened and he started to sweat as he remembered walking with them. Suzie was tired. She was a fantastic mother but if she hadn't slept she found things difficult and she found Luke difficult most of all. And on this day Luke was behaving as though he were a three year old in a busy shopping centre on a Saturday afternoon. Surrounded by people bigger than him, too hot and too bored, all he wanted to do was escape. To run somewhere. But his mother held his hand tightly – too tightly – and as he struggled against it her grip became tighter and sorer and her irritation grew.

As Oliver drew Suzie's attention to something she let Luke's hand go and he darted away. It took Suzie the best part of ten seconds only to realise that his hand was not in hers. When she looked down to her left he wasn't there. Her eyes looked quickly to Oliver and then to Euan and then about her, darting from one place to the other but not able to move quickly enough for her. She panicked almost immediately. Luke didn't run off, he stood silently and hung his head in a huff if he was unhappy. Luke didn't run away. Oliver and Euan became part of the search party as they scoured the shop.

What happened next was told in detail later to Euan by the police and several witnesses. Oliver only told him, initially, that he found Luke and brought him back. But Luke told them immediately how Oliver "hit the bad man" and his breathlessness, red hands and bloodied shoes were suddenly explainable. Oliver had gone downstairs, on the hunch that Luke may have gone onto the elevator as he would happily go up and down them for hours. As he reached the bottom he saw, just about to exit the building, a man with a little boy. But something wasn't right. The boy was struggling, resisting. His clothes looked like Luke's. Oliver raced down the escalator, sprinting to the exit. He got there after the man had left. Oliver ran out and heard a faint cry to his left. Had he not heard that cry then Luke may have become another missing child statistic, a face remembered on anniversaries of the disappearance. He followed the noise and saw the same man with the same child.

Oliver sped after them. Had the man known Oliver was chasing him then he certainly would have reached the car before him. It was only when the man heard the heavy breath and feet close to him that he knew he was being pursued. As he turned Oliver was almost on him right away. He let Luke go. Oliver grabbed the man and ran his head into the nearest car. The man cried out in pain. Luke scuttled away. "Behind me, behind that car and stay," Oliver yelled at Luke. He then turned back to the dazed man, who had fallen down by the car. Witnesses say they saw a man looking as if he were jumping then kicking his car. In truth Oliver would have killed the man. His pleas for mercy made Oliver's feet move harder and faster as he kicked his hatred and disgust into this crumpled figure of a man. He heard bones break and he saw the man's face begin to dismantle as he booted and punched him. The only thing that made him stop was Luke, creeping out from behind the car, crying in horror at what he saw in front of him.

Oliver picked him up and took him back to Suzie who sobbed with such huge breathless gasps that they took her to hospital. It was a few hours before she could simply cry, her heart broken with the sudden intrusion of darkness. Euan cried too, for Luke and for Suzie and for the fear of his horrible imaginings. But he cried mostly for Oliver, who that day in that place had saved a life. He had to go to Nice to find him. It was the least he owed to a man who every day he felt proud was his best friend.

The Capo took the call from Davide. "Just to let you know, we have a watch on this guy Oliver's wife."

"You found him?"

17

"No, we haven't found him. We still don't know where he is. We're pretty sure he's still in France. But we got the surname and it was easy to find where he lives. You want us to keep watch on the wife?"

"Yes. What's she like?"

"Too good for him."

CHAPTER 2

Euan first of all had rung Alastair though was not hopeful that a sports journalist would be able to take off to the south of France for a few days. Against that was set the strong history Ali had had with Oliver. They had been friends since University and unlike so many people who had drifted apart, they had stayed strong. Euan's hope in fact was that the strength of the friendship between the five of them would mean that when he headed for Nice it was with Ali, Ellis and Aidan. They had gone to football and rugby matches, on trips, golf days, to concerts together and usually all found time at least once a month to get out for a drink. At a time like this, and quite what a time like this was Euan remained unsure of, he knew that he did not have to make the appeal to a sense of loyalty. It would be instinctive and keenly felt without any appeal. Yet he realised how odd a request it remained: "Man lost, probably south of France, let's go and find him." And the more Euan thought of it, the more concerned he became. This wasn't Oliver.

Ali proved to be as concerned as Euan. "But someone must have heard something from him. People don't just disappear, do they? Have you phoned the police? Has Helen?"

"Helen has covered all these angles. She's worried, she's very worried. Can you come with me?"

"Yes of course. It seems… almost an emergency. We must go, we must go." He changed his emphasis to "must" on the latter occasion, as though there was no decision to take.

Ali put the phone down. 'I owe him', he thought. And as he sat down and started to watch the television he remembered Oliver's part in his marriage.

Lesley and Ali were still just going out. It was a month or so before they got engaged. Ali knew he wanted to get engaged and he was sure, as sure as you can be in these situations, that Lesley felt the same. Then one night she came round to the flat and said she wanted something else. Someone else. Ali struggled to believe her, at first thinking it was a perverted wind-up. And she sat there, looking beautiful. That hurt him more than anything. That she'd appeared to put make up and perfume on just to get rid of him. She'd dressed up to dump him. Then he

19

thought that maybe she had seen the other guy just before or was seeing him that night after she dumped him. He pleaded with her, begged, almost stopped her leaving the room. He cried and howled at her but she went off, leaving him to contemplate his life without her.

Ali didn't really drink. Not in the Scottish sense of the word anyway. But that night he drank. He drank till he could drink no more. He always thought that if anything like that ever happened to him that he would pray more, focus on what God expected of him and stay strong. He didn't expect that his crutch might lie in a bottle. But then again he could never have foreseen the bottom falling out of his world like that. A couple of hours later Oliver phoned. Just by co-incidence, it seemed. Oliver could tell anyway that something was very wrong. It was almost impossible not to. Oliver came to the house quickly, so quickly it seemed he had been just round the corner. Ali wept for what felt like hours.

He stood up now and walked through to the kitchen where he remembered looking at knives in the kitchen drawer and thinking: 'if I had any courage I would press them through my wrists.' The thought of life without Lesley was unbearable.

Oliver listened for what seemed all night. He stopped Ali drinking, not early enough for Ali to truly experience the awful feeling of the room spinning, his head spinning, his whole world spinning away. And the sickness that went with it.

Ali sat down and he remembered, as clear as you would any event that defined your life, the strange thing that Oliver said to him. The thing that changed everything. After Lesley walked out that night, they were probably the only words he remembered from the whole night. He said: 'You need to be a bit more you. Keep her feet warm, don't set them alight. There is no one else.' And the thing is, he was right. When Ali thought of Lesley being the girl he wanted to marry, he would tell her of the exciting things that might do together – of living together, of making love every day, of making love on the kitchen floor and of going to Paris for the weekend at the drop of a hat. It wasn't that such romantic impulses were somehow wrong to her but they were not how she defined him. He was warm and comfortable, like an old familiar jersey. It was as though he was trying to impress her and it sounded very false to her. She wanted someone safe and steady. She didn't want to be impressed. Oliver could apparently see what Ali couldn't.

Ali phoned Lesley the next day, they had a long conversation and of course it transpired that Oliver was right. There wasn't anyone else. She thought it was the easiest way out. Ali and Lesley have now been married for eight years and have two children. But Ali knew, and at a time like this was acutely aware, that Oliver had saved his marriage with Lesley.

He faced the thought that Oliver might be dead. It was possible. An accident unreported. Maybe he'd gone somewhere where nobody knew him and something had befallen him. When the mind moves from one degree of pessimism to another, the possibilities for disaster begin to avalanche. Could he be in trouble? With whom? Anyway, Oliver could talk. He was a good talker, a great convincer. He could talk his way out of anything. He seemed to have been born with the ability. He could carry people with what he said and the way he said it and Ali smiled to himself as he remembered Hamlet. He would joke about it with Oliver even now. Whenever Ali would listen to him bring others round to his point of view he would look at him and say 'There speaks Hamlet.' And they would share a knowing smile.

'Hamlet' related to a tutorial at University. They were discussing Hamlet and it was clear the tutor was right into this, leading the way and telling the tutorial group to have their own interpretation whilst also making it clear that his view was the right one. He said Hamlet was a character full of melancholy, who delayed so much he put everyone in danger and who, though he had some beautiful poetry to speak, didn't really have much in the way of redeeming characteristics. Oliver sat, thinking, his fingers tapping. Eventually the tutor was quiet and asked for opinions and Oliver said that the problem with Hamlet was that he was torn between two religions. And the whole tutorial laughed at him, a soft snigger more than a hearty laugh. He set his hands out in front of him.

'Look,' he said, 'where has Hamlet been? In Wittenberg. What's he doing there? Studying. Studying what? Well this was about 1602 or round about that time and remember what put Wittenberg on the map: in 1495, Martin Luther strode up to the door of the cathedral and pinned his 95 theses on the door. This was the hot bed of Protestantism. It's made clear later in the play that Hamlet is 30 years old. So if he's 30 years old, and he's in Wittenberg, I'd venture that he's probably a teacher…the ideas of mature students and lifelong learning not being quite as popular in Wittenberg then as they are now. So what, well'….and at this point the tutor sat back and smiled, as though here was clearly an undergraduate worth listening to, probably an unusual experience….'Hamlet sees a ghost. And not just any ghost but the ghost of his old man. That would probably drive most of us a little mad but for him it's much worse. What are ghosts? They are spirits who walk the earth until they get out of purgatory and are sent to heaven or hell. Purgatory, and the indulgences that were issued by the Catholic Church to limit the amount of time your relatives spent there, were one of Luther's main criticisms of the church.

So as far as a Protestant was concerned, purgatory doesn't exist and so those unclean ghosts that walk the earth don't exist either. Can you imagine how a Protestant teacher or preacher must feel then, on witnessing this ghost? Hamlet doesn't delay, and he's not mad either, but he's a religious man and he's made a thinking man's decision to follow another faith. He's in Wittenberg, for goodness' sake. And then comes this ghost which shakes the foundations of his belief system. Look at the things he says: "From whose bourne no traveller ever returns." Well, that's the point, something has returned and he's now in this spiritual maze.'

Ali recalled Oliver's style, the wonderful way that he asked questions which suggested there was actually a choice in the answer. But they were wonderfully rhetorical and his Platonic structure was compelling. You couldn't disagree with anything he said, or answer any question he asked in a different way.

Ali looked around at the rest of the folk in the tutorial group. They weren't sniggering now. They had been blown away. He could have sold them anything. Even the tutor. Ali could recall it almost word for word, even after all those years. How often were you blown away by one of your peers, after all?

When Euan phoned Aidan he came round straightaway, his concern and worry matched only by his disbelief. Aidan was a theatre director and as much as you could ever say someone looked like one then Aidan did. He had long brown hair that was beginning to grey and you could tell was going to thin on top quite quickly. You could also tell that Aidan would continue to let it grow at the back and that soon he would have this odd look of wispy long hair that told of a man determined to go through middle age in defiance. He had very distinctive features: a long, pointed sharp nose, chiselled jaw bones and a flat chin. He had a small face and the long hair with such dramatic features made his face look at times like a collection of objects. This was particularly pronounced in the winter.

He always wore clothes that never seemed to quite fit. His

omnipresent blue blazer was worn, slightly tatty and a size too big. His trousers were usually too long and his shirt usually too small, probably because he had refused to recognise that he was getting fatter. Alone of the friends, he smoked. Usually cigarettes but not exclusively. When he was younger, Aidan usually spoke of being into "the experience" of life which tended to mean the excess of things. And when he was younger Aidan could do "excess" very well, whether it involved drugs, women or drink.

Aidan knew Oliver because they had rented flats next door to each other years ago. They became close friends because of similar recreational tastes – sport, drink, the arts in general. They had remained close friends and Aidan was very much part of the group of friends that Euan was putting together. Aidan had known the others for almost as long as he had known Oliver.

Aidan married early, which should have toned down the excesses, and remains childless despite many attempts over the years. He and his wife had gone through every treatment available and emerged only with a bundle of disappointment. He would have resigned himself to it being God's will had he not denied God vehemently. He described himself as a "zealous atheist". Strangely this never really led to any awkward moment between himself and Ali – they respected, valued and loved each other and their choice of belief, or non-belief, seemed a matter of insignificance to both of them. What united them was much greater and stronger than the little that divided them.

Aidan sat opposite Euan, listening to his concern and to his plan.

"How is Helen? I mean, what does she think has happened?"

"Oh she hasn't got a clue," replied Euan, spreading his arms in front of him. "She's absolutely lost. That's why she's so worried. It's not Oliver. If there's a problem, he's a talker. For him to break off contact is…" He left it hanging, the consequences too chilling.

"Then we must find him." Aidan put his tea down and looked at Euan. "It's the least I can do. I mean, I owe him a lot. More than a lot, sometimes I feel I owe him everything. Do you remember when my dad died, about ten years ago?"

Euan narrowed his eyes. "I remember your dad passing away and going to the funeral. I remember how bad you looked and I remember the four of us talking about it after. Olly didn't say much….didn't say anything that I recall." He looked up at Aidan. "And then you seemed to be ok after a day or two. I mean, relatively speaking. How, what happened?"

Aidan sighed. This was still difficult for him, but necessary. He needed to restate it for himself and Euan had to know how important Olly was to him. "My dad was a good man, a great man, and I thought he was God when I was growing up. Most people think that of their dad, don't they? But by the time they become teenagers most folk think their dad is a complete bloody idiot – from the benign hand of God to some stupid old twat in six years. It's normal, I think. Well I never thought that, I always thought my dad was great. He never got all nasty and dictatorial like I saw my friends' dads get – don't do that, you can't watch that, you can't stay up till that time, what are you doing with that girl, you're spending too much money, etc. He always had time for me and we were……well, friends I guess. In fact I think he was probably my best friend. He always seemed able to get me things too – I mean when you're young you take these things for granted but as I got older and he got me quite….well, quite big toys and such things, I did wonder a bit how he managed to do it. Dad worked as a sales rep for a timber company and it's not exactly the most lucrative of jobs or professions. He used to go away on business quite a bit – usually the Baltic States and Russia – which seemed to make sense as that's where they bought the wood from. Mum worked too but as a secretary and as I got a bit older I felt that we had more money than we should have had. I was at a fee-paying school and my friends….well, their parents did other things, worked in a bank, doctors, lawyers, where it was more obvious there was wealth.

But when you're fifteen or sixteen such things don't really prey on your mind too much. Maybe there was money from elsewhere, maybe they'd been left some money, I don't know. I remember mentioning it to mum one day and she was non-committal, just saying 'Your dad does a great job running this place, I don't know where I'd be without him.'

Then one day I came home from Uni for the weekend. I hadn't bothered to phone and let them know, I drove down and sure enough they were pleased to see me. I remember dad and I sitting that night, watching tv and drinking some special 22-year old malt whisky that he'd opened cause he said he was so happy I'd come. We talked about anything and everything and I felt …so lucky I suppose that at nineteen years of age my dad was one of my best pals. Then I could see his eyelids begin to droop and he said he had to go to bed. I stayed up, watching tv and suddenly thought of a photo of me and him that was taken years before at a football match. Arms round each other, scarves on, smiling…and in that instant I had to have that photo to take back to Uni with me. So I trudged up the stairs…well, sort of staggered up the stairs really…to my room and rummaged about but couldn't find it. Then I remembered that there was a place in dad's study where a lot of things like old photos were kept so I went back down again and raked through the places I thought they might be but it wasn't there. I wish, almost every day, that I'd given up then and just waited till the morning. I could easily have asked him. But the whisky, the glow I felt and having had a great time chatting with him made me want that photo like nothing on earth. I remember thinking 'I'm going to find this photo tonight if it's the last thing I do.'

So I looked on his desk, around his desk then started to dig into the drawers. They were big and deep and the top was full of papers of shipments, of different marks of timbers, address books of agents and suppliers over in Russia. But I figured that the picture – it was quite old – wouldn't be on the top anyway so I began to dig deeper, to take the folders out and see what was beneath. And it was mostly older papers and what seemed pretty irrelevant stuff, old data on exchange rates, etc. Until I got towards the bottom of the last, the deepest, drawer. Then there were a few different folders. They were different colours and of a different make to the ones above – plastic as opposed to the plain card ones that dad seemed to keep most of his papers in. And they looked newer, much newer than the stuff above them. There were four or five of these plastic folders.

For some reason my heart began to beat a little more quickly as I took the folders out. They didn't fit with the other material that was in there and I felt that something wasn't right. I still remember a part of me thinking 'Do you really want to open this?' I slid the top of the folder open and saw some writing on the top in a language that I didn't understand. But when I lifted that paper I saw pictures of girls. Young girls, beautiful girls… pictures of them and underneath details of where they were from, a date, the name of a British guy and a city in the UK. Delivery dates. I looked through them, one by one, and they were all the same format. But the number of them and their ages…it was horrific seeing smiling face after smiling face looking up at you…"

Euan listened, his eyes widening slowly "People trafficking? Smuggling girls?" he said softly.

Aidan looked back at him, his eyes moist. "Yes, smuggling girls on boats from Russia over here. For the purpose of……Christ, can you imagine, my dad being involved in that, can you imagine?"

He stopped and wouldn't catch Euan's gaze. "But Euan, it got worse.

I looked at all the folders and they were mostly full of photos of girls. I looked at the dates, hoping they would be years old but they were all within the last month or so or over the next year. Then in the last folder there were a few handwritten notes. They were in English – not perfect English but intelligible and were clearly written in a woman's hand. They were all addressed to my dad and the messages were… I think some of them will stay in my mind forever: "as always you are the fantastico, the sealing of the deal is always the bit I am most looking forward to. Get inside me again" and "Hope that Lolo and I did the good for you tonight, playing the tune on the pipe" and "No one has the love like you, love. I am old and lucky you even look at me, the young girls make good satisfaction for you. Younger is better!" I couldn't read the woman's name properly, maybe Natalya, maybe not but in that moment, or these five minutes, everything I believed, everything I felt, every joy I'd felt…they all seemed manufactured and false. My dad was a people trafficker who shagged – probably raped – young girls and prostitutes. How can you know such things and stay the same? My whole life felt like a lie, who I was and what I was felt false, all my thoughts seemed wrong, as if they somehow belonged to someone else. So I left, there and then. I got back in the car and went back to Uni that night. Probably wildly drunk, well over the limit, though I never felt as sober in my life.

I never spoke to my dad again. He tried to get in touch with me that week, there were calls and I think him and mum even came up. I don't know, I crashed a lot of different places that week. And then he died, just after that. A heart attack but I will always wonder if he knew. I think he must have and I think it killed him that I knew. That's where Oliver came in and I think he probably saved my life. I remember being down home with the family but I had to come back up here for a day or two before the funeral. It took time to release the body in any case. So I came back up here and I remember feeling when I got here that life was too painful. To think, to talk, to arrange things, to engage with other people was too painful. I'm not talking just about dealing with dad, but general stuff. I couldn't focus, I couldn't concentrate… it wasn't even that I was walking about in tears, it was much more… I'm not sure how to describe it, maybe more fundamental than that. I think I probably made a decision there that I didn't want to live anymore. I did the only thing that you can really do when you are thinking things like that – I decided to drink and drink until I couldn't think anymore.

I had been there for a while, sitting in the pub and things were beginning to numb when Olly appeared from nowhere. I didn't want him there, I didn't want any company, I knew that later I was going to do something to make me not live anymore and I wanted to be alone with myself. I thought Olly was quite a sensitive guy but he didn't take any hints that night. I didn't look at him, hardly answered him, told him to go away a few times quite blatantly but he wouldn't go. He kept telling me he wasn't leaving. We could talk or not talk, laugh or not laugh, smoke or not smoke, cry or not cry but he wasn't leaving. And eventually I crumpled. We went back home and I'm pretty sure I cried into his arms all night. Somehow I felt protected. He listened to me – to everything – all night. To how I felt such hatred and love in the same instant, to how my dad was now someone I felt I never knew, to how I could have loved someone so much who was so evil. And he said 'Sometimes good people do bad things for reasons… reasons they can justify even if only to themselves. Doesn't change how much they loved us.' I can't say that after that night everything was all right because it wasn't. But what had changed was me. The feeling of nothingness slowly went away. I still miss my dad today desperately and I still have such twisted complex feelings. But had Olly not been there that night and simply appeared, I'm really not so sure that I would be here now. I always wonder where he came from – was he just walking about the streets looking for a bar to go into? How did he find me? I often wonder… anyway, if he's in any trouble, I'm on the plane with you."

Euan sat, visibly shocked by what he had heard. "Jeez, Aidan, I never knew any of that. You didn't… you didn't have to tell me that, it must be so painful, I'm sorry."

"I don't want to make you feel awkward, I only want you to know that I'll do what I can to help you find Olly and if that means we are on a plane tomorrow then let's go."

"Yes," said Euan, "I think it does. I need to see if Ellis will come then we can go. There is a flight from Edinburgh tomorrow to Nice."

Ellis was tall and permanently bronzed, even if he had not enjoyed the benefits of two weeks in the sun. He had dazzling brown eyes, a large oval shaped face and large busy eyebrows that he was always threatening to eventually grow into. Unashamedly middle class, he had hands which looked as though they had never done a day's manual work in their life. Ellis would always dispute this, saying that he was sure he had dug the garden for his dad once during a school holiday. He worked as a fund manager, investing other people's money to try and make them more

27

money, and he was very wealthy. Ellis was married with two children: he had married Yvonne seven years ago and the children were six and two. He gave the impression of being permanently optimistic about almost everything.

"He's what? What do you mean Euan? He's where? What the hell's he doing in the south of France? And he's just got lost?"

"Well, truth is, Ellis we don't know where he is. We don't know if he's still there or if something else has happened, maybe he's been injured or something, we don't know."

"But if he'd been injured we would surely know – hospitals and so on? Police?"

"Helen has tried those and we've got nothing. But we have to find him. He can't just have run off and left Helen… and Terrence."

"No, no I know, I know. It doesn't sound like Oliver. So what do you want to do?"

"We're going to go and try to find him Ellis, and we want you to come. We'll leave tomorrow and we don't intend to come back till we've found him."

Ellis was silent. "That might cause me a problem or two…" Euan could hear Ellis' mind start to work and go through mental gymnastics on the other end of the phone. "Hmmm…might have to move that… would be difficult… I wonder if I could join you in two or three days' time?"

Euan was hesitant. "Well, if you want, of course, if that's best for you… but who knows where we'll be, we don't know what's going to happen. Maybe we'll find him in a day and we can sit about that lovely beach in Nice… but maybe not…"

"Yeah, sure, of course… ok, ok, I'll come. I can re-arrange stuff, this is important. Anyway, I'm owe Oliver one, he beat the shit out of that guy who was going to attack me in the pub a few years ago, do you remember?"

"Ah yeah," said Euan, "I do remember that. I think that guy had a knife."

"Yeah, he was angered by me talking quite loudly. Well, angered may be a bit of a euphemism….I think I'd had a few and, as you know I tend to get a little louder when I've had a couple. I heard him muttering about 'posh twat accent' but never paid him any heed… I was quite a bit bigger than him and anyway these things never usually develop. But he got more and more uppity so I think I got louder and louder – and probably posher and posher. And with no warning he came at me. Ran me against the door then through it and I fell over outside. And I heard him say 'I'm going to slit your fucking throat you fucking yob' and he went to his pocket. Then out came Oliver, jumped the guy, got him to the ground and I heard the tinkle of a knife on the ground and saw this huge steel blade. And I thought at the time 'Christ, who brings something like that out with them, he must have had the intention of doing something like this to someone.' And Olly went for him. Dragged him up from the ground so he could punch the guy. I've never seen someone's fists move as fast as Olly's did that night. The guy could hardly make a noise for all the blows that Olly rained down on him. Then when Olly let him fall to the ground he booted him until we had to stop him, almost pull him off. And then – it was really odd – Olly just walked away, quite calmly, as if nothing out the ordinary had happened and started talking about football or shagging or whatever it was we'd been talking about in the pub before this mayhem ensured. Bizarre. But yeah, I'll come – you book the flights and we leave tomorrow?"

"Yes," said Euan. "You, me, Aidan and Ali. We'll leave tomorrow and we'll find him."

Euan put the phone down and looked at Aidan. "They're all in. It'll be the four of us. That's good."

"Yeah, that's great," said Aidan. "So, what's the plan? I mean, say we find him and there is some odd but rational explanation for all this. Do we just bundle him on a plane and bring him home? Do we leave him there? I mean, what…?"

"I don't know," Euan replied, puzzled. "It just depends, doesn't it? For the life of me I can't see a rational explanation here. But one thing's for sure, we won't be bundling him on a plane."

"No? How do you know?"

"He can't fly. He won't fly. He only got out to Nice in the first place by train, it took him ages."

"He can't fly? Really?" Aidan searched through his mind for some confirmation. "Did I know this? Is it a recent thing? I'm not sure I knew that."

"No, it's not recent. He's never been able to fly since I knew him. Helen says he's never flown in his life. It's all down to claustrophobia I think."

"Claustrophobia? He's not claustrophobic is he? I've seen him in lifts, in closed rooms."

"Yeah, it's not acute but with him it's down to feeling he's spending a long time in an enclosed space. So he's never really bothered about lifts. It all comes from something that happened when he was a kid apparently – the wooden horse. Did you never hear about the wooden horse?"

"The what?" Aidan looked at him as if he was deranged.

"When he was younger…very young, about four or five….one of his friends had this wooden horse. It was a huge thing apparently. I think the intention was that you sat on the thing but the manufacturer has obviously thought it could be used as storage too so the bottom opened up and you could put stuff in it…all the stuff that a four or five year old plays with. But of course four or five year olds also think it might be a good idea to put themselves in it and it used to be used quite a bit when they played hide and seek. This was ok, I remember Olly saying, if you hid in it yourself and you could hold the door shut. But one day he had hid in it and a couple of guys came up and, for a laugh, decided to shut it from the outside. Then they ran away because that's what five year olds do to amuse themselves I guess. Olly was trapped and for a couple of minutes he was laughing but then he said he heard silence and he felt the trapped space begin to get warmer. He couldn't see daylight and he couldn't get fresh air from anywhere. He tried to stand up but the horse was too sturdy for him to move it. He tried to topple it but no joy. So he did all he could do which was shout. And I think, from what I've heard, that's what stayed with him till this day – the shouting, the heat increasing, nobody coming, the desperation, the sweat. Without really understanding why, I think he knew he was going to die. Then he cried and shrieked as the oxygen began to run out. Eventually it was his friend's mum who heard him and got him out. The boys had run away and expected Olly to come and find them. So the thought of an aeroplane is to him…you know, like being in that horse again…that breathlessness and feeling that he's going to die."

The Capo looked at the meal that had been set in front of him. He was always impressed when associates knew what he liked, cooked the way he liked it.

"It's just beyond medium rare, I hope it's as you like it."

The Capo licked his lips as the taste of the first mouthful struck his taste buds. "It's beautiful," he said. "Very beautiful. And it is very good of you to meet with me. Your hospitality," he waved his arm airily around him to take in the stunning view that spread out across the balcony they sat at, "already convinces me that we shall have a fruitful collaboration."

"Oh," said the official, "please let me correct you, it is very good of you to meet with me. And I am willing to do what I can to ensure that we both come out of this happy."

"Mutual satisfaction," said The Capo, motioning with his fork. "I take nothing. Everything is mutual." He looked at the man sitting opposite him and smiled. "I think we understand one another."

The official raised his glass and said: "To us. And to the future" and they exchanged nods as the glasses chinked together.

The Capo put down his glass and his tone changed to the rather expressionless, matter of fact and dull voice that it did whenever he addressed matters of business. "I need….I want…several things to happen and I think it is best if I simply tell you what they are." The official nodded and replied "Of course" but The Capo did not wait for his approval or consent. "I need the contract for the building of the hospital to go to company Y… no dubiety, you know who I mean by company Y…and I need the contract for the new build of the University to go to Company A. I appreciate that Company…the other one, you know who I mean… are favoured on both of these but they cannot receive either of these contracts. They have done me dishonour and disservice in ways that you do not need to know. I think my word should carry enough for you in this. You need to make this happen. Can you make this happen?"

The official looked at The Capo and was struck by his blank look. His eyes seemed dull and lifeless, as emotionless as a robot's might be if programmed to kill. Suddenly he felt threatened, and realised what type of man he was about to shake hands with. He smiled, not at The Capo this time but down at the tablecloth. All he could think was "This guy has the power to have me killed in an instant, probably so that I am never found again." He looked up and caught The Capo's stare.

"Yes, I can make it happen. It will be difficult for me to do this… "

The Capo cut him off. "I will pay you well for your difficulty. Difficulty can always be bought or easily got rid of."

"Then yes, it will be done. You have my word."

The Capo looked at him and stretched out a hand : "And your deed too. Ok, within two weeks."

"Ok," said the official. "Within two weeks the contracts will be awarded to the companies you wish."

"Very well. And you," said The Capo to the official, "are about to become a very wealthy man." The official's eyes could do no other than focus on The Capo's hand as it brought out note after note after note from his jacket pocket until the official had lost count. 'No wonder there is a crisis in the Euro zone,' the official thought, 'this guy's got the lot.' The notes were handed to the official, their brightness temporarily blinding him to the knowledge of who he was dealing with.

"And now," said the official. "I have arranged some entertainment for us. I hope you will enjoy. I have tried to get what I have heard you enjoy the most."

At the wave of the official's hand five women walked in to the room. All of them had long red hair, all of them were six foot if they were an inch, all of them had full figures bursting out of see through black lingerie. The only differences were in age and The Capo's educated eye placed the youngest at about twenty, the oldest at about thirty. This is how I'll die, he thought, lost in the absolute excess of sex. He let the woman come to him as he sat at the table. One kissed his neck as two began to work down the zip of his trousers and gently massage. He felt a need shoot through him as his back arched and he sighed an almost imperceptible sigh. The official smiled and left the room.

When The Capo was finished he joined Davide in the back of the car. "That official," said The Capo, "we need to keep an eye on him. I trust him – so far – but I need to see what he's up to, where the weaknesses are in case we need to exert any pressure. I can't afford to kill him yet, it would make things difficult."

"It's done," said Davide. "Is there anything else you want to know?" He passed across a large brown folder.

"Oh, I'll look at this later. Is there anything that I should know now?"

"Not much," said Davide. "I think Jean who owns the restaurant on the front is taking in more money than he is registering and I think Frank's casino is genuinely in trouble so I think his reduced payments are right. In fact, I think he is paying over 12%. And some friends of that guy Oliver are coming to Nice to try to find him."

"Tell Frank he doesn't need to pay me anything till he wants to. Frank's terrified of me, he always had been. It's good, it makes him loyal. So I must be loyal to him too. Give him money if he needs it. Jean is a crook but he's a petty crook and if he's paying less it's probably just 11%.

We'll leave it until I have run out of more important things to do. If these guys are coming to find Oliver then it's safe to say we don't know where he is either yet?"

"No, we haven't found him yet." The Capo looked across at Davide. "Sorry."

"It's ok. He may know he has to hide. How many friends are coming?"

"We don't know exactly. Our information is a bit sketchy but I think three."

"Ok. Well they should stand out. They should stand out like statues."

As the car drove away The Capo realised that this Oliver was one of the few people in this part of the world, if not the only one, that he wanted to know something about and didn't.

Anthony knew something was wrong and he knew that Helen knew that something was wrong. As he watched her go through her morning routine – up, shower, Terrence ready, breakfast of toast, muesli, orange juice and coffee then out – he could see someone else, standing opposite the house, looking into it. In the same way that an artist will recognise the beauty in a rival's work, or that an angler would discuss with another which fly to use in which condition, Anthony knew that the round faced man looking into Helen's house was no idler. This was a man looking at Helen with the same purpose as him. And as he looked through his binoculars at her at the window, he saw her look at the fat faced man and the expression on her face changed. She knew she was being watched. He was hit by several instinctive thrusts at the same time – a rival was a threat, too big a threat, Helen would prefer this other man, Helen had to be protected against him.

He wished too in that moment that Helen had done something, like the others, to disappoint him. Like Jessica, the first woman he had yearned to take home and the first woman he had built a room for. But as he followed Jessica and studied her routine, learning as he went how easy it was to adopt little disguises to make himself undetectable and unknown to her, he discovered things that began to disgust him. She drank to excess, she took sexual partners wherever and whenever she could find them, she clearly cared little for other people and he quickly came to the conclusion that though she had been good to him she would not be deserving of him. Lucia disappointed him too, as she clung pathetically to a boyfriend who worked his way around all her friends.

He remembered her pleading with him more than anything, the way she trampled over her self-respect by holding her hands in front of her, wringing them in despair, begging this horrible person to "Don't leave me, don't leave me, don't ever leave me." How could he respect and value such a person?

But Helen had never deflated his opinion of her, had done nothing to cause his obsession to falter. Instead his desire grew every time he saw her and her beauty enveloped him more. The desire to own and control her engulfed him more. However, Anthony was nothing if not logical and he realised how difficult it would be to take her if she was being watched by a rival, probably with the same intent as his.

Anthony then looked down the street for any other threat. All he saw were parked cars, the same cars that had been there for the last two to three weeks. Except one. He lifted his eyes from his binoculars and looked at a black car, parked slightly away from Helen's house. He looked at the registration number and checked it against those in his book. It was a new car. He looked back through the binoculars, trying to see if there was anyone in the car. Then he saw a man get out and look around him with a casual air. But Anthony saw his eyes rest particularly on Helen's house, focus on the distance between the path and the door then look purposefully at the front window. Then just as quickly he looked away again and crossed the road to meet a woman who had walked from the end of the street. They shook hands and the woman pointed to a top floor window. Anthony put his binoculars down. He's going to rent a flat, he thought, right opposite Helen. And because he was a connoisseur, Anthony knew instinctively that this man was a threat to Helen too.

Helen forced herself to eat breakfast in the hope that exercising her routine may be a comfort to her. But just as she wasn't sleeping properly neither was she eating properly and the food that she did manage to eat was without taste and choked down.

During the night all she had thought about was Oliver. She hadn't dreamt about him, in the way we do when the random unchecked thoughts come to us, but had spent much of the night thinking consciously of him and of them as a couple. What had he done? Was it believable that he could be in any trouble? What did she really know about him? About his work? And she became uncertain of everything,

not because she had any real evidence but because she realised how little Oliver knew about her. Why should she know more about him? Perhaps he was a very good liar and what was happening now was always meant to happen. Whilst, of course, rationally it did not make sense logically it made perfect sense and Helen's logic began to piece together how easily Oliver may have lied, covered things, given her false information. Even the work number that she had phoned and his so-called boss that she had spoken to, could that have been a name and number that Oliver had given her and had he always been planning this deceit, this disappearance? Maybe he's not even in Nice, maybe he never was......
but surely he had to be, she had spoken to him in the flat there, she had phoned the number, hadn't she...or had he phoned her... surely she had phoned the number there sometime since he had been away. But even if she had, it could have been redirected. If he had planned this then that would be a little technicality.

And as Helen questioned her life with Oliver up to this point, she gazed out of her bedroom window and across the street. She wasn't looking at anything or trying to look at anything but was consumed with thought so deeply that she noticed nothing. Until, that is, the man standing opposite changed his stance and she realised that he had been there for a while. With fear now, she looked directly at him and saw him looking directly back and she stepped back from the window, her heart quickening.

That look had not been one of curiosity or of casual observance. It had not been the look of someone who was standing about, waiting to meet someone else. It was the threatening stare of someone who had been looking for her and at her. She got down on the floor. 'Christ,' she thought, 'what is he mixed up in?' The thoughts that raced through her mind all linked the man outside the window to Oliver's disappearance. They have him, now they are coming for me and Terrence or maybe he has sent someone to watch me to make sure I don't chase him or try to get any money out of him or maybe he is into something so bad that he wants me dead because I know something or maybe he just wants me to feel threatened and watched. Maybe I am about to be kidnapped and they will hold me until he does what they want him to do. Maybe he has told them about Terrence and me and they will take us.

There was one thing she felt she had to know and could discover. She grabbed the phone from above the bed and crawled over to the window. The man was still there. Well out of his sight, she stood up and hid herself behind the curtain where she was sure she could not be seen. She dialled the first number on the phone, the flat in Nice which she had tried again that morning.

She watched the man opposite. By pure coincidence Ambrose felt his phone vibrate in his pocket. He took the phone out and immediately saw it was a sales call from his mobile supplier who had been trying to sell him something over the past week. As Helen put the phone down he hit the button to ignore the call. For Helen it could not have been clearer had the message been painted across the sky: her phone was tapped. She recoiled in horror and the darkness consumed her.

CHAPTER 3

"But that's not the name on this reservation, madam. That's what I'm trying to say to you. The name on the reservation and the name on the passport are not the same."

"My name is Kletchkova. I booked my ticket. I entered all the details. Why is this a problem?"

"It's a problem because your passport says K-L-E-T-C-H-K-O-V-A but this reservation says K-L-E-C-H-K-O-V-A. They are different names. I can't use this reservation to let you travel, you will need to buy a ticket in the correct name."

"I need to buy another ticket? How much is another ticket?"

"I don't know madam. You will need to go to the sales desk over there." She pointed vaguely. "But the flight is full I think."

"The flight cannot be full if you are not allowing me to travel on a reservation I have already made. There must be at least one space. That is logical, I think." The woman's anger was evident in her voice and she was struggling to retain control.

"Yes madam. Now, please, if you could go to the sales desk, they will be able to help you."

The four friends waited behind Ms. Kletchkova. Euan shook his head and looked at his friends. Aidan shrugged his shoulders, Ali and Ellis looked at the floor, wry smiles on their faces. They went forward together but their check-in passed without incident: all their names had been entered correctly, they all had passports, and they all had to pay for the luxury of putting a suitcase in the hold of the aeroplane.

"You know," Euan announced as they made their way to Security, "I've thought of doing that in the restaurant. Saying to folk: 'Ah, you want to use a napkin, that's extra. You want to use a chair, that's extra. You want to use a knife and fork, that's extra...and you want a different knife and fork for each course? That's double extra. You want to go for a pee? Extra. And you actually want the food on a plate? That's extra.'"

The line for Security slalomed like a snake in front of them. A slow moving snake, full of people who didn't smile and hardly talked. It was as if when people joined this line they entered a Kafkaesque world where everything they were and everything they thought was under suspicion.

The friends inched and edged closer, seeing as they did people taking off jackets, jerseys, belts, shoes and emptying bags of liquids, computers, clothes. People in uniforms made unsmiling demands and everyone obeyed. The friends did as they were asked and proceeded through the scanner which Aidan set off. He shrugged his shoulders as a stranger demanded he stretch his arms out and then touched him in places where only women he had slept with had touched him before. With a nonchalant nod of his head, the stranger bid Aidan to be on his way.

The others waited for him. Only fifteen yards away they could see the Departures hall.

"Excuse me sir, I'm from UK border control, are you travelling alone or with others?"

Ellis was quite clearly with his friends but thought better of giving a sarcastic reply. "I'm with my friends, these three guys here."

"Where are you flying to sir?"

"Nice."

"And what's the purpose of your visit?"

Ellis thought about it. And he thought about telling the truth: 'Actually, I have no real idea. We're going to try and find a friend who seems to have vanished off the face of the earth. Do you think you might be able to help us in this?' and then thought better of it. "Oh, we're just a few friends getting away for a few days."

"And do you have large amounts of money with you?"

Ellis thought it a stupid question. There were cash machines everywhere, weren't there? What did it matter how much money he had? "No," he said. "I'll change some sterling for Euros through there" and he pointed to the promised land of Departures that was tantalisingly close, "maybe three or four hundred."

"Very good sir. Thank you. Enjoy your break." And Ellis felt like asking him what purpose this had served. I could have millions of whatever currency in my suitcase, he thought, even in my hand luggage.

Euan looked at his watch. "Ok, it seems to be on time so we've got an hour and a half in this place. Beer? Food? Beer and food?" The consensus was beer and food, on the basis that anything they wanted on the plane they would have to pay for and would probably be of minimal gastronomic quality anyway.

The bar was quiet and the friends sat down near a couple who were sitting together but not talking, drinking or watching the television. Ali asked: "Have you booked a hotel Euan, or do we find something when we get there?"

"No, I booked a hotel, called the Boscolo. It's near the centre. It's not so cheap but I reserved four rooms for two nights. I didn't know what to reserve… "

His friends nodded in tacit approval. "It defies belief, doesn't it," said Ellis. "Oliver I mean. I can't believe he's just disappeared of his own free will. Something must have happened to him. I'm apprehensive… scared…of what we're going to find. He would surely be in touch if he was alive. Wouldn't he? Wouldn't he? And that's going to be devastating for us but how are we going to tell Helen?"

Euan raised his hand. "Guys, I've thought this through, I feel the same as you Ellis, the same as all of you I'm sure. I'm pretty convinced that what we're going to discover out there, if we discover anything, is going to be unpleasant. I'll deal with Helen, I'll speak with her. Maybe not till we get home, she'll need someone near her."

"You think he's dead, don't you?"

"Probably," said Euan, "but there is a big 'but' there. And the 'but' is why don't we know? If someone dies the first thing you get is the next of kin being informed. That's three days. Surely the police would have found out who he was within three days. He has some folk over there that know him, they'd surely put the police in touch with folk in Edinburgh. Could he be lying dead in the flat for three days and nobody's found him? Is that credible? Apart from the fact that he's fit and healthy, someone over there would surely have gone round to check? Or is there something obvious that I'm missing here?"

Aidan fiddled on his mobile phone. "No," he said. "I've thought about it a lot and 'disappearing' isn't Olly. He's a good man and he loves Helen and Terrence so much, they're his life."

Ali said: "The only other alternative is that he's hiding. From whom, I don't know. Why, I don't know. But I thought about it, what if I was in this situation, what would make me break contact like that and the only thing I could come up with was if I was in some sort of danger. Then maybe if I got in touch with anyone it would put them in danger too. That's all I could think of."

"But what sort of danger could he be in?" Euan said, half pleading, half shouting. "He's unremarkable, he's so uncontroversial, he works for a company that makes those little war figures for Christ's sake. Toys!"

"Yeah, I know, I know all that," said Ali. "It makes it all the more confusing. I wonder if it's something to do with a woman?" He held his hands up. "I know, I don't want to think it either."

"Well, yeah, you've maybe got a point there," said Ellis, slowly. "Remember that dinner we were at a few months ago, do you remember that woman who virtually chased him about the place all night? Helen was going mental."

The dinner had been a fund raising event for a charity with which Euan had an affinity. He regularly donated to them and occasionally arranged events such as this to help them raise funds, usually once or twice a year. These dinners were always well attended: as a restaurateur, Euan was always talking to his clients and was a very popular host. He also had boyish charm, foppish good looks and affable smiles in spades. The success of these dinners was helped by his clientele being wealthy with a significant amount of disposable income.

The five friends and their partners had shared a table and passed a pleasant if nondescript evening until the dancing started. The Scottish country dancing began to engage the crowd and in one of those dances that sees partners constantly changing, Oliver ended up beside a beautiful woman who was about five years older than him. Ellis looked at him, looking at her. Everyone who went to an event such as this made an effort to look their best, from the guys who made sure their bow ties were straight to the women who'd booked themselves into the hotel for the night so they didn't have to travel any distance once they had prepared themselves. But no one had made an effort quite like this woman. Ellis looked around for her partner, a husband who was maybe looking for her. He noticed that Oliver wasn't looking for her partner, just looking at her and smiling, listening to what she was saying. She reached for him as the band started to play a waltz and Ellis saw her talking to him almost constantly, smiling and Oliver smiling back. He saw Oliver's hand on her back, firmly placed, maybe too firmly for someone he had just met. He saw the woman touch her hair, pull back from Oliver so he could see her neck and her figure. Oliver smiled. From what Ellis saw, he never looked for Helen once. Helen was sitting with the others and Ellis looked at her. She was trying not to watch what was happening but when she did he could see her lips tighten and her eyes, in a flash, narrow. Ellis struggled to understand how Oliver could look at anyone except Helen. She looked beautiful, bejewelled in a black dress which hugged her as though it had been painted on in parts.

Eventually the dance ended and Oliver sat down beside Helen but she turned away from him and the woman came over to sit down beside him. To most people, thought Ellis, this would be a distinctly uncomfortable situation. But Olly seemed more than happy, smiling and turning to Helen, bringing her into the conversation. All the time the woman seemed to edge closer to Oliver and take up more of his personal space. At some point the woman got the hint that she was the reason why Helen was sulking and she went away, leaving Helen to tear into Oliver without really caring about who was around them or who was listening to them. Oliver just listened and watched Helen and he looked so content that Ellis wondered if he done this just to see Helen get to this state. He looked at her almost in wonder, even in awe as her eyes flashed and her hands did everything but hit him. Most guys would have said "It's only a dance, I was just being friendly, leave me alone" but Oliver clearly knew it was much more than that. So maybe, concluded Ellis, he did this just to get her to that state. And when she had burnt herself out he looked at her with such desire and longing. She tried to look away and to resist, perhaps even to make some attempt to take control. But he gently turned her face back to him and softly raised her chin till she was forced to look at him. He gazed into her eyes and Ellis could almost see her melt in front of him. Then he took her hand, stood up, put his arm round her as she did to him and they briskly walked away with their heads full of nothing but desire for each other.

"Yeah," said Euan, "I remember that dinner. And I remember all the times we had at school…nights out, discos….so many women… well, girls I suppose at that time. It was great being with Olly because you were pretty much guaranteed a result. I usually got "the friend" but given the women that he went with, the friend was usually a stunner." Euan smiled and allowed himself to be indulged by some sweet memories. "Still, I don't think he's gone with a woman. He would have told somebody, surely. Maybe one of us if not Helen."

In this way, by discussion and memories, trying to call to mind something that might help them to understand, the friends tried to rationalise the situation. Inevitably, however, their attention was drawn by the discussion taking place at the table next to them. The man and woman had sat without talking much to each other, watching the golf on the television and slowly having a drink. Then the waiter had brought a menu and the man quickly announced that he wanted fish and chips and another beer. His wife or partner or friend put down her menu and sighed. The friends at the next table quickly concluded that she must be his wife.

"Do you think that's a good idea? I mean, really, is it a good idea? You know that fish batter sits in your stomach and the problems you have digesting it. And chips are too heavy to eat when you're going on a plane. Why don't you have a nice salad or something light? And do you really think having another beer is a good idea? That'll make you spend half the flight in the toilet. Why don't you have an apple juice or water or something that isn't going to dehydrate you and give you a sore head?"

The man nodded his head in assent and said: "that's probably a better idea, yes. Ok, I'll have a salad and a juice."

The man scratched at his arm. "And you'll need to watch that rash in the sun," said his wife. "You'll need to cover it up, you can't let the sun get at it. And we will get some cream too because we don't want it to spread. I'm still not sure this is a good idea, I don't think the sun agrees with you and you need to be careful."

"I can always sit in the shade and read my book," said the man, searching for a solution.

"Yes. And we'll need to be careful with the food too. And watch what you're drinking. No alcohol during the day. And nothing with ice in it. Just bottled water, we can buy some when we get there. And you need to make sure you get plenty of rest, you need your sleep. And we won't be hiring a car or doing anything like that that gives us any stress. It's going to be a relaxing break."

The man nodded in agreement. You could tell by the way he nodded that he had done this kind of nodding, to this kind of comment, for years. And as they listened in that delicate way that we do when we have to make the people we are listening to not suspect at all that we are listening to them, the friends looked at each other. Ali's eyes opened wide and Aidan stood up quickly, frightened that the laughter he felt building up inside was going to explode so quickly that he couldn't get out the way in time.

"I'm going to look in the paper shop," he blurted, almost running out of the way before he allowed the laughter to get the better of him. He wondered how the poor guy put up with it. Though, he thought, he seemed quite happy. He wasn't exactly complaining.

He looked about him and was struck, as he always was in an airport, by how characterless and soulless it was. A bit like a prison, he thought, except you could buy quite expensive things. He was also fascinated by the range of the social spectrum that passed through here. As he walked past one gate he could see people whose average age must have been

about eighteen, people who, had they been that age twenty years ago, would probably never have dreamed about flying anywhere, ready to get on a plane to somewhere in eastern Europe. He looked at them as a "backpack brigade" – people who evidently had virtually no money but who'd shoved some things into a bag and grabbed a boyfriend/girlfriend and decided to have a travel experience overseas. They all looked happy…
…or at least content. Couples that smiled at each other, a boy playing with his girlfriend's hair, one reading with his legs stretched out over someone else, one's head on someone else's shoulder, another couple standing talking to each other smiling into each other's eyes. They all had the look of people who were escaping but more than that it was as if they realised they were escaping…escaping, if only for a little while, from conforming.

Then at another gate sat guys in suits either on their phones or playing with their phones. Aidan touched the phone inside his pocket, to make sure he hadn't left it on the table in the restaurant and realised that he belonged much more to this group than the one he had passed at the other gate. He also realised that the people who were at the previous gate would be at this gate in ten years' time. He walked slowly by, walking up to the window and feigning interest in what was outside. Close to him one guy was getting particularly animated on the phone. He was clearly the boss of both the person he was talking to on the phone and the guy sitting next to him. Though he spoke quietly he spoke with force and Aidan couldn't help but hear his conversation.

"I don't care about the Israel story. It doesn't matter what they've done. Get it on page five if you think it's interesting. But it's not page bloody one. Page one is that stupid twat having an affair… yeah, yeah, I know what the news editor thinks but he's not paid to make this decision, I am…….No, No, that's where you're wrong, it's not public interest because the public aren't interested….listen they couldn't give a flying fuck in a high wind about what the Israeli army might have done or who they might have bombed. They still think Gaza is a football player. We put that on the front page we make them feel stupid… well, yeah, they might BE stupid but it's hardly our bloody job to reinforce it… no, the shagger is public interest, it's what the public want to see and what people want to read about. Yeah, ok, ok.." There was a lull in the conversation and he turned to his colleague beside him. "This business is about psychology. What do people want. What makes them happy. Do you think Joe the trucker, who buys the paper in the morning and looks forward to reading it when he has his break, is going to look forward to reading about bloody Israelis bombing something? Of course not. Is he going to want to read about some overpaid footballer shagging his brains out while his wife and kids sit at home in ignorance? Of course he is because then he sees this rich twat fall over. He's human, just like me. For all his money he's going to be going through hell. His wife's going to hate him, like mine does sometimes. He's going to want to be with his mates, like I do sometimes. But give him bloody Israel bombing somewhere and he can't relate to that. He probably doesn't know where the fuck Israel is." The man beside him nodded politely, as if he knew that was his job. He did it very well.

"Hello, hello, yeah, what is it," said the boss, turning back to the phone…"No, we can't have two stories on page one! Put that prick on the phone, what the hell's his game? He said what?" He turned to the man beside him and said: "Freddy in news apparently told the defence minister that he would do all he could to get the Israel story on page one. Bit of government elbow there. Freddy needs to know who pays his wages – and it's not this bloody government." He went back to the phone. "Freddy? Oh, it's still you. Well tell him it's not going to happen. I couldn't give a toss what he's promised anyone, page one is the shagger. We decide what the headline is, not the fucking defence minister. And tell Freddy he better push a cushion down his pants because I'm going to boot his arse up and down the office when I get back." He pushed the 'off' button on his phone and turned to his colleague: "When the fuck does this flight leave anyway?"

Aidan walked slowly away, taking his phone out of his pocket and pretending to react to something as he did so. He wondered what the guy would have said if he'd gone up to him and said – 'My friend is missing in the south of France, do you think that might make any page in your newspaper?' Maybe the rules in the crossword competition….

He walked down the concourse, noting that even the police who strolled around with guns looked bored. He wondered exactly how they filled their day. Then he saw a bar/restaurant type place which seemed to appear in the middle of the concourse. Most of the other shops and eateries were clearly at the side but this one was plonked right in the middle. It seemed expensive, offering caviar and champagne and he quickly imagined how some of those kids on that flight to eastern Europe might react if they looked at some of the prices here and how the staff behind the bar might react if they saw them waiting to be served. There

44

were not many people at this bar but those who were, unsurprisingly, dripped money. Two guys on their own at the other side from Aidan and two guys who were together quite close to him. He didn't stand or sit at the bar but sat down quite close to it, taking out his phone to pretend to be as "in demand" as everyone else whilst listening to what the two men were saying.

He was immediately fascinated by them because they were so obviously important people. One guy had grey wavy hair, a loud assertive tone, a stomach whose size immediately indicated that he knew what the good life was and that southern English brogue to his voice that spoke of an expensive education. He wasn't a government minister but he sounded every bit as polished as one. The other guy was dressed in a suit which cost a good four figure sum. Aidan knew nothing about suits but even he realised the guy's clothes reeked of opulence and excess. His thick black hair was combed back and gelled down. He was tall and broad but not fat and he was the kind of guy that if he came near you would have filled your personal space right away. Aidan hated him on sight: it was as if his very appearance took all the failings you'd felt in your life and rammed them down your throat in one go.

The fat one was talking: "It needs a little rebalancing overall. I think we need to make the shift to holding more in Sterling than in the Euro. It's a bit unstable, things are maybe a bit uncertain. Sterling is a safer haven."

"If we begin to do that," replied the suit, "there will be a reaction. I mean, others will do the same."

"Well sure maybe, but it's not going to collapse the Euro. It'll push its value down a bit, the exporters won't like it, tourists might."

The suit looked at the fat one with a knowing smile. "You're speculating, aren't you? You want to put the Euro in play?"

The fat one drank from his champagne and savoured the first taste, letting out a sigh of contentment. "I love this place. Not this airport," he said, looking around him. "I mean this restaurant. Isn't it glorious? That you can get food like this" – he lifted his fork with caviar on it and waved at some indistinguishable seafood –"in an airport." He looked at the suit. "A word or two in the right ears…and you know the right ears… see what happens. Money to be made." He announced it as though it was a call to arms.

"There's another thing," said the suit, pushing his hair back as he thrust his head forward. "We're trying to get the lending side to be a bit more liberal. Their average credit card limit is £7,000, the highest mortgage they give is to 95%, personal loans are almost a thing of the past. They are not for moving. What would it take for them to see things our way?"

The fat one swirled the food around in his mouth, savouring the taste. "I can fix that. Well, you know, if not fix then get some changes there. We need to be more sympathetic to the situation people find themselves in. They don't have any money, they'll go to some two bit cash outfit that'll give them a loan till pay day. They should be putting that on their credit cards. See, that average figure of £7,000 means nothing, nothing at all. Because you know and I know that the people we really want to get will have a credit limit of about £3,000. We need these people to be desperate to use their cards, to go on holidays they can't afford to get away from the crappy situation they find themselves in. And as for the mortgage….well you know what I think. It's a knee-jerk reaction. House prices won't fall any further, we all know that. If we give them 100%, 105% we're going to get our money back even if they default. Ok, transaction cost, selling the house cost, but that's minimal. What difference does it make if it's 95% or 100%? It's still our house if they can't pay the bloody mortgage."

The fat one drunk deeply from his champagne glass. "There's so much to be made out there, Bart. We're running away from it because of all the crap. People need money, people want money in times like they're in now more than ever. It's as old as the crucifixion. People want things they can't afford, it's what we do, it's where we make money. You're dead right. We need to give them a little more, open their eyes a little more to the promise of what they can have. Look down this airport, look in these shops," he said, pointing down the concourse. "There's iPads, iPods, iPhones, kindles, there's £100 whisky, perfume, designer clothes shops. And people are trapped here, surrounded by goods that are more than they can afford but they want to be able to afford because they're either going on holiday or half excited because they're going somewhere to escape their crap life for a while. You don't get Primark selling clothes in an airport, do you? Of course not, because that's the life they leave behind when they come in here. Everyone wants to be something they're not, wants to have things they can't afford, be someone better than they are. These shops dangle things in front of them but we're the ones who say 'you can have it'. You can be that guy." He poured himself more champagne. "I'll get you those credit limits uplifted, and those mortgages upped. Don't you forget to whisper in those ears."

Aidan stared at his phone, grateful that there was so much on them that it allowed anyone to appear busy even if they were only flicking back and forward through messages. And the image that he couldn't get out of his mind, as he looked up and watched the two guys smiling, laughing and indulging, was of puppets being twisted and danced one way and another.

The guy who had tried to sleep with one of The Capo's mistresses jogged along the front of the Promenade des Anglais as he did at six o'clock most mornings. Like most mornings, it was quiet and he met few other joggers. Like most mornings he gazed at the natural wonder of the bay as he jogged along, relishing the quiet as the rest of the world began to wake up. Unlike most mornings, however, two pairs of binoculars were trained on him as he ran along the front.

"You're sure he knew Angelique was mine?" said The Capo.

"Yeah," said Davide. "He kept at her most of the night. I think she was flattered in the first place, you know how women are, but she told him that he had to stop, and she told him of her connection to you. It didn't bother him. So we got her miked up and….well, you can hear what he's said yourself if you want, I've got the tape." The Capo shook his head. "Well, anyway, he said how he'd heard of you, thought you were a fool, didn't know how to run a business. He kept at her, trying to dance with her, touching her, trying to grab her. She managed to get to the toilet and escape."

"Do you think she liked him?"

"If you're asking me if she was innocent boss… I've seen the video and without calling for help she couldn't have done much more."

"So she's clean," said The Capo to himself, as if he were dismissing something that was at the planning stage. "This guy, I don't care what he thinks of me or what I do. People can say anything about me, who cares. But he can't touch anything of mine and expect to get away with it. Go to this guy's house tomorrow morning and take his wife and kid. I don't want them harmed but I want him to think they have been harmed. I want him to have to wait for a while so say you'll phone back in a few hours and he better be there. Then take the wife and kids to the Workshop and tell him a car will come for him. Hood him and take him to the Workshop. I want him to think his wife has come to some harm. Smear her lipstick, tear her top, her clothes. Don't touch her, but I want him to think she's been raped. I want him to know that I can take anything of his and do anything I want to it. Then take the wife and kid away and take them back home. I'll come to the Workshop and deal with him."

"Do we need any plastic?"

The Capo seemed unusually indecisive and paused for a bit. "You know Davide, you can't really blame someone for wanting a shot at Angelique. Men have died for less. But he tried to take something that was mine when he was told he couldn't have it and that deserves punishment. Maybe we'll make it so he'll never bother any woman ever again. Even his wife. Ask the Doctor to come. I think I'll leave him alone with this guy for ten or twenty minutes." The Capo continued to watch the man jogging as he began to disappear from view. 'Enjoy your jog,' he thought, 'it'll be your last for a while.'

He continued to look through the binoculars, at anything and everything that moved along the promenade, at the gentle waves of the morning ocean as they lapped onto the stones of the beach. He loved the peace of the morning. "Capo, the situation with that family problem is getting worse. They beat Henri almost to a pulp and he's in intensive care now. Jean is asking for you to take revenge, appealing to your good nature because he is one of your oldest and closest friends. What do you want to do?"

"I don't mind a war, Davide, but not over a stupid bloody woman." He paused. "Jean is right, I trust him as I would my own wife and son, but I don't believe I owe him a murder or two. It is insane that this should escalate further. But then Jean is… " The sentence hung in the air, unfinished, as though The Capo was unsure exactly what Jean meant to him or what his level of commitment might be.

The Capo put his binoculars down. "Davide, tell our friends in America that I will come next week. Start of the week. I don't want to go this week. There's this prick to deal with," he pointed outside in the general direction of where the jogger had gone, "and there are a few things I'd like to be straight about before I go to see them. I need to know they can deliver what they say they can deliver. They might just be punks who got one lucky score. Can we get them checked out? Do we still have anyone in Chicago?" Davide rocked his hand back and forward and scrunched his face up. "Ok, well do what you can. Get someone out there if you have to, to keep an eye on them. There's a lot in this for us but we don't exactly need it and they seem too keen. Maybe they do need it. Or maybe they need us, and that's what worries me more."

"Sure, it's done."

The Capo walked into the next room and noticed that last night's girl was sitting up watching television. She looked at the pile of notes beside the bed. "You know," she said, "I would have done all this for free. But since you've paid me I think I still owe you something." The Capo allowed himself to be pulled back into bed and gasped as her tongue danced around his mouth and her hand caressed between his legs.

The four friends sat on the plane, three together and Ellis in the aisle seat opposite. The first twenty minutes had passed without incident but things had gradually become a little bumpier and it clearly wasn't going away. With one particularly strong buffet, the seatbelt sign went on and the clinical sound of metal against metal was heard throughout the plane. It was a sound Ellis always hated. It sounded harmless and mechanical but hid fear and apprehension, like the cocking of a gun foretold of an impending horror. Ellis hated turbulence. He flew a great deal with business but didn't enjoy the travel experience and every inconvenience, like a delayed or cancelled plane, a busy airport or turbulence, became magnified. He looked around him as the plane began to rock and sway and made you feel as though you were on a boat, going up and down with an uneven rhythm. He felt like he was being tossed about, played with by the winds and looked for acknowledgement of the danger of this in the faces of his friends and the travellers around him. They all looked blank – they looked blankly at their books or out the window or had blank expressions on their faces with their eyes shut listening to music. Ellis tried to rationalise the situation, as he usually did, by thinking that he would never even notice this movement if he was on the ground. The movement was much greater in a car, but we didn't think about it. Except we're not in a car, something screamed inside his head, we are 35,000 feet up in the air. In this fragile piece of metal that's getting tossed about by the indifference of the winds.

The plane continued to be bombarded by winds as it struggled through clouds and lost a bit of height. Not much, but enough to make Ellis' hands grip the armrests and for a woman behind him to let out a little gasp. To make matters worse, the pilot announced that they were going through this turbulence, it would last for a few minutes, but that there was nothing to worry about. When a pilot tells you there is nothing to worry about, Ellis figured, you should worry. He felt his legs begin to shake, gently, imperceptibly and his fingertips began to tingle. He felt his heart rate quicken. Still the buffeting continued, out of control, at the mercy of the elements. It was easy to realise, he thought, how people years ago saw bad weather as a sign of the Gods' anger. Not that many of the ancient Greeks would have made it up in an aeroplane, he thought. But he couldn't make himself laugh or think of anything funny even if he had wanted to try. And he began to feel anger at the pilot, for not being able to do something about it. Surely they could climb, they could go down, they could do something to escape these conditions. He picked up his magazine and tried to appear interested but with another huge buffet he closed it and looked around him again. Ali was reading something and smiling to himself with a nonchalance that Ellis found offensive.

Ellis wondered if Ali's Christian faith got him through this without it bothering him at all. God'll save me. Ellis had been brought up in a Protestant family but his faith had waned since almost the first day he went to church and by the age of thirteen he had turned against it. Now he was non-committal, live and let live, whatever works for you, but when it came down to it, when he was in some sort of danger, he wondered if his faith would return. But all he could think of was the pilot getting them through this and of the power and indifference of nature. He thought of flight AF447 from Rio to Paris in 2009, the one that fell out of the sky because the weather was bad, and thought that the weather was simply bad because it was bad sometimes. There was no logic, no reason, no grand plan, no God to anything. It was the random indifference of nature and events. Ellis didn't really feel, even at his lowest point, that the plane was going to fall out of the sky or that anything would fall off it. But it could have happened. And the fact that he was on it, and that there was someone like Ali on it who believed in God, didn't make one bit of difference.

When Ali felt turbulence like this, he preferred to stay in his own world with his own thoughts and avoid conversation if at all possible. Of course it was a worry but for him the worry was a test. It was one of these times when God revealed his power and Ali recognised the power. It was how he reacted to it that defined who he was and his relationship with God. What does He want me to think and how does He want me to feel? And Ali thought of those much less fortunate than himself, of the starving in Africa, the drug addicted, those whose houses were swept away by floods, whose children had been kidnapped, whose loved ones had died young without any obvious reason. Those who were going through so much more agony than him. Affirmation is strength, he thought, and the strength of his belief felt like a warm blanket around him. The buffeting was God's presence, God's existence, sending him this to test him and make him stronger. He looked at his friends and Ellis across the aisle seemed edgy, his hands not relaxed, holding on too tightly. Aidan looked as though he was sleeping, probably having smoked some dodgy drug in the time he went for a walk in the airport. Euan listened to his iPod, eyes shut but fingers tapping, though they looked tight, unrelaxed fingers. Ali's faith didn't make him feel better or above anyone but at that moment he felt his friends were missing this beautiful and comforting presence that brought him relative peace and stability. Ellis, he felt, had this great chasm where fear had taken root and grown. And that was what he felt he wanted to give to his friends – not to save their souls but to give them something that would turn that chasm into something warm. Something that would take away the fear. And as the buffets continued, he smiled to himself as his self-satisfaction grew.

And as for Oliver…maybe he had run away, maybe he was in danger. But Ali had prayed that they would find him well and that dialogue had given him hope. It was one of those few times when his dialogue with God had been of the "I need you" nature. Ali spoke with God a great deal, sometimes in his own head as if he were talking to another perfected part of him but he preferred to talk out loud. It forced him to rationalise his thoughts, to prepare them for scrutiny and inspection, as though it were a test and he was in competition with others. This morning Ali had spent twenty minutes talking with God, talking about Oliver's beauty, his value, his importance to Helen and Terrence, how he enriched people's lives and how he – Ali – needed help, support and inspiration in finding this lost soul. Ali knew that God could never tell him anything, but what he knew for sure was that God was listening.

Eventually, the buffeting stopped, the seat belt sign was taken off and Ellis allowed himself to exhale slowly. He looked around his friends and the rest of the cabin for a shared sense of togetherness, a collective mopping of the brow, but was met with expressionless faces. Suddenly he felt like talking and reached across to Ali, asking him about work, Lesley, anything. The words didn't matter, all he was saying was "I'm still alive and I'm happy about it."

They checked into their hotel and agreed to shower and meet downstairs for a meal and a drink before addressing what they were going to do now they were here. As Euan got into the shower he wondered, for the first time, if they had done the right thing. Maybe, perhaps maybe, Oliver didn't want to be found. It wasn't a rational feeling but a back of the mind unease, one of those horrible thoughts that leap at us from goodness knows where and make us doubt things for reasons we can't express. Everything that was rational in him told him that this was someone very dear to him who was in trouble. It was his sister's husband, reason enough alone for him to come. But the nagging doubt was not rational, the part of his mind that feared maybe he didn't know Oliver as well as he thought. When he thought back and put a few small incidents together, that feeling grew....

Like the time when he was sure – as he still was – that Oliver had slept with one of Euan's girlfriends at the time he was engaged to Helen. It was nothing he'd found, there was no proof, it was just the way they were with each other. A smile into each other's eyes, the way her hands held him rather than rested on him when they danced together to a slow song and the way she cupped her hands around his when he lit a cigarette for her. Little things which gave strong hints of a much closer physical intimacy. Euan remembered asking him and Olly seemed genuinely offended, saying "Do you really think I'd do such a thing? To you and to Helen?" But he never answered the question and Euan thought 'That's exactly what I would have said if I'd slept with her.' Then there had been that issue Helen had had in her job, when she was being bullied and thinking of taking legal action. Olly had hardly seemed interested and Euan recalled he had spent more time with her than Olly had. Even Helen remarked how she'd expected a bit more from him. Olly seemed to feel that it had been in Helen's imagination, that by having a quiet word with her boss it would all go away and that taking legal action was a ridiculous over reaction. Yet Helen had been so affected by this; frightened to go into work in the morning, the sound of the shoe clicks of one colleague alone putting her into a state of anxiety, taking prescription drugs to help her through the day. Helen spoke at the time of how she felt almost rejected by him because he refused to validate her feelings. Then the person got a move and Helen began to feel better almost overnight.

And there was the time, too, when Euan knew that he lied about a business trip. Helen told him that Olly would be in Aberdeen overnight but Euan saw him that night at an expensive restaurant in Glasgow. Olly was clearly with another guy and two women and Euan had watched them carefully from a position where, unless Olly had turned his head around 180 degrees and lifted it up, it was very hard for him to be seen. Though they seemed like two couples, in truth they didn't behave like couples. They didn't smile very much, there was no touching that Euan could see, all their body language spoke of reservation rather than intimacy. It was as though it were a business meeting rather than a romantic meal. It was puzzling, but what Euan knew for sure was that Olly had lied to Helen and if it was only a business meeting then why would he need to lie?

"Little things," thought Euan as he went downstairs, "little things. Well," he thought, as he steeled himself for the action that he had set in motion, "even if we do discover things that Olly would rather we didn't, this is still the right thing to do. Definitely."

The friends entered the hotel's bar. Nondescript French music played throughout, loud enough to hear but not loud enough to be an annoyance. The dazzling cream carpet, embossed wallpaper and large plush seats that invited you to sink into them gave the place a very warm and inviting feel but also told you that it was going to be an expensive night. Two waiters loitered about, waiting for custom and the four friends were met with an immediate smile and asked where they wanted to sit. Though the bar was quite small they had plenty of choice as the only table taken was occupied by a single female, engrossed in her phone. Waiting for someone, Euan presumed.

The friends sat down and ordered sandwiches and beer. Their conversation didn't get very far before they heard the woman at the table close to them take a call, get angry, cut the person on the other end of the phone off and start gently sobbing. The friends looked at each other and Ali made his way across to the woman. He sat down beside her and put his arm in the direction of his friends at the other table. After initially shaking her head, the woman nodded in consent and she made her way over to the table and sat with the four friends. She looked down at the table as she continued to gently sob then looked up, giving a feeble smile.

Euan noticed right away that she was a beautiful woman. About thirty five maybe, long black hair, brown eyes which had lost some of their sharpness due to the dark circles the tears had revealed, a small mouth with full lips. A tiny delicate nose and high almost pointed cheekbones gave her a very striking appearance and Euan knew that he would remember her face for a long time, even before she told them her story.

It took her a while to tell her story – why would you tell four absolute strangers such a story after all – but on the other hand it felt very unburdening for her to talk to people who didn't know her and couldn't have had any involvement in her situation. Her name was Josette and….

"I was married to this man, Francois, for five years. He was a lovely man, at first. We knew each other at school but we didn't… I mean, he wasn't my boyfriend then. Then we finished school, we moved away to different Universities and ended up back here in Nice. We met, by accident, out with different groups of friends at a restaurant and we recognised each other. He was very beautiful, very handsome and I liked him right away. And then he got in touch and we saw each other, dated, then got engaged after maybe a year. I always thought, I always said to him was he sure it was me, was he sure I was the one….he liked going out quite a lot, I didn't, he liked doing sporty things, I didn't and I thought he was maybe…well, maybe too handsome for me. But he said 'yes, yes, I love you, you are all I want'… you know how men say such things.

Then we're married, which is great at first, and then things begin to get a little less great. Small things at first, like he doesn't kiss me in the morning when he leaves, doesn't wave and smile as he walks away up the street. Then he works longer, he goes abroad on business a bit more, he seems a bit more distant. We don't go out as much, somehow it's not so easy to get time to do these things like make the time for each other that we used to. We had a conversation or two, as people would do – do you still love me? Is there anyone else? But all the time he said no, no, things are ok. The thing is though he was always attractive to women. I knew how attractive he was, I knew how much he loved the attention of women. Did I trust him? I think yes, absolutely, until he began to give me reasons for not trusting him. The coldness, not wanting to be with me, not wanting to make love….what would you think? I try to throw myself at him and nothing happens, you feel rejected. I think I thought then, there must be someone else. So I tried to find out things – I didn't follow him but I checked his phone, I phoned his work, I phoned the places where he said he was when he was overseas on business. And all the time he was there. Maybe there was someone else there too, I don't know, but I did begin to think I was possibly wrong. But then why was he so much colder?

Then one day it happened. He disappeared. As though, for a week, he had vanished off the face of the earth. I couldn't get an answer from his mobile, his work, his family...no one. I even travelled to a couple of the places he went on business, thinking maybe something had happened to him and that he was maybe lying in a ditch, or an unclaimed body in a hospital. Nothing. It was the worst week of my life, I don't think I slept more than a handful of hours the whole week, I don't think I ate anything. I could feel my clothes begin to slip off me by the end of the week. Then, a week to the day after he disappeared, I got a letter. A short, unemotional, matter-of-fact letter which told me he had been 'beguiled' by another woman (I didn't need to know her name), was so much in love that he found it impossible to find the words to describe it, that he felt sorry for any hurt he had caused me, but basically that he was happy and it would be nice if I was happy for him. He added that it hadn't been working for a while, hoped I'd find the happiness that he's found, said he'd collect stuff when it was convenient, etc. This letter, his letter seemed like an afterthought. An obligation. It was so short and... .functional. Then I thought of all the other people who must have been in on it...his family, his work colleagues, his friends, all feigning hurt and distress, all those people combining to trick me and to make me feel stupid and pathetic. I looked at the envelope and saw the post mark was relatively local but I wasn't convinced he was living locally – if he could make that many people cover up his disappearance and keep things from me then I felt equally convinced that he could arrange for a letter to be sent from a small town up the road. I also became a bit obsessive about the other woman – who was she, what did she look like, what did she have that I didn't? And my hurt began to turn to hatred and my thoughts were full of things I would do to him if I ever saw him again."

Josette stopped and took a long drink, almost gulping it down. Ellis motioned to the barman to bring her another and it arrived before she started talking again.

"I made, looking back, a big mistake. I told my family how much I was hurt and how I would quite like to have seen both of then dead. But Francois in particular. I should have played the grieving woman spurned, rejected for a younger and prettier version. But my anger fuelled their anger. As a family, we've always been close and both my older brothers and my dad thought it was their job to protect me. This ranged from beating the shit out of a guy who tried to kiss me in the playground to setting fire to a car garage that had overcharged me for a service. It was also clear to me from quite a young age that my dad had some influential friends, people who he could rely on to help him. Once when I was young he got me tickets for a concert here – a sold out thing, sold out for months and a couple of days before I said I wanted to go and suddenly there were a couple of tickets there. He said 'Your dad knows people who can fix things,' and gave me this huge smile. I didn't really care or think about it – I was thirteen, who cares about where the ticket comes from when you're thirteen – but over the years I could see that if we wanted something we tended to get it. And many of my friends, and others, didn't. I also… I mean, my brothers…I still don't know what jobs they do today. Oh, I know what they say they do, what they tell me they do, but it's not what they really do. I don't know what they really do.

You see, the more you see about the way things are around here, the more you see that things are controlled by maybe a few people. Is it a family? Organised crime? Mafia or something like it? I don't know, these are just names, aren't they? But what I do know is that if I, say"….and she pointed at the guy at the bar…."want that guy sacked then I could probably mention it to my brother or my dad and it would happen. They know people who can fix things. They probably work for people who can fix things. And that's why what I did was wrong. Because when they saw me upset and hurting they felt my hatred and asked me if they could do anything to help and I kept saying 'I want the bastard dead. I want him to die for what he's made me feel. This worthlessness…I want the bastard dead. And I want his whore dead too.' But I wasn't only talking to my family. I was talking to my family knowing they had influence.

I guess hundreds of years ago people used to pray to the Gods, didn't they? And if it happened the Gods must have smiled upon you. Maybe they sent a strong wind or no wind, whatever. But it felt to me – and I knew it when I was saying these things to my family – that the Gods were standing right next to me. Deep down I knew they could make this thing happen and deep down I knew they were no idle words of anger. They knew people who could fix things…

A few days later my brother came round and showed me the photos, photos of François stabbed goodness knows how many times, his body covered in blood. I had never seen a photo of a dead body before, to see one of someone who had a few weeks ago been your husband shook me to my core. I trembled and all I could think of was how much I wanted him back and I'd never ever have him back. Maybe he would have tired of the whore, maybe there would have been a chance for me if I'd waited.

But now there was no chance, his mutilated body lay lifeless and abandoned. I looked through my tears to my brother: 'And the girl?' He shook his head. 'That wasn't sanctioned,' he replied. 'We could frighten her, so we did and we could threaten her, so we did.'

And you may think that was that but it wasn't. It isn't. Right now my other brother lies in a hospital, in intensive care. It turns out that the woman my husband ran away with wasn't younger at all. She was a few years older, a divorcee who had been married young, had a child young and then spilt from her husband. She has a son, about eighteen years of age who must have come home to see his new step-dad dead and his mum terrified. Turns out that he must have known people who can fix things too and he must have spoken with them because within a few days my brother had been taken at night as he left a bar near the centre of Nice, bundled into a car, driven to the outskirts and they set to work on him with a hammer. My brother is strong, very strong, but there were three of them working on him, literally hammering him. The doctor told me that he somehow managed to protect his head. Had he not done that he would have died as there were broken bones all over his body and a scale of internal bleeding that they hadn't seen before. I cannot imagine what he went through…what he went through because I said something that I should never have said to him. And now of course my other brother and my dad are plotting a fresh hell of new revenge, they are talking of killing the woman and her son, the men who battered my brother, realising that it will lead to an all-out war between….I don't know, families, organisations….

My call….the call you heard me just take….that was my dad, telling me what they are going to do to these guys…family honour, the things that people like that talk about. It's… you know," she sobbed quietly as her head bowed; "I wish I had my husband back. I should have been more thoughtful about what I prayed for."

Euan moved towards her and put his arm around her as she sobbed. He looked at the anxious faces of his friends. They all seemed to realise that something which they had thought difficult had become much, much harder. And much more dangerous.

Ambrose watched Helen through his binoculars. She stood by the upstairs window, staring out of it, with the light on. She looked worried, staring at the phone as if it held some hidden meaning or fear. She also looked irresistible and his binoculars rested on her chest and the flesh that moved invitingly at the top of her t-shirt. Then lower, down to her trousers, resting on the inviting V in between her legs. Ambrose felt himself begin to stiffen and felt that he had to do this tonight, now. He put the binoculars down and went into the kitchen, grabbing a knife. Short, very sharp, absolutely functional. He was uneasy about taking it because when you take things like that you might end up using them and he didn't want to use any weapon on her except his hands. It was only as back up, he convinced himself. He shoved it crudely down the back of his trousers, threw a jacket on over himself and started to make his way out of the flat and across the short distance to Helen's house.

Anthony moved quickly, coming out of the car from behind Ambrose's left with a clipboard and pen. He crossed the street quickly and raised his phone to his ear, pretending to have a conversation with some imagined boss about the success of his canvassing. He hastened down to a house that was three doors along from Helen's and ensured that Ambrose could hear him as he was about to push open Helen's garden gate. He glanced across at Ambrose and smiled. Ambrose had never felt as close to actually killing someone as he did then. But he looked around and realised that although it was getting dark, there were numerous windows around him and someone was bound to see. This guy wasn't worth it. He could wait, he could surely wait, maybe later tonight, maybe another night, maybe two. He paused at the gate, like someone caught in the act. He couldn't go to the house now. He looked at the gate, the number on the house and then looked around him. He caught sight of the street name and then looked at his phone, slapping himself on the head as if he had just come to the realisation that he was in the wrong street.

Helen had turned the light off when she had gone to take Terrence out of his bath. As she dried him and got him ready for bed, something had made her go back into her bedroom. And as she walked in she saw out of the window the man who she knew had her phone tapped standing at the gate, about to come in. Then he stopped and she realised that he must have seen someone or something that made him pause and turn back.

'They are coming for me,' she thought. 'Without Euan here, who can I turn to?' She watched the man walk down the street then cross the road, walk back on the other side and go into one of the flats not far away from her. Helen felt more abandoned and threatened that she had ever done in her life, as though she was waiting for something horrible to happen to her. 'No Euan here, no Oliver, only me......and Terrence.' Somehow the need to protect rather than be protected kept her mind on preservation and she locked every window and door before she lay down. She held on to Terrence till she almost squeezed the life out of him.

A few hundred metres away Anthony was content that he had deterred The Other Guy. He looked at his phone and deleted the message that he had been about to send to Helen: DON'T ANSWER THE DOOR.

CHAPTER 4

Anthony worked through the night. After preparing his plan, he prepared the table and rushed round to one of those 24-hour supermarkets to get everything he needed to make her the perfect meal. Three courses, it would be, for by about seven o'clock she would be hungry, the shock would have worn off and she would have spent long enough in her room to know how much he loved her. So he would start with something light, maybe salmon, then rack of lamb, cooked slowly so the juice flowed out of it when she ate it and then a soft light mousse. Then he would take her to bed and he imagined her smiles, falling into his arms, in a state of bliss as he made love to her. He felt a tingle go through him as he allowed himself to think of possessing her physically but it was quickly banished. Impulses got in the way of rationality and there would be time for physical desire tomorrow, for now it was a distraction.

Helen worked at a University and Anthony knew, generally, which mornings she went there and which she preferred to work at home on. He guessed – correctly – that having a child meant that her employer gave her some flexibility over her hours and he also guessed – correctly – that she spent quite a bit of her time working from home. What Anthony didn't have to guess about was the amount of time Helen spent at her computer in the study: he knew she was there for quite a bit of time on most days, even at the weekends. Anthony also knew that her subject area was engineering, though quite what her particular specialism was he remained unsure of. It did seem a bit discordant when he first found this out and he never quite reconciled how such a woman as Helen could be interested in something as mechanical as engineering.

Helen took Terrence to school then took herself to work. Anthony did allow himself to think, as she left Terrence, that this was the last time she would see him and he felt a slight twinge at this. However, he quickly reasoned, Terrence was in the way, he wasn't important and Helen had to be saved, there was so much danger around her. Anyway, Helen had parents, they would be able to look after him. Helen belonged to Anthony. Not to her son or to a disgrace of a husband who had deserted her. She belongs to me.

Anthony reached the University car park and was met, as he knew he would be, by a barrier. But Anthony was not a man who had left much to chance and he gave the name of two of Helen's colleagues, saying he was working with them on a research project, and he was allowed to enter immediately. He shook his head as he smiled to himself. These people, they think they are putting measures in place to make people secure and safe but you can drive a truck through their pathetic systems. If someone was important to me I'd have much more in place than this, and he thought of the locks on the door and the many small almost imperceptible cameras he had in Helen's room and around the house. Even in the bathroom. Somehow the idea of seeing Helen in the bathroom, when people think they are alone and in the most private place, shot desire right through him.

He had to be careful with his choice of parking space. He was going to lead Helen out with a gun at her heart so anywhere too near to the main entrance was public, maybe too public. But the walk to the car was dangerous, it was the only conceivable time that she could escape him. In the car the doors would be locked and she could not open them from the inside. She would be strapped in to her seat but even if she escaped the strapping there would be a barrier of unbreakable glass between her and him. He expected, at first, that she might prove difficult, she may even want to escape so he had to be prepared for that and make sure she didn't go anywhere. There was something appealing about seeing her despairing, shouting, screaming.

Anthony found a suitable spot near the side entrance to the building where previous observation had revealed that fewer people tended to go in and out. He knew Helen had no class today and he knew that she had her own room but he could not see her room from the outside and gave her five to ten minutes to settle herself in before he decided to go after her. "Our destinies, combined destinies," he felt as he checked his appearance and rammed his gun down into the top of his trousers. He stood up and got out the car to check his appearance in the mirror but Anthony wore quite loose baggy clothes and there was no sign of the concealed weapon from his outward appearance.

Helen had entered the building and was met by Jenny, a rather flustered and harassed Jenny, almost as soon as she'd set foot inside. Jenny was quite flustered at the best of times and prone to over-dramatisation and as Helen watched her face redden and her words quicken she realised she didn't have a clue what Jenny was saying.

"Woah, slow down, slow down…"

"Oh sorry, Helen…." she stopped to catch her breath. "Like I said, my computer is broken – they think it's a problem with the hard drive – but it's not going to be fixed until at least this afternoon or maybe tomorrow. I need to get that… I must get that….research update in, you know the one I got funding for. It's about a week late as it is and I'm going to get my backside kicked, I know. But I need to use a computer and I need one with access to the departmental drive – can I borrow yours?"

"Oh, is that all?" sighed Helen, thinking of her own waking hell of a lost husband and being under observation everywhere she turned. "Of course. Anyway, I've got a class this morning – I told Harry I would take his class this morning, he's got a hospital appointment. So the room is free, no problem."

Helen had thought she should at least appear interested. She didn't really like Jenny very much and tended to feel quite guilty that she didn't because Jenny was the sort of person who would have done anything for anyone. Yet Helen found her a bit too animated, a bit too bouncy when she was happy, a bit too flappy when she was in a panic, a bit too open when she was down about something. They should have probably been good friends – they were a similar age, had broadly similar interests and had a similar sense of humour. They looked quite alike too, from the back. Jenny had a build very much in Helen's mould though was maybe an inch shorter, and had the same sort of golden hair. But even by her own admission, Jenny wasn't beautiful. Whereas Helen's features were sharp, striking and unforgettable, Jenny's face was round, fat and a little too rosy.

"So what's the project about again? I know you've told me before but I'm afraid I forgot."

However, this time it was Jenny who wasn't listening. She thought of all the things she needed to take to Helen's room – memory stick, research folders, those two books, anything else…broadly aware that Helen had asked her a question, she said: "Oh, it's that stuff for the Scottish government."

Helen remembered that the department had been awarded a research contract by the Scottish government, something to do with oil, and she recalled too that those involved had to sign Secrets Acts to not reveal anything about the research. However, the government had awarded the department two or three contract recently and Helen mistook Jenny's airy response for secrecy. Jenny was working on a relatively simple traffic management contract which had no secrecy attached to it at all.

"Ok, well, I'll go to my room now, get my stuff for the class and wait for you there. I'll give you the key then. You'll be there in two hours when I get back?"

"Oh yes, sure, of course," said Jenny. "I may be longer than two hours, is that ok?" and she made a scrunched up face of apology.

"Yes, no problem. It's ok."

Anthony entered the building after a short wait. He had walked in this building before, several times, but never with the finality that he strode into it today. He strode confidently and with purpose, with his head held high and the hint of a smile on his face. He took the lift up to the 2nd floor, Helen's floor. He glanced at his watch. Five past 9. Maybe give things another five minutes. Just to let the crowds die down. So he pushed the button for the 4th floor and walked about. Anthony had a brown folder in his hand so wasn't worried about being seen or discovered – someone with a folder or paper in their hand always looks busy, looks as if they are going somewhere.

He paced around, avoiding the gaze of anyone who came near him. He had tried to dress as anonymously as he could so had put on clothes that he thought would merge into a student background....faded jeans, a black jacket, training shoes. The only thing that might have told you Anthony wasn't entirely comfortable was the beads of sweat that started to trickle down the sides of his head. He got back in the lift to go to the 2nd floor. "This is normal," he told himself. "Perfectly normal. Of course you must get nervous about this, when taking her back and making her mine is so close. If there were no nerves there would be something wrong. It's normal." And he tried to push his mind to think of Helen and him together that night, enjoying the meal then later enjoying the physical union.

But as he got out on the 2nd floor he had to pause to catch his breath. His stomach somersaulted and the place felt suddenly very hot. He couldn't take off his jacket but he quickly realised how odd he was now going to look if anyone saw him. It was so hot and this guy still had his jacket on. He walked along the corridor, as he had done many times before, to Helen's room, but his steps were slow and leaden, heavy and full of anxiety. And he suddenly felt his scheme was mad, he'd never manage to take her out with a gun held to her, it was a crazy idea, she would scream the place down. His legs began to shake and tremble as he forced one in front of the other. By now the sweat was dripping off his head. But for every instinct telling him "NO!" there was also a voice saying "if you don't do this now, then when, this is perfect, it's been planned to perfection, the idea is perfect and she is perfect, this is the thing that turns your life around and you get to own the thing that you want."

He came to Helen's door and it was very slightly ajar, as it usually was. He could tell she was alone, sitting at the computer with her back to the door, facing the window as she had been so many times before. 'This is how you imagined it,' he said to himself, 'this cannot be better.' The corridor was quiet and he stood outside for a minute, trying to gather his thoughts and calm his mind. But he felt his heart race and his stomach felt like bursting with the pressure of the gun against it. 'I've never even used a gun,' he thought, 'I don't know how to. And you won't need to,' came another voice, 'get in there with the gun and lead her out and live the rest of your life. Think of her, every night, on top of her, fucking her, that beauty owned and possessed by you.'

Anthony stood at the door and saw his cold, sweaty, clammy hand tremble as it went forwards to grasp the handle. His body shook. Sweat continued to drip and he felt his clothes begin to stick to him. The door pushed silently open. The figure in front of him did not move. Anthony knew he had to move forward quickly, he couldn't give her time to do anything. So he knew his next step was the be-all. Now was his last chance to set his foot back, to step back into the corridor and accept that this was too much for him.

With a lunge he moved forward into the room and realised something was wrong when it was too late to do anything about it. As he lunged and ran at what he thought was Helen he saw that her back was shaped slightly differently, the arch of her shoulders was much more of a slouch, the hair was very slightly darker than golden and it was an inch or so shorter. But these thoughts came to Anthony in the blink of his eye and by that stage he was standing beside a girl, his gun in hand, as she stood up and started to look behind her. He saw her face take on a look of horror, as his did when he saw that this was not Helen. She must have shrieked, he figured, she must have shouted but he could hear nothing because all he could think about was Helen. She must have known he was after her, she must have planned this somehow. And in his horror he must have heard Jenny shriek. "Silence the bitch, silence the bitch now!" And he drew his arm back to his chest and hammered the side of the gun across the side of Jenny's face. Jenny slumped, making a thud as her body crumpled when it fell to the floor. He saw blood gently trickle from some part of her head but would look on her no further.

Anthony looked around him, realising very quickly that all he had touched was the door handle. He listened for voices outside and heard nothing, only the gentle humming of the electrics that you get in big buildings. He stuffed the gun inside his trousers and went quickly to the door, wiping the handle with his shirt. Then he began his retreat. His immediate thought was that he had killed the girl and that now he must get out of here undetected. Stairs, not the lift. Not many people used the stairs, they were a bit out of the way. He knew he must not be seen by anyone as he felt sweat drip from him. Would they find that? Sweat? Could they get your DNA off that even if it had dried on the floor? He kept his head down and walked as briskly as he could without running...
.get to the end of the corridor, turn right, go along, some people there, cough a bit and they won't see you, won't think anything of it, people cough all the time, get to the stairs and now safe. He ran down the stairs and walked out of the building's main exit. It was always busy, so many people milling around, no one would notice one guy. And he got to his car then quickly sped out of the car park, the slight screech of the wheels going too quickly round a corner picked up by Helen in her classroom with the window open. As her class did an exercise, she watched the blue car hurry out of the university and smiled to herself as she thought: "yeah, sometimes I'm in that much of a hurry to get out the place too."

As he travelled away from Helen, Anthony tried to understand what had happened. How could she have known? He never doubted, not for an instant, that she had known and had made a plan to be elsewhere. And she must have put a double in the room deliberately too, knowing that this other girl was likely to be taken instead of her. Helen must be very cunning, very devious, very cruel to have set another girl up to be kidnapped. He tried to figure out how she knew and when she knew – had she been watching him when he was unaware? He tried to think of all the things he had done at home, such as covering the walls with her pictures, setting up the cameras all over the house, buying clothes for her, spending all the money on the underwear he wanted to see her in... could she have seen him doing these things? Could she have been following him and now had him trapped?

Anthony's first instinct was that he had had a lucky escape and should forget about Helen. She had beat him at his own game, she was better at it than him. But he couldn't forget about her. The need for her was obsessional, the desire for her absolute. It dominated everything he thought and everything he did. He couldn't imagine anyone else taking her place. Maybe he had to lie low for a bit, maybe that girl was dead, maybe he had to stay away from his house for a day or two because they would look for him, but as he drove on and on towards nowhere in particular, he became more resolute than ever that he must have Helen.

Helen's class finished and she decided to give Jenny a bit more undisturbed time and went for a cup of tea. Her mind inevitably went to Oliver. She had heard nothing from Euan as yet and asked herself what she genuinely expected – was it really believable that Euan would have gone across to Nice and found Oliver within a few hours? Oliver may be nowhere near Nice anyway. She stopped herself crying but the fear of where he was, what had happened, and her life without him consumed her again. "At least we are doing something," she thought to herself, "and with the guys who are there, surely they will find him or find out something about him." And she tried to let optimism banish her worry.

When she reached her room the door was closed but not locked and when she opened it she couldn't see Jenny. 'Odd that she would go out without locking the door,' thought Helen. As she went into the room, carrying her materials, she dropped her memory stick and as she bent down to pick it up saw what looked like blood on the floor across by the chair. She went quickly to it and saw Jenny's huddled mess of a body, lying lifelessly with a little dried blood on the side of head. She screamed, an involuntary shriek of anguish at the state of her colleague.

"Jesus Christ, Jenny, Jenny!" Helen shouted as she slapped Jenny's face. In a still, small moment of calm amidst the nightmare around her, she instinctively tried to take Helen's pulse. Though no medic, Helen was sure that she felt blood flow through Jenny's wrist and she watched closely as Jenny's chest gently raised and lowered. 'She's alive, she's alive!' thought Helen and immediately dialled 9-9-9.

As she waited for the police and ambulance to arrive she looked at Jenny, trying to figure out what had happened. All her clothes were on so she hadn't been raped. Her purse was still on the desk and Helen opened it, noticing that there were credit cards, bank cards and about £25 in cash there. It hadn't been a robbery. Helen then wondered if any of Jenny's work was missing. There were books on the table, a memory stick in the machine but of course there was no way of Helen knowing if that was all the material that Jenny had brought to the room. She quickly concluded that it had to be something to do with work. Whatever had happened to Jenny, it was quite obvious that she had taken a blow to the head. Helen couldn't see any other marks. But the blow was a significant one, clearly delivered with a weapon of some sort to cause the mess that it had made to Jenny's head. Who delivers such an injury? And did they hope that she was actually dead? Or did they not care? Helen thought suddenly about the conversation she had with Jenny earlier… the research was about oil, it was secret, maybe it was something that someone was willing to do anything to get information about.

As the ambulance took Jenny away Helen went with her and the police to the hospital. She became more and more convinced that someone had tried to kill Jenny because of the work she was doing. And quick as a flash she thought of Oliver and the man who was tapping her phone and realised that her entire existence, whether at work or home, was surrounded by dangers and threat. She felt consumed and frightened, as though the entire world was in a state of perpetual night.

The four friends reconvened back at the hotel at 11.30 in the morning and compared their findings. Between them, they had very little. The police knew nothing about where he might be, they had taken a call about it from a woman in Scotland a few days ago. He was now on their missing persons list and they were actively trying to find him. The people at Oliver's work, the place where Oliver should have been working in these days, likewise knew nothing of his disappearance and had gone round to the flat where he was staying. No response. They added, however, that the cleaning lady had been round in the last two days, tidied the flat and had noticed nothing amiss. No dead bodies lying on the floor, nobody hiding in a cupboard anywhere. Aidan did learn that Oliver appeared to have gone to a corporate night out in Monte Carlo a few days ago and this seemed to have been the last time anyone saw him. He had been the company's sole representative as the boss of the office in Nice couldn't go. He'd gone with a supplier who said they'd no idea what happened to him. Aidan concluded that the search must therefore move to Monte Carlo and a hotel called The Hermitage. Ellis had been round the hospitals in Nice and not one had any admissions of any British citizens below the age of 70 and none recognised Oliver's picture. Euan had even gone around some of the major hotels with Oliver's photo, asking if a man who looked like this had checked in. He wasn't always sure he was being told the truth but no one came back with any positive identification. The search seemed to be leading to a puzzling and premature dead end, with Monte Carlo being the only conceivable lead.

"Then we shall go there this afternoon," said Euan. "Maybe he's there, maybe a crash coming back at night…", he let his thoughts flow out as they came to him…"maybe he started to feel ill, checked himself into a hospital…I mean it's credible, right?"

His friends nodded, thoughtful. Ellis said "I know we went to his work, and they're as puzzled as we are, but have any of you heard him talk of anyone else down here?"

"You mean colleagues?" Ali looked puzzled.

"I mean anyone. Colleagues or acquaintances or friends or people he met in a bar or people he did business with. He's been here before, a few times, I remember him talking about it to me last year, I think…and the infernal time it takes him to get here and back because of the train journey."

"Ah yeah of course," said Aidan, "I just learned that he can't fly."

"You didn't know that?" asked Ellis. "It was because he got stuck in that bloody wooden horse when he was young."

"Yeah, yeah, I know now."

"Does anyone remember him talking about anyone? I know it's clutching at straws but anything that can give us some lead."

"We might be better going to Monte Carlo," said Euan. "I think that's our strongest lead for now."

"It is, that's true," said Ellis. "But we're in Nice now. If there's anything else we can do here we should do it."

There was a brief pause. Ali said: "I remember him talking to me about football down here, saying some guy in the office here could get me a ticket for almost any game you'd want to see in the south of France. I think his name was… Pierre I think….but then he was in the office, wasn't he, and you'd have spoken to him anyway. Did he talk to any of you about what he did down here? Who he dealt with? Agents? Customers? I remember him talking a bit about getting a deal or something but it's not easy down here…."

"Ah yeah, I remember that….Clotilde! I remember that name, it's an unusual name. I remember him talking about a woman called Clotilde that he did business with…she was difficult but he thought he had her measure…tricky negotiator…good at her job…pretty, I remember him saying…Clotilde….God, unusual surname too…" and Euan looked around his friends for support and affirmation.

"Clotilde!" said Aidan. "That's the name of the supplier, I'm sure. That's who he went to Monte Carlo with."

"Oh Christ yes," said Ellis. "Clotilde, yes, I remember her. He called her "the posh totty" didn't he, she had this unusual surname...'de' something....Clotilde de Banso, Bansette or something. Do you remember?"

"Yeah, yeah," said Ali, agitated and excited, "I think it was de Bresseau, something like that.."

"That's it! That's her, that's her name," exclaimed Euan. "There can't be too many Clotilde de Bresseaus here!"

"But the office said she knows nothing," said Aidan.

"Oh you're probably right," said Ellis, "probably right....but let's at least try to find her. She may know something. And she's been the last one to see him. She's worth a shot, isn't she?"

The search in the telephone book revealed three de Bresseaus but only one beginning with a "C".

"She might be married though, maybe it's her husband's initial we should be looking for. Does anyone remember if this woman is married? Did he say? Think!"

"I can't remember," said Ali. "I don't think he said. But if you ask me what my thoughts are, thinking back to the little I heard of her, instinctively I would have said that she wasn't. But who knows?"

"Well let's try the "C" first. There are only another two de Bresseaus. We could try them if we have no joy then leave for Monte Carlo tonight if that returns a dead end. Agreed?" Euan looked around him and saw a general nodding and silence, which he took for consent.

"Ok, this rue Cassini, where is that? Aidan, can you ask that guy at the bar?"

Aidan returned quickly. "He says it's near the port."

Ambrose decided that the best thing might be if he stayed away from the rented flat opposite Helen. Maybe only for a couple of days, until suspicion passed. He didn't think the girl would go to the police but she might and she certainly wasn't so drunk that she wouldn't remember where she had been. It wasn't that his need for Helen had dissipated as he had kind of hoped it might – indeed, it was probably stronger as the substitute seemed unsatisfying and inadequate – but he was apprehensive of police involvement, being caught, even being put away. Then he would never get Helen.

The inability to get anywhere near Helen the previous night had left him with a sense of frustration and anger so intense that he knew it demanded release. Had he been keen on drinking to excess he would have got drunk but Ambrose was rarely drunk and so the force of his feeling had to be unleashed in some other way. He needed a woman. The need to force himself onto another and to dominate her took control of him. If she consented, that was fine, though he would probably prefer it if she didn't. He thought of picking up a prostitute, someone in as much need as he was but for a different reason, someone who'd let him do exactly what he wanted. But Ambrose felt hatred at that moment. Hatred for Helen in particular but the feeling was easy to generalise and he wanted to do something to someone who didn't really want it done to them. He wanted resistance, he wanted to use force, he thought of using his strength, of hitting, of forcing his way into a girl who screamed at him to stop as he did it.

Where could he find such a girl? Ambrose was not inexperienced in picking up a woman for a night. He knew a few clubs, a few pubs and he also knew how to be appealing and attractive. He could fake it quite well. He tried a couple of pubs without any joy but the third one seemed to hold more possibilities. Like the others, it was quiet but he saw two women together in this one. This was hopeful. He looked across, smiled, looked away, smiled again and a quiet understanding seemed to develop. If they were not at all interested they would probably have got up and left, he reasoned, and so he did what he usually did in such situations – find out what they were drinking and send a drink across. If they didn't ask him over then he knew he had to move on. But after sending the barman over to them with a bottle of Pinot Grigio, and a decent tip for his help and advice, Ambrose was beckoned over with a smile.

His immediate concern was that they might think he was looking for some liaison with both of them. Ambrose had never experienced this in his life and was not at all interested. He could have been overpowered by what they wanted to do. The two women sitting opposite him could easily be termed The Pretty One and The Not So Pretty One. She wasn't ugly as such, he thought, but she was clearly in the shadow of her friend. The Pretty One was blond in a gentle sense, with a long thin white neck and little make up. She looked like she didn't have to try very hard and she knew it. The Not So Pretty One had dark tousled hair, wavy in places. Some people might have thought it looked attractive – that sort of "just been slept with" look, figured Ambrose – though he personally thought it looked as though it needed a good brush. Her face was quite square and featureless and Ambrose thought that it should have been put on a diet, especially given that the rest of her was shaped quite well. He looked at the things that people in his situation, at that time, in that place, would look at – surreptitious glances at their breasts, at their eyes and how often they made eye contact, faces, hands, how often they smiled, the way they inclined their heads, body language, did the hands go up in front of their face, were there any barriers being put up? But he also looked at their arms, did they look strong, would they be able to resist him? They found extra strength when they were under threat and Ambrose didn't want someone who looked strong to begin with. But they both passed that test as they were both quite petite, relatively thin and both wore reasonably tight fitting tops the outlines of which showed straight "up and down" arms, as Ambrose called them. That meant that the top part of the arm was as thin as the bottom part below the elbow.

Ambrose immediately decided that The Not So Pretty One was the one that he wanted because he figured that she would be easier to capture. In this type of situation, he thought, The Pretty One must have got most of the attention which would have, in some way, pissed off her Not So Pretty pal. How grateful would she feel if it was her getting the attention, he thought. Ambrose didn't care about the woman that he got that night. He couldn't have Helen so it really didn't matter if the woman he did have was pretty, ugly, fat, thin, blond, brunette, etc. It mattered that she wasn't strong. And the easier the better. So he made sure she was the one he was sitting beside, she was the one who he touched, at times ever so gently, almost gliding his hand across her arm as they shared a common understanding. She was the one who he looked at the most, who he smiled and laughed with the most. Maybe an hour of this, he thought, an hour of listening to her work and her life, and nodding and smiling, another hour of this and we should be ok, we should be there.

About an hour later The Pretty One got up to go the toilet and Ambrose looked into the eyes of The Not So Pretty One and said: "Jackie, I think you're great. I'd like us to get to know each other a little better. Could we take Linda home then maybe go back to mine? There's a nice bottle of champagne there, it's been on ice for a while…"

Jackie smiled, as though he had given voice to a thought that she had been unsure how best to articulate. "Sure," she said. "That would be great." And that's what they did. The girls spent some time whispering together, away from the table, but Ambrose could see Linda almost congratulating her friend and Jackie's almost constant beaming smile.

71

Ambrose looked at Jackie and for the first time since he had been in this pub with the girls he began to feel himself about to lose the façade of control. He could feel his hands tearing at those trousers, ripping that top off her, guzzling at her breasts, forcing his tongue into her mouth, shoving his crude fingers inside her…

"Shall we go?" Linda brought him back to the here and now. 'Just another half hour he thought. Control, for another half hour.'

When they got to the flat Ambrose sensed she was hesitant. Perhaps the reality of this was beginning to make her anxious. 'Good,' he thought and sat her down in the living room as he went to lock the door. He checked all the curtains were drawn but also ensured that all the windows were shut. He wondered when he would do it. He had promised her champagne and whilst she had clearly had a drink she was not drunk. She didn't have to be drunk but some general fuzziness would be a good idea.

"Here we are," he said, handing her a champagne glass and sipping at one himself. He watched her chattering and wittering in her nervousness. He didn't listen but smiled in acknowledgement, watching the glass and what she had drunk. Maybe a glass and a half he thought…champagne can have quite a quick effect. When he refilled her glass he stood behind her as she sat down and massaged her shoulders. She closed her eyes and let his hands work their way into her flesh. It was a sure and firm touch, relaxing yet stimulating, calming and arousing at the same time. His hands moved in broader circles, wider than her neck and shoulders, down the front of her top, near the top of her breasts, then stopped and moved towards her back, then back again down to the front of her breasts, under her bra and she almost lay back, willing him to continue.

Ambrose went round to face her and raised the champagne glass to her lips and she drank as instructed. He kissed her, gently at first, till he felt her move her body towards him and into him and then he became quicker and pushed his tongue into her mouth. She gasped, but it was a gasp full of the pleasure of surprise, not of fear. She opened her mouth wider and let her tongue dance around his as it thrust harder. He pulled her top over her head and shoved her bra down, kneeding roughly at her chest and again she gasped a sigh that he knew was one of anticipation. His hands fumbled with the button on her trousers and then the zip before he ripped the trousers off, taking his body away from her to use both his hands. He quickly kissed her again lest she see the mixture of anger, excitement and obsession that was clear in his wild eyes. Then his hands pulled at and ripped her underwear and he felt her sigh for the first time to be one of concern and hesitancy. 'At last,' he thought, and really set to work.

With her underwear off his hands thrust inside her and she tried to move away. But up to this point she had been very excited and his fingers moved easily within the moist flesh they surrounded. He quickly took off his own trousers and began to force himself on top of her. The taste of champagne in his mouth already felt stale to her.

"No," she said. "Not like this, not like this, please."

"Exactly like this," he said, and drew his free right hand back before slapping her across the face. "Exactly….like…fucking…this," he repeated as he began to thrust inside her. Her gasps were now cries as he threw himself inside her completely.

Her face contorted in the humiliation of what was happening to her and she tried to move, gently at first with a wriggle then more forcibly, to try and escape and push him off. Ambrose hit her again, not caring this time if his hand was open or shut, and he saw blood flow from her nose. He moved inside her more quickly and wanted her to resist. The feeling of domination and release when he hit her was a beautiful and soothing one and he battered her again as she tried to move her legs and twist him out of her. As he thrust again, with more force, he saw her breasts jiggle and move and he instinctively bit at one around the nipple. She cried and hit at him and he let go a volley of punches into her face and abdomen.

Finally he released himself into her and immediately felt dissatisfied. Suddenly what he lay on top of was a Not So Pretty girl who wasn't Helen and who he now had to get rid of somehow. As he looked at her underneath him, sobbing now, he hit her again for the anger and emptiness inside him. For the first time he felt a bit in danger. 'She knows where I stay,' he thought and as he looked at her he realised that he had made a mess of her. She was bleeding, already red and swelling in places. He felt no guilt or pity, only anger and a bit of anxiety now that she might go to the police. He must make sure that didn't happen. He looked in her face and she tried to turn her head away from him, still attempting to push him off. He grabbed her chin with his right hand, his fingers drilling their way into her skin and held her head firm while he spoke.

"Look at me. Open your eyes and look at me." She did as she instructed. "Now listen to me. You tell anyone about what really happened here tonight and I will kill you. Do you doubt that I would do this?" Jackie shook her head but said nothing. "I'm going to take you away in the car. You'll lie down in the back seat and won't raise your head till I tell you. I'll leave you somewhere and you'll find your own way home. Nod if you understand." Jackie duly nodded. "Now get your fucking clothes on before I want to do it again."

He watched her as she moved gingerly, redressing herself. He walked with her to the toilet as she got some paper to catch the blood as it ran from her nose. "You try anything, you try to run away here or try anything against me, I'll batter you to within an inch of your life." Again, she nodded in consent. Trying anything against him was the furthest thing from Jackie's mind. She simply wanted to make it through the night alive.

He did as he said he would, leaving her somewhere a few miles away from his house, and far enough that she would not be able to retrace the route. But of course she had gone with him in the car to the flat originally and, even though she was distracted and laughing with him at the time, he still felt sure that she would have had a good idea where she was. So maybe he should lie low for a couple of days. Helen wouldn't be going anywhere, would she? Stay away for a couple of days, maybe in a hotel across in Fife, down the borders, somewhere. He thought back to Jackie and how unsatisfied it had made him – indeed, the only bit that had really excited him was the effect it had had on her when he slapped and punched her. That and, of course, the feeling of pushing himself inside her as her increasingly desperate arms and fingers tried to repel him off. And he smiled as he thought of Helen's arms and fingers doing the same, even hitting at him and striking him, as he relentlessly violated her.

The two men watching Helen for The Capo took a call from Davide.

"Any update? What's going on with this woman? Any sign of her husband yet?"

"No," said the most senior one. "The oddest thing is that she hasn't used her phone. Her landline I mean. We've got a tap on it and she's not used it at all. Not for a day or two anyway. If it was you in that situation, wouldn't you be phoning friends, phoning anyone to try and find out where he was? Apart from two nuisance calls, she's not received any calls either."

"Maybe she's using her mobile, do you have a trace on that?"

"No, not yet. We don't see her on her mobile much at all either. It's like she... almost isn't interested, doesn't care."

"Any visitors?"

"No, but……"

"But?"

"Well," said the most senior one, "there are things happening that are a little odd. They're maybe nothing. But one guy, a round faced guy, he stays a few flats along, we saw him make to go to her door last night then he stopped and made as though he had made a mistake. We've seen him stand opposite the house and stare at her. It's been quite blatant."

"Who is he? Maybe he's connected to her husband and is keeping an eye on her, to make sure she's ok?"

"That's possible. And then there's another guy, quite an odd looking guy, who seems to be about the street a lot. He doesn't live here. He wears different clothes, I've seen him dressed as a postie and we spotted him looking through binoculars trained on the woman's house."

Davide thought for a minute. "Do the two guys acknowledge each other? Have you seen them together?"

"No, they've never spoken as far as we can see."

"Then I think they are probably working together. They have probably both been activated by the husband. They are probably both operational. They may not really be that aware of each other. The husband…….he must be significant if he can call on two guys to guard his wife. But we need to know what the husband is saying to her, how they are communicating. You need to get a tap on that mobile."

"Ok, we can do that. I think she goes to work… we haven't followed her when she's gone to work, as you requested, but we can do that….we'd have to distract her, take her phone for an hour or so."

"Yeah," said Davide, "we might need to find out what they're saying to each other. She could easily be talking with him at work but I appreciate it might be harder for you to get a tap on that. I thought this guy Oliver was a two-bit, someone who hit a guy he shouldn't have, and he'd be home within a few days. But maybe there's more to this… more to him….than I first thought. He's clever and he's powerful, that much is clear."

"There's something else Davide……" the senior one paused, not sure of the overall significance of what he'd seen. "This afternoon she came back in a police car. She'd gone out, we assume to work, as normal. But then she came back a couple of hours or so later, without the boy, in a police car."

"In a police car? What's that about? Was it to do with the boy?"

"No, I can't think it was because the grandparents brought the boy round a bit later. He looked fine. And they looked…well, it looked as though they were comforting her. They stayed in the house for a good half hour, she made them tea. She looked quite worried. We thought maybe she'd reported him as a missing person and….or maybe she saw an accident…"

"No, I can't see the police bringing her back from that. Possible, but unlikely." He thought for a minute. "Unless he's asked her to do it… .unless he knows we're watching her…maybe he asked her to do something or say something to the police, to make sure they brought her back in a police car, to make sure that we saw it. Maybe it was all for us, maybe to try and scare us off, make us think the police are looking for the two of you." Davide stopped and sighed, a quick sigh of frustration. "This is becoming a pain. I'm all for you taking this woman and finding out what she knows but Capo isn't keen on that. He doesn't want her touched just now unless we're going to kill her. But I'll try and work on him a bit. I think we're dealing with someone who is more of a threat than we first thought, who is much more clever than we first thought, and we need to find out what this bloody woman knows. And where is her bastard husband? Why can't we find this guy?"

"You've had no joy then?"

"No," Davide almost shouted in frustration. "We know his friends are here, we found what hotel they are staying in, but it's clear that they know nothing just now. They're like four guys on a wild goose chase."

"How is Capo about all this? Is he upset we haven't found the guy?"

"Oh he doesn't care that much about it, which is good for us. He's doing a favour for Paul…who isn't worth the favour, I can assure you. He's a jumped up, self-important twat. He's like one of those little yappy dogs, yap yap yap, but there's no substance there. Shout "boo" at him and he'd run away. Capo's only doing him a favour because he laid on some special hospitality. So Capo's not so bothered. But you know what he's like, he might suddenly become bothered and we need to have answers."

"It feels like we don't have many answers right now."

"Yeah, I know, I know… ," and Davide sighed again, not with frustration this time but with the resignation of someone who was being forced to do something he didn't want to do. "Let's stick to it. Try to get this woman's mobile and get a tap on it. Don't touch her though – not yet anyway. And watch those two guys closely because they're feeding back to this Oliver, I'm sure of it. If you can find out any more about them, great, but don't touch them either. We don't want them to know we're watching them." As an afterthought, he asked: "What's she like anyway, this woman?"

"She's lovely," said the most senior one, his voice softening as he smiled. "She's very beautiful. Gorgeous face, figure that makes you glad you're a man. Henni and I have to fight to take turns to watch her."

Davide smiled to himself. "Well, you never know your luck. If we do get to take her, you might get a shot at her before you have to kill her."

CHAPTER 5

At times, Oliver's looks were so distinctive that you might have thought him a film star or a male model. It wasn't that he looked like anyone in particular, but he could appear so attractive that people often thought he was "someone famous". His dark complexion, black hair, soft warm smile, glinting eyes and slim build gave him the look of a Heathcliff you could take home to meet your mother….that's if you trusted your mother not to want to steal him away. Added to that he was open, funny, engaging, vulnerable, with that little degree of self-confidence that could never be mistaken for arrogance. He had soft small hands that he used to caress the air when he spoke and a wonderful deep but quiet voice. He wasn't tall and this seemed to emphasise everything that was remarkable about his other characteristics.

Oliver had known from an early age that he was very attractive to females, and known from a slightly older age how attractive he was to males too. But it was only females that had interested him and, as a single man, he behaved very much like a confirmed heterosexual man would behave. Since school, though, there had always been Helen. Somewhere, always Helen. He probably knew he would marry her from about a month into their relationship. But they were both too desirable to not want to be distracted and to not experience the brief sparkle that they might feel with others. Yet they always came back, after arguments or dalliances or chance encounters, to each other. Always.

He thought about Helen now, as he lay on the bed, fully clothed, wishing he could phone her or do something to let her know where he was. Maybe not that he was ok, for he was very far from being ok, but that he was at least alive. What would she be thinking? She would surely think he had died or been involved in an accident. And he thought of Terrence and how he missed his son's boyishness, wanting to play tig or hide and seek or kick a ball. He heard his son's laugh, saw his blond curly locks, his smile…

The bedroom he lay in looked as far away from being a prison as you might imagine. The doors opened out on to a little veranda where you could sit, have a drink or a meal, and watch the world go by on the bustling Rue Cassini below. The room was sparkling and clinical white, clean and pristine, with framed pastel drawings of people, faces and places spotted around the walls, clearly things that had been drawn by the person who lived here or by someone close to them. Oliver knew next to nothing about art but these were careful, well-structured and well-proportioned drawings, full of beautiful people with expressions which told of their humanity on their faces. There were also framed photographs, mostly of friends, groups together, one framed and signed photograph of a film star and above the bed a painting of a view out of a bedroom window which swept down across lush green grass to a twinkling azure ocean. It was the kind of view you would wake up to in your wildest dream. Oliver concluded that it sort of went with the room, which was beautiful and homely, probably professionally designed and yet personal.

The bedroom door opened and Clotilde stood in the doorway, smiling. She had the longest dark hair and soft beautiful red lips that never lost their moist feel, not even in the winter when everyone else's seemed to crack. She had a wide mouth which seemed to stretch ear to ear when she smiled and made it look as though she was smiling with her whole face. Her skin was soft and deep, a full brown colour, absolutely unblemished. She smiled at Oliver and held a plastic bag up. She shook it gently and Oliver could see the logo of a big expensive department store on it. She held her index finger up to him, telling him to wait a minute as she went into the bathroom.

Oliver began to tremble inside. An inner panic, an almost, by now, Pavlovian response to Clotilde's knowing smiles. It was going to happen again. He had begun to tell himself it was rape. It was against his will. It was a violation. He had pleaded with her not to do it. What else could that be if not rape? But still she penetrated everything about him. And he knew he couldn't stop her. So where could the mind go except to try and rationalise? Pretend she is Helen. Close your eyes, tight, tight and pretend she is Helen. But she was not Helen. Helen's sensuality was subtle, betrayed by a sway of the hips. Clotilde slapped it in your face. Her sexuality attacked and butchered him.

When she reappeared Oliver could see that her lips were redder and could smell that she had put perfume on. Clotilde had changed into the underwear that she had bought for him: a black bra, lacy at the top, in which he could see her soft dark nipples begin to protrude; black stockings that clung to her long legs and guided his eyes gently to the see through black thong. She turned around for him, slowly. Clotilde had the shapeliest backside that most men were ever likely to set eyes on and she knew it. It was full but not fat, a heart shaped thing of beauty that Oliver would rather have stared at and passed comment on as it catwalked down the street than see it like this, in front of him, trapping him as it did now. She gently moved her legs apart to let him see inside the darkness and as she did so she began to, ever so gently, bend over and Oliver could see the smallest fissured bits of black hair escaping round the edges of her thong. She was excited already at the thought of him, the preparation for him, and the feel of the thong pressing against her had sharpened her anticipation of what was to come.

She was attractive. He could not deny that, even to himself. He didn't try to. Very attractive. Physically. But when you are being raped even the most beautiful thing can be distasteful and repulsive. It is the price of safety, he told himself. It is the price of staying alive.

She stood back up and turned slowly around. Oliver could see her nipples were harder now, pressing against her bra and her smile was full, telling him of how she possessed him and he was at her will. He did as her eyes instructed and took off his trousers and shirt and she could see an already familiar shape. Every erection had shocked Oliver, shocked him to the point of self-loathing. He cursed that his prick had not rejected the jailor. Oliver had expected that he would somehow fail to get an erection. Every time he had expected it. Instead his body reacted to new sights and touches and sensations in a way that made him despise himself. Her smile was now wider as she crawled onto the bed, offering herself to him whilst at the same time knowing she would and could take as much of him as she wanted. Clotilde raised herself in front of him and all he could see were the two dark and creamy nipples coming towards him, all he could smell was Clotilde's perfume, all he could touch was her silk skin as she lifted his hands and made them glide across it, and all he could hear was her breathing and murmuring, murmuring then breathing and her soft sighs in his ears.

Did it really matter now how often this happened? They had done it once, so did it matter if it went on for another two, three or twenty times? If Helen was betrayed, could he betray her more than once? Oliver wanted to feel sick as his hands moved on her, wanted to spit at and bite at the nipples in front of him. He wanted to turn her murmurs into screams. But of course he didn't. This was the price of safety, this is why I am still alive.

She peeled his underwear from him, gently caressing him and slowly at first putting him in her mouth. He closed his eyes and felt only her rhythm as he seemed to go deeper and deeper into her mouth. Its warmth smothered him as she began to quicken and her hand began to move up and down on him and he knew that if she continued it would only be a few minutes before he was ready to let go. Let it happen now, quickly now……but she wouldn't hurry these things and she stopped suddenly because she wanted him inside her body this time, to feel herself shudder, to be breathless, to orgasm on him.

She lifted her head and as she towered over him and dominated him he felt her hair cover his face. She moved her head back and forward, to and fro, till he was covered by the soft darkness. Helen used to do that, he used to love that, getting lost in Helen's hair. It made him smile, a little lost memory of happiness… Clotilde began to lower her silken body onto him, shifting her knickers to one side as she positioned him inside her. He moved inside her entirely almost immediately and she smiled at him again –"That's what you do to me," she whispered in his ear. She guided Oliver's hands to her breasts and, their hands together, they ran them over her breasts, massaging them gently, running their fingertips over her fine nipples before she brought his head up and forced him to take them in his mouth one after the other.

She moved her head to kiss him and he knew she was almost ready. He could feel her being aroused outside as well as in as she slowly grinded along him. He quickly ran his hands over her back and her hands cupped his face with some force, not letting him move while her tongue explored his mouth. She ran his hands, pulled them, further down, further down, onto her cheeks and she pulled herself into him, deeper, deeper. She glided harder across him, her body pinning him down. As he felt her begin to get closer, her sighs became longer and louder and she grabbed his hand and thrust his fingers into any opening she could find. Instinctively he felt the beginning of the rush as his fingers pushed and curled and she began to come, breathlessly at first and then with a loud and high-pitched cry. Shudder upon shudder seemed to pass through her as she almost shook on top of him. Oliver silently ejaculated inside her. He had to. It was the rule. It was not done until he had given himself to her.

He was silent. He closed his eyes and tried to think of his beautiful wife. Every time is a betrayal he thought. Every time is a betrayal. This is another woman's body that I have been inside. Sometime soon, surely, he would fail to get an erection. But then what might she do to me? Throw me out, out to my death… And Oliver came back to the same thought, the same thought that he had had since the first time they had done anything at all a few night ago… I am damned here, I am damned because there must have been pleasure in it for me, I am damned because I got hard, I am damned because I could have jumped out the window or tried to kill her. I must have wanted this, I must somewhere have wanted this. It was a thought process which eventually might lead him to throw himself off a high bridge. But Oliver wasn't quite at that stage just yet.

He opened his eyes, after having them clenched shut for what had seemed like an age. She sat proudly on top of him, some hair sticking to her face with sweat though, from beginning to end, this had taken no more than five minutes. Sometimes it was like that with Olly – sometimes five minutes, sometimes half an hour, sometimes longer. All were fantastic… different, but fantastic. But she knew when she was buying the underwear, she could feel herself excited at the thought of him seeing her in it, this was going to be quick. And she already knew that Oliver, in the afternoon, was at his most receptive – and that usually meant a quick flash of wonder.

She lay down beside him, almost demanding to be cradled by him and he knew that sometime in the future, maybe in an hour when she felt he had the energy back, she would want to do this again. Otherwise she would have thrown a t-shirt on. Oliver's eyes quivered shut in silent protest.

He put out his arm and she grabbed it before curling into him. She put her arm across him and she kissed his chest.

Oliver didn't really know, didn't truly know, if he could trust Clotilde. She had saved him, she had saved his life, she was saving his life but this situation……this situation was one, one where she was raping him at will, no human being could think that was normal or be happy with having someone who loved them only because they had to, only because they were a prisoner. So there was something different about her, maybe something damaged, something wild. Be careful. On the other hand, I must get out of here…

"Clotilde," said Olly, hoisting the question gingerly. "How long do you think I need to stay here? I mean, you know, before it's safe to… " It was left unfinished.

"You mean before it's safe for you to leave me? Who knows Olly… but I can't imagine why you would want to leave me."

"Clotilde….I….I have a wife. And a child. Who must wonder where

82

I am. I need to let them know at least that I am ok. And when they might see me. You understand that. Don't you?"

Clotilde was very matter of fact. "Yes, I know you have a wife and child. But I also know that you have half the Mafia looking for you. If you try and go home now you'll be killed. You're safe here, I told you that. They don't know me. You're only safe here."

"But why not a phone call? Is that so dangerous?"

"Yes! You know what these guys will be doing right now? They'll be trying to find out every call that's been made to the UK over the last three days to trace the source. They'll have access to everything, every mobile operator, every land line, everything. And anyway if you phone over there you'll put your wife in danger. She's maybe in danger already. These are ruthless people. You're safer here, with me." And she hugged him a little tighter.

"But Clotilde, I......I can't stay here, in this flat, day after day, not going out, for how long, for ever?"

"No," she said, and leapt upon him, putting her elbows on his chest. "I've thought about that. I've thought about it a lot. We can move somewhere. Not France. Maybe Switzerland, maybe north Italy. Easy for me to get a job, maybe you too. Just us. Just the two of us."

"And Helen? And Terrence?" And me, he felt like saying too.

"You'd forget them Olly. Not at first, sure, but you would. I'd make you. Haven't we been great together, these last few days? Imagine how it could be. I have. I've thought about nothing else. I used to think...you and I...one night would have been good but now, there's a chance to have it all, to have everything. No one would treat you like I can Olly. No one can give you what I can."

Olly slowly shook his head and said softly. "You can't mean that. This is only three days, only three days we've spent with each other. We don't even know each other. And I love Helen. I'd die for her. I'd die for Terrence. You can't think this way Clotilde... "

She looked at him. "Olly, these bad people......I'm not on their radar, I've never had any reason to be. But I know of them. I knew Paul was well in with them. All it takes is a call from me, Olly. Just one call...here he is, he's there, you can take him away. If I can't have you...... Listen, you knew when you came with me that I wanted you. I've not stopped wanting you, I want you even more..."

"You said you could keep me safe. For a day or two. I thought that was all it would be...."

"Are you saying you don't want me? You've seen me the way you've seen me the last few days, having done the things we've done, made love to me as many times as you have… were you faking it?"

Don't trust her, don't trust her, don't tell the truth…"No, Clotilde, no. Since first we met I thought you were…gorgeous, sexy and I'd be lying if I said I didn't find you….well, desirable. But it's….I'm sorry, but it's not my life… "

" So just fun then?"

Oliver could not imagine that any dictionary in the world could define the fear and coercion he had felt over the last few days as "fun". He didn't remember the last time he had truly eaten. "Fun, yes, but 'just' no….Clotilde, if there wasn't Helen or Terrance then maybe yes I'd be planning what you're planning, thinking what you're thinking….But there is my family and I must, somehow, return to them."

At this point he thought Clotilde might start to sob and she was silent for a while. However, her silence wasn't borne out of sadness or distress and instead she was mulling over in her mind whether to betray him or not. Though she had hinted to him that she felt used she knew that this was nowhere being the truth. If anyone had done the using, it was her. She adored Olly, found him funny and charming, attentive and handsome, sexy and thoughtful and when she saw a chance to 'have' him for a while she leapt on it, thinking only of the consequence that it might lead to something permanent. In the short time that it had taken her to make a decision about him three days ago, she had seen the possibility of a life with him. Even if she knew that he might not have chosen to be with her by himself, without a little persuasion. But if that life didn't happen, and she wasn't convinced at first that it could, he would be hers for a few days, perhaps weeks. Almost imprisoned. He wouldn't be able to resist her physically, she knew that, and she knew she wouldn't disappoint him. So, yeah, she thought, it was my sexuality that I used to trap and keep him here. But Clotilde had made love to enough men to feel that Oliver wasn't only 'going along with it'. He was usually as hard as a rock and quick to get there. And at other times they talked, they laughed and joked….he would be reflective at times, and Clotilde slept so unusually well that she had no idea if he spent some of the time during the night when they weren't making love thinking about his wife and child, but she convinced herself that this was a guy who was happy with her. Who responded to her. This guy, she felt, genuinely felt, is in love with me. You can't fake that….and she thought again of how easy it would be to leave the flat, make a call on her mobile, tell them where he was, and close the book on him. She realised, and fully appreciated for the first time, that she might be happier sending him to his death than she would be sending him back to Helen's arms.

"Oliver, do you love me?"

Oliver had expected this question for about a day now and still had no idea how to answer. Not because he didn't know the answer – he loved Helen – but he was fearful of what Clotilde might do.

"Clotilde......I... if I wasn't married......"

"You can love two people Olly. I'm not asking you if you love Helen. I know you love Helen. I appreciate she is a very beautiful woman. I'm asking you if you love me."

"I......really....I don't know. Clotilde, you have to realise, the conditions that have brought us together, they're hardly normal...I mean..."

"Then you're not happy here?"

"Who could be happy like this, hiding away, frightened almost literally for their life... maybe, maybe you too, for keeping me in hiding."

Clotilde stayed within the protection of his arm, moving her head more onto his chest. "I only ask because I wanted to know if you felt the same way about me as I feel about you. Leave aside the situation you're in here, leave aside Helen – could we have had a life together?"

"But Clotilde if I say 'Yes' then you will think we can have a life together. And we can't."

"How do you know what I think? Or what I might think or will think? It would comfort me to know that you loved me." She didn't really mean it, it wouldn't comfort her. But she wanted him to at least be interested in how she felt, she wanted to explain to him how he filled her with such excitement and longing and it felt wrong to do that to someone who didn't care much for you.

She terrified him. She had brought him here, locked him up, overpowered him in every sense he could think of. Raped me, for Christ's sake. He could only think to flatter her... he could flatter her... .perhaps vanity may be her weakness. "Honestly, Clotilde, I don't know. And I mean that, truly. I really think you are a wondrous person. But this situation it's so fucked up, so fucked up.." He paused briefly, raising himself to look at her. Change the subject... "But I don't understand how you're....well, alone. You're incredibly beautiful, you're lovely, you're funny, you're great to be with...what is it that's wrong with you?

Why isn't there a boyfriend, a husband? I mean, has there been? A husband I mean? A long-term partner?"

And she felt warmer and happier inside and felt like crying for the first time. He had told the truth, he really didn't know if he loved her or not. This wasn't only frolic after frolic, sex a la carte, he was interested in her, really interested. She thought she'd make sure.

"Are you interested? Or flattering me?"

"No, not trying to flatter you. I'm interested. Girls like you tend to get snapped up quite quickly."

"Oh, I guess things never happened the way they do in story books. I've had lovers, boyfriends, one-night things, the odd longer term thing, I even lived with a guy once but it was suffocating. My first love was at the end of school....well, end of my school days, he had left... I was 18 and I thought he was great....you know, guy a bit older than me, handsome and I thought yeah, maybe he's the one I'll lose it to. And he was, but it wasn't a pleasant experience..."

"I think it rarely is..."

"Well, yeah, maybe, but it was for him. And I think he was the person who really convinced me that I was quite attractive. I'd seen, you know, going through school the way people....the way boys....looked at me... sometimes in the street people looked at me too. I was pretty then....but this guy...he frightened me a bit... when we did it for the first time, it was sore for me, you know, a painful feeling and I wanted him to stop a bit, slow down, but he began to push all the harder when I tried to get him to slow and he must have seen the pain on my face then when I looked at him I could see this look on his face and he kept saying 'I have to fuck you Clotilde, this is so beautiful'. But this wasn't desire, or love, it was something deeper, like some desperate need to possess me. And he was strong. So I wanted to push him out but instead I hugged him, I wanted to scream but instead I sighed, I wanted to hit but instead I held him, bringing him closer into me. Soon he had finished what he came to do and he said 'Ah Clotilde that was so beautiful, I never thought I would fuck someone so beautiful'. And it really hurt...physically and every other way. I didn't expect choirs to be singing but for your first time you don't want to be fucked, you want someone to make love to you, to hold you, to care about what you're feeling. So I didn't last long with him, he wanted to do it all the time, telling me I was so beautiful, telling that fucking with me took him to such pleasures. But it never gave me any pleasure and I had to grit my teeth a few times with him until I realised

I wasn't gritting my teeth because it was sore physically, it was because his presence inside me began to repulse me.

And then there were a few others....university things... I studied Sociology and the guys you get doing that...maybe there's something not quite right with them, they think too deeply. One guy I thought was great only wanted to be my friend, I was too much out of his league... what's that all about by the way, you people have a league... then another obsessed over me..."

A general conversation, something generic, some talk about anything that wasn't about "them". That would be good. "Hah," said Oliver, laughing, "yeah, of course we have a league and don't tell me you don't too. And it's purely based on looks and anyone who says otherwise is just a liar. You gravitate to your own equivalent......medium, five to six out of ten girls go out with medium five to six out of ten guys..."

"What do you mean? It's not a class thing? Your country gets a bit obsessional about class, it must be a class thing too?"

Oliver thought for a bit. Maybe even beginning to relax. "I don't think the class thing is what it was....landed gentry will probably marry landed gentry but I'm not sure I could really define for you what working class and middle class are any more. And is it down to money? A plumber will probably earn more than a teacher or a lecturer... so what does that say? Probably nothing. But no, five out of ten is about looks, nothing else."

"So," said Clotilde, looking at him and smiling, "this guy must have thought he was maybe six and I was maybe seven?"

"You've got the idea," Oliver replied, "but perhaps not the application. I'd venture he thought he was about four and you were about eleven."

She kissed him on the nose. "Well, anyway, one wouldn't go out with me, one almost stalked me. I had a few people asking me out, I'd occasionally go and I could tell quite quickly it wasn't working, you know that way when there isn't a spark. But I did go with one guy....great sex... he was the first to, you know, give me an orgasm. It was a great relationship that because we didn't love each other – we liked each other a lot – but we both wanted to have fun and that was good. Then he went away and that was the end of that.

Then post-university and my move to England where I must have lived for about three, maybe almost four years. A few guys I suppose but nothing serious... no one I wanted to get serious about. Then when I came back to France I moved in with a guy not that long after, I must have been 26 or 27…but he was possessive, too possessive. Always ran to take any phone calls, got angry when it was for me, didn't want me to go out to see friends….he always seemed unhappy, as though everything I did made him unhappy, everyone I spoke to was a threat to him. He wasn't like that at first but when we lived together…oh dear, terrible. Sexually a bit of a yawn…And you get to thinking there will be someone for you it's only a question of time…but eventually you begin to think, 'but where am I going to meet them?' You get into work and your social circle narrows, you meet fewer people, your expectations get a little higher because you know the next one will probably be the one rather than just someone to have fun with…and the years go by and you get into a routine where you are probably quite happy with the way things are, or at least you convince yourself you are." She paused. "And then you meet someone you can't have but who you know is the one for you and you see the chance of a life you'd almost denied yourself. Children, family holidays, the whole dream…."

Oliver sighed. Not a sigh of frustration but more one of sympathy. She started up. "Oh, you think I'm talking about you, don't you? I'm not talking about you."

"Oh… ok… I thought .."

"No, I'm talking about Martin. I met him a few years ago. I used to co-manage a hotel here and he was a guest, a regular guest. It wasn't a small hotel but not so big that you wouldn't get to know regular clients and so I asked to meet him one day, to say thank you for the business, find out a bit more about him and the nature of his business. He was a lovely man and I felt a spark there, you know the spark I was talking about… something that I hadn't felt with a guy for a long time. Not sure if he was my…what did you call it…eleven out of ten…but I liked him. We talked, about him and his business at first but then just about him. He was married, no children… this didn't have any effect on me at all at the time. It didn't deter me. I remember thinking….'maybe you are married but you can have something better'. So I was attentive, finding out where he did business, who with, how often but mostly what he did at nights and he seemed to spend them in the hotel or walking along the promenade, watching tv in the hotel or people watching outside. I offered him dinner, compliments of the house, I would be happy to take dinner with him and I could see in his eyes, a quick flash, that he had….well, if not the same then at least a similar feeling to me. I dressed for him that

88

night…maybe, you know in your language maybe I don't think of myself as ten out of ten but I think I faked ten that night. Even the staff knew there was something different. You could tell he'd done the same. By the end of the first course there were those knowing little touches between us, affirmations of intent I think you might say. And of course things led where we both wanted them to go and we had a beautiful night with a couple of bottles of champagne and no sleep.

But I knew then that this wasn't the end…it wasn't just a night for him either…and there were another two nights before he went home. He came back the next week but this time there was no business for him to do and we spent the days doing the things that people who are falling in love with each other do… sunbathing, splashing in the sea, walking, going to Monte Carlo. The trips got more frequent and I remember when I began to think I could have it all. I turned to him at one point and said 'Does your wife not ask about the increase in the number of trips?' And he looked at me and said 'I don't want to talk about her. She's nothing to me. Let's think of us and what we can be.' I thought…this could be it…ok he's married, a bit of fall out…but I love him, he loves me it's clear…and I saw us together, maybe a few years, then children… it wasn't that I allowed myself to dream because I'd dreamed about such things before, it was that I felt it would be more than a dream. This was what was going to happen. I really believed, then, that he would leave his wife. But, obviously, he didn't."

She stopped abruptly and Oliver wondered if it was to make sure he was still awake. But he had become engrossed in this and so much appeared to have been left unsaid.

"He didn't? Why? I mean, what happened?"

"Well, it seemed he would. He came down once and began to push me a bit on what I really felt, could we make a go of this. And I said that I loved him and would do pretty much anything he asked except let go of him and it seemed that was what he wanted to hear. He got to the stage of talking of details that I hadn't even thought of – divorce settlements, monies he would and wouldn't have after the divorce, what he might do if he stayed here, would we stay in my flat, what would he do for a car… you know, pretty detailed stuff and when he left I was absolutely convinced this was going to happen.

Then he returned but he didn't return when he said he would, it was a week later. I don't know if he'd spoken to his wife or if something else had happened…I've often thought that maybe she had become pregnant and he didn't tell me…but it was clear that he had come to tell me that it was over, he couldn't go through with it. I couldn't believe it. It was as if he had set fire to my future, our future. I don't remember the reasons. That evening was the worst of my life and I felt almost unable to breath at times, suffocated, as though he had choked the life out of me. And that's the last time I saw him… but it was the last time his wife saw him too."

Oliver sat up, as though he had been hit by lightning. "What do you mean, 'the last time his wife saw him too'?"

Clotilde paused, and she already regretted saying what she had said. It was as if she somehow had to assert herself, to show that she ultimately had control and not this lothario who had played with her emotions as though she was a rag doll. Do I tell him? Should I tell him?

She inhaled and exhaled, listening to the sound of the breath going in and coming out of her body. Tell him, she thought, the words that she had used were ambiguous enough that she could lie anyway.

"Well, when I said that what I meant was that it was the last time she saw him as he was then. That night….the night he told me…we were supposed to be going to dinner with a friend of his or a business associate or something and he had asked me to get their address a few days before. After we spoke that night he still had to go and see this person but clearly I wasn't going to go….I had the address but excused myself for a minute, went away and wrote down a different address. One in not such a nice area. I have a brother…he's…well, he's my brother so I love him as my brother but he's sort of fallen on the wrong side of the tracks. Used to be a drug addict but now deals and…well, these people, these kind of people, they can look after themselves. He stays in an area here called L'Ariane… no tourist would go there, it's dangerous. So I sent Martin off to L'Ariane to see my brother, unwittingly…and when he was on the way I phoned my brother and told him what had happened and that it might be nice if Martin was given a bit of a reception. I've often wondered what would have happened had my brother not been in that night….Martin would still have ended up in L'Ariane, alone, so maybe he would have got beaten up… anyway, my brother and his friends played around with him a bit, a bit of facial reconstruction. He assured me that by the time Martin was sent home his wife may have had trouble recognising him…."

Oliver was breathless and frightened, and tried to tear himself away from Clotilde. "You did that to a guy? Jesus Christ Clotilde, what the hell are you going to do to me?" She almost pinned him down and looked at him.

"Calm down Oliver, calm down. He lied to me. You haven't. You have promised me nothing. He promised me a life and then took it away. No one could endure what I did without taking some revenge."

But Oliver remained in something close to a state of shock. "For Christ's sake Clotilde, you can't do that…you can't deal with things that way… things happen, we all get hurt…" He was terrified. The fear that had lingered was rammed inside him. He had to, he had to, get out of here…

"Do we?" she said, her eyes flashing in anger as she pinned him to the bed. She was on top of him again but this time her face was full of threat, her actions full of power. "Do you get hurt like that Olly? Does Helen fuck other people, promise them a life and throw you away? I don't think you'll ever know how I felt that night so don't fucking lie there, holding me, and tell me you know how I feel. You can sympathise, tell me someone will come along, make love to me or fuck me in any way that you want and take the most pleasure in it, you can think I'm cheap or a tart, you can hate me for being in love with you and the trouble that brings with it for you or you can think of me as your little toy but do not ever, do not ever, tell me that you know how I feel by saying 'we all get hurt'!"

She shouted the last few words in his face and then fell in a heap as her head slumped onto his chest. Then, softly, "Don't tell me how you know what it's like to be in love with you….or what is was like to be in love with Martin. You can never know what it was like to wait for the next visit, or maybe a phone call saying he wasn't coming back, to feel as though you were almost stealing someone, then seeing that you'd done it, both together, achieved this freedom….then it's thrown in your face and the world implodes. Don't tell me you can say you understand that by saying 'we all get hurt'. Olly touched her face, expecting to feel tears but Clotilde had not cried. "No human being could have withstood that without wanting to take some revenge."

It wasn't that he didn't agree with her in principle. But wanting to take revenge and actually doing something about it to the extent she did changed her from the mere jailor she had been to someone with the tendencies and behaviour of how he might have described a psychopath. He thought it best to say nothing directly. "I know," he said gently. Now he was lying beside, lying with, someone who was desperate and damaged. Such people are dangerous, even without Clotilde's sense of justice. Hell hath no fury indeed…

She was motionless as she lay on him. Then she lifted her head and kissed him softly on the lips, a kiss without passion but full of love, slow and with purpose. "I love you Olly. I just wanted to be sure you knew that. I can't expect you to know what these words actually mean to me and the depth of feeling that's inside me for you. But my life would be complete with you. Maybe it would have been complete with someone else, it probably would have been complete with Martin. And if Martin and I had worked then maybe there would have been no need for you. But that didn't happen......and how I felt then...and how I'm going to feel now, or soon, when you go away....do you really have any idea how I'm going to feel? I mean, Olly, that's really what I want you to experience. I want you to know how empty I'm going to be. How there's going to be this smiling shell on the outside, who'll go to work and do the things that people do to get through the day, but who inside is going to be drained and empty and numb. What am I going to actually feel when you go? You make me feel, you make me alive, I feel as though I'm sparkling and twinkling. It's not just you that you will take away with you Olly, it's me too. My sense of feeling....feeling anything. I want you to experience that. I don't want to hurt you, I don't want anyone else to hurt you, but I want you to know what I will be without you. And more than anything I want you to feel it. But you won't, you never will, never, never...."

There was a philosophical hook he could cling to, make this less personal, less about us. "We never can, can we? We're all islands. Maybe, essentially, unknowable. And no, you're right, maybe I never will know how you feel, or how you might feel because I'm not you, with your feelings and hopes and fears and desires. I honestly wish I could, I deserve to feel it, I should have your pain and more...."

And she kissed him again but this time with open mouth and they both knew where that would lead. When she made love to him again it was slower and she didn't want to orgasm quickly. On top of her, he was forced to move inside her and she smiled at him, at his tightly shut eyes, a smile of understanding and resignation, a smile which at that moment told of her never wanting this action between them to end. She stroked his hair and spoke to him softly, whispering words of love to him in French that he barely understood as his hands slid dispassionately up and down her long neck. She wondered if this would be the last time that he would be like this with her and she wanted to take it all in, him, his movements, the little sighs he gave her that told of her nirvana, this room with him in it, its brilliance, the gentle breeze blowing the curtains that she could feel over her body and of him being inside her and feeling their bodies moving together. Whatever else they may have done in the time he had spent there, this time she felt they truly made love. For twenty minutes – it felt like a day to Oliver – they moved together. It felt like one rhythm to her until she began to move a little harder, push herself into him and gently orgasm, her eyes closed and mouth open with his hands faintly caressing her face.

He lay on top of her for a while until she glanced at the clock.

"Oh, shit!" and with the exclamation she almost bolted up. "I need to go into work for something, I told them I'd be in for an hour or two today. There's something needs to be tied up."

She hurried into the bathroom, dressed herself quickly and applied whatever needed to be applied to make it look as if she hadn't been doing what she had been doing for much of the afternoon.

"Olly, don't go out. Trust me on this one a bit longer. But they are probably still looking for you, maybe even watching this flat. We'll talk about it when I get back... I know you have to go, I know.... But honestly for your good and not mine, I don't think today. We can talk but maybe early tomorrow morning....you can even take my car for a bit maybe...anyway, let's talk......but please be here when I get back, for both our sake's."

"Sure," he said, "where would I go anyway?" He held his hands and arms up in resignation.

She smiled at him and kissed him on the lips before she left. As she walked downstairs, she thought that she had only lied to Olly twice. Well, only twice that day, maybe more since he had been staying with her. Once was about Martin. The truth was that his wife never did see him again because his dead body had been burned somewhere to the north of Nice. He was still registered as a missing person. And it seems his wife had known nothing of his plans to leave her because Clotilde had spoken with her when she came with the police to the hotel. She knew then that she had done the right thing: if his wife had never known anything then Martin must have told her nothing. Which saved Clotilde from suspicion but indicated how shallow the things he said to her were.

The second time she lied, and she consoled herself with the fact that she hadn't really lied because she had promised him nothing, was when she gave Oliver the feeling that he was different and wouldn't be harmed. As she went down the stairs and out of the front door, she thought that she would wait twenty minutes or so, enough time to ensure she felt the same way, and would then phone her brother and tell him where Oliver was and where he was going to be for the next hour or two.

As she walked down the street four men walked past her, clearly tourists, probably wandering away from the port area looking for a quieter bar or a cheaper café. She didn't register them at all but they registered her and as she walked past them four sets of eyes were pulled into her, into her tight black trousers and white top, as she made her way down the street.

"Ok," said Euan, "I think this is the one… that seems to be the number……let's ring the buzzer and see…"

But they had no need to ring any buzzer as a delivery man came whistling down the stairs and held the door open for them. Clotilde's apartment was on the first floor and soon the friends found themselves staring at a bell with "C de Bresseau" marked underneath.

Inside Oliver heard the doorbell ring and instinctively got down on the ground. He crawled from the bedroom out towards the hall and immediately thought he wouldn't answer it. He was about to crawl back into the bedroom, under the bed, when he thought that it could be innocuous…maybe a delivery of mail, maybe something harmless… anyway, there was a peep hole…if it had been someone coming to kill him, they wouldn't ring a doorbell, would they? He crawled back towards the hall, silently, listening to see if he could hear any voices. The nearer he got to the door, the more he heard murmurings, voices….voices which sounded vaguely familiar but he realised that it must be that way that language sometimes plays with our senses. Sometimes it took a few seconds to realise that people weren't speaking your language but another one which had similar sounds. He listened again and heard a clear "let's go, we can phone later, it's still afternoon."

"Jesus," he thought and raised himself up so he could see out of the peephole. Whatever he was thinking, and whatever he thought he might see, it certainly wasn't Euan, Ellis, Aidan and Ali. He ripped the chain off the door and almost threw the door open.

Whatever Euan, Ellis, Aidan and Ali were thinking, and whatever they thought they might see, it certainly wasn't Olly. The four of them stood, mouths open in unison as though it were a ghost in front of them.

Euan was first to break the silence. "Olly, what the fuck…"

Oliver grabbed him. "Get in! Quickly. All of you. Quickly!" And they scurried past him and into the bedroom.

Olly ran quickly around the bedroom, picking up the few of his clothes and possessions that Clotilde had gone back to the flat to get for him a few nights ago and began stuffing them into his bag.

"Guys what are you doing here? You're not safe, we're not safe." He spoke quickly and looked at none of them directly as he scurried about, trying to find all of the possessions of his own that he could.

"Not safe?" said Euan, looking about him at a dishevelled bed, Olly throwing some clothes on and running around like someone trying to distract attention from....something. "What do you mean, 'not safe'? Not safe from whom?" and, sitting on the bed, he bent down and picked up the black thong that Clotilde had discarded. "Is someone going to shag us to death?"

Olly stopped, briefly: "This isn't what it looks like," he said.

Ellis looked around him. "Well, that's a relief... but then I have absolutely no idea of what this actually looks like. Olly, married Olly with wife and kid, in some bird's flat for three days... looks as though he has been having a good time," he nodded at the thong which Euan proudly held aloft, "he looks as happy as a dog that's discovered it's suddenly got two dicks...no, Olly, mate, you'll need to fill me in, I have no idea what this looks like. I might need to know what it looks like first before I can believe you that it's not what it looks like."

Oliver looked up, sweating a bit from both the hurried movements and the situation. "What are you guys doing here? How did you get here? This flat? How?" he looked at them as though he was owed an explanation before them.

"Helen was – is – worried sick," said Euan. "By the way, someone phone her and te...."

"No!" Oliver shouted. "Don't phone. Don't touch the bloody thing. Not just now. I told you, you are not safe. Tell me about Helen, how is she? Terrence?"

"Yeah," said Euan, looking around him, "she's worried, she thinks you're lying dead somewhere. I think you might be when she gets a hold of you. Well, I spoke with her and after some discussion we all decided to come and find you." He said the next words with force and they were absolutely unequivocal. "And bring you home."

"And this flat? How did you find this flat?" Oliver was glancing around, aware now that he had everything he needed, double checking that he had his passport, some money....

"A hunch...we thought we remembered you talking about some bird called Clotilde…very pretty…….say, Olly, this girl wasn't wearing a white top and quite tight black trousers, was she?"

Oliver nodded. "Wow, well I think we just passed her in the street….so what was going on? Had you set up house with this Clotilde? Were you going to tell anyone? Helen? Terrence? Fuck's sake Olly," Euan said, suddenly getting angry, "have we really come all this way to find out that you've moved in with some French bit? Couldn't you have slept with her for a night like the rest of the world does? Helen is worried sick for Christ's sake – why couldn't you have phoned?"

Oliver looked around him and motioned them to the door. He was ready to leave this room where he had been a prisoner. "Guys this will take some time to explain and we don't have much time. I was at a dinner on Saturday night and got into an argument with the wrong guy. That argument had a physical consequence and this guy chased me and tried to attack me. I hit him in the eye with the blunt end of a knife and I think I blinded the guy. As I ran away from this guy… it was a quiet area, I thought there was no one about… Clotilde stopped me and said she had seen what had happened and did I realise what trouble I was in and with whom. She told me this guy Paul was very well 'connected' – I don't know what that means but she made it sound very threatening and dangerous…she said they would know who I was, where I worked, they would find me…they knew I was from the UK, they could monitor calls, if I phoned I'd put people in danger…I needed to lie low for a few days and that I'd be safe at hers. And that's what I've been doing, I've been here for three days. I haven't gone out, made a call, done anything…she told me we were safe…I was safe….here but who knows, they may even be watching now. It's why you're not safe, it's why we shouldn't make calls…"

Ali asked "So what does 'lying low' involve these days, Olly? Her underwear is about the floor, you're here in what I guess must be her bedroom, where you've probably been sleeping…she's probably been sleeping….the last few nights.."

"Listen, I'm telling you the truth. If I wanted to leave Helen for Clotilde don't you think I would have told someone? Christ sake guys, do you really think I'd abandon my wife and child? Have you any idea how much I've missed them. What a hell this has been?" It sounded as though he was starting to break.

"Olly mate," said Ali, "I haven't got a clue what to think right now. If you told me two days ago I'd be in Nice, in some girl's flat, trying to bring

Oliver home… I'd have thought you'd had the oxygen to your brain cut off. So you leaving Helen for some French girl doesn't seem so mad."

Aidan had been quiet, looking around him, remembering that brief glimpse they had caught of what appeared to be Clotilde. And he saw her, here, in this room and he could see that girl with Olly and that was what led him to ask the question that the rest of them were, by now, beginning to think. "Olly, were you and this girl…was it more than your minds that met? Did you exchange bodily flu-ids?" He drew out the last word, almost pronouncing its two syllables as two different words.

Olly looked around at the expectant faces and knew that he would not tell the truth. "Guys, it's not important….what's important is the situation we're in now. We need to get out of here and get back home. We don't know if we're being watched. We don't know if our calls are being monitored. We don't know if every move we make is going to be reported. We are in serious danger here. You're in serious danger. Let's leave this 'did you fuck her' crap till we can talk properly, shall we?"

Euan looked at him. "If I believe you Olly…and I'm not sure I do… but even if I do…I still want to know what the relationship between you and this girl was…or is. And you can say that in about ten seconds."

"Okay, okay….she saved me from what could have been the death of me, literally. You want my opinion? I think she liked me…likes me…I'd be lying if I said she didn't give me some indication over the last three days that she was there for me, in all sorts of ways. But think of me being here, for just a minute, will you….away from Helen, from Terrence, unable to call anyone, worried sick for them, for me too, wondering if the next noise would bring something terrible behind it. You think I slept at all feeling like that? You think that, even if I'd wanted to, my prick would have stood up at all? I don't think I could have got an erection if you'd put a group of supermodels to work on me for a day. So, guys – task in hand…we need to get out of here and decide how the hell we are going to get home."

"Surely we can go to the airport? This time, surely can you fly?"

"I can't fly. You know that, I can't fly. Maybe it's best if you fly back, I'll have to find another way, I won't fly."

"No," said Euan. "We go back together. Together. We left our luggage in a place by the port…we didn't know what might happen here, we thought maybe nothing, and we thought we'd go to Monte Carlo and maybe stay there to try and find you,"… he paced up and down, pausing and thinking…."we need a car…or a train…."

"Or a boat," said Olly, and the others stared at him. "We could get a boat somewhere away in another direction…they know where I'm from, they know where I'm going to try and get to…but if we got a boat to say…I don't know….Corsica….and we left from there…no one would be looking for me….us….there."

"Corsica?" said Euan. "Are you joking? A little island miles away….we've got to come back to the mainland to do anything anyway… mental idea, Olly. I think the train… "

"No," said Ellis. "You're a prisoner on a train…if what Olly says is right then we would have nowhere to go, we're stuck….and I don't fancy the chances of five thirty-somethings trying to jump off a moving train. We'd have bloody heart attacks at the thought of jumping."

"Ok," said Ali, "looks like we've agreed on the car. But we don't have a car. Do we rent one and take it home?"

"No, no," said Oliver, "we need to buy one. A second hand one maybe….and better it's from a private sale than from a garage."

With that Oliver ushered and pushed his friends and their inquisitive eyes out of the room. He took a last lingering look at its whiteness, felt its airy breeze on him, listened to the noises that drifted up from the street and smelt the smell of Clotilde as he closed the door. He felt very close to tears. The past three days had been a vacuum where horrible imaginings were somewhere in the background, distant enough to be put, literally, to the back of his mind. But now he was going out, out into a place where he felt he could be a sitting duck, a target that someone picked off for their fun at a moment that suited them. And these guys who had come here….he wasn't really as shocked as he seemed, he had expected something, but probably Helen. Instead these guys that loved him dearly had come… and though he was glad they had come, he was scared for them too…what sort of danger had they put themselves in for him?

As Oliver closed the door he noticed the flowers that Clotilde had bought three days ago, after the first time she had, she had, no, he thought, she didn't rape me… they had fucked. These red roses that had looked so beautiful and full and deep red…they were already beginning to wilt and die. The outsides of the roses were already turning brown, a little crispy now, not soft and waxy to touch. Oliver knew if he touched the roses now they would simply disintegrate. He looked at their heart and inside the roses the core was tighter, darker, shrivelled. He couldn't be sure, but he thought that this morning when he had glanced at them they had still been red and full and very much alive.

Oliver and his friends went out into the corridor and his eyes were everywhere at once – above him, beneath him, to the sides… They shuffled downstairs until they came to the door. Aidan took out his mobile phone.

"DON'T," hissed Oliver, in a whisper that was louder than a shout. "Don't text, don't phone, don't e-mail. Not yet, not yet. Where are we going to go when we get out of here?"

"We're going to walk down the street," said Euan, "like five guys on holiday might do. If something's going to happen then it'll happen. But if your Clotilde is right then maybe you have been safe for the last few days and maybe these guys don't know where you are. So we should be ok. Olly," he said, as though the thought had just occurred to him, "you're not taking the piss here, are you? I mean…it is mental…I feel like I'm in some half-assed film…guys like us don't have bloody hit men after them. My biggest concern is normally if my vegetable deliveries are fresh enough and now I'm being hunted by bad guys… you've not made all this shite up to have a few days with this woman? I mean if you have I'd be pissed off, I'll tell you that now, mighty bloody pissed off…and a bit jealous if she's the one that we saw… and I'd get a bit angry at you, maybe shout at you, call you a cheating bastard asshole or some such epithet, but I'd forgive you and we'd have a bit of laugh and a few beers getting home. I mean, I'm only saying…if you've been taking the piss, now would be a good time to tell us before we all make our way down the street like fucking grouse on the 12th of August."

Oliver laughed, because Euan was right. This did have the mad landscape of a dream, one of those dreams that are so realistic you wake up feeling you're still being chased, or you did that terrible thing that you'll be punished for, or your teeth are still missing.

"Honestly guys, what I've told you is what has happened. I wish it weren't, I wish I could've changed it, I wish I could go back a few days and not have come to this bloody place. But I can't and I'm in this situation and now you're all in it too. It's not a nightmare we're going to wake up from…but I've no intention of dying here and neither have you and now that we're all here we're all going to get home, all of us, together."

They all looked at him and surprise gave way to quiet nods of confidence between them. "Anyway," said Ellis, "I'm sure we've been in worse situations than this before."

Euan's hand was on the handle of the door and he turned to look at Ellis. "I'm not!" he burst out. "Jeez Ellis your life must be one adventure after another if you've been in worse situations than stepping out into a street wondering if some mad French twat is going to shoot you because your pal had a fight with someone. Bloody hell, I know working the stock market is difficult but I didn't think it brought daily challenges on that scale. Or are you Batman in disguise? Actually, that would be very helpful right now...."

"Ok, maybe not, maybe not......trying to be positive...."

"We'll be ok," said Oliver, with a calm authority that he didn't really feel. "But we need to get out of here and we need to get a car. Some of the cafes by the port area have small ads in them... let's go and see if there are any....maybe a long shot but it's worth a go...we're in plain sight in a café anyway, in a busy place....unlikely somebody is going to shoot five guys in a public place." But inside he thought: 'they don't need to shoot five, they only need to shoot one.'

They opened the door and tried to appear as though they were walking with confidence down the street...from Euan's purposeful stride, to Ellis' pretend nonchalance and affected swagger, to Ali's forced casual looks about him as though he was a tourist taking everything in, to Aidan's fixed stare in front of him, to Oliver's inability to take his eyes from the ground beneath him, they looked to all the world exactly as they were – five guys on edge, trying to distract themselves from the inevitability that something dreadful was going to happen. But if you could have seen their eyes, they were remarkably uniform: whether they were blue or brown or green they were all frightened, timid eyes, that moved quickly here and there, never resting on anything too long.

They reached a café near the quayside and sat down. The walls seemed to be full of small ads but, if you had put the five of them together, you might have got a stuttering conversation in broken French between them so comprehending what was there was not going to be easy.

"We can ask the waiter, the owner, surely," said Ali, "or don't they speak much English here?"

"It isn't Paris, Ali," Olly said, "almost everyone here speaks some English and they usually don't hate you for not talking French."

Euan looked at them but focused on Oliver in particular. "Listen, I don't care about the risks...there's something we....there's something you...must do. You must phone Helen. Use my phone...."

Helen wasn't in the house when her mobile phone rang. She was in a

100

friend's, having taken Terrence round to play with one of the boys from his school. It was a welcome distraction, being in Rachel's world, listening to the mundanities of how she coped with three children under five and how she felt her husband was doing things like working late to avoid bath time, feeding time, such responsibilities… He's probably having an affair, thought Helen, and she thought of telling Rachel about her and her lost husband, her brother and the gang of four, finding a colleague almost dead on the floor. But sometimes it all seemed so unreal to her that she felt it wasn't happening and this was one of those times. She looked at Rachel, her animated, pained face, worn down, almost exhausted, her black rimmed eyes, her dank hair and pale skin. But Rachel was only tired, because her eyes still sparkled and she only wanted someone to share her troubles with. Helen felt lifeless in the face of Rachel's animation….I couldn't move my hands the way she does, I don't have the energy….I couldn't make those expressions with my face, I don't think I have muscles that would move that much. As she looked around the room, smiling patiently at Rachel, she saw two vases of flowers on either side of a high mantelpiece. One was full and clear and a mixture of dazzling reds and yellows, new flowers, recently cut….and the other was filled with what must have been bright white roses, dying now, their edges beginning to brown, their leaves crumpling. They wouldn't, they couldn't, react to water or food, they had passed that point where you would really have cared about them and Helen imagined them the next day, their brittle leaves in the bin. They wouldn't dazzle anyone any more, their beauty had burned out. And she suddenly felt within her what seemed like a crashing wave of such infinite sadness that she cried out and couldn't stop the tears which began to stream down her face.

But before Rachel had time to ask her anything, her phone went. Euan! Maybe something, maybe something good…

"Helen?"

Christ, that's not Euan…and again, "Helen?"

"Olly?" She barely got his name out before she surrendered and, for what seemed like an eternity to her, she couldn't speak or think or make any noise except cry.

"Helen….I need you to listen to me, listen closely….I can't imagine what you've felt… but I couldn't help anything that has happened. It's been for the best that I haven't been in touch. I'm in trouble here, I had to stay hidden for a few days, I got into a fight on Saturday and hit someone, maybe blinded them… someone I shouldn't have hit, someone who has friends who can hurt me, who are after me I think. I have been hiding, trying to hide for three days… but the guys have found me and we are coming home. We may still be in danger. I can't stay on the phone long, I've been told calls might be being monitored, so we can't phone so much, we can't keep in touch, if I can phone I won't phone the house……maybe best even if I phone you at a friend's house. I'm not sure I should phone your mobile. How are you, how are you?" And with the repetition he emphasised the last word. His voice had been calm and soft and quiet throughout.

Helen was a mixture of tears and laughter and anger and confusion. Later, she would think of all the questions, of all the things that didn't make sense but at that time she had heard Olly's voice and he was alive and he was going to come to her.

"Oh Olly……Olly…," and she surrendered again, sobbing and gasping, short little breaths of life returning to her. Then she almost shouted at him, in anger and relief and joy "I thought you were dead you stupid bastard!"

"I know…I know… but I…," and he stopped because he knew that the chances of him dying were surely much greater now than they had been when he was with Clotilde. I can't tell her all of this is done, it feels so far from being over.

"Olly, someone's here, someone's watching me, the house…," she stammered out the words. "I think they have the phone tapped… "

"Don't use it Helen. Keep away from the house as much as you can. If anything happens to you…….Oh," he said, with a loud exclamation, "how's the little one, how's Terry?"

"He's fine, don't worry, he's fine…I've told him you had to stay for a few more days… he knows something isn't right though, he can tell…"

"Helen, I love you. I love you and we will get through this. I have missed you, I have missed you in so many ways…I miss you so much…. But we need to be careful. Maybe stay at your parents?"

"No," she said, with a quiet determination, "if they can trace me to our house and put a tap on our phone they can do the same wherever I go… and anyway I don't want them in danger. Jesus Olly, I wish you'd never gone there…" and she gave way to tears again.

"Yeah, me too, me too…you have no idea….I love you Helen…. I must go now, I must go… I will speak to you again when I can… "

Thankfully the boys had been playing upstairs and had heard nothing of the conversation. But Rachel had and as Helen looked at the blank concern and confusion on Rachel's face, she felt the least she owed her was an explanation.

Clotilde paused before she phoned her brother. She had waited twenty minutes or so, wondering if she could really send Oliver to what she knew would be his death. 'But I can't have him,' she reasoned, 'so neither shall his wife. The thought of him can't hurt me if he's gone and I'll always have the memory of those few days of happiness... like his wife will have only memories of happiness. We're the same then, each with our memories of him.' But she paused because she loved him and it could be hard to kill the ones you loved. 'This has been done before,' she thought to herself, 'by stronger and more powerful women than me, since ever two women wanted a man. Old as the Bible, as stories of the Gods answering one prayer and rejecting another, and I can do to this one what I really want to do to him.' And she phoned her brother. But by the time her brother arrived at the flat Oliver was quite long gone and her brother decided to wait for a while before he told his sister. Sometimes, she could be a little too dark and a little too dangerous.

The Constable waited patiently outside the room where Jenny lay alone, waited as he had done for the last two and a half hours. Eventually the doctor and nurse came out.

"She's conscious and we believe she's fine. We need to keep her under observation, with the head there are a few things that might go wrong over the next day or so, but she is ok. Go easy on her though – it was a significant blow that she received and the pain in her head and face is quite intense. The painkillers will slow her down a bit. But it's ok for you to question her. The nurse will stay with her and will let you know if she thinks Jennifer needs to rest."

"Thanks doctor, I will try not to be too long. But what has happened here is something, unfortunately, we must pursue as quickly as we can."

Jenny looked as though someone had smashed a wrecking ball into the side of her face. She was a mixture of black and blue and red, of dark dried blood and of little fresh spots where the wound refused to close over completely. The Constable had a rough idea of what had happened but had no idea of motive until he actually saw Jenny, when he concluded, quickly, that it must have been attempted murder.

"Hello Miss Drysdale. I'm Constable Barclay but please, call me Stephen. I'd like to ask you a few questions, if you feel you're up to that."

Jenny nodded, slowly, and Constable Barclay could see immediately that the doctor had not exaggerated – the painkillers had made her very slow and he expected that he would not get very much out of her tonight.

Jenny described suddenly seeing a man, seeing the look of panic on his face, his dark hair, black glasses, medium appearance, slightly unshaven….not an attractive man….but what she remembered most was his frightened look, as though, as though he was almost horrified to see me…

"And this was in your room, which is on the…."

"No, Constable, I wasn't in my room, I was in Helen's room. My computer had broken down and she let me use her room whilst she took a class."

Constable Barclay stopped. "You weren't in your own room?"

"No. Is that important?"

"I don't know, maybe….maybe." He searched through his notes. "I can't find a record of that, I don't think we knew you weren't in your own room." He could see Jenny was beginning to flag and the nurse pointed to her watch. "Ok, sure," he said. "Jenny, last thing… do you know of anyone who might want to hurt you in this way…someone who has something against you, would want to do you harm?"

Jenny looked down and then gently shook her head. "No Constable, I don't."

Constable Barclay left, thanking Jenny for her time, saying he'd be back tomorrow if that was ok. The nurse told Jenny she would leave also, but she could simply press the buzzer that was close to her right hand if she wanted anything. Jenny nodded and managed a smile which hurt her face.

She lay on her back on the bed, knowing that it would have been impossible for her to sleep and wishing the nurse had stayed. Maybe tomorrow she would tell Constable Barclay the truth, of how she knew who it was who had done this to her and why. She closed her eyes and saw Tom, Tommy, again….the student who had flattered her, who had told her how interesting she had made the classes, how he wanted to be just like her, doing what she did when he left University, enthusing and inspiring people as she did. He would come for coffee in her room and at first they would talk about tutor/student topics and essays and exams but after a few visits the talk became more general, more personal, until she began to know more about Tommy and he began to know more about her. He excited her, not only because of his enthusiasm for her, but his appearance….dishevelled almost curly hair that crept over his head like a wild garden, making her long to run her hands through it, sparkling little almost innocent blue eyes, soft rosy skin. And it was clear that she excited him too. Then on the days when she knew he was coming for coffee she would dress up a little, maybe a skirt, maybe a little more make-up, perfume. And he could see the effort she'd made and she knew he knew what she had done. Which gave an inevitability to what happened and he would go round to her flat or they would meet in other places, even going away for a couple of weekends to hotels far enough way to make them feel safe.

Jenny should have told her boss, she realised that, but she wanted this to be kept a secret and so did Tom. The dangerous liaison was kept between them and Jenny satisfied herself that her ethical code remained unblemished. She hadn't given Tom any explicit examination details, she hadn't helped him anymore than she would have any other enthusiastic student.

Then suddenly and without warning Tom ended it, as perhaps 19 year olds are wont to do. Jenny was devastated and realised how much she had grown to like, perhaps even to love, this guy who was funny, who could be so charming, who could make love three or four times a night. He tried to be nice to her but basically explained that he had found someone his own age, was happy, that he was sorry but had had a lovely time. These things happen, etc, etc…

But Jenny felt wronged and she felt hurt and she felt taken for a ride and she wanted revenge and stupidly she took an action that she would never really forgive herself for. Tom was a bright student, one of those who looked to be of First Class calibre. But he failed Jenny's programme of study and it took his average to below that of First Class standard. Of course, he had not failed it, the paper was probably worth about 70% but Jenny never even bothered to read it, marking it at 20%. She made sure the paper wasn't subject to any second marking or external assurance procedure and by so doing she determined the grade that would be on Tom's transcript for the rest of his life. It made her smile inside and for a while she was entirely convinced she had done the right thing.

Then Tom came to see her, all fire and bluster, knowing what she had done. He exploded like a thunderstorm of anger and frustration and she quite enjoyed seeing him hurt. 'Good,' she thought, 'now you know what it's like to feel hurt.' But when he had calmed down he said to her something that chilled her: "I'll get you back for this. I'll make sure some harm comes to you. You absolute bitch, I'll make sure you pay for this." These words had not been spoken with the same anger as the rest of what he threw at her that day. They had been quite calm, his eyes fixed on her, his finger pointing at her.

And she knew now that this is what had happened. Someone that Tom knew had come to punish her…to hurt her how badly she didn't know…but they must have followed her that morning, followed her closely, to know she was in Helen's room and not her own. And that look of surprise on the guy's face…was it because she wasn't pretty and he wondered 'How did Tom get involved with this ugly thing' or was it because she was a small quite delicate little thing and he felt bad at having to pistol whip her like he did. She was certain that he didn't want her dead though – if he had wanted that then she would already have been dead for there had been ample opportunity to shoot her.

Jenny sighed, sighed because everything in her head hurt physically and sighed because of the self-loathing that seeped through her. She couldn't tell anyone what she suspected, what she knew, let's face it, had happened to her earlier today because to do so would mean she would surely lose her job.

As Jenny lay in all sorts of pain, Constable Barclay went back to the station and spoke with Amy Phillips, the police officer who had taken Helen back to her home.

"Yeah," said Amy, "we knew it was this other girl……this Helen's… room. Do you think the guy was looking for something and expected the room to be free?"

"No," said Constable Barclay. "I think he might have hit the wrong girl. I think he was expecting to find someone else. I think this Helen… she was the one he thought he would see."

Officer McLean, sitting across from them, lifted his head at the mention of the name 'Helen'. He looked at Constable Barclay. "You think Helen…this girl Helen…is she in danger?"

"Who knows? He had a gun, didn't he, what else might he have a gun for? We need to talk with her, this Helen, soon – she may still be in some danger."

Officer McLean tapped a pen against his chin, puzzled and thoughtful and not a small bit worried. He looked at his mobile phone and couldn't understand why he hadn't received even a message.

CHAPTER 6

Between the five of them, they had managed to make clear to the waiter that they were looking for a car......a second hand car, most important feature was that it had to be able to carry all five of them. Thankfully for them the waiter's English was better than their French and he explained that one of his friends was selling a car...maybe not the most beautiful car but functional...

The waiter phoned his friend and a hurried conversation took place in French. "Ok, he says ok....about 2,500 Euros for the car but if you can talk well maybe you will get it for less...I will write down his address for you...bon chance. I will bring your coffees."

Ellis threw some Euros on the table. "Forget the coffees, we have to go now. You have been very helpful."

Helpful, yes, thought Oliver, maybe too helpful and since he was wary of everything and everyone he looked at the waiter as a prisoner might look at a judge who had sentenced him to death. Perhaps every waiter in every bar in the area was looking out for someone of his description...

Ellis ran off to find a bank and returned with enough money to buy the car and then some. "Right, let's get a taxi to this guy's house or flat or wherever he stays and get out of here as quickly as we can."

Oliver held the piece of paper in his hand with the address on it. He opened it and didn't see the address itself but only the district at the bottom – L'Ariane. "Shit!"

"What? What is it?"

"It's supposed to be a bad area....I mean I was told it was a bad area, I heard of someone who got beaten up quite badly there."

"So what?" said Ellis. "We're not going to be there for very long, it's not as if we've booked a hotel there for two weeks. And I'm happy to throw over 3,000 Euros at this guy if it gets us out this damned place."

The five friends sat in the taxi without making conversation. The weather was warm, stiflingly warm, one of those days when it seemed to get warmer the longer the day went on. They were squashed together, a couple of them with luggage on their knees, and they could all feel the sweat almost everywhere on their bodies. Euan no longer doubted the main gist of Oliver's story…maybe he has over exaggerated here and there, but he could see Olly was clearly very frightened. In fact, he thought, I don't think I've seen him like this before. Olly always seemed in control, self-assured, not scared, not someone who might run away from anything. And Euan realised, maybe for the first time, that Oliver wasn't tall. He wasn't tall at all.

Aidan sat, quietly, desperate to use his mobile phone, at least to let his wife know that he was safe if nothing else. He wasn't sure if he believed Olly's story but he was absolutely convinced that Olly had lied about Clotilde. 'I deal with actors all the time,' he thought to himself, 'and he was definitely acting.' He also felt that Oliver's first reaction when he saw them was, if only for a split second, one of anger. He didn't want them there. And if he's lying about Clotilde then he could easily be lying about the whole story. 'If I wanted to disappear for a few days and get up to what he's been doing, I'd make up some hugely over the top cock and bull story too,' thought Aidan. Part of him was angry at the thought of having been dragged out here because of a lie and part of him was jealous, as part of him was always jealous, of Olly.

Ellis wasn't sure of Oliver's story either but he took it seriously enough to want to get out of the area as soon as possible. He wouldn't have been shocked if Olly had told them, sometime later, that it was really just about Clotilde…but then to make up such a story, no one would do that, would they? Anyway, he could see the fear in Olly's face, in his expressions, even in the way he spoke more quickly than he normally did.

Ali felt out of his depth. He was shocked at finding Olly in the flat because the flat smelled absolutely of intimacy. Her thong was by the bed he had been lying on and the whole place had the feel of a couple's togetherness, sexual togetherness certainly but more than that and it shocked him that Olly could have betrayed his wife and child. As for the story…the problem for Ali was that he did believe it, at least some of it and he believed that at least Olly, if not all of them, was in danger. He prayed quietly and inwardly for help…for help out of this situation but also for the strength to deal with what might happen to them.

Eventually the taxi came to a halt and the friends looked around them. They were on the edge of a built-up area which was clearly a place where outsiders were not welcome. Some of the windows on some of the houses were boarded, some with metal where windows used to be. There was no human presence on the streets. The friends didn't get out the taxi until they saw three people come out of one the flats and come to meet them.

The biggest, and clearly the man who had been friends with the waiter, was called Guy. He was fat, with a huge black beard and a featureless, smile less face. He must have weighed at least twenty stone, thought Oliver. He had thick white hands, fat fingers and wore a white vest, very much like British people used to do in the 1960's when it was a sunny day. He grunted. Oliver thought about holding out his hand to greet this massive presence but then thought better of it and simply nodded. Oliver thought – and he struggled to stop himself smiling as the thought came to him – that this man looked very much like the gruffalo character that he used to read about to Terrence for his bedtime story. The man pointed to his left, meaning that they had to walk somewhere to see the car. Perhaps, Oliver assumed, a garage. But this was L'Ariane and he remained conscious of what had happened to Martin.

Behind Guy walked two others, a girl of twenty years who was gruffly introduced as Natalie – "my girl" – which the friends took to mean as daughter and Jacques, a lumbering bulk of a boy about the same age introduced as "her boy". Natalie was very pretty and Ellis wondered as he looked at her how on earth this brute of a man could have been involved at all in the production of this lovely girl. He smiled at Natalie and she smiled back. The lumbering hulk of a boyfriend looked at the smile with a frown and his dark eyes met Ellis' with an unsubtle "back off" stare. This emboldened Ellis and he smiled broadly at all three of them.

Jacques had arms, noticed Oliver, that were too long and gave him a gangly unseemly gait. This, combined with his small open mouth, little head and huge shoulders gave him the appearance of someone who, as Ali would say, "didn't have the lights on upstairs". Ellis looked again at the girl and the boy and couldn't understand that connection either. With the right make up, a bit more money, perhaps a bit more time spent in front of the mirror, Natalie would have been stunning. She sort of skipped gently along in an almost see through white cotton dress, humming a song as if she were in her own private world. Ellis could hardly take his eyes off her. 'She could never have chosen a monkey like that,' he thought and then began to wonder if it was an incestuous family thing….or perhaps it was her brother and they had misheard Guy. But no, as she glided along Jacques put his thick tattooed arm around her, again more in a statement of 'Don't even look, let alone touch' than as a loving gesture.

They turned a corner and moved to a more secluded place where the friends could see a blue Renault car. It looked fine and big enough for five and Oliver felt like saying there and then – 'Let's see if it starts and just buy the thing'. Guy led them towards the car without words and Natalie skipped along, Jacques almost prohibiting her with the restraining arm around her waist. Oliver suddenly panicked, looking around him for places where someone with a gun might hide, for as they walked closer to the car he began to realise they were headed into a cul de sac. But he saw nothing…buildings, sure, but the angle they were at would have surely made a shot impossible. He looked at the three people that led them down the road…two brutes but surely even they could not expect to beat five guys without help. Perhaps there was help, people hiding behind garages maybe, maybe close by… and he began to sweat again, not the sweat that came from the sun's heat but the cold clammy sweat that came from fear.

As they neared the car, it became clear that Natalie could speak quite a bit of English and she acted as a sort of translator for her father, though she added smiles where he glowered and looked at Ellis whereas Guy hardly took his eyes from the road. Jacques tried to keep his arm round her but she moved a bit away from him, freeing herself, and Ellis smiled at her all the more. Jacques stood with his back to a garage and turned round to put the key in it. Immediately Oliver wondered what was in the garage and Natalie must have sensed his fear for she turned and said "Oh, ok, don't worry, he looks just for the car's….em…papers, documents, if you want to buy." But he didn't open the garage and the five friends walked round the car, pretending to be interested in it. Ellis would look at the car, stroke parts of it gently… the bonnet, the doors, the boot… and look at Natalie as he did so. He didn't need to check Jacques' response, who by now was beginning to boil and silently rage.

Ellis looked at Natalie and nodded to the inside of the car. "Sure," she said, "of course you must try it inside."

Ellis sat in the car, feeling the steering wheel, smelling the acrid stench of old tobacco. Still, the car was clean now and Aidan would probably love the smell. Guy became slightly animated and exchanged quick dialogue with his daughter in French.

"Um…he wants to know why you……why you want this car. Are you in difficulty?"

Ellis looked at her and smiled. At that moment he didn't have a clue what to say. "Difficulty? Now what sort of difficulty could you imagine five guys like us might be in?" She smiled sympathetically. "No," he said, "no difficulty. But we want to tour around the place......maybe go to Monte Carlo, maybe go to north Italy, Switzerland....we have a few weeks holiday and we thought we would use the trains but it's quite... restricting...so we wanted to get a car, not too expensive....then we are free to do as we want."

She translated and she must have translated well for the retort from Guy, through her, came back: "why not hire a car?"

"We thought about that," replied Ellis, "but we don't know where we might finish. Maybe France, Switzerland, Italy. Hiring a car... well, you need to give back to a certain place at a certain time...this car...we can use then try to sell on when we go home... if we can't sell it then it will have done its job for us anyway. Say," he said, again looking at Natalie, "where do you recommend we go? Where should we visit?"

"I'm sorry? I didn't understand..."

"To visit, where is nice to visit...."

"Ah, yes, I see. Monte Carlo is nice, very near and in Italy, if you go... Genoa, Portofino... Switzerland the mountains are beautiful...Geneve... em, Geneva.."

"You don't fancy being our guide, do you?" Ellis grinned at her. The comment was half-whispered and he didn't expect that she would have heard it.

"Oh, em, I have work here, I work..." and he saw her blushing as Jacques came closer, like Guy not exactly sure what was being said. Jacques tried to pull her arm away, to take her away from the car and nearer to him.

"Easy tiger," said Ellis, staring at Jacques, "just a friendly conversation..."

Natalie loosened herself from his grip. "Forgive him, he is a little... em..angry...no, not angry...well, he is not so good in these days."

'Can't imagine he'd be good in any days,' thought Ellis. He looked around his friends and motioned to them to sit in the car. "See what you think boys." And he looked at Natalie. "Can we start it up, maybe even take it for a little drive?"

She looked at her father and he barked something in French. "Um, yeah, that's ok...but for one person to stay here.."

"Of course," said Ellis and both Oliver and Euan stayed as Oliver insisted that he should not stay on his own. They smiled at their French acquaintances but only Natalie returned a watery half smile. Jacques stayed by the garage, as though he were a guard in front of something of great importance, and Oliver feared that he might open it at any time and unleash some form of hell upon him. Natalie couldn't stand still, a pretty picture in constant motion, humming to herself, her dress billowing slightly in the breeze. It was inevitable that his eyes were drawn to it – to her – as, with the sun behind her and the almost transparent dress, there was a stunning feminine silhouette in front of him. Without trying, and Oliver could be quite good at trying, he could see tight white underwear. He glanced back to Jacques and could see those dark eyes boring into him, knowing what he had done and what he had seen. He looked towards Guy the gruffalo, a frowning monster of a man and he whispered to Euan. "I wish they'd hurry up. Then we can throw 3,000 Euros at this bunch and get the hell out of here."

"Maybe we should ask them how much they want for it," said Euan. "Might speed things up a bit." Oliver nodded. "Um…how much do you want…for the car, how much?"

Natalie looked at her father who almost shrugged his shoulders before speaking with his daughter. She confirmed the amount with him and confirmed the amount to herself in English. "2,200 Euros." Oliver immediately felt there was something not quite right here. They had been told 2,500 so he found a pen in his luggage and wrote down the number '2,200' before showing it to Natalie and her father. "Yes," she confirmed, "that's right, yes." Odd, he thought, very odd. These are people who don't look as though they have tuppence to rub together, you would have thought they would have wanted to negotiate a higher place……but Guy's shrug of the shoulders, it was the only sign he had given so far that he was actually human and it was nonchalant, like the price doesn't matter. He looked at the three of them again, for some evidence of money in their clothes, something in their appearance which didn't say that these were poor people. Guy and Jacques, with tatty vest and dirty t-shirt, old jeans and flip flop shoes…there was no money there… Natalie's dress didn't look so expensive and apart from her flip flops the only other thing Oliver could see was her underwear. Even if it was silk……

This was strange. Oliver wondered what might happen if he gave the impression that the price was higher than expected. "Oh," he said, and grimaced a little…."I thought maybe 2,000…but I guess, well, maybe that will be ok…but I thought 2,000.."

Natalie translated and Guy nodded his head almost without taking notice of what was being said. "Ok. He says 2,000 is ok." No it's not, thought Oliver…

The friends returned and Ellis gave a thumbs up as he drove the car back to the exact same spot that he had taken it from. "Ok, we'll take it," he said, "now to agree the price…."

"It's ok, that's done, 2,000 euros," said Oliver, starting to take the luggage to the boot of the car.

"2,000?" said Ellis. "Are you sure? That's odd…"

"Very. Very odd. But let's get on with it and get out of here," said Oliver, beginning to move more quickly. He was starting to look like a man who was a bit desperate and it was clear that Guy and Jacques were beginning to notice.

Guy called his daughter over and after a quick conversation she said: "he asks if can he see a passport. From one of you is ok. In France we must see identification when we sell a car."

The friends looked at each other. "Sure, of course," said Ellis with a smile, taking his passport out of his bag and passing it to Natalie. Both Natalie and her father poured over it, lingering for quite a while on the last page, looking at the photo then looking again at Ellis. Guy nodded silently.

To Oliver, who was continuing to attempt to put all the luggage into the boot, this was increasingly concerning. 'Just give him the bloody money,' he felt like shouting at Ellis. He motioned the other guys to the car. Ellis, meanwhile, was absorbed with Natalie and as they confirmed the fee of 2,000 Euros Ellis held his hand out to her, as one might when concluding a business deal. Behind him, Jacques shifted nervously and Ellis could almost hear him breathe. Natalie took his hand and Ellis held it softly in his own, more a hand hold than a handshake.

"When in France," he said, and leaned in to Natalie to kiss on both cheeks. At this Jacques shouted Natalie's name loudly and certainly Natalie seemed to want to feel Ellis' lips on her cheeks, smiling and turning first her right cheek to him. Guy shouted something quickly at Jacques and motioned him towards the garage. Oliver watched as Jacques quickly opened the door of the up-and-over garage and went inside. Instinctively, as he loaded the last piece of luggage in the car, Oliver looked inside the garage.

What happened next happened in a few frantic seconds. As Ellis slowly kissed Natalie and breathed her in, as the rest of the friends began to get into the car, Oliver saw a shotgun lying on the floor of the garage. Jacques seemed to be making his way towards it. With speed that came from the adrenalin pulsing through him, Oliver leapt to the garage and slammed the garage door, trapping Jacques inside.

"Ellis, get the fuck out of here, they're part of it!" he screamed at Ellis.

Ellis withdrew from Natalie and threw himself across the short distance to Guy, the speed of his attack and the force it mustered throwing the huge man off his feet and he fell over, slowly toppling, hitting the ground as a dazed heavyweight fighter might. Natalie put her hands to her mouth as Ellis rushed to the car and, with Oliver in the driving seat, they screeched off. Oliver had taken the key to the garage with him and threw it out the window after a few hundred yards.

"What did you see, what happened?" asked Ellis and he spoke for all of them as no one had seen what Oliver had seen.

"Shotgun, in the garage. That guy was going for it. I saw the gun, lying on the ground. He was virtually bending down to get it."

"Shit!" said Ali. This was becoming horribly real, guns on a hot afternoon in the south of France. What might these people do, where does this end?

"But it's not....it doesn't.... I don't understand then." Ellis spoke quickly. "That big guy was surprised when I rushed at him, you could see it in his face. Maybe he was trying to get those papers that Natalie said we needed... oh, shit, we didn't pay them, I didn't pass the money across... we've effectively stolen this car.."

"I'm not going back there!" shouted Oliver. "We have the address, we can post them the money if we feel that badly about it. But I'm sure the guy was going for the gun, I'm sure of it. Where the hell are we going? How do we get out of here? Does anyone have a road map of this place?"

They headed back towards Nice and found that the first garage they stopped at had a road map and they took the chance to fill up with petrol and every conceivable type of non-alcoholic liquid along with sweets, crisps and snacks of indeterminate origin. They decided that they would take the train across the channel and so they must head towards Paris, taking the E15 from Avignon and the E80. There had been a hurried debate about whether it was best to take the main motorways or the back roads and the motorways had generally won but with the caveat that they should probably turn off and stay in smaller hotels, B&Bs, pensions etc if they had to stay. The general idea was to travel through the night but they recognised that a hot car without air conditioning was not exactly conducive to rest and if they had to stay for a night or even two then, as long as it seemed safe, that was fine. It was a small price to pay considering the forces that Oliver had convinced them might be in pursuit.

"Are you sure there was a gun there Olly? Aidan asked. "I was looking in the garage and I never saw a gun."

"Yes, yeah, there was, on the floor, on the right hand side as you looked in, towards the back....and that lumbering hulk was heading right for it..."

"Was he moving quickly?"

"Quickly enough," said Oliver though in truth, when he thought about it now, Jacques didn't seem to be moving with much speed at all.

Back in L'Ariane, Natalie had seen the key being thrown out of the window and had run down the road as the car sped off. She picked it up and sped back to her father, who was still trying to get up. He leaned on her and raised his massive frame up from the ground. By this time Jacques was banging on the garage door and she quickly opened the door to let him out. He sprang out, his eyes furiously searching for "the English bastards" who had locked him in the garage. When the three of them came together they tried to make sense of what had happened.

Jacques – and Guy – had forgotten that the old hunting rifle was even in the garage. It was broken in any case. It was so remote from their thoughts that they did not associate it at all with what had just happened. And it was very difficult for them to process what had just happened as they spoke with each other in quick French, their Gallic temperament emphasising their gestures, making their confusion and anger self-evident and dramatic to anyone who might have seen the conversation that developed.

"These guys were not thieves," said Natalie, "they weren't poor, they looked wealthy..."

"They bloody were thieves, they stole the fucking car!" exclaimed Jacques. "And anyway you could not think anything bad of them, you would have gone with them.." and what he muttered under his breath sounded very much like 'prostitute'.

"We needed to get rid of the car, at least it is away," said Guy. "Better to have got some money for it, yes of course......but I agree with you Natalie, they did not look, they did not behave like people who were thieves. I think the one who got you in the garage Jacques, I think he was frightened."

"Thieves can get scared," said Jacques.

Natalie had a thought, a fear, one which emanated from her stomach and forced an involuntary gasp from her. By the time it was audible to others it was almost a scream.

"What?" Jacques looked at her in confusion as she started to cry with deep sobs. She struggled to breathe.

"What? Tell me, what?"

"The money," she said it in almost inaudible gasps. "I think… the money….still in the car."

Guy turned pale. "No, Natalie, no, no! It must be in the house. I told you days ago it was safer now, you must have taken it out.."

Natalie shook her head and her tears flowed more freely. "No. I thought…there was a call to my phone….there was no one on the other end but I was scared…I thought I was being watched, being monitored… I didn't want anyone to see me doing anything…for all these guys know the money could have been in an account…but if anyone saw me, shifting it…."

Jacques looked at her. "And you remembered this now? You useless bitch!"

He looked as though he was about to strike her when Guy came between them. " Ok Jacques, ok, no violence between us.." Natalie almost screamed at him, "It's my money anyway you big idiot! It's me they paid, it's me who's in any danger. If it's lost then it's my money that's lost."

"We're in this together Natalie," said Jacques. "We're in this 150,000 Euros together."

Guy said, "Maybe these guys who stole the car….maybe they were from the Defense. As you said Jacques, we needed to get rid of the car anyway, they knew it was ours, they knew the registration…maybe it was a loose end for them and maybe they knew where the money was."

"No," said Natalie, "I don't think so, I don't think so…these guys didn't seem like thieves….they had something to hide I think but what? Who knows?"

"Then," said Jacques, "we must go after them. They have 150,000 Euros beneath the compartment in the boot that they don't know about."

"How will you do that, you iron head?" Natalie almost shouted at him.

"I saw they were from Edinburgh. The guy's passport…next of kin was an address…I remember it…it was a wife I'm sure. Jacques, are you still friends with the guy in the police?"

"Friendly enough that I can get an eye kept on the car, that they can look out for it…but not much more than that."

"Do you think they are going home? Maybe they were right when they said they were touring… maybe we should wait for a day or two… "

Jacques and Guy looked at each other, silent nods of assent. "Ok, we wait. For a day or so. See if we hear anything. If not, we then go across to Edinburgh to this bastard's house and wait for him. In his fucking front room if need be."

When Clotilde's brother told her that Oliver was not there, about an hour or so after he had discovered this for himself, she made out to him as though she was angry but inside she was relieved. She knew that he had escaped, though she doubted if he knew from what. It could not have gone on much longer anyway, even if she had not wanted him dead – at some point the French police would have become more seriously involved. People like Oliver didn't go missing, not handsome respectable people.

As she returned to her flat she contemplated its emptiness and how large it was going to seem without Oliver there. She thought of the things that were going to hurt her, like his smell on the pillow, his shape in the bed, the lack of his presence when she woke up…if she was going to get to sleep in the first place. She nearly allowed herself a tear as she thought of him.

It was not an empty flat that she found when she returned, however, and she had barely walked through the door when she was grabbed by what she thought were two men who placed a black cloth over her head and roughly bundled her into a car. She was breathing hard, and at times struggled to take in enough breath through the cloth, but she never said or even tried to say a word. Instead she wondered how these people had got her. She could not conceive that her brother would have betrayed her. But if not him then only Olly….and that simply didn't make sense. Olly must be the one they really wanted, not me.

She was led out of the car with the cloth still on, upstairs in what even from inside this crude bag seemed like a big house as she could hear the echo from her shoe clicks reverberate around a large area. She had no idea where she was and had stopped trying to follow the route the driver had taken after a few minutes but she could now hear the gentle lapping of the sea. The cloth was pulled off and she looked out across a breath-taking view, the sun still glinting and flickering off the water.

A man she did not know came and sat down opposite her. He carried authority in every step he took and after he sat down he simply stared at her for a while, his hand cupping his face, with a superior smile creeping across his lips. She stared back and thought, for probably the first time, that she was going to be killed quite soon. Apart from the initial fear, which forced her eyes to look around and behind her for an escape route, this did not fill her with as much panic as she expected it might. Before he spoke, her last thought was how depressed and empty she must be that the thought of dying did not fill her with horror... my being feels already dead she thought..

The Capo could see from the way her eyes moved and the quick terror that registered that she thought she might be killed before the evening finished. It was a look he had seen more times than he cared to remember. Then, suddenly, she seemed to relax.

He held his hand up to her, showing her the palm, in a symbolic gesture of surrender. "Rest assured my dear, you are not going to die here tonight. Well, if you do, it will be due to natural causes and not down to me. I am sorry for the blindfold... .but it was necessary, as it will be necessary when you are taken away from here." He looked at her, her face, her body. "Excuse me, would you mind very much if I asked you to stand up please?" She did as he asked and as he twirled his index finger she turned around. He motioned her to sit down. "You're a very beautiful woman."

No death, thought Clotilde, but maybe rape? Perhaps that's what I'm destined to be, the whore of some sort of Godfather type. Instinctively, she thought, let's get this over with, and it's not going to be rape if I consent. Instead of sitting down she grabbed her top and began to pull it over her head, leaving her standing in front of The Capo with a white bra. The sunlight shone on her and The Capo was dazzled, putting his hand up to his forehead. She mistook his silence for encouragement and began to undo her trousers until he held his hand up, with force this time, not surrender.

"No," he said softly, "that's not why I brought you here."

She put her top back on and said calmly: "you're not going to kill me and you're not going to fuck me. What is it that you want to do to me?"

"Would you be very offended if I said information?"

"You could've called for that."

The Capo smiled. "I know you had a man staying... Oliver...with you for some time. I need this guy. I want to know where he is now."

Clotilde felt she could deal with this in two ways. She could either tell him very little, answering his questions with short if truthful answers, or she could give him huge answers, full of information, much more than he needed, perhaps even full of lies to see how much he actually knew and, more of a puzzle to her, where he knew it from.

"Why do you need him?" He stared at her, without words telling her that he was the one who asked the questions. "I ask the question because he seems a harmless guy to me and I would like to know what he's done wrong before I might be giving you information that could send a man to his death…though, by the way, I really have no idea where he is now."

"I need to talk with him. One of my partners has told me that this guy, Oliver, blinded him in a fight. I need Oliver's side of the story before I… "

"Before you what?"

The Capo raised his hand, this time with authority and Clotilde decided to talk and try to give him more information that he could process.

"I've known him for a while, quite a while, maybe three to four years now. He does business down here quite a bit, he used to stay at a hotel that I helped to manage, my co-manager at the time still runs it but I decided to move on and do other things. The hotel trade here, you know, it's difficult, it's competitive…uh, anyway, we sort of forged an understanding between us you might say and the number of trips increased until over his last few trips the stays got longer and he started to stay with me in the flat. He's stayed with me about three times now I think…" and she lifted her eyes up and to her left as she pretended to count… "yes, three times I think and this last time, he'd been there for about eight nights, nine days and now of course he's away, you know that. He's married, he says he's married to a girl back home and he has a child, a little boy….But you want to know where he is now….well, I don't know…I assume that if you don't know then you don't have him… I went out this afternoon, I had to go into work….well, I try to take time off when he comes over here so we can spend so much time together but I had to go in for two hours this afternoon. Then, when I left, I phoned my brother to tell him about the leaking tap, my brother is good at fixing things, and I told him that Oliver would be there so don't be alarmed… but my brother phoned back to say the tap is ok now but Oliver was not there. No sign of him, no clothes, almost as if he had never been there. So this upset me as you can imagine and I went home…when I got through the door your goons got me and now I'm here….so, to answer you, no, I don't know where he is or why he has gone."

"You have no idea why he might have left so quickly?"

"Maybe his wife? Maybe something has happened with his family?"

"My associate was injured by Oliver on Saturday night. Were you with him?"

"I don't think……oh, yes, I was, we were at the thing in Monte Carlo…"

It was about the only test The Capo had. If she had said she had not been there then he would have known she was lying. But this all sounded terribly believable and he began to curse himself that he had promised Paul he would do something about it.

"And… "

"And…nothing…we went to this dinner, a big corporate thing, expensive…"

"It is at this event that my associate said he was injured, blinded by Oliver."

"Really? Well I can't……well I wasn't at the same table as Oliver….we didn't go as partners, it was a corporate thing and we were split up, our tickets were for different tables…but I remember…well I think we left quite early…I just recall him coming up to me to say we had to go, he wanted to go."

"And he didn't say why?"

Clotilde held her head down and blushed. "The truth? He said he couldn't look at me any longer in that red dress and not want to make love to me."

Again, thought The Capo, totally believable. 'I don't think I would be able to go twenty minutes without wanting to make love to you,' he thought. "But you told the police the two of you left separately."

"Yes, I did."

"Why?"

"That was to the police. I wanted to protect him. I didn't want him found by people……people like you."

The Capo smiled. "Yeah…people like me."

Clotilde had told lie upon lie, story upon story, aware that it could have put her life in danger. All to try and ascertain from where this guy had got his information. Had it been from her brother then he would surely have stopped her by now, telling her that he knew she was lying. So if not her brother, then from whom? He can't have had the flat watched, he can't even have known of her existence before tonight otherwise he would have come and taken Oliver away or killed him.

"But he didn't tell you about the fight he had?"

"A little. He told me a little."

"So where has he gone? Why has he gone? Has he done this before?"

"As I said, maybe something has happened at home…"

"He didn't phone you? Wouldn't you phone someone to say you had to go…or leave a note…"

"Maybe he did leave a note….I didn't get far into the flat before your boys kidnapped me… maybe he knew he was in trouble…."

"But how would he know? I mean, why leave now?"

"How would I know? How did you know where he was?"

Clotilde didn't get an answer and she didn't expect one. Instead he looked at her and smiled, gently shaking his head. "May I ask you a personal question?"

Clotilde opened her arms in front of her. "I was ready to take my clothes off in front of you and you could have done anything to me. I think you can ask me anything you want."

"You're in love with this guy, Oliver…" Clotilde nodded. "But he's married……so don't you feel a bit like…he's probably only into the sex bit with you…don't you feel a bit like his whore?"

Clotilde had never felt like anybody's whore. Since the first time, that Saturday night when she got him home and forced him into this, she felt infinitely more powerful and in control than Oliver. "Maybe he's my whore. Maybe the sex bit is what makes me love him. Anyway, now it looks like he's gone so I guess I'll just have to find myself a new whore…."

The Capo sighed. Beautiful women like this, mixed up in this nonsense….as Clotilde sat opposite him, he toyed at times between killing her and asking her for a date. Was she telling the truth? Who knew. Always a sucker for a beautiful woman….He might have the flat watched, the line tapped, some work colleagues (for there were always some) primed as informers and some staff in some places looking out for her with a specific male companion, but he felt there was little point in killing this beautiful woman.

"Well, good luck in that search. Miss de Bresseau, I must ask you to leave now. Unfortunately you'll be bundled back into a car with a blindfold the same way you were as when you came here…"

"Are you going to kill me?" She asked the question as though she was asking if it might be ok to smoke.

"Two things: I told you when you came here that you would not die tonight and I am a man of my word. Secondly, if I'd wanted you dead then you would already be dead. But I need to talk to this guy. I will not have him killed indiscriminately, I don't have snipers looking for him....but if you hide him, knowing what you know now, then that might change the way I see you. Don't give me a reason to want you dead, Miss de Bresseau. You're a very beautiful woman." Two men came and stood behind Clotilde. "Now go with these men before I want you to take your top off again."

Clotilde smiled at him, not a weak watery smile but a confident full faced sparkler of a smile with flashing white teeth and that full mouth. He held up his hand to the two men behind her as she stood up and The Capo nodded to them in assent. She leaned across to him. "What's your name?" she asked. But The Capo looked at her only, her soft black hair gently blowing with the breeze from the sea. "Well, anyway, this is for you...," and she leaned across and kissed him on his right cheek, so close as to be almost on his mouth.

As she walked away with the men, she thought of how she had wanted Olly dead and had activated her brother to carry this out. But yet she was relieved when Olly had escaped and she had lied to try and stop this man finding out information that could have put Olly in more danger. Somehow, though she couldn't have him and the flat would be empty when she returned, she was glad that he seemed to be safe. And, just before the blindfold was put on her, she saw The Capo's garden full of hundreds of roses, yellow and red and pink and white, all bright and vibrant and looking as though they might live forever. For the first time that day, she cried for the loss of Olly.

As the car drove away, Davide walked over to The Capo. "Do you want her killed?"

"No. But I can't say I trust her so monitor. He may come back to her. I think he knows he's in danger....she seems almost ignorant of it... if he knows he's in danger he'll get out... what did the original message you got say?"

"It was brief, as I said. Only an address in rue Cassini, he's there, staying with a Clotilde de Bressau."

"Do you trust the source?"

"Didn't come to me directly, it came through one or two people. I don't actually know the source. Want me to find out?"

"No, no." He suddenly sounded angry. "Do you think someone else has found him before we have? Before I have? How is that possible?" He smashed one hand into the other. "I'm pissed off that this thing is taking up so much time. This guy's wife?"

"Just the same, he's not returned there.....we are struggling to get a tap on her mobile."

"Hmmm...." The Capo was right to an extent, he was pissed off that this thing was taking up so much of his time. But he was more pissed off that he had wanted Clotilde and had stopped himself from having her. Part of him toyed with getting the guys to bring her back. "Fuck!" he shouted loudly. Davide looked at him, it was unusual for him to hear his boss lose his temper. "Tell me what else is going on Davide....please at least tell me the doctor managed to castrate that bastard who wanted to fuck Angelique......."

Tom sat with his father, watching the news on tv. Tom and his father often sat together, watching something, but didn't often actually communicate. Sometimes his dad would comment on or shout things at the tv and Tom would nod or laugh inwardly or very occasionally add his own comment. 'That must be what happens when you get older,' he thought, 'you shout at the tv...but it's an inanimate object....it's like clapping at the cinema.' And he figured that it was one of those things that people did as they became more powerless to change things, they shout about how rubbish they think things are. Or write letters. His dad was always writing letters, getting into epistolary debates with other similarly deranged people in national newspapers. Tom shook his head at the very thought.

The news on the television was indicating that there was a heightened level of alert, something which seemed to be measured in colour codes. It seems that things had moved to a colour that was very close to red, from what Tom could see and the reporter was telling of increased security, lengthened queues at airports, check-in in plenty of time. Government ministers gave interviews with sonorous faces, even the Opposition supported the government in this fight against "those who seek to destroy our way of life."

"But what I don't get," said Tom, "is that the government think they are winning. Look at the queues, look at the hassles....they've probably picked up a little bit of information that some bad guy has leaked, just so that we all get inconvenienced like this." He pointed to the screen.

"There won't be any threat," said his father, without emotion. "It's only to make us feel in danger and to then make us feel protected. Think about it. If there was an increased danger, if there was an actual chance we were going to be bombed, would you really tell the perpetrators that you had found out about the threat in a public way like this? Of course not, you'd keep quiet about it, go about your business discreetly and arrest them. But doing this," and he waved his hand at the screen, "this keeps us in fear, keeps us in check, let's you know who's in charge…"

The story ran for a few minutes and changed to something about a flu bug, something which had emanated in a district of southern China, a mutation of something from animals. Seemingly it was potentially lethal, had killed a few people in China, possibly spread across various parts of the world now by aeroplane travel…

"We should ban aeroplanes," said Tom. "Statistically, it would cut down both the terrorist threat and the threat of getting some scabby disease from a Chinese chicken… "

"That's another thing," said his dad, "don't you think we've always had this type of thing happening? Flu being spread from one part of the word to another? But now we get words like 'pandemic' and 'epidemic' and no one knows what they really mean but they frighten people, the connotations of these words…….they're emotive, people get scared… another way of keeping us scared. You know what Tom, these things seem to get more prominence when times are bad. Right now we've got high inflation, fuel prices getting so high you need to be a Saudi to fill your car with petrol, we've got an experiment, a failed experiment, in a single currency that's costing billions on a pretty much monthly basis, we've got public services being cut and we've got little or no wage increases. These are conditions for a revolution! But what do we get on the news… things to frighten us, to make us think about dangers that will kill us, of terrorist groups attacking us. You notice how they never say the attack is specific to an aeroplane because you have to be vigilant, you could be attacked anywhere at any time, a bomb in a city centre….and if the terrorists don't get you then the killer animal flu will. So people don't think about the inflation, and the rising mortgage and the fuel price… they think about what they might catch from a door handle, or from a guy at the bus stop who's sneezed because exhaust fumes got up his nose…or what sort of bomb's in that bag or trolley that someone has left in the supermarket because they forgot to get something about ten aisles away. Tom, your chances of getting bombed, or getting the next round of animal flu or some life threatening disease…well, you've done statistics, what are the chances?" It was a rhetorical question and Tom did not have time to answer even if he had wanted to. "They're about a thousand to one, maybe ten or twenty thousand to one. But your chances of getting hit by a cut public service, or higher fuel cost, or a higher mortgage because billions and billions of pounds were given to a set of institutions who couldn't do their job properly...infinitely higher, wouldn't you say? Don't get me started on all this" – 'I think I already have,' thought Tom – "it's all about making people think in a certain way. Distracting their minds. If you think about what's happening over here," and his dad threw his arm across to his left, "then you won't think about what's happening over here", and he threw his other arm over to the right. "Government disinformation......been going on, in one shape or form, since Mount Olympus."

Tom looked across at his dad. This was an unusually long outburst and Tom wasn't sure if he should validate it with a nod of the head. 'Maybe best to keep quiet,' he thought. Then he changed his mind and nodded his head vigorously as his dad looked across at him. 'Change the subject,' thought Tom....

"I em.......I got a rejection today... a letter, saying I wasn't going to be asked for interview."

His father looked at the tv and didn't raise his eyes to catch Tom's. "Nothing else? No reason?"

"I phoned...and at first the person I spoke with gave that usual, you know......high quality of graduates etc....so I said well, was it down to other attributes, work experiences, was that what they were using to define 'high quality' because I thought....well, you know, a high 2:1 is a decent qualification. Then she was a bit non-committal but when I pushed said that 'no, no my other attributes were fine'....but the quality was so high that they were able to put a criterion of 'must have First Class degree' against the job spec and so......."His voice trailed off, as though he need add no further comment.

This time his father did raise his eyes and they flashed at Tom's in thinly disguised anger.

"I don't know what to do about it, dad. I appealed to the Uni about the course but they said I can't appeal a mark on academic grounds. I asked if my paper had been second marked, had been seen by an external examiner and they said that all the usual quality assurance principles had been adhered to. I know my paper was good and I know it was her, I know she gave me that mark for spite..."

"Why the hell did you get involved with her in the first place Tom? She's your lecturer for god's sake…."

"I guess….well, I guess….I mean, I liked her….she was nice… "

"I hope she was good in bed. I hope it was worth screwing your life up for."

Anger flashed through Tom. 'Yeah,' he felt like saying, 'she was good in bed, what's it to you?' or, 'why, are you jealous?' but of course he said neither.

"I'm not saying she's blameless, of course she's not," said his father. 'Here we go again,' thought Tom. "A person in her position….are you the only one she's seduced?" 'What an old person's word,' thought Tom, 'seduced'. Was I seduced? It sounds quite nice, I hope I was.'

His father suddenly raised himself up. "Surely some of her colleagues knew about this… your friends…if you went to her and told her that you were going to go to the Principal, that you had information from various sources to support your claim that she had been biased against you because of this affair…she must have to declare that. If you're screwing a student, you must have to tell someone, don't you? You're involved with someone….like you must have to declare when there's a family member on your course or programme or whatever it is."

"Oh yeah, I'm sure you do," said Tom. "But that's the thing dad, nobody knew."

"But they did! We knew. Your friends must have known. Her colleagues must have known. What about the places where you stayed, hotels….they must recognise people….are there credit cards, receipts… did she pay?"

"Yes," said Tom. "She paid. But I can't go about asking for credit card receipts that aren't mine. And I can't exactly ask the police to investigate. As for her colleagues… nobody knew, she kept it secret, I'm absolutely sure of that. Wouldn't you? And as for my friends, and you….well, you and mum are not exactly neutral, are you? Neither are my friends. She'd deny it. She'd have to or she'd lose her job."

"There must be someone," his dad said, getting agitated and increasingly excited, "someone who saw you together."

"Oh, tons of folk saw us having coffee together….in her room or in the Ref…."

"No, no, no…I mean in a hotel, wherever you stayed. You must have eaten… "

"Room service," Tom interrupted.

"Well you must have walked in and out the bloody place together! And you must have looked an odd couple, the sort that people might remember. You said she was in her 30s…"

"She was…she is……but she looks quite young…I don't know. Do you really think it's worthwhile trailing around the… whatever it was, four or five hotels where we stayed all that time ago….about two, maybe three months ago…to see if anyone remembers a couple they might have seen for twenty or thirty seconds…."

"Didn't you have breakfast?"

"Room service."

"Jesus Tom, did you ever go out the room?"

"Not much," said Tom truthfully and smiled in recollection at the memory of more sex than anyone his age had the right to experience. At times her appetite for him was voracious and for him, being with a woman who had, as he used to say to his friends, 'been around the block a bit'….she gave him a lesson in his own sexuality and gave him sensations in places where he didn't know he had places. Every time with her they seemed to discover a new orifice.

"Don't you think it's worth a try?"

"Honestly, dad, no, I don't. I think the only one who can change this is Jenny. And she won't. She can't. I tried to appeal to her better nature then the last time I saw her I threatened her and that doesn't seem to have had any effect."

"What did you threaten her with?"

"Oh, I don't know…probably should have made her go on an aeroplane or travel to southern China…I can't remember, I said I'd get her for it, I'd punish her… who knows, I was angry, they were just empty words… I don't think I could threaten anyone with anything really…"

"Tom, you were an arse. An arse who did a stupid thing. But you're young and that's about the age when people do stupid things. She's done something that is getting pretty close to being illegal. At best, she must have broken every ethic in the book. She should pay for what she's done to you. You should have got a First, Tom. I know it, you know it and she knows it. Now you're getting turned down for interviews you should be getting because this stupid cow made a decision that you are going to have to live with for the rest of your life. She should pay for it." And again, more quietly, in a more determined manner. "She should pay for it."

"Dad, let it go….most jobs ask for a 2:1 minimum….I've got a high

2:1….it's annoying on a personal level but I really don't think it's going to affect my chances too much."

His dad was silent. "I can't agree with you, Tom. No one should be allowed to affect someone else like that, through spite." He paused for a minute. "Have you heard back yet from that job with the six months in New Zealand? You really wanted that, didn't you?"

"Yeah, I still do, that would be great, six months over there. No I haven't heard back from them. I phoned yesterday and they said they've not chosen the applicants for interview yet so, here's hoping…"

The HR director of that company and the manager of division sat with the list of applications. They both had one candidate who they felt was a question mark – should they ask him for an interview or not? The HR director pointed out that the prospective interviewee candidate had only failed one course and that overall his profile looked good. However, the manager of division pointed out how significant that particular course was in the overall remit of the job the applicant was applying for. It was like an applicant applying for a tax position when he had passed everything else but failed tax. Anyway, argued the manager of division, the rest of the candidates had First Class degrees whereas this candidate only had a 2:1. The HR director countered by saying that had performance in the course that was failed been at the same level as the other courses then the candidate would have merited a First Class degree. Exactly, concluded the manager of division, he did not and that area is vital to the job.

The HR director of the company accepted the argument and nodded her head. The manager of division left the room. The HR director picked up Tom's application and tapped it against her chin, deep in thought. 'Odd profile,' she thought. 'Odd result. There's a story to tell there, I'm sure.' And as she placed Tom's file into the pile marked 'non-interviewing' she thought for a brief moment, as she sometimes did, on the magnitude of the decisions that they took at times like this.

CHAPTER 7

After a while, Oliver's looks into the rear view mirror became less furtive. He didn't relax as such, none of them felt they could do that, but he became less conscious of a car racing after them....or of someone slowly overtaking them and putting a bullet in his brain as they passed. They also realised that they were probably going to have to stop for the night, somewhere. They were too hot, beginning to tire and the car was simply awkward. It was old with scratches and holes in the seats, with that smell of smoke which seemed to seep out of everywhere, even with the windows open, and it was difficult to get comfortable.

The more Oliver thought about it, the more he was unsure of what Jacques had been trying to do. Had I not seen the shotgun, he thought, I don't think I would have said he was moving towards it. But I did see it......and he was going in that direction.

"Did anyone else think those three were dodgy? Was it only me? It's just that now, when I think about it, I'm not as sure as I was back then." Oliver asked because he was interested but also because there was a silence there, a silence which was becoming increasingly awkward to him as the awareness, and the guilt at what he had dragged them into, began to pinch at him.

"The money thing was odd," said Euan. "But that doesn't mean anything, not really."

"The three of them were odd. The big guy looked like an inbred mutant...and for him to be with that cracker of a girl... that doesn't make sense at all...and the father....his supposed daughter didn't have any of his features, his characteristics... I don't think they had the relationship they said. The two guys had probably captured the girl and were sharing her... or the big lumbering one was maybe the son of the big fat one in the vest...maybe she was the sister and maybe he was the father and maybe they were both shagging her in some sort of incestuous domestic Gallic bliss......" Ellis tailed off and the others looked at him, wondering where his imagination might take him next. "Well," Ellis retorted, "I'd find that easier to believe than them being out to kill us."

Ali said: "They were strange, unusual. But the only vague threat I felt was that they might rob us. They weren't people who looked part of any….what might you call it…syndicate."

Aidan had been quiet, thinking things over, taking in what he had seen, making conclusions and he concluded that if they had not 'been on the run', so to speak, then the behaviour of these people would really not have seemed that strange at all. There was the natural caution of people who're selling and people who're buying a car, there was the language barrier, there was the added complication of Ellis fancying the girl and being quite open about it. No wonder everyone was edgy. "Olly," he said, "I don't think there was that much that was so unusual about these folk. A bit odd, maybe. But you can find 'odd' in any city, in any house pretty much. And the folk who're after you… if they are so close then they would have got you already, they would have known where you were… but clearly they don't because you are here, we are all still here, and we haven't been under any threat at all since we came out that girl's flat. Not really. Is there a chance that maybe…maybe this is all in your head? Maybe someone has convinced you that people are after you and they've got you looking all over the place for things… well, things that aren't there."

Oliver thought for a minute. Could he have been misled? "I don't think so… I….the guy I hit, the guy I blinded….I don't think he was exaggerating… and Clotilde……she had no reason to lie." But he realised now that Clotilde had plenty of reason to lie and it would not have been entirely unusual for an upstart like Paul, the man he blinded, to exaggerate his own sense of importance and the extent to which he was 'connected'. 'Have I really been this duped,' he thought, 'because Clotilde wanted me?' Would she, could she, have lied about the danger I might be in to have those few days….well, maybe as many days as she wanted… Christ, if that's what's happened…and again he felt a sense of betrayal, a sense that he hadn't questioned it enough, a sense that he had been a willing sinner.

"What happened anyway?" asked Ali. "How did you get in this situation at all?"

"There was a dinner on Saturday night, last Saturday," said Oliver, beginning his story. 'I may as well tell them everything,' he thought. "It was a… big sort of corporate thing….an important one, a posh one.."

"So how did you get an invite? You didn't come here for the dinner, did you?"

"No, no, I didn't…I came here to fix up contracts for buying the base

130

metal for the figures for the next two to three years. That's where Clotilde came in, she's one of our major suppliers. There are one or two others but the guys in Nice – and we ourselves in the UK – wanted it fixed through Clotilde's company if we could. They're a big outfit, less risky...some of the others could have done it more cheaply but they're getting squeezed and we felt....well, maybe they won't be around too long. We can all offer things on the cheap if we have nothing to sell. So that was the main purpose in coming here. And I went with Frederick, the guy who runs our office here, on the Wednesday...or was it the Thursday...maybe....I can't remember... anyway, it doesn't matter...we went to fix the contract with Clotilde's company. We met with her and her boss over this lovely lunch and the boss said to her – 'why don't you give Frederick and Oliver the two tickets we have for Saturday?' We didn't know what they were talking about but it was a big gala event, a charity dinner at this lovely Hermitage hotel, a black tie affair, lots of famous people to be there apparently. But Frederick couldn't go, he had something on and eventually we decided that Clotilde and I would go. The two tickets weren't together, though....I think Clotilde's company were late in trying to get these things and so they had to take what they could get. But the way she spoke – the way her boss spoke – it was maybe a good event for their company to be seen at. And it was going to be a great dinner, a beautiful dinner, casino, beautiful views etc. Personally, I didn't want to go....you know these things are not really me..." the four friends looked quickly at each other, all of them concluding knowingly that this might be exactly the sort of place they imagined Olly might be and that it was 'really him'......"but we had secured a major deal with the company and it seemed a decent way to celebrate that.

So Clotilde drove me to this thing on the Saturday. I was a bit surprised, I thought she might drink and that maybe we would get a taxi or a train but she said the trains could be unpredictable at night and that taxis cost a fortune. I didn't know what she meant by that, "unpredictable"...whether she meant they were late or whether she meant that you might be in danger on them at night. She came to the flat to get me and came upstairs...that surprised me a little, I was going to go down to the car...but she came upstairs to get me. She looked... .she was very dressed up.... and I wonder now that maybe... well, it's only a thought...but maybe she wanted me to see her like that rather than seeing her in the car. She had this red dress on..." And he recalled at the time how it made him a bit uncomfortable. It was a big event, an important event, we would all dress up for it, but she walked around the flat he stayed in as though she wanted to be seen. By him.

And now, for the first time, he began to think about every way in which Clotilde may have deceived him and his mind had not yet worked things through fully enough for himself that he could present his story to others without pausing and reassessing its significance. Specifically, he wondered if Clotilde had been trying to seduce him from the start of the night. Which led him to thinking if she had tried to seduce him before and he thought through all their previous dealings, in an instant trying to find anything that was more than mere flirtation. But he couldn't find it. She was beautiful and she knew that he thought she was beautiful and at times he had looked her up and down and she knew it. Her smiles, her affectionate touches, her clear eyes and the way she let her eyes travel wherever they wanted to let him know she found him attractive too. But so what? These things were not unusual and Oliver could see from the way that other men looked at Clotilde that they cannot have been so unusual for her either. Yet when he saw her in the red dress she really did look like someone who had made an effort....by coming upstairs to let him see her, Oliver convinced himself that the effort was for him. She made sure she turned around too, so he could see the way the dress glorified every curve and every movement and she made sure he was behind her as she sashayed her way through the flat, parading her subtle, thumping sensuality.

"Anyway, she drove to this thing. Monte Carlo isn't so far away and it was a nice drive....God, that seems like years ago, when you were with someone and spoke about things like work and the weather and...stuff... ," and he thought of the things they spoke of, ordinary normal things, not things that were charged with anything. There were no 'innocent' brushes of hands, nothing that was out of the ordinary...and it was dark by this time so however appealing her legs may have been, however much her dress may have been riding up to show him the tops of stockings, he couldn't have seen it anyway. No, he thought, maybe I was wrong, maybe she wanted to see the flat, see where the company put me when I was over here...

"...and so we arrived and she parked her car...I think someone parked it for her and we went in and had a glass of champagne as you do at these things. She had told me on the way that I probably wouldn't know anyone...and that that was ok because she wouldn't know anyone either. But I shouldn't worry as pretty much everyone would speak English. Well, she was right in the second thing, everyone did pretty much speak English, but not in the first as she seemed to know lots of people. As we briefly stood together quite a few came up to chat, as though…" and he thought about it carefully, looking back, reassessing, thinking of the way people reacted when they saw her…"as though she was some sort of long lost friend." And he thought again, remembering the people who had come to see her, who kissed her on the cheek three times, not little kisses of greeting where the head was turned away but kisses you gave when you knew someone and turned your head into them…"or a lover they hadn't seen for a while." His friends looked at him as he drove. "All the people that knew her were guys. Not one girl. All guys."

He said it quite slowly and quietly as the realisation came to him. It was one of those moments, maybe a moment of epiphany, when you realise you know nothing about someone. You see a veneer, a front imposed by social norms of work and respectability, but then you're with that person in a situation where these barriers are stripped away and you get a glimpse of a tiny part of what's underneath. And it surprises or shocks you a bit, in the way we tend to say: 'Oh, I didn't quite see him doing something like *that.*' The thing that struck him the most was that all these guys seemed almost in awe of her, the way you might be if you had slept with a film star. At the time he hadn't noticed it so much, mostly because he'd looked around the room, breathing in the heady atmosphere of opulence, ball gowns and crude wealth. It seemed to fill his senses, the noises of polite laughter, the chinking of glasses, the touchy-feeliness of these people, but most of all the beauty of their fragrances which all seemed to combine into one fabulous scent. 'This must be what heaven smells like,' he thought.

"After a few minutes looking around this place….jeez, it was fabulous, the sort of place where you'd imagine they might have a scene from a James Bond film…there was a call to be seated, dinner would be served shortly." And he thought back to walking over to the notice board with Clotilde, she took his hand as she guided him towards it, again something he hadn't really registered at the time.. 'Ok, you're at table five and I'm at table eight…ummmm…I can see the names of the others you're with there and….no, no, I don't think I know any of them.' Oliver smiled a watery smile. 'Hey, it's ok,' Clotilde smiled and kissed his cheek, 'be yourself and you'll charm the pants off them. Literally.' And she gave him a playful childish wink. 'I'll come find you after the meal…we'll go home, or dance, or go gamble…whatever you want….enjoy yourself, Oliver, have fun. Hopefully it'll be a good night, one to remember.' And she squeezed his hand and off she went. But though she had touched him and kissed his cheek, it didn't have intimacy as much as reassurance, he felt then as he felt now that she had been trying to make him comfortable, to let him know he at least had one friend in this rather daunting place.

Oliver could see Clotilde from where he was sitting. In a sudden flash, he had the strongest feeling, the clearest image of himself and Helen, sitting in a restaurant in the old part of Nice, drinking beer and eating pizza and listening to music on a bustling Saturday night in the south of France. He felt terribly homesick. Yes, for Terrence too but mostly for Helen. It would be great to have had her here for the weekend....to have lain about the beach, drunk wine in the afternoon, eaten together at night...held hands, been a couple... it was hard sometimes to be a couple. You were somebody's father or somebody's husband....I want her here, being my lover. And me hers. As he sat down and smiled at the others at his table he saw only Helen.

He was at a round table with nine other people. Quickly, he realised that there were four couples and one other single guy who Oliver immediately termed "The Spare Part". He looked like the kind of guy who would never look at home anywhere...bespectacled, with a mouth that turned down and gave him a constant look of sadness, a soft rather dumpy nose and fat cheeks, he was clearly only here because he was wealthy. He was sitting opposite Oliver, the farthest away he could be from him at a round table, which was good because Oliver imagined that it would be like drawing teeth trying to have a conversation with him. He told Oliver his name – as they all did when they introduced themselves – but Oliver never heard it and didn't bother to ask him to repeat. The guy sat on the edge of things all night, never initiating a conversation, never smiling. Oliver thought of where the guy might be at home, what was it that he did where he became 'someone'? Professor? Some trader of things who sat in a back office? Or born rich into a huge family business, bullied by a domineering father and a passive mother? The guy made what seemed to be an expensive dinner suit look like something the cat had dragged in. His straggling brown hair hung in separate strands around the collar, Oliver thought he saw specks of dandruff on the collar and the guy's eyes lacked any interest and enthusiasm, just dull lifeless forms. Oliver flirted between feeling sorry for the guy and wanting to jump start him.

Then there were the four couples. To his immediate left sat a very attractive guy, his short grey hair giving him a dignity that was strengthened by his large hands and commanding smile. He spoke clearly and was very fluent in English and Oliver noticed how his mouth seemed to almost exaggerate the pronunciation of every word as it widened and stretched. He was called Charles and was a lawyer though by the glint from his small gold cuff links and the time he took quizzing the staff about which wine to choose, Oliver guessed that he was a pretty successful one. That is to say, a pretty rich one. Next to him sat his wife, Astrid, almost an archetypal Nordic beauty with flowing blond hair, blue eyes whose sparkle would have eclipsed that of the sea as it swept into the shores of Monte Carlo, and a soft and lilted accent when she spoke in English which told of exactly who she was and what she had done – been born and raised in Scandinavia then lived in France for several years. Oliver wondered, as he watched her, what people like Astrid did with their days and one of the first questions he asked her and Charles was if they had children…at least, he thought, that might give her something to do. Turned out they had three, aged between seven and two but despite Oliver asking a few interested questions they seemed disinclined to talk much about them. Perhaps they didn't want to bore us with the tales of children, he thought….or perhaps they have a nanny and haven't got a bloody clue about anything to do with the children.

To Astrid's left sat Brigitte and her husband Roland ('but you can call me Roll or Rollie'….actually, thought Oliver, I'd rather call you Roland….) Roland worked in the financial markets but Oliver never really determined in which market and wasn't sufficiently interested to find out. He didn't like Roland on sight – the guy was loud, had quite obviously already had a few too many glasses of champagne, was balding and had swept what hair there was over his head but most of all Oliver didn't like him because he kept referring to Oliver as "our Englishman". Everything he said that involved Oliver referred to his nationality, everything that he brought Oliver into the conversation with had some sort of comment like "I wonder what the English perspective is on that." Oliver told him at least twice that he was Scottish, not English, but that wasn't what bothered him so much as being constantly made to feel an outsider. What was the guy trying to do? Demonstrate superiority? Make him feel uncomfortable? Oliver soon began to imagine that it might be a good idea to smash Roly-Poly in the face to see if he bled.

And girls who looked like Brigitte……how did they end up with oafs like this? She was charming and beautiful but quiet and Oliver quickly concluded that her quietness was no surprise. Roland was a guy who had an opinion on everything, not that it was ever expressed as an opinion but instead as the objectivity born of fact, and Oliver imagined that, beyond the obligatory "yes dear," she must struggle to get a word in edgeways. Oliver wondered, and as he did so wondered also if others had a mind as contorted as his that it would think such a thing at such a time after seeing people for so little time, what sex was like between them. He saw it as the Oaf on top, everything pretty much at his request….almost rape…no, perhaps that's unfair…but he bet the Oaf didn't hang around much to make sure she was satisfied. He looked at Brigitte and wondered when she last had an orgasm. Part of him wished he had the strength to say it out loud, it would give him an excuse to leave. He glanced quickly across to Clotilde and he saw her talking, laughing, and what seemed to be nine other pairs of eyes at the table watching her.

Next to Brigitte sat The Spare Part and the body language between them was quite amusing to watch. The Spare Part almost defied anyone to analyse his body language because he seemed to compress his body into such a small area that, beyond the obvious discomfort, it was hard to see him make any gesture or to see him shift consciously or subconsciously in any direction. Even when he ate, his arms seemed to hardly come out from his body and his head was so low that there seemed to be no distance from his hand to his mouth. Brigitte was almost always turned away from him and towards her husband…perhaps listening to the Oaf was going to be easier than trying to initiate a conversation with The Spare Part. When they did talk Oliver was pretty certain, even with his limited knowledge of French, that they were talking about the weather.

On The Spare Part's left sat Vincent and his wife Valerie. Oliver liked Vincent straightaway – he smiled a lot, clearly never took himself too seriously, paid a great deal of attention to Oliver and seemed keen to learn about him and what he thought of the south of France, and had one of those faces that was full of expressions. Almost as though you could see the character, the true character, in the way his lips, his mouth, his eyes and his nose reacted. Oliver liked watching him, even when he was talking to Valerie, and you could see his eyes widen or his mouth open as she told him something. They went together very well, he thought, Valerie and Vincent, they looked like a couple and seemed so together that Oliver couldn't quite see either of them with anyone else. He saw them as childhood sweethearts, perhaps even the boy/girl next door and he wanted to ask them how long they had been together, when they first fell in love, how many others – if any – there had been for either of them. They were both made more attractive by being together. You couldn't really look at either of them without looking at the other one because the one would always either be talking with or looking at the other one or would immediately engage them in the conversation. It wasn't in the least annoying, instead it was quite touching to see. Oliver thought of Vincent on his own, maybe in an airport, walking…and of how those expressions and the free way in which his face gave a clear view of his soul simply wouldn't be there…and he saw a different guy, without Valerie an expressionless, almost lifeless façade. And when he saw them making love he heard them giggling and laughing, he saw them caressing each other, a mutual exchange of pleasures where the giving meant more than the receiving.

To Oliver's immediate right sat Elaine and to Valerie's immediate left sat the guy who called himself Paul. It was clear to Oliver, as soon as they both sat down, that something was not right between them. Perhaps they had had an argument on the way there, perhaps they had not been getting on for a while, perhaps one of them had done something to piss the other one off. You couldn't tell – and in truth, thought Oliver, I don't think I want to know – but something unpleasant had passed between them. They were the last to sit down at the table and they arrived in a rushed and flustered manner, he adjusting his hair and she touching her earrings and adjusting her dress. When they sat down they did so without smiles and Paul simply said their names, not giving Elaine a chance to introduce herself nor wanting to hear the names of any of the others at the table.

Paul and Elaine almost immediately, gently but perceptibly, turned away from each other. Paul shook hands with Valerie and Vincent and Elaine turned to Oliver. She said her name and held her hand out, not in a firm confident "let's shake hands" way but more in a "I'm presenting my hand to you, take it in yours" manner. Oliver held her hand, which she immediately turned down, and as soon as he took it Oliver felt as though she was asking him to kiss it. He didn't, giving the hand a limp shake whilst feeling how soft it was as her fingers gently touched the palm of his hand when she withdrew. He looked at her and her full eyes were gorging on him, her lips breaking into a smile. Oliver smiled back, a polite and nervous reaction.

Like everyone else around the table – certainly every woman – Elaine was beautiful and spoke English with that French lilt that so many French people do. She had bobbed black hair that shone, little diamond earrings and a flowing figure-hugging black dress. The dress was one of those dresses that Oliver thought must present such a challenge to woman – it was stunning and she looked a picture in it, he admitted, but he bet that when she got home that night her first words would be "I couldn't wait to get that dress off!" It was strapless and the material was gently plaited across most of the dress until it came to the cups, when it faded out presumably to emphasise what was in the cups. I wonder what she was thinking of when she bought that dress, thought Oliver.... The dress pushed her chest up a little bit more than she clearly liked as she seemed to spend a bit of time, at first discreetly but then more openly, pushing and pulling and prodding herself so that she fitted into the thing with a bit more comfort. But it certainly had an effect and the cleavage that it enhanced was soft, brown suntanned skin that you knew went over her whole body and that moved gently whenever she changed her position at all, almost whenever she spoke. It pulled you in ways you could not ignore, a bit like the way an alcoholic might stare at a bottle, knowing that was within could ruin you but that the pleasure involved in getting there might just be worth it.

She asked him questions, interested questions, what he did, who he was, why he was here, was he married and she never lifted her eyes from him. He asked similarly interested questions of her and as she spoke to him she let her eyes travel over him, his face, his hands but mostly his eyes. Sometimes she would make as though she couldn't hear him, or that the band playing in the background were too noisy (they weren't) and she would lean in closer to him, allowing him to lower his head to hear her and take in a full view of her cleavage. As the evening wore on a bit she adjusted herself once or twice when she did this and Oliver concluded that this could not be a coincidence. His uncertainty and discomfort was allayed slightly by the fact that he felt she was a woman who was, right now, quite a lethal combination of someone who had had a bit too much to drink and had a need for some sort of attention since she wasn't getting any from her husband. That meant she would have craved attention from any male that was sitting next to her. This is not about me, he thought.

In Oliver's experience, tables at that kind of event rarely had "table" conversations. People chatted in little groups of maybe even up to five but rarely did conversations bring in the whole table. There were good logistic reasons why that might be the case. There was a reasonable distance across the diagonal of the table, which meant that including everyone would be difficult without shouting and with a band playing in the background it made physically being heard a bit harder. Plus, when people have had a drink, it's quite hard to get nine people to shut up and let only one speak. "Sub" conversations tend to develop and the group discussion is gone. However, this was a little different in that they did manage to have a table conversation....or perhaps it was a table listen as it seemed that the Oaf wanted to do all of the talking. He was initially only talking to Charles and Astrid but the ostentatiousness of his gestures and the volume of his voice couldn't help but draw the attention of the others. He changed to talking in English when he saw Oliver was listening...."I will speak in English for our Englishman here, I would like to know his thoughts too…"

"What I'm saying is that we should be rid of the European experiment, it is a waste of everything. Most of all, the biggest waste of money. Do you know that we gave money to the Spanish recently, to Spanish banks? Billions of Euros. I think they need even more but that's not my point, my point is that we have given money to something that doesn't work. It's broken. If something has to go bust then it goes bust and something else, someone else comes in to take the place. That's our system. But instead we support these failed institutions… and you know," and he started pointing around the table, to ensure he had the attention of everyone, "and you know that to pay the Spanish, the Italians had to borrow money. That's crazy. But it's not the really crazy bit. The really crazy bit is that they had to borrow money at a higher percentage of interest than they will get back from the Spanish. And they had to do this, because they belong to this…stupid, corrupt club… Englishman..," he pointed towards Oliver.

"Oliver, actually… and I'm Scottish…"

"Ok, ok, Oliver…in your country your people will work longer until they get their pensions, their child benefit will be taken away from them if they earn over….I can't remember the sum….and you'll charge for people to go to university. All to support a failed currency and failed institutions. Some people – stupid people – they say….and we have plenty of them here in France as you do in England I'm sure… they say politics will not and does not and cannot affect the lives of people. Hah! It is just nonsense. These people affect us whenever they take a cent of tax from us….we will have to work longer in France too…" He paused to gulp some wine and Oliver interjected.

"But our government's money has gone to supporting our financial institutions, not the Euro...."

The Oaf pushed his hand out, silencing Oliver and his interjection. "It's the same thing. Your government gives money to the banks so they lend money because that's what banks do...but they don't lend money to businesses or people for mortgages anymore because if they go bust the bank won't get the money back...no, no, they lend money to countries like Greece and Spain and Ireland who can't repay...so central banks and the European Union give these countries more money so they can repay.... so, directly or indirectly, it all supports the Euro." He slowed down slightly. "Just think for a bit on the changes the Euro has brought to us, the way it has changed lives, the way business had to adapt to charging new prices...the cost involved...just think of the effect on people, on ordinary people...and tell me, was it, is it worth it?" He paused.

Charles interjected – "I am pro-European, very pro-European....if you have a sense of history...what happened in the last century must never happen again." He looked round the table. "The original intention of the group in 1948 was always for monetary and economic union, you know."

"Oh come, come!" The Oaf was, if anything, more animated. "We are unified enough now to prevent us killing each other again. We have learned from that mistake. Indeed, we must not make it again. And imposing a currency without there being a country is a disaster. The EU has sovereign states, it's not a federal arrangement. The Greek government can do whatever they want to, we can't tell them what to do! There is no European country so to have a European currency leads to the disaster we have now. Listen, if this corrupt experiment cost nothing, fine, they do what they want...politicians...fine let them play. But the effect on your business, my business, his..." and he pointed to Oliver "life, the age to which he works, we work....the effect on businesses when banks won't lend to them because they're already too exposed to what happens in the Euro zone so investments don't get made, people lose their jobs, we stay in recession...all these things, people don't join them together, they don't see the horrors of the effect this failed experiment has on all of our lives." And he gulped again from a large glass of wine and stretched across to refill his glass.

He continued but by this stage the sub-conversations had started to develop and Charles had turned to Oliver and asked about the feelings towards Europe and the Euro "in your country". Oliver didn't really know how to answer: the differences between Scotland and England were significant, probably Wales too for all he knew, and he broadly indicated that when times were fine there was less noise about money being spent on things like supporting the Euro but when times were tough… people perhaps saw problems closer to home as being more pressing and worthy of attention.

"Despite myself," said Charles, "I hate politics. I want to love it and I would like to be involved. But I hate the waste of time, the waste of money, the way things take so long. Sometimes, democracies are the best adverts for dictatorships, aren't they? I hate paying tax but I pay it and I think my company will pay more tax than it has to because I feel it is a duty, it comes with being a citizen of this country. But I hate the way they think they know best, it's like the church used to be…it's more subtle, less obvious, but it gets to the level of telling us units of alcohol on wine or any drink, of telling us not to work beyond a certain number of hours a week because we may get stressed. Like the way the church used to try and control people, you know….the church used to be very strong, the Catholic church I mean….you know no sex before marriage, be frightened of God and it tried to control the way people thought and the way they behaved…I think of politicians as the new church…"

"I've never been religious," said Oliver, "but I think all churches tried to do the same. Still do in some cases. What was it the Jesuits said…give me a boy till the age of seven and I will show you the man…something like that…that said, I think perhaps churches, Christian churches….that have so little political power these days…are perhaps better places to belong to now. But the politics stuff….we get the warnings on alcohol too, smoking has pretty much been outlawed, if you see someone you think is cheating their benefits there's a number you can phone to be a whistle-blower, and you know that if they need to they could tap into every phone call you've made, every text message you've sent, every web site you've looked at…."

Astrid leaned across. "It's the little details that I don't like….that maybe change your life a little bit. There seems to be a desire in France now to be rid of…what's the word in English…" She turned to Charles and mentioned a word then turned back to Oliver. "…to disinvent the car, is that right?" Oliver nodded his head, the sense of agreement adding vigour to his movement. "So, you know, we see things change…so yesterday you could turn right there but today you can't so you need to

141

travel a much longer way, much farther, to go the same way. Public transport here is ok I think, maybe… maybe better than your country… but still not so great that you would want to sell your car. So everything is made harder for you if you drive the car…so you travel longer, the journey takes longer, there are more cars using this road because you had the cars that were using it anyway and the ones who are using it now because they could not turn right before. And changes like this, they happen all the time….almost every day it feels, little by little, things change, your routines change, they're taken out of your hands…." And she shook her head with a look of resignation and a shrug that indicated you simply had to put up with it.

Oliver was ready to reply because he felt he had quite a bit to add here. Edinburgh had been a city of roadworks, tramworks, gasworks and general potholes for, it seemed, as long as the first dinosaur had roared its way into life and the changes that came about on the roads – roads that became one-way streets, roads where you couldn't turn right, roads where you couldn't turn left, roads where you couldn't turn left or right – seemed to happen overnight, every night. However, The Spare Part leant across to Astrid and spoke in French to her and Charles joined in. Whatever he said interested Brigitte and the Oaf got up and, presumably, went to the toilet.

Most people had, by now, finished their desert and it was at that stage where things began to break up slightly. Some people got up to talk to others at other tables, some walked away from the tables to make calls, some went to the toilet and drifted into conversations with people as they got there. Vincent and Valerie were engaged in a conversation with each other, Elaine and Paul were quiet, still gently turned away from each other.

Elaine turned towards Oliver and started talking with him. It could have been about anything and Oliver didn't remember the focus of their conversation at first. But perhaps he wasn't meant to, because Elaine leaned in as she spoke to him, kept adjusting herself but not in the quick almost flustered way she had before but more slowly as though she wanted to focus his eyes on her hands and what they were doing. This must have gone on, Oliver thought, for about twenty minutes. He did not remember a word of that part of the conversation, only the way she looked at him with full inviting eyes and the soft brown flesh of her chest as she presented it to him.

When he did begin to remember the conversation, however, was when he looked up from her and saw Paul, staring at him, clearly with hate or something close to it in his eyes. Paul's eyes were narrow, his mouth tight, lips tense and Oliver looked at him then immediately looked away though he could still feel that burning sensation. Paul must have started at him for a full two minutes. Oliver didn't move away and Elaine moved closer to him, once or twice drawing her chair in. It was also clear that Elaine had had, by now, a bit too much drink: not so much that she was completely drunk, but she was beginning to slur her words and any inhibitions she may have had had been lifted.

Suddenly Paul pushed his chair back and stood up. He leaned across to Elaine and shouted in a gruff whisper something into her ear. He pointed at Oliver as he did so, his face again full of barely disguised rage. He then walked away.

Oliver smiled. "Is something wrong?"

She shook her head. "No, no, he's just being a…" and she thought for a minute and smiled. "I don't know the word in your language…" And she placed her thumb across her middle finger to make a hole of her hand and then moved her hand up and down quickly.

"Ah!" said Oliver, "….you mean he's being a wanker…"

"Yes!" she exclaimed, bringing her hands together in a celebratory clap. "My husband's being a wanker! I like that word, wanker, it suits him… actually, my husband is not just being a wanker tonight, he is a wanker most of the time…"

'I don't doubt that,' said Oliver under his breath.

"He was nice once, you know," she said…"He was nice before. Before I married him. And a little bit after I married him too. He was kind. He can still be kind…he isn't horrible to me, he doesn't hit me or anything, it's only…." and she tailed off as though the reasons were either so obvious they didn't need explanation or were so difficult they couldn't be explained.

"Only……what?" Oliver offered, having glanced across at Clotilde and seen her engaged in conversation. She's not exactly ready to leave, is she?

She grabbed his arm. "Well maybe that's what happens when people get married… But it's not the same for everyone, is it? No, not for everyone. Look at the two that were sitting next to us, over there… " she threw her arm in the direction of Vincent and Valerie…"they still love each other. They look like they might eat each other. I'd like to feel like that about someone. But I don't think I could feel like that about anyone.

I don't think it's only Paul. I think being married to anyone….you know, after a while……you'd be thinking……this isn't what it was……I need something new…."

"Well," said Oliver, thinking of Helen and thinking of Helen being here and them having that weekend…"maybe you need to do new things, go new places, do things together you haven't done before. Get the odd time, maybe the odd weekend away from the children. To stop, you know, things getting…"

"Boring?"

Oliver smiled. "Maybe that's the human condition. Maybe that's our essential struggle. Against routine. And routine can be boring. But sometimes it's comforting, it's the warmest blanket wrapped around you and it says 'No harm can come to you'. I like that."

"You know what I think," she said, her eyes darting all over him. 'She has practically undressed me,' Oliver thought.

Oliver didn't reply. He was going to hear it anyway. By now there was nothing subtle about her movements and she was lifting her chest towards him as she adjusted herself.

"In life we are encouraged to be what we can be, to be as much as we can. To try our best and to strive for more, to want more. That can be a personal thing, a spiritual thing or a material thing. Maybe mostly material these days. You know, you work harder to earn more money to buy more things for you, for your family….to provide more, to make them happier. We don't really stop. Not till we maybe retire. But what I mean is, if you're the vice-President you want to be the President. If you're the assistant boss, you want to be the boss. I think it's the way things are….perhaps in your society more than mine but the attitude is still strong here. This kind of ' you can always do more' attitude… " She paused to take a drink.

"And that's a bad thing?" said Oliver, unsure as to where she was going.

"No, no, I'm not saying it's bad…well, too much, yes it's bad …but the 'push' is a good thing, I think? Ambition is not a bad thing. Anything, taken to excess……yes, it's bad….but that's not really what I want to say… " She paused and Oliver watched as she picked the wine glass up gently between her thumb and middle finger…

"What I want to say is…somehow that same…what might you call it, logic… well, that same logic doesn't apply to love. With love, you should find someone and stay with them. You don't think of getting more…

Love doesn't have ambition…you don't strive for more, for more people, to be with more than one person. You're supposed to find one person and that's the way you stay, happily in love forever."

She looked at him again, softly and with warmth. Her beautiful brown eyes rested on him. "Everything else….the other things in your life… you get taken, pulled, in that different direction. Always more. But the desires we have for other people, we should not want more."

"I'm not sure I understand you." And he was right, he didn't. But what he didn't understand was whether she was having a conversation about how complex relationships can sometimes be, a rational discussion in the abstract, or whether she was trying to use the conversation to try and seduce him.

Elaine didn't take her eyes away from him as she spoke. "Let me try and explain then. My situation, ok? I think at first, I liked to have the eyes of others….of other men….on me. At first……at first after we were married….it was saying 'You can look at me and you can want to have me but you can't and so….' And so I got to feel good. But then not so good because I didn't want only eyes to look at me. After a while….how long, I don't know… I don't know……you think……I wonder how it would feel to be touched by someone else, to touch them, to feel them everywhere on you, inside you…and what you have seems not exciting, it seems like the same thing every time, the same person who doesn't change.

You see, there are different parts to me, at times it feels like so many different parts. I want to be seen as a beautiful painting, one that you look at every day and see a different thing. Maybe you see a brushstroke you never saw before, maybe the expression on the face looks a little different on different days. Maybe the picture looks different when the sun shines on it, maybe it is different when it is hung in the shade. When there is a light on it, it sparkles and everyone in the room looks at it and comments on it. Different people see not the same things in it…maybe someone sees a beautiful lady with a soft round face, maybe another person sees someone strong and confident…but everyone talks about it, in some way they are all attracted to it and like to look at it.

And I want to be this person in the bedroom, to touch places and make a man feel such things as he's never felt before. To be the one who they say of – 'she was the best'. I don't want love, or admiration when I am that person, I want to be the best fuck……to be the best everything that goes with it… that they ever had. I want to do everything to them and I want them to do everything to me and for it to feel always new, never repetitive.

And I want to be this figure, like a statue, that people look at and respect. Now I am married to this guy," she waved her hand dismissively towards the toilet, "and I am his. I am owned by him. That's how it feels. But I was independent once. I did a degree in Physics, I had a decent job…I wanted….I want people to admire me for the things I can do, the expertise I have…or I had. To look at me, at a statue of me and to think that I did something good……

These things, all these different things……sometimes I feel I want all of them every day." She bowed her head and Oliver wondered if she was going to cry. She lifted her head slowly.

"So, Oliver, how often do I have desires for other people? Well, when they touch these… buttons. I have these desires when someone looks at me as though I am something rich and strange that has captured them…. I have those desires when someone talks to me as though I am myself and not part of him, of Paul…… And I have those desires when someone wants to sleep with me and give me such pleasures…… And I have those desires when I want to lose myself in someone as much as….well, as much as… " And she smiled, a smile full of deceit and destruction.

She drank from her glass, her thirst unequivocally quenched. Oliver reached for his glass and almost gulped down what was left in it. He looked at her with an uncomfortable, slightly startled, smile. How do I get away? He was about to rise, to say he had to go the toilet….

She leant across quickly and trapped him there, talking more quietly, almost whispering to him. "I have on this….I'm mean I'm wearing this….underwear….I would like, I want you to see me in it. I would like to watch you watching me dress, undress, putting it on, taking it off… I sometimes see images like this and they seem so real….as though I can see someone like you watching me. It's black. I'm wearing stockings. If you put your hand up the side of my leg here you can feel……do it now, you are so close to the table that no one will see…." And she took his hand and forcibly thrust it up the outside of her right leg till his hand went past the soft silk of her stockings and onto her leg. He immediately pulled it down.

"You see? And maybe now you'll have images of me, think of how I feel to touch, putting hands inside my underwear, inside me… I wonder if the thought of me excites you as much as the thought of you excites me? We've talked, we've spoken to each other, but the words…….do they mean anything? Have they meant anything? When you think of me you'll think of the image of me, of touching me, of having your hands on my underwear… the words haven't been as significant. Our lips have moved but it is really our eyes that have talked. Put your hand there again…" and she grabbed and pulled his hand swiftly and almost wrenched it to in between her legs. She parted her legs slightly. "You're touching me," she whispered in his ear. With force, Oliver pulled his hand away.

"Now when you watch my legs, or see me cross or uncross them, you know something of what is underneath. You know what is moving with me….and what I want you to have." She leaned across and kissed him on the cheek. It was a gesture that could be taken for one of friendship, especially in a country such as France where it was a common occurrence. But this was no gesture of friendship. She raised her left hand to touch his right cheek as she kissed it. Oliver closed his eyes and put his head back. He felt utterly trapped. He clenched his mouth and his teeth, his body tensed and tight. When he opened his eyes he still felt Elaine kissing his cheek, lingering, and for one brief moment he thought she was going to kiss him on the mouth. He moved his head with an almost violent speed away from her and as he did so Paul came, almost running, towards them.

He did not make a public scene and neither did he shout so loudly that anyone else could hear. By this time the table was empty, it was only Elaine and Oliver who had remained talking to each other. The rest had dispersed. So no one else really heard what Paul said. All the time he looked only at Elaine.

"You fucking bitch, you whore…what the fuck do you think you are doing? Playing with this fucking idiot behind my back, when I am gone for only 5 minutes." He looked as though he might hit her as he towered over her but he never lifted his hand to strike her. He had, however, grabbed her on both arms and the imprints on her flesh were obvious as he took his arms off her.

He turned to Oliver. "And you, English, fuck off. Fuck off away from me and away from my wife. Fuck off now, before I have you shot."

"Nothing has happened," said Oliver. His words came out with a calm authority. "We were only talking."

"I know what I saw, you bastard. My wife nibbling on your ear. Don't tell me what to think. I'm telling you, fuck off now. I have this tart to deal with."

Oliver left the table and instinctively looked for Clotilde. He couldn't see her where she had been sitting as her table, like his, had dispersed. He then decided to go to the toilet but made a decision not to go to the nearest one and instead to find one further away, to be by himself for even a few minutes.

He walked for what seemed like ages to him, finding himself alone and walking down a large corridor which seemed to have function rooms on both sides. Eventually he found a toilet, a deserted toilet and looked at himself in the mirror for quite a while. He wished he could have cried. These people were aliens to him, he wanted that blanket that Helen gave him, I want to be back home, sitting at the end of the sofa with Helen's feet in my lap after Terrence's bedtime story. I want to be massaging them gently – Helen had quite beautiful feet – I want her to be shouting the nonsense that she does at the television when it's rubbish or when the news comes on or when some lunatic can't answer an easy question on a quiz show. I would settle for even watching one of her girly films, films that made him usually pretend to be asleep…but it wouldn't have mattered because she would have been there, a glance of her would have been the security he needed. But instead he was here, in this supposedly beautiful place with these supposedly beautiful people. Just get out, find Clotilde, plead with her better nature to get home….we've given her company quite a bit of business, she must be own me one….

He probably could not have known when he walked out the toilet how his life was going to change. Or maybe, somewhere deep in his subconscious, he did. Outside, it seemed as though Paul had almost given up on his search. But Oliver came out the toilet as Paul came down the corridor towards him. Instinctively, Oliver turned into one of the first rooms on his left, which happened to be a function room that was set for some sort of event – probably a wedding the next day. There was a long rectangular table at the top of the room and other circular tables, which seated ten people at each table, around the room. There were stiff white table cloths, sparkling silver cutlery and wine glasses on each table. At the end of the room were stairs that went up to a gallery above which seemed to be connected to elsewhere, perhaps the floor above.

Oliver was glancing around quickly, almost furtively, for an escape route and could see himself running around the tables with Paul chasing him and realised how stupid this seemed. "Tell him," he thought, "nothing happened."

Paul came in the room and Oliver stood in front of him, his arms open in front of him, in a defensive gesture.

"I'm sorry if I have offended you. Truly I am. But nothing happened between me and your wife. Nothing. We spoke, we talked….about ordinary things… nothing more…."

"Your hand was up her skirt, you bastard. And she was kissing you." Paul had been walking towards Oliver, forcing him to retreat. When he stopped Oliver's back was almost pressed against the table behind him.

"I complimented her on her dress and on the way she looked. I said I thought she looked very nice and she was wearing a beautiful dress. Maybe that was wrong, maybe I should not have said it….I meant no harm, but if you think it was inappropriate… then I'm sorry." He gingerly held out his hand. Paul ignored it.

"That's not what she says. She says she was leaning across to whisper in your ear that she wanted to sleep with you and that you seemed to like the idea." He began to move with menace towards Oliver. Oliver could not move back any further. He held his hands in front of him again.

"There's something between you, between the two of you….it's none of my business, I know…but it's clear you weren't happy… and I think she might be saying that to you maybe to get at you….you know, to make you angry. But that is not what happened. She did not say that to me. You have to believe me on this. She didn't say that."

Paul held up his hand. "I only have your word for that. And I don't trust you." And again: "you had your hand up her skirt!"

Oliver dropped his hands to his side. "Well, I don't know what to say to that…….maybe your eyes deceived you. I do not remember that."

Paul moved towards him, till their faces were so close that Oliver could smell the alcohol off his breath, could see the dull emotion in his eyes.

"What's between my wife and me is between my wife and me. It's fuck all to do with you. Are you really saying"…… and he moved his head more in towards Oliver until their lips were almost touching……
…."that I can't trust my own wife? Because it's funny, that's what I'm thinking too. I'm thinking she's a no good whore who wanted to fuck you. And I think you wanted to fuck her too. And had I gone away or gone home I can see the two of you here or some other quiet place, fucking each other. And I don't like the thought of someone else fucking my wife, you English bastard." And he touched, but didn't hit, Oliver in the stomach though Oliver knew the guy could have belted him with everything he had if he wanted to.

"You don't want to cross me, you fucking upstart. You don't need me

149

as an enemy. And right now, you feel like my enemy. I can have you battered to within an inch of your life for that. You dirty little bastard. Do you think it's ok to do that? To come to a dinner like this and put your hand up another man's wife's dress? You'll pay for that."

Oliver shook his head quickly. It may have seemed as though he was forcing a reaction, that he was frightened but inside he felt quite calm. "That didn't happen."

"Well I can believe it did….the way in which you were all over each other…I'm warning you, I can have such things done to you……" he leaned forward as he spoke, forcing Oliver to lean back on the table. As he did so his hand instinctively grabbed a knife. "….though maybe I don't need to, maybe I could give you a go myself…." He drew his arm back. Oliver was defenceless. His arms were on the table and his entire body was open to whatever force Paul may throw at it. Oliver acted quickly as Paul's arm went back and he thrust the blunt end of the knife towards Paul. He wasn't aiming for any particular part of Paul's body, and he used the blunt end because he thought he had no intention of stabbing him. But as Paul's arm came down so did his head and Oliver shoved the knife forward with force. It met Paul's right eye as his arm was descending and Oliver heard a sickening squelch then a high pitched scream, one of absolute terror. He couldn't look upon Paul but he saw the knife still stuck in Paul's eye socket and blood on the ground.

He must have heard a noise from somewhere and looked up above to the gallery. There he saw Clotilde, holding her hand to her mouth and motioning him to go up the stairs at the end of the room. Meanwhile Paul's screams got louder as he stumbled around, falling to the floor in agony as Oliver raced up the stairs. Clotilde grabbed him as he reached the top of the stairs, keeping her hand over her mouth. She glanced back, certain that Paul had not seen either of them. She almost ran with him, holding his hand, almost pulling him with her, until they reached a place where there were other people. She started to walk and then let his hand go.

"We must get out of here now. We must get out without being seen by anyone if we can." And she seemed to make an elaborate detour around the room where their dinner had been and after a short wait outside her car arrived. Clotilde visibly exhaled as they began to drive away. Then she turned to Oliver and exploded.

"What the fuck are you playing at, Oliver? What the hell are you doing with that guy's wife? She was all over you! What did you think you were doing? Flirting with…….it was more than flirting….you were all over each other....do you know who that guy is? Do you have any idea what sort of trouble you're in? That guy... he has connections, he knows people... "

"You know him?"

"No, I don't know him. But I know of him. He's a.......not a gangster... but...he's involved in things, with people, that are on the wrong side of what's legal...."

"I thought he was boasting, being a big guy....he said he could have me shot...."

"And he probably can....he probably can... But Christ Oliver, what were you doing with his wife?"

"You saw what happened?"

"Yes, I saw...I watched you most of the night...."

"Then you know nothing happened! She....I don't know, she must have fallen out with her husband... she was really flirty... ...but it's not like we slept with each other for God's sake.... I tried to get up a few times, I tried to get up to say I was going to the toilet at the end, anything to get away from her. But she pinned me back"

"Well, it didn't look like that." She sounded.......she spoke with the indignation that a spouse might feel....she sounds jealous, thought Oliver.

"Oliver, you're in trouble here. I mean I think you blinded that guy. You're not safe. Did you tell them who you worked with? Why you were there?"

"Yes, yes......I don't remember if I gave them the actual company name...maybe I did..."

"Did you mention you were with me?"

"No." He was definitive about that. She had been at another table quite a bit away, it made little sense.

"Then you cannot go back to the flat. They will find you. Stay with me. We will go back to your flat, now, and grab your stuff. But we must be quick. And then you can stay with me. They don't know me and they will not know we arrived together. You have to stay low for a few days, maybe a week, I don't know. And no calls. Most of all no calls. It's the one way they will find you right away. You've no idea how easy it can be for people like that to get access to calls made to the UK from this part of the world... narrow that down to Scotland – they knew you were Scottish, right? –".... Oliver nodded...."then they would find you in a heartbeat."

Oliver's head was swimming. Swimming with fear, swimming with exhaustion, swimming with the sound of the knife squelching its way into Paul's eye, swimming with the image and sounds of Paul as he fumbled and squealed...

"Are you sure Clotilde? I mean, really sure? Am I in danger?"

She looked across at him as she drove. She was driving at such a speed that he wished she had not looked across but instead had kept her eyes on the road. "Of course I'm sure! Oliver, you blinded this guy who thinks you fondled his wife. He's a serious guy, a seriously powerful fucking guy. He has friends in high places, high dark places. If you stay where you are, they will find you. If you go home now, they will find you. You must lie low; give them a chance to let it all die down. That is your only chance of safety."

Oliver turned to his friends in the car. "So that's what happened. That's why I was fleeing...or hiding. And that's where I've been since Saturday night. Hiding in Clotilde's flat. Dreading every footstep, every voice outside the window. A prisoner... "

Euan turned to him. "Ok. But we will get you home Olly. We'll all get home. Maybe this guy... maybe he over exaggerated his own importance. And are you sure you blinded him?"

"I saw the fucking knife stuck in his eye, Euan! I don't think he was holding it there for effect. And I wasn't hanging around to ask him if he was alright."

"Ok. But so far nothing has happened to us. The people we bought the car from... I don't think they were part of this gang, mafia or whatever they are...I think you're safe now...we're safe now." He paused. "And what did you and Clotilde do for those three or four days Olly? Or is that none of my business?"

We're best friends, thought Olly, but he is my brother-in-law. I can't tell him, I can't tell them, the truth. If they have any sympathy for me in this whole horrible story then they will lose it. I don't want to be seen in that way by them...as a......traitor......that they're come all the way here for a...cheating no-good bastard....I don't want to take from them the image they have of me...But most of all if it had to be admitted then it had to be admitted to Helen first.

"Euan, there was nothing between us. I need you to believe... I need you all to believe....there's nothing between us. Was she attracted to me? Yes, truly, I think so. And of course she is a beautiful woman. But she has done a selfless thing, perhaps putting herself in danger, to try and protect me. We did not sleep together. We did not make love. I can't help the way it seems, or the way things look. But you're my best friends and I need you to believe me."

Euan nodded. "Think Helen will believe you?"

"Yes," Oliver replied quickly. "Of course she will. Of course...."

"Then so do we," smiled Euan. "Though, speaking as we might have done a few years ago," and he looked round at the rest of the friends in the car, "we reckon you might have missed a trick there. That Clotilde looked like an absolute shag... "

Oliver smiled, an inward smile of happiness that his friends had believed him and of resignation that he had told a lie to cover his deceit and betrayal. Images, images.......as the conversation went through a lull, he remembered the rest of what happened that night. Yes, they had gone to his flat and picked up all his stuff, they had moved quickly, they had returned to Clotilde's flat, they had sat down and she had poured him a drink.

And as they drank together his head began to swim less. As they drank together his mind somehow managed to focus only on what was in front of him. And he became quickly aware that there was a danger, more clear, more present, than the guy whose eye he had bashed about. Clotilde... as she kicked her shoes off, as she sat opposite him and her dress began to ride up – deliberate, or not? – as she pulled her chair closer to his, as she pretended to be motherly and protective by holding him to her in case he felt as though he might want to cry, to get rid of all that emotion, as she did all that he knew, absolutely, that she wanted him. And he knew that he was in her debt.

Clotilde lifted his head and kissed him fully on the lips. He didn't react. "Clotilde....I can't do this...I can't do this. I'm married, I'm married to Helen....I miss her and I miss my son. I can't be this person with you, this person who can forget my life and the people who make my life what it is...to sleep with you."

"Oliver, you have no choice. Think about it. You have no choice. Work it through. From where I am standing, you don't have too many alternatives."

And she unzipped her dress and let it fall to the floor, standing in front of him with stockings, suspenders, bra, almost assaulting him with her body. "Clotilde, please, please...."

"Hush, hush...let your body tell me it doesn't want me...let your body tell me." And she leaned over him, unzipping his trousers and feeling him hard within a few seconds. "Your prick won't lie to me. It isn't the obvious hypocrite that you are."

"Please, I'm begging you…" Did he have any alternative? Oliver will probably ask himself that question till the day he dies. And he will always answer the same way "Yes, of course I did, I could've ran away." But at that moment running away meant death, being captured, meant something horrible beyond imaginings. Being here, with her….meant doing whatever it took to survive.

The first time she did it to him it was frantic, frenetic, a flurry of fast sharp movements, one body furious for the other. She orgasmed quickly and with a quiet rage, and would not rest until she had brought him to orgasm too. That seemed to mean more to her than anything else. Oliver didn't think anything of it at the time, but, as he remembered now, the first thing she said after he orgasmed inside her, the sound that came first to his mind was of Clotilde's soft gentle voice almost whispering: "Enfin. Enfin, tu es mien."

CHAPTER 8

Ali looked around the car at the others who were all quiet now. Olly continued to drive, Euan in the front had his head back on the headrest and it seemed as though he might be sleeping and both Aidan, next to him and Ellis across from him looked blankly into space. Probably as confused and shocked as I am, thought Ali. He wondered what he would have done in such a situation as Olly found himself in… he would never have been in such a situation, never have allowed that woman to get so close to him. He would have walked away. But Olly…… Olly was different. For as long as Ali could think back, for as long as he had known Olly, Olly had always been this attractive guy. Devilishly attractive guy. And he knew it. That's the part Ali found very hard to relate to. Of course he had been, at times, jealous of Olly and of the way that he attracted women with sickening ease. They seemed drawn to him, almost in awe of him. He wasn't arrogant either, never the big-headed boaster who would talk of his conquests. It was as if……well, Ali tried to reason, as if it was almost something Olly had to live with, like a….like a…well, not a curse exactly, but a burden. Had Olly really been able to resist that girl Clotilde for three days? Well, Ali thought, he was probably terrified…… she probably went to work….and Olly for all his charm knows the difference between what's the right thing to do and what's not…

Ali thought about Lesley. He hadn't phoned yet but maybe when they stopped, he would. He would like to think that he missed her and the boys but things had been so frantic since they got here that at times it felt as though he had not had time to think. So he thought of her now, of her little smile, her soft touch and warning to "be careful" as he left, her constant busy-ness….Lesley seemed to be in constant motion most of the time, always something to do, or to tidy, or to clean, or to sew, or to cook. He thought how……how boring it all was compared to Olly… how boring but how safe. Safe was good, that was fine.

He wondered how Lesley was….really was… how she saw their life. If he asked her she would say what she was supposed to say or else she would say she was so busy she never had time to think of anything else. But really, how was she… Lesley never shared Ali's religious views and he had accepted long ago that she never would. What she thought,

155

though, and what she believed, about the way to live, the way to behave…
they were so close to Ali's. He knew she sometimes resented the amount
of time he spent at church – she occasionally, when she was feeling
slighted or ignored or upset, would refer to it as his "hobby" – but at the
same time she did understand how much a part it was of him.

And he thought how in the last few weeks, maybe the last month,
she had seemed a little less…stressed….a little less busy. She had rushed
about a bit less. And Ali knew it was because of the lull in his job that
came at this time of year. He was at home more, his hours less irregular,
deadlines less looming, his tension levels much lower. They had more
chance to be a couple, to walk together and talk together. Hold hands.
She had smiled more….and he smiled to himself as the thought of her
made him happy.

He was, however, mistaken. Lesley had been slightly different over
this last month because she was affected by the attention of a new
member of staff, a divorcee of similar age to herself who had made clear
their interest in her from an early stage. It was subtle and almost bland at
first, compliments on the way things were done with such efficiency, to
comments on the way Lesley's work, specifically, was well done. From
that to comments like "nice earrings", "lovely perfume", "that colour
really suits you" to having coffee together at break times. The divorcee
had an almost reserved charm and revealed parts of themselves slowly in
an undramatic manner……little stories about things they had done, no
overly gushing emotional outbursts…it was all very gentle….and the
questions about Lesley had been gentle too… lots about Ali…it was really
only two work colleagues who liked each other, talking. And that's what
she had convinced herself at first, that it was just two people who had
become friends. But the "friendship" was one that made her eager to get
to work, that made her think about what clothes she might wear, that
made her pick up one, two, sometimes three different pairs of earrings.

Then the divorcee suggested lunch….it made sense, they said….there
was quite a bit to talk over on some particular aspect and getting out the
office, having a working lunch, that would be a good way to get on with
this without the phone going or there being e-mails to answer. And of
course it made sense…and of course Lesley had done this kind of thing
many times before…so she couldn't say no…she didn't want to say no.
And the lunch had been relaxing and stimulating and exciting and they
had spoken about work for about all of five minutes but by that stage
both of them knew that work wasn't the real reason why they had agreed

to have lunch together. But nothing was said, nothing was hinted… lots of smiles, happy, relaxed, inviting smiles…and only one touch. The divorcee had got up to go the toilet and returned. However, they couldn't get to their seat. It was a small restaurant and there was a waitress standing serving a table opposite which left no space. So the divorcee stood behind Lesley and waited for the waitress to move. But at that time the person sitting in the chair behind the divorcee got up and bumped them, knocking them forward. Instinctively, hands reached onto Lesley's shoulders and instinctively she welcomed the feel of those hands on her. They lingered awhile and the touch seemed so fair and gentle and when the divorcee sat back down opposite Lesley and apologised Lesley said "Oh no, it was nice" without even thinking about it and both of them blushed and both of them knew that something had changed.

After a day or two they did talk about it. They had to. The attraction they felt for each other was….almost out in the open. Lesley felt as though she had rubbed the lamp and, being out, the genie couldn't easily be put back in. But it was a difficult conversation for both of them because neither of them had felt attracted to a woman before and had you told Lesley a few weeks ago that she would go to bed wanting to be touched by a woman she would have probably hit you. But she told Tess how she wanted to touch her and be touched by her and Tess told her similar things, how she had fought against it, how she had thought that the feelings that she was having were those of friendship. But one night she had decided to "self-pleasure", as she told Lesley, and her thoughts were full of Lesley touching her, bringing her to orgasm and it was then that she fully understood that her feelings went beyond friendship. It was the next day that she had to put her arms on Lesley in the restaurant and it was a touch which she would remember for the rest of her life. "I have never before touched a woman and felt my body tingle," she told Lesley.

Nothing had happened. Yet. But they were making plans, plans for a night away, plans which Lesley knew – and which she told Tess – she may never go through with. But she wanted to. For herself, she wanted to feel alive, she wanted to feel unfrozen, more than what she was to those around her.

Ali closed his eyes a bit, thinking of Lesley and the security that their relationship brought him. "I'm lucky," he thought to himself, "I'm very lucky… "

In the front, Olly yawned and turned to his friends. "We have to stop. We need to find somewhere to stay the night. But, I was thinking, not somewhere just off this motorway, that's where we might be expected to stay, you know, if people are looking for us. I thought we should maybe turn off, find a small town…something like that…what do you think?"

"Ok," Ellis leaned forward. "Sounds good." He looked around him, outside the window. "Where are we anyway?"

Euan looked at the map in front of him. "North of Valence… how far north I'm not sure….but headed towards Lyon…between Valence and Lyon.."

"Well," said Ellis, "turn off at the next exit and drive till we find somewhere where you think we won't get shot."

"Or kidnapped and shagged to death…." Aidan added.

Even Oliver laughed.

"Yeah," said Ellis, leaning back, smiling, "That French filly Natalie could take me there any time she wants….getting bonked to death by her would be like dipping your dick in warm honey…….fabulous and sweet as hell but it's ultimately going to get pretty messy… "

"Here! Turn off here. Before he gets even more lost in that image… "

They travelled for a few miles and passed a few villages. "Too small," "nowhere to stay," "looks like a backwater hell hole," until eventually they came to a place which seemed about right. Perhaps somewhere between a town and a village in size. But more than that, there was clearly, as Euan so accurately put it, "something going on". That "something" looked as though it were a festival, perhaps a village celebration day and as they travelled towards the small centre they could see more people on the streets until, as they got closer, the crowds got larger and there were traffic diversions in place.

They decided to find somewhere to stay and have a look at the village celebrations. Though initially anxious how the appearance of five foreigners might seem, Oliver was quickly assured by the others that the danger must be slight….no one had seen them, no one had chased them….and Oliver's doubts about what Clotilde had said, and why she had said it, continued to ferment.

The place where they found to stay was a surprisingly big hotel for the size of the little town. "Oh," said the receptionist, "we are a decent stopping place for people going from the north to the south… if they are going to Nice or Marseilles or somewhere they tend to get past Lyon and think of stopping….where are you gentlemen going? Are you here for our fete?"

"Um, no, no, not for that," said Oliver, "we're on holiday."

"Ah, lovely, where have you been?"

"Oh here and there… down south a bit, in Marseilles… we thought we would get a car and travel north…"

"A boy's holiday, yes?" and she gave them what seemed to be a knowing wink.

Better she thinks we are gay than we are running away from something, thought Oliver….though what did she imagine about there being five of us…and us getting five separate rooms.

"Yes, no wives allowed! Tell me, the fete….what is it, what's it for?"

"Oh, it's a town… I'm trying to think, I lived in England and I saw that many of your small towns did the same sort of thing but I can't remember…what did you call it…ah, yes, gala day, it's like a gala day! It's our town gala day. We have sports and dancing and there is story telling… it's a good atmosphere, it goes on till late at night so maybe you won't get to sleep until it's finished anyway…there is lots to eat…lots of wine to drink…"

"Ok, thanks," said Oliver. "Then we shall definitely go."

The first thing they did was eat. Not a huge two-hour meal but a light 45-minute salad-type break with a little of what seemed to be a local French wine. At this stage they were still a bit away from the main centre where there was clearly quite a bit of activity taking place and their conversation was often punctuated by shouts and screams from nearby.

When they first saw the centre they saw two men, local men quite clearly, with trousers on and scruffy white vests and boxing gloves, boxing each other in an elevated boxing ring. They were clearly both tired – it remained very warm – both had blood creeping rather than seeping out of parts of their nose and it was obvious they were, if not friends, then at least on friendly terms as one would enquire after the well-being of the other if a punch was landed. Oliver guessed this must be somewhere near the final as the men looked so tired and sweaty, their vests caked with little bits of blood in places, that this could not be the first fight of the night.

Ellis rubbed his hands. "This gets better and better. A chance to see the French knock nine bells out of each other, I would have paid to watch this."

Aidan looked around him. He felt hot and tired, sweaty and dirty. He wished he had had a shower before they came out for the meal. He wafted his shirt a bit, trying to get some air on his body but also trying to find out if he smelled as much as he feared he might. The boxing ring had little specks of blood on the canvas, some fresh, others which had clearly been there for a while and were growing darker now. There were many people standing ring-side, cheering and laughing, glasses in their hands. How many….he broadly looked….well, hundreds certainly. This was clearly a family event as he could see some families standing together, others a husband and wife keeping a look out for their children who might be playing in the small children's park adjacent to the main square. As Aidan looked around him he saw that it wasn't a main square exactly, but it was certainly the middle of the town. What he noticed most of all was the span of age groups that were covered here… clearly, it was a town event that you went to regardless of whether you were 7, 17 or 70.

In some cases, groups of young girls stood together, adolescents, teenagers, girls with those tight shorts that girls around the world seemed to wear these days, with overt make-up, beautiful thin girls who were really too young, thought Aidan, to make the kind of statements they were making and to attract the kind of looks they attracted. Especially, thought Aidan, from people like me. And likewise groups of boys, similar ages, a fusion of hormones and hair gel, boys trying to outdo each other and be the best in show. And then young couples standing together, loosely holding hands, older couples, men with their arms round their wives' shoulders. They all seemed happy. But it was more than that, thought Aidan as he looked around, they all seemed healthy…their skin was unblemished, their figures small….there was the occasional old man you might call fat but for the most part these were healthy, beautiful looking people.

And the smells…beautiful smells of…well, concluded Aidan, of France. Of the glory of cooking mixed with wine, of hot barbeques, of the French countryside which enveloped them from all sides. Of French tobacco… of a hot warm summer night in the middle of France…. Aidan drew it in, not intoxicated by it but a little overwhelmed by it, as though, after all the madness of the day, they had arrived in some brief nirvana.

It transpired that the boxing match they had seen was the first semi-final. There was still a wrestling competition to take place after that and names were still being taken for those who wanted to compete.

"Great," said Ellis. "I'm up for staying here until we fall down. Or until the bad guys get us…"

"Yeah, let's stay and see what happens, it's a nice event, nice setting," said Ali, looking around him.

"But you won't be reporting on this, will you?" asked Oliver laughing.

"No, I don't do boxing…too much brute force and ignorance…"

"Is that you or the boxers?" They laughed amongst themselves and must have looked to the outside world as if they had not a care in the world. They attracted no curious glances, no awkward looks and as Oliver gazed around him his fears began to recede and doubts about Clotilde continued to grow. He smiled, outwardly and inwardly. For the first time that day he truly felt out of danger.

The friends were standing quite close to the ring, watching what appeared to be the second semi-final being fought between two quite young men of the town. As with the previous fight, this appeared to be between two men who didn't actually want to hurt each other. Oliver watched as, at the ringside to his right, two girls stood together, almost hugging each other at times, giving different whops and cries and he quickly concluded that the girls were the partners of the two men fighting in the ring. Just along from them stood a group of maybe four or five couples…perhaps the two girls were with them, perhaps not… but the males in the four or five couples were loud, shouting encouragement or abuse at the men in the ring. Oliver wasn't quite sure which it was. And the girls, their partners, seemed drunk.

One of those males in particular was a big man, towering at six foot three, maybe six four, thought Oliver… he had long blond hair that kept falling over his eyes and which he would continually have to sweep away. He had on a tight blue t-shirt which showed off his biceps, bulging whenever he moved his arm. Oliver guessed that his arms would bulge in any t-shirt. Beside him stood a girl, quite tall but thin, and he occasionally enveloped her with one of his arms. However, whether she was not a fan of blood sports or whether she was disinterested and bored by the boxing, she casually looked around her quite a bit, taking things in, Oliver thought….either that or keen to get away. She was the only person here who you might have said looked bored.

Then she saw Oliver and Oliver saw her, seeing him. She was pretty in an understated way, he thought. She looked to be without make-up but she had a rosy glow to her face. The glow could have been down to the alcohol or it could have been natural. Long black hair hung about a white sleeveless top and Oliver also saw dark, deeply dark, brown eyes. She looked away and so did Oliver, a casual glance that strangers walking down the street may pass at each other.

But from the corner of somewhere, from either his eye or perception, he felt something. As though eyes were on him, watching him, studying him. He vowed not to look up. But in the same way that it is hard not to imagine a pink elephant when told specifically not to think of one, Oliver eventually looked in that general direction. The dark blaze of her eyes met his and she smiled in an almost coy way, as though she had been caught doing something she knew she shouldn't have been doing. Oliver felt uncomfortable. We should go back to the hotel......But he looked at his friends and they were happy, relaxed, enjoying themselves. I have led them into enough misery today, don't look back at her. The girl, her curiosity as to who this stranger was no doubt fuelled by red wine, turned herself slightly, trying to dislodge her partner's arm, making him feel she was uncomfortable with the position it was in. He took his arm away, his entire focus still on the fight and she wriggled a little further away from him.

During the break before the final the group she was with left but they returned. Not to the same place but nearer, much nearer, to Oliver. He coughed uncomfortably and again looked to his friends. And she began again, looking across to Oliver, her smiles more overt now, warmer. He didn't return them, he hardly took his eyes from the ground and didn't even register the fight, but he could feel her and he could feel her watching him, almost haunting him.

At some point the Hulk turned around and saw her head turned away. Not sure of what she was doing, he watched her for a while, turning his head now and then, and realised what was happening. He didn't really take in the fact that Oliver wasn't playing ball, nor did he really take in Oliver's eyes being rooted to the ground in front of him. Nor could he feel Oliver's discomfort, discomfort that was now making him begin to sweat. Oliver never felt it but the guy glowered at him and put his arm firmly round her, pulling her into him with unequivocal force.

After the boxing finished the wrestling was due to start and it transpired that the wrestling event was a three minute challenge. Competitors would pay (money to charity of course) to wrestle against the Champion – if they lasted three minutes they could either stay on or get their money back. Likewise, of course, if they actually managed to win. A win came either through a submission or a "pin", where the opponent had their arms and back pinned to the floor for a count of three. Oliver watched as the Hulk stepped into the ring as the Champion and from the little Oliver could gather from those around him the guy was a bit of a local hero.

The girl looked across at Oliver as the Hulk got into the ring and he briefly looked up, threw her a nervous smile and gave a suitable expression to indicate he was impressed. She waved her hand across her face, as if to say he had nothing to be impressed about. She was now standing effectively on her own.

Oliver also watched the Hulk as he wrestled his way through the evening. He was strong, certainly, but he was slow and his stomach had begun to drip over the top of his trousers. He didn't have much trouble disposing of the first two or three challengers – his strength saw to that – and he then had the chance to have a break, to sit in the corner and take on water, to be fanned down by what appeared to be a trainer.

Oliver turned to talk with his friends and they laughed and commented on the event and were clearly enjoying it. The Hulk went through another opponent or two and as the boys' chatter paused Oliver looked round himself again, relieved that he had had his attention engaged elsewhere and grateful for not having felt the girl's eyes on him. But as he did so he saw right away that she was next to him, standing, smiling. He jumped, almost physically jumped, and his first reaction was one of fear. She must have seen his face lengthen…his eyes widen….his mouth open. She laughed, putting her hand over her mouth as if to suppress a giggle. She said something in French.

"I'm sorry," said Oliver…."em….je m'excuse….I don't…je ne parle pas francais… em……. English….Anglais?"

At the same time the Hulk seemed to have run out of opponents and the announcer's voice boomed out over the crowd, looking for an opponent, anyone who would take up the challenge to live for three minutes with this great fighter. Was there anyone who was man enough to take on this Champion? The Hulk stalked around the ring like a caged tiger, almost crouched and ready to pounce or maybe to eat someone, his hair almost covering his face, his torso by now almost covered in sweat. Who would be the last competitor for this great Champion, he's already beaten five opponents and was now so tired that someone who was man enough would surely have a chance.

The girl leaned in to Oliver to try and make herself heard and Oliver bent his ear towards her to try and hear her. "Yes," she said, "a little. You are here on holiday?"

And Oliver was about to respond to her but at that time the Hulk had caught sight of his girl talking to him and he grabbed the microphone from the announcer and shouted something in French at Oliver. The announcer, having found something to get animated about, appealed to the crowd to encourage Oliver to get into the ring and they started clapping and cheering for him to go, universally smiling at him.

Euan had been standing to Oliver's immediate left and didn't understand what this was about. He hadn't seen the girl, didn't know anything about her looking at Oliver over the last half hour or so and hadn't even realised that Oliver was talking with someone else. With the rest of his friends, he turned to Oliver and Oliver shrugged his shoulders.

"Olly, what the fuck....you're not going to wrestle that guy are you? Why does he want to wrestle you?"

Oliver stood back and his friends saw a girl standing next to him. "She was looking at me...and then she has come over here and asked if we're on holiday. That's it, that's it, that's all. She's that guy's girlfriend......."

Euan ran his hand through his hair. "Is this... have we all walked into some dreadful fucking soap opera... you're going to wrestle, and get killed by, some big bastard for talking to his bird when we've spent the last few hours.......running away from some guy who's going to kill you because you were talking to his bird! Olly, you're a one-man fucking war zone!"

"It's ok, I'll go up, get beaten in 20 seconds....don't worry... "

"Don't worry! You've told us we have to stay low, we're being hunted by all sorts of low life...and now you're going to put yourself in this public position where the whole world can see you...."

"It's ok," said Oliver, slipping his shoes and socks off, then his shirt. "I'll be back here before you know it."

However, even Olly knew that that wasn't quite right. Olly was fit and he was quick and he was reasonably strong. Not as strong as the Hulk, sure, but the Hulk was slow and the people he had wrestled couldn't move quickly enough to avoid his gripping bear hugs.

As he got into the ring Oliver waved aside the announcer. He didn't want to draw attention to not being French and he gave the impression that his focus and concentration was on the task in hand. If I can get him angry, though Olly, he won't think straight. As long as I'm quick I will out think him....Before he went to shake or touch hands with the Hulk he deliberately and slowly glanced back to the crowd, to where he had been standing, and smiled at the girl. It was a provocative gesture that wasn't lost on the Hulk and as Oliver leaned forward to touch his hand he smiled at him, a wide beaming smile, which the Hulk met with a grunt as he swept hair from his eyes again. He looked angry, Oliver thought, angry and perhaps a little wild.

Oliver certainly tried his best to bring the Hulk to anger, firstly by dancing around the ring to frustrate him. When he had created enough space to allow himself to glance to the crowd he would smile towards his friends, to let them know he felt in control and to let the Hulk know that he felt he was in control. As the Hulk got closer Oliver could hear his breathing, almost like a growl, rhythmic and dangerous. When he grabbed Oliver it felt at first like being sandwiched in a vice, the monster's arms wrapped around him like steel grips. But as Oliver had thought the stomach was the Hulk's weak point and he would always find a way of digging his elbows into the Hulk's gut and then feel himself being freed as his opponent grunted or cried out.

At first Oliver had only wanted to last three minutes but after the first minute or so he realised the Hulk was tired and angry. The anger may help his opponent overcome the tired part, thought Oliver, but it would impair his judgement and force him to make mistakes. I could win this....

Oliver let the Hulk come at him, grappling and grabbing again, trying to take any part of Oliver's flesh. Oliver darted quickly to the right, forcing the Hulk to move to his left, then just as quickly back to his left. The Hulk quickly tried to shift his balance back to his right side to grab Oliver but Oliver was ready for the move and, knowing the Hulk would be off balance, rushed behind him and pushed him with quick force. The Hulk wouldn't have fallen over had it not been for the sweat that he and others had dripped on the canvas but as he tried to catch his footing he slipped and fell. It was the first time that night that the Hulk had been on the canvas. But this time there were no smiles from Oliver to the girl at the side of the ring, no taunts. He sensed a chance and ran at the Hulk as he began to try to raise himself from the canvas.

Oliver grabbed him around the top of his arms and pushed the Hulk back. Oliver was trying to almost lie over the top of him and to pin the Hulk's arms and back to the canvas but he knew he would have to be quick to do it because the Hulk's strength, even after five or six rounds of wrestling, was enough to throw Oliver from him. So he virtually tried to lie on top of the man but with a huge roar and a massive lift of his right arm the Hulk managed to throw Oliver off him. Now Oliver was vulnerable: he was on the ground and if the Hulk turned quickly enough Oliver knew he was finished. If that guy gets on top of me, he thought, I'm as good as dead. The Hulk tried to reach across to grab Oliver and bring him nearer whilst Oliver tried to turn himself over to escape the enormous hand that came towards him. The hand slid across him, missing the right side of his stomach that would have meant Oliver was dragged closer to the Hulk. But it did catch his trousers and pulled him across the canvas.

Suddenly Oliver could see the Hulk above him, threatening. His face was hardly visible because of the mass of hair sticking to it and Oliver thought how he was grateful for that, the last thing he wanted to see right now were this monster's eyes. The Hulk's sweat dripped on him and Oliver raised his hands and turned his head. Perhaps because he had so much hair hanging about him, the Hulk didn't properly see Oliver's left hand come up and Oliver managed to get his hand onto the Hulk's throat. The Hulk instinctively raised himself, lifting his hands from the canvas and to his throat. With equal speed Oliver raised his free right hand to the Hulk's throat. His intention was not to hurt the Hulk..if I can get his hands away from me then I can wriggle away and stand up again… time must be getting on, we must be almost past two minutes…

The Hulk grabbed at Oliver's hands, forcing them away from his throat. Because the Hulk's hands were clammy and sweaty, however, it wasn't difficult for Oliver to slip them free. But the Hulk quickly grabbed at them again, holding Oliver's right hand by the wrist this time and Oliver felt his wrist squeezed until he thought his hand might begin to pop. For the first time since the fight had begun he wanted to say "submit!" But, sensing that, and seeing his obvious discomfort, the Hulk made to quieten anything Oliver might say by trying to put his hand over Oliver's mouth. As the Hulk moved his right arm Oliver moved his left one up, to try and stop the movement. The Hulk caught it and Oliver wriggled and moved it, summoning up all the force he could. Eventually it was pushed out, almost squeezed out with the force of a bullet. Oliver couldn't stop the momentum of movement the action had given to his hand and he felt his thumb slam into the soft part of the Hulk's right eye, catching the sweat on the side of the Hulk's eye socket and drilling itself into the Hulk's eye.

The Hulk immediately recoiled, his screams reaching far into the night sky and across the peace of the French countryside. His hands shot up to his face and Oliver turned away, quickly standing up and wiping his mouth. By now he was breathing heavily. The referee crossed his hands in front of him, indicating the end of the wrestling match. Oliver went quickly across to the Hulk, bending down beside him, apologising, saying it was a mistake, he couldn't help it, the way his hand came up, the speed of it… But as Oliver spoke quickly in English no one really understood him and in return the Hulk spoke…or maybe shouted, Oliver wasn't sure…quickly in French and Oliver could not comprehend him either. What he did understand was that the referee had called for medical assistance, maybe a doctor, maybe an ambulance. One thing Oliver was sure of however, was that there was no blood… nothing on the canvas, nothing on the Hulk's hands.

A doctor arrived very quickly…whether someone in the crowd or someone who had been called Oliver wasn't sure…but he looked at the Hulk, asked him to raise his head to the sky, saw the eye clearly and nodded calmly. He spoke quickly in French with the Hulk and the referee and then Oliver asked if he could tell him in English if there was any lasting damage.

"No, no, it is not something that will stay with him long. Maybe for a few days he will wear a… something on his eye to cover and protect it… but it is a common injury here for rugby players…like when they…" and he made a motion with his index finger to show someone trying to gouge someone else's eyes…"you know it's quite common. His eye is hurt but there is no…" he made a motion to show a scratch…"well, there is none of that on his eye. He will have a bruise, for a week or two it may be a not very pretty colour….but he is ok."

"Thank goodness! I'm sorry… really sorry….I mean it was a mistake… "

"Oh, I could see…we could all see that……sometimes these things happen. Always for the fete I make sure I don't have anything to drink, I am usually called to help somewhere. Though normally it is with the boxing! Don't worry, he will be ok."

Oliver leaned down to talk to the Hulk who was still sitting on the canvas with the referee. Two of his friends, male friends not quite as big as him but similar in size and scale, were with him. Oliver touched his shoulder and apologised. The Hulk didn't lift any part of himself to try and engage with Oliver and he didn't say much to him, save some brief comment in French. By the look on the faces of the Hulk's friends, Oliver concluded that it was not very nice. It was only when he decided that he should leave the ring that Oliver realised that the girl had not come into the ring and as he lowered himself down he saw her, talking with the group she was originally with. He walked towards her.

"I'm sorry… I am sorry….it was a mistake."

"I know." She smiled a watery smile. "I should go to him now. It is his own fault. He is big and stupid and thinks he is as good as he was a few years ago. Maybe now he will think more......"

Oliver made his way back to his friends who weren't sure whether to shake his hand or to wrestle him themselves.

"Remind me never to fall out with you Olly," said Ellis, "I kind of value both my eyes......"

They laughed and spent several minutes standing there, laughing almost despite themselves. They then took the decision to do as most of the other people seemed to be doing, heading to some specially constructed small stage a few hundred yards away to see a play or some kind of performance. They didn't feel the angry stare of the Hulk's friends on their backs, a stare full of desire for revenge and retribution, as they walked slowly away.

It wasn't clear what sort of a performance there was going to be. The stage itself was small, very small and though quite elongated it lacked depth and it was hard to imagine more than two people on it at the same time. But if not a play, then what? At first two mime artists came on....their performance was, as far as the group of five friends was concerned, mercifully brief, though the locals seemed to holler and hoop and applaud their way through the silent nothingness.

When they went off an announcer came on, introducing the next act.

"I wonder," said Ali, to Oliver, "if it's going to be The Murder of Gonzago?"

Oliver laughed. "Aye, maybe if I had a word with them they could adapt it...and instead of murdering Gonzago and sleeping with his wife, the guy would blind him...... "

"And not sleep with his wife?" Ali put his emphasis quite distinctly on 'not'.

Oliver barely registered the comment, instead watching as two performers playing something that resemble a lyre came onto the stage and went through a few songs which, at first, sounded interesting and different but which by the third song in were sounding samey and hideously dull.

Ellis turned to his friends. "Riveting stuff, I must say. Should we go back to the hotel?"

At that point the announcer came on to introduce the next performer. From the little they could gather, this was to be a narrator or recitor, dramatising a story or a poem. He was a small man, maybe in his mid-50s and he looked at first to be intimidated by being on stage, alone, in front of what remained a group of a few hundred people. But when he started his narration it was clear that this little man, with wide expressive hands and a face that looked as though it held hundreds of tales, was not at all nervous. He made the stage his home as he paced up and down it, telling his story to people at the front and to his left and right, at times looking over the crowd at the front to make sure he had the full attention of those at the back. He had a glorious booming voice, at odds with his slender appearance, and his voice almost caressed the words before he let them out. He immediately engaged everyone, from the seven year old to the seventy year old.

Whatever the matter of the narration, it was clear that the form was poetry. Casual rhymes slipped from him with the ease that only comes from one who lives and breathes what he does. As Oliver watched him he thought it was like watching a recital of something like Tam O'Shanter given by a professional. Something that forces you to realise the power and the enduring drama of the spoken word. Even the five friends, who really did not have the faintest idea what he was saying, could not take their eyes off him.

"I wish I knew what he was on about," said Euan, as much to himself as to his friends. "What a performer."

At that point the doctor came to stand beside them. "Do you understand our town poet?" he asked.

"No," said Euan. "But he is a fantastic performer."

"Well, maybe I can help you. My English is ok...not great, not perfect, but it a great story, a sad story but a very traditional story for our village. No one knows who wrote it in the first place and no one really knows if it is true but we all like to hear it. Every year now... he used to change the poems he told... but every year now people want to hear only this one.

It is about a man called Julien who was a man of this town. He was a good man, a very good man, even when he was a child he did things like raise money for the poor...he helped the sick in the hospital...and he was the perfect child, helping his mother and his father, good at school, a clever boy who worked hard. And he liked to play sports, he was a great team player and a good sportsman. Of course he had a chance to leave the town... he had many chances....as he got older and kept doing well at school there were offers from companies in Nice, in Paris... chances to go to University.... but he never took them, he always said this was his town and these were his people and this is where he

169

belonged. This was to be where he would live his life and where he would die.

He was a man who was... .handsome and attractive... that all the women wanted to marry. It was the talk of the women of the town, how they could make a situation so that they could ensure their daughter would be the one he would choose. And they would do things, almost try to set traps to get him to fall for their daughter or to make him feel obliged to marry their daughter. But he was a good man and he only ever had eyes for one girl, the girl who lived next door to him when they were children, the beautiful Adrienne. They say she stole his heart when he first set eyes on her. They played as children, in sandpits and on swings and they studied together as schoolchildren. When her mother got sick, when he was only eight, it was him that she turned to, it was Julien who would bring her back from school and help to cook for her father when he came back from work at night. They were inseparable. What they had was almost beyond love, as though they were almost meant to be together from the moment they were born. And they both seemed to know it.

Anyway, they married and it was the most wonderful celebration for the town. Even those who had wanted to marry him, and those who wished it would have been their daughter, were happy for him. They looked like... it was the happiest day of their lives. And he stayed here as he said he would...everyone wondered, because Adrienne was so beautiful, if they would go to Paris or to a big city. But they didn't. Then along came a son and then soon after him a daughter, two beautiful children, always smiling, who looked just like their parents.

Julien worked here, he managed things...he had a car garage, a few little shops...people often wanted him to be part of things that they did because he was such a help. There was the story of the greengrocer who was going to go bankrupt because of some competition and Julien worked with him, worked in the shop with him for some time, gave him money, made sure the business was safe...he didn't take a penny. He sort of... .kept the community of the town together, maybe even he made the town a community. He made people look to each other, to care for each other...

And then one day the men came calling, the bad men as the poet calls them in his poem. He just calls them 'the bad men'. The bad men......
.well these bad men... see, he's talking about them now, watch his face, it's almost as though he becomes Julien when he tells this bit....look how his face goes so red with anger...you can almost see his fury...."

It was true. The little man's face had changed colour, almost changed

170

shape. He looked out darkly upon his audience, staring at them with anger and hurt and hate. His face seemed much bigger too, all-encompassing, as he almost ran from one side of the stage to the other, spitting out his venom.

"These bad men......we don't really know who they are or who they were....maybe an organised crime syndicate, maybe Mafia, Camorra, who knows...maybe Italians who'd come into France from the south, maybe southern French who knew about what went on in Italy....and these guys came in and spoke to Julien and asked for money, protection money, to protect him from people like them, to protect businesses from people like them. And Julien said no because it was wrong and he told them to go because they were 'the bad men' and this was a good town, this was a town where decent and good and true people lived. They would get no money from him.

And they went away and everyone was happy and Julien was the hero who had saved the town. But they came back....the bad men came back the next week and the week after that and the month after that...and always Julien's answer was the same...they were the bad men who had no place in this town of good people. Some say they saw him fight these bad men, some say he knocked one or two of them out...but he always sent them on their way and always the town would rejoice.

Then one day they came and said to him that they would talk to him no more. They would find other ways of getting their own way. They would defeat him by striking at things they knew meant something to him. So he gathered the people of the town together and told them to be ready, to defend themselves, to all help each other....these people might come and set fire to their shops so we must be ready...they may try to steal our business so we must be ready and we must support each other... .they may try to rob us so we must be ready.

But Julien was too good a person, his soul was too beautiful, too white, that he could never truly comprehend the bad men or the darkness they brought. He could never think as they thought, he could never see what sort of evil they could do. One day his son was taken from school, snatched from under the nose of his wife as she went to collect him. She was battered to the ground and though she survived they all said that the blow she got was so hard and merciless that it could have killed her.

Then they came to talk to Julien and the bad men felt they had much more to bargain with. So they said to him that he would get his child back unharmed if he would pay up, if he would only be like everyone else. But Julien wasn't like everyone else and he said he would never pay, the town would never pay. And they said they had no choice… they had no choice but to get rid of the problem….and they brought his child to him and told his boy that he must hug his daddy because it would be the last time he would ever see him…and the boy hugged Julien and they wept and the boy went away and went free and the bad men took Julien away……"

The doctor paused to wipe his eyes, which had moistened. "……and after that no one ever heard anything about Julien again. We assume he died, we assume the bad men killed him. But, as the poet says," and he pointed at the little man whose face was now tranquil, his animation soft and subdued, "we have his spirit, we have his beauty, we have his memory and, if we live as we all can, we have his soul…"

He paused, applauding with his hands above his head as was everyone else. Some flowers were being thrown at the poet. "Every year now he tells this story and every year we all come to see the same story, to hear the same story. It's the highlight…"

"Is it true?" asked Aidan. "Did the guy exist?"

"Does it matter? Is it important?" asked the doctor. "Maybe the idea is the important thing…. did the Greek Gods exist? Did Christ? What matters is that we believe or think that we want it to exist…and so it does. And so we want the spirit of Julien to be in this town so perhaps it is. Maybe originally he was only some nice guy that someone liked who got into a fight with someone over something…maybe something honourable like not paying protection money, maybe something over a woman, who knows….and then that story gets blown up to be what it is now….a fable, almost a parable…"

"Except in this one," said Aidan, "the bad men win…."

"I think that's the whole point… maybe if we had that…call it the spirit of Julien….if we all had that spirit of Julien then the bad guys wouldn't win…"

He paused. "Anyway, it's a mere story, only a poem. I hope you enjoyed our fete. And be assured my friend," he said, looking at Oliver, "…that man you fought, he will be fine. You've done no damage."

The crowd began to disperse and it became clear that the evening's entertainment was finished. It was almost midnight. The friends decided to try and find a bar for a quick drink – only one – to round off what had been a more eventful day than any of them could have wished to have ever experienced.

Oliver thought again of Helen. Where was she, what was she doing now? How was she feeling? Was Terrence in bed? And he imagined what they might be doing right now if he were at home....probably nothing in particular, maybe watching a film, maybe talking about their day... Somehow her days were always more interesting than his. Even though, as she said, she would usually "only" be looking after Terrence, she seemed to do more interesting things than him with more interesting people and he loved when Helen would go into a monologue about what she'd done and let her thoughts flow like a true stream of consciousness. She'd say what she thought about others, get side-tracked from her story about little things that had happened or she'd seen, what some parent had said to a child as she was walking by, how she thought it was not the right thing to do and how it reminded her of this other time that she'd seen something... and off she went, down a random walk of a road that led all over the place till she never got to the point of what she was telling him in the first place. He loved those times...and sometimes he'd ask her a question and that would get her going down another alley. Helen's humanity was beautiful. When she expressed herself, when he could watch her talking and being herself, only to him, he could lose himself in watching her flick her hair or in the way every emotion that she was feeling in what she was saying was clear on her face. He could sit with an almost idiotic grin, looking at her, feeling his good fortune at being with her and she would ask him what he was smiling at but inside she knew he was smiling because he was happy being with her. He was smiling because he loved her.

There was a brief lull. "Wasn't that storyteller great?" asked Ali, looking around his friends.

"Maybe you could get him across to your place Aidan......he'd sell out, even speaking in French....he was wonderful. In fact you didn't even need to know the story, you could tell from his face how much he was... .well, living the story really...," said Ellis. It was high praise, for Ellis rarely went to the theatre unless by coercion, was close to hating what we might call "the arts" and whose definition of culture was an action film with shootings and killings and the more the better.

"He was fabulous," said Aidan, "it's the singer and the song thing, isn't it? The nature and content of the song inspires the singer to greatness. It's maybe the story that made him so good at narrating it. But he was so... expressive, wasn't he? You couldn't imagine a voice like that coming out of such a little man, nor the range of expressions and

173

emotions… it was as though he was truly inspired by something…"

"A great actor," Ali added.

"I don't think he was acting," said Aidan. "I'm around actors quite a bit and you can always tell……maybe I get too close and can see the person before they start to act… but you can tell the act is an act. Maybe it's good or maybe it's bad…but it's still acting. This guy, though… seemed more than acting….his fury and his sadness and his expressions….," he tailed off, unable to find words to suitably express what he had seen.

"Maybe that's the thing with a great actor," said Ali. "They're so good that you don't know when they are acting." There was silence, briefly. "Must be awful living with someone like that, though – you'd never know if what they were saying was……well, true. You'd never trust them! Maybe it's a good thing that, like you said Aidan…you know the person before they start to act, you can see when they are putting on a show."

Oliver was silent, looking into the distance. And suddenly he was hit by a sad thought that took him from his mental warmth. He thought of how no one knew him, of how no one would know what he had done over the last few days or of how he could be capable of doing such a thing. Not these friends. Not Helen. Maybe… maybe he truly didn't know them either. It was a thought that was both comforting and disturbing.

CHAPTER 9

Again, Helen had not slept so well. Again, her night was broken and disturbed, little snatches of sleep rather than long undisturbed hours. She was full of the visions that occupied the mind when it is in the state between dozing and dreaming, between waking and sleep, between being frightened and feeling safe. Unpleasant images they were too, those of her not being able to move, of Olly being shot by a man with a rifle as he crossed a street in the bright sunlight of a French afternoon, of cameras and microphones and guns trained on her, the house….

Olly was alive….at least he was alive in the afternoon when I spoke with him, she thought…and that brought a little comfort…but questions had shot through her head with such a speed that she struggled to articulate them. Why was he in danger? How could he have blinded a man? Olly was not aggressive, how could he have got into a fight? Who was after him? How could he lie low? How did his friends find him quickly but the guys who were after him hadn't? Were there really bad guys? But if there weren't, who was watching her and the house? Who had her phoned tapped? And was Olly still alive now? Sometime he'll phone she thought… sometime soon he'll phone…he has to. She thought of phoning him but realised it was pointless: Olly turned his mobile on infrequently anyway, Helen was sure it would have been switched off now. And though she wasn't sure what to make of what Olly had said, it could put them both in danger. And Terrence too.

It was about 7:30 in the morning and Helen looked cautiously out of the window, looking for the guy she thought was monitoring the house. She hadn't seen him last night and she didn't see him now. When she thought about it, his attempts to watch the house had been quite blatant, unsubtle. But she couldn't see him, which was no surprise as Ambrose was sitting in a bed sit across the water somewhere in Fife, convincing himself that he could go back today, maybe later today. The two men who were hired by The Capo continued to watch Helen but they had been asked little about her by Davide after their conversation yesterday and were getting close to thinking that the whole surveillance might be called off. They had not seen at all the two men who Davide believed had been employed by Helen's husband to watch over her and ensure her safety.

Perhaps they were in hiding… perhaps they had left……..perhaps Davide had got it wrong… or perhaps they had been replaced by another man, or another two men, whose presence had not been detected yet.

Helen thought too of Jenny and the horror of the attack on her. She wondered what the exact nature of the work she was doing was, what was the detail of the material that was so damaging or dangerous that someone would try to kill her? And she thought of how Jenny must have felt, how terrified must she have been when a man came into the room, hitting her……and again she wondered of the way Jenny must have been watched and monitored. They must have followed her movement, her every movement, to know that she was in my room, thought Helen… so how long had they been monitoring her and what had they taken? And Jenny….harmless, thought Helen, completely harmless…

She heard the noise of Terrence waking, put on her façade of smiles and sunshine, and washed, dressed and fed him. She took him to school and returned to the house, trying to settle down to do some work at home. But her mind was at times too active, at times too tired to let her fully engage with the material she was trying to deal with and she found herself sitting at the table in the kitchen, papers in front of her, cup of coffee after cup of coffee, pen in hand, trying to read and take things in but rereading abstracts and introductions again and again. Words lost their meaning for her. What might have seemed clear last week was now worse than hazy. She seemed to have lost that fundamental understanding between the word and its meaning. She could read the words but what they said made no register, as if….as if her mind was saying that it was shut to this kind of activity. Cannot compute. She sighed.

The doorbell rang.

Her first reaction was fear. She scurried through to the living room, going the long way round to hopefully see someone standing there before they saw her. She saw a police uniform…who might it be… is it…… .then she wondered if it was a real policeman. She opened the door with the chain still on it and asked for I.D. which Constable Stephen Barclay showed her.

Helen didn't know if the I.D. was genuine or not – and how easy must it be to fake I.D.- but, given the attack on Jenny, it seemed logical that the police might want to talk with her and they had said as much yesterday. Anyway, this policeman did not look at all like the man who had been watching the house, she would recognise his face, she was sure. She invited him in.

"I'm Constable Stephen Barclay, Mrs Elphick......"

"Please, call me Helen."

"And I'm Stephen. Well, em....Helen....I'd like to ask you a few questions about the attack on your colleague yesterday, the attack on Jennifer..."and he rustled some papers... "on Jennifer Drysdale."

"Yes."

"Jennifer....she was in your room at the time, wasn't she? Why was she in your room?"

"She... well, I had a class, I had to take a class for a colleague...."

"Was this a class you have regularly, every week, every two weeks...?"

"No, no, it was for a colleague who had a hospital appointment... quite last minute... but it was lab work tutorial stuff...not difficult stuff for anyone to take really..."

"So why do you think your colleague might have asked you to take it? What was your colleague's name, by the way?"

"He's Harry, Harry Meades....I....well, I don't know, I mean Harry and I work quite closely...why not ask me?" Helen paused, a little unsettled and a little curious. "Is it relevant?"

"Mrs El....Helen... we're not entirely sure what's relevant and what's not right now. Anything unusual is...... " He left the sentence unfinished. "Anyway, Miss Drysdale......."

"Oh, yes, well, Jenny asked me if she could use my room....if my room was likely to be free...her computer had broken down and these things can take time to get fixed...she was in a hurry to get something done."

"What was it?" Constable Barclay looked at Helen as though he thought she knew the answer.

"What was what?"

"The something she had to get done."

"I don't know....but I wondered......it sounds too dramatic almost saying it... but I wondered if that's why she was attacked. We won a Scottish government contract, it was quite important. I think Jenny was working on it and I think the nature of what she was doing... maybe she was attacked for what she found...or was beginning to find."

Constable Barclay mused this over and looked at Helen. "We thought of that. But I asked Miss Drysdale earlier this morning what she had taken into your room and what she had taken was exactly what was found. Anyway, she said she was working on some very low level traffic research and couldn't see anyone wanting to read it, let alone steal it. I guess someone could have….oh, I don't know, taken photos of screens with an iPhone or a camera……but it's not likely. No, that's not likely at all… "

"No? Why?"

"Because it's too risky. You hit someone, maybe kill them, you don't know, then hang around for a few minutes to find stuff on a memory stick then take pictures. And your colleague said she always gives her files unusual names…she says she remembers things by song titles…so it would have taken a long time for someone to find what they were looking for. You don't do that after you've battered someone. Anyone might come in."

Helen paused, putting her hand to her head and running her fingers through her hair. "Well, I don't understand then…I thought….I thought someone had been watching her, someone who wanted to access what she was doing… I thought it had been planned by someone who knew what they were looking for….so if that isn't what happened…."

"Oh that may be what happened, that may very well be what happened. Do you know anyone or any groups of people that might wish Miss Drysdale harm? Anyone with a reason to frighten her… to maybe… " and he paused.

"……to kill her you mean?" Helen finished the sentence.

"Well Mrs El… sorry, Helen, that's odd too. She was hit by a pistol, a gun, no question. She saw the gun and the mark that she has on her head is in every way consistent with being hit by a gun. But if the man… .and we are assuming it is a man but of course…….anyway, if the assailant wanted her dead, and had a gun, why not simply shoot her? He could have shot her as he went into the room, she had her back to him and she had left the door slightly open. No, I don't think whoever entered that room had the intention of killing anyone." He looked at the floor and seemed as though he was talking to himself more than to Helen.

"Constable Barclay…" he looked up at her quickly… "Stephen….I can't think of anyone who might want to harm Jenny. She was…she is… she can be a bit of a pain, always jolly, I mean I don't…I'm not great friends with her….so maybe I'm not the best to know if anyone might want to do her harm. We're not very close."

"Uh-huh. She got a boyfriend you know of?"

"I don't know. As I said, we're not really very close. I'm sure she could tell you that."

"Oh she has. But I'm asking you."

"I don't know."

"No rumours, no scandals......she hasn't done anything like have an affair with the Principal...."

"I wouldn't know. Nothing, really... nothing." That wasn't quite true. There had been rumours of Jenny and the odd student, Tom was the most recent, but they were things that people spoke about when had grown tired speaking about anyone else. There was no evidence, it was really people having a laugh. This Constable didn't need to know anything about that.

"Well then it is odd, isn't it, why anyone might want to harm this... inoffensive, jolly girl?"

Helen looked at Constable Barclay and she felt that he was looking at her for an answer. She shrugged her shoulders and drank from her coffee. He looked, almost stared at her, in the silence which ensued.

"So, Constable......Stephen....what happened in this case? Why was she attacked?"

Constable Barclay looked at Helen, mulling over how many of his thoughts he should share with her. What he felt were unsubstantiated things, fears... but the more he heard about why Jennifer Drysdale was in that room, the more he thought it was such a last minute thing that the attacker could not have known. And so the more he thought that the attacker had hit the wrong girl. Now of course they did not look alike... .Jennifer was almost nondescript and this woman sitting opposite him was shapely and, though she had clearly barely slept, was still beautiful. But their hair was of a similar colour and would have looked the same from the back which could be the only view the attacker had, their height was similar...... He didn't want to frighten this girl but Helen's face was haunted, her expressions were pained, she rarely smiled, something was clearly making her very anxious. He didn't want to frighten her, but...

"Mrs...sorry......," and for the first time since he had come into the house, he smiled...."....Helen... Do you know of anyone that might want to cause you harm?"

"Me?" Helen almost pulled both her hands into her chest. "What? Me?" She seemed genuinely shocked by the question, thought Constable Barclay, and he noticed the way her eyes widened and her expression became slightly more desperate when he asked the question.

Constable Barclay said nothing. "You think someone wanted to attack....to kill....Jesus, to attack me and what......got the wrong girl? Are you... is that what you think?"

"I'm considering possibilities, that's all. Only what might have been possible. All these changes, the manner by which Miss Drysdale came to be in your room… it was all so last minute…"

Helen looked around her, quickly and in an increasing state of anxiety. "But that's not…….it doesn't make sense….so why attack Jenny?"

"Whoever attacked would only have seen a person sitting at a desk. Not a face."

"You think they mistook Jenny for me?" Helen was almost incredulous. "We look nothing like each other!"

"From the back you do. Similar colour of hair, weight… oh, I agree from the front, facially of course… " He watched as she put her head in her hands. "So, Helen, do you know of anyone who may want to harm you?"

And Helen told him about Olly and his disappearance but she didn't tell him about the man who had been watching the house and she didn't tell him about the phone tapping. The Constable asked questions about Oliver but seemed to be aware, as people in that position doing that sort of job tend to be aware, that Helen was not telling him quite everything. She is looking down and to her left a bit too much, he thought…too defensive, hands across her face…she struggled to make eye contact consistently, began to shift in her seat a little more, scratched herself a bit more, her head, her neck….he could see quite a red blotch on her neck now, irritating her, it wasn't there before. If you ignored the words and watched this woman, he thought, you wouldn't believe a word she said. But what he was getting from her voice wasn't the fear of discovery, it wasn't the poise of someone with something to hide….it was someone who was frightened and a little desperate. Of course her husband is missing…though he had called her he was clearly still in some potential trouble… but her voice spoke of someone who perhaps now only realised how terrifying a situation they were in. For some reason she feels she cannot share that with the police, thought Constable Barclay. So although Helen professed she knew of no one that may want to harm her, the Constable took the opposite message. But who, and why… As the conversation progressed her answers grew shorter, her avoidance stronger and he decided to leave it, perhaps he would come back in a day or two.

Helen, feeling cornered, tried to ask a question of her own. "Tell me….do you have any idea who did this?"

"Right now we don't know. We have a couple of descriptions but they may be of people who have nothing to do with this……if we had cctv footage of the car park it would have been easy to monitor who might have left at around the time of the attack but we don't have that unfortunately....we have a few things to follow up on but really, trying to find something unusual, around a busy University... " Again he left his sentence unfinished. "That's why it's vital we have as much information from people like yourself, to catch this character before....well before they do more damage. They maybe didn't get what they came for." He paused until he was sure Helen's eyes were on his before he said: "perhaps next time they will."

Helen looked down. He stood up to go and she went with him to the door. As she held the door open for him he looked at her, physically closer to her at that time than he had been during the entire conversation. "Be careful, Mrs Elphick. Be careful. I hope you know what you are doing."

Helen looked down and tried to dismiss his comment with a shrug of her shoulders. "Here is my number....just in case you need it." And before he left he handed her a card which she immediately slipped into her pocket.

She sat down, almost sank down, into the chair. It seemed illogical to her that something could have happened to further intensify the fear she woke up with that morning. But it had and Helen put her head in her hands and, as she made noises over which she had no control, she came, in those 20 to 30 minutes after the policeman left, the closest she had ever come to a nervous breakdown.

The five friends slept in the next morning. Not Oliver himself, not really. He genuinely did not know where he was when he awoke at about 4:30 and initially looked about for someone in the bed. But the feeling of imprisonment did not last long. Between trying to go back to sleep and trying to make sense of the last few days, he began to think of their journey onwards. Surely now this would be a straightforward journey, probably get to Paris later today, get the Eurostar across to London, get back home. Somehow, despite what Helen had said about maybe being watched, home signified absolute safety. It would be all over when he got home.

Oliver dozed again, drifting between sleep and something else till about 9.30 when there was a knock at the door. Between them, the friends realised that they were going to miss breakfast in the hotel and made a collective decision that the best thing to do was to have a relaxing French breakfast in one of the cafes near the centre and then journey to Paris. If they got there in time, they might get a Eurostar today…if not then tomorrow morning.

They checked out, paid, loaded the car with luggage then made their way down the street for the short walk to the centre of the town. It did have a strong feel of the "morning after the night before" to it… there was still quite a bit of litter on the streets, plastic glasses were spilled about the place and work appeared to have begun on dismantling the stage. As the day before, the weather was warm, the sunshine sparkling and the smell of the newness of the French countryside surrounded them.

As the five of them sat down at the café, Cyrus and his friends watched them through binoculars from a distance. Cyrus had, by now, a large patch over his right eye and had spent a very uncomfortable night, his eye at times weeping then at different times nipping but quite consistently preventing him sleeping. He had agreed with his friends last night that they would get this guy, rough him up a bit….and the fact that he had a few friends with him was so much the better because Cyrus knew that his friends were bigger and stronger than the assortment of individuals that were keeping the Englishman company.

Cyrus had told his friends how the guy had started smiling at his girlfriend, ready to steal her away. And if that wasn't enough he had fought dirty, trying to hit me in the bollocks said Cyrus, trying to grab me there and hitting me in the eye…when he did eventually get me it wasn't the first time he had tried to do it…he was a dirty fighter, needed to be taught a lesson. He had quickly roused his friends to a similar state of anger as his own and they had agreed to follow them to their hotel, to wait for them in the morning and to confront the group of five before they left. Now, as they spotted the friends in the café, they decided to wait until the friends had finished their breakfast then make their way towards them.

Cyrus' friends were all almost as big as him. Four other men with a physique that looked like a mixture of shot putters and basketball players, they were all tall and strong. They had unforgiving faces which had left signs of previous confrontations, fights, little altercations. But not many signs of defeat. Together, they looked like a group you would cross the road to avoid. Their arms hung about them when they walked, almost prowled, and their smileless faces made eye contact something to be avoided. They also, each of them, carried a knife. Originally, this was

182

justified on a "just in case" basis but of course when you had the knife with you, and you really wanted to make a point, a strong point, just in case the guy you were trying to convince hadn't quite got it... So, yes, the knife had been used, to slash, sometimes to defend, sometimes to mark, sometimes only to threaten. And Cyrus thought that was all it would be today. He wanted to batter the Englishman till he peed blood but not in the centre of the town, away down the fields....and the knife might be needed to persuade the Englishman and his friends to walk down towards the fields.

Oliver and his friends enjoyed a breakfast at their leisure. Ali phoned home, Ellis texted....Oliver thought about phoning Helen but was a little wary, maybe wait till a bit later, that's quite a bit of contact with home from the same area. It was still possible there were people after him who might detect this. They paid the bill and then sat for a few brief minutes, taking in the weather, the quiet morning bustle as people went about their business.

"When in France...," sighed Ellis, leaning back and putting his hands behind his head as he began to people watch. More accurately, to woman watch. His head was turned with stunning regularity as female legs and shorts and miniskirts passed by him more often that he might have thought possible for quite a small town like this.

Oliver stood up and stretched. With reluctance his friends stood up too.

"Right," said Oliver, "Let's......." And that was as far as he got before five guys appeared from nowhere and stood beside him and his friends. Oliver and his friends quickly looked up, Oliver immediately recognising Cyrus as the Hulk from last night and two of his friends as guys who had come to help him. He recognised the look of hostility and venom immediately as one that Cyrus had shot at him last night from the canvas. Cyrus motioned the friends away from the café and they all crossed the street. Cyrus and his friends then made an open circle around Oliver.

Oliver stood, looking around him. Not a word had passed between anyone. "What do you want with us? If you have trouble then it is with me, not my friends. Leave them alone. And send your goons away. Just you and me." But it was all lost on Cyrus and his friends, none of whom had stuck around or paid attention at school long enough to learn any English. Cyrus smiled, a smile of darkness, and put his finger to his lips, motioning Oliver to shut up. Cyrus looked around his friends and they each drew a knife, pressing buttons so the blades shot out almost simultaneously.

"Jesus Christ, steady!" shouted Aidan. Cyrus motioned that Oliver and his friends should walk and keep walking and one friend of Cyrus walked closely behind one of Oliver's. Cyrus himself walked behind Oliver, talking and shouting at him though Oliver understood nothing of what was said. However, when he had seen the knives come out he was gripped by the fear that this had very little to do with the previous night's wrestle. This was about the attack on Paul and Monte Carlo and the guys they were trying to run away from. Big gangly idiots in some French town don't have knives, he thought, they simply batter you if they want to batter you. And he began to dread where they might be being led to…to some place, or some guy who would exact revenge on all of them for what he had done in a moment of haste at a dinner. Christ, thought Olly, as they were marched down the street, we could die here. We could all die here.

They walked for what seemed an eternity. In reality, it took about fifteen minutes to get to the fields on the outskirts of the town. During that time little passed between Oliver and his friends. Each was following his own thought process that led to a similar brutal finale. Cyrus and his friends grunted and laughed in French at or to each other, but it was French that Oliver could not understand a word of. He also felt that their lack of comprehension of English was genuine, not faked, and that there was a chance he might be able to talk with his friends, to try and say something so they could find some way to get away from these Hulks. But what, but what… Oliver became increasingly desperate as they moved more into the countryside, more convinced that they were going to get half beaten to death in some field before being taken back to the south of France. Once more he felt guilt and regret… stopping in that village, the girl, at fighting this guy……

Perhaps the best hope lay in outrunning the Hulks. But he couldn't turn and tell his friends to take off. The respective Hulk that trailed each of his friends was too close for that….they could easily reach out an arm and stab before the runner got away. An opportunity would need to come their way. Which meant he would have to make one. Oliver knew his friends were quite fit… maybe Aidan was less active then the others but still……Oliver remember how slow the Hulk was in the ring and the Hulk's friends were similar in the sense that they had too much around the stomach and could surely be outrun by guys who weighed about half their weight and had half their bmi.

Oliver saw, ahead, something which could be their only opportunity.

As they headed down more fields, over gentle hills and towards what looked like a wood, there was quite a bit of sand ahead of them, maybe 200-300 metres ahead of them. Maybe the field had been prone to flooding and the farmer, or whoever owned the field, had put sand on it to soak up the water. Oliver could see that it was drying now, however, and it gave him a thought... perhaps each of them, bending down quickly, scooping or throwing sand in the face of the respective Hulk behind him might give them enough time to run, to run quickly enough to get some space and distance between them. He looked around him for something else, for stones, anything...but there was nothing. The sand got closer, now maybe less than 100 metres in front of him.

Oliver coughed. A loud almost chocking fit that attracted attention. When he finished he looked across his friends and mouthed: "Sand. Face." Neither Cyrus nor his friends had registered anything. They had seen Oliver cough and his head bow. Natural enough. His friends carried on walking, almost marching, same pace, eyes in front of them. But each of them had noted what was said and each saw, very close now, the sand that Oliver was talking about.

The sand got nearer. Oliver knew his friends were going to take a lead from him and he knew that they were all going to have to move with such alacrity, to effectively bend down and scoop up then throw sand in one motion. Oliver rehearsed the move in his head as they got closer. As he advanced he counted that the sand may last for about five or six steps so he decided to make the move on the third step. By that time the Hulks would have stepped onto the sand themselves, there was a chance, depending upon the shoes they were wearing, that they may lose their footing. But there is a chance we may do that too, thought Oliver. He felt sweat on his temples, he felt his hands become clammy, his thighs began to quiver a little as he went through the action again and again. Bend, pick and throw...bend pick throw...no, quicker than that, quicker......

He set his first footstep onto the sand and wanted to pause. His left leg then went forward, however, the second step completed. He felt the sweat almost dripping from him, the beautiful breakfast that he had enjoyed only half an hour ago swimming all through his system, up, over, under, down... As his right leg was raised for the third step he screamed "Now!" and bent down to scoop up as much sand as he could. When he turned he saw the Hulk, his hair beginning to creep over his face, but with a confused and almost beaten expression on his face. As Oliver threw the sand in his face, and pushed at him with all his might for good measure, he knew that he had a real advantage.

He briefly saw Cyrus stumble but did not wait to discover if he might fall. Instead he took off and only then looked around him for his friends. Ellis and Euan sprinted beside him, Aidan behind and Ali just behind him. He also saw a fleeting image, one that would stay with him for a long time, of two giants on the ground and three others roaring as their hands scraped at their faces. As he briefly looked at his own hands he realised how lucky they had been. Yes, the sand had been dry but not 100% dry which meant then when it got onto your skin it stuck. This was fine if it were on your hands, a bit annoying and nothing more, but in your face or eyes it was a different story and it meant that the hands that tried to get the sand away were increasingly covered in sand which accumulated the more you tried. Effectively, the problem got bigger the more you tried to scrape the sand away. The five Hulks stood, frantically trying to get their eyes clear of sand, but their predicament had given Oliver and his friends a good few seconds of advantage and they raced clear, sprinting their way into woods.

As long as there was a path they kept running but when the path began to taper, when it became hard to run three abreast, they had to stop and make a decision about what to do. Aidan wheezed the most, a heady mixture of cigarettes, lack of exercise and an ever increasing waistline making him begin to feel quite sick. Lactic acid swirled around him as he gasped for breath.

Oliver held his hand up. "We can't.......keep going this way. We must....go back. So we have to either turn back and lose them or hide and wait for them to... to pass."

Euan looked around, his eyes darting one way and then the other. They were surrounded by trees, the terrain was undulating a little but there was no obvious place to hide. He ran to his left, telling the others to stay where they were and returned a few seconds later. "There is a cave... I think there is a cave....it looks like a cave....down over there... ...opens into a field a bit, there are some sheep... but quick, let's try it, these guys can't be far away."

They sprinted to the cave. Sure enough, there was a clearing and it looked as though there was another field, or at least a large area within the woods where there were no trees or foliage. Sheep grazed by the cave and seemed almost disinterested as the friends rushed towards it.

Oliver went in first. The entrance was relatively small in height and not very wide. Not so small that you had to stoop to get in but Oliver imagined that the Hulk and his friends may find it uncomfortable, they might avoid coming in here… However, when you went inside it was a bit like the tardis as the cave, which effectively looked as though it had been chiselled into the side of a small hill, opened up into quite a wide area. For some reason a few sheep had made it inside, searching for the grass which grew in abundance outside. Oliver looked about the cave quickly. They couldn't hide on one of its sides… Though it darkened they would be easily seen. He went in a little deeper and noticed, on the left hand side, what looked to be a small tunnel. It was slightly raised but you could step into it although it was small and narrow and Oliver had to bend down as he walked into and along it. It was dark, pitch black and without any light, and Oliver inched himself forwards until he could see a little chink of light ahead. When he made it to the small light he realised that the tunnel came out further down in the cave. It didn't make sense he thought, why would someone have built this little tunnel which didn't go anywhere except further down the cave?

Still, it gave him an idea and he quickly returned to his friends, telling them about the tunnel and suggesting that it was a place they could hide. "We need to lure them in here, down to the part of the cave where the tunnel is. We're hiding in the tunnel, or at least at the edge of it…and when they're all in here, looking for us, we can scurry back up the tunnel and get away. The tunnel is safe, there is nothing in it that's dangerous, there aren't any paths in it that go anywhere else. So although you won't be able to see anything you need to keep going. It only goes on for a minute at most. But by that stage they will be hopefully looking for us down the cave, it goes on for quite a bit more. We can make noises, we can speak to each other, not so loud that it is obvious but loud enough to bring them down here and hopefully past the tunnel ……actually, it would be great if we had a recording of our voice, or one of our voices, that we could leave somewhere and play, so they thought we were still here…."

"We could do that," said Ali. "We could record a voice…one of our voices…onto a phone….but we'd have to leave the phone…and they'd have access to everything that was on the phone…"

"No," said Aidan in a fast whisper. "No, let's try this tunnel…unless we have any better ideas…"

Euan turned up his bottom lip, deep in thought. "There are some sheep there. We could get underneath the sheep and…you know….sort of cling onto them…underneath….and get out as they went out the cave. Do you think that might work?"

The friends looked at each other. "I don't think that would work for five normal guys, do you? And anyway, they would have to be bloody big sheep."

The friends went into the tunnel, each travelling its length and familiarising themselves with it to make sure they could scramble back into it from the other end. Then they waited. For what seemed like too long, they waited. Perhaps the Hulks had simply given up. Suddenly, however, they heard the noise of various people at the entrance to the cave, people who had the same voices, the same tones, as the Hulk and his friends. The friends knew they could not be seen from the entrance of the cave, it was too dark for that, but the deeper Cyrus and his friends travelled the more likely they were to spot something.

Oliver looked at where he and his friends were sitting. It was almost around a small corner of the cave, where it began to widen. It wasn't a big enough corner that it would hide them and they would be easy to detect in any case but looking quickly around him it gave him an idea. He needed light to make sure that his instincts were correct and that could be dangerous, the light could easily draw attention to where they were. Gently and silently, he took out his mobile phone. It cast a small amount of light around him. Oliver held it up above his head, hoping that the little light it gave off was enough to illuminate what he wanted to see. He made the quick decision that it was. The way the cave opened out, Oliver instinctively felt that if he made a noise, bouncing it off the wall down to his left, it would appear as if the noise was coming from much farther down the cave. This could entice the Hulks much further in and if the friends made their way quietly then they could slip away without suspicion.

Oliver heard the Hulks' heavy footsteps, crunching as they made their way down the cave. I cannot leave this until they are too close, he felt, then they will realise how close the sound is. So he listened with strained ears. The Hulks were making their way slowly but their heavy feet and loud voices almost telegraphed where they were and Oliver knew, at the pace they were going, they would take a minute, maybe more than that, to get to the friends. He could also hear what sounded like a large stick or iron bar being trailed against the side of the cave, so that the Hulks could find the friends if they were lying down in the darkness.

The Hulks started to shout, loud roaring noises that rebounded and crashed off the walls and seemed to seep through the bodies of the friends. Aidan jumped, terrified by the power and force of the voices. The shouting wasn't in the form of specific words, only brutal disturbing noises which, in such contained surroundings, bombarded the cave with the omnipresence of the Hulks. It felt as though they were everywhere. Meanwhile they began to hammer the stick or bar off the wall, sensing that they were getting closer to the friends. All five of the friends sat cowered, their bodies reduced to as small a size as they could contort themselves, silently shaking. They held each other fast, scared of losing each other in the chilling darkness, but also because each was terrified of being alone.

Oliver motioned to his friends to be quiet then looked again at the wall to his left. In a throaty whisper he pronounced the word "Tu". He was careful not to move his body, not to rustle his feet. And again, gently, "tu". Cyrus stopped. He was the only one who had heard something. Quick French dialogue ensued and Oliver knew that if he was going to say something else he would have to say it quickly or they would begin to get so close that disguising his voice would be impossible. He motioned the first of his friends to be ready to get into the tunnel. If we are caught in here, he thought, we really have no place to go. But whereas Oliver could feel the anxiety of his friends, could hear it through their quick breaths and sense a shaking hand grabbing his shirt, he felt suddenly steeled. This was about getting home, home to Helen and Terrence and his life. He trained his ear and again looked down the cave wall, looking for the place he wanted his voice to hit. He made vague vowel sounds, soft but gruff, then finished with "Tu".

This time all the Hulks stopped and conferred quickly. When they resumed they did so with increased pace, convinced that the soft whispers they had heard came from much further down the cave. They were not yet upon where Oliver and his friends were when the friends decided to pour themselves into the tunnel. By the time they passed, Oliver and his friends had scuttled quietly into the tunnel, each of them confident enough that they could crawl up it in silence. This was perhaps just as well as by this time the Hulks had begun to use a light from one of their mobile phones to shine in front of them.

By the time the Hulks passed the entrance to the tunnel all the friends were in it and Euan had almost reached the end. And by the time Oliver, the last one through, had reached the end the Hulks were deep into the cave, much deeper than Oliver and his friends had ever been.

Euan was the first to arrive back at the start of the tunnel. As he did so he looked back to his friends and relaxed as he thought they had all managed to make it. He popped his head out and caught a quick flashing sight of one of the Hulks, standing at the front of the cave. Euan immediately withdrew his head, putting his hand behind him to stop Ellis pushing further on. He drew Ellis to him and whispered in his ear that there was a monster waiting for them at the exit. Euan drew his head forward again to catch sight of the monster, convinced that he had not allowed the monster to see him. Oliver was at the back of the group of five friends in the tunnel and Euan tried to slither past his friends, cutting his hands and tearing his shirt on the little jagged bits of rock on the side of the tunnel, to get to Oliver.

"We need to rush him," Oliver's voice rasped in Euan's ear. "We need to rush him and shut him up. Rush at him, knock him and tie a rag round him to gag him. If he shouts, we're dead. You and Ellis rush him…make a noise to get him to come near you. Then you have to knock him over. Quickly. Or we're dead…"

"So no pressure then," said Euan, tearing a part off his shirt that was large enough to be effective as a gag. He moved back to the front of the cave, noiselessly and slowly squashing himself against the side to move past his friends. He told Ellis to charge at the monster when they managed to get his attention.

Euan peeked out. The monster walked across the front of the cave from one narrow side to the other, looking more bored than alert, more at his phone than down or across the cave. Euan picked up some gravel and let it fall to the ground. It wasn't a loud noise but it was unusual and it attracted the monster's attention. Amidst the increased shouting and shrieking of his friends further down the cave, he had heard something, probably a sheep against the wall over there though the sound didn't quite reflect that of a sheep's hooves on the gravel. Maybe there's a bit of a cliff over that side, some gravel slipped down it…. As he neared the tunnel, a tunnel which he had not known was there, the monster saw the opening to something…looks like a tunnel….shit, we never saw that…

And then he was hit by such a force that he was knocked back and lost his balance completely. His head hit a rock on the ground, rendering him briefly unconscious. Euan and Ellis had hit him almost simultaneously and pushed him with every ounce they had. When he fell, the only noise had been the clunk of his head on the ground behind him. As the friends poured out the tunnel Euan tied a gag round his mouth. There was no resistance and Euan knew that something was wrong but he felt a rapid heartbeat from the prostate but lifeless form and figured that there was some concussion but nothing more serious.

As soon as they got to the start of the cave Oliver said "Now run!" But Ellis stopped him and pointed at a large boulder that was sitting off to the left of the cave. "Let's see if we can push that thing in front of the cave. It's not tall enough to cover the cave but it's wide enough to stop anyone getting out….getting out quickly anyway. The bastards would have to climb over the top. And look, there's a slight hill going down. So if we can push it, it would roll right into the centre of the cave. And it would be hard for them to push it away because they'd have to shove it uphill…."

Oliver looked at the rock. You certainly wouldn't have been able to push it on your own but five guys, well, probably…

"What about the sheep?" asked Aidan. "They'll be trapped."

Ellis looked around him. "Never eaten lamb Aidan?" he asked. There was a brief silence. "Oh come on guys," Ellis said. "This stone isn't going to trap these monsters in there for ever. Or the bloody sheep. The five of them will shove it out the way easier than climb over the top of it. But it's going to buy us time we need to run away from them so come on……" And he started to push the stone.

Within a few seconds all the friends were pushing at the large stone which, as expected, moved quite quickly with the force that five bodies were able to apply to it. Guiding would have been much harder, however, and they were grateful that the stone rolled naturally around to the entrance of the cave and covered it almost to the perfect place that Ellis had imagined. Certainly, it was impossible to get round either side of it and though there was space to get over the top it would take some time to climb over it. "Now let's get away from here, quickly, back to the car." The friends took off in a run again but this time not in such a desperate sprint. Before long they were out of the woods.

As Cyrus went deeper into the cave his stomach began to sink. They are not here, he thought. They are not here and they have tricked us. And he looked around him at the blackness as he went deeper but more slowly into the cave, into what seemed to be the heart of an impenetrable darkness. He stopped and shared his thoughts with his friends and they ran up, up towards the entrance of the cave. But where they expected to see light coming in there was none. As they got closer and closer there were still none. Then, a flash of light across the cave, a little touch of illumination. Cyrus reached it first and his shadow cast a reflection on the wall of a massive figure, enormous and giant-like in scope. He looked towards the stone which blocked the entrance and stared at his friends. They ran towards their friend who lay on the ground, gagged and motionless. But with some slapping and shouting he came round and told them what he could remember of what had happened.

They all vented their anger by cursing, throwing things, shouting at no one and anyone but Cyrus simply stood there, head bowed, with his huge shadow on the wall. He shook his head. "Always this way," he thought. "This is how it always is for me. Never the winner. Twice I should have beaten that guy. Twice he beat me. He was more clever." And he realised that the position he found himself in was a perfect physical metaphor for how he saw himself……always out-thought, a stature and standing which intimidated others with its size but always finding himself trapped in the darkness. "She doesn't love me either," he thought. "Maybe she is scared of me…"

His friends began to look for ways around the stone, to try and climb over it. But there were no easy footholds and they realised that they were going to have to push it out the way. The four of them began to try and look for a position from where it was easiest to push until they realised that Cyrus was not with them. He stood away from them slightly, with his head bowed, until they called for him to come and help them. With reluctance, he trudged forward. 'What's the point,' he thought, 'maybe we're best to stay here in this dark horrible big cave. I feel quite at home here.' But of course he joined the effort as his friends summoned up their strength and the rock began to slowly move.

When Oliver and his friends reached the car they piled in and headed back on the road towards the motorway. By now it was well after the middle of the day and Oliver immediately revised his idea about getting to Paris by early evening. He also realised that he had to share his thoughts with his friends.

"We have to get rid of this car. We have to get another one. These guys had us watched, probably from last night. I'm sure they knew where we stayed. So they would have seen us loading the car. They will be looking for the car. They'll know the registration."

The friends were silent. Ellis spoke first. "Do you think these guys were….are….connected with what happened in Nice?"

"Of course," Oliver flashed a look back at him. "Yes, of course. I think these guys were either taking us away to beat the shit out of us and deliver us to someone higher up the food chain or kill us themselves, who knows? They had knives….did you see the size of those blades?" He was quiet. He mistook his friends' silence for scepticism. Their silence was actually a result of exhaustion and the natural relaxing of adrenalin which tends to prohibit thought and speech. Each was in his own world of thought and threat. "You don't think they were part of all this? Of course they were! You think it's normal for a guy to get beat at wrestling then, with his mates, watch where the guy who beat him stays… monitor them the next morning with his huge friends…then follow them and threaten them with knives and lead them into the woods to do… well, to do God knows what. You think that's normal behaviour?"

Put like that, thought Euan…… he has a point. But still… "But these guys….they were…well, they've not exactly shown themselves to be the brightest…"

"Maybe you don't get too many criminal geniuses in small towns in rural France," Oliver shot back at him. "I'm convinced they were part of this, completely convinced… the more I think about it the more convinced I become. So we get to Lyon or somewhere near Lyon and we get rid of this car, we get another one, I don't care where and I don't care about the type of car. As long as it's not this one." It was said as a statement, not a question, and the resultant silence Oliver took for consent.

He sighed deeply, tired and with a headache that almost seemed to drill into the side of his head. Briefly he thought of Clotilde: 'I'm sorry I doubted you….'

"No," said The Capo into the telephone. "The other team will win that match. You know who I mean. I have friends, friends I need to impress, friends in Asia, who will be putting a lot of money on the other team. And I believe in a healthy rate of return for my friends. I don't care what you have to do or who you have to pay… try the referee, he has been obliging before…or talk with the manager of the team who have to lose." He suddenly started to become angry. "I don't care what you do. But know that if the other team don't win then I'm going to hunt you down and I'm going to have you killed. So arrange it. It's one match, it's not as if it's a whole league or tournament. Can I now put the phone down assured that you have seen things my way?" He must have been duly assured as the phone went down with a thump.

Davide walked in and stood in silence as The Capo kept his head down, looking at the phone as if it might jump up and attack him. "Well, what is it?"

"It's Paul. He's phoning from a police station. He says they're threatening to lock him up. He needs your help."

"What's he done?"

"It's Elaine. He has hit her, quite badly I think, she's in the hospital… the police have arrested him. He wants you to help him, to get him out."

"To get him unarrested?"

"Yes."

The Capo knew he could make one call and Paul would be free within the half hour. But this guy had caused him enough time over the past few days and Paul being locked up was maybe a good idea. Then again, he was a friend, he has done me such favours….

"Shit! He's an idiot!" Then he sighed. "But I suppose being an idiot is not a crime." He was thoughtful. "Ok, but we are going to see him. I want to talk to this guy and ask him what the hell he is up to."

When Paul saw that The Capo himself had come he almost kneeled in supplication. He grasped The Capo's hand with both of his hands and bowed his head. "Thank you, thank you… "

"You're not out of here yet Paul. What the hell are you doing? What's going on? Did you really hit Elaine? And look at the state of you…"

To be fair to Paul he could not help the ungainly patch that covered his eye. It was large and all-consuming to prevent any possible infection getting in. But he had cried, tears of rage and frustration and hurt and this had led to puss oozing down and through the cover. He still had his eye, just, but it was in such a state they said he should get used to seeing through only one eye for at least a year.

His shirt was open and there were scratches on his chest that looked like those of a woman's fingernails. There were similar tears down the other side of his face, the side of his good eye. His hair was a dishevelled mess, an arrangement of peaks and troughs that a teenager may have paid a fortune for at a stylist.

"Yes I hit her. We had a fight, a big fight…I've never hit her, I've never hit a woman before…"

The Capo knew this to be a lie. He looked at Paul with eyes lacking both emotion and compassion.

"I got out of hospital, I was in hospital for a couple of days, maybe three days. Then since I've got out she was there at the house but she was different. She started accusing me of seeing other women…she was accusing me, can you believe that, after what she did with that bastard on Saturday night….and she was drinking, she was getting drunk. She's a stupid loud bitch when she's drunk at the best of times. Earlier this morning she went at me, asking me how many women I had been with, saying she was glad the English guy had practically blinded me, how she'd rather be with him than me. Who could listen to talk like that and not react? Who could remain cold and….dispassionate? So I slapped her, a little slap, on the face. And she went mad, she went really mad, attacking me, scratching my face, scratching me everywhere, ripping my shirt. Then I fought back and I hit her, I punched the whore everywhere I could. I heard her cries but I kept going. She deserved it all. What she said to me, what she did with that bastard, what she would have done with him if I hadn't been there……no woman can do these things or talk like that, no woman of mine. You would have been the same Capo, you would have beaten the shit out of someone who had been so disrespectful."

The Capo ran his hand over his face. He couldn't imagine hitting a woman. Shooting one maybe… He shook his head. "I can get you out of here. Charges dropped, no problem…."

"Oh thank you Capo…"

The Capo held up his hand. "I'd do that because you're my friend. Friends help each other. Friends are honest with each other. The real issue is that you have not been honest with me." He simply stared at Paul and by so doing silenced the indignant interjection. "I was told this guy, the Englishman, Oliver….that he threatened your business, that he was working against me for a rival…" Paul looked down, down to the ground. "And that's not true. He works for a company that make war figures. He's inoffensive, he's nothing, he's a nobody. You want me to get him because your wife fancied him……"

Paul looked up. He held his hands up. "Yes, if I'm honest, yes I exaggerated….I exaggerated to try and make sure you would help me. But you're wrong if you think he's a nobody. He is connected. He's connected to those that work against you. I know this. I know it. From what he does, through his work…" Paul threw his hands in the air as if this were so obvious that it did not require further explanation.

The Capo knelt down beside Paul and lifted Paul's face so that he could look into his eyes. "You are my friend. Friends help each other. I would have helped you anyway. Why don't you tell me the truth? Who is he connected to?"

Paul paused. "I can't tell you definitively because it is what others have told me. I have not seen it for myself. But I trust what I have been told. Trust is so important. I'm asking you to trust my judgement. Have I ever let you down?"

The Capo sighed. "And Elaine?"

"I saw this guy, at the dinner on Saturday, talking to Elaine. They were sitting next to each other at the table. She was all over him and he was all over her. Then it looked like they were kissing. I got angry. He almost ran away and when I spoke to Elaine she said she was flattered by him, he was charming, he was a much better man than me... then she told me he had had his hand up her dress...."

"And you believed her?"

"Twice. So I had to find the guy, I was going to beat the shit out of him. And when I found him he was retreating, defensive, clearly lying. Yes, I believed her. Yes. Then I got him against this table and he rammed this fucking knife in my eye...."

It was what The Capo assumed had happened. He said, more to himself than Paul, "this guy is a bit of a ladies' man..."

Paul ventured a question. "Do you know where the guy is?"

The Capo sighed again. "Not exactly. He's not crossed any border so he's still in France. Unless he's swam somewhere. I think he has some friends with him and I think they may have left Nice. But they have not flown anywhere, he hasn't been anywhere near an airport. We'll find him...." As an afterthought, he added, "But we know where his wife is, she's in Edinburgh, she's under surveillance."

Paul became more animated. "That would be great. If I could get his wife, if I could hurt him in the way that he's hurt me... I'd rape the bitch......then he'd know what it feels like."

The Capo turned to him quickly. "That's your problem, Paul. Too emotional. You let your emotions rule everything. Had you dealt with this with cold dispassionate logic you would have got Elaine out of there on Saturday night. Now we're in this situation, this problem...which is what it is because you lost your temper..."

"I know, I know...but if I can't get him could you let me at his wife. Please?"

The Capo was silent.

Paul tried another question. "What were you going to do to this guy... .what are you going to do to this guy when you find him?"

"I was going to talk to him. Stabbing you with the blunt end of a knife…it's defensive. So I want to talk to him. And when I talk to him I will find out if he works against us. I will find out the truth on that. If what you say is true then I will kill him. If not, I will let him go."

Paul felt his heart become much lighter. With The Capo on his side he knew that he would win. Paul put his hands together, as one might do when praying. "Please, Capo, let me go to Edinburgh. Let me watch this bastard's wife. Give me an evening, one evening, where you turn your back. Please, I'm begging you. I can do things, I can still give you things…"

The Capo's curiosity was aroused. "What sort of things?"

"Young sort of things… some eastern European, some Brazilian… .your own personal playground…."

The Capo smiled. "I think we understand one another."

He put his arm round Paul and walked him out of the cell and to the front desk where Paul was signed out. The Capo passed an envelope to the man on the desk whose heart skipped a beat when he felt how thick the contents of the envelope were.

CHAPTER 10

It was early afternoon and Jacques paced up and down the hall, waiting for a call back. He hadn't slept that night and had paced up and down the street. So much money, their future, his future… He could have killed Natalie, how could she have been so stupid. And now these guys, these guys who they were so quick to sell the car to, who had known what had happened….they must have watched Natalie for days. They must have been from the same Mob who paid her off and wanted their money back. But they seemed….they didn't seem like Mob. He banished the thought. We must have that money back. We must. And by the time morning came Jacques had convinced himself that they would have the money back come hell or high water, even if it meant chasing some guys in the Mob, even if it meant going across to Edinburgh. Natalie had earned that money for what she had seen, she had earned that money for what she had done. It was hers. Theirs.

As soon as he knew his friend's shift was likely to start, he phoned the police station. He wasn't exactly a friend, not a close friend anyway, but surely he would help. And when Jacques explained that his car had been stolen and he was desperate to know if it had crossed any borders, his acquaintance was certainly keen to help, indicating that he would alert all the police forces and keep him notified if anyone tried to trade it in. He could ensure they would be stopped – somewhere.

"Ah," said Jacques. "Ah that's good, I think… but you see, the thing is, it's a …well, to me they stole the car but perhaps they don't see it that way. There was a….dispute, an argument…over money…and I don't want to waste police time over something like this. Much better if I knew where they were and could go and talk it over….man to man, you know? It's a little favour I'm looking for."

"Ok, I think I understand. I can tell you if the car is spotted or if it's crossed a border or anything unusual. But I can't be of much more help than that…."

"Oh, that's great, that's good…. And we know the name of one of the men and where he stays, would that help? Would you know if he crossed a border?"

"Yes, yes. Give me the name and I will call you back…………"

When his friend phoned back there was nothing to report. Nothing. The car had not crossed any border. The man had not produced his passport for anything nor had he used it to get out the country.

Jacques spoke with Natalie and Guy. "We must go. We must go to Edinburgh. We take a car. If we fly we have no flexibility. My friend could phone at any time. They may be in France, they may go to Italy to escape and if we are stuck in Edinburgh then we are stuck, we can't move anywhere fast. We must get this money back."

Natalie was resigned to its loss. "It's the Defence, it's the Mob. They paid me and now they want it back. It's so simple. We can't go chasing these people."

Guy spoke quickly and with authority. "Natalie, the Mob would have killed you for what you know. They would have killed you as quickly as they would look at you. They wouldn't come, pretend to be English, have a British passport, live in Scotland… they wouldn't do that, what's the point? And to them, 150,000 Euros is nothing, nothing at all. If they wanted you they wouldn't have paid the money in the first place, they would have shot you somewhere a week or so later. No, no, these guys… ….I am not sure if they even knew what was in the car at all."

"Of course they did!" Jacques almost screamed. "They were nervous, they knew. They knew. And more than that, they knew that we didn't know. That one who was getting close to Natalie, he knew she hadn't taken the money out of the car and wanted her mind distracted, away from thinking about the car and about him instead… "

Natalie blushed and bowed her head. Guy looked pensive. "Then let us try to find them. If they were as nervous as you said they were then maybe they are small time, opportunists who happened to see something and maybe watched us, who knows…. But first we must get a car. Jacques, see if you can borrow one from a friend. In normal circumstances I would have had 2,000 Euros to buy one but that money never quite materialised, did it… "

The friends travelled north, heading towards Lyon.

"Are you really convinced that we need a new car?" asked Euan.

"Yeah," said Ellis, "I'm not sure about that. If these guys were really connected to Mafia or something wouldn't they have shot us or led us somewhere with guns? I don't know much about organised crime… .well, I've seen *The Godfather*, all three films….but they don't fanny about

199

with knives, do they? This was just a fight, just a fight we got into because of an accident."

"No," said Oliver. "I don't think so. Not at all. There was too much of a threat there for this to be just a fight. And they couldn't tell us anything because they didn't speak English so it's clear to me that they were going to take us down the woods, beat the shite out of us, then get us taken back to Nice. Or maybe someone from Nice was going to come." He paused, turning round to try and see his friends. "Can't you just indulge me on this? Let's get another car."

They sighed, looking around at each other. Ellis looked at the money he had taken out to pay for the car yesterday. "Well, we have all this cash I guess…it's bound to buy us something."

"It's Friday," said Aidan. "Will there be places open on a Friday afternoon?"

"Use your phone," said Oliver. "Just google… car sales, Lyon… we are getting pretty close to Lyon.."

They found a Citroen garage that was open all day. "Hopefully they will sell second hand cars. We don't want a new one."

And, when he was asked about the men who couldn't speak French a bit later, the garage salesman would say he thought they were "odd. Strange…and odd." Odd because they didn't want a new car, odd because they didn't want an old car, odd because they wanted a car, any car. People who look around them for someone chasing them are people who want any car. Odd because they had no car to trade in, odd because they didn't really pay much attention to the sales talk and how to get a better price and a better deal. Odd because they had to have the car that day, they couldn't wait until Monday. Odd because they looked odd – British guys in a hurry to buy a car on a Friday afternoon in Lyon. But they did look wealthy. Not rich, the salesman would later say, no, not completely filthy rich but wealthy. They had vibrant faces, clear eyes, they looked like they were used to being around money. They were nice enough. They had to have a car but buying a car isn't like buying your next meal. And of course, when the salesman was asked for the registration number of the car he gave it to the men who were asking him.

The garage didn't have much in the way of second hand cars but the salesman was able to get them something through an acquaintance or two and the friends had to wait around the garage until the car was brought to them. It was a long wait. Oliver paced up and down the showroom, looking at the same cars again and again, looking inside the same cars, thinking of how this day was now lost and they were going to have to stay in Lyon or near Lyon or something. Paris was still 300 miles away and even if they travelled there would be nothing to get them across the Channel until the next day. He sighed. He sighed because he was frustrated and he sighed because he was sad. The nearer he got, the further away home seemed.

He thought of Helen and Terrence and thought of what they might be doing, the three of them, over the course of a normal weekend. Oliver would have played football before lunch on Saturday, eaten and then it was time for him and Terrence to do "boys' things" on a Saturday afternoon. Sometimes this meant going round the park, watching local teams play football… Terrence loved when it was windy and the goalkeeper kicked the ball and it would end up curling back, that could keep him laughing for hours….or sometimes going to the swing park, maybe the zoo. Oliver had tried a couple of times to get Terrence to go for a walk, just a walk, but a walk without purpose was nothing to Terrence. You walked to get to somewhere, like the park or to a soft play centre or to the cinema. You didn't just walk. And when Oliver would suggest it Terrence would just look at him and shake his head, the actions of a 50 year old in a four year old boy. "Daddy, you've no idea… "

Helen would be on her own on Saturday afternoons, time she loved to meet friends or read her book or to do anything that involved her only thinking about Helen. Then the boys would return, they'd have dinner….though Terrence treated dinner as you might a landscaped garden in that it might look nice but you didn't really want to spend the time on it to get it to that state. If he sat at the table for five minutes without wanting away it was a minor miracle. Apparently this was normal behaviour for a four year old but it could drive Oliver and Helen to distraction. Oliver missed them both with such a sense of loss that he felt the emotion begin to build inside him. And he longed to be sitting beside Terrence and trying to get him to sit down and eat, he would have given anything to see Terrence's cheeky little face trying to get round his dad by putting on his "You can't give me a row, look how super-cute I am" face…

Oliver realised then that he had to phone them both. If I'm quick, and if I phone Helen's mobile… He went outside the garage and paced up and down the street, as always looking around himself. Then he dialled Helen's number and almost cried with relief when she answered the phone. She cried with relief when she heard him. He told her where they were and what had happened….not about Cyrus and the other monsters, she didn't need to know that, and not about stealing the car, she didn't need to know about that, and not about Clotilde because it wasn't time to tell her about that, he would do that face to face. You can't tell someone on the phone that you have betrayed them when all that you feel for them is absolute love. But he did tell her about last Saturday and all the details of how he thought he might have blinded someone. And he said he lay low on the advice of a work colleague over there and he told her he'd stayed with him, that he was in hiding and he told her of all the things that could happen to him if he were caught. And she told him about someone who she thought had been watching the house… .though no sign of this guy over the last day or so….and she told him about how she had told Euan and how Euan had acted so quickly to get everyone together….and she told him how Terrence knew there was something wrong but she didn't know how or what to tell him because she didn't know the "hows" or "whats" herself.

Then she told him of the attack on Jenny and the policeman coming earlier that day to talk to her about it and the policeman wondering if Jenny had not been the person that they wanted to attack.

"What?" said Oliver. "Jenny was attacked when she was in your room?"

"Yes."

"And the police think the attacker might have wanted to attack you?"

"Well, they don't… I don't think they know so they have to consider that possibility. Who would want to attack Jenny?"

"Who would want to attack you?"

Helen was silent, thoughtful. Then she asked: "Is it possible that this is part of what you're mixed up in?"

Oliver felt cold. He was standing in the sun but he felt a cold shiver pass through his body. Then he felt his reason and rationality return. "It would have to be a stupid hired hood who didn't know one girl from the other. But then… Listen, maybe it was supposed to be Jenny anyway. From what you have told me about her, she's a bit of a dark horse. She's probably got quite a few skeletons in the closet."

"Yes," said Helen though she was not entirely convinced. "I miss you. I miss you so much. Get home, get home…even if your friends have to knock you out to get you on a plane, get home. Come home to us." And she started to cry, tears not of relief but of fear, tears that came because there was no other way to express the deep anxiety that went through her. He is in danger. And maybe me too. They talked some more, Oliver

202

trying to calm her and fill them both with the hope that soon their lives would return to being simple and that soon he would be home. All would be ok when he got home.

When they did eventually get the car, which this time they ensured they paid for, it was early evening and they decided that it was best to take the old car to a place where it could be legally parked and leave it. They would then find a small hotel or B&B either in or around Lyon and have a meal. Fetes and wrestling were to be avoided.

They drove away from the centre of Lyon and found themselves by the river Saône. As they pulled further away they could see that there were streets, side streets and main streets, where it didn't cost to park. Streets where they could leave the old car.

They parked the two cars together and got out. Ellis and Aidan, both very thirsty, had each grabbed a can of juice and drank them almost in one gulp. The others shifted all their possessions from one car to the other, checking to ensure that they had taken everything. Whilst this relatively quick process was going on, Ellis took the can that he had emptied and put it on top of a wall that was about chest-high and adjacent to where they were. By the looks of things the river was on the other side of the wall but Ellis never checked what was on the other side of the wall when he put the can on top of it. He turned to Aidan who let it be known his thirst was quenched by letting out a burp that could probably have been heard in Paris.

"Beauty!" nodded Ellis in approval. "Right Aidan mate....put your can on the top of the wall and the first one to knock their can over wins."

Aidan walked up to the wall and, as he placed his can on top of it, thought he could hear something, some noise, maybe voices, on the other side of it. He looked down but couldn't see anything though there was certainly a noise coming from somewhere. He shrugged his shoulders. Probably the river gurgling. He placed his can far enough away from Ellis' so that, hopefully, they would not hit each other's by mistake. It was easy to come to an idea of how far apart they should be because in the middle, on the other side of the wall, was a sizeable tree and you could put the cans at an equidistant space from the tree by imagining it to be in the centre.

"Ok ready...," said Ellis and threw a stone at his can. It missed by the proverbial mile, skewing off to the right and making Ellis thankful that there was only a river, and no houses, behind the wall. Aidan's first attempt was little better, flying above the can to such an extent that an aircraft warning might have been appropriate.

"Ok," said Ellis. "This time, let's try throwing together, maybe that will inspire us."

The drop on the other side of the wall was quite significant, it fell about twenty to thirty feet and was not on the same level as the street. This was a wall you would not want to fall from, you could not tell how far you might fall. On the other side of the wall, down so far on the other side of the wall that neither Ellis nor Aidan could have known, a meeting was taking place. A secret and furtive meeting of a gang of teenagers, most of them 15 to 16 years of age, who were about to experience illegal drugs for the first time. They were nervous, excited, everyone building himself up with more braggadocio than the other, everyone playing The Big Man.

Ellis and Aidan threw their large stones together, this time with a touch more success than their previous attempt. Aidan knocked the can off completely though Ellis managed to whack the tree in between the cans. The effect on the stones, however, was remarkably similar. They were both weighty and, having been launched at a fair pace by both throwers, now took on significant momentum as they travelled southwards. The boys sitting beneath the wall had no warning of what was heading their way until the stones landed on the heads of two of them with such a force that both Aidan and Ellis could hear the unmistakeable sound of screams coming from behind the wall.

Teenagers getting their first hit don't always think rationally. Even if they had thought rationally, they may still have wanted to physically confront whoever was attacking them with stones. But in the state they were in, with every sense heightened and adrenalin charging through them like a herd of rhinos, they wanted blood. These could be people after their drugs. These could be people from a rival gang, wanting to rob them or fight them, knowing that they had taken drugs and might be in a weakened state. Whoever it was, whatever it was, get the bastards!

Aidan and Ellis looked over the wall and saw people below, people who looked up, pointing and shouting in French when they saw the perpetrators at the top. It was one of those instances when they both realised that reasoned conversation might not be an option. It also became clear that there were steps, not far along from where Ellis and Aidan were standing, steps that led down to where the boys had been, steps which it was clear from the huffing and shouting that could be heard, that the boys were using to get back up. Aidan looked across at the car and realised that they probably wouldn't get back there in time before the unruly mob descended on them. To make matters worse, the other three had started to walk across to Aidan and Ellis and were now more than half way to reaching them.

"Run!" Aidan yelled at his friends. "Run, this way!" And with Ellis he ran away from where the mob would come up the stairs but also away from the car. Oliver looked around and quickly heard shouts from people climbing the stairs. "Oh shit!" he said and, grabbing Euan and Ali, ran towards Ellis and Aidan. They ran beside the wall, looking for a place to jump over, but it was too steep, it still wasn't possible to see the ground on the other side. They surely had seconds only on the wild youths behind them. Fifteen year olds with their senses heightened can run quicker than thirty-somethings and the friends knew they had to do something quickly. No one looked back but body after body piled up the stairs, almost all of them skinny as athletes.

Then Oliver saw that the wall gave way to a railing and he could see the ground beneath. It was about ten feet of a drop he thought but we must do this. He fell down first and as he looked he couldn't see the gang but he could definitely hear them. By the time Aidan dropped down, the last one to lower himself, he couldn't have been sure if any of the gang had seen him or not. The friends quickly made their way back along the direction they had come as there was more foliage and it was easier to, hopefully, stay hidden. They also made their way back a little, away from the wall, as the river was not as close as it first seemed. They crouched, silent save for the panting and the thumping of their hearts. Oliver put his index finger across his lips.

Up above, the gang didn't know what had happened to their attackers but the process of elimination was not a difficult one. As the wall gave way to the railing, the stretch of pavement was quite long and straight and it would not have been possible for all the friends to have got to the end of that without being seen by the first gang member. So they must have jumped over the wall. They can't have run the other way....at least it was very unlikely...the ground was quite open and there was little to hide behind. They would surely have been seen. The ten to fifteen teenagers then had a conversation between them that involved quite a bit of shouting and swearing but which didn't last very long. Views ranged from leaving things alone to trying to find these people and teach them a lesson to keeping a look out at the top of the wall. The two who had been hit by the stones – and how had lumps to prove it – were most for initiating a hunt in the manner of Roger and Jack looking for Ralph in *Lord of the Flies*, with sticks pointed at two ends.

They decided to walk back alongside the wall, not to go down into the riverbank because there were probably too many of them to make their way along the little paths there, but they were going to arm themselves with as many stones as they could and throw them as they went back along by the wall. The distance to the river was not so great, there was nowhere for these people to hide.

The friends could hear most of the conversation but didn't understand a word of what was being said. They did understand the noise of stones being picked up and guessed then that the youths were going to make an attempt to smoke them out. Slowly, and conscious of the potential that the action had to make a noise that might be heard, Oliver lowered himself on the ground until he was flat and suggested, through motioning with his hands, that his friends might choose to do the same. Up above, the youths began to line up along the railings and the wall and, on the shout of the one who clearly seemed to be the leader, began throwing stones into the foliage below them with all the ferocity of a Mediterranean thunderstorm.

Oliver knew, but couldn't communicate to his friends, that on no condition must they cry out. They could be hit many times but to say anything, to let this angry mob know where they were, could have terrifying consequences. The first barrage of stones rained over and around them, the boys above being a bit too forceful in their throws, maybe throwing for length rather than down into the foliage, and Oliver could hear the stones zip past them and into the river. Quick urgent shouts above and the tactics changed, this time stones thrown with more force down into the foliage and Oliver saw one bang Euan on the back of the leg. The friends covered their heads with their hands, gentle and quiet movements that seemed incongruous to the speed and violence with which the stones came at them. Most of the friends were hit, somewhere, at various times. And although the youths up above did not know they had connected on many occasions they had a sense, an overall feel, that they were in the right place, throwing and hitting the intended targets.

Oliver knew he needed to do something to distract the attackers. He squirmed down the slight incline that led towards the river. There was a slight break in the foliage as you got to the river and he knew, looking up, that you couldn't be seen at the edge of the river from where the attackers were. But if you moved into the river, more than a few feet, then there was a clear line of sight to the road above. If I can throw some stones over there, way over to the direction where they had come from but past where they had originally been, then perhaps they will hear the noise and be distracted. It may give us a chance to get back along towards the steps. And if I can throw more stones as we get there then they may think we have gone even further along that way. He looked back towards his friends, stones still zipping their way around them, on them, past them. We can't stay like this much longer...

He picked up a stone that lay next to him and launched it, quite high but low enough to avoid the boys seeing it, and it landed past the stairs, past where the boys had run up. Up above, one or two of the boys heard something and the leader shouted at them, fast words of furious French, and they sprinted quickly towards the sound. Oliver knew that when the five of them moved they had to do so silently and behind the foliage. But they must move because only by moving would they be in any position to throw a further stone. Oliver motioned to his friends to follow him and they each moved as quietly as they could, each one feeling some bruised and battered part of their body. They inched forward, close to the riverbank, ensuring all the time that they could not see the road above and so could not be seen. The shouts of the boys became slightly more remote and the friends could hear again the boys start to bombard an area with stones, this time thankfully well away from them.

After a few minutes they reached a point where Oliver felt he could throw another stone. He was helped by the fact that the distance between the wall above and the path below became greater as you continued in this direction so their chances of detection, in theory at least, were less. The friends got to a stage where they were quite close to the boys, could hear their shouts and could see the stones flying not too far in front of them. They could also see the shape and outline of the steps up above, the steps to safety, not far away. Oliver looked around him. He was covered and safe, he was sure of that, but would he be able to throw the stone without it being seen and only heard? And could he throw it so that it did not touch any foliage before it landed? He picked up a stone. He was nearly in the water. If he moved back much further there was a risk he might be seen and if he moved into the water there was danger there too as it was fast moving and, beyond maybe one or two steps inwards, it wasn't possible to see the bottom. Oliver put his foot on the edge of the water. He looked across, confident he could not be seen. He looked outwards, towards where he wanted the stone to land. He practiced the action of throwing, reasoning that he could throw the stone round the nearest foliage and it would land as far away as he wanted it to land, missing everything else on the way. He reasoned it... but actions and reason are different things. He rehearsed again, pulling his arm back. Maybe a bit further into the water, that would help... But he could feel his foot begin to lack support in the shallows of the water.

Oliver drew his arm back and launched the stone. It missed the foliage in front of him and landed almost exactly where he wanted it to. The attackers paused. He quickly picked up another stone and tried to make it go a bit further. This time it hit some foliage on the way through but the boys up above didn't register. What they had heard were two quick noises which sounded like someone standing on or snapping a twig as they tried to run away. In a cacophony of shouting, the boys sped off up beside the wall, away from the steps, and as they did so the friends tried to make their way in silence towards the steps.

Oliver didn't know but he reasoned that, if the friends could make it to the top of the steps undetected, they would be able to get back to the car and drive away without any further trouble. The boys were quite far up the river by now, they would surely never be able to get back to the car in time. The friends reached the bottom of the stairs and could hear the attackers throwing their stones again but quite a bit away. Oliver gathered his friends and told them he would go first and they should follow close behind. When he got to the top of the steps he would let them know if it was ok and they should run to the car. They should run as though their lives depended on it... which they sort of did....

As Oliver reached the top he looked out to his right, where the attackers were. He saw a group of twenty boys about 500 yards away, their arms full of hatred as they drew them back and whizzed what seemed an endless supply of stones into the ground below them. He looked across to his left, to the car, and he knew that the five of them could run there more quickly than the youths could run the distance between to catch them. He motioned to the friends behind him to be quick and sped to the car himself.

The boys throwing stones heard nothing and did not look back. The friends were not detected as they sprinted back to their car. But what Oliver didn't see in his quick glance back to the car, what he couldn't have seen, was the one boy who was kneeling down on the other side of the car, trying to break in. He was the one who had introduced the others to the drugs, one who already had a need for the sensations it brought him, and who was already finding that his "income" didn't quite match his expenditure. So you had to take what chances you could and he wasn't interested in throwing stones but had more of a thirst for a car whose owner wasn't there…it might have cds to sell, someone might have left a wallet in it… hell, he could wire the thing and take the whole bloody car away. But he was having trouble getting into this one and that trouble was magnified when he saw five men running around to get into it.

Oliver looked at him as he ran round the other side of the car. His initial instinct was to run away, run back, until he realised there was one boy here, one boy and five of them. After a brief pause Oliver ran at him and then Euan ran at the boy too. The boy took off, all his drug-induced nightmares coming at once, took off way into the distance. But he made a noise as he did so and the friends piled into the car, anxious that the less pacifist wing of the Lyon youth would by now have been alerted.

As Oliver started the car he looked up but saw nothing coming towards him. The small road they were on meant that they would have to pass their attackers to get out. Gently, he thought, gently. He looked at his friends. Ali, sitting beside him in the front seat, had bleeding and bruised hands. Euan had blood on the front of his shirt. Though Oliver couldn't see it, Aidan had a bad bruise on his leg and had been hit right at the bottom of his back too. Ellis looked ok but had taken various hits to the body. Collectively, they looked like they had walked off some boat that had been tossed about in a Force 9 for a few hours.

The car moved forward and Oliver saw the boys, still throwing stones but by now becoming confused as to how they had not seen anyone. He saw one or two run further up. As the car slowly passed them Oliver saw one of the boys look round at them. The flash that the boy caught was of Ali's bloodied hands. Oliver saw the boy's expression change, from a quick puzzled frown with knotted eyebrows to one of discovery. But just as the boy was about to scream to his friends Oliver took off, hammering his foot to the floor and the car screeched away, getting out of there before the boys could either give chase or, Oliver had hoped, spot a registration number. And quickly the friends were away, out of sight, turning anywhere, in any direction that took them onto a faster, bigger road.

For a few minutes they didn't care about which direction they travelled. For a few minutes each of them nursed his own injuries, injuries that were both physical and mental. For a few minutes there was silence. When Ellis broke the silence, he didn't know whether to laugh or scream. Instead he nodded sagely, almost to himself and said: "Sweet fucking Matilda……this is as much fun as a rodent in your arse…."

Oliver laughed. He laughed because it was funny and he laughed because he felt together with his friends. Odd that what they had experienced over the last day had been so horrible yet he felt as close if not closer to these guys than maybe at any point…"Boys, boys… you can't blame that one on me… " he looked round his friends, at Ellis in particular. "And personally, I stopped trying to hit a can with a stone when I was about ten."

"Yeah, no doubt," said Ellis. "Your pursuits have certainly been more adult, that's for sure."

The friends stifled a giggle.

Aidan looked up from his phone. "So… what are we going to do now? Where are we going?"

Euan looked around him. "We stay here, somewhere, tonight. As last night, maybe a smaller place, maybe on the outskirts on Lyon. We're in no state to travel right now, we need rest. We probably need medical attention. But we can't go to a hospital so we stay here, go out to eat… we have a relaxing night. If that's at all possible."

After realising they had taken a road which headed south, they managed to negotiate themselves around the correct way and then made a mistake and took the wrong road, the E611. The error was rectified quickly but they decided that it might be best to stay somewhere to the eastern outskirts of Lyon. It would be easy enough to get back on the E15 tomorrow morning when hopefully they would make the rest of the journey to Paris.

They checked into a small hotel with a friendly welcoming face behind the desk and all quickly showered. The welcoming lady had given them the odd unusual look – after all, they were blood stained with dirty clothes and they looked for all the world as if they had been rolling about in the dirt for the last hour or so.

Each of them looked at their scars and bruises. They were all lucky that they had been in a position where they could protect their heads and, because of that, their hands were chipped and battered. But other parts of their body had taken a hammering too. Oliver had been hit on the back, the ankle, the arms. Everything moved, nothing was broken, but bruises and lumps appeared almost as he looked over himself and he knew that it was going to be a difficult night and that he was going to feel the real effect in the morning.

Ali was worried, more worried than the others. As one who had never had a fight in his life, he had stepped into another world for the last day or two and he was terrified of it. Knives pulled on him, stones thrown at him by people who would have probably killed him had they got him into the open, Ali was frightened and anxious about how much of this he could take. He tried to rationalise, to see God's will in the test he was undergoing, but his resolve was quivering. He maintained a calm exterior but the bruises that he felt all over his body, the blood where the stones had crashed into his body, all made him question what sort of purpose there was right now in God's specific actions.

The smiling welcoming lady recommended to them a restaurant called *A Clemence*. It was nice, small enough to be welcoming but large enough that they wouldn't feel alone…beautiful food, people say it is one of the best in the area. Good value too. The friends made the ten-minute walk, quite a difficult ten minute walk in some cases, to the restaurant.

They were struck immediately by the beautiful smell as they opened the door to go into the restaurant. It was hard to describe… yes, it was the scent of wonderfully rich cooking but it was more than that, it somehow smelt fresh and new. Once there in your nostrils, the fragrance stayed, almost dancing around your senses. After the madness of what had happened earlier this was a wonderful calming sensation, almost as if your senses were being softy and warmly massaged.

The lady in the hotel had been right in one thing but wrong in another: it was small enough to be welcoming but when the friends walked in there was no one else in the restaurant. They had the entire place to themselves. Euan knew how much this might make him about turn if he were at home. Psychologically, it's never ideal. But on this occasion the friends had been almost imprisoned by the beautiful smell. They also needed somewhere to sit down and eat.

After a minute or so a woman appeared from the back of the restaurant. She smiled as she walked up to them. Clemence was a beautiful woman. She was nearly 50 now and moving to the twilight of her beauty. When she was younger she could have turned every head whereas now she tended to turn the heads of men who were about 25-plus. She walked in a studied, definitive way, quite slowly, one foot deliberately placed in front of the other. She walked as if she were walking down a catwalk. She walked as if she wanted to be watched. She wore a dress with flowers on it, all multi-coloured and blooming, which was emphatic without being obvious, flattering without being overt. She had flowing red hair, no doubt dyed thought Ellis but who cares about that, little brown mischievous eyes, a seductive smile that invited you to look wherever you wanted. The dress at the top finished in a V and she wore a chain that had a tiny red heart at the end. Both of these drew Ellis' eyes into her cleavage and he assumed that this could not be an accident.

She spoke with them, smiled with them and flirted with them. Gently. She explained she was Clemence, this was her restaurant, anything she could do for them, if they wanted anything that wasn't on the menu she would do her best to please them. The friends ordered what proved to be some beautiful and wonderful food, full of tastes that zinged on the senses, full of tastes that were so unique at times they all felt they were experiencing food for the first time. All accompanied by some of the most wonderful French wine. After the hell of the afternoon, this felt as though they had reached Valhalla and she was one of the Valkyrie taking them on the final journey. By the time dessert came they were all in such a relaxed and blissful state that their conversation was full of smiles and laughs and stories of past times, past happiness, of such male bonding that you envisaged a group hug was close.

Clemence began to clear away their dessert plates. "Café?"

"Sure," said Ellis, "but only if you sit with us." And he cleared a space at the table then pulled a chair across from another table. The friends all shifted round a bit to make space for her. When she brought them coffees she sat down with them, smiling, eager to seem flattered by their attention.

"What's your story then?" Ellis asked.

And, in her very good English, she told them that she was a divorcee, her husband had left her for a younger woman a few years ago, maybe four years ago now. He was rich – he is rich – and he gave her a good settlement, a lot of money, so much that I don't need to work again if I don't want to. So she decided to open up this place. She'd always loved cooking and it was her dream to have a restaurant, only a small one, where she could do her own things, make her own dishes, but not have the stress of knowing that she had to make money. But it does make money she said, it's good, even though it's quiet tonight, it does quite well. It's hard work but she mostly loves it....few staff and those who do work there are her friends.... I'm happy, she said, after a year of feeling sorry for myself, thinking why me, what did I do wrong... the things people think...I'm happy.

Ellis looked at her. She certainly looked happy. She looked happy, too, knowing Ellis was looking at her. It wasn't only Ellis. She had reeled them all in as she told her story, each one of them, and they sat watching her with different shades and forms of desire. Even Ali.

She stood up, looking inquisitively at the coffee cups. With their affirmation and their attention she paced her walk across the floor, away from them. She felt eyes on her hips, her neck, her legs, she felt their pull to look at her like the force of a magnet. She smiled to herself as she picked up the coffee and walked back towards them. She imagined five little lap dogs, eating out of her hand, licking it as she bent down to feed them.

She poured the coffee and sat down. "Is it ok if I smoke?"

"Hell, it's your restaurant, you can do whatever you like. Cigarettes indoors, whatever…," said Ellis, smiling at her.

She lit up and inhaled, exhaling slowly. Sitting next to her, and smelling what had come from her, Ellis knew the truth of what she said next. "It's not a cigarette."

Aidan rubbed his hands. "Oh now we're talking. Prime fresh weed in France. We should all have some. To celebrate our escape. From the bastards with the stones. And from the big bastards with the knives. And from the bastards who're screwing Olly – sorry Olly, pun intended.."

She laughed. "It's not exactly…it's not completely weed either. It's my special mix. To relax. To make you feel all nice and cuddly after a nice meal. If you want to try, you can try. I want you to. And if you are celebrating something then you all must try this – and I will get you champagne too, on the house, if there is a celebration."

"Well," said Olly, a bit embarrassed, "it's not exactly a celebration as such. We had a couple of… you could say adventures that we would maybe rather not have had."

"But you've escaped, right," said Clemence, exhaling the smoke around the table. "So, celebrate!" And she threw her hands up in the air and smiled.

Ali smelt the smoke and would have instinctively turned away from it. However, this did not smell like ordinary cigarette smoke. It smelt good, pleasant. He was sure he had smelt it before… in fact he thought it smelt, in a stronger form, it felt like the smell that they had first smelt when they came in the restaurant. Enticing, beguiling and smothering as it blasted the senses with its appeal. 'If that's what its smoke smells like,' thought Ali, 'then I went to smoke it. What does it feel like, what

213

taste does it give you?' This, from a man who had only ever tried a cigarette once in his life, from a man who had never touched an illegal drug, from a man for whom a glass of red wine was an indulgence.

She smiled again as she inhaled deeply, passing the object to Ellis. Ellis looked at her, at the object, at the end of the object where her lipstick left a tell-tale rouge promise and Ellis grasped the object to his mouth, sucking the goodness from it into him. He blew out the smoke with a sense of regret, his eyes shut and his head skyward. Euan was next. He looked at Ellis, who by now seemed to be in a state of post-coital bliss, and thought: 'Why not? After all we have been through, why not?'

Aidan watched Euan, expecting him to cough and splutter his way through inhaling, but it was a slow and clam intake and Euan exhaled with a smile. Aidan took the object hungrily. His experimentation had been wider than any of his friends and was something that he still indulged in whenever the opportunity arose. Even as he put the object to his lips he knew that it was not weed, not anything he had smoked before. There was weed in it, he could tell, as he twirled and sniffed the object around before putting his lips onto it. He tried to take in as much of it as he could, which wasn't difficult to do as it tasted sublime. He passed the object to Oliver who looked at it with caution. Oliver could see that it was having an effect on the others but it seemed to be a good effect. He would have rejected it had he not felt that Ali, sitting next to him, would definitely try this heady relaxing concoction.

Oliver turned to Ali. "Are you going to try this?"

"Why not? Just a little… seems to be relaxing and after what we've been through….one little draw on this thing can't hurt.."

It wasn't a line of logic that Oliver associated with Ali. But then it had hardly been a normal couple of days and maybe he needed a release. Maybe that's what we all need. Oliver looked across at Ellis who by now was smiling at, and smiling with, Clemence. He put the object to his lips and drew in a quick breath. As he did so he felt something go through his body. Quite what he couldn't articulate, he didn't have words to even describe it, but it seemed to relax him and make everything around him seem more beautiful than it was. And really, Clemence was quite beautiful enough before he inhaled anything. Ali drew in twice, the first a short intake to see if he was going to cough but when he didn't he drew in longer and sat back on his chair, a smile on his face as his head began to feel soft and weightless.

Ellis grabbed the object again, taking in its beautiful taste and wanting its sensations to fill up his body. Clemence took another draw, blowing her smoke out slowly into Ellis' face.

She stood up. "All of us," she said, turning around in a slow pirouette, "all of us can have some fun tonight. All of us. Together. Five of you, one of me. But one of me will be enough for the five of you, I promise." She looked at Ellis and held out her hand. He took it and stood up, waiting only a second or two before kissing her quickly on the lips then nuzzling hungrily into her neck. She put her head back and his hands scurried over her body, one hand vanishing under her dress, under her bra. The friends watched and Ellis knew they were watching and Clemence knew they were watching and everyone was happy with the situation. Their minds suitably adjusted, all were lost in what seemed to be a blissful state. Her hands went down his back, pulling his shirt out of his trousers with some force. They then quickly moved round and she deftly undid his buttons and let his jeans fall to the floor. Her hands first went round to his backside and she dug her finger nails into him and he gasped as he was pulled closer to her. By this time his hands had pulled at her dress, lifting it up, until his fingers were inside her underwear, touching, stroking and arousing her as they moved gently inside and outside her. She put her hands round to grasp him and shoved his underwear to the ground. He stepped out of the garments that lay around his ankles as she started to move her hand up and down on him. He took her underwear off and she whispered to him: "in plain sight. It is better to watch."

She moved with Ellis, their bodies almost together, to the next table. She almost threw the chairs out the way and sat on the table. Ellis' hand moved again to between her legs and she spread her legs wider and threw her head back. He lifted her dress until it was above her waist and lay her on the table. Her legs went further apart. He slipped inside her and he began to move to her rhythm, slowly back and forward, his head soft and without memory or conscience, his desire to be in the moment absolute. She stimulated herself outside, her fingers going back and forward inside the wet black hair, as Ellis stimulated her inside and before long Ellis could feel her come almost in waves…waves of noise, waves of motion, waves of ecstasy…and as he felt himself about to climax he felt like a fifteen year old, discovering the joys of his prick for the first time. In fact, this was even better than the first time he had ejaculated. This was a taste of heaven wrapped up and rolled into a couple of smokes and a woman who had made sex new.

Ellis had known his friends were watching and his friends had watched without realising what they were watching. He almost collapsed on the table as Clemence tidied and dressed herself, put her underwear back on and walked slowly beside the table. Her arms rested on Aidan's shoulders. "Your friend will need to sleep, maybe to rest, for a minute or two. So we shall have things to do when he rests..."

She began to massage Aidan's shoulders and her fingers undid the buttons of his shirt. She sat down beside him to undo the other buttons and then took his shirt off. She ran her hands over him, over his chest, his face, his hair. Slowly she touched herself and put fingers inside herself then drew them out and put them around Aidan's mouth. Then she forced them inside his mouth and he feasted greedily on her taste. She tasted as beautiful as whatever it was that he had smoked. She stood up in front of him and placed her hands on his shoulders to let him know that she wanted him to remain sitting down. She drew her dress up, up above her waist, and moved her crotch closer to Aidan's face. Aidan put his thumbs into each side of her underwear and dragged it down. He knew what Ellis and had just done with Clemence and he didn't care. He realised that there may be all kinds of fluids there and he didn't care. He wanted to savour the taste of this woman, to lick and kiss and suck softly at her, to feel the taste of her throughout his body. He wanted all his mouth on her and he drew her into him, guzzling on her as his tongue darted everywhere into the wet warmth that she presented to him. Like Ellis, this felt like the first time...the first woman, the first time. He felt her fingers join his and they were at once inside his mouth and inside herself.

She stopped suddenly and took off his trousers. Without touching him she straddled him on the chair and he eased inside her. She held onto the chair and rocked herself forward and backward. Aidan peeled the top of her dress off and shoved her bra down, bringing her breasts into him and running his tongue around the outside of her nipple. She sighed, her sighs getting longer as she rocked into him, pressing her body into his as he went deeper inside her. Then within a minute she was there, her glory and joy perhaps even greater a second time as she rode Aidan till her body lost its convulsions.

After staying on top of him for a brief moment she took herself off him and started to touch him. Then, with one hand moving up and down him, slowly at first, she put her mouth over him and he could feel himself surrounded by all the warmth in her throat as he moved further into her mouth. Her hand quickened, as did her lips and mouth going up and down on him, till all he could feel was a beautiful blur of soft warmth. When he came inside her mouth he did so in what felt like a torrent, as though all that desire had been stored up for years and years. She hungrily ate at him, drinking everything he could give her. Like Ellis he fell back almost into a sleep, his head swimming with nothing but the senses and flavours and tastes of Clemence.

She disappeared with haste and came back just as quickly, again fully dressed. She had something in her hand, maybe a small bottle of liquid. By this stage Ellis was awake again, drawing on the cigarette. Ali and Euan were sitting as they were, having been aroused by watching two of their friends enjoying this beautiful woman. Oliver alone sat unaroused, knowing that something was wrong, realising for the first time that they had been drugged by something more than a casual draw of a chemically-enhanced cigarette. He, alone, saw what was happening for what it truly was, disturbing and threatening and a situation from which they had to escape. But he felt paralysed. It was almost as if he couldn't talk. He tried once or twice, when Clemence was away in, he supposed, the toilet, to shout to the others and to tell them to run away but words wouldn't come. And he realised, as his friends sat or lay around, that they seemed to be in a similar state of paralysis. No one was speaking, almost as if no one could speak.

When Clemence returned she knelt down beside Euan and started to run her hands up and down his legs. She put her mouth on him and kissed him, her tongue pushing its way inside his mouth. Euan had the vague feeling that this was going to be unpleasant but she tasted of mouthwash and the thought went to the back of his mind. He returned the kiss, his hands quickly on her neck then on her dress then under her dress and under her underwear and on her breasts. She pulled his trousers and underwear off in a speedy gesture and he smiled at her, standing up together with her. He briefly felt the absurdity of him standing there, naked while she was fully clothed apart from a slightly dishevelled dress. As she kissed him again he put his hand up her dress, no underwear, and inside her. She turned around so that she had her back to him. She felt him hard behind her and lifted her dress up above her waist. She whispered to him: "I need to feel something different this time. Use the lotion if you have to." And she took both his hands and put them behind her, making sure that one was working on the front of her and the other was working on the back. Euan felt his fingers slither into her warmth wherever they were massaging, whether they were gently rubbing and pressing outside or whether he pushed fingers into her from outside. She felt wet everywhere.

She reached her hand behind and grabbed him, gently pressing him against her. As he slid inside her she gasped and he felt her recoil slightly then she put her hand back and tried to pull him into her. As he went deeper Euan could feel himself ready, almost too ready, she felt so tight around him that every movement was heightened, every sensation one that could make him ready to ejaculate. Her own hand was intertwined with his between her legs and when she came he felt her tighten around him almost in spasms and she screamed in a way that he had never heard before and would never hear again. It was a scream but a scream of bliss, one that threw out all the joy the body felt into one wondrous sound. It was a scream that you would make when you had had the best fuck of your life, thought Euan.

Clemence seemed, once again, to get herself back to a state of near perfection and closed in on Ali. But Ali's smile to her, though genuine, was nervous and she saw him shaking slightly, his temple almost dripping sweat. No, she thought, this is not a fair exchange, if he's resisting then there is always the next one....But the next one was Oliver and he kept his head down, averting her gaze, and avoided looking at her. So she looked around again and settled on Ellis who had by now almost finished smoking whatever it was that they had smoked. He felt ready to take on the world. Most of all he felt ready to screw for Scotland.

"You ready again, soldier?" she said, her eyes inviting him more than her words.

"Fuck yeah! Fuck... yeah!" Ellis shouted into the air. "Let's go through the back this time." With Clemence taking his hand they disappeared through the back of the restaurant. The rest of the friends could hear their various states of arousal, screams and cries and laughs at points. They sounded in a state, or close to a state, of permanent orgasm.

Oliver looked up and around the restaurant. The paintings on the walls seemed to be moving towards him, the whole room looked as though it was in constant motion. He felt as though he was sailing, waves taking them gently up and down. Things that had been stationary did not seem stationary any more. The chairs looked as though they were slipping over the floor, the tables looked to be made of rubber, bouncing off each other. Then he heard noises. Noises of animals: he heard dogs growling and barking and panting, he heard the mee-ow of cats and he heard horses whinnying and neighing. He looked up above, below, tried to look out of the window but all he could see was his own reflection there. Where were the animals? He looked at his friends. Surely they must be hearing this too? Euan and Aidan looked ready to sleep, their heads almost falling off, but Ali was trying to run away, pointing at something in front of him. He then threw himself under the table. Oliver thought Ali was saying something, shouting something, but he couldn't hear him. Oliver closed his eyes. Still the sway of the sea, still the noises of animals. Then suddenly he heard Ali's voice rising above everything:

"The fucking wolf! Look at the wolf!" Ali ran around the restaurant, banging into tables, knocking over chairs, staggering and flopping like a drunk. Oliver managed to grab a hold of him, told him to shut his eyes and try to think of something, of anything, else. Euan and Aidan, sparked and now alive, saw and heard the animals too but neither of them cared. They saw and heard pigs grunting and sheep baaing as well as the dogs chasing the rest of the animals but to them it seemed the most natural thing.

When Aidan spoke they could all hear him. When Aidan spoke the swaying had begun to die down. And perhaps because he spoke the animal noises and images began to disappear. Aidan's head was still warm and soft but a coldness, a firm and piercing coldness, was beginning to return.

"This is like… it's like….we're trying to get somewhere and we can't get there…it's like that song…" and he searched his memory…"ah fuck it, I don't know what it's called… *standing in the dock at Southampton…* "

Oliver looked around him and could see his friends quite clearly now. But he was unsure of where they were, unsure of why they were there and unsure of what had happened over the last few hours. It felt as though the part of his mind that did all that stuff had shut down and another part had taken over, a rather strange and unusual part over which he had little control.

Oliver looked at Euan, who was by now nodding his head, either at the song that Aidan was trying to remember or another one. His mop of blond hair bobbed up and down. "Fuck me Euan, you look exactly like Boris bloody Johnston…"

"*Trying to get to Holland or France……*"

But Euan was lost in his own thoughts, his hand tapping the table. "I said, hey Euan, you look like that Boris bloody Johnston."

This time Euan looked round and smiled "Boris – ma man!"

"*The man in the mack said….*"

Ali stared in front of him. He spoke to no one in particular. "I wonder when it first rained. The first time ever. And I wonder what the first cavemen thought when he saw his first sight of rain. He must have thought the sky was leaking…."

"He must have thought the Gods were pishing on him…"

"….*you've got to go back*….or is it 'you're gonna get attacked'… I'm sure it's the Beatles, I fucking hate the Beatles… "

Ali looked at Euan. "Why do women wear make-up? With other beasts it's the male who gets dolled up. You know, the peacock and stuff. It's the male who shows off. Who started females wearing make up? They've no business doing that…"

Oliver was overtaken by a pressing desire to make his thoughts public. "I want to be a spacemen. Seriously. Flying above earth, looking down on it… "

"*You know they didn't even give us a chance…* "

Euan said. "I've never tasted human flesh" and sank his teeth into his arm. He felt no pain.

Aidan shouted: "*CHRIST, YOU KNOW IT AIN'T EASY*… It is the Beatles….shit!"

Euan looked across to Ali. "Ali mate, there's no fucking God. Just wanted to tell you. There's never been one. It's all a big fucking con. They mess with our minds, these bastards. Can you fucking believe they would do that? Only God there is is woman. Women are fucking Gods. I'd pray at a different holy fucking temple every day if I could."

Ali stood up. "I hate fiction. I wish it had never been invented. People reading about other people. That doesn't make any sense."

Oliver looked across at him. "It's the fucking shadow. It's the shadow on the wall…" and he started laughing, almost uncontrollably…"my shadow's better fucking looking and more interesting than me…."

"…*you know how hard it can be…*", and Aidan stood up and his body started to sway…"*the way things are going….*"

Euan stood bolt upright, quickly. "Songs! Fuck! Here's mine… aye diddley dee, a wanker's life for me…"

Ali looked down, a resigned look on his face. "You get bored with sport. You really wonder what the point in it all is. Golf? Hitting a ball in a bloody hole. Football? Kicking a round object in a net…and we get all excited about that? People fight over it! And as for rugby….touch a ball down over a line, kick it between two posts….we pay people to do that…" He mimicked the actions of the sports as he went through them.

"...*they're going to crucify me*...... I still don't know what it's called, anyone know what the song is?"

Ali turned to Oliver. "You slept with Lesley..."

"That's shit!" said Oliver. "I haven't even seen Lesley. She's not even here you fucking idiot!" Then he stopped and rubbed his head. "I don't even know a Lesley. Deny it, anyway..."

Euan's eyes widened as though a light bulb had just popped up above his head. "Olly fucked the French bit! Jesus, the ass on her....woooohoooo!"

Oliver threw his arms in front of him. "I haven't slept with any women. I didn't go with her. All you bastards went with her...."

"Christ I remember more of the bloody thing...I can't get it out my fucking head now....*Finally made the plane into Paris...* it's John Lennon isn't it...or is it the Beatles....was John Lennon in the Beatles?"

Euan said to the room. "Olly, my mum fancied you like hell. She probably still does. Did you ever dip your wick there?"

Oliver heard the question but didn't really understand it. He laughed. "Dip your wick, that's funny....does that mean my cock is the candle or the wick? Fuck...a wick is tiny...and there are some odd shaped candles...."

"*Honeymooning down in the Seine*....no, no one would sing that, would have to be *by the Seine* maybe...fuck, guys, this is our song...whatever it is, whoever sang it... that's where we were, we were by the Seine today... are we honeymooning? Oh fuck yeah, of course, Olly you got married didn't you? Where's your tart then? Where is the stupid bitch? Dishcloth she's called... what a fucking name...see when you're bored of her though, throw her over to me....you can be a right cunt at times Olly, no offence, but the women you get...I'd mud wrestle a Russian to get a sniff of the leftovers at your table..."

"Can you imagine," asked Ali, "a colour darker than black? For a few years now I've tried to imagine that. A colour that's darker than black – that's really dark, isn't it? Think about it for a minute."

Oliver stared across at Ali. "Then what the fuck are you a sports journalist for if you hate sport?"

Euan continued: "She did, she really fancied you. Every bird I've known fancied you. Even mine... could I be you Olly? For a day or two? I wouldn't, like, go with my own mother or anything, that's not the reason....Christ how fucked up would that be, a Freudian fuck me... "

"Someone....some twat *called to say 'You can make it ok'*....and then what does it say….*you can get married in somewhere in Spain*… something like that….*Christ you know it ain't easy*…."

Euan turned to Olly. "We're mates. Tell me, how many birds have you slept with?" Euan almost ran across to the table and put his face in Oliver's. Not in a threatening way but in a way that demanded an answer.

Euan looked at him. "When…today?" replied Oliver, and he collapsed in laughter. Euan's arm had started to bleed. He looked at it and couldn't understand why, despite the deep imprint of his own teeth.

Ali looked around him, part of him trying to take in where they were and what they were doing there. He shook his head. He then bent down quickly and took off his shoes, throwing them past his friends and at the wall. "I hate shoes. All shoes. Especially mine."

Aidan registered the shoes flying past his head but it seemed to be the most natural thing. "There's still more to go…at least another bloody verse… I can't remember all that…..*from Paris to the Amsterdam Hilton*… "

Ali looked around him. "Where's Ellis?"

Euan went up to Ali and put his arm round him. "He didn't make it, son. Ran out to hunt Charlie down and caught in a fucking ambush. Bastards. He was a fucking hero, a legend. But now the fuckers have blown his fucking head off – we're a man down, son. Have you got what it takes now to forget him and get through this? Remember, the fuckers are everywhere…"

Oliver leapt up. "Aw shit," he said in an American drawl, "we're in a forest full of fuckers… " he looked around him, pretending to hold a gun. "We're almost surrounded by the enemy…." He shouted across to Aidan : "Get your gun ready, we're surrounded by Afghanis and fucking Vietnamese… they've already shot the cock off Ellis and they're running around with it…it's a sizeable fucking trophy if a bit diseased…"

"Shagging in our beds for……no, it wouldn't say that, would it… *sleeping in our beds for a week, the newspapers said*…"

Ali looked ahead, straight ahead of him, like a rabbit that had been caught in the headlights. "I don't know where I am. I don't know why I'm here."

Euan started his own song……"we're only here to drink your beer and shag your fucking women…"

Oliver started to clap his hands then quickly realised he didn't know the words to whatever derivation Euan was trying to sing. "Ellis has always been a cheating cunt, don't you think? I'm only asking, throwing it out there…you know, for debate. I think so anyway."

"..*what you doing in bed, I said we're only trying to get us some* sleep…or is it *peace*….fuck, I hate The Beatles….*"

When Ali stared his monologue his friends were barely listening. They remained, for the first few minutes anyway, in a numbed state where concentration was difficult. But as the story wore on, and the shadows on the wall became darker and longer, they listened. By half way through the story Ellis had returned, physically exhausted but kind of mentally alert, and they all sat in silence and listened to what Ali had to say. At times it wasn't clear to them where exactly they were, or why they were there, or why Ali was telling them what he told them. But the story gripped them and made them think only about what they were being told and forced them to focus only on the words. The story went in. Unlike much of the rest of the evening which they would struggle to recollect, the story went in.

"I'm a cheat and a fraud and a liar. Before I was a journalist I worked with a company…doesn't matter who, no one needs to know that, you wouldn't want to know that….but we sold building stuff. Stuff you might use to build houses. It was a big company. I used to check invoices. Check that what the customer wanted was what they had got. You see, we weren't computerised for sales then so you had to check that what was despatched was what the guy had got. Then the invoice could be entered into the system.

Our stock take was always a mess – some items up, some items down. We were so disorganised, the yard was a mess, things got damaged. And the girl who entered the stuff on the computer was crap. You'd have been better with a dog. So you see you could drive a truck through everything…the processes, procedures, everything… Then one night there was a social thing, a customer thing and one customer who had a bit to drink chatted to me for a while and he came up with this idea. He said at first it was only the two us talking. The idea was to send material to him, not huge amounts that would attract attention, but reasonable amounts here and there….I would lose the paperwork before it was invoiced, he would sell off what he'd been sent and we would split the money. I was quiet at first. But I was thinking it over and he could see that. I should have smiled and told him….oh, that hypotheticals don't work in the real world or something like that. My sense of what's right and what's wrong should have stopped me from even discussing it.

But at the time….I was struggling to get a job in journalism, quite a few knock backs, didn't get to interview stage, it was…it is….very competitive. And there was Lesley too…and she likes money, she likes to be comfortable and so I went away and thought of it. I didn't sleep that night. Then I phoned him and we met and we discussed it. He said how easy it was, he'd done a similar thing with people at other companies, he thought I might be up for it. I always wondered why he might have thought that….did I have a certain look about me or did he take a chance?

I did fight it. I prayed, I looked for help and guidance…but either God failed me or I failed him…and I told the guy that we would go ahead. And it worked so easily because he was a big customer and in amongst the larger invoices the ones worth a couple of hundred here and there got easily lost. Of course it was a chance… but only a small one because the organisation really wasn't so joined up that you'd get the transport manager asking about whether a particular item had been invoiced. What did he care? And the sales manager wouldn't have seen the order until it came to invoice… and if there was no invoice…

This went on for a while, a few months. And I got greedy. I spoke with another customer, a casual conversation, the same way it had been put to me and he was game and we did the same thing, a few hundred here and there. By this time I was taking quite a bit of extra money. Of course you never really knew if your "partners" were giving you 50% but you never really cared about that…you'd meet for a drink once a month and get three or four hundred pounds in an envelope. And when you've got two customers doing that…

Now, I wish I'd been discovered, I wish I'd been found out. I never had the courage to admit what I'd done, never had the faith to go and say what I'd done. I needed the money too much. It felt justified, it felt right. So you see I'm a fraud. I'm a cheating no good fraud. I'm not what you think I am, what you think of me isn't the right thing. The worst thing is I felt I could justify it – sometimes, I still do – I felt like I could justify it to the God inside me. I could justify it because I needed the money. I needed Lesley. And sometimes my conscience would stab at me but it felt too right to be doing something wrong. All for love…

I know it was wrong but I'll never admit it. Not to Lesley. But my God knows how I've fallen and knows that I'll always be worthless and a cheat." He turned to Oliver. "And if you did sleep with Lesley then that's the price to pay, isn't it?"

Oliver raised his eyebrows and his hands, speechless.

They got back to their hotel that night, somehow. Between a stagger and a woozy walk they managed, after a wrong turning or two, to find themselves back at the place where they had set out from earlier that evening. None of them really knew, then, what had happened that night. Their chemically-induced inertia was wearing off and the cold rationality of normality was beginning to return. Just not yet completely.

They stood together in the entrance to the hotel. Ellis looked at his friends. "What the fuck happened tonight?"

They stared at the ground. Oliver put his hand across Ellis' shoulder. "Sleep," he said in resignation. "We need to sleep."

CHAPTER 11

None of the friends had any idea about what time it was that they went to bed. None of them had an idea of how long their night had been and already any memory that they had of it was beginning to fade. It was as though the part of the mind where those memories were would become very hard to access. Even as they went to bed they remembered a beautiful meal, being served by a beautiful woman, then something that Ali had told them about his deceit and ultimate fall. Ellis alone thought that he had engaged in some kind of sexual activity. For Aidan and Euan it was a pleasure that, not remembered, hadn't truly been experienced.

As Oliver went to his room he knew that something wrong had happened and, though he had blackouts and lost hours, he was convinced within himself that he had not been the perpetrator. When he saw Clemence now, in his mind's eye, he was sure he would have remembered if he had touched her, if he had kissed her, if she had made love to him. He didn't remember what was said between them and, though he struggled to recall where Ellis had been the whole night, he didn't automatically think that he had been having sex with Clemence all that time.

Like his friends, when he eventually put his head down on the pillow, still fuzzy with the remnants of a potent hallucinogenic smorgasbord, it was about two thirty in the morning. Unlike his friends he stayed awake for a while, thinking over the events of tonight, of the last few days, of the dangers. In another light, these recollections could have been humorous but in the refracted view of this man dealing with 'coming down' they were ghastly and fearful. Stones had battered his body and could have killed him: a guy had held the steel of a shining clinical metal blade so close to him that he could almost feel it scything through his skin: he had been drugged by a woman who could have done anything she wanted to him, to all of them. Maybe she had. Then there was Paul, a bastard madman with the Mob helping him, chasing me, chasing us, with people everywhere trying to find us and kill us. And on top of it all was Clotilde, a woman who in a different time and in a different place he may have liked, even loved, but who had been a rapist, a jailor.… A woman who made him betray himself, Helen and Terrence. He wondered if he would ever see Helen and Terrence again. It was the first time he had had that thought. Up until now it had been a question of... when I get back, when I run away from these guys, when we can get across the Channel.... Now, there seemed to be too many 'whens', too many conditionals. Oliver wished he could have been like Ali, to have had his belief and faith in a benign being watching over him. He needed someone to tell him it would be ok.

As he drifted into sleep he dreamed in the strongest of images and clearest of visions. He saw Mandy, smiling bubbly Mandy, a girl at University who had liked him more than he liked her. She had offered herself to him one night, a kind of end of term alcohol binge type of thing, and he said 'no'. He regretted saying 'no' that night as he lay awake in bed ; things had been rocky with Helen and she wanted a break for a bit and he had been happy enough to take pleasures anywhere he could find them, so why not with Mandy? As he lay awake in bed that night he remembered thinking that he would set it right tomorrow, there was always a tomorrow. Except this time there hadn't been a tomorrow and his friends told him the next day that Mandy had been hit by a car that morning. She had no chance and had been killed instantly.

Images dragged themselves into his mind, for tonight they were neither hidden nor stopped. Images that he had never seen, or had never allowed himself to see, before. What did she see before she was hit? Did she get sight of a car and the driver's terrified eyes, both of them knowing the car was going too fast, before she was thrown into the air? Did she know in these split seconds that she was going to die? And did she register the thought that it was somehow my fault, thought Oliver, because if I had been with her we would still have been in bed? What was her thought, her very last thought....a thought unsaid, that no one would ever know.

He saw the other people, the friends who cried and wailed when they heard that she was dead. Oliver couldn't cry. He watched the group therapy, the open catharsis as tears were shed, intimacies were shared, hands were touched, embraces exchanged, sympathy expressed. But it felt fake to him and he saw himself standing naked amongst them, standing in the middle of the floor with a blank expression on his face. How can it be so real to them? How could grief come so quickly? It still felt like a sick joke that he could not understand. Perhaps Mandy would come bounding from behind the sofa. They couldn't see him, naked, and though he was watching them he didn't truly see them either. His head turned around and around from his central point but their faces, in grief, were all the same. They did things exactly the same. I can't understand any of this... Mandy was too alive to be dead.

Then his mind flashed to the crematorium and these colours and images were bright and vivid and fresh. He waited outside, alone, as the others busied themselves somewhere inside a small waiting room, hushed conversation in respectful low voices. Forced smiles. He saw lush green grass, small trees sprouting leaves for the first time. Yet there was no wind. No sun. He remembered thinking at the time, the long-banished thought now forcing itself up into his mind, that the essential ingredients that moved life didn't nourish this place. But still it grew, this place of death, this sick freak, this unreal landscape full of silent nightmares. It took its life from death, nurtured by death's long straggling fingers, fingers that stretched around it and protected it and claimed it.

He walked into the crematorium, seeing himself now as the last to enter. In the images that came to him nobody saw him and he stood at the back beside some people he did not know. Where were his friends? He didn't cast eyes anywhere to look for them. He simply stood, detached from everyone, everyone detached from him. He heard the sound of muffled sniffles and the noise seemed to come from everyone; young, old, fat, thin, all reinforcing to him that he wasn't engaging. He was staring ahead, into a void. The organ started, the minister entered and behind him came the coffin, a gold plaque in the corner, Amanda J Johnstone and dates that he never saw. But he remembered the glint from the coffin, the glint as it was carried up the aisle and a freak lay of light reflected from it and into his eye. It blinded him then as it blinded him now, as he stood again watching those unreal letters on that terrible container. With his detached stare he wanted to walk beside the coffin, to open it, just for curiosity, just to make sure that it was really Amanda in there. Because it still wasn't sure, it still wasn't certain, he still wasn't convinced that she was in there.

As the coffin disappeared away from him he gasped, shocked in that moment that he would never see Mandy again in his life. He'd never be able to change his mind, to have a chance tomorrow. All there was of Mandy now were sweet memories. And when he thought of her he didn't actually see her or her lovely little-girl-lost face but he saw her in the image of a sprinkling of gold on black canvas. Something an artist might use to brighten things up. That's what she did, he thought, that was her. She brightened things up. In a group, or alone or in a class, wherever...

he remembered smiling at her, smiling when he knew she was there. Smiling because she made things brighter.

So why's she away then? What's the point in that? He listened to the minister speak. He listened to the way he spoke and heard the minister describe the mystery, in the way that he saw as religion's property, as "God's will". It was God who had robbed them of her. It was God who had taken the gold dust away and made the canvas blacker than it had been. Had it been a serial killer then he would have been hunted down, maybe by vigilantes, but this was not the work of a serial killer. This was the work of a benign creator who saw it appropriate to take this girl for one of his own. How fucking cruel, he thought. To give her family this beautiful girl for 20 years then to say "sorry, need her back." This is decayed logic, rotten to its very core. We would worship something that evil…. He heard the minister say 'In my father's house there are many rooms. If it were not so I would have told you' and he wanted to stand up and say that Mandy was rooted in life. She didn't want a pretend room in a mythical palace.

It was all too twisted and full of evil. This religion, this Christian view, it was full of evil. How could you believe that of something you worshipped? No, let us know that Mandy was taken not by the Divine but by the random anarchy that is termed the way of things. The same Godless, lawless, arbitrariness that gave one child the surroundings of comfort while another one struggled for food and water , that raged wars in some parts of the world and not others, that made madmen cultivating the lunatic hit one person with a bullet and not another, that made one ship sink in a gale and another one sail right through it. Anyone could give life, it could be an accident after one night or it could have been meticulously planned. And anyone could take it away too. No one deserved to live and no one deserved to die…not 6 million Jews in a Holocaust of unleashed hell, not the victims of some cleansing activity. It just fucking happened.

The minister biographised Mandy's short pale blaze of a life and people cried. Still Oliver couldn't and wondered for whom they cried. Not for Mandy surely because she couldn't hear them. She was dead. Did they cry for themselves, for the loss of something that young and free and happy? Or was it because it brought them closer to mortality themselves? Because it made them think that one day the sun will continue to shine for hours, days, weeks and months after they were gone, through decades when the last person to have known them, to have kept their memory alive, will finally die too? Then what would be left but this....well, the man got it right...this quintessence of dust...

He watched the coffin go down, down into the depths of the heat. He tried to free his mind from the horrible connotations and flames and wanted to see Mandy again, wanted to hold her before she finally went away, to kiss her goodbye. He re-thought his rejection of her and where they had shared a gentle hug of understanding he saw instead a tight embrace, her face full of acceptance as her hair billowed around both of them. He saw her smile softly at him as she walked slowly backwards away from him and he stood, unable to move. Mandy was dead. But as she let go of him and moved away he smelt her distinctive fragrance in his nose, he felt his hand slide along hers. And she seemed so very very real.

What might she have done, this beautiful and promising and clever and sexy young woman? Would she have worked in an insurance company, maybe her potential thwarted, maybe have to take a job to pay the bills and never get to do what she truly wanted to do, whatever that might be? Or would she have done what she wanted...painted pictures if that was her thing, or been a banker? To whom has she been lost? What boy, all brash and showy or coy and innocent, was her type? Who would she have married? And kids she would never have.... I could have changed all that. I could have given her that future if I'd gone with her. Why didn't I do that? Because now....because now she's died in public with all the dignity of a dog.

At the end of the service everyone manoeuvred out of the crematorium, soft shoe shuffling their way out past the bereaved family. The crying was universal. Oliver still knew that other people couldn't see him and he walked on the outside of everything. He walked away from the others when he got outside, across the verdant full grass. He stood alone. Then he saw the sun come out, and it shone all over the grass and trees and then the wind started to blow through the leaves and it was only then, at that point, that he started to cry.

Oliver didn't know if he was awake or asleep or in some state in-between. But he realised that he was unable to resist the thoughts that began to think him. They would simply throw themselves into his head, launched without mercy like the stones that had physically battered him earlier that day. Relentless, endless......

He saw his father, at the end a fumbling delicate shadow that tottered from one step to the next, gaunt and thin and eaten. He wondered what had really killed his father – a cancer or the death of his dreams? I didn't know him, not the complexities of his silence, not the triggers of his anger, not his aspirations for me or mine, not what made him brood or made him bitter.

His father had last spoken to him three or maybe four days before he finally passed away. Oliver tried to look for some significance or message in what passed between them but of course there was nothing there. It had been a normal conversation at that time where his father's mind drifted effortlessly from one thing to the next, randomness combining thoughts that went across years but which played themselves together in the fragments of his memory. Oliver would smile and nod and ask a question which prompted another diversion but it didn't matter, none of it mattered, because they were at least talking and smiling and together. The happiest he saw his father was sitting up in that hospital bed, being served food by some beautiful young nurse, smiling at her with all the coyness and reserve of a polite 15-year old with desire pumping through him. As though, then, that his mask was down, finally down, after years of trying to be someone and something that he found almost impossible.

He wasn't a giant of a man any more. He didn't tower over Oliver with everything he did, like a black cloud, and frailty freed him from omniscience. In those last months we were friends….was it too much to even say equals?

Oliver had been frightened of his father and frightened by his father. Sometimes by the silence and the cold steel stare, sometimes by the raising of his voice or the grip of his arm, sometimes by the tone of his voice. He never wanted to be his father but he admired him for many of his values – his hard work, his ability to deal with people he clearly would rather not have dealt with, his everyman status and the way he saw the managing director and the labourer as the same. His father was a provider. He was the product of a generation that prided itself on providing. Man provided. As best, and as much, as he could. His father had lived through World War II rationing, undertaken the character enhancing national service, lived through the liberalisation of everything in the 1960's and saw the excesses of the Thatcher era in the 1980s. The man could have, if he had wanted to, been a one-man story of the development of British society. He was part of that ethos that drove the post-war generation – "we shall give our children the things that we never had." No one really stopped to ask the children if that was what they actually wanted but that didn't seem to matter – there was money to be made and children liked to have money spent on them. And perhaps the desire to be heard was lost in the presents bought to compensate for there being no one there to hear: perhaps the need to be friends was lost in the time it took to be a successful adult which made the effort it would take to enter a child's world impossible: perhaps the longing to have an interest shared with a parent was too easily lost in the need to relax oneself after the efforts of getting through the day, striving for the next promotion, to provide more and more....

So it probably wasn't his father's fault that they never really understood each other. How do you explain to someone who loved national service that you would rather read a book? How do you explain to someone whose silence could be days long that it might not hurt to open up a bit? How do you explain to someone whose life defines him that he was maybe chasing the wrong dream?

When his father stopped working he became a living paradox. He had lost his very reason to live yet became more interested, more interesting, more vulnerable and more alive. And more ill. As if the one could not exist without the other. Oliver cursed him then – and his brow furrowed in his drifting state of sleep now – for resigning himself to accepting whatever illness might come his way and accepting the inevitability that it would kill him. Though more interested in others, the lack of work could not make him more interested in himself. Oliver wanted to throttle him at times, wanted to open his eyes to the beauty that might be in a simple thing such as a walk round the park, or a book, or in things such as his grandchildren....which he would always ask about and play with if he could but limit his involvement to the hour or so a week that they forced themselves into his company.

Will I be like that, Oliver wondered... a damned foolish old man who was old without being wise? Was I, am I, him already....me at this age like him at this age, dominated by a warped and twisted idea of perfection through the looking glass? And Oliver thought of the things he sometimes said that he said only because his father said them, of the things he did because "that's just what you did" but were really done because his father had done them that way. He saw similar characteristics, similar quirks... So what is left that is me?

And as his mind regressed he remembered a long-ago conversation with his father after Sunday school one day. Oliver never knew if his mother or father went to church but he was dutifully despatched to

Sunday school which was vaguely ok as he knew some of the children but there had been a bit too much talk for Oliver's liking and not enough play. As the memories shone inside him he remembered sitting there one Sunday, listening to the attractive smiling teacher talking about God and his inherent goodness and his son Jesus Christ and how Jesus is with us all the time and knew everything we were doing. For a four or five year old, Oliver struggled to get his head round that, how one guy would know everything about everyone. And why he would want to. And then about how we could pray and our prayers might be heard, but they might not…and even to a four or five year old there seemed to be little or no correlation between the two actions.

"Dad, I don't understand….in Sunday school the teacher was talking about how Jesus is with us all the time and knows everything we do and even everything we think. How can he know that?"

"I don't know Olly."

Oliver was puzzled. He believed his dad pretty much knew everything.

"Jesus knows what you're thinking…and what I'm thinking… how does he know that? And I'm frightened because sometimes I don't think nice things about people. Will Jesus do bad things to me?"

It was clear from the pause that his dad had clearly thought this over for a while. And he knelt down beside Olly and put his arm round him. Olly could still feel that gentle touch on his shoulder. This was serious, Olly knew, because his dad never knelt down beside him, he much preferred to stand above him and look down.

"Olly…….religion, Jesus, God…….it's not something that we can prove….it's…"

"What does 'prove' mean?"

"'Prove' in this sense means that we can't show that it definitely exists. Like we can prove your clothes are yours because they have your name on them. God is……well, it's something that people can believe in or not believe in… but we can't prove it's true."

"What do you believe? I'll believe what you believe."

"You have to make up your own mind, it's your choice."

"What do you believe? Do you believe that Jesus knows everything we think?"

"No, Olly, I don't….but maybe somewhere there is a God, maybe……"

"I don't like Jesus. Why would anyone want to know what I think?

If I think a bad thing, but don't do it, it's not bad is it? Do you think bad things?"

"All the time."

"You're not bad!" And Oliver remembered how animated he became, as though he had worked everything out. "So it must be wrong. I don't want people to know what I think. I don't want people to know what I think." He repeated it, as if he had affirmed something to himself and freed himself from a lifetime of angst.

"Daddy, did you go to Sunday School when you were young?"

"Yes, I had to. We were made to. When I was young, you didn't choose whether to believe in God or Jesus, you had to believe. You would be a bad person if you didn't believe."

"So…did you believe in Jesus then?"

"I don't know. I don't think so. But I didn't question it. You just did it. It was the way things were, it was the way things worked. Most people…everybody… went to church. It was a way to keep everyone the same."

Oliver paused. "But not everyone goes to church now, do they? Most of my friends don't go…."

"It's different now. Times have changed since I was a little boy like you." And he added, as an afterthought – "The important thing is to be a good person."

"Can I be good even if I don't believe in Jesus?"

"Of course you can."

"Good, because I am scared of him. I don't want him to know my thoughts. So if I don't believe in him then he can't know them." He paused. "And I don't want to go back to Sunday School." As Oliver remembered it now he realised the significance of the conversation for two reasons. It was the first time he had used his own sense of reason and logic to come to a conclusion that was right for him but, more than that, it was one of the first conversations he had had with his father about something of importance, be it of a personal or theological nature. With regret, he also realised it had been one of the last.

Oliver twisted in his bed, his head still full of fervent remembered images, conversations held years ago that came back as though they were yesterday. He was sweating but not feverish, uncomfortable but definitely not awake, restless but still dreaming. Then he saw his father on his deathbed, the family gathered round him, saying goodbye, and he wondered what his father could see, if he actually saw anyone who was there, and then suddenly he was gone, his face left in an expression of peaceful horror. The image burned into him, the clear eyes, sallow skin, fading paler almost by the second, the vision of a soul and spirit vanished. It was inhuman yet somehow tender too to see someone with whom you had lived your life, someone whose thoughts you felt at times you could almost think, breath their last. Reason never defeated that image. However much you knew he had been put out of his misery, however much you knew that he would have wanted it this way, however much you might try to convince yourself that he had had a long life…"a good innings"…you could never get over that image when death took over and claimed this soul that you had wanted to stay with you for ever. That you thought was immortal. That image was unknowable, unfathomable….who could rationalise the moment when life became death? Who could reason when one of the pillars that you stood upon was now taken away? Who could explain to you that the hand that had been warm to touch was suddenly going to get cold?

Oliver tried to hear his father's voice, to see his expression, to watch him eating and he could see them all, more clearly than at any time since his father had passed away, but still dulled by the distance of memory. He tried to remember other conversations, photographs but they seemed distant too. Until suddenly, as his mind raced from memory to memory, his father's face, smiling, began to appear in the centre of his vision. This was a fresh image, full of colour and life. Oliver shifted his head on the pillow, trying to get away from it. But forward it came and as it came closer Oliver saw the expression begin to slowly change. As the vision began to fill his space till he could see nothing else, he saw the smile metamorphose into something expressionless before, as the face came closer and closer, he saw his father's eyes begin to pierce into him, his mouth tighten, his face change to an expression of unease. Not anger, Oliver thought , no, not anger… but he's going to go at me over Clotilde and this unholy mess we are in.

The face stopped in front of him and Oliver was calm. He lay still and waited. He felt certain that the face in front of him was going to speak. For a while it didn't. It seemed to look at Oliver as though it had not seen him for years, up and down, a faint smile…

Oliver went to speak first but his father's head silenced him with a gentle nod.

"Olly… Olly…….what a mess you are in. Over a woman. " And his father smiled at him, as though it was the most natural conversation that

235

they had had a thousand times before. "Clotilde was wrong, she was a mistake. She is dangerous."

Oliver didn't know what to say. But, having been whirled into a state of either semi-consciousness, dream, hallucination or simply pure imagining he did the only thing he could and spoke back. "I didn't choose Clotilde. She….she chose me and I couldn't……."

"I know that you probably had little choice. It's not important. If you can tell yourself that and believe it then you will tell Helen and she will believe it. But you have awakened forces and feelings that I hope you will never realise the consequence of."

"What do you mean?"

"You must be careful of what you will discover. About yourself and others. Be careful. We don't know ourselves as well as we think we do. You made love with another woman. Tell me you were raped. You cannot. You betrayed your wife and son and you are convinced that you have done something you could not have avoided. So who are you? Maybe you don't know who you are or what you have done and you will carry that burden with you for as long as you live. But you are not the only one. You are not the only one who is not as he seems. You are not the only one who is unreadable. We are all wearing disguises. You must beware of what you will find when the disguise is removed."

"I don't understand…..I made a mistake, that's all it is, that's all it was…and you… you don't need to think any more of it than that. We all make mistakes."

"Your mistake has started a fire that you won't put out. People after you. People want you dead. And people are not what you think they are…."

Flashing through Oliver's mind went a long-remembered line… "Nothing is but what is not…"

"You're being tossed about on the sea, Oliver. Adrift. It's all out of control. You're out of control. Don't trust, you're only seeing the mask."

The picture began to fade, the clarity dimmed. Oliver's first thought was that he was not strong enough for this. Take me with you, old man. We can talk over in a heartbeat all the things we should have spent my lifetime talking about. Don't leave me here in this place where there is danger in every smile and deceit in every nod. But his father's vision faded quickly and Oliver's mind soon returned to its more normal state.

When he awoke in the morning his pillow was wet with tears, tears he could not remember crying. His head was full of things he could not easily recollect…why were Mandy and his father right at the front of his thoughts and what made him think Ellis had been involved in some inappropriate dalliance last night?

And why, when he met his friends in the hall to check out of the hotel, did he feel uneasy in their company, as though he was only truly seeing them for the first time?

CHAPTER 12

Davide stood in front of his boss, waiting. The Capo was on the phone and he was silent, his hand running through the side of his hair with increasing speed. This usually meant some trouble or agitation. Davide had come to know it as a "tell". The Capo was imagining inflicting some damage on whoever he was talking to and this was its physical manifestation. That, or he would occasionally smash the phone.

"You can buy elections here or there or anywhere. USA 1960, the greatest democracy in the world. Don't tell me I can't influence what happens in Paris. I could buy Paris ten times over. If electioneering doesn't work, there are other ways. Don't make me tell you what the other ways are. You know the other ways. It's simple, a voice in Paris is a voice in Brussels is a voice in Germany. It has to be this way, we can't buy an elected politician any more, those days are gone. It's not that they can't be corrupted, but that they leave too much of a money trail. They're stupid, poor and stupid, they can't hide their glee or getting a few francs… .Euros…to spend and away they go. Don't buy the idiot, buy the system that elects the idiot. We need this election. So you do what you have to do. But make sure that when all this posturing is done that we have who we want where we want them. So we can be heard. Because you and I, we deserve to be heard. We are good for people. We are good for the country. But most of all, fix it because if you don't fix it I'll have you killed. Then I will find your wife and I will kill her too. And I will make sure that both your son and your daughter will never have sons or daughters of their own. I am trying to make my position here very clear, so that even a fucking idiot such as you can understand me. You understand me? Ok, good. Get it done. I don't expect to hear from you any time soon."

He slammed the phone down and gently shook his head. He then pinched the top of his nose with his thumb and middle finger, his face screwed up in frustration. "Davide, when you have finished telling me whatever it is that you are going to tell me, get me Arabella. This tension needs an outlet and she loves to fuck me when I am angry."

"Yes boss. I have some news on the guy Oliver and his friends. It seems they are travelling north, probably towards Paris, in a car they bought in Lyon. What do you want me to do?"

"They bought a car? Who from?"

"From a car garage in Lyon. Our enquiries… what we heard…was that they bought a second hand car. They were in a hurry. The assistant remembered them right away, they didn't seem in any desire to hide their identity. He thought it odd, four or five British guys buying a car like that."

"Where are they now?"

"We know they stayed in Lyon, or near Lyon, last night….but they started out late today and seem to be heading on the E15-E60 straight to Paris."

The Capo thought for a minute. "Beaune is on the way isn't it? Simone and Charlotte owe me a favour, a big favour……ok, get Alain on the phone for me now."

The Capo paced up and down, not in frustration or anger but in curiosity. This guy Oliver became more and more intriguing but also, apparently, less and less threatening. At times, I'd want to blind Paul with a knife, thought The Capo. I want to meet this guy, I want to talk to him. I'll probably let him live.

The phone was passed to him quickly. "Alain… good good… yes, all well…… I need you to do something for me. I need you to make sure that certain people have dinner tonight at your restaurant. They won't have a hotel or anywhere to stay and you'll direct them to Simone and Charlotte. They will listen to their singing and Simone and Charlotte will take over from there. How do you ensure they have dinner at your restaurant? I will give you the car registration number and you must find a way of stopping them. You are on or near the main road, aren't you, so this shouldn't be difficult. No, listen, I don't want to have to answer questions on this, spare me any details – find a way of stopping them. Put glass on the road under their tyres. Or close the bloody road if you have to, that is easily arranged. But get them into your restaurant, feed them well, send them to Simone and Charlotte and you will be rewarded in the usual way."

He put the phone down and looked at Davide. "Get the girls. Tell them it is the usual deal. But drug these guys, don't kill. They can scare if they like. You arrange something to get these four or five guys back down here….helicopter, train, car, some bloody thing so that I can see them sometime tomorrow down here. Might even get his girl back here – it'll definitely make him talk if he sees some harm coming to her. Or someone else fucking her. Go, go….now send me Arabella and tell her to bring her toys…have you seen the expression on her face when she feels them? Tell her she's got five minutes to get here or else she'll be wearing her toys permanently."

Anthony had let stubble develop for the past couple of days and wore a different pair of glasses. He had dyed his hair but it was maybe a bit too light brown. He wore an ill-fitting baseball cap and looked exactly like what he was – a man trying to disguise his appearance. He had retreated, scared and out-thought, for two days. If the police do not come here within two days then I am safe. He thought little of the girl he had hammered in mistake and didn't care whether she was alive or dead. Her only meaning to him was that hitting her would certainly have brought the attention of the police. And Helen may have told the police about him because she must have known about him to outsmart him like that, outsmart him to the extent that she chose someone who was so like her from the back to sit in her room and pretend to be her.

But the police never came. So maybe she really didn't know that much about me. Maybe she doesn't even know where I live. She hadn't even bothered to see where her new home would be. But still, it did mean that she knew he was after her and that he would have to be more discreet, less detectable. Do something to blend in but you have to stay close because you need her. She needs to be with me.

During his observations, Anthony had noticed that no regular window cleaner came around Helen's street. I need to see inside the house. I need to see inside the house because there is more of her in there that I have not seen but I may need to get inside the house to take her next time. So if I can see what her house looks like inside, I can see the size of the rooms, the places to hide. And as he looked along the row of houses he realised that he may not even need to see inside Helen's house – she may not want her windows washed and he wasn't really sure that this disguise was good enough – because most of the houses were built in the same way, to what seemed to be a very similar specification.

In any case, he could almost tell the plan of downstairs from the studying he had done at night. It was easy to creep into her garden from the neighbour's house that her back garden backed on to. He had been doing that for quite a while. You could slip in there across a small fence then climb into Helen's garden quite easily. He had crept around, pinning himself to the outside walls of the house, feeling comfortable and excited there. Somehow he always felt excited when his foot touched the grass in Helen's garden. Excited in every sense. Then sometimes she left clothes outside to dry and he had breathed them in, daring himself to take her skirt and blouse to help him become a part of her more but he had restrained himself as people tend to notice these items going missing. But not so much underwear and he could almost hear the thump of his heart as he stretched up and first took a bra and pair of knickers from the washing line. Later, on other occasions, he would take socks, a thin strapless t-shirt, a camisole top, a black thong...things that he laid out in her room in his house. Sometimes he devoured their smells, sometimes he laid them on the bed, put there for all the world like she was going to put clothes on when she came out of the shower.

So when Anthony came back to Helen's street it was with ladders and window cleaning material and he started at the end of the street, working his way along, ringing door bells and asking if a window cleaner was required. He didn't reach Helen's house on that first day but he built a very clear picture of what upstairs in her house must look like: large bedroom then there was a hall and he could see another three doors leading off the hall, one must be a bathroom...the main bedroom itself had two wardrobes in it, both built in, both common to all the houses that were built the same way as Helen's. Should I take a picture, he wondered... to get the dimensions right. He had taken pictures of what was downstairs and had a perfect to-scale drawing of dimensions.

"Excuse me, could I have a quick word with you please?" Anthony felt a gentle shake on his ladder and looked down to see a policeman standing at the bottom. Panic, sudden panic. Nowhere to run...

"I'm sorry to disturb... ," said the policemen as Anthony made his way gingerly down, "...but we are making enquiries about an assault a few days ago and wondered if you had seen anything out of the ordinary. Someone in your position, a window cleaner, maybe you have seen something unusual."

Anthony was silent.

"Have you?"

"Have I what?"

"Seen anything unusual...new people here... anything out of the ordinary...."

"When?"

"Anytime in the last few days, last few weeks." Constable Barclay looked at the man opposite. He was nervous and agitated. But he was probably frightened that he was going to be questioned over something such as tax evasion.

"No. No. I am new here too. I normally work another area. And anyway, I have been away for the last week. In Yeovil. Seeing my sister. She's ill...."

"So...how long have you worked here, in this street?"

For the first time Anthony looked at the police officer. "This, today, this is my first day."

"Ah. Well, I'm sorry to have disturbed you."

Anthony was beginning to relax and felt that, in this situation, it would be natural to show a little curiosity. "Was the assault here? In this street?"

"No, not in this street. But perhaps involving someone who lives in this street."

"Ah."

"Say, you don't happen to know anyone here, in this street, do you? Who recommended that you come here to try for business?"

He's fishing, he's just fishing, he doesn't know anything. "Oh, no one. I thought I'd try somewhere else because I don't get so many people in my old area. So I thought...try here..."

"Why here?"

Anthony paused and his pulse began to quicken. "Well, you see, if I'm being honest with you...two reasons...it looks quite a rich area and if you look at the houses they are similar, the windows are quite easy to wash."

The guy looked uncomfortable. Surely now not because of tax evasion. Constable Barclay smiled at him, waiting for some form of eye contact, some form of mutual understanding. But the man looked down and shifted uncomfortably from one foot to the other.

"Aye, you must see a lot of things, cleaning windows... "

There wasn't a question there and Anthony continued to look down, averting the eyes of the policeman which were now beginning to burn into him.

"Oh, no, no, not so much..."

"How long have you washed windows?"

This time Anthony looked up. "Oh for a couple of years. I lost my job. Banking, you know, the banks laid people off. But I was quite good with my hands, quite practical." Anthony knew he had to give the policeman something because he was pushing and prodding, from one way then another.

"Listen," he said, looking directly at the policeman, his eyes almost pleading. "I do this work and most of it, a lot of it, is cash….you know cash in hand……if you're here to ask me if I declare everything then no, I know I haven't done that. I will. I will make good what I haven't done well…."

Constable Barclay held his hand up, satisfied that he had found the source of the discomfort. "Between you and the tax man, my friend. I don't want to hear it. Now if you think you see anything out of the ordinary, whatever it is, however trivial it might seem, you give me a call on this number." And he handed Anthony a card.

"Sure officer, thank you. Yes, of course."

And he made his way back up the ladder with small steps, shaking softly as he went. Watching him, Constable Barclay did think it odd that a window cleaner seemed so uncomfortable on a ladder but put it down to a decent man being frightened by the thought of prosecution for tax evasion.

Constable Barclay sighed. Maybe his idea was a flight of fancy. Maybe he should listen to his colleagues and focus on the girl who was attacked. After all, it was pretty clear that she was hiding something. But as he drove away, and began to consign the thought of Helen to the back of his mind, he couldn't help but feel that he was deserting someone who was in imminent danger.

It was quite late in the afternoon by the time the friends had awoken, managed to get something to eat, then began to travel north. None of them had much in the way of recall about the events of the previous night. Over what was more lunch than breakfast, Ellis had been the first to speak about what had happened.

"My head is fuzzy this morning, how are yours? What did we do last night? I remember having a meal, it was gorgeous, and then I don't seem to remember much… that girl, that woman who ran the restaurant….I think I remember…did she not come onto you Ali?"

Ali thought, blushing with a half-remembered longing, a dull memory of seeing Ellis going at Clemence on the table. "No, I think she came onto you….or maybe you came on her…" And they laughed, an uncomfortable laugh. "I'm sure I saw you and her doing stuff… things… " And he looked around at his friends. "Did I dream that? Did anyone else see that?"

Oliver said: "I think a lot went on last night. I think we were drugged. I don't know why. We've not been taken, we've not been captured. But I think we were drugged and I don't know if we'll ever remember what happened."

"Christ!" Euan shouted. "I have an image, maybe I dreamed it, but an image of that woman's back, she's bending over the table and I'm going away, bashing away inside her." He looked around his friends. "That's not true, that didn't happen, did it?

Ellis laughed. "Wishful thinking I suspect. She was very pretty. We'd all have liked a shot. Who would have wanted to drug us? If it's your Mafia boys, Olly, then why didn't they take us? Or take you?" He stopped to pause, thinking through his own comments. "Maybe she's a woman who does that sort of thing…."

"We were definitely drugged," said Oliver. "Absolutely. None of us can remember what happened. I can remember getting home…….and I remember you, Ali, telling us……telling us something……you remember?"

Ali's hands went up to his face and he bowed his head. His cheeks burned with shame. "Oh I didn't, I didn't……I am so ashamed… "

Oliver interrupted and spoke with authority. "Guys, we forget about last night. Whatever happened, happened. Maybe over time we will remember more. But I think it would be a good idea if we never mention again what happened there, or what we think might have happened there. We had a bad experience and we escaped from it. We have had a few bad experiences here and we have escaped from them. So, maybe no more about last night. Maybe we will all remember things that we would rather had stayed hidden. Maybe we all said and did things that we regret. But we were drugged. So maybe it wasn't 'us' that did these things or said these things. So try to forget about it. And we don't talk about it again." Inside himself, Oliver knew that a genie had been let out of a bottle. What he didn't know was whether the others had realised it too or whether there was any conceivable way he could ram it back in.

There was nodding. And general silence. Great, thought Oliver, silence is consent…. Then Ellis spoke. "That's fine Olly – but if I ended up shagging a bird as stunning as that Clemence was, I want to remember every bloody sensation and every sound she made." He looked around the car at his friends' faces. "But of course I'll keep it to myself……."

Aidan thought it might be quite a good idea to change the subject. "Where the hell are we?"

"Just coming up to a place called Beaune," replied Oliver.

Alain was 45 years old but he didn't look anything like that. He had all his hair, none of it had yet started to go grey and a healthy diet combined with exercise and a relatively stress free existence had left him looking about ten years younger than he was. He was handsome too, short tidy black hair and large brown eyes complemented his chiselled jaw and sharp cheeks bones that made him very distinctive. He looked immediately like someone you could trust. He looked like someone you would call "one of us". He was soft spoken, a gentle soothing voice which was always calm, never raised, and he was detailed and structured in his approach to everything. Alain never seemed to be hurried by anything: attentive, direct, responsive, alert and interested but never hurried.

He had married young and that had probably been a bad idea because he had a lifelong affair with women that had not been quashed by being married. Opportunities came his way quite often and he had taken them, at first the odd casual one-night thing, convincing himself that it meant nothing, but later longer term things, lasting across a few months. He seemed immune from detection and over the years his wife seemed to have no idea of the kind of sub-life that he was living. Maybe because, he figured, however many other women he may have been involved with, his physical desire for his wife had not abated. It had been unaffected. It wasn't as if he was looking for something specific in other women that his wife was not giving him, it was as though his being always needed something in addition to make it complete. One would never be enough.

He had fallen in with The Capo about five years ago. He had been asked to do a favour and had been well rewarded and he liked his relationship with The Capo because he never felt exploited by this huge, powerful and brutal figure. The Capo never asked him for money. But then again Alain had never refused him a favour. That was something you didn't do. So when a favour was asked, however difficult it might be, you had to do it. And you'd get a sackful of money for your trouble.

He could have done without the favour tonight and was very tempted to refuse. Because tonight he had planned a secret rendezvous with Emmanuelle. He had told his wife that he was going to his restaurant, as normal, but he had planned instead for Emmanuelle to come and to close the restaurant. The two of them could either stay there or go somewhere else. If they went somewhere else he would tell his wife that there was a catering contract which he had to take care of…he had to take care of personally because of illness. Alain had so many excuses that seemed to work again and again…

He had been anticipating Emmanuelle all day. Alain had experienced different women....French, Asian, American, tall, short, fat, thin but no one quite as young as Emmanuelle. She was sixteen and the daughter of his best friend and what she knew about how to please him shouldn't really have been known until she was at least ten years older. She had soft beautiful skin, the face of an angel in orgasm when he pleasured her, warm moans that sounded like no noise he had heard a woman make before. On the odd occasion when conscience did eat at him, he battered it away by reasoning that there was no way he was her first, he was probably about tenth given the things she knew how to do. Someone that young, that beautiful, whose very thought excited him....having to postpone was difficult and he could tell she was disappointed too, fearing a brush off or rejection. And her tone had concerned him because she was young and impetuous enough to make trouble, to tell people such as her father...she wouldn't do that, she couldn't do that...

Alain prepared the restaurant, putting posters on the walls and setting the kind of ambience that should force his clients to ask the questions they were required to ask. If they didn't, well, there were always the posters and he could refer to them himself. Then he made the calls he had to make to the people who could do what The Capo wanted and within a while the roadblock had been arranged. Davide had sent him a message with an estimated time of arrival. He had the registration number. All there was to do now was wait. And think about the pleasures of Emmanuelle that were to be denied to him that night.

"What's this? A traffic jam?"

Oliver looked ahead. Everything had stopped. "I think the road may be blocked. Or maybe it's a traffic light that I can't see. But it's not moving."

Ellis got out the car and looked ahead. It was clear that the cause of the hold-up was not clear. Nothing was moving ahead. Ellis shrugged his shoulders and put his arms in the air. "Who knows? Maybe it's an ambush set up by these guys in Lyon who want another chance to stone us to death."

They sat for perhaps ten or fifteen minutes without moving. The frustration level began to ratchet up, noticeably. It was hot and they had thought that, with a little luck, they could have made Paris for a late crossing. But as that possibility began to vanish in the oppressive stifling heat, so the feeling grew that this journey was turning into a nightmare from which they were never going to wake.

"For fuck's sake," said Oliver, to no one in particular, banging his fists on the steering wheel. Aidan took the opportunity to phone home, his attitude to communicating being more cavalier than it had been a day or so before. But Oliver still did not want to phone Helen, too frightened of his phone being tapped and her being watched and so he got Euan to phone his wife who then phoned Helen at work. And all, relatively, seemed fine. Except Helen did not really appreciate how it was taking so long to get to Paris and get home. None of the wives did. So they concocted a story of dodgy cars, breakdowns and long sleeps, wrong turns and journeys that ventured towards Switzerland rather than Paris and unhelpful French people giving them confusing, or plain wrong, directions.

Another fifteen minutes passed. No movement. Most of the friends stood outside, as indeed most people in front and behind were doing, watching what was happening. Or more accurately what wasn't happening. Oliver alone stayed in the car, watching, listening to the radio, trying to control his fraying temper. He looked around him, realising that on another occasion this would be a nice place to stop and walk about, another beautiful part of a beautiful country.

The first he saw of Alain was when he popped his head in at the window on the passenger side with Euan beside him. "Listen to this guy," said Euan, "this is a good idea."

"Hallo…I see you are English…British, sorry… em, this traffic situation is bad, there is a road block a few kilometres ahead which the police will need to clear. It may take a few hours but the police are saying they may close the road tonight, depending. There are other ways to go but the way the traffic is right now it is almost impossible to access those other ways. So I think you… I think everyone…is stuck. I have a restaurant here, it is quite close by and there is a car park at the back… you could drive up the pavement and park in the car park….you can relax and have a lovely meal, look here is the menu, you can see if there is something you like…if not, I will make something for you….and then you can do as you wish. Are you staying here tonight?"

Oliver sighed. "We were hoping to get to Paris tonight but I think that may be optimistic now."

"No sir, I think you may have a better chance of walking to Paris tonight."

He looked at Euan and at the others who had gathered around this rather pleasant Frenchman who seemed to be very kind and helpful. "Well," said Alain, "maybe I could even recommend you a hotel or two if you want. But first why don't you come and see if you like my cooking. We don't have too many British guests here and it would be my honour to see if my cooking can make you happy."

Convinced, Oliver drove the car slowly on the pavement and around into the car park. As Alain walked back he wondered what it was these guys could possibly have done to upset The Capo. On the face of it, they looked as far away from the type of people The Capo was involved with as you could possibly imagine. Harmless, middle class, out for a boys' holiday…and most of all completely unsuspecting. The people The Capo tended to be after usually knew there was someone after them.

The friends walked into the restaurant, pleased to see that on this occasion they would not be alone. Indeed, the restaurant was quite full – evidently the owner had seen the opportunity in the huge tailback to do some touting for business. They looked around themselves, Oliver feeling a touch nervous at the prospect of another meal in a French restaurant.

Aidan looked around his friends at the table. "This is a nice restaurant. It's going to be a nice meal in a nice restaurant. Forgot our meal last night. This place smells different. It looks different. And we're not alone in here. So let's try to relax, get a few bottles of whatever wine this decent chap recommends, and take it easy. We're going nowhere tonight." He looked outside the window at the stationery traffic. "Nobody's going anywhere tonight. So, let's relax and enjoy. Come on, we'll probably be home tomorrow and all this will be over. We've had a hellish time. So let's enjoy each other's company tonight." He raised his hand, clasping an imaginary glass. His friends did the same and they exchanged warm smiles, arms round shoulders, back slaps and came close to achieving a group high-5. Alain remained confused because they looked like a group who believed their troubles were at an end. And they seemed genuine, warm, lovely people….how could they be mixed up in something with The Capo? He shrugged. Orders were orders; he would do what he was told….

As they anticipated from the first sight of the menu, the food was gorgeous and the wine divine. They took their time, three courses spread out over three and a half hours of talking and remembering, incidents recalled from the last few days and from years and years ago coming together to reaffirm their friendships, their belief in each other.

Ellis looked around himself, at the multiple posters on the wall which seemed to be advertising something involving two girls who looked identical. Beautiful, he thought, identically beautiful. They must be twins. And whatever they were doing, the event was tonight. Curiosity got the better of him.

"Excuse me… excuse me…Monsieur…"

"Alain."

"Excuse me Alain…these posters that are around your walls here… what are they advertising? None of us speak very good French."

"Ah, our singing twins! Our beautiful singing twins! You should hear them, they are beautiful, their voices are…." And he made as though he was trying to find words to describe the beauty of their singing but there were none in the language that were descriptive enough. "They are singing tonight, you can go and hear them, they will sing in one of the venues close to here. There is always a little space, I am sure you will get in….in fact, I may have some tickets still here if you wish… it's not at all expensive… in fact, you have given me so much business tonight, and I am so grateful, you can have them for free, no problem."

He went away and quickly returned with five tickets. "And the girls actually run one of the hotels I was going to suggest you might stay at. Well, it is a mansion, owned by their parents, it is a touch on the outside of our town but only five minutes from here to drive to, it's easy… .especially now that the traffic has gone down. It is a beautiful place with such big rooms, you would love it. You could drive there, check-in, walk back in to town and see the girls singing." He looked at his watch. "You still have an hour before the show starts, plenty time… "

Ellis looked at the poster, smiled at his friends then looked back at Alain. "What a great idea! These twins… do they have names?"

"Of course, of course they do – Simone and Charlotte."

"Simone and Charlotte"….Ellis repeated. He looked again at the poster, trying to see any difference, however small, between them. He looked at Alain. "Which is which?"

"Ah," said Alain, smiling, "no one really knows. They say Charlotte has a… what's the word…a little spot that is dark skin, a little round dark piece of skin…."

"A mole?"

"Yes, I think so… a mole. They say Charlotte has a mole at the very top of her leg," and he pointed to the inside of his groin, "… they say she has a mole there that Simone does not have." He paused, sensing five pair of eyes on them. "Oh, so they say, I mean I wouldn't know…"

Ellis laughed, it being obvious to him that Alain very much knew. "Well, Alain, here's hoping we get the chance to discover if you're right. I can think of nothing better than watching these beautiful ladies singing then trying to find out if what you say is true."

They paid, leaving a handsome tip and followed Alain's instructions to the mansion on the edge of the town. None of them were fit for driving but, they reasoned, five minutes would be ok. The mansion was beautiful, in spacious grounds, and they were checked in by a lady who had more than a passing resemblance to the two girls they had seen in the poster.

"You must be Simone and Charlotte's mother," said Euan.

The woman smiled, a warm engaging smile. "Yes, I help them run this place when they sing. But I don't stay here, I stay in the town." She looked around herself. "This place is too big now for me to help with. Oh, that reminds me, you must take your key with you because I will leave here in an hour or so and there won't be anyone here till the girls come back. They stay here. And there won't be anyone else here till the staff come in about half past four or five in the morning. So if you don't have your keys and you come back before the girls, you won't get in. Your room key will fit the outside door so don't worry." She paused. "I have managed to put all of you upstairs, upstairs is nicer, the rooms are bigger and you have a beautiful balcony to stand out on and welcome the morning sunshine in tomorrow….if you are not too tired. Will you go to hear my daughters sing?"

"Yes," said Oliver. "We have been told they have very beautiful voices."

"Well, I am biased, they are my daughters and I am so proud of them. But you must judge for yourselves and tell me tomorrow."

She walked with them upstairs to their rooms. As instructed, she had given Oliver room 12. Room 12 was between the rooms where Simone and Charlotte slept. She opened it for Oliver. "Ah, I think you have the best room. Look at the view and the balcony." The room opened out because it was on the corner of the building and the soft warm air filled it. It was beautiful and spacious with delicate paintings on the wall, a big en-suite and a large soft double bed that Oliver could have sank into. He stayed and looked around as the others were shown their rooms, wishing that he could lie down here and fall asleep for the next twelve hours. But Aidan was right – they had had a beautiful meal, they were going to hear some singing that would probably take their breath away but most of all he owed it to them to do something they wanted to do. To have a night of relaxation amongst the madness that he had dragged them through to find him.

They walked back into the town and arrived in time for the start of the girls' show. The venue itself was quite small, more like a jazz café than a nightclub, with a few seats though most people were standing. As the friends pushed their way in, through the crowd at the door, they saw some space near the front and made their way there. The place was a little too hot and they were a little uncomfortable but it wasn't oppressive and they stood and waited, along with the others, waiting for the twins to appear, occasionally mopping their brows or fanning themselves with leaflets. Thankfully waitresses came round to take orders for drinks otherwise there would have been no wine, beer or water as it was quite hard to get to the bar. To get to the bar and return carrying five drinks would have been an adventure that none of them were up to.

Then, five minutes after they were due, the twins came on. They had some musical accompaniment, maybe a harp, a guitar, a bass, a violin or a keyboard at various points but the accompaniment tended to fill in the space between the singing. It was clear that the main event was their singing.

Before they opened their months Oliver was stunned by their appearance and their attire. They were beautiful girls. He started from the bottom up. Black high heel shoes with a subtle diamond-like sparkle on the outside of the shoe, sheer black tights or stockings (who might know?) and a tight red dress with a high split, split almost all the way up to the top of their legs. Then on, up further, flat stomachs and gentle chests, sleeveless dresses, strapless. The tops of their dresses curled round their curves, hugging them. They both had a very similar colour of sun-kissed skin, as though they had stayed in the sun for the same amount of time. Did everyone do that here? Long necks, stretched and graceful as they opened their mouths to sing and then their faces....full warm red mouths with rows of brilliant white teeth, eyes that danced and darted and invited you in, long beautiful soft straight brown hair shot through with a few subtle blond streaks that shone and sparkled like little glints of gold as the light went on it and through it. Smiles, the same smiles, that would have brightened a winter's day. Girls like this were the reason caveman drew on walls, they were the reason why painters picked up brushes, the reason why poets would always write poetry, the reason why people might die rather than lose their love. Oliver looked at his friends and they were utterly rapt and enchanted before the girls had sung a note. Then they opened their mouths, together…as they did everything, together.

The sound they made was like nothing Oliver had ever heard before. It was a soft lilt, soft yet full of power and charm, that held you firm. Oliver heard its beauty firstly in images: when they started to sing he immediately saw himself driving through Glencoe and looking around him at the fierce beauty of the remote and breath-taking landscape. He saw rugged peaks of wondrous mountains, heights that dragged you in and made you want to dive into them, to ascend, and to gaze with all your wonder on the stunning sights below and its natural danger. These were voices that could have floated you to the edge of that danger and made you want to fly, to take off and spread your wings over all that you could see. These were voices that would have hypnotised you to the point of self-destruction.

Then he saw Helen's face, smiling, for if she were something sung she would be this beautiful and awe-inspiring. She could touch you to your very essence the way these high notes seeped into your mind and made you feel a virgin of your senses, previously untouched and unexplored. His mind flashed to the best of times that he and Helen had made love, bodies moving together, loving each other and in that gentle sway he heard the voices of the twins, making themselves part of the moments that defined your best as a human being.

Their voices lifted him until he saw himself in the purest blue in the sky, not floating or moving, only existing in this oneness with nature. He felt air on him and around him, blowing delicately through him, till nature filled him. The sound took him to a state where he felt he could see everything, know everything, as though hearing these voices sing beauty in this way unlocked something that man had striven for years to get to. What he heard was religion and belief and sensation all combined and explained in the places that these bewitching voices pulled your soul to.

When they had started to sing Oliver had immediately closed his eyes. He didn't know why. Perhaps it was in order that he may see the images more clearly. Perhaps with one sense being closed off, it would heighted his ability to hear. But as his eyes remained closed he suspected it was perhaps for another reason, perhaps because if he looked at these beautiful girls he would be drawn in evermore to the places their voices took him. He fought it, he fought it for about five minutes, but eventually gave in and watched the girls as they smothered him and the others with the noises that enraptured them. Now there were not so many images in his head. He tried to see Helen and the barren beautiful landscapes but they weren't there anymore, their memories distant and remote. His eyes couldn't move from what was in front of him. For the girls' beauty was now part of their song. He could not hear the wonder of their voices without seeing the wonder that was them. They moved as one. Each rhythm was as one. Each move of the neck, each open mouth, each note, each gentle move of their hips, each move of their hands was as one. As their voices invaded him so his eyes were forced to gorge on them. As the notes played themselves into his head and touched his own innate sense of being so images of them began to smash away at the others of landscapes and his wife. As they dominated everything he heard so they dominated everything he saw or wanted to taste. His desire for them became absolute. He neither wanted to feel it nor felt happy to feel it. Everything about this spoke of danger. But this wasn't a feeling that you could discard, wasn't a mild sensation that kept niggling at the back of your mind. This was an addict who was desperate for a hit, who would have killed his own mother for the next hit; this was the first sight of sun for a blind man who never wanted to go back to the omniscience of darkness; this was the promise of a waking heaven amidst a furious hell. You could not go back.

Once opened, Oliver's eyes became impossible to close. When he could, he would look at his friends, struggling with the same pulls and tears at their being, eyes tightly shut in some cases, eyes wide open and hypnotised in others. Occasionally he would see the girls look at him, at them, across, smiling knowingly but for the most part they looked straight ahead with an other-worldliness to their gaze. It was fitting, as Oliver had never experienced anything like them in this world.

When they finished Oliver didn't know if they had sung for six seconds or six hours. It didn't seem to matter because the effect would have been the same, he was certain. When they finished he didn't know how he had managed to stop himself from walking or running up to them, trying to capture the root of the overpowering desire they had filled him with. When they had finished he wanted to talk but he could not say a word, none of them could. They were people who had dabbled in things they shouldn't have and were frozen by the results, as though they have started a Ouija board experiment that had resulted in the glass flying around the table. As though they had heard voices they should not have heard, as though they had discovered things that should not have been known by mortal people.

After a while the club began to empty and the friends sat down at a table, none of them ready for the walk home. The least they needed was a drink. Euan had called for white wine as they struggled to come to terms with the spell that still seemed to hold them. For fully five minutes they did not speak to each other. When they did it was with the awkward reverence of people who did not know whether they should talk about how much they had been disturbed and amazed or whether it was something that should not be admitted, something which stunned and shamed, like a one-night stand without any inhabitations where betrayal was smothered with further betrayal.

Ellis was trying very hard to be Ellis. "Phew that was something, that was really something, wasn't it? Weren't they? Don't you think?"

His friends nodded their heads. Aidan said what he felt. "I've never heard anything as beautiful as that in my life. These girls should be world famous, they should be......"

He paused as he looked up. With the club becoming quieter by the minute, the girls had come back onto the stage, still in their dresses. They walked to the table where the friends sat and smiled down on them.

"Can we join you for a drink? Please?"

They must have seen five wide open mouths, goldfish at feeding time. Ellis was the first to react, standing up, offering to get the girls a drink. But Simone – or was it Charlotte – insisted no, they would buy and she came back with another bottle of white wine for Oliver and his friends and a bottle of red wine for her and her twin.

The friends chatted with the girls as best they could. It wasn't always easy for they remained almost as bewitching in a social occasion such as this as they were when they were singing. Still they seemed to laugh together, even little mannerisms like touching their hair, showing their necks, they seemed to do as one. Oliver sensed they looked upon him and at him more than they did the others and their attention made him uncomfortable. It made him uncomfortable because Oliver felt very strongly that these girls were not normal human beings. Their voices had done things to his soul that no person had ever done before. They had punctured and slayed him with notes, with sounds. These were not normal people, they could be dangerous. So their looks to him and at him, which in a different time and in a different setting might have flattered him, made him uneasy. And we are staying at their hotel, close to them…

Which they also seemed to know because when they stood up they said – though probably it was only one of them that spoke – "You are staying at our place tonight, aren't you? Perhaps you can walk us back there, back home? I hope you won't be too offended if we change our shoes into something that we can walk in."

On the way back Oliver could feel his senses begin to relax a bit. Ellis had even managed to get his arm round one of them on the pretext that it wasn't warm anymore (it was) and he didn't want her to get cold (she wasn't). By the time they got back and had another drink with the girls he was feeling better about it. His senses felt numb and he began to feel very tired. Looking around his friends he could see they were fighting sleep too. Their heads began to droop, their eyelids a bit too heavy to resist much more. Even Ellis looked tired. Odd that we should all be so tired at once, thought Oliver. But it wasn't an uncomfortable or worrying or disturbing thought. The lethargy that had come to his senses didn't permit his thought process to go as far as finding it disturbing. It was easily rationalised by the events of the past few days. But as they all trudged upstairs to bed they individually struggled to get one foot in front of the other and they each felt consumed by an unfamiliar and absolute need to sleep.

Oliver barely had removed his clothes before he sank down into the bed and was simply overpowered. He had no idea how long he had slept before he was awakened by the noises on either side of his room. To his left he heard what seemed to be the growl and fury of a dog barking. It wasn't a curious or frightened bark that he heard but instead a low, constant growl of anger and hatred, punctuated with deep and fierce barks. His immediate thought was for the safety of Simone – or was it Charlotte – next door to him. But as his head came up from the pillow he heard a noise on the other side of him, his right, from through the wall that his bed was against. This was the noise of water rushing, not the gentle lapping of the ocean on the shore but the wail of a storm wind through high crashing waves that would have consumed you. This water was wrathful and dangerous. Now feeling much more awake, Oliver jumped out of his bed, his pulse quickening as the adrenalin once again filled his body with the need to flee. He rushed to the balcony, half expecting to see a tidal wave coming towards him even though he realised that would have been impossible. But there was nothing outside, outside looked safe. He looked down from the balcony and his immediate thought was to jump but it was too far, his legs would have struggled to take the impact of such a jump.

The noises began to get louder and the dog's sounds more savage. There were no cries but it sounded as though the dog had captured something, a person or another animal, and was killing it with the swift snap of its jaws. The noises were terrifying, noises of danger and death and Oliver could not comprehend what was happening. If it had taken one of the twins, surely there would be screaming. If it was the twins' dog and had captured something in the house then they would surely be shouting at it to let go. But there were no human voices, none. Only the guttural growl and roar that became louder and louder, more and more threatening with every passing second. And on the other side too the noise of the water became louder, closer, more threatening, more likely to engulf Oliver and submerge him and his room.

Then, for only a second or two, the dog was silent and Oliver thought of getting out the room. He reached the door handle and tried to turn it but the room was locked. There was no key inside. Oliver knew that he had not locked the room when he came in, the key was still in his jacket. As his hand turned the door handle he heard the noise of the beast scratching and scraping at the door, then its growls and its horrible sickening low barks. The growling got louder, the scratching more intense, till he imagined that sometime the dog would scrape away at the door so much that it could jump through its remnants. Oliver ran again to the balcony. No, he thought, nobody could make that jump and not sustain an injury. And if I jumped what about the others, what about them? In quick flashes, nothing more, he tried to understand what was happening but he couldn't. What was going on? Had the girls been killed by a dog? Was it their dog? And where the hell was the water coming from? This was the stuff of violent destabilising and unfamiliar nightmare. I cannot, I must not, be awake.

Oliver felt himself move closer to the wall beside the door, feeling its cold touch on his body and thought, amidst the dog's hellish scraping and pounding and growling, that he heard voices. Female voices. He looked towards the door and saw the handle begin to turn, slowly. As the door edged open he expected to see the beast bound in and start to feed on him but as it edged wider and wider there was no beast though there remained the sickening and fearful sound of its growls. Oliver scuttled to hide behind the door. Whoever or whatever was turning the door was doing it slowly until they could see the entire room from where they stood. Then Oliver heard a voice, a female voice, say: "Probably jumped. Check. Then we can pick him up."

The twins prowled into the room, pacing slowly, their bodies crouched. Oliver saw them from the back and did not know, at first, that it was the twins. They looked bigger, their bodies looked physically bigger. And still he heard the hideous noise of the dog but no physical dog. The twins slouched like animals towards the balcony then, as though sensing the same thing at the same time, turned to look at what was behind the door. The light that came in through the balcony was too little to allow Oliver could see them quite clearly. But it was definitely their form, their hair, their broad shape.

They both had their arms and hands extended, ready to capture their prey, and Oliver noticed the length of their finger nails, huge extensions whose shadows stretched over him. Then he looked at the wild, wide, terrifying eyes, manic with animal fervour. But most of all he saw the teeth. What had been rows of beautiful white teeth earlier in the evening were now gnarled and fanged, points on each one like little individual shark's teeth. They looked at him the same way as he imagined that terrifying wild dog might have looked at him. They paced towards him, slowly, their arms extended, their claws ready to grab him should he move before they had taken him.

Oliver wiped his arm across his eyes, not believing the evidence in front of them. The twins, now making noises that would be more appropriate to a wolf or a lion, closed in on him with sick, dark smiles on their faces.

"You must still be sleepy. Give in and let this happen. You don't have enough to get past us."

Oliver didn't feel sleepy. Adrenalin was surging through him. Amidst the fear and terror that they must have seen on his face there was also a brief look of confusion.

"You were drugged. Your friends too. Something from the Benzodiazepine family. Pathetically easy." Oliver didn't know if it was one of them talking or if it was both of them but they moved closer with each syllable. They couldn't pounce on him yet but he could see the sharp points of their finger nails as they moved closer and he could, in a quick flash of an image, see how easily they would pierce his flesh. He could see the saliva almost dripping from them, like dogs when the dinner bell had been sounded. And then their eyes, wider and wilder as they got closer, not human. Feeding time. Oliver knew there was a very good chance that he was going to, literally, be ripped to pieces. But they had spoken, there was perhaps some chance in trying to talk back to them. Even if he could delay and shout on the others. But still he heard the noise of the dog and the hideous noise of the water, could he really shout above that?

"Wait," he said and tried to put his hands up. "Why? Why me? Why us? What do you want from us?"

The twins looked at each other. Again Oliver wasn't sure if they spoke together or if only one replied. Their voices were beginning to sound blurred in his head. "You don't know?"

"No, fuck, no, of course I don't know."

"You have wronged someone you should never have wronged. Now he may get you, eventually, tomorrow, if there is enough of you left. But he said that we get to play with you tonight. And we know how to play." Again they shared a sickening smile. Oliver was struggling to comprehend what the fuzzied voices had said. He was struggling to think straight. As the danger in front of him increased he sensed he was less able to fight it.

"Who did we wrong?"

"Not 'we' but you. We don't know and we don't care. All we know is – we get to play."

Oliver's mind quickly flashed back to Nice. But it was impossible, it was impossible that these girls in front of him could be connected to Paul. He tried to get the thought out of his mind. The girls edged closer, more crouched and their arms extended.

"But if only me then let my friends go…"

"No. We will deliver all of you. As we have been told to do. But sometimes delivery can be difficult. Because people like you resist. You get casualties. Our Capo understands that sometimes things get out of hand."

Oliver's mind was foggy and confused. With his eyes still on them he ran his hands along the wall, in desperation searching for anything that he might use to throw at the animals in front of him. There was a table beside the bed, a small table, and he remembered there were a few things on it. Maybe ornaments, a bottle of water, a lamp, something. But he wasn't close enough to it to get anything so he knew he had to try to manoeuvre his body to being a little closer. They had to be careful, almost imperceptible movements for he was in no doubt that whatever creatures stood in front of him had the instinct of animals. My only chance might be dialogue.

"Where is that fucking dog?" Oliver asked, his voice shaking and his body visibly beginning to tremble. His state was evident to the girls who inched ever closer. But their movement gave Oliver a chance to slowly move towards the table.

"Oh she's about, somewhere. We were wondering, my sister and I, whether you might prefer to be savaged by the dog or to drown. It's easy for us to do both… "

Then came another voice that sounded like the same voice. "I prefer to see people drown. You should choose drowning. We would play with you for a while then when we've had our fun we make you re-born by letting those waves that you can hear claim you. It is beautiful. The sight of a handsome man like you breathing his last is a fantastic sight. It would be good if you could watch. Your eyes will get desperate and you will try to draw air in quicker and quicker. And you will draw in more water as your lungs fill up. The death state of drowning is unfortunately very quick. Unfortunate because I would like to watch it for hours."

As she spoke Oliver felt, it was a small and almost imperceptible feeling, that the bodies of her and her sister were slightly less crouched. Not that they had relaxed exactly but it allowed him valuable inches of movement till his hand was very close to the table, till he could almost grab whatever was on there.

Still his body shook. If they saw him shaking then they would see his small movements less. And, as he inched to his right the space was darker…unless they could see just as well in the dark. Try to keep them talking.

"But I can't understand why I can hear the dog but I can't see the beast." Gentle, soft slight shift along, less than a shuffle but more than being stationary.

One of the twins hissed at him, venom almost shooting at him as though from a serpent. He recoiled, almost throwing his head back against the wall. "Maybe you hear what you are frightened of. Maybe the noise is in your imagination."

'No it fucking isn't' thought Oliver. "No! Where is the dog? If you are going to kill me or play with me or do something to me that involves my life being in danger, tell me where the dog is." Closer, until he felt his hand touch a bedside lamp. Pick it up and throw it….

"Maybe you shall meet her. Do you want to meet her? She has feasted

259

on many like you before. Usually one leg, maybe an ankle. Then we have to stop her. It is difficult to stop her…." As the voice continued, swirling and indistinct and dangerous in his head, his right hand grabbed the lamp and he knew he had to do it now. Don't think about it, don't wait for a lull, do it when she or they are speaking, do it now….

If Oliver had been drugged, and he didn't doubt that they had all been drugged, his body overcame the tiredness and disorientation and confusion for a few vital seconds. The survival instinct overpowered him.

He grabbed the stem of the lamp and noticed as he did so that the lamp had no shade. In one movement he lifted the lamp and threw it at the monsters in front of him, who were by now almost close enough to reach out and grab him with their talons. As he lifted the lamp his fingers inadvertently pressed on the switch and as he picked and threw the lamp it flashed on the twins and their faces lit up in front of him.

At first he felt transfixed and rooted because what he saw in front of him shocked him to his very core. What he had thought was saliva dripping from their mouths was not saliva but blood, fresh and warm and shockingly light in its redness. He could see the blood smattered across their white fangs too. They were both naked and blood was smeared on their bodies, as though they had rolled around and smothered themselves in the death of something they had killed. In that brief moment when Oliver took it all in he realised then that they must have killed one of his friends. At least one, maybe more.

Oliver still heard the noises of the dog and of the water, still both hellish and chilling in their effect. They were somewhere outside. But he had to take the chance. The flex from of the lamp was long enough to allow the lamp to actually reach the twins. Oliver didn't aim it as such, his actions were too quick for that, but if he had aimed it he could not have picked a better spot as it flashed into the very small space between the twins rather than hitting them directly. As a result they both instinctively turned towards each other, banged into each other very briefly and Oliver sensed his chance. He darted to his left, well wide of the despairing swipe of one of the twins' flailing arm. He made it to the door in less than a second and slammed it shut, as he did so seeing the key in the lock outside. He quickly locked the door before he heard the beasts within batter and hammer and growl and hiss at him. Outside, as he briefly looked down he heard where the noises had come from, two cd players still blasting their noises, one of the hellish hound and the other of the tsunami-like waves. Relief briefly passed through his body until he realised that he must get out of here, and must discover what sort of a state his friends were in.

He first rushed into Euan's room and tried to wake him but he was fast asleep, submerged and consumed. Oliver ran to the bathroom, filled two glasses with water and threw them over Euan. This had the desired effect and Euan shot bolt upright, startled and shocked.

"We need to get the fuck out of here now. Those girls have drugged us and have been told to either kill us or take us back to Nice. They're covered in blood, I think they've killed someone. We need to all get together and get the fuck out of here. Now."

The speed of Oliver's speech, his breathlessness, and the terror in his voice all made Euan move with a speed he never knew he had. He didn't ask any questions. "Wake the others. Throw water over them. Don't even try to shake them. Throw water over them." Euan woke Ali and Oliver woke Aidan. They were fine. There were now no noises coming from Oliver's room. Where were those bitches? And as they all gathered he realised that it must be Ellis that they had killed. But he went to waken Ellis and Ellis was there…startled to be awakened by water thrown over him but physically in the same state as when he went to bed. Only very fleetingly, as they ran down the stairs did Oliver wonder where the blood had come from and where the twins were now.

Their car was parked slightly away from the mansion and to the right side of it as they exited. Oliver could see it as he went out though his fear was that the twins might have done something….water in the petrol tank, something in the engine maybe. Perhaps an explosion as he turned the key. But there was no other way of escape.

As they started to sprint towards the car Oliver heard the shrieks of the twins coming from his left. It was impossible. How could they be down here, on the ground? They could not have jumped from the balcony in his room, no one could have done that, surely… not without breaking legs or back or something. But the twins shrieked as they started to run round to the front of the house then they stopped and let the leash off the huge beast that was running with them.

"Sprint!" yelled Oliver at his friends and all of them flew as fast as their feet could carry them. Oliver looked back and saw the monster advancing on them. As descriptions go, and Oliver tried to avoid focusing on or even thinking about it, you would have to call it a dog. But it was bigger than the largest dog Oliver had ever seen, when it barked its mouth opened wider than any dog Oliver had ever seen and it made a noise that was the very essence of terror. It was the same noise that had been outside his room and that had fuelled his fear that he might be eaten alive. And, though huge, the monster moved with a speed that defied its size. Even as he sprinted away Oliver wondered where it had come from, a genetic freak bred by these hellish bitches or something else, some hideous mutant cross breed that had been natured and nurtured on human flesh. One thing Oliver was certain of: if this bastard thing caught them, it wasn't going to stand around and merely bark at them for a while, it was going to devour them.

The distance between the mansion and the car was not large but with the monster gaining at every step it felt like a mile. Instinctively, Oliver didn't see any way they could all make it to the car. Maybe he would, maybe another one or two. But not the five of them. Somehow they would have to deal with it. The only thing he could think of was a spray… there was an air freshener spray in the car, he remembered seeing it rolling around on the floor…but if the car is locked I will never have the time to open the door and pick it up, I don't have time to play around with a key, all of us will be savaged by this brute. Did I lock the door? I don't think so….

As he made the last steps to the car he saw the hound closer, quite close to Ali, maybe within a few seconds it would be there. He grabbed the passenger door. It wasn't locked. He flung it open and grabbed the can. Immediately Ellis and Euan had reached the car and threw themselves in the back seat. Aidan would make it too, maybe… but Ali… Oliver ran towards the dog, making a distraction from Ali and a few seconds were all that Ali needed. He was now close, very close to the car and like Aidan almost threw himself at it. The dog turned to Oliver, still bounding and very close. Oliver bent down and in the same instant pressed the spray at the dog. He felt pathetically inadequate, a man armed with air freshener. However he had shifted his position well and knew that the spray would be carried by what little wind there was. As the dog tried to leap at him the spray went with as full a force as it could into its eyes and the noise changed from a bark of death to a high pitched, delicate and vulnerable yelp as it stopped and its paws came quickly across its eyes in a very human-like gesture.

It was enough for Oliver and he ran round to the driver's side, the beast still fawning over its poisoned eyes, and he rammed the key into the ignition. He stopped for the smallest of instants, wondering if this would be his last breath. Would there be an explosion as soon he the key clicked round? But he couldn't wait, he had to take the chance. The hound wouldn't be disorientated forever and again the twins were silent. God knows where they might be or what else they might have in store. All these thoughts, not even thoughts, mere flashes, impulses, shot through Oliver's head in the fractions of a second he delayed before finally turning the key. The car started. Oliver revved it to a ferocious level and it skidded in the stones as it began to shoot off. Then, from what seemed like nowhere, Oliver felt the car being hit by the force of what seemed to be a massive wave.

The strength of the water shook the car, almost knocked it onto its side. Oliver looked around, frenetically searching for where the deluge could have come from in these peaceful, flat, dry gardens.

"Oh sweet fuck!" yelled Euan. "Look at those bitches!" Oliver looked across to his left and saw each of the twins standing with what seemed to be a cross between a hose and a water cannon, firing them at the car. These things were so big and so wide that the twins could hardly hold them. Water shot out of them with a force and speed that defied belief. These things must have been used to do things like quell riots. They would literally have taken your head off. They battered the car again and Oliver yelled: "Get down, get down! If the windows break, we are dead."

Oliver also felt the water battering the front of the car, on the engine. We must get out of here. If they flood the engine we will never escape. The shock of the initial hammering had forced him to stall the car and he tried to restart it as twins stumbled ever closer, carrying these enormous weapons as they came. After a couple of turns it started and Oliver, instinctively, wondered about driving straight at them, keeping his head down, and letting the car plough into the demonic bitches. But the water would surely break the windows.

There was a small wall on either side of the main drive up to the mansion and Oliver knew that he had to go down the main drive to get out. Though small and nothing to a human being, he couldn't have driven the car over the wall. The car would probably have got stuck and cars only fly over walls like that in movies with super heroes in them. To get to the main drive he had to get past the twins. We have to take the chance, he thought… there is no other way. Soon the water is going to get in the engine, soon we are going to be stranded here, maybe even die here tonight…given those alternatives our best chance is to drive straight at them.

Oliver told his friends to put their heads down and he put his down as he drove straight at the water and its source. He tried as much as he could to make the car zigzag so that the water didn't hit one spot continuously and he occasionally tried to look up, over the wheel. He tried to put his foot down to the floor but knew also that he could not go too fast when he couldn't see where he was going. If the car went over the edge of the wall they were probably dead.

He felt the water pound and batter the windscreen, a horrible deafening noise that told of the creaking strain and pressure of a windscreen that was visibly buckling. He swerved and swerved back, the car skidding as its wheels cut deeply into the stones beneath it. Its movement slowed and the change in direction was so clunky that it was telegraphed and the twins read it, smashing the water into the car again. Oliver glanced up above the wheel. The water seemed to be coming even quicker and harder and he felt the wing mirror fly off. We have to do this quickly…… In an instant Oliver put his foot to the floor and hammered the car straight. The noise was sickening and full of death, a horrific death engulfed in ferocious water. His speed increased. For the first time the twins were affected and Oliver saw one on the fierce jets fly over the top of the car as she adjusted herself. Oliver hammered more and looked up as he saw the car batter into one of the twins, her naked body smeared with blood thrown into the air as she clung onto the massive hose.

Oliver reversed the car quickly to get back to the drive and spun the car round till it faced the exit then sped off. He looked into his rear view mirror and watched incredulously as both twins raced after them with their water hoses. There was a small barrier at the exit to the mansion and Oliver raced through it, snapping it clean as they made their way away from the mansion.

Drugged and sick, chased and hunted, terrified to within an inch of their lives, Ali encapsulated what the rest of them were feeling when he asked Oliver to stop the car and retched for what seemed like an age by the side of the road.

Oliver got out the car and walked slowly up and down. He had started to cry and didn't want anyone to see him. He told himself it was a reaction – to the singing, the sounds he had heard, the hellish twins, that dog or beast or hellish creation, that hideous water… it was a reaction to all that. But it wasn't. Oliver cried because of Helen and Terrence. But he didn't cry because he thought he might never see them again. He cried because he knew that, by his actions either tonight or previously, he had effectively killed them.

CHAPTER 13

Simone held a quick conversation with Alain about who should inform The Capo and when. They agreed that it should be Simone or Charlotte, since they had screwed up, and that it should be done quickly since there was going to be a helicopter at the mansion in a few hours ready to take five drugged British men down to Nice.

Simone phoned Davide, hoping that she would only have to deal with the consequences of failing and waking him. But Davide transferred the call: The Capo would want to hear about this first hand he thought and then, with a smile, turned over and tried to fall back to sleep.

"They did what? You let them what? I thought you and your sister could make a celibate monk beg to fuck you! And then you what? You frightened them and they escaped? Who are these guys? Maybe I should hire them to work for me, they seem to manage to show how inept my people are at every fucking turn. And you wake me up to tell me this... .I don't suppose you'll be competent enough to know where they were going, do you? Paris...yeah, well fucking done, a blind man with directional dyslexia could have figured that out. I mean after Paris...you don't know....what the fuck do you know? I thought you knew how to sing, to hypnotise, to fuck and to maim. Can you do any of these? Oh, you sang quite well... great, we'll get the bastard on the phone and you can sing sweet nothings to him till we catch him. No, no, I don't want you to do anything else....you'd probably fuck that up as well....what were you going to do anyway? Run after them all the way to Paris with your water pistol? Listen to me you stupid bitch. People in my organisation don't fail me. I'd have accepted if you killed the idiot by mistake, if you'd taken your work a bit too seriously. That happens. It's not good but it happens. But to not be able to capture five guys who you're telling me had little or no idea they were being hunted, who allowed themselves to be drugged and who didn't seem to have any fucking idea of what they'd walked into... Jesus Christ, how fucking stupid are you and your fucking idiot of a clone sister? Now I've got to spend more time trying to get this guy who I'm beginning to feel more benign towards every day. No, don't try to speak, fuck off until I need you again. And if you fail the next time I'm going to take your long pointed nails, the paint you put on your teeth and that big bastard dog and see how much of them I can use to maim you and your arse of a sister."

He paced the room. The Capo would have loved to have let this guy Oliver simply go. He was clearly quite resourceful and if what Simone had told him was true and he and his friends had genuinely not suspected anything then did this guy really know that he had done something wrong? As he thought about it, The Capo certainly felt better disposed to this unknown, this Oliver, than he did to Paul. But Paul was an acquaintance, a like-minded individual who had some influence and who The Capo could use. Also this guy Oliver has become very good at escaping me and The Capo realised it was almost becoming a matter of pride or a battle of wills that he should eventually get hold of this guy. Once he had endeavoured to do something, The Capo didn't like to fail. He tended not to lose. Not at table tennis, not at poker and definitely not in anything that involved anything to do with business.

As Davide had expected, it wasn't too long before he received a call. "Davide, these girls don't seem able to do even half of what they boasted that they could. I'd ask you to get the doctor to do something permanent to their voice boxes but… honestly, they're not worth the trouble. These guys – and this Oliver in particular – are still free. From what the girls said they didn't know there was anyone after them. They must know now, given how much the girls screwed things up. I think they must be headed for Paris and if they've any sense they'll change the car before they get there. No, no, I know they won't be able to buy one but they could easily ditch it and steal one. Even if they don't, it might be hard to catch them before they get on the train. The girls said their plan was to take the train so we have to assume they heard that right.…though you'd better check the ports too…and the airports… we are dealing with girls who I now realise I can't trust to wipe their own backsides. What I'm saying is I don't know if we can deal with this from the French side any more. They will have a few hours on us. But it takes about 2 hours and a bit to cross the Channel by train and it will be easier to get them when they arrive. They may also think they have escaped everything when they make it to the UK. So activate our guys in London. Find out what train… if it is a train…that they're getting…or have got….and let them deal with it. No, no, don't kill, I want the guy back here….certainly him and preferably his mates but definitely him….I think I might offer him a job actually. What? No, no, not really. His wife? I don't know. Paul wants to

266

rape the woman so best leave her where she is for now; I don't want her half killed by a monster if I can help it. Keep a watch on her. I may need to use her as bait but she's not done much wrong. No, leave the twins for now....I'm sure my anger will cool down....or maybe I should visit them......perhaps the fact that they're a great fuck might make up for them having the same brain power as fucking pond life."

The friends journeyed north, conscious of trying to get to Paris and out of France as quickly as was possible. For the first half hour few words were exchanged, a collective state of shock having consumed them. This must be what post-traumatic stress disorder feels like, thought Ali. It wasn't that one thing that had happened though that one thing of being chased by a huge dog and almost drowned, that was bad, but it was everything....the stone throwing, Clemence and the restaurant and what he had told his friends, stealing that car from these people, the guys with blades chasing them into a cave. It was everything, it was too much, too many things. All these things, within such a short space of time, all these things that made you feel your life was in danger. That made you feel that you were going to die. You really can't take very much of that. Not if you're a sports journalist and your normal idea of danger is the venom of a football manager or a golfer who didn't like your last question, or your last article. I don't know how much longer I can go on with this sense of danger. But you had to try to stay strong, if only because everyone else was trying to do the same. Don't let the team down. He'd been sick, terribly sick, but that catharsis over you had to get back to being positive. We are nearly at Paris. We are nearly home. And then we'll be safe. Whatever was after them, it wouldn't chase them back into the UK, of that Ali had no doubt.

Ellis had tried to put everything that had occurred over the last few days together. "Olly, what's been happening here? Do you think everything that's happened to us has happened because of what you did in Nice? That can't be right, can it? That woman Clemence, those guys throwing stones, even that big daft wrestler......do you really think they were all connected with Nice?"

Oliver paused for a bit. His thought process hadn't quite got that far. Instead he had thought about how rational he had seemed, even to himself, when dealing with that dog. I knelt down and invited the savage beast to leap at me......he hadn't started to try to put things together. "I don't know. Maybe we've been unlucky. But tonight….last night….that was definitely connected, these hellish bitches said as much. Which then leads me to think……how did they know…You know, how did they know where we would be? How did they know we would stay at that hotel? Or was that their good fortune?"

He looked across and round at his friends, enquiring. But only Ellis was consciously awake. The rest were asleep or trying to sleep.

"I think about what you told us quite a bit Olly…the guy you blinded and all that….and it doesn't seem right, something doesn't click that we would get chased like this because of that. Those girls could have killed us. It seems an over-reaction, don't you think? And I wondered if that girl you stayed with, Clotilde, maybe she was connected too and you… well, you know, 'rubbed another man's rhubarb'…

Oliver thought. "But if Clotilde had been connected then why didn't she give me up? I was there for about three days. She had me terrified that if I went out I would have been captured. No, I don't think she was connected, I think she was more of a good Samaritan. And I didn't rub anyone's rhubarb, not even my own…."

"So what was in it for her? Would any normal, rational human being have taken in someone who the Mafia or Mob or whatever were after? Who the hell would do that? If she knew what she told you, that the guy……Paul….if she knew he was well connected, why protect you when she must have known that they would probably have killed her for protecting you? Who would do that, really? Maybe you can tell me… .what was in it for her?"

Oliver thought about it and from Ellis' perspective the question was certainly a reasonable one. It wasn't a rational thing to do. Oliver wasn't sure what to say.

"Listen, Olly," said Ellis, looking at the other bodies in their states of snoring or slumber, "this is a conversation between you and me. If you and that Clotilde were living high on the hobby horse and shagging like rabbits, that's fine, no one knows except you and me. I won't say anything – to Euan, Helen, anyone. But I'd find that easier to accept than her taking you in and putting herself in such danger because she's a nice person."

Oliver paused. "Well……she……absolutely you're right, of course there had to be something in it for her. She made it clear to me she wanted me, she wanted us, to be a couple. At first it was just the chance to have some time together to, you know……but then as the day went into another and then another it was clear she wanted us to be together,

268

for me to not go home and try to forget about Helen and Terrence. And it was clear… she's dangerous too, she had some previous guy half killed from what she told me."

"Did you sleep with her?"

Oliver said nothing.

"Olly, mate, I saw her. I didn't realise it was her but the four of us saw her walking down the street. She was stunning with a figure to die for. I can still see her arse swaying. Christ, I would have slept with her in a heartbeat. Did you?"

"If I say yes you will think things that I don't want you to think. It was a terrible time for me. I did what I had to do to survive."

"You didn't enjoy it? Are you telling me you didn't enjoy it?"

Oliver didn't blush often but he blushed now. In the darkest hour before the dawn, as it was, Ellis couldn't see him but he blushed bright red. "I didn't exactly struggle to get an erection…." He said it quietly and thoughtfully.

"I fucking knew it! You don't need to say any more, I think we understand each other." He's one of us, thought Ellis, he's like me, exactly like me.

"No, I don't think we do. I hated every minute of it and it sickens me now when I think of it. You have to know that if I didn't do what that girl wanted, she made it clear that she would have picked up the phone and I would have been dead within the hour."

"Oh, I believe you," said Ellis, "but it is fortunate for you that all she wanted to do was fuck you. I mean, if you take your conscience thing away….it's not exactly twenty years hard labour, is it?"

Oliver felt vulnerable and saddened. He had felt his betrayal of Helen and Terrence wound him over the last few days but was managing to begin to reason it away. Yet there was Ellis, tearing at his protection, taunting him with it and daring him to say he hadn't enjoyed it. Oliver changed the subject, flashing back at Ellis. "Don't you remember what happened a couple of nights ago? At that restaurant?"

Ellis smiled. "I was drugged Olly. We all were. But not that drugged. You think I wouldn't remember shagging someone as stunning as Clemence?"

Oliver was shocked. "You remember that? And did you know what you were doing at the time?"

Ellis nodded, slowly, in recollection. "Yeah, pretty much. I don't think there's a hole in her body that I wasn't in at some time."

"But you….your wife….the girls… "

"Olly, for fuck's sake….I've been married for years. Yvonne's pretty and all and sex is still good but come on, it's what guys do, take the odd night where they can get it."

"I don't!"

"No, you've done something more than that, haven't you?"

Oliver shot a glance at him. "Was that, you know, the first time you have……"

"I have what? Been disloyal? Slept around? What do you think?"

"I think maybe no."

"Then you are maybe correct. Olly, these business trips overseas, it's sort of par for the course, you know. Honestly mate, it's nothing major. No long term affairs……ok, a couple of girls across in…let's be broad and say Asia….a couple of girls there I might have seen a few times. But it's just sex, it's harmless. Bloody hell, Olly, are you telling me you wouldn't have gone with one of those twins before they went schizo? I was desperate to shag one of them. But I was too tired. No surprise really given that we'd been hit by another drug. But, sure, I would have gone there. Away from home, Olly – you don't get caught. And your secret is safe with me. As I know mine is with you."

Oliver liked Ellis. He had liked him since he first met him. Ellis had always been a bit of a big shot – those who didn't care much for him used to refer to him as "the Great I Am" – but he was funny and warm and though most of the time the centre of attention somehow he was charming with it and could be very self-deprecating. Vulnerability is always appealing, attractive even, and Ellis was quite good at emphasising his vulnerability. But this was quite shocking and Oliver struggled to believe that Ellis took pleasure wherever he could find it.

"Really? I mean, truly? Is that what you think? You're not …… exaggerating…."

"Olly, if anything… under exaggerating… "

"Fuck, Ellis, I thought I knew you…."

"What, I was one thing and now I am something else? Come on Olly! Don't pretend to be naïve! Maybe you don't know me but that's not because you've suddenly discovered I've shagged the odd women or two who happen not to be my wife."

"What, there's more? You may as well let it all out now…"

Ellis looked suddenly thoughtful and serious and even his tone changed from a slightly mocking disbelief to being sonorous and weighty.

"There's always more Olly…" He looked up. "I think we are getting near Paris. What do you think we should do with this damned car? They must have its registration number at least. If we take it across to the UK it's going to be quite easy to spot."

"Yeah, I was thinking about that and I have an idea. It's…well, there's a vital part missing. I think we can dump the car in a station car park or anywhere where it might take a day or two to discover it. They'll know where we're going, I'm sure – I mean we told these crazy twins when we were talking to them anyway – but we don't need to advertise it by leaving the car somewhere where it shouldn't be. And we really need a car at the other end and that's my problem, that's where there is a bit missing. It would be great if we could walk out and get another car to drive us home. I don't think we should get a train from London to Edinburgh, it's too constricted if they do know where we are, and we could drive the car home in a day, traffic permitting. But to get a car we'd need to hire one and you can imagine the influence that those bastards might have. I think we'd be found quite easily, they'd know what we'd done. So what's the alternative? Well, we could steal a car but I couldn't hot wire a chicken curry and I don't think you or any of the others are criminal masterminds so……"

"Hold on, hold on, it's a good idea. You're right, by car is best. I can get us a car, no problem."

"You can? How?"

"I've got quite a few pals down here, quite a few guys that I use, who I throw some business to. They're all bloody loaded, they could leave us a car in the station car park."

"That's… even if that's possible, they won't think that odd?"

"Oh, of course they'll think it's odd. But don't worry, I'll make up some believable lie about some stag do gone wrong….tell them I'll bring it back next week or something……Christ, that has to be more believable than the truth."

As they entered Paris and headed for Gare du Nord, Ellis phoned a friend or two in London and was successful at the second attempt. One friend's wife was away at her parents in France for a week or so with the children, the car was sitting there doing nothing, it would be left in a car park at St Pancras International, exact location would be texted, key was under the sun visor. It was hideously easy. As the sun began to rise on what seemed to be a beautiful morning in the city, the other friends awoke or at least stretched themselves out of their slumber and listened

271

to the plan. A cautious optimism ran through all of them except Oliver. They all felt, except Oliver, that their problems would be over when they got to the UK. They all believed, except Oliver, that no person or organisation would have the enthusiasm or the contacts to pursue them overseas, back into their own country. They all considered, except Oliver, that they had reached the end of an adventure which had terrified them in a way in which no previous event in their lives had prepared them for.

After leaving the car in the nearest car park, the friends walked to the station and had a brief conversation about buying tickets for the train. Ellis won the argument and the tickets were bought with his credit card. He won the argument over Oliver, who had wanted to pay cash, because: whoever was after them probably didn't know Ellis' name; there would be plenty of British people here buying things, unlike other things they had done in France where they had been more conspicuous; they couldn't readily find a cash machine and didn't want to draw attention to themselves anyway by withdrawing large amounts of money; most of the friends felt that the people chasing them were about to give up the fight so it didn't matter how they paid.

The first train they could get was at 08:37, which meant an hour or so wait, but at least the breakfast they had of the obligatory croissants and coffee felt like their last breakfast in France. They began to talk of last night, the horrific experiences of the dog and the water and Oliver told them more fully about the sounds and how he was awoken, at the sheer terror of being woken up by noises that made you fear you would either be savaged or drowned or both. Then they tried to share their fears and relive the feeling they had of how they were going to die, trying by reason to defeat feelings that they all knew were going to scar and haunt for years, perhaps for ever. Having stones thrown at you and being drugged were one thing, but being savaged by a wild animal for fun was enough to shake your state of being to such an extent that some parts of it were altered forever.

Sitting beside each other on the train, or at least close enough to engage in conversation so that no one else might hear, they continued to share their angst and try to make it more normal by making it public.

"I can't get over," said Euan, his mop of blond hair now slightly dirty, straggly and unkempt, "the change in those girls. Their voices…the most beautiful noises you'd ever heard…and then we walked home with them, they were just fabulous. And so beautiful physically too…and then the next thing you know they are savages, monsters. It's unbelievable."

272

"No indication at all that they were anything other than these beautiful girls, absolutely charming. I still don't know how they transformed into these ghouls. Or how they got involved with......with the people who were after Olly in the first place." Aidan sounded confused and bemused, as though the whole experience had bordered on the paranormal.

"Who knows," said Ellis, almost philosophically calm. "Who knows......goes to show you, you never really know anyone, do you?"

Ali looked across at Ellis. He had registered everything but had been staring out of the window. "What's that supposed to mean? Are you suddenly going to turn into a monster......Jekyll and Hyde-like? The bloody Wolfman?"

"No, I mean... ach, I'm not sure what I mean...I could have sworn at least one of those twins was well up for a night, you know......and then this madness happens... you realise that you didn't know anything about them at all."

"I thought they were well into us. Definitely you Ellis," Aidan added. There was a brief silence.

"You know the scary thing," said Euan, "the scary thing is that it doesn't have to be people you've just met and you think you know that can really surprise you. It doesn't have to be people like those insane witches. I heard this story a few weeks ago, one of the waiters at the restaurant was telling me it about someone he knew. Don't know if it was a friend or a friend of a friend...maybe it was him... golly, makes you realise that you don't really know anyone."

There was another brief silence. "Well tell us then!" pleaded Ellis. "Come on, we've still got about two hours left on this train wondering if some guy is going to run in and put bullets into all of us. Least you can do is try and make the time pass a bit quicker. Because I'm not at all interested in trying to read a French newspaper." And he tossed the paper beside him onto the table.

"Ok, sure. If you're interested. It revolved around the guy's wife. Like I say, I heard it from the waiter, it was a story at the end of the night when the restaurant's shut and we're standing around, tidying up, having a drink or two. So, anyway, he told me that he had a friend – so it was probably all relating to himself I guess, but anyway – he said he had this friend who wasn't sure about his wife's fidelity. Oh, nothing major he said, a few little things of how she might talk about men at work, how she started wearing different make-up and longer earrings... "

"Hold on a minute," said Oliver, "you've lost me a bit. Longer earrings….longer earrings mean what, what's the significance there?"

"Well I think… I mean I think he thought…that was a sign of a more, maybe a more flirtatious woman. Longer earrings…"

Oliver looked at his friends. "Really?" Ellis shrugged his shoulders. Ali's face was completely blank as if he had no idea what an earring was. Aidan nodded. "Sure, yeah, I can go with that."

"Shit," said Oliver. "If I ever get home then the first thing I'm going to do is start to measure the length of Helen's earrings." He paused. "Seriously, you reckon there's a correlation between earring length and marital fidelity? Seriously?"

"What if a guy wears an earring?" pondered Ellis. "If he buys a longer earring is he putting it about a bit?"

"Jesus, guys," said Euan raising his hands. "I don't know! I'm just telling you the guy's story. I'm telling you what he said! I didn't expect to have a bloody examination about it!"

"But you didn't think this weird enough to pass comment…or ask a question?" Oliver looked confused.

"No! It was about half past midnight. I probably wanted to go to bed. But this guy's now telling a story so I'm thinking – 'Oh, I better listen to this, I don't want to be rude'. I'm not going to ask a bloody question about everything. Fuck me….earrings…who the fuck cares about bloody earrings…"

"I think the last pair of earrings Helen bought were quite long," said Oliver, more to himself than to anyone else.

"You don't buy her earrings?" asked Ellis.

"Jesus, not all of them," said Oliver. "She's got enough to build a bloody mountain of the things." Oliver thought briefly. "So hang on, hang on, those women that wear those really long dangly earrings, you know the big round circle things….they're up for anything, are they? Jesus, I never knew…"

"Fuck, Olly," said Euan. "I don't think this is science…."

Ellis interrupted. "Hmmm, he might have a point, I think girls – women – with longer earrings are… well, they're being a bit more flirty, saying 'Hey, look at me' a bit more…"

Euan shook his head and looked at his watch. "Okay, maybe someday I'll host a programme called 'What's the fucking significance of earrings' but not now so can I tell the story please?"

"Oh sure, sure, on you go," replied Ellis.

"This guy had noticed little differences. Maybe she used to wear tiny earrings and now she was wearing big dangly ones, who the fuck knows, but there were other differences like I said. And he had doubts about her. Just little things that made him think…hmm, she's changed a bit. But there was nothing overt. He admitted that he got to the stage of checking her phone…nothing…but still wasn't convinced. So he wondered what he might do as….as a sort of test, you know…"

"He should have taken her to buy earrings," said Ali. "If she bought a long dangly pair then what more confirmation would you need?"

They laughed together, even Euan. It felt like the first time they had laughed together for years. "Well he didn't do that. The stupid fucker should've but he didn't. Instead he did something else. He managed to get hold of quite a few photos of some attractive guy…how, I'm not sure…he said it was through someone new who had started at work, they became friends and he 'adopted' the guy's photos from facebook. I've no idea how that might work but anyway he adopted them to make an entirely new character, inventing a name and a whole career for this guy. A whole life. Then he followed his wife to make sure she went the places she said she was going. So if she said she was going to the gym he would follow her to make sure. He would check the amount of cars in the car park to see how busy the place was. If she said she was meeting her pals for a drink then he would check that too. He never discovered anything nasty, no horrible secrets. She didn't say she was doing one thing then go and meet another guy. But he wanted to make sure that she was where she said she was. Then he started to put his plan into action.

He started by sending the odd message to her as this guy, a fictional guy with his made up facebook page and false e-mail. Scary how easy it is to be anonymous these days. Anyway, he started sending her the odd message, very flattering, along the lines of "saw you at the gym last night, well done on the work out," that kind of thing."

"That must have had her eating out of his hand," said Ellis. "As chat-up lines go, I've heard better."

"You know what I mean. He was chatty and flattering without being creepy. She didn't reply to him, not at first, but the husband noticed that she started to go to the gym a bit more. Instead of going twice a week she would go three times a week. He chose to send her a message when he saw the car park was quite full, when the gym was at its busiest. Probably so she wouldn't be able to see, by some basic process of elimination, who had sent or was sending the messages. He tried again, staring with an "ah, I hadn't seen you there at the weekend before." And eventually, of course, she replied. At first she was quite cold and non-committal – how do you know who I am, who are you, have you been watching me, that's a bit spooky etc. But he replied with very believable answers – he had seen her sign in so knew her name, had checked facebook and found her, didn't watch her exactly but couldn't help noticing her, she's very pretty etc. Then he took it a bit further by asking a bit about her…what did she do for work, was she married, what sort of things did she like. And she replied, saying that yes she was married – but that was the one and only time she mentioned her husband, if you can call that a mention – and yes she did work in medical research and she liked doing the things that people liked to do….meet friends, have a drink, go out for a meal, go to the cinema.

But then, and as he saw it quite crucially, something changed. She began to ask him questions. What about you? What do you do? It was at that point that he began to struggle a bit to believe it was his wife because, thought they spoke to each other, he realised that they didn't – at least she didn't – ask him many questions. He would come home and talk about his day and she would appear interested and she would nod and frown where she was supposed to but she didn't ask much. Yet she was actively interested in this guy, she was asking him questions, she was asking him plenty questions. So he made up some alternative reality for this guy, working in 'banking and finance', divorced, quite wealthy but also quite clearly a bit lonely. And also quite clearly very handsome.

Then it began to get slightly tricky because she looked for him at the gym and would say, occasionally, that she hadn't seen him, didn't he normally go on a Tuesday, etc and he would be forced to say that something came up, unfortunate, because otherwise he would have come up and said something to her. Maybe they could have a meal one night, or a drink, after the gym? She agreed. But again something came up. By this time the messages between them were at the rate of about four to five per day. These people were getting close, very close.

Their communication had also got beyond merely being suggestive. He had paid her a compliment on her body, which she had accepted. Then he said a bit more about her shape and started using words like 'sensual' and 'sexy' and again she accepted and returned that she hadn't felt sensual or sexy for a while. Temporarily torn between pursuing the charade and sitting down with her face to face as her husband, he pushed the fantasy….he began to mention underwear he'd seen in a shop and how he would love to see her in it, how he imagined her in a certain dress and how he would like to peel it off her and let his hands dance all over her, slowly let the dress drop, touch her everywhere....you know the sort of thing. Well she was very into this, replying that no one had made her feel that way for so long and how she longed to feel wanted, sexually wanted, again. And that really should have been enough for him. Because if she'd said she hadn't felt like that for ages then he kind of knew what he set out to try and discover – that there hadn't been anyone else before. But of course he was now stepped in this far too far to step back and walk away.

So he decided to ask the question he really wanted to ask her from the time he first set out on this venture. 'Why don't we meet at a hotel? Yes, sure, I'd like to spend the night with you but we can have a meal and if it's not working then you can go and we'll say nothing more about it. And if it does work then we can....see what happens.'

At first she didn't reply and in the day before she did reply he noticed that at home she was uptight, edgy, quite quick to lose her temper. He asked what was wrong but she said nothing, just hormones. So, guys, beware the hormones excuse, it covers a multitude! Anyway, he made things really easy for her... said he had to be away on business next Wednesday, exactly the date that had been proposed for the liaison. So she went back to her suitor and said 'yes, ok.' And when he got the message he realised that she had said 'yes' without having met him, without having had any proper conversation with him, without any confirmation that the guy in the photo was anything like the guy she was going to meet."

"Jeez," said Ali. "She did that? People do that sort of thing?"

"I guess they do. It's a different age now. People date people they meet over the internet, or social media... people date like that all the time. Maybe, as he figured after she said yes to meeting this guy, maybe that wasn't the first time she had done this. It had seemed quite hideously easy.

He wondered what he should do. Should he turn up himself and surprise her? Or could he persuade the guy at work, the guy whose pictures he'd 'adopted', to turn up? To tell him what he'd done, let him in on the secret and see how far he might take it. He wrestled with the problem for a while. And he decided to go himself. To take a chance, a big chance, by getting there early, being in the room, then telling her to come up to the room. So that she was almost finding him in the bed. So that she'd only know it was her husband when she went into the room. Maybe she wouldn't go straight up to the room but he was prepared to take that chance. After all, if she was prepared to even go to the hotel then she had committed some kind of overt act that he felt was, at best, dishonourable..."

"Dishonourable?" Ellis interjected. "Dishonourable? What sort of a word is that? She's a cheating bitch! If she set foot in the hotel she's a bloody cheat!"

Oliver looked at him was a sense of disbelief but Ellis' sense of injustice still burned.

A brief pause. "So, anyway, they'd agreed to meet at about 7.30ish so he got there at about 6, made himself at home, got an ice bucket for the champagne and positioned it so it would be the first thing someone would see when they came in. He had a long relaxing bath and then he waited, waited to see if his wife was going to betray him or not. He waited for what seemed like an age. By 7.45 there was nothing......no e-mails, nothing. He hadn't given her his mobile number, all communication went through e-mail and he wondered if it might be a network thing, maybe he should e-mail her. Then at 7.50 he got an e-mail – 'I'm here in the lobby but I can't see you. Are you here or have you taken fright?'

He replied, giving the room number and suggesting that she come up and see if she liked what she saw. If she didn't she could turn around and walk away. The door was open. He then tried to get himself into a position where he might be able to see her but she wouldn't be able to see him. However, that was impossible. Should he either stay in bed or stand at the door? He decided to stay in bed, in which case she wouldn't see him until she had stepped quite a bit of the way into the room. The door opened. He pulled the covers up to his head. He could hear tentative steps. Then he heard the door close and could smell a subtle but distinctive perfume, something he had never known his wife to use before. He was both hurt and excited, almost simultaneously. She stepped further into the room and he could hear her take off her coat, slowly. He managed to peek through the covers and could see, from the chest down, his wife's body in a long, tight, black dress. She must have been looking straight at the bed now, he thought, she must be able to see someone hiding. I will have to do this now. She has come this far – to be in the hotel bedroom of someone she has never met. Jesus, he briefly thought, I could be anyone......I could be a rapist, a killer...and my wife is that happy about her life with me that she has taken this chance.

As he pulled back the cover to reveal himself his wife did not immediately see him. She didn't immediately see him because at that moment she was turned with her back to him, unzipping her dress and pushing it gently down to the floor. He looked at her from behind: black stockings, lacy black underwear that was as soft and fragile as dental floss, black bra...all on what he had to admit, looking at her, remained a beautiful body. He wanted that moment to last the rest of his life. He saw, in that picture of his wife, the sexual urge and desire that he first had for her, that he hadn't felt for longer than he himself cared to remember. And also because he knew that when she turned round their lives were going to change forever. He feared that it could only be for the worse. How could it not be when the first conversation you were prepared to have face-to-face with a stranger was probably after you had had sex with him?

She turned around and he saw first that her bra and thong were see-through and, when she saw his eyes on her, the first thing she tried to do was cover herself up. One hand instinctively went across her chest, the other went to between her legs. When he thought about it later, that hurt him more than anything else – that she wouldn't want her husband to see her in that sexy underwear. She screamed, a little yelp of discovery, as her eyes widened and she rushed to put her dress back on.

What happened? Well, they talked....they talked maybe too much because the first thing he wanted to do was make love with her and maybe if each of them had fucked a fantasy in that instant it might have acted as a spark. Instead they talked and tried to reason away what had happened....they had been married a while, you can take each other for granted, she hadn't felt like a woman for a long time, maybe they needed to make more of an effort. But each of them knew then that something had changed. She had been amazed then later appalled by the extent to which he had made this fabrication, this alternative guy, to entrap her. It wasn't the kind of thing that husbands and wives should do to each other and she felt that somehow comprehending him was now beyond her. For his part, his indignation was around her going freely with another man, one she had never met, one who could have been anybody... almost as if......well, almost as if she was betraying him with the first thing in trousers that showed an interest in her. And I remember how he finished the story, even if it was late at night, he said: 'it was almost as if we got to the stage where we agreed that each of us now didn't have the ability to know the other one. Unknowable. Each of us. Can you believe that? After being married for 8 years. Unknowable.'"

There was a brief silence. "Are they still together?" asked Oliver.

"I don't know. I only heard the story a week or two ago. Seems like a lifetime ago, right enough. But it made me think of those girls. I don't think I'll ever know how they could have gone from being one thing to being something... something I guess none of us can understand."

There was silence as each of them was again taken back to the previous night's nightmare.

Ali said: "I remember once Lesley saying something similar....not about me but about one of her friends. It was a good few years ago. She had been shocked, she thought she knew the girl. The girl had...oh, I can't remember, maybe split up with a partner, maybe it had been a one night thing, I don't know... but she had fallen pregnant and she decided to have an abortion."

"That's not so shocking," said Ellis.

"Well it was to Lesley. They were good friends and the girl was really anti-abortion, didn't see how people could do it, that was a life that was being killed, abortion was murder, it was a heinous crime that she reckoned people should be put away for. She was the kind of girl who always supported these far right groups in the States that propose making abortion illegal and who attack abortion clinics......thought it was a murderous horrible act basically..."

"Ok, ok, you've made the point," said Ellis. It was out with an anger and frustration that he could barely control.

"Well.......," said Ali, though his eyes and indeed the eyes of all his friends were on Ellis, whose head was now down to avoid their gaze. "Well anyway she decided to have an abortion and Lesley said how it shocked her, she said she thought she knew the girl but ultimately....she didn't know her at all..."

But by this stage no one was listening. All eyes were on Ellis as he looked to his left, out of the window. Oliver could swear he saw tears in Ellis' eyes. Yes, surely, his eyes had reddened. And moistened.

"......so she didn't know her at all.......Ellis, mate, everything ok?"

Ellis was seen as an unemotional, generally uncomplicated character. Two dimensional in his deeper moments. What he was experiencing just now seemed close to a breakdown. He held his head in his head but the movement of his body and the sounds that he made belied a sobbing....a deep and unrestricted sobbing.

Oliver leant across and touched his friend on the shoulder. Perhaps this was a reaction to the last few days. They had been through hell. We all have our breaking points. Maybe it was easier for him that things come out like this, rather than being stored away and hidden. "Hey, Ellis, it's ok. It's been a horrible time. Don't worry."

Ellis' head was still down but he shook it. "It's not the trip. It's not that."

Then he was silent. He raised his head as his sobbing stopped. "Then what?" Oliver asked. Oliver looked at the friends round him. "You're amongst friends. If we can't share what we're feeling after the last few days we've had together, then......."

"I had an affair."

None of the friends looked at all shocked. Euan shrugged his shoulders. Ali opened his arms in front of him as if to say 'yeah, and so?' and Oliver looked distinctly puzzled, given the conversation they had held a few hours ago.

"But not only that. When I was engaged to Yvonne, only engaged, there was a girl in the office, she was my PA at the time... she liked me, it was clear that she liked me. She was very tidy, very pretty. She thought I was this....big important guy, you know. She flattered my ego and I suppose I liked that. She wore great clothes as well, she really got dressed up to come into the office. I remember a colleague saying that on the days I was going to be away, or on holiday, she never made as much of an effort. So I kind of knew it was for me. We'd occasionally have lunch together – working lunch I called it at first – but we didn't do much work. We'd talk about things, stuff.......got quite suggestive at times, it was obvious that she was interested. And I was engaged so I should have had my mind on other things, on other women....on Yvonne... but it wasn't easy with this girl almost offering herself to you.

She used to ask about the wedding a lot – when was it, how were preparations going, might she get an invite. It was funny because though she was asking me all these questions about me confirming that I was spending my life with this other woman, the subtext was different...... you know, she'd say things like – 'oh, that sounds great, you'll be so happy together' and she'd cross or uncross her legs so that I'd see a flash of stockings or something. It wasn't a coincidence.

Eventually what was, I guess, inevitable happened. I had to work late, genuinely work late and I needed help so she stayed. By about half past seven the work was done and we were both hungry. Yvonne was out that night anyway, this girl lived alone, so we got some food delivered to the office and opened a bottle of wine. We had a lovely meal, lovely wine and afterwards we tore the clothes off each other and satisfied ourselves of a desire that had been burning for a few months. It was great, I mean....in the office...great. Recommended. So this continued for a bit, we found ways of getting alone together in quiet, there was even a trip to the US that she, of course, had to come on and it was...well, it was what it was.

I asked her a couple of times, the first time before we did anything on that night in the office, if she was on anything, protection-wise, and she told me not to worry, of course she was. And rightly or wrongly I've always been convinced that a sexually transmitted disease is something that happens to other people so I didn't wear anything. For a month or two things were great..."

He paused, lost in the memory. "I mean, I know it was wrong, I knew I shouldn't be doing it but it all felt so good that I didn't want it to stop. I didn't love her but I liked her and she made you excited just looking at her. We laughed a lot too. And I think what happened between us was a fair exchange of equals looking for the same thing so – no robbery, if you know what I mean. Then she dropped this bombshell. She looked serious and said we had to talk. My first thought was that she'd met someone and was going to have to call it off which would have been fine and my conscience would feel a little lighter. But that's not what she said. She said she was pregnant. I was speechless. I literally couldn't say a thing. There must have been about 500 thoughts rushing through my head at once. Two were out before I could stop them."

"But you are on the pill. Is it mine?"

"The pill...well...," she said, "I may have been less than truthful about that. And as for it being yours....what else do you think I'm getting up to? If there's you then there isn't room or desire for anyone else."

"I told her to get out. I needed time to think. And all that day I could see my life, the life I had seen for myself with Yvonne, seeping away. And I wanted that life. Yvonne was – is – gorgeous and I needed her. You have to understand that this woman was going to take all that away from me. She was going to destroy my life. So I made a decision. I was going to see her at the end of day to tell her she was going to have to have an abortion. Then I thought that she hadn't actually said she wanted to keep the baby, she may have been looking for help from me, so maybe all would be well anyway. We could easily be discreet about it.

But she didn't want an abortion. That was the last thing she wanted. She was horrified that I would even suggest it. She became...angry, indignant, even furious at me...how could I suggest that. She didn't talk about 'my responsibilities' or anything like that but she made it clear there was going to be this living reminder of our fun time together. It couldn't happen. It simply couldn't happen. So I tried to persuade her, calmly, that this was wrong. I felt anything but calm and she sensed it. She pushed me further, saying how there would always be this baby. When I married Yvonne I could think of the baby and then I said something which... something which I should never have said..."

Ellis again put his head down and took time to compose himself. "She thought I was quite a big important guy, like I'd said before, she thought I was someone. So I guess I played on that. I told her that if she didn't have an abortion then I knew people... I knew people....who could make life very difficult for her. She asked me if I was threatening her and I simply said 'yes'. I told her that she was going to hand in her notice and leave. She was going to have an abortion. And she was going to move to London where I could find her a job quite easily. If she stayed here, if she decided to go ahead with the baby....perhaps she wasn't safe. She lived alone...."

He stopped again. "What I did was...what I said was... evil, worse than evil...."

"But," said Euan, "in that moment, understandable."

"But indefensible," said Ellis and no one could contradict him. He was silent.

"What happened?" asked Aidan. "Was that it? Did she leave or did she stay?"

"I got married to Yvonne. So I guess I got what I wanted. She – the girl – she handed in her notice the next day. She left, as I had asked her to do. She got an abortion, as I had asked her to do. And she got a job in London doing a similar thing, as I had asked her to do."

"And she never got back in touch? She's not sitting there in the background ready to pounce?" asked Oliver. "I mean...maybe it was for the best for her too. How old was she...early twenties maybe...", Ellis shrugged his shoulders and nodded, "...bringing up a kid on her own... not ideal...maybe it wouldn't have been the joy she imagined it. Maybe it's for the best."

Ellis looked up, his eyes very red. "Oh," he said, his voice quivering, "I doubt that. A month or so after she moved to London she was found dead in her flat. She'd hanged herself. I killed two people. Two people. Two lives that would have been still here had I not said what I said. Maybe, if I am any woman's husband, I should have been hers. And do you know what I think, do you know what haunts me…." His sobbing was louder now, deep heaving sighs shaking his soul. "I think of the kid. How old would he or she be? When would their first day at school be? What would they be like? She was beautiful – would it have been a sweet candy-floss type girl with her stunning features or one of these beautiful boys who have their mum's features… Who knows… who knows… how do you miss what you have never had?"

The question hung, rhetorical and unanswered. As with most of the journey, the world outside the window was dark as they passed through the tunnel. Briefly, the lights on the train flickered and the darkness was omnipresent. Oliver couldn't see his friends. He couldn't even see Ellis who was sitting next to him. But Ellis was already in a different world, one in which Oliver would find it very difficult to find him.

CHAPTER 14

"The car's abandoned? Where? In Lyon? And....where did they go, did they get another car? Ok, ok, I understand…so they bought this other car in Lyon and left our one. Where are they going? North, yes, that's exactly where we thought they would go. Probably to Paris. Great, thank you, thank you, please let me know if you find out any more, this is fantastic, it helps."

Jacques put down the phone. He had only, within the last hour, managed to find a friend who was prepared to lend him a car for a vaguely undetermined period of time. Now there seemed to be a purpose, there seemed to be somewhere to actually go. He turned to Guy and Natalie.

"The car has been abandoned in Lyon. In some backstreet. But they bought another one and are headed to Paris. Maybe Calais. We have the registration of the new car. My friend will tell me when they get a definite location. But this is good news… "

"So we go to Lyon and find the old car and we'll find the money…," concluded Natalie.

"No!" Jacques shouted. Guy also shook his head. "No, they have the money. They have taken the money. There is no point in us looking for the old car – the police maybe have it anyway – because these guys changed cars specifically to try and throw us off their tracks. They knew we had the registration number so they took the money and changed the car over as quickly as they could. This has all been premeditated. Now we have a car we have to find these guys. So let's go towards Paris and hopefully we will get an update on where they are exactly on the way."

Jacques was clearly quite pleased with himself and hopeful that the cash would be retrieved. But Guy noticed that there was something else in voice, not panic or despair exactly, but something like concern, maybe even fear.

"That's all?" Guy asked. "Your friend told you nothing else?"

"Well he did say something else…he said that we are not the only people looking for these guys…there is quite a high alert on them from some people, important people.."

"What does that mean? Why would other people be after them? Have they stolen money from them too? And what important people, who are they?"

"I don't know. My friend doesn't know. He said: "Ah, you're not the only one asking about these guys. One of my colleagues already spoke with the garage in Lyon. Be careful, these are serious guys that are after them. They must have offended somebody important.""

"Important?" Guy screwed up his face, as if he was trying to induce a physical manifestation of what that might be. "Important like a mayor? A President?"

"Well, no, I don't think that kind of important. The impression I got was… underworld important, Mob important.."

"Oh shit!" said Guy. "The Mob know they've taken the money and they want it back. They know we don't have it." Then he thought for a minute. "Jacques, I think we have to accept defeat on this. We can't compete with the Mob. They'd kill us as soon as look at us. And as well as that they seem to have a day or two's start on us. Let it go…."

"No!" Jacques almost shouted. "All of us, for all our lives, your family, my family, we've been poor. Stuck here. Eating things we don't want to, living where we don't want to. This is our chance to have something different. All of us. If only for a while. We know it wouldn't last forever. But that money represents a decent little flat in a nice area, it's the hope that we can get out of this horrible bloody place. I'm not giving that up. If they want to kill me then they'll have to kill me. We are getting that money back, even if it means going across to Edinburgh, even if it means fighting the Mob for it. It's our money." He said the last three words as though they were three distinct sentences, each with their own emphasis.

"Ok. Ok."

"Let's get our stuff together quickly and get going. Let's head for Paris and I will keep in touch with my friend."

"You don't want to stop in Lyon, just to see?"

"No. It would delay us and there's no point. I am sure the police have taken the car and impounded it. These are clever guys. They know what they are doing. They have the money with them. The more I think about it, the more I think how clever they have been, how much they must have watched us, waited for the right time…"

Natalie took herself from the room. She was not optimistic about the chances of recovering any of what she saw as her money and had no desire to journey across Europe. But that wasn't why she left the room. She left the room because a message had come through on her phone from someone she had called "Unknown Source". Not exactly a proper name but anonymous enough if Jacques happened to ever look at her phone as she imagined he did on a fairly regular basis. And although Unknown Source had sent her quite a few messages, and vice versa, she always deleted everything that had been sent and everything that had been received, except the most recent text, in the inbox. That way, if anyone did happen to see it, it was a random message that had been sent to the wrong number.

She had met Unknown Source in a work capacity. Natalie was a waitress in a hotel: she was a good waitress and the hotel was four, four and a half, five stars, depending upon the year, the effort and who did the judging. The uniform suited her, making her look efficient but feminine, work-like yet graced. Natalie knew how to smile and could smile very well and always with the eyes, never looking as though it was forced or insincere.

She often got offers, some requests kinder than others, some a bit more blatant and she had stopped telling Jacques about them almost as soon as she had started to tell Jacques about them. He became jealous and angry and would explode. She really should leave him, she didn't really like him let alone love him, but he'd been very good about the whole Mob thing and the money over the last few months and it would have been too awkward. So not now, maybe some time in the future, sure, but not now. He didn't want to have sex that much anyway so that saved the physical bit. It was truly dreadful. She hated him on top of her, he was fat and heavy and always seemed to smell, but if she went on top of him it took him so much longer. She used to think about her shift, the people, see if she could remember the Specials from earlier today, from yesterday, from this day last week…come on you big oaf, just let it go, you must be ready now…Horrible.

So when someone charming came along it was quite difficult to turn them down. Someone she found genuinely charming, that is, not someone who merely flattered her because they fancied a fling with a waitress for a night. Unknown Source had really charmed her very much. The first thing Unknown Source had said to her, maybe three or four months ago, when they had been sitting in the hotel, was how good she was at her job. Unknown Source had watched her scuttle about quickly, smile, take orders with her keen, fresh eyes, listen to everything, remember little things about people. Unknown Source had been in the hotel trade and wished she could have had Natalie working for her back then. It had made Natalie blush, a stranger saying these things about you, to you. Very flattering. Then she would see Unknown Source more often and they would smile and talk to each other till one day Unknown

Source asked her if they could have a drink after work. Natalie agreed immediately: staff tended to hang about at night after work anyway for a drink and a chat so it wasn't as if she had to make some special justification for coming home late.

It was clear from about five minutes into their first conversation that Unknown Source had an interest in Natalie that went beyond that of her ability as a waitress. It was clear from about five minutes into that conversation that the interest was personal. Unknown Source commented on her hair, her finger nails, her beautiful young face, her figure that must send pulses racing, the way she carried herself. She remembered Unknown Source looking at her in the eye, making sure she caught her full on and saying: "You're a very stunning, beautiful girl."

Natalie was thrilled. Thrilled and exited and a little shocked. The person sitting opposite her was beautiful too. But this person reeked of money, class even, and everything about this person, from the way they smelled to the way they looked to the tanned colour of their skin, told of an existence that was a world away from Natalie's. Natalie didn't know what to say. All these thoughts but this person, this situation, I don't know what to say. With her heart beating faster, in the nice way so that you can feel it and you're fully aware of your own existence, she said the only thing she could think of to say:

"Um.......well, you know my name but I don't know yours.."

The person sitting opposite her held out her hand for Natalie to take and briefly they held hands rather than shook. Wow, thought Natalie, the skin, so soft.... "I'm Clotilde. Clotilde de Bresseau."

Well, Clotilde de Bresseau, thought Natalie, what on earth do you want with me? But it was very clear very quickly what Clotilde de Bresseau wanted with Natalie and as the evening wore on Clotilde made her desires overt. "I'm not gay, Natalie. That is to say, I'm not solely gay. I'm what you might call bi-sexual. It has always seemed such a shame to me to give up the chance of a beautiful woman for a one-dimensional guy. And let's face it, when it comes to giving any sort of pleasure beyond a rose or chocolates, most guys are one-dimensional..." 'On a good day', thought Natalie...." Do you know what I mean?"

Natalie nodded but in truth she had no idea what Clotilde meant. Natalie was beautiful but it was a beauty that had never been encouraged or fostered. It existed despite Natalie rather than because of her. She was never in situations where she was fought over or where she was "in show" because, to her, these kinds of things happened to other girls. Natalie didn't know very much about boys – there had been one, maybe two if you count a drunken fumble when she was seventeen in the woods, before Jacques – let alone anything about girls. She had never felt attraction to a girl or a woman before. She had never really felt much in the way of attraction to a man before.

Nevertheless she agreed because she wasn't sure where this conversation was going, or where they might end up, but she was thrilled from her fingernails to her toes and she desperately wanted to follow her instinct. "Oh, yes, yes, I know what you mean." She hoped she said it with enough confidence that Clotilde would believe her.

"And, as I've said Natalie, you are a very beautiful woman. So…," and she paused.

"So….," said Natalie, unsure of what she was supposed to say and do now.

"So, what do you think? What do you say? Have you done anything like this before?"

'Anything like what,' thought Natalie. 'Is she asking me on a date? Is she saying she wants to sleep with me now?'

She stumbled. She could hear her heart thumping. Clotilde must be able to hear it too. "Have I done….with, you know, a woman…" And Natalie thought – she later reflected on how strong the instinct was – if I say 'No' then maybe she won't want me anymore. Maybe I should lie. Because I want her to want me. I want to be wanted by her. I want her.

But the converse of this was feeling pressure, pressure that she couldn't have coped with. 'If I say 'yes' then she'll think I know certain things when I don't. I'm virginal, horribly virginal, and she has to know that. If she walks then she walks…'

"….No, I haven't been with a woman.." her head was down, as though she was a little ashamed. "I've really not been with many men…."

"Would you like to? Because I've had you in my thoughts for the last few weeks and they're not going to go away. I think you're gorgeous and I love the thought of us being together, our bodies being together… Listen, I have an idea. Why don't we try it and see? If, at any point, you don't like it or you don't want to be there or this is too awkward for you then you can walk away. Ok? But I really like you and I think you really like me. We could make each other happy, I'm sure. It would be a shame to not take that chance."

'Yes,' thought Natalie, 'it would.' "Ok", she said. "Ok…….um…… when?"

"Tonight?" Though Clotilde had asked a question it wasn't really a question, it was more a statement of fact. "We could go to a hotel or you could come to my flat, whatever you prefer."

Natalie knew how easy it would be to make an excuse to Jacques and to her dad. Staff were always ill or not turning up and it wouldn't be the first time she had had to cover for someone on the night shift. That would be easy. But she didn't have money to go to a hotel, she couldn't afford that. Yet to go to this woman's flat seemed a bit too much, a bit too soon. How to articulate that....

She paused. Clotilde held her hand up, as though she had been able, though the frenetic drumming of Natalie's heart and her little awkward movements, to read what had been going on inside that pretty little head.

"Don't worry, Natalie. I have money. If we go to a hotel I will pay. Honestly, it's nothing. Don't have concerns over this because I don't. Maybe we should go to a hotel…wine, some champagne…would that be nice?"

Natalie smiled and melted and her heart was normal again. But everything else on her body began to tingle as this fresh, new woman held her hand to help her up when she had no need of it, just to be closer to her. This woman smelt of freedom, of the discovery of wild and beautiful flowers that you could only see after you went deeper and deeper into the forest.

"Yes, Clotilde, I think that would be nice." She felt relaxed with this woman already, able to show her vulnerability and have it returned with an embrace. "But this is new for me…I mean I think I will be nervous……"

"Oh don't worry. Be yourself. And, as well as tasting beautiful, champagne is great for turning those nerves into something bubbly and wonderful."

And that night had been bubbly and wonderful. Any anxiety Natalie had felt was stripped away by Clotilde. She was comforting and warm and beautiful and relaxing. She made Natalie feel as though Natalie was in her own home and had done this more times then she cared to remember. Natalie was also taken to places her senses had barely dreamed of. Clotilde's touch was gentle but firm, soft but assured and her deft fingers and later, her mouth, took Natalie to breathlessness and the unrestrained shriek of what felt like a first orgasm.

It wasn't all one way. When they touched Natalie wasn't sure she wanted to kiss until she felt Clotilde's soft hand on her face and her full lips press softly against hers. Instinctively she opened her mouth and let

Clotilde inside and Clotilde's tongue danced and glided around her mouth. Still standing up, Natalie let her tongue touch Clotilde's and run around her wondrous lips. She felt a desire for the woman, a sexual desire, pulse through her and she instinctively drew her left hand round from Clotilde's back to her front, where she began to tentatively fondle Clotilde's chest. Clotilde ripped her own top off, took off her trousers and they moved to the bed. Natalie undressed as she moved towards the bed and when she lay down she was over Clotilde, kissing her and her hands were the first ones to work, disappearing inside Clotilde's knickers as she pulled down her bra and started to kiss her chest, which smelled new, like the grass after the rain and storms have gone and the sun has come out again. Clotilde was first to orgasm, a shuddering juggernaut of a bolt that shook Natalie as much as it shook Clotilde, loud and long and glorious.

Natalie wasn't really aware of the exact details from there. They were probably awake most of the night but it felt like about an hour or two. Time got lost amidst talking, champagne and what felt like orgasm after orgasm for both of them. When she left that hotel she remembered thinking to herself: 'I came in here a girl and I've gone out a woman.' She looked different. She felt different. And all over her was the scent of this woman who had reshaped her.

Things continued from there. Natalie wasn't sure if it was a relationship, an affair, a love story, what… She felt they had been very open with each other: she had told Clotilde about Jacques and Clotilde had told her that she was pretty much a free agent, looking to take whatever she could find wherever she might find it until she felt like "settling down", whatever that meant. The closeness only went so far, however, and Natalie told her nothing of the trial, or the pay off or the money involved. And when Clotilde had something else on she didn't have to explain to Natalie why she might not see her for a few days.

About a week ago, however, she had sent Natalie a message saying she had someone staying with her. An old friend. May be staying for a couple of weeks so may not be able to see you. Ok, thought Natalie, though she was immediately saddened at the thought of not seeing Clotilde for a couple of weeks. Still, she could always text or phone her and the communication, always friendly, continued between them. At the start of that week Clotilde had seemed happy, really happy, and Natalie figured that the old friend must be an old boyfriend or girlfriend, things had clicked, ok that's good for her. Then came the hassle with the car being stolen by the English guys and she didn't know what to say to Clotilde. She wanted to tell her. As well as being what you would call a lover, she had become a best friend. But she had made an agreement with her father and Jacques that they must tell no one about the money, they would have enemies everywhere if they did. So at first she didn't. But as the days moved into each other she felt the need to talk with someone about it. And over the last two or three days Clotilde had seemed less happy, her texts less frequent. I wonder if she is bored with me…

Last night she had phoned Clotilde, telling her not quite everything but that these English guys, five of them, had stolen their car. But it was strange, they were strange, they didn't seem as though they were thieves. Should I tell her what was inside, thought Natalie? Maybe had they been face to face she would have but the impersonal nature of the phone stopped her.

"They stole the car? That is odd. But your boyfriend….you said he was a big guy…didn't he stop them?"

"He couldn't, it all happened very quickly. Anyway……. Anyway, how's your friend?"

"Oh, away. He… left." Clotilde seemed very curious about the car being stolen. "And these guys were from England, were they?"

"Yes. All of them. I saw the passport of one of them. From Edinburgh….well, that's Scotland, isn't it, but it's kind of the same country."

"What?" Clotilde almost shouted down the phone.

"Yes, Edinburgh….oh shit, I can hear Jacques at the door, I have to go, talk later, bye."

It had kept Clotilde awake almost all that night. Was it Oliver? But there had been quite a few of them, Natalie had said. Where had the rest of these people come from? Were they Olly's colleagues from the office here in Nice? Impossible surely, they would have spoken French…or even if they had spoken English it would have been with a French accent. Perhaps it was a co-incidence…maybe these were four or five random guys…or maybe some folk had come over here to look for Olly. But if so how could they possibly have found him? Did they take him from my flat? Olly hadn't used his phone was he was in her flat, she had checked, so unless he got in touch with them when I was away and they got over here within the hour or so I was out – no, clearly impossible. They couldn't have come over here to look for him and got lucky….

But more to the point, Natalie now maybe had some lead on where

Oliver might be. And Clotilde knew that she still wanted him – perhaps dead if he wasn't hers, alive if he was. How might she find out if it was Oliver? Then she remembered she had taken a couple of photos – one of him lying on her bed when he wasn't looking and one less furtive one of them both at the event on the Saturday. If I send these to Natalie, perhaps she can confirm…

The message that Natalie received from Unknown Source that made her leave the room came with two attachments. She wanted to open them in private. It wouldn't be the first time that she and Clotilde had sent each other pictures of things that you wouldn't want anyone but a lover to see. Accompanying them was the message: "Was this one of these guys?" Natalie felt a little surge of disappointment. Whatever was in those images, it's safe to say there was going to be nothing of Clotilde. They took a while to open: one of a very handsome guy sitting on a bed, alone, Clotilde's bed she recognised, and the other of Clotilde and this handsome guy together at what appeared to be some very high class function. Clotilde looked stunning. As for the guy…yes, a bit more dishevelled when he was here, a bit more rundown, a bit more nervous but absolutely, yes, the same guy.

"Yes," she texted back. "He was one of them. But I don't understand. You know this guy who stole our car?"

"Yes. It's a long story. Do you know where he is now?"

"No. Jacques and my dad want to try and catch them. I don't think it's a good idea."

"To catch them for stealing a car? You said it wasn't worth much anyway."

"No. Why would your friend want to steal our car?"

"He – they – may have been in trouble. Maybe he felt he had no choice. Who were the others that were with him?"

Ok, so maybe Jacques and her dad were right. Maybe they needed the money and had known about the car all along. How? Well, who knows… "I don't know. Just three of four other guys. Your guy was quiet. Is he a boyfriend?"

"It's a long story. But I would very much like to know where he is. There are things unresolved between us. Things that don't affect you and I but which still need a resolution. Can you keep me informed?"

"Yes. What will you do?"

"Find him. Edinburgh or France, I don't care. But find him."

"Ok." Natalie was taken aback, and not just a little hurt, by Clotilde's

293

apparent need and desire for someone else. Clotilde's next text was warmer. "It's ok Natalie. There is much between me and this guy that we have to work out. But I need you and I want you. Find a way to get here tonight if you can."

That would prove to be difficult as they were planning to leave that night. She tried to talk with Jacques and her father but there was no talking them round from their plan to leave as soon as possible. Natalie then asked if she couldn't stay here, they didn't really need her did they... but a fierce scowl from each of them was all it took to send Natalie scuttling to prepare a suitcase.

Clotilde sat in her bedroom, staring around the white walls, pensive. This was dangerous. It would be dangerous for Natalie and her assortment of relatives too but Clotilde was not going to tell her friend about the Mob being after Oliver. They would have to take their chances there. But to give chase on Oliver, when he clearly hadn't chosen to stay with her, when he was being hunted by people that could find anyone wherever in the world they might try to hide, that was dangerous. He has already rejected me. And if I get caught up with the Mob I can't imagine their head guy is going to be quite so friendly next time. But, she thought, I still have a few cards. I can sit down with Olly in front of his wife and dare him to deny what has passed between us. I can describe the way he makes love, the way he feels inside me, the things that he can't resist, the manner in which he touches, even the way he sometimes can't catch his breath when he's kissing and has to pause and his wife will know, for all his denials, that he was mine. And he can be again.

She looked down at the bed where she had made love to him and ran her hands over his side of the bed. 'Now,' she thought, 'how should I get to Edinburgh? Should I get a plane or should I drive like the rest of the world appears to be doing?'

The train journey seemed to take an age. This was due in part to delays, a slow service and the need of the friends to feel that they were home and safe. Oliver was the one who spent more of the time bringing Ellis back to something like his normal self. But it hadn't been easy and Ellis's face suddenly had looked different to him. When he wasn't smiling his face looked burdened and sad and old before it should have been. And grey.

After a brief conversation they had agreed to keep communication with home to a minimum until, at least, they had reached St Pancras.

Communication may be easy to spot from a train and Oliver had a concern about how much watch was being kept on their relatives. All of their relatives, not only Helen, who he knew was being watched. So, without wanting to alarm his friends that their spouses may be in danger, Oliver managed to persuade them to wait to send texts or phone.

Aidan had managed to get hold of a newspaper, a tabloid, but still the first chance that any of them had really had to catch up with anything that had happened back home for a few days. An almost post-coital tristesse had subsumed them and that, with its accompanying silence, made Aidan quite keen to change the subject to something that could distract them.

"See that politician," he started. "Playing about with some young girl, she's only seventeen but there's a picture of her there, look...," and he opened the paper to show them all, "....but she doesn't look seventeen, she looks about twenty seven and look at her. Sex on legs."

He continued to read the story and narrate the best bits to his friends almost at the same time. "Well, it seems he got involved with her at some function, oh it was his daughter's eighteenth birthday party... this girl he got involved with is the daughter of one of his best friends apparently...and one of his own daughter's best friends....this gets better and better. They got involved and got caught, literally, in the bushes. But from what it says here no one grassed them up at that stage. So he managed to carry on this affair for some time....he said he was giving her help with her homework, from what it says here... maybe with Romeo and Juliet, though he's not done very well at taming the shrew..."

He laughed. "It says here that he 'used to eat ice cream with her when they were doing her homework then liked to have her put the ice cream on her breasts so he could lick it off'..."

Oliver was the first to react. "Really? What flavour?"

"It doesn't seem to say... I'd guess vanilla, he seems a boring sod just looking at him. But can you imagine that, ice cream... on your body... that's got to freeze! Where's the pleasure in that?"

He looked around his friends. Euan and Ellis looked down with a tinge of embarrassment on their faces. "What?" said Aidan. "Do you smother your women in ice cream?"

"She's occasionally put ice cream on me," offered Euan. "You know, down there..."

"Ice cream on your dick? Fuck! I'd jump through the roof! And that's nice? You like that?"

"Hey," said Ellis, "don't knock it till you've tried it. I've played around with food a bit. Can be quite nice together. Food and sex, two essentials really, your main ingredients of life. Having them together is good."

Aidan looked at Olly. "Fuck a dee doo dah! What do you think?"

Oliver looked puzzled. "Food…eating food off a woman…or her eating food from you. That's weird. That's seriously weird. There have been some women I'd like to eat – but that's a different thing, isn't it? As for ice cream on your dick – that's sub bloody human. That's almost a torture!"

"Anyway…," Aidan continued, "as you can imagine his wife found out about this cozy little arrangement and was none too happy. I think the seventeen year old told her which is even better. It says that… they've got an interview here with a friend of the wife apparently…"

"That means it's made up shite," said Ali. "Trust me."

"Yeah," said Euan, "but who cares? It's going to titillate and it's going to sell and everyone will believe it because it's in black and white. So what does she say, this friend?"

"Well," said Aidan, "it says that this friend said that he and his wife had a storming argument and she booted him out…but when she was out he got the locks changed and she was left knocking at the door. Neighbours noticed the situation. Then it got increasingly petty… "

"*Then* it got petty," said Oliver. "Seems to be at the 'petty' stage already."

"She left very abusive messages on his phone, he stopped the insurance on her car so she couldn't drive, she destroyed most of his clothes when she did get back into the house, he cut the heels off her shoes and…oh, you beauty, according to this friend 'he defecated in her training shoes so she couldn't even go the gym anymore.' What a guy!"

"Wonder if it was in the left one or the right one……either way, must have taken a bit of balance…poise….accuracy…"

"Olly! You're not going to tell us you've done that before? That's a step way beyond the ice cream challenge."

"No, just thinking it through…"

Ali said. "It's a pity, though, because that's the way he's going to be remembered from now on. I've not worked for a tabloid but when they say 'a friend' or 'a friend of a friend'….you're on dodgy ground, you know? It's probably a lie. And that guy…I thought he was ok. As politicians go, he was pretty good. He did a good job in the Middle East, he seemed to genuinely bring folk together there and the social stuff that he did here was pretty good too. Bank reform, benefit reform, the way he got Unions on board. I thought he was a pretty good politician. Rare, nowadays. But when people hear his name now, all you'll think of is this guy who shit in his wife's shoes."

Ali hadn't meant it as a joke but his friends almost exploded in laughter. Euan was the first to speak. "God, that's funny.' What did you do today? Well, I solved the Middle East peace crisis. And what are you going to do tomorrow? Take a dump in my wife's shoes then eat ice cream and jelly off a seventeen year old's mammoth breasts.'" And they laughed again.

"How are the mighty fallen," said Oliver, more to himself than anyone else. He looked out of the window. "We are not far away. It can only be a few minutes before we get in."

They were silent, each individually sensing that the train station was a place of unease, perhaps even danger, for them.

"I've got an idea about what we should do here," said Oliver. "See if you agree. I think that you, Ellis, and someone else should get the car. You say it's where... parked in a car park somewhere..."

"Yeah, it's in the Renaissance hotel car park, across from the station. Dead easy to find, so I've been told."

"Ok, well I think you and someone else should get the car and the other three of us can get food from here and meet you. Should we meet you on the car park or on a road?"

"There's a road called Midland Road that the hotel seems to be on. You can't miss it. It's the main road. We can meet there, across from the hotel. I might not be able to wait on that road, I might need to drive about a bit so wait if I'm not there."

"Ok," said Oliver. "I think that's better than the five of us going to the hotel, I think that looks....conspicuous. And anyway, this way will be quicker. I don't think I'll feel safe until we're out of here and well on our way."

"I think we're safe," said Ellis. "If they were going to get us, it would have been in France."

"Maybe," said Oliver but he didn't really believe himself. "Ok, so," he said as the train came to a halt. "Euan, you go with Ellis. Ali, Aidan and I will go get some food and drink to keep us going on the journey up."

As they got out the train Ellis and Euan were at the front with the other three behind. As they started to walk Aidan realised his shoelace

297

was undone and bent down to tie it. Ellis and Euan walked on, oblivious to the fact that their friends were now quite a bit behind them. Not that it would have seemed to be significant to them anyway. Oliver stretched as Aidan tied his shoelace, taking the opportunity to look around himself to see if there was any obvious imminent threat. He couldn't see anything or anyone that was an overt enemy but when you are anticipating that danger might come from anywhere then you suspect everything and anything, everyone and anyone, from the old man with the crumpled hat and the Zimmer frame to the young girl with the large rucksack and the loose fleece. From the boy and girl holding hands and laughing to the two women walking together. But looking around him, in front, to the sides, Oliver felt as safe and out of danger as he could allow himself to feel.

The two men had been on a carriage that was about three or four behind the one Oliver and his friends had been on. As soon as they descended from the train they were in radio contact with the spotter who was sitting somewhere up above, watching as people started to walk from the train into the terminal.

"Ok, we can see your man. He is still with his friends. There are a lot of people there so wait. Wait until they get closer to the main concourse. You can take them there."

"And there are five of them?"

"As far as I can see. Slow down, slow down a bit, one of them seems to have stopped, go slowly, you don't want to end up in front of them."

The two men slowed down. They had rehearsed on the train what they would do, it was relatively simple. One of them would cover the guy on the left-most side, the other would cover the guy on the right-most side, they would make their guns visible and bundle the guys back on the train for Paris. Someone else would take over when they got to Paris and there would be additional presence on the train to help them. No force should be required, the five guys were to be returned unharmed. It was made clear to them, however, that the main one was the one called Oliver and they were given a few recent photos to ensure that they got the right guy. Even if the others escaped – which would be very much frowned upon – but even if they escaped, they had been told in no uncertain terms that if they came back to Paris without Oliver, they'd be sent to exile in Corsica or given a similar 'reward'.

"Ok," said the spotter. "Getting to the main concourse......getting there....not long...are you ready?"

"Yes. Can you see them?"

"It's busy, still busy, but I can see the main guy, he's there alright. There's a big crowd. Be subtle. Gun to the side and a whisper in the ear rather than a shout. Don't make a scene. I can't see any police but they will be about, I'm sure. I haven't been told that they will turn a blind eye so we have to assume that they won't. Ok, nearly, nearly...."

The two men moved forward, advancing through the people making their way to the concourse. They brushed past those in front of them with indifference, knocking and bumping and raising the odd frown. They both moved with one purpose alone. Until, as they passed the first carriage and came to the main concourse, they could see Oliver in front of them. His four friends in front of him. Now the crowd began to thin, just a little, but enough to give the two men enough space to make their move. They exchanged nods. One moved to his left and other to his right so they were walking alongside Oliver, Ali and Aidan. It was only as one of the men covertly drew his gun that he realised there were only three of them, not five as he had been told. But with the gun drawn he felt he had passed the point of no return and pressed it softly into Ali as his friend did to Aidan on the other side.

One of the men spoke as they walked, in a gruff voice that was loud enough for everyone to hear.

"There are guns pressed against you. We have been instructed to use them if you present us with any difficulties. We are happy to use them in a public place such as this. Have no illusions, you are going back to France. Alive or dead. Nod your head gently if you understand this."

All three of them nodded. The two men exchanged glances. One looked at the other with quite desperate, enquiring eyes and mouthed 'Five?'

The other one nodded. "We know that there are five of you altogether. Where are the other two? Answer briefly, please, and let us continue to walk slowly."

Oliver spoke. His thoughts came quickly, as they had to. Perhaps because they came quickly much of what rushed through his mind was unstructured stream of consciousness rubbish that he couldn't use. But amidst that he knew that their only hope lay in the car. If they could get to a situation where Ellis and Euan could see them with these guys, and Ellis and Euan were in the car, maybe that could be used to their advantage. So there would have to be an element of surprise, these guys who were marching them back to Paris couldn't know there was a car waiting.

Olly thought about denying it at first, saying there were only three of them, to give him a bit more thinking time. But it would be obvious to everyone in this organisation or Mob or whatever that was after them that there were five of them. Oliver spoke slowly. "They had to get something at a hotel nearby. We're going to get food. And then we're going to meet them on a road outside to get a taxi altogether. We were going to get a train from another station in London."

"Where are you meeting them?"

"Outside. On a road outside of this station."

"Which road?"

"Midland."

This had bought Oliver a bit of time to try and think of an answer to the question he knew they were going to ask him. It was the guy on the other side who asked it and Oliver pretended he didn't hear at first to allow himself to breath a bit more.

"I said, 'What was it that your friends needed to pick up at the hotel'?"

"A mobile phone. We thought that our calls were being monitored. So our friend borrowed someone's phone on the train and asked one of his friends here to leave a phone for him at the hotel at the station. That way we thought we might communicate with our families without wondering if you and the rest of the French underworld were listening in."

"Your families are being monitored."

Oliver didn't say anything. Ali and Aidan looked shocked, as though a fresh horror had entered their heads for the first time. Oliver thought that engaging them in conversation might be a good thing: maybe they would find out something they didn't know or would get an idea of the trouble they might face if they managed to get themselves out of this situation.

"Are you monitoring our families? Really? You know this, do you?"

Neither of the two men said anything.

Oliver tried again. "When you take us back to Paris, is that where we are supposed to stay? Or are you taking us anywhere else?"

The two men said nothing, instead keeping themselves focused on where they were being led. They both had become conscious that Oliver had slowed his walk, especially when he asked a question.

"You'll find out soon enough. Keep walking. Keep moving to the place where you are going to meet the other two."

Oliver quickened slightly. "Do you know what it is we are supposed to have done?"

The one on the right answered. "We don't know. We don't care. We are told to do something. We do it. We get paid. We get well paid."

"So… if it's about money then you'd take some more money than you're being paid to let us go?"

"No."

"No?"

"No."

"Why not?"

"We let you go we get punished. We get no more work. You're going where you're going. If you don't know what you've done then you talk about it with someone if you behave well enough to get back to Paris in one piece."

They continued, out into the bright sunshine, into the same day that they had left behind in Paris a few hours ago. Oliver knew they had to go to the rendezvous place. The two men were close enough on each side of Ali and Aidan to shoot them. They couldn't even think of trying to run away, it would have been impossible. They were now in a wide open space and Oliver could not see where a distraction would come from. They would have to rely on Ellis and Euan and Oliver thought, as they moved towards crossing the road, that he didn't know at all what he might do in the same situation if he was in their shoes. Would Ellis and Euan even know that there was something wrong?

Fortunately for Oliver and his friends, Euan and Ellis realised very quickly that something was wrong because they saw the three friends cross the road with a man on either side of them. It was obvious to Euan and Ellis immediately that these men represented danger – they held their hands tight in their pockets, holding onto something, they were studying the three men they were walking beside and not the road in front of them and one was talking into what looked like his wrist. Euan saw them first, the shifty uneasy gait of discomfort written across both of them.

"Fuck!" he exclaimed, "Can you see, Ellis? Two guys have got them, look."

Ellis looked. "Yes, I see. I wonder what has been said……Let's drive up the road a bit, give ourselves time to think, then we can double back and turn around…"

"Ok. I think the guys must have told them where we were going to meet….so they must want all of us or else they would have taken Olly…"

"Yes. Why not only take Olly, you're right……so they're coming for all of us… wonder if these guys know we'll be in a car…what did Olly and the others tell these guys, do you think?"

"Well," said Ellis, "even if they know we are going to meet them in a car, they don't know which car exactly. Unless they can read the texts from my phone but let's assume they can't. So we at least have that on our side. They don't know which car. Ok, so, what can we do, what can we do…."

Euan thought for a minute. "Don't stop the car. If we stop the car then we lose any advantage we have. Our only chance is to try and go for one of the guys and hope that in the confusion Olly and the guys can clock the other one. Think of it. Did you see how these guys were walking Olly, Aidan and Ali? One was on one side, one was on the other… like they were trying to circle them. So maybe one of them will be on one side, one of them on the other… our only hope is to drive and try and get on the pavement and hit one…."

"It looks like they have guns," said Ellis. What's to stop them shooting us?"

"Nothing," said Euan. "But….if we can get behind another car, or better a truck or a bus so they don't see us until the last second, they won't know it's us until we get on the pavement. And we'll see them as we drive past them on the other side of the road. We'll see if one of the Mob or whatever they are is on the outside, if we'd hit one of them first."

"Either that," said Ellis, "or we throw something at them."

"Yeah," said Euan, "I thought of that…but what? Even then, we'd pretty much have to knock them out. No, let's drive down, turn at the bottom or as near as then wait for a bus or a van to get behind."

They went down the road, passing their friends and the captors, watching them closely as they drove, recognising that, as expected, one of the captors was on the outside and would be first to be hit. They also noticed how close all five of them were standing to the edge.

At the bottom of the road they turned and waited for a large vehicle to appear, something which they could follow. Both recognised the disadvantage of staying hidden was that they could not see their friends or what was happening, if anyone had changed where they were standing or if they had moved further up the road, but they realised they simply had to take that chance.

A large lorry appeared, trundling slowly, and Ellis, despite the traffic following it, managed to pull in right behind. Its lack of speed was a blessing as it almost meandered up the busy road, its engine revving and noisy. Ellis stayed as tight to it as he could, anxious that he should not be seen. 'It must be soon,' he thought, looking only to his left, touching the brake now and then to stop himself hitting the monolith in front of him.

"Coming up," said Euan, who had climbed into the back of the car and sat on the left to give himself a better and closer view. "You need to veer quickly in about four seconds...."

"Now!" Ellis veered when told. He increased the speed of the car to get it over the edge of the pavement and to try and take out the first guy. He had to be neutralised and he had to remain neutralised. The car revved and bumped over the pavement. Ellis kept his focus on the five men. He steered the car straight at the man who was only a few feet away from him. The man had little or no time to react and Ellis could see his startled face as the car hit his body. Instinctively the man had drawn his gun and as the car ploughed into him his gun went up in the air and landed away from the man as he fell to the ground.

A few things then happened at the same time. Euan threw open his door to find the gun that had been thrown into the air. As he did so he saw the man who had been hit, lying on the ground, trying to get up. It was clear that the man was shocked and dazed but probably not badly hurt. However, he was vulnerable and Euan threw a punch which knocked the man down again and kicked him in the stomach as he fell. Euan couldn't recall punching anyone in his life before and his hand seared with pain. He saw the gun lying nearby and quickly picked it up, holding it at the man who was lying down. But he was now simply moaning and seemed to be no threat.

Euan looked across at the others. Olly and Ali had struck at the other man as the car had driven into the first one and the other man was knocked onto the ground. He too had attempted to reach for his gun but had only managed to get his hand on it before Oliver was down on top of him and Ali had thrust his knees onto the guy's arm until he was forced to let go. Ali now held the gun, the first time in his life he had held a firearm. He waved it around, first to his left where he saw Euan pointing one towards the other man who was lying on the ground, then to the guy who they had attacked.

Ellis had also sprung out of the car and, seeing activity on both sides of him, didn't know where to go or what to do first. But he quickly realised that his friends had overcome their adversaries, except for Aidan who seemed to stand in the middle of it all, almost in tears thought Ellis.

Olly hammered away at the man beneath him, a man whose power to resist had been taken away from him with the force of the surprise of the car ramming into his colleague. When he felt his gun being taken from him he knew that his only chance of remaining alive was to keep resistance to a minimum. Oliver had no desire to kill the man but there was more than a desire to remain safe in the punches that he threw at the increasingly helpless form beneath him. In the man that he was hitting, Oliver saw whoever was after him, whoever was insane enough to set dogs on him and try to drown him, whoever was evil enough to hunt him across France and back into the UK. Every punch that Oliver sank into the man was a punch against The Capo. They got harder and fiercer as the fear that Oliver had felt over the last week externalised itself. He spoke between batterings.

This"… hammer… "is"…….that must be his nose broken…."for… your….fucking…….cunt … of…a….boss… … .Tell… him……to…… leave……us… the….fuck… alone……"

The man beneath him was now a mess of blood and spit. Ellis ran across and hauled Oliver off.

"For Christ's sake, Olly! How much trouble will we be in if we kill these guys? Leave him the fuck alone."

Oliver was trembling, his voice quivering as he screamed at the man below him. "You fuck off! Leave us alone! This is done now!" He physically shook and Ellis put his arms around Oliver, anxious that they were going to be seen. They had been lucky, Ellis quickly recognised, because the car on the pavement had pretty much hidden what had taken place. It had all happened very quickly but even so, soon someone would stop and they had to be away before that.

Oliver seemed to be weeping and shouting and grunting all at the same time, as if every emotion that he had felt over the last week had no dam to prevent it avalanching out. His rage and fear and terror spewed forth as Ellis bundled him into the car. His hands shook, his eyes were wild and distant and full of the primordial that can only possess when you have been taken past your limit.

"Hold him," Ellis said to Ali. "Hold him and make sure he breathes."

Ellis started the car. He looked to his left. Both men were still very much alive but in very different states. One of them almost scratched his fuzzied head, looking at the car and still wondering what had happened.

The other tried to sit up but it was clear his head spun. Blood covered his face. Ellis reversed the car as soon as he could see a break in the traffic then sped off up the road. By the time the men were out of Ellis' view in his rear mirror no one had stopped for them. Therefore no one could have seen the registration number. Could the men themselves have seen it? Possibly, but it was all so sudden…who knows?

One thing Ellis certainly knew, as he sped off, was that this was not the end. To do what they had done, to the kind of people they had done it to…they had probably now truly awakened a monster. 'We should have taken a gun…we should have taken their guns,' he thought. But beyond an air rifle in their teenage years none of them had touched a firearm and the thought was chilling and appalling.

He looked at the seat behind him. Oliver was now quivering as opposed to shaking, sobbing as opposed to giving voice to those hideous guttural ululations. He wondered if each of them had what it took to get home. Emotionally, physically……both the mental and physical strength to get home. They were only about 400 miles away, it was a day's drive, but Ellis knew that it was a distance which would get farther as it got nearer, much in the same way that a dolly zoom shot would destabilise your perception of what might be in the foreground and what would be in the background. And the distance they had to cover scared Ellis in much the same way as the vertigo might, except he saw danger as not above or below but potentially all around. This would be a journey where they would have to have heads spinning at 360 degrees, constantly. He felt his head dizzy already, dizzy and numb and sore. He wanted to see Yvonne and the girls. He tried to see them, to find them in his mind's eye. But what he couldn't shake from his head was the vision of himself back in Nice, lying in some abandoned warehouse, kicked and shot like a dog by some hired hood. As though he had meant nothing to anyone. Whose body would be thrown away or maybe left there. Just like a dog.

CHAPTER 15

Sitting alone, away from Helen with a little apprehension still more at the forefront of his mind than he would have liked, Ambrose began to think of what he could – what he should – do next. He was wary of turning up at the door, a travelling salesman or a researcher or someone who needed to use the phone…….he might be seen forcing his way in. There might be someone else in the house, her kid might have had friends in, anything really could go wrong. But he craved her as one would crave the next hit, though in his case the hit remained literal rather than figurative.

It was something he never questioned. The instinct, or the need, or the force as he thought of it, was too strong to question. It could therefore not, or ever, be wrong. He knew that he should say it was wrong, when you were in company for example and the conversation might turn to force or sexual violence as it could do occasionally, but these were things people said to put a polite veneer on their impulses. Things we say to reflect the kind of society we think we live in. To convince ourselves and others we have moved away from instinct to the logic and rationality of reason. Things like not being stereotypical, treating everyone the same, pretending men and women could do the same jobs for the same money…all things, believed Ambrose, that we say in public but which we know in private are nonsense. How had it come to this? Where we ran a society based on some nonsensical ideal where the least common denominator had become the most valued? The whole thing was based on catering for minority interest. Desire is natural, God-given even, and the strength of desire is a vindication of God's will or the way it should be. The feeling he got when he thought of Helen's body beneath him, grasping and pulling at her hair as he became one with her, feeling the force of his hand on her face and his teeth on her nipples, that feeling was a natural God-given high that had to be exercised. Nature is this way. We can hide and pretend we are something that we are not but it will out and his desire for Helen was never likely to have been abated by Jackie or a hundred Jackies. Like a few stones in a stream, other women might make him channel his desires off to the side in a slightly different direction for a part of the journey but he was always destined to flow straight to her and into her, relentless and sweeping and engulfing.

Then he had had an idea. Something to lure her out, bring her to somewhere where there might only be two of them, where she could be overpowered there and then or bundled into a car and threatened till she went with him. He knew what she did and where she did it and the basics of what her work involved and so sent a letter, from the Scottish Qualifications Agency, requesting that she be part of a think tank on curriculum and syllabus design for her area. The remit was to try and ensure that the design of school material at the higher level reflected the skills, attributes and knowledge that Universities would expect from a student entering first year. Sitting alone, killing time as he was doing, it was no problem for Ambrose to find official logos, letterheads though getting what appeared to be a valid e-mail address required a bit of help from an ex-colleague whose past was so murky that he could not afford to ask questions. The letter was sent off, highlighting a place where they should meet (six of them, a working lunch at a Chinese buffet restaurant that Ambrose knew was closed on the detailed day) and asking for confirmation by e-mail. Short notice apologised for, it was next week, but would really appreciate the input from professionals such as yourselves. If she said 'No,' then...well....she said No and maybe he would have to be more direct. But if she turned up... she could be threatened and thrown into his car or there was an alleyway nearby.

She said 'Yes'. She would attend. Less than a week away. Less than a week to wait. The thrill went through him to such an extent that he fantasised about another Jackie before Helen, a warm-up kind of thing, something to keep the hunger at bay. But that might cause complications and the route of self-pleasure would exorcise today's ghost in a much more clinical manner.

Davide was surprised at The Capo's reaction. Surprised because The Capo was very calm, almost as if he had expected something like this. He didn't pace the room or run his fingers through his hair. No signs of agitation, no "tell". Davide thought that, yes, probably, it was a smile that had crossed his boss' lips. It didn't look like a sarcastic one either.

"What do you think, Davide? Should I accept that I am beaten? Beaten by a guy I don't care much for? Who's probably done nothing wrong? Who we've probably frightened the life out of over the past couple of days.... Should I just let the poor bugger go?"

Davide was confused. His position was to make things happen. He wasn't a consigliere. Was The Capo testing him? He wasn't used to questions which weren't rhetorical. And that was a problem because he wasn't sure if these questions were supposed to be rhetorical…or were genuine questions to which his boss was seeking a considered response.

"Yes boss. I mean…I don't know, boss."

"No. You don't know. Neither do I." He picked up an apple from the table and sat down. He stretched his feet onto the table and began tossing the apple in the air, catching it every time. He spoke as he continued this action. "You see, the people we normally involve ourselves with… they're like us… they're not very nice people. Most of them… are horrible. They're fucking criminals. Now this guy……he's a decent sort…he's shagging away down here….when he's on business… but so what….he's married but it's not exactly a crime……indeed, it's compulsory practice… he gets into this argument…makes a mistake……escapes from here, escapes from the twins… now it seems he's given our boys waiting for him in London the slip… you have to admire him, don't you?" He caught the apple suddenly and looked across at Davide for an answer.

"Yes boss."

He stood up. "Yes boss….well, maybe you're right. But he's a challenge now, a real challenge. Because all I know is that he's driving in the UK, probably headed back to Edinburgh, in a black car. These lunatics we hired didn't even manage to recognise that each car has a registration number, which makes them easier to find for someone like me. I mean, he's really going to stand out, isn't it? The whole bloody country is black over there, they never see the sun. And it's his home, not mine. Which makes things a little more difficult for me. But we're not going to go to America this week anyway and I'd quite like to meet this guy so let's put out feelers in the police over there. Oh, and could you bring Ms de Bressau back in here – minimum force Davide. I need to know if she's been back in contact with him and given the failure of our 'professionals'" … it was laced with sarcasm…. "she's about the only lead we've got."

However, Davide found Ms de Bressau impossible to find. She wasn't at work and Davide's contact there had said she had taken a few days holiday and said she was going to stay at home. Maybe she was a bit down with the English guy leaving. But when he went to her house she wasn't there and the house was that well-structured tidy way that people leave it before they go on holiday or are away for a few days. Davide rummaged about a bit until he found what he wanted – her medium size suitcase was no longer there, there was less underwear in her drawer than there had been a few days ago and most of the toiletries in her bathroom were away. Ms de Bressau's car was not to be found anywhere near her flat nor was it in any airport car park. Wherever she's gone, he thought, she's going by car and it isn't a simple overnighter.

This time, The Capo reacted in exactly the way Davide expected. Not angry, or upset, or at all questioning of Davide's competence or of his contact network to know where she was going. It was still a free country, sort of. "Intriguing," said The Capo. "I wonder if she is following her star, wherever it might lead her?"

"Maybe she is away on holiday," Davide offered.

"No, Davide. People going on holiday tell people where they are going. This girl has told no one anything that we know of. She's disappeared. She's probably wanted to disappear. I wouldn't bet on anything that I don't know the outcome of and that's why I would wager a few Euros that she's journeying to Edinburgh. But that's strange...."

"It is? If this guy is from Edinburgh..."

"Oh, that's not what's strange. It's strange she's taking the car. She can fly from here. If her car isn't anywhere here...."

"We would have found it by now. Cameras, police observations... we would have found the car if it was in Nice."

"Well then, Ms de Bressau... why drive? Unless...unless... ah fuck it, who cares? But it may be that we need to get ourselves to Edinburgh to meet this guy...and probably his wife and lover as well...Make sure the plane is ready to go and that we have a pilot on standby, just in case. And hire someone to kill those two fucking idiots who screwed up in London. Make sure that the ones you hire this time are more competent than the clowns you hired the last time."

Davide didn't respond at first. Then he added: "We have something on our side, boss."

"Which is....what?"

"One of our sources....the source has actually come through another source and not to me directly....but this source is someone quite close to this guy Oliver."

"Really?"

"Yeah, look," and he passed his phone to The Capo. The message read : "My contact told me that they will keep us informed. The contact says they are at least partly aware of the movements of this guy Oliver. Probably his friends too."

"What's his name? The source, not the guy who sent you this message."

"We have always made this anonymous. Our people – our sleepers abroad– go by false names too. Your request. Remember?"

"Ok…but get back in touch with this guy and tell him to put pressure on his source. I don't want to fly across to Edinburgh and find out that this Oliver is halfway to Mongolia… "

Ellis was driving and had chosen the A1 to go north. Oliver was calm now…tired, drained but calm overall.

The events had passed Aidan by as though they had been happening in a dream. Someone else's dream. He had felt rooted. His body hadn't told him to move, his actions and senses had been dulled and he realised now that all it might have taken was a stray shot and he would have been unable to get out the way. Leadened and heavy whilst his friends had moved with the speed of a spark. He said to no one in particular: "What do you think these guys meant? Do you think they are watching our families? They can't even know who we are, surely? That must have been a lie?"

Ali responded. "Listen, we booked flights. We went through customs. Can't be difficult for people like that to find out who's come in, who's gone out, who's on what flight……It didn't sound like an idle boast when he was telling us, it sounded very….matter-of-fact, business-like."

Oliver had to phone Helen. Even if there was a risk, even if she went to her parents' or next door, he had to phone her. Without causing concern or fear…

Helen heard her mobile phone ring and she ran to it. Olly.

"Olly? Olly? Where are you?"

"Helen? Oh it's you! God, it's good to hear your voice." He paused, almost as though he couldn't believe she was really there, alive, at the other end of the phone. "We're in England. We crossed this morning, we're journeying up today, we should be home later today". Even as he said it, however, he wasn't entirely convinced that they would be.

"Oh thank God!" she almost sobbed.

"How are you? How is Terrence?"

"We are fine, both fine. He keeps asking where you are, wasn't it today you said daddy was coming home and I have to keep making an excuse because that's what I thought too. What's kept you, what's happened? Has someone been after you?"

Oliver was suddenly silenced, as though a guilty secret had been exposed. "Em, no, no, no one's after us. Not that we know of anyway. It's been difficult...we had a car breakdown, punctures...they're not exactly helpful where we were and without a spare tyre or a garage nearby...it was difficult, it's been very difficult...," and he paused, fearing his emotion may overpower him.

"How do you have a car now? You're in a car now, I can hear it, aren't you? How did you hire a car on a Sunday?"

"Oh, it's not a hire, we haven't hired a car... " and he paused, not quite sure whether he should tell her the truth. It sounds suspicious, even to me he thought.

"So...what, how have you got one, have you stolen it?"

He laughed, an embarrassed laugh. "No, no, not stolen. Ellis managed to borrow one from a friend of his."

"Borrow? You've borrowed a car?"

"Well, his friends are loaded, they're not going to miss a car....how are you, what's been happening?" He really wanted to ask – 'Do you still think you are being spied on?'

"Oh, not so much. The police were here again...em, asking about Jenny, remember I told you she was attacked....well now they're trying to dig into her private life and see if there's any motive there...going to try and talk to some students maybe...they don't think she was mistaken for me anymore so that's good.." 'I wouldn't be so sure,' thought Oliver.

"You said before, you remember, there was maybe somebody, someone watching...are they still there? Is the house still being watched?"

"I don't know. I haven't seen anyone in the last few days, not the guy I saw before. But I'm starting to wonder, maybe...if no one is after you and that guy attacked Jenny and didn't mistake her for me....maybe that other guy wasn't watching the house at all. Maybe I just thought he was, maybe I over reacted." Oliver didn't believe it for a minute but he would much rather Helen felt safe than frightened, whatever the reality might be. And the reality for him, horrible to imagine, was that the house was going to be watched much more intensely than it had been before and Helen could be taken at any time.

"Well," said Oliver, "it would have been a very natural reaction to have. And I'm sure you're right. We are almost home now. This guy that I hit, maybe blinded, he's got friends but I'm sure they're not going to come across the Channel after us. We're safe now." He didn't believe it and the way his friends looked at him made it clear that they didn't believe it but Helen accepted it with a deep sigh.

"I know," she said, choking back tears. "I know. But I won't feel you're truly safe until you're all back here. How are the others?" she asked, almost as an after-thought.

"Oh fine, fine, everyone's fine. They're all still here, in one piece…" He wanted to say something ordinary, some phatic communication that people have when they are far away and distant from each other. "What will you do today?"

"Something with Terry, whatever he wants to do. Then I need to do some work and some preparation for this syllabus seminar thing…."

"What syllabus seminar thing?"

"I heard about it a day or so ago. Said I'd take part. They want a think tank, maybe 5 or 6 people, to talk about how we might have input into Higher, Advanced Higher syllabus… "

Oliver interrupted. "When's that?"

"Tuesday."

"When did you find out about it?"

"A day or so ago. Letter said it was last minute kind of thing to involve the Uni academics… ."

Perhaps it was Oliver's too heightened sense, perhaps it was the over-reaction born of the experiences of the last few days, but this did not sound right. It did not sound right at all. Then again, it was Tuesday. Surely to God they would be home by Tuesday.

"Who else had been asked? Anyone you know?"

"No……I mean I don't know….why?"

"It sounds….odd. You always tell me that things move very slowly in your world yet here is this thing…within a week of getting the letter… .it's odd, don't you think it's odd?"

"Well…I didn't think anything….I suppose it is a bit quick. But then…what is it? If it's not an invitation to a think tank group then what is it? What's the point of the letter?"

The thoughts raced through Oliver's mind. 'To get you on your own, take you away…abduct, kidnap…if they took you in the morning then we wouldn't know they had taken you till the end of the day…you wouldn't be registered missing for a whole day…oh, clever….this isn't going to stop even when I'm home….it's going to go on and on and on until they eventually get me or my family..' Eventually he said – "I don't know. I don't know. But it sounds strange."

"But it can't be suspicious! You've said this mess is all over."

"Yes." Without conviction. "Still, it would do no harm to find out a bit more about it. See if any of your colleagues were asked. And phone the organisation – not the number on the letter you've got but at their main number, ask to be put through to who's dealing with this event…"

"It's Sunday, they won't be in. Olly, you're scaring me…"

"Let's be sure Helen. Let's be sure. No harm in being sure. And we'll discover I'm being stupid and that's fine. No harm done. It'll only be a couple of phone calls."

"You don't want me to go, do you?"

"It's not that at all. I….it sounds a bit suspicious, that's all."

"Suspicious… maybe, ok, I'll check, I'll check, ok? Christ Olly, the whole thing has been suspicious…you away, not getting home, blinding someone…you've never hit anyone Olly, how did you suddenly blind someone? This has all been unreal." Her tone was heavy and her voice betrayed her. She did not understand. She could not understand. Two weeks ago everything was normal now she had been made to feel frightened about a letter.

Oliver sighed. "I know. I understand. When I get home…"… 'if you ever get home, she thought..'…."when I get home we shall talk about it and everything will be peaceful again. I promise you."

Peaceful. Helen thought many things when she thought of Olly but when she heard that word it sounded as jarred and awkward as metal on metal. Peaceful……have things ever been peaceful? Glorious, at times wondrously glorious, at times desperate, a few regrets, much excitement…but peaceful? The word swirled around her head as she agreed with Olly – what was the point disputing a mere word when she felt she understood so little of him – and put the phone down.

Helen sank into the chair. She wondered, in a frighteningly rational and logical way, how much more of this she might be able to take. She didn't feel emotional and was certain that her blood pressure would have been 'normal'. But there must be a limit to this – a limit to expecting him home and him not coming home, a limit to being able to accept that there had been punctures and breakdowns, a limit to feeling yourself in danger in every sphere of your life, at work, at home, in bed, in the shower, on the phone… . There must be a point at which your mind said that it won't deal with all this and, in the interests of self-preservation, goes mad or something. Just shuts down. Like your body gets rids of toxins by being sick, your mind must do something similar to get rid of toxins. She wondered what would happen to her. Because even though Olly was now in the country, this felt far from over.

She listened to Terrence's familiar sounds upstairs, fighting wars and quashing rebellion with soldiers the size of ants who somehow managed to fly through the air at each other. Baddies became goodies very easily, insurrection dispelled with toys jumping on the heads of other toys. She smiled to herself, his yells and screams strangely comforting, the only blanket around her as she sat alone.

Inevitably she thought of Olly. But not the Olly that had gone to France a couple of weeks ago. She thought of the Olly she had first met at school, her charming prince, her knight in armour, dulled if not quite shining, as she escaped the attentions of the school bully. The bully… what was his name again… anyway, a big ugly guy whose face always seemed to be a fine mix of spots and general, abstract, unspecific redness…he had wanted her and had tried charming her and then threatening her, cornering her one day in the playground, his arm over her against the wall as she stood with her back to the wall. He tried to take her long golden hair in his other hand when she started laughing at him. Laughing because behind him this guy Olly, her brother's friend, was making faces, emphasising and exaggerating the ugly state of the guy's face, crossing his eyes, puffing his cheeks. The bully turned round and, seeing Olly, immediately swung at him. But Olly had read his intention and quickly ducked, pushing the bully as the force of his attempted punch threw him forward. The bully stumbled and fell and all those around laughed, a great sight to see this guy get something of a comeuppance.

Olly spoke to her but not quite with words. She remembered his smile, his clear white smile, and she remembered him holding his hand out, his fingers almost caressing the air as he gently moved towards her. Yes, she was ok, no the guy hadn't harmed her. Then she remembered him talking to her for the rest of that break, sitting on the wall together. She had no idea now what was said but she absolutely remembered that that was when she had fallen in love with him. When they used to talk about how they got together they always spoke about The Conversation on the Wall.

They were, she reckoned, about sixteen when they started to go out. He was her first. She wasn't so sure about Olly and she had never truly asked him. Why not, she thought? Maybe I didn't want to know the answer. But that first time when she was nervous and twisted he had been

314

smiling and calm and....experienced...as though he knew exactly what she was going through. And he was gentle, softness itself as he moved inside her for the first time. She felt it – Christ, and how – but he could not have been more sensitive. He said to her then that the first couple of times would not be much fun but after that... he felt sure she would feel things that would refocus her life. He said that when he was 16. And he was pretty much correct.

You can't go through your teenage years and not attract the attention of the opposite sex. You can't go through your teenage years and not actively want the attention of the opposite sex, Helen thought. And certainly not if you were as beautiful as Helen or as desirable as Olly. She attracted attention wherever she went, that full shape and sensuous sway as she moved could melt a stoic, and at first she turned everyone down and spurned everything because there was Olly. But she never truly trusted Olly. Not really. She believed him when he said he loved her but she never believed that, in Olly's world, this meant not having a casual fling with anyone else. When they talked about their friends, or people splitting up, or people who strayed, Olly would usually express surprise that they had split up when one of them had slept with someone else because "it was just sex." But when she went back to that first time with Olly, that was as far away from just sex as she could reasonably conceive. He cared about nothing except her that night. If he really valued "just sex" then he would have been different, wouldn't he? He would only have thought of himself and that night he had only thought of her. In fact, sexually, he had been more or less devoted to pleasing her....so how could it be "just sex" when there was clearly emotion and love and everything wrapped up in it for him?

They went to different universities, Olly had almost insisted on it. "We'll get through it, we'll be stronger for it, we'll have our own space but we'll also have each other and when we're finished then we can have our future together." It had sounded rational, reasonable even and of course she had believed him at the time but now she wondered. What had he done? Did he want to have his cake and eat it? What's the point in having it if you can't eat it anyway? Perhaps that's what he was doing. But he never told her anything. Oh, she had doubts and some things remained unexplainable but then Helen knew she could never be Snow White herself. The thought began to prey on her almost as soon as she got to university. It was like looking at all the chocolate in the shop and imagining the different tastes on your tongue whilst you were on a diet.

You were only going to say 'no' for so long before you would surrender. How would someone else be….inside her… on top of her? She didn't, she never, thought or pined for love or understanding or conversation. She wanted to feel what it was like to have sex with someone else. There was nothing to compare Olly to. He may have been the best lover in the world but everything is relative and you can't know what a Ferrari is unless you have also driven a Ford Focus.

She accentuated her beauty. She drew stares. She wore things to parties that emphasised her shape. She started to wear mini-skirts. Though quite small, Helen had long legs, chiselled and moulded to something so close to perfect that no one would notice the difference. She wore underwear that made her tingle when she put it on, the soft sweep of silk on her skin as it slipped over her. Underwear that she wanted to feel someone touching, hands over it, underneath it, teasing it or tearing it off. She could probably have had anyone, any student, any member of the teaching staff, probably any female as well as any male.

The first one was a lovely sweet guy, someone who realised how lucky he was. Not a cocksure, arrogant bragger but one who she almost had to tease into bed with her. And he was good and he was nice and he made her orgasm and it was all perfectly acceptable but he wasn't Olly. He didn't say the things Olly said nor did he seem as comfortable with her, as though he had known she was out of his league and thought he better make the most of it before she changed her mind. She tried to reassure him and it worked, up to a point, but when he smiled it was as though he was smiling to himself, not at her. And when he finished it was as though he didn't know what to say or do. He tried to make out that he had had too much to drink but they both knew it wasn't true. One of the reasons she had chosen him was because she knew he had hardly drunk anything.

She should have felt guilty and she sort of did the next day a bit. But she felt more frustrated than guilty. It hadn't been the best of experiences. It hadn't really lit the fire. She drove the 200 miles to be with Olly the next day to feel what the fire was like and sure enough he could take her places within herself that her conquest the previous night couldn't even reach out to touch. Olly thought it strange that she had said she was coming but when she got there… well, she thought, he said he thought it strange but he never asked much. It was if he knew something like this might happen. Maybe he even knew exactly what had happened. He was full of smiles, full of devilish charm and made love to her almost as soon as she stepped foot in the flat. As if he knew that was what she had come for.

There had been others as curiosity tumbled upon curiosity. Even a lecturer, but that was a quick romp over a desk that sounded much more fun than the uncomfortable mess that it was as he bent her over and grunted and groaned. The thing she remembered most about that was looking at what was on his desk as he shoved himself into her from behind, seeing the marks her friends had got for their essays, laughing at the surreal nature of what she was doing.

One or two had got close to being as good as Olly. But they were guys that she didn't actually like and it was hard to make love with someone you didn't like. Not impossible though and she drank from one well for over two years, on and off, off and on. He wasn't her type, though Helen never knew quite what her type was. He was big and brash, loud in voice and personality with a smug self-satisfied grin like the cat that got the cream and knew it, as he often did. He made her feel as though she was lucky to have him, as though he was doing her a favour. She wished she could have ducktaped his mouth shut and let only his body talk. Because he could move inside her in a way that made her gasp, he could touch her with a sensitivity that belied his entire personality and he could kiss her as though it was the first time she had felt the soft warm lips and tongue of another explore her mouth. And when he took his tongue to other parts of her and let it slide and glide, soothe and move, she felt her back arch and pleasure fill her body. If only he were mute he might have been a genuine rival to Olly.

On the rare occasions that she was lonely she wondered about Olly. What did he get up to? Who did he see? She wondered about telling him, she wondered about splitting up with him, maybe that was what they should have done. She hinted to him occasionally that there had been others......the odd comment that most boys might have picked up on, about how she'd seen someone and they were handsome or how she had been complimented or how she looked or how her and some guy had done something like go shopping together but Olly never took the bait. If he pursued it, it was to ask what she had bought or what degree the guy was studying or some such banality, never to ask if she fancied him or if anything had happened. He was either trusting or knowledgeable. But you shouldn't really do what she did, go with other guys as she had, and stay in a relationship. Or if you did have this open thing then surely you had to talk about it. They never did.

317

When university finished they came back to each other – mentally, physically, sexually – and she convinced herself that she had tried as many avenues as she wanted to and that Olly was pretty much perfect for her. No one had taken her to places that were in any way substantially different to where he had taken her. And, she thought, he understands me. He loves me. I understand him. I love him. But as she thought about it now, she realised that she really had no idea what Olly had been up to for those four years. How many women he had slept with…how many men? No, I don't think so…but I don't know, I never asked. Suddenly this seemed like a chasm between them more than a shared understanding, a silent secret. Christ, how could we be such strangers to each other….

Then there was the post University years as they got jobs and, after a few years, moved in together. And things were good. They were both content. Well, she knew she was content and he had seemed content. But that whole thing about 'settling down' was wrong. Who settles? What settles? It's made to sound as though you stop thinking, stop being yourself, stop doing and thinking the things that you did before. As though part of you is somehow lobotomised. 'Settle down'. What do people, ordinary people, do when they 'settle down'? That's what they spoke of, when they moved in together, how they had now settled down and talk inevitably began to turn towards marriage and they thought of things like The Conversation on the Wall, how they had been in love with each other for so long, how they had survived arguments, separation, differences of opinion but they were always there for each other and always wanted to be there for each other. They were never going to want anyone else, they were made for each other. All their friends said it too – if Olly and Helen weren't ones to get married then who on earth could possibly feel confident about choosing a partner for life. So, she thought, it was inevitable. And I did love him, I do love him…but I did love him back then in a way that, in a way that….he was almost part of me. I couldn't have rejected him without rejecting a large part of myself that had made the choice to keep with him, again and again, throughout these years. 'Olly, I am you….such a large part of you is also part of me, I define myself by you… of course I will marry you.'

Then after two years of marriage there was the research student. The guy had been on an exchange thing from Italy and was at Helen's university for nine months. He was handsome, an almost archetypical Italian dark swarthiness about him, with a ruthless smile and eyes that looked as though they were undressing you. Perhaps that's only how Helen saw it. The first time he looked at her she could feel the attraction he felt for her...his eyes resting on her, his smile manufactured for her with that tactile Italian way of touching her almost every time he spoke to her. As with Olly that long time ago, she really had no idea what Enrico (he became Chicco very quickly) said to her, nor what she replied. But she felt the somersaults in her stomach when he spoke to her and she began to feel the beginnings of the need to fight the feeling that pulled her towards him. This was different. She was married. But it was also different in a much more frightening way. She had never been attracted to anyone that made her feel like this when she had been at university.

At first she tried to avoid him. As she sat remembering, she began to convince herself that she had done everything in her power to stay away. She had refused his offer of coffee, she had said she could not help him on a couple of occasions when he had asked and she had asked someone else to be his guide and mentor for the time of his stay. But that could only go so far and she had to go to his research presentations because he was studying in her area and she had to talk with him about the little lecturing he was undertaking because it was for one of her classes.

When they did talk she felt elevated, taken away from where she was now and lifted to some place outside of it where the everyday didn't exist. Where the normal rules didn't apply. When she spoke with him she felt him manufacture opportunities to touch her, a hand on the shoulder, a brush of his hand against hers, opportunities that she welcomed as she moved her body closer to his. You wouldn't have needed to have been an expert in body language to have seen a mutual physical attraction – bodies almost contorted into each other, legs crossed into each other so the feet were almost touching, hands almost touching, heads inclined into each other. When they spoke she felt as though she was standing against a wall of water, trying to stop it as it came rushing onto her and through her. I know, she thought, I am going to surrender. And as hundreds of thousands of others have no doubt felt in the same situation, she contemplated that it couldn't be wrong, could it, to feel this way, to feel light and lifted and excited, to be taken to such sensations, that couldn't be wrong, could it? She tried to think of Olly but he stayed at the back of her mind. The dam that didn't function when she felt herself trying to hold back the water certainly worked when she tried to put thoughts of Olly to the back of her head. Of course if she did anything it would be wrong...sort of wrong....but if you didn't think about it then it couldn't really be that wrong, could it? Something that you don't perceive can't be as real as something that you do perceive: conscience has to be there to make you a coward and if it isn't then you can be brave.

As a compromise she told herself not to pursue him. But if he asked again… for a coffee, for anything… would she really want to resist? And if she didn't want to then she knew she didn't have the power to pretend to. Sure enough he did ask for coffee and sure enough she went. She hoped that the chat would be brief, small-talk. But this wasn't small-talk and he was unsuggestive. No double entendres. This was much, more worse. He wanted to know about her and he asked questions and she asked questions and then an hour had passed and then two and then almost three. When she went back to her desk she could neither focus nor concentrate, she kept thinking of other things she wanted to ask him, kept imagining his touch on her, his smile as he made love to her. He doesn't only want to sleep with me, she thought, he wants to fall in love with me.

She should have refused his offer of another coffee. It was easy to say that now, looking back with the benefit of hindsight. She should have said how she felt about him, how dangerous it could be (he knew she was married after all). But then you couldn't admit that, could you, she thought? Because nothing had happened, nothing had taken place. It had been two colleagues being friendly, having a coffee. You couldn't go up to someone and say 'I'm not doing that with you again because I'm married and I don't want to fall in love with you.' They would think you were odd, she self-justified. So they coffeed again, a week after the first time. The conversation was a bit deeper…… partners, choices, likes, dislikes…general but somehow specific and very personal. Again, she thought, I should have taken the chance to have told him about Olly, how great Olly was…is….how much I was…am…in love with him. But she didn't. She swept over him with the speed of an air brush, as though she had closed the door of the room that the elephant was in. He would never again be spoken of. And Chicco did the same with his partner, wife, whichever it was Helen never really knew, back home in Italy. These were two people who would have preferred to have had no past before they spoke with each other.

The third time they met they spoke about what existed between them. He didn't profess undying love, he didn't beg her to have a night with him and he didn't flourish her with compliments. He was frighteningly rational, almost calculatingly clinical in what he said. "Helen, I feel this way about you….that I want to be with you…I want

320

to spend the night with you, to make love with you…to hold you and to kiss you. I don't think this feeling is going to go away. I have tried to make it go away. I appreciate, I understand this is dangerous and if you tell me you are not interested in me then we can stay as friends and have a coffee together. But I want you, I need you, to know how I feel. I need you to know how strong my feeling is for you." She remembered him pausing and slowly finishing his coffee. "And I need to know what you think about me. Because I think you have similar feelings. But perhaps I am mistaken." He was dark and clinical and very very dangerous.

She remembered feeling as though she were on the edge of a cliff, the wind battering at her, almost pushing her into diving. What was below looked warm and beautiful and inviting, a cool clear blue pool. Behind her was a terrain barren and grey, grass that didn't grow. The road that had been trodden didn't invite her back. The road not yet taken was enchanting. 'Settle down'…but settling down looked lifeless. Jumping looked life-affirming, necessary. But she wondered then as she wondered now if it would be one cliff, would this be the one and only time she jumped or would it be something that she did again and maybe again? Was it that the path of dead grass and grey landscapes would always seem as if it was strangling and suffocating her?

She took her time before she replied. But she knew what she wanted and she had known what she wanted since her eyes had first met his. So she didn't say what she ought to say or what the little voice of reason told her much later she should have said. That voice wasn't there at that time and not being audible it didn't exist. Instead she told him that she felt the same, that she wanted to take their relationship further, that she wanted a night with him and not just dark fumbles and gropes stolen behind a locked door at work.

Such things are never hard to manufacture. A night away, a conference or a meeting held in some place far enough away to necessitate an overnight stay is always enough to convince the partner and Olly accepted it all, no doubt in his mind that she was away for the night engaging in some academic activity that was as close to absolute boredom as he may ever wish to go. She felt no guilt, only excitement. She felt only that what she was doing was right. Her greatest fear was that when she got there, when they could be in each other's arms for the first time, when he touched her or when they made love, that she might recoil, that she might be hit by an as yet undetectable wrecking ball of guilt hammering at her.

It didn't happen. When he touched her he was as soft as his lilting voice, when his hands glided over her she felt in his power as much as she did when he spoke to her and transfixed her with his eyes, when his lips touched hers she felt his warmth over her and through her. She wondered if making love would be hurried and rushed, two people with a passion for each other ripping off clothes, desperate to belong to each other after so long waiting. It wasn't like that. Everything was gentle, almost slow, and as she sat in the chair now she raised her hand up from under her top towards her breast, remembering how he took a long time, his hand moving slowly as though he wanted to take in every inch of her, before it rested on top of her bra. Then he moved it gently and slid his fingers underneath, the wait making her gasp when his deft fingers eventually started to play with her nipple… almost rubbing it between his fingers, gently and with caution. He lifted her top over her head and undid her bra, kissing her nipples, licking around and over, his small mouth making them feel every sensation as though it was a touch rather than smothering them in his mouth and numbing any sense she might feel. As she lay back on the bed she felt his hand move up her leg, inside her skirt but again this was a slow deliberate movement as though he wanted to feel everything. Almost despite herself, for it seemed so inappropriate as to be almost evil, she felt her hand on her chest, massaging gently….Terrence was still fighting battles upstairs, she was out the view of the window…It's an escape, a little escape…

His fingertips massaged as they moved and she opened her legs wider as he moved closer. His hand crossed the top of her stockings and he touched her outside her underwear, gently pressing the silk against her. Then his hand slipped underneath. She had never felt so wet in her life, not for Olly, not with Olly, not with anyone. As his finger slowly moved she felt almost embarrassed, as though she should apologise…….then he began to slide his finger up and down, a little quicker and a little harder and she knew that it would not take too long like this before she was ready to orgasm. But she desperately did not want to orgasm in this way and she grabbed him, pulling him up and almost tearing the trousers from him, throwing them down. She hitched her skirt around her waist and guided him inside and as she remembered him sliding inside her she put her hand down into her trousers, just jogging bottoms, no need to take anything off, and she felt as warm and wet as she was the first time he went inside her.

After that she only remembered trying to delay the inevitable. He moved inside her with grace and with…it was almost an elegance. Without speed, without force, without noise but with a smile on his face and with eyes so dazzling and wonderful that it felt like making love on an almost spiritual level. Somehow it was the more sensuous and stimulating for that. This didn't feel like any sort of sex she had felt before. He pressed against her as she felt his rhythm inside her, a pressure that was like cotton and she tried to replicate the feeling with her fingers, by now become more furious inside her underwear. She ran her hands over his back, soft unblemished skin, and through his black hair…it was like running your hands through white fluffy clouds. All the time the pressing against her, his movement, she knew she could not delay much longer, as she felt now as her fingers began to bring her close to the same state again. She dug her nails into him as her body began to shudder and she made noises that she would never have recognised as her own, noises that were primitive and desperate and virginal. She didn't know if they were screams or gasps or sighs and she gently moaned to herself as she felt herself taken to the point of climax again, a little breathless now. She felt him and she heard him smiling at her, she could see when she opened her eyes the pleasure he had taken from taking her to such a state. 'I want to do the same for you,' she thought, but she didn't know how. She didn't have a clue what to do to him. But she didn't have to do anything. As her hands caressed his face, his beautiful boyish face, he moved himself slowly into a slightly different position and he increased his speed, just a little. She could at last hear something from him, the almost breathless noise of his breathing, silent intakes and expulsions which graced her ear. His hands moved quickly on her face, the only thing he did quickly all night, as they slid around her cheeks, gently over her eyes, around her mouth, down to her breasts and as his fingers gently moved on her nipples she felt him shudder inside her. Without voice or noise he exploded into her with a force she hadn't felt, with a quiet passion that, being silent, was so loud it shrieked and yelled at her. He lay inside her for a while, they didn't speak but smiled at each other, held each other. And after a few minutes, surely too short a time she thought, wanted each other again.

And so it went on. The night was punctuated by conversation but they made love more times than she had thought physically possible – was it really six, was it more? – and every time seemed distinct and memorable. The affair, for it definitely was a love affair, continued for a few months until they both knew it had to end. He had been fun and adventurous. She had dressed up for him – coquettish schoolgirl mostly. It was different and exciting. But it had to end. Either that or they split with their partners…and they both knew there wasn't really a choice. He was going to return to Italy. It was best they ended it before he was due to return, best to deal with any emotional fall out when they could at least talk with each other about it. Of course they had other nights, equally as thrilling, equally as exciting.

She wondered when she was going to have to deal with the guilt but it never truly came. If it came at all it went through twisted paths to get to her, manifesting itself in an insecurity around Olly and any attention he might get from a female. And sometimes she thought he played on it, going out of his way to make himself more attractive to any female when Helen was there, almost trying to goad her, make her jealous, force a reaction. She often wondered if he knew. Nothing was ever overt. He never asked her if she had ever had an affair, or was having an affair and she never asked him. Still,   Olly knew her like no one else, sometimes knew her desires and fears before she did. When walking down the street together Olly could often look at a guy and say 'You find him handsome, don't you?' And though she might deny it, he was always right. She tried to do it with him, with girls they passed and he would always tell her that she was right but she knew it wasn't true, he was saying it to make her feel she was correct.

After Chicco there hadn't been any others. Not till recently. She had met Officer Chris McLean a couple of months ago, a conversation struck up at a bus stop in the summer. They had much in common – his son was at her University though not a student of Helen's, they had been at the same school though he had been a few years older, turned out their fathers had known each other through working in the same company. When you're attracted to each other you'll always find lots that you have in common and conversation built on conversation and a coffee soon followed. He wasn't Chicco but she knew she might slip again with him. Maybe it was the attention, maybe it was a spark, maybe it was simply because he was attractive but she knew he could take her to the edge of that cliff again and make her want to dive in. And she did but this time with less vigour, less sense of something she felt for the first time. This was more cautious. But still they managed to steal nights here and there… Terrence would stay with his grandparents when Olly was away or she would take the odd holiday and they could spend a day together when Olly was at work and Terrence at school. It didn't have the inherent sense of wrongness that she thought she might feel but it didn't exactly feel righteously and unequivocally right either. When she thought of Chris her first thought wasn't of love or guilt or any really strong emotion. Thoughts of him tended to be met with a sympathetic sigh and the realisation that she didn't have time for this, it all made her too tired.

They had made love a few times and it was, as these things go, ok. But he made love as though he had been married to the same woman for twenty years and had just seen the view through another window – fast and selfish and unrestrained. The first time was always about him but the second time, if she waited and if he managed it, she would find that she could get as close to pleasure as she was likely to get. She wondered now why she had done this and why she kept it going. She didn't love him. The sex was ordinary, it was better with Olly. But he was interested, he made her feel special and a little bit bright and sparkly. In amongst a school run and a job and running a house, he seemed like a small ray of light, something to look forward to, a little colour in amidst the grey. It was that that made her feel guilty. Thinking of the grey around her. She didn't feel that guilty about sleeping with Chris or about spending time with him. She felt guilty about thinking her life needed this lift. She had a beautiful son, she had a beautiful husband whom she loved and whom she knew loved her. Why was it not enough? These were things that people wanted, that they needed, to 'settle down'. Why didn't she feel content at 'settling down'? She should. And that brought guilt. That stabbed at her. Whether she went with Chris or anyone else wasn't as important as the desire to go with Chris or anyone else. She felt guilty about feeling the desire, not about exercising it.

Conscious that she had brought herself to orgasm whilst thinking of a virile Italian that she had had an extra-marital affair with, she wondered if she and Oliver had too many secrets. We may be part of each other but it doesn't mean we know each other. She felt that at crucial times she didn't even know herself. As for him....too attractive for his own good at times. And she was convinced he had slept with Lesley. Poor Ali. Lesley had almost tried to tell her one night, a drunken girls' chat where layers were peeled away, and Lesley had spoken of him with a twinkle in her eye and a blush on her face. But when asked directly she put her head down and said nothing, changing the subject as soon as she could. We're all wearing disguises, thought Helen. It's just that some of us can do it better than others.

CHAPTER 16

With Oliver having phoned, the rest of the friends felt justified in making calls in a more open and unrestricted way. There was no rational reason for feeling they were safer than they had been: indeed, collectively they felt that they were probably in more trouble now than they might have been before, and they didn't doubt that the power and influence of whoever they had got themselves involved with had spread across the Channel into their own country. But they were in their own country. Surely it would be harder to monitor calls. All of them doubted if the hired hoods had managed to even see the number plate. They might be very hard to find.

So Ellis phoned Yvonne and the girls, Ali phoned Lesley, Euan phoned Jennifer and Aidan phoned Sarah. They told roughly the same lie – tortuous journeys, unfortunate punctures, breakdowns in the middle of nowhere. There had to be some semblance of commonality, the wives and partners could, maybe would, talk to each other. They had agreed that they might tell the truth, or at least their own distinctive, censored and manufactured versions of the truth, when they got home. If they got home.

Apart from the conversations with spouses and partners and children, the car was a silent place. It felt an uneasy silence, one born not of exhaustion or even tiredness, but of apprehension, distrust, even anger. Oliver looked around at the faces of friends that he thought he knew but who he had now dragged through some horrible mire. He wasn't sure he recognised them much anymore. They probably didn't recognise themselves and blamed him for forcing them to see things, both outward and inward, that they may never have wanted to see. And as for the experiences......he had taken them closer to death than anyone should ever feel at their age. Deep down, however they might try to assuage him that it wasn't his fault, he knew and they knew that it was. He wondered where he might have been without them. What if they hadn't come? He would surely have tried to escape. And he might have failed or he might have been caught by whoever was after him. Or by Clotilde. That wasn't what scared him, however. What scared him was wondering how long he would have taken to have been turned by Clotilde. How long until he would have accepted it, in the way hostages are reported to side with their captors? How long before he would have thought of Terrence and Helen less and less? That point existed, he realised it had to exist somewhere. How long before you give up fighting a battle that you know you are going to lose?

When Ali clicked the phone dead after talking to Lesley he was almost in tears. Ali was solid and dependable, sometimes a rock. At first the others thought nothing of it. Oliver looked at him, closely, as his head bowed and almost buried itself in his jacket. Quiet sobs. Oliver, as you might expect, felt guilty. He didn't know what to do and tentatively stretched his arm round Ali. He expected Ali to throw it off but no, Ali almost drew himself into Oliver. Oliver closed his eyes.

"Ali, I'm so sorry. All this… all this….hell. It's my fault. To have put you and everyone through this…"

Ali held his hand up. "Oh," he said, between sobs. "It's not that. That's been awful but we've got through it… through it together. It's Lesley… she…" And he began to sob again.

"What? What is it?" By now three sets of eyes were on him and Ellis was looking through the mirror at him.

"What, what?" said Oliver quickly. "Is she ok? Is she hurt? Is something wrong?" He wanted to ask 'has someone got her?' and that same fear rested in each of them as they urged him to talk.

"No, no, she's not hurt. But she's not… she wasn't… "

"She wasn't what?"

"She's not herself. Something's not right."

The others sat back. They thought they knew immediately what was wrong. It was Ali that wasn't right, not Lesley. He was shaken and not himself. So they didn't switch off as such but tried to convince him that it wasn't her it was him, think of what he'd been through, all that horror that he couldn't share with her yet, trying to normalise all that, to pretend this was a trip with the odd puncture and breakdown was difficult and he would be feeling his own sadness, not hers.

Ali had stopped sobbing and looked puzzled. "No, guys, I don't think so. She seemed…happy…."

"But that's good!" Oliver almost shouted. "Better she's happy than feeling like Helen, scared to almost move."

"But whenever I'm away she's uptight. And I'm away a lot. She's always uptight. But she wasn't uptight. She….she didn't ask any questions. She always asks questions….she spoke about herself, about work….I don't want to know about her work right now. And I asked her what she was going to do today and she was…… airy…"

Euan looked at him. "Airy? What the fuck does that mean? Airy? What's airy?"

Ali glanced across at him. "You know, airy….you say something airily you're trying to hide something…as though you didn't expect the question and you lie about the answer by saying the first thing that comes into your head."

"Why would she lie?" asked Oliver. "You're mistaken Ali, you must be. She'll be uptight and she'll be trying to make you less uptight, to try and sound as though it's….I don't know, business as usual…"

"That's not Lesley. Business as usual isn't Lesley. She's not a drama queen but she finds it hard to hide her feelings. If she's happy……you know she's happy. If she's uptight she talks more quickly, the questions come one after the other. And she was happy. It was if she was….well….almost relieved when I said we wouldn't be home till late tonight at the earliest. As if there was something she was going to do today…"

"Maybe there is," said Euan. "That'll be it."

"Then why not tell me? We don't have secrets."

'Yeah you do,' thought Oliver. 'You've got a few hundred from the last few days alone. Everyone has secrets.'

Lesley's was that, if her husband wasn't going to be back, she would spend the day with Tess. Going for a walk if the weather was nice, sitting in town having a drink or a coffee if it wasn't. Two girls, two friends having a chat the way girls do. So why hadn't she told him? When he asked she should have said….but the instinctive desire to hide the attraction she felt for someone else from her husband caused her to stumble to a lie and she knew he thought what she said was odd. He would be home soon enough though, maybe too soon, and she was more excited about the thought of time spent with Tess.

Ellis tapped his fingers impatiently. The journey had been slow and the traffic heavy. Now they seemed to be stuck in a jam. He fiddled with the radio, trying to find something local that would give them an idea of what was going on. He looked at his watch. Already mid-afternoon. He looked behind him. Tailback as far as he could see. He couldn't see that much in front of him except the back of a couple of lorries. He looked round at the others who all seemed so self-absorbed that he wondered if they saw at all what sort of mechanical mess they were stuck in.

"Guys we're going nowhere. Nowhere fast. Look."

They looked around them. As the car had been stationary for a few minutes Aidan got out and looked in front and behind, as many others were doing. Everybody looked at everyone else, shrugging their shoulders. "We're not moving," he said, dropping back down into his seat.

"Yeah, well, we needed you to tell us that," said Ellis. "I was hoping you might enlighten us as to why we're not moving."

"Because the traffic's stopped," said Aidan. They couldn't help themselves laughing. Except Ellis, who threw open his door and got out to see for himself. He could see nothing, only lines and lines of cars, most now with their engines turned off. Never a good sign. The others watched him stride up past the lorry to a car ahead and knock on the window. A brief conversation ensued with Ellis nodding his head quite a bit though as soon as he strode away from the car he started to shake his head.

"Fuck's sake!" he exclaimed as he sat down. "There are roadworks ahead, maybe a couple of miles ahead, but the road's closed now because there's been a bad accident. Maybe two lorries, one guy heard it on the radio. Police are at the scene but it's quite bad, maybe a fatality and so...."

"And so?" asked Oliver.

"And so we're here for a while. The woman said the police are trying to divert everyone off at an exit before this crash. But there are roadworks on this exit too so it's going to be a long bloody process..."

Oliver shot up. "Shit!" he said. "Remember what happened the last time we got stuck in a traffic jam. In France. In that place...Beauane I think. Remember?"

"But," said Euan, "but that was a co-incidence. That restaurant guy coming round, it was a coincidence."

"It couldn't have been a coincidence!" Oliver almost shouted, as if it had just dawned on him. "It was all deliberate, all manufactured! Don't you see?"

Ellis looked around him. "You think this is manufactured? I don't think so. This is a motorway. There are thousands of cars here."

"We're sitting ducks," said Oliver, quietly and almost to himself. "We need to get out of here. Right now."

"Be my guest," said Ellis. "Take the wheel if you think you can get us out of here any quicker. But it looks like the very definition of gridlock to me." He turned the pages of a map that his friend had left in the car. "Even if we get off that turnoff the traffic is going to be heavy. It's going

329

to take us ages to get back to the motorway. Why don't we get off the motorway and find a service station when we can and kip down there for the night? It'll be much easier tomorrow."

Though it was something that none of them wanted to do it seemed the best plan. They all sent text messages home, comfortable in the knowledge that at least this delay would be one their families could verify. Of all the spouses and partners, only Lesley didn't reply, too excited by the implications of what she had read. Maybe, Ali thought, maybe she didn't get the message. Sometimes there's a delay. Sometimes it can be very difficult to get the right reception. That's what had probably happened.

It took a couple of hours to get off the motorway and onto the slip road. The traffic moved at a pace that never demanded the use of any gear above first. Even the slip road was slow and winding, tortuous and akin to sitting in a car park that was strangled to the point of absolute stagnation. By the time they reached a hotel by the side of the motorway it was nearing six o'clock. As days go, this one was ranking as close to hellish as they could bear. But the best was yet to come.

The five friends trooped into the hotel and requested five rooms.

"Oh, no, we don't have five rooms free, we're almost fully booked." Lucy at the desk wore a badge which had a little smile on it and also, very conveniently, her name. She seemed to take pleasure in there not being five rooms.

"Ok Lucy," said Ellis. "How many rooms do you have?"

"Um....I'll check," said Lucy and started to do things with the computer which involved her fingers moving very quickly. Whatever she was doing seemed to take a while and her concentration was etched into every fibre of her young face. 'She's about 20', thought Ellis, though he was too mentally exhausted to figure out if he thought that was a good thing or a bad thing.

After what seemed like an eternity, and with an ever growing queue of people behind them, Lucy declared that there were two rooms. She seemed quite pleased with herself, as though she had just managed to build the rooms herself. "Yes, two, you can have them." And she smiled again, ruby lips and white teeth.

"But my dear....Lucy...," said Ellis. "There are five of us. You can see us, look..." and he counted round his four friends... "I'll even introduce them to you, see, this is Ali, this is Euan, this is Oliver and this is Aidan..." Each of them said hello and gave Lucy a little wave as their name was announced. Somewhat embarrassed and by now reddening in the face, Lucy waved back. A stilted wave that looked as though she was being controlled by a puppet master.

"Five of us. Five guys equals five rooms. Are you really telling me that in this great big hotel you don't have five spare rooms?"

"Yes…em, I don't remember your name… but yes sir, we only have two spare rooms. But one of these rooms has two double beds. The other one has one double bed. So maybe three of you can go in one room and two of you can go in the other?"

The friends looked at each other. Ellis leaned across the desk. "Lucy, my dear….I don't think you understand the gravity of the situation. These are my friends. I would probably die for them. In fact I almost have. But some things are beyond the pale. You can't ask me to share a room with them. Look at him…," and he thrust his index finger towards Euan. "He snores. Louder than thunder." Then he pointed at Oliver. "He sleep talks and sleep walks. It's like spending the night in a bloody horror movie. And he moans and groans." Lucy started to laugh. "It's not funny my dear, believe me. And….," with that he thrust his whole hand towards Aidan. "You fart. A lot." He turned back towards Lucy. "He farts." By now Lucy was crimson and had developed an uncontrollable fit of the giggles. "And as for the other one," said Ellis, pointing at Ali, "he steals all the bloody covers." He turned to face Lucy triumphantly as though he had made his case and, having done so, the evidence was incontestable. Her case must have crumbled.

Lucy could hardly raise her face to look at Ellis and when she did she couldn't help but laugh again. Ellis leaned across the desk, his face now close to hers. "Lucy……little Lucy, come on dear, you can do better than that. Don't make me spend the night with these monsters. You've no idea what we've been through together, me and these guys. Give us one night away from each other. I might kill one of them and you wouldn't want that on your conscience, would you? Come on, please, I'm begging you. We'll pay double."

Lucy wiped her eyes. "You wouldn't need to pay double. I don't have the rooms. But given what you've said, I'd pay now to watch how you and your friends are going to spend the night together. I'll give you the keys, here. The rooms are next door to each other. Maybe you can swap rooms during the night…" And she laughed again.

"Oh God. Lucy, may your God forgive you for what you've done. I'm going to have to spend the night being walked on, talked at, snored at, in the cold or farted on…maybe all five, who knows, I might get lucky…"

"Well," said Lucy, "you can stick toilet roll up the snorer's nose. There's plenty in the room. And the walker… the rooms aren't that big, he won't be able to walk far and you could gag him….you can wrap yourself in the covers so your friend can't steal them…and the guy who….who….well, the wind guy, you can maybe give him a pill or something."

Ellis stopped. "I can do what? I can give him a pill? Do you get pills that can stop people farting?" He turned to Aidan. "Did you know about this? All these years! Did you know about this? You could have stopped it all with a pill. You absolute bastard!" He turned back to Lucy, who had gone crimson again and had hidden her face behind her hands.

"Right Miss Lucy, we're not leaving here till you give us the name of that pill." Lucy was almost breathless. When she showed her face it was to wipe tears from her eyes. Her stomach was beginning to hurt.

"I said… it was the first thing that came into my head……I don't think such a pill exists…really I don't…. though there is a chemist over there, you might ask…"

"Ah, Miss Lucy, you're like all the others. You say things to get us interested but when it comes down to it it's all just hot air." Ellis smiled at her as she almost spontaneously combusted behind the desk. "Well," he said to her as turned away, "I'm going to see if it can be me and The Snorer. From what you say that'll mean sharing a bed. Look at him," and he pointed towards Euan as Euan pulled his stomach in, put his chest out and arched his arms in the way a strutting body-builder might. "What a fine figure of a man, don't you think? Actually, dear, don't answer that. But tell me this…do you think I'll be able to resist him? All night?"

Lucy looked at Euan, giggling again, and handed Ellis the paperwork. "Well, you never know," she said. "He might not be able to resist you."

No, thought Ellis. Far enough. She's about twenty. "Ah, Miss Lucy, you know how to make an old man very happy! But I warn you now… actually, will you be here in the morning?" Lucy nodded and said "Yes, I finish soon and come back for the early shift tomorrow." "Well," said Ellis, "you won't recognise me. I'll have dark circles round my eyes and I will have aged about twenty years. Your fault Lucy," he said as he walked away with the others. He pointed his finger at her as he left. "Your fault."

After a brief debate, during which each of the friends denied having the nocturnal habits that Ellis had ascribed to them, they decided that Ellis and Euan would share…which meant sharing both a room and a bed…and Olly, Aidan and Ali would share the other room. Quite who was going to have the pleasure of a bed on their own was a discussion which was to be left to later, with perhaps the drawing of straws being an option should rational negotiation falter.

The friends each had a shower, lounged about a bit and were grateful to see familiar television. Though they had only been away a few days it had seemed like ages and a time during which home had seemed light years away. The 'familiar', however banal, was comforting. They walked the short distance across to the nearby service station where what passed for a restaurant awaited them. Perhaps naturally, they took a more than normal interest in their surroundings, in the food, in the people who sat near them, across from them, away from them, anywhere. But everything seemed normal, or at least as close to normal as you might get without people trying to kill you. A few older couples, a couple of families, a relatively noisy rabble of youngsters. No tables of groups of men on their own, apart from their own one, no tables of even two men together. It was louder than you would have wanted and the children made more noise than you might have deemed acceptable and the noisy youngsters shouted and swore and drank a bit more but so what? No one, it seemed, was talking into a radio, monitoring them. There were no guns trained on them.

For what they ate and for what they drank they paid too much. But the pricing policies of UK service stations somehow never came up in what was quite a warm and engaging conversation. Each of them looked forward, despite the obvious trickiness of the predicament, to a night's sleep and so when they left the restaurant they did so as five guys, tired and maybe a little drunk, the same as any other group of people in that place at that time. The evening's routines of teeth brushing etc were conducted with haste before Oliver almost grabbed Ali and declared that he was going to sleep with him. Aidan could have the other double bed to himself. Euan and Ellis initially both wanted the same side as they both "always slept on their partner's right" but it was resolved by a civilised toss of the coin. It didn't even need to go to best of three. They went to bed at peace… maybe apprehensive, maybe even fear at the back of the mind, but they had accepted what had happened that morning as part of the past and had managed to lock it away. For now, anyway. And they all needed a good night's sleep.

It must have been about two hours before the battering on the door next to Oliver started in earnest. At first he didn't hear it. But it got louder and louder and was accompanied by shouting and yelling, so loud and indistinct and gruff that Oliver wasn't sure at first if it was even in English. Then he heard some unmistakeable swear words. He shot up in bed, the only one awake at this point, initially terrified that the banging was at his door. But he quickly heard that it was going on next door. It sounded like someone was banging to be let in. He looked at Ali and Aidan, who continued to sleep. He relaxed from the fear that consumes you when you feel it is your own life in danger to that of there being a more potentially hideous situation happening around you. At worst it would mean no sleep. The banging continued and the shouting. 'Well,' thought Oliver, 'if the place is full as Little Miss Rosy Cheeks said then let someone opposite come out and say something. I'm not getting involved.'

Which is fine as a first point of defence but it continued. He felt Aidan stirring across from him in the other bed, shooting up with the same panic that had forced a reaction in Olly initially.

"Guys? You awake? What the fuck's going on?" It had been said very quickly and he leapt out of bed.

"It's ok, it's next door. Next door the other way, not Euan and Ellis." By which time Ali had begun to toss and turn and eventually consciousness seeped over him.

"What is it? What?" he mumbled, shooting up.

"It's ok. Next door. I don't know what's going on but it's not anyone that wants us."

The shouting and the banging increased. It sounded like a female voice, high pitched, angry and emotional, loud and abrasive. The words she spoke came out as a string of swear words.

"Just folk drunk," said Ali, turning round and trying to get himself back to sleep.

However, it sounded as though the door was being physically battered in. It seemed as though the girl, if it was indeed a girl, was literally trying to batter the door down. When you listened carefully you could hear someone shouting back, someone clearly on the inside of the room next to them.

Olly knew he could only take it for so long before he would say something. He thought of phoning Reception. But their reaction would probably be to call the police and did we all really want that hassle? And whoever was chasing them may have connections there. Perhaps a quiet word would help, maybe that would be enough.

He went to the door and opened it slowly, edging himself out to have a surreptitious look at the person who was making enough noise to wake the hounds of hell. Unfortunately the girl was looking at his door as Olly was peeping round it.

"What the fuck are you looking at? Fuck off!"

Oliver held his hands up. "Nothing, nothing. I wanted to ask...... could you turn it down a bit please? There are quite a few of us trying to sleep."

"Fuck you and your sleep!" she yelled at him. She was anything but a pretty picture. Dressed in a bright pink shell suit that she was almost bursting out of, her platinum hair in two Shirley Temple-type bunches that failed to give her the desired femininity and her face covered in a mixture of running mascara and smeared lipstick, she looked as though she had been dressed by a two year old then thrown into a hedge. To cap it, she wore white training shoes or running shoes or whatever they were that she had never bothered to tie the shoelaces of. And even from this distance she smelled of someone who had probably been drinking for about the last twelve hours. Conservatively, Oliver thought. As he looked her quickly up and down she returned to the door and began hammering again.

"You fucking bastard you let me in! She's fucking in there with you. Let me in you fucking cunt!" Oliver wondered if he should go up to the door and gently knock. He couldn't contemplate a whole night like this. The again... Jesus, he thought, I've survived devil dogs and she-wolves, going up to ask folk to be quiet should be a relative doddle.

He walked towards the girl. "Excuse me...em...sorry, what's your name?"

"What the fuck is it to you what my name is?" she barked. He continued to walk towards her. Simultaneously whatever presence was in the room must have heard the change in voice, from yell to bark and as Oliver got closer to the room the door opened.

A head thrust out of the room, male, wide eyed and shaven with a tattoo on the neck that Oliver did not want to rest his eyes on for too long.

"Excuse me...," Oliver started.

"Who the fuck is this cunt?" The man directed his question to the girl. "Did you pick this fucker up?" then he turned to Oliver with menace in his eyes and his finger raised. "If you've fucking touched her I'm going to fucking kill you."

'Yeah, well, get in line,' thought Oliver. He held up his hands. "Listen…em….sir….em…I…my friends and I……we only want some sleep. I was coming to ask if you could keep the noise down. Just a little. Please?"

"You," and he pointed at Oliver. "You – fuck off. If I see or hear from you again tonight I'm going to kick the living fuck out of you." He paused and said quietly but with no small amount of force. "Do you fucking hear me, you mincing cunt?"

Oliver held his hands up but said nothing. "And you, you fat fucking whore..," he turned to the girl, grabbed one of her bunches and literally pulled her into the room.

Oliver returned to his own room. Ellis and Euan had woken up, heard Oliver's voice and immediately feared the worst. When Oliver told them what had happened there was an immediate sense of relief, tempered by the fact that they were probably not going to get much sleep.

As they spoke the noises from next door began to change. From the initial shouting, almost shrieking of both the male and female, things began to change. There had been a noise, almost like a thud. The friends looked at each other. They waited again for shrieking and swearing and sure enough the male voice continued in the same vein. But the female's voice had changed. She now sounded pitiful, maybe crying. Her shouts were not those of anger but of desperation. It was hard to imagine what was going on; though easy to hear voices and noises, especially loud ones, the walls had an effect similar to talking into a pillow in that everything that came through was muffled. Distinguishing individual words was almost impossible. However, as Oliver looked around his friends, he was convinced the girl was crying for help.

"She's not shouting in anger. Listen. The girl needs help." His friends looked to the floor, as though either the carpet or their feet had become objects of fascination. "Come on guys! We can't listen to this." It almost seemed as though a rhythm was developing and Oliver imagined him battering her or punching her every few seconds.

"It's probably nothing. It's probably how they get off," said Ellis in a very matter-of-fact way. He didn't want to be dragged into anything with these people. They were trash. Let them get on with being trash.

"What do you want to do Olly? Go back to that door? That guy threatened to kill you." Aidan said it in a tone of voice that suggested he thought Oliver had lost control of his mind.

"Yeah, and there's five of us. Only one of him."

"Well you go then!" shouted Ali. "If it means so much to you, you go. We're right behind you."

Oliver looked at his friends and shook his head. He walked out of the room and along the corridor, along the short distance to what seemed like another world. The noises became louder, her sobs more despairing. Oliver stood at the door and realised that, because it had been slammed shut with such force, it had not stayed shut but bounced very slightly open. He knocked but the noise inside meant that the knock was not heard. Gently, he prodded the door open, slowly, with his foot. The only light came from the street light outside as the curtain had not been properly drawn across. What he saw, however, was unmistakable enough. The woman was lying face down, naked on the bed, spread-eagled. The man sat above her, over her. Oliver couldn't tell if he was having sex with her but every few seconds he would raise his right fist up into the air and bring it down on her in some part of her body…her back, her buttocks, her legs, her neck. He almost shouted at her in time with the rhythm of his actions and Oliver thought that his words must have hurt as much as his punches, whoever she was and whatever she had done. "You….mean… fuck….all…to anyone… no one… will….ever….love… you… you've……got……two…….fucking……….breasts……and…….a…… cunt….that……no one……wants…."

It was when Oliver heard her stop crying that he spoke. "Stop this! Stop this now!" In the next room Ellis had heard Oliver's shout and came out to stand behind him. The man on the bed now saw two men in the doorway.

"You fucking bastard. I told you I'd kill you. What do you think, you think this useless slut needs your help? She loves this, she stays with me to do this stuff to her. She's a hopeless cunt, she's not even human."

Oliver moved slightly forward. The man moved his hand to reach for something at the bottom of the bed. Oliver saw the movement.

"Leave her. Leave her alone." His eyes were on the man's hand as it stretched. Oliver thought it was probably a gun. But the light from the street lamp flashed on the man's hand as it made contact with whatever it was he was searching for and Oliver saw it was a mobile phone. 'What the hell is he going to do with a mobile phone?' thought Oliver.

The girl looked across at Oliver, fear and resignation in her eyes. As the man picked his phone up he shouted to Oliver: "Do you want a shot of her? She's all fucking yours mate. Small fee involved. Money back if you're not fucking satisfied. Your cunt of a mate can have a go at her too."

He pushed a button on his phone. "Mal mate, get the fuck up here now. And bring the others. Trouble here. Been threatened. Don't know who the fuck the guys are but they might be Rizzalos. Fucking now mate. Here. Don't waste time talking to me." He clicked his phone off and pointed at Olly. "You better get the fuck out of here if you don't want to die. My mates will be here in a minute. Now fuck off!" he screamed. "And you can take the useless slut with you if you want."

Oliver shook his head and moved Ellis back towards their room. "Get dressed," said Oliver. "Quickly." Ellis and Euan dressed and returned as they were bid and not a moment too soon. They made the safety of the other room before what seemed like an endless stream of youths came piling down the corridor. After a quick conference with their friend next door, the friends could hear the gang converge outside their room. At first they were relatively quiet, polite even. "We would like to have a small conversation with you gentlemen about your interest in our friend's relationship with his tart. So open the fucking door!"

Oliver whispered to Ellis – "How many?"

Ellis shrugged his shoulders. "God knows. Ten? Fifteen maybe?"

"Christ," said Oliver. He looked around the room, up to the ceiling, in the toilet, even under the bed. Nothing, nowhere….he went to the window. They were on the second floor but it would conceivably, in an emergency, be possible to jump from here. And as the banging on the door commenced with the force of what appeared to be years of pent-up aggression, this began to look increasingly like an emergency. He pulled his friends over to the window and look questioningly at them. There was a unanimous round of enthusiastic nodding.

The banging outside had changed. There was now a rhythmical thudding, as though one or two or maybe three of them were taking it in turns to charge at the door to try and knock it down. The shouting had increased and it sounded horrific, a lynch mob who had been taken to the height of their anger. Perhaps there were only ten of them but it sounded as though there was a football crowd, desperate for blood and vengeance and the feeling of boots on flesh. The words were indistinguishable as they all shouted at once and the noise was much the worse for that. The door began to buckle, the lock beginning to give way as Oliver eventually threw the window open. Their luggage was thrown out quickly first then Aidan went because he was the most apprehensive. But with a leap and a quick roll on the grass beneath he was fine.

Oliver went last and he managed to launch himself from the window before the door was finally beaten down. He had drawn the curtain across and tried to close the window as much as he could. As he hit the ground and rolled then started running to the car he could hear the door being almost ripped from its hinges and the demons pile in. He looked back up but the demons tore around the room first, throwing over the wardrobe, battering over the bed, finding nothing. By the time the friends had made the car one of the gang had decided to look through the window. But he didn't equate a car starting with the guys they were hunting actually escaping and even if he had there was no way of catching them.

The one who was clearly the leader said: "Knock on every fucking door if you have to. Wake every cunt in this hotel. But we will find these two pricks and kick everything alive out of them. We're going to send the fucking Rizzalos a clear fucking message that even they will understand." He went back to the room of his friend who had made the phone call to him. "Dave, mate, how did this all come about? Did she get herself involved with a Rizzalo?" He pointed to the girl who was still lying naked on the bed.

"No!" yelled the girl.

Mal leant across and grabbed her hair, pulling her hair back quite violently. "I asked you fuck all. You shut the fuck up till I ask you a fucking question." Each word was spoken through gritted, fierce teeth.

Dave thought for a minute. "Who the fuck knows? She gives everyone the gravy, you know what I mean mate? These guys...they could have been Rizzalos, maybe not. There was one guy complaining about the noise, then another fucker appeared with him. Maybe there were more of them somewhere....and those bastard Rizzalos are sneaky fuckers.."

"You," said Mal, now turning to the girl. "What the fuck have you got to say for yourself?"

"I was trying to get in. He wouldn't let me in. He was with that other girl and he was hiding her in here. I wanted in. This is my room!"

Mal looked enquiringly at his friend and Dave shrugged his shoulders. Mal slapped his friend on the shoulder. "Couldn't exactly blame you mate." He looked at the naked woman lying on the bed. His eyes looked questioningly at Dave. Dave nodded. "Be my fucking guest."

Mal took his trousers off and, after a brief time massaging himself, began to lower himself on top of the girl. "Some people might call this rape," he said with quiet fury into her ear. "But you can't rape a fucking tart like you." To an extent, she thought, he's right… he wasn't exactly the largest in the world and though he pounded into her with all the anger he felt at not capturing those guys who he thought belonged to a rival gang, she hardly felt it. Even when he finished off by ramming himself into her ass it was quick and sudden and it had been, all in all, the least unpleasant five minutes that she had spent that evening.

For the first twenty minutes the friends simply drove. When it became obvious there was no one behind them they stopped and drew a collective breath.

"Ellis," asked Oliver, "earlier today, when we checked into that place, did you pay? Or are we going to have a hotel chain pursuing us too?"

"I paid. For breakfast too. Though I think I'd be quite happy to skip that…"

Ali said. "Were these guys anything to do with……you know, what happened in France?"

Ellis looked at Oliver and Oliver shook his head. "I don't think so. No, I think we have to put that one down to our good fortune to be in a room next to a bunch of fucking nutters……But that poor girl, Jesus…."

"You don't get involved with people like that unless you want to," said Ellis. "She's not worth another thought Olly."

"Bloody hell Ellis, did you see what he was doing to her? It was horrific."

"So what do you want to do, Olly? Go to the nearest police station? Come on! Forget about the bitch, she isn't worth a thought."

Olly wondered how many people had thought that about the poor girl. It's her own doing, she's a bitch, she's a whore. If it was her own doing, what had made her so desperate to belong that she had fallen in with such a gang of monsters?

"If you're going to feel sympathy, Olly, feel it for us. For yourself even if not for us. Think of what we've all gone through in the last few days. In the name of friendship." What Ellis said hit Oliver like a punch that a boxer might throw after the bell had sounded. When your guard was down and you were vulnerable. Whatever Ellis might have meant, it said to Olly – 'This is all your fault.'

Ali changed the subject. "What are we going to do? We can't drive all night, surely. We're all knackered, we've not slept properly for ages…"

Ellis looked at his watch. "It's two o' fucking clock in the morning,

Ali. Where the hell do you think we are going to sleep? And anyway, those bastard neds might well find us, who knows what they're doing now?"

"No," said Oliver. "He's right. Find a layby and stop the car. We'll rest even if we don't sleep. Even if it's only two or three hours. The way we all are right now, we can't drive. There's still too much alcohol in the system and we are all too tired. Those guys aren't after us, they're probably still turning over the room."

Olly was right, the gang that had tried to attack them earlier were not after them. Not as such. But the gang had had an informal meeting at getting some sort of vengeance against the rival gang that had tried to molest their woman, and a stealth plan to attack the Rizzalos was hatched and planned and drawn up in detail with the precision and fury of a clinical military campaign as dawn broke the next morning.

Officer Chris McLean had been a policeman for over twelve years. He enjoyed his job, mostly. Sometimes there too much paperwork and sometimes you felt like a political football but it had the sense of order, discipline and, to an extent, routine that he had been so comfortable with in the army. He would have stayed in the army, had he had a genuine choice. But a wife of eight years and two relatively young children meant that he had to take something that was less likely to catapult him into a war zone and leave them stranded, alone. Coming out of the army was a compromise and it was something he never let his wife forget, whenever they argued.

He kept himself fit, undertaking the same regime of running, weights, gym and swimming that he had done since his early teens. He hardly ever drank. He had been handsome as a youth and had retained his boyish grin and distinctive features. His eyes were clear and light and blue, his hair short to emphasise the narrow beauty of his face, his ears and nose almost what could be described as dainty. Even with his clothes on you could tell there was not an ounce of fat on him. His hair, beginning to grey now, gave him a dignity to add to his impressive demeanour.

He had thought, through the years, that he probably could have had a few affairs. Probably. Had he been interested and had he made the effort. Somehow he never had. Maybe it was because of the effort involved, maybe there was some latent sense of loyalty to his wife, maybe it was something else, who knows. Helen, however, had affected him in a way that he hadn't felt before. She was beautiful and sexy and desirable. So he pushed things....from the initial conversation, to coffee, to another coffee. It had, he thought, looking back on it, been ridiculously easy. Even making love, they had got there quite quickly and he wondered now if had all been deliberate, if it had all been too easy. Maybe she was part of it.

"It" was the blackmail. Officer McLean was being blackmailed by person or persons as yet unknown for planting evidence in the home of a known drug dealer. Photos had been sent to Officer McLean, photos which showed him taking a bag of powder out of his pocket and placing it in a toilet cistern. The photos clearly showed Officer McLean putting powder in somewhere as opposed to taking it out of somewhere. He didn't feel at all bad or remorseful about it, only anger at the existence of the photos. They knew – they all knew, every police force in the country knew – that the guy was a drug dealer. He was, however, very slippery and notoriously difficult to catch. Two or three of them took a decision one day that they would catch him, by fair means or manufactured.

However, what Officer McLean and his colleagues didn't know, and could not have known, was that the dealer had stopped dealing. He had stopped dealing about two months before the material had been planted in his flat. The man who supplied the dealer had accepted that his 'customer' now wanted out of the game and had promised him protection. It had all been amicable and the necessary dues had been paid. The supplier, however, when he had first gone into business with the 'customer', felt that honour might only be expressed by the mouth and he never went into business with those who he didn't truly 'know'. Hence he had cameras and cctv installed in his 'customer's' house and had no problem now in identifying Officer McLean as the rogue element.

When he received the first envelope Officer McLean kept it quiet. The note inside asked for the relatively small payment of £500 though it was made quite clear that this was the first instalment. He was told to leave the money in a certain location at a certain time and he did as he was bid though he also left a note explaining that he was not a wealthy man and this couldn't go on much longer before he would have nothing left to be able to pay with.

Other photos came, similar ones, with him in the same location, planting drugs in different parts of the house, asking for more money. It was then that he decided to go to his colleagues, the two others who had been involved in the operation, and ask their advice. They realised their vulnerability also, it would surely only be a matter of time before they received photos and demands, so they suggested they take the material to forensics. Perhaps they could enlighten as to who might be behind this, maybe a stray fingerprint, something......because beyond a West London postmark, there was nothing to be identified or distinguished about the envelope with a typed address on it or the A4 size black and white photographs or the typed note inside with instructions on it.

Forensics kept all the material for a few days, which was usually a good sign. If they came back after a day or two it usually meant there was nothing. Alfie came to see the three of them, together. "There isn't much to go on, we are clutching at the proverbial a little bit...... but if you look beyond the postmark, which leads us to London – and obviously the actual posting of this envelope took place in London – then you start to examine the paper the photo was produced on, the note, the envelope itself. Little traces on the envelope itself tell us that the envelope was inside another envelope – so, sent to London to be posted from London, but not initially posted from London. At least, probably not. The paper itself doesn't tell us much but the paper the photo is on is typical of French manufacture..."

"Which means it was posted from France?" said Officer McLean.

"Well maybe, but not necessarily. The paper can be bought in this country too. The paper the message and the instructions are typed on – nothing in the typing of course, it could be any computer – is again just a little thicker than normal. Tiny amount thicker than what we might call 'standard' here. It again leads us to France. My contacts abroad say more typically used in the south of France, though they have no idea why."

"So your view is......". Officer McLean motioned with his hands, trying to get Alfie to come to a conclusion.

"My view is I don't know. Off the record, it might have come from France, maybe the south, but the chances of the same paper being used over here must be quite high. Or another country for that matter. So there's nothing there that would stand up. You couldn't take any of this to court and expect it to hold water."

"No, sure," said Officer McLean, appalled at the thought that any of this might get anywhere near a court room. "What about the envelope?"

"Standard. Can be bought here, France, pretty much anywhere."

"No sign of any fingerprints?"

"Nothing on the inside. Outside, yes, but the position they are in would be very much the position the postman would have the letter in to stick it through the post-box. Not the place you would have held the envelope if you were putting stuff inside in. No evidence of saliva either, just water. Gentleman," said Alfie, looking around his colleagues, "whoever did this, whoever sent this….they're professionals. They're not fortunate opportunists. Whoever sent this was prepared for it to be forensically examined."

Officer Mclean didn't tell anyone else, outside of his two colleagues, what had happened. Not his wife, not Helen, not anyone. And his two colleagues, suspecting strongly that they were next, did not share their secret with anyone either. They had, between the three of them, to find a way of getting the case dropped. That wouldn't be easy as those above them were already excited at the thought of a conviction of a notorious dealer.

As he lay with Helen one afternoon when Oliver was working and Terrence was with his grandparents, she began to ask about his wife. What was she like, what did she do, her character, did he still love her. Officer McLean did not particularly like talking about his wife with Helen. When he was with Helen he would have liked to forget that his wife – and the life that he lived when he left Helen – existed at all. So his answers were quiet brief. Not curt as such, or rude, but hardly expansive and he changed the subject to the first thing he could think of at the first opportunity. Her husband.

He didn't really listen to what Helen said. She didn't talk about her husband in glowing, thrilling terms, it was a bit more matter of fact than that. But she was happy to talk about him. Childhood sweethearts, university, saw other people during that time, came back together, he works with a company that makes war figures, travels to France for a week or so at a time, occasionally further, loves his son……

Officer McLean sat up, a sudden almost violent movement. "He travels where?"

"All over sometimes. France mainly. They have a production plant there, I think. Or something. I'm not as interested as I should be…"

"France?" he interrupted. "France where?" Officer McLean was agitated and tried to slow down his speech. It was hard, however, for him to hide the growing anxiety.

"The south mostly. Paris sometimes. But mostly Nice."

"Nice?"

"Yeah, Nice." She paused, wondering at his interest. "Have you been there?"

344

"Yeah…well, no, not really…….passed through it." His mind was racing. Things were racing through it with such a pace that they could hardly find their form in words. At first he thought the blackmailer was her husband because he was having an affair with the guy's wife. But the blackmailer had never mentioned the affair and if he wanted to issue a threat it would have been about going to Officer McLean's wife and telling her about the affair. No, no, if this guy was the blackmailer then he was, as Alfie had said, a professional. Not an opportunist. This guy was part of something else. That was the first time he wondered if it was all a trap. Had Helen got close to him to find out more about him – the blackmail, would he pay the money, to get inside information from him? Was this part of the set up? These two – and it surely couldn't have been them acting alone, they must be part of something bigger – had got him. The husband had probably set up the cameras in his house, maybe they had had him watched for a while, knew his routines, knew when he would be out….he went to France 'on business' and posted the things and her job was to find out what his reaction was, maybe get information on the case, was it to be dropped, etc.

He lay there, all these thought zipping through his head, Helen yacking away about whatever she was talking about. He threw her the odd "Really?" or "Sorry?" to try and feign interest and keep his new knowledge hidden away from her. But he felt frightened and curious and saddened. He was sad because he realised that Helen's interest in him was purely professional. It probably wasn't even her husband, she probably didn't even have one…. She's beautiful, it was always unlikely such a beautiful girl would be interested in me and her making even a bit of the running made so much sense now. He was frightened because he felt surrounded by a sudden and evil force that he felt envelop him. Whatever he had done had disturbed an individual or an organisation that was very powerful and clearly felt no anxiety about taking on the police. Perhaps organised crime, very well organised crime. People that could make him disappear. And much as he wanted to stand up for what was right, Officer McLean did not want to be 'disappeared'.

Forced to stop his mind thinking and not able to face a conversation yet with Helen as though he knew nothing, he did the only thing he could think of and practically jumped on top of her. He didn't notice if she orgasmed; he didn't notice if he orgasmed. He was thankfully aroused enough by her body to maintain being hard but he jumped on top of her to give himself thinking time.

She hadn't reacted to his surprise and interest at France….but then why should she? Would she even know the material had been posted from there? Maybe not, it was a minor detail. So she probably suspected nothing. She probably thought he was in the same state of ignorance as he was when he arrived at the house. Play along, he thought ….play along. His immediate thought had been to stop seeing her but that would have sent a clear message. Anyway, he had almost professed love for her, she knew how much he liked being with her and they made love like rabbits. It wouldn't have been at all logical for him to stop it. I suppose I could have had an attack of guilt he thought but still, it would send the wrong message. No, best to stay with her and perhaps feed her false information…maybe in times of pillow talk to let slip the pressure he was under because of the blackmail…begin to control the nature of what information was fed back to the 'husband', the organisation, whatever it was.

It all made sense. Even earlier, talking about her husband… people doing the sort of thing we're doing don't talk about their spouses, they want to forget they are alive. It's clearer and clearer… she's a plant.

She got up from the bed and smiled at him then took a quick shower. When she returned she put on new underwear, a luxuriant and life affirming blue colour.

"Wow!" said Officer McLean. "That is beautiful. Very beautiful. As, of course, is what's inside."

Helen did a little playful twirl, letting him see the full three hundred and sixty degrees. She smiled at him. "My husband bought me it. It's expensive. I know because I checked on line, I knew the make was not cheap. It is nice isn't it?" And she twirled again.

"It must be a lucrative business, those little war figures."

"Well," she said as she came closer to him. "He had a bonus. Not huge, but still enough for him to blow a few hundred pounds on this. Worth it, do you think?" And again she smiled at him, a coquettish, roguish, knowing smile.

Officer McLean tried hard to smile. It was forced and very difficult. 'I would have been better buying them for you myself,' he thought… .'I've effectively done that anyway.'

CHAPTER 17

Surprisingly, not least to the friends themselves, they managed some sleep. Five of them, lumped together in a car that would have been more appropriate had it been about double the size, somehow contrived to sit out in differing degrees of discomfort and reach a suitable level of bodily equilibrium. If someone did snore than it didn't wake the others. And if someone did want to sleepwalk, there was nowhere to walk to. From the outside it was not a sight that anyone would have found aesthetically pleasing: fully dressed guys reposing themselves, half leaning on each other in some cases, filling a too-small space with the unmistakable stench of stale beer. It was no surprise that Ellis, who woke first, was overcome by the immediate need to open the window.

He stepped out of the car and stretched himself, looking at the others in the car. His body felt as though it had been squeezed into a metal box for the evening. His shoulders hurt, his neck ached, his back felt as though it belonged to someone else and his legs trembled gingerly as he put one foot in front of the other, recovering slowly from the pins and needles that had seeped into his body about four hours ago. He looked at the others and thought about banging the roof of the car, a little bit of fun, to see how they reacted. Perhaps it was a potential trauma too far, however. After the sisters, the gang from hell, the stone throwers and the one-eyed monster and his mates, someone would probably have had a heart attack. But he was keen that they get on their way as soon as possible so initiated a few noisy stretches, barked out a few yawns and began to whistle. Soon enough, there were five bodies outside the car, like squashed rubber balls trying to get themselves back to the shape and the state they were supposed to be.

"We need petrol," announced Ellis. "And we need to stop in Leicester."

"For petrol?"

"No. We need petrol. And we need to stop in Leicester. Two things."

"Why do we need to stop in Leicester?" Oliver asked. He sounded annoyed – another potential diversion, who knows what sort of fresh hell might be waiting for them there – but he was also curious.

"Ah, yeah," said Euan. "I forgot about that. Well, when we were in that hotel room, before these crazies attacked us, before we went to have dinner even, Ellis thought it wouldn't harm us to have……well, what would you call it……I suppose it's a weapon."

There was a sense of urgency in Oliver's voice. "A what? A weapon? What does that mean? A weapon? A gun? We're stopping so you can pick up a gun? You know people in Leicester who have guns? What the… "

"Ok, ok," Ellis interrupted. "It's not a gun, ok? Alright? It's not a gun. It's a stun thing. An electronic weapon. It doesn't kill, it stuns. For a while."

"Taser? A Taser thing?" asked Oliver.

"Yeah, that sort of thing. It can't do us any harm to have something, can it? And it's not a gun, it can't kill."

Oliver's head ran rings around itself. Aidan and Ali looked nonplussed, as though, amidst all the madness of the last few days, this seemed as normal as eggs for breakfast. "Ellis…what…you know people who have Tasers? How is that possible? What sort of friends do you have?"

"It's not that bad Olly, come on. It's probably useless against the maniacs who are after us. But it might be something….a small something. I don't know the guy….well, I do know him but he's more friend of a friend…I phoned a couple of friends and they both recommended this guy. I don't think we really want to know what else he's into, he's the kind of guy who has more secrets than a high-class prostitute, but I phoned him, we reconnected and he said he'd give us the thing for free if we wanted as long as we got it back to him. Sometime. My friends said he lives on this dodgy estate but I shouldn't be fooled by that. He's loaded apparently. The estate probably represents the bulk of his client base, I would guess. Don't ask. We'll get in, get out as quick as we can…"

"Yeah," chimed in Ali, "that's what we thought we were doing when we went to France in the first place. Now, about three hundred years later…."

"Guys," said Ellis, as he started the car. "It'll be ok. But first we need petrol or we're going nowhere. And some delicious and nutritious breakfast from the culinary beauties that are on offer in the petrol station. I don't want to stop in another service station for a sit-down meal quite yet, in case that mental gang have made some attempt to find us. Oh, and of course the French maniacs who might be anywhere between here and Edinburgh and Nice."

They pulled into a petrol station off the motorway and Oliver got out the car to fill it up with petrol. It was still relatively early in the morning and Oliver was a little surprised to see another car across from him. An insomniac maybe... At first the car had not caught his eye but as he went to take out the petrol cap he looked across and saw a blazing red car, very sporty, distinctive and which shrieked money. Perhaps even a Ferrari. The car stood on its own. He looked to where he thought its petrol cap might be but there was no one. Then he heard laughter and saw a woman inside the car, the window down, on her mobile phone. Very much a human manifestation of the car... beautiful, distinctive and shrieked money. Long straight blond hair, suntanned, fingers adorned with two or three rings which sparkled and dazzled. An almost perma-smile when she either spoke or listened and even from here Oliver could see flashes of almost perfect, sculptured white teeth. She held her head high as she sat in the car, in what seemed a bit like a jolting, strutty and uncomfortable position but which was undeniable in its superiority. 'She not only thinks she's superior,' thought Oliver, 'she knows she is.'

Then she started to talk and Oliver paused. It was a quiet morning, there was no wind and they were far enough away from the motorway that there was minimal noise of passing traffic. He could hear everything she said. He pretended to fumble with the petrol cap but instead focused his eyes and his ears on her conversation.

"Things are good, very good. His business is still fine, going very well. Gets us to Barbados next week and there'll be the usual ski-ing at New Year. What's that? Oh, well, a lot of it is newspaper talk, I wouldn't say he, we, have been affected as such, things are still good. Oh yeah, the children are still good, Lucinda is away on a school trip this week to somewhere abroad, I can't remember where, maybe France. And Johnny junior is very much into horse riding so we've had to get a horse for him, have it in stables. Oh, I'm sure it is a dirty business but we don't have anything to do with that. The stables clean it and feed it. I don't think that's my role in life, dear. We all have our strengths and weaknesses. Yeah, yes, I know..." And she picked up a coffee next to her and started to drink from it. Oliver felt desire and jealousy and inferiority all at once. Somehow that feeling manifested itself not in a desire to slap her or to simply fill up the car and ignore her but to sleep with her. Somehow that seemed to be the perfect leveller. But it wasn't really a desire to sleep with her, more a desire to shag, even to fuck he thought...to bring her down to my level. Imposing, dominating, taking, penetrating appeared to be the immediate way his mind tried to reassert his, if not superiority, then at least equality.

She continued. "Oh God, yeah, well, I remember, yes, he got rid of her. She was ..well I didn't like her. I didn't like the way she looked at me, you know that up and down look and the way she dressed, well, it takes a woman to know a woman and I knew what she was trying to do. So I asked him to get rid of her and he did. So that was good. Sorry, what? I don't know, he never said there was any hassle about it, she went and that was that. What was that? Oh, yeah, he's ok, he's fine, he's good, he's been away a bit because there's something he's transferring to China. So he goes away there a lot, goodness knows where. I'm sure he tells me but I don't quite listen......what was that... yeah, he's moving something over there from here. Well, it's cheaper, whatever's involved is about a quarter of the price, it makes sense. More for us! I know he asked the guys here to take a cut, maybe 30%, maybe 50% but they wouldn't. Bet they're regretting now, no job to go to...yeah, ha ha that's funny, maybe they should go to China..."

Oliver was transfixed. He felt a bit like a voyeur, watching this woman reveal her inhumanity as she laughed her way through a conversation of broken dreams and broken people. He wondered what had been the original basis of the mutual attraction between her and her husband. Back in the day when they first met. Had he looked at her and seen a reflection of the self in the mirror? Had she looked at him and seen the man she would have been? On what level might they fuck? A financial one? Or on one where they could at least look down to see what was beneath them, a level full of glass floors with no ceilings?

"Oh, well, yeah, you'll know all about that...him and a few others... .it even made the papers. But he won the case, the tax case. He got a good lawyer and a great accountant and he's paid...well, not very much let's say. Well, it's only right, isn't it? You can't kill people like Johnny and his ambition with crippling tax so he...well, you find ways of getting round it, don't you? We had a cracking bottle of champagne that night. Oh, yeah, I know, yeah, but he's got a couple of mates there....hey, if Alan needs help with that, Johnny can....you know he has influence there so let me know. Oh yeah, thanks for asking, he got that contract, so that's good... well, I don't think luck had much to do with it but yeah, it's good, all's rosy."

She sipped at her coffee. Oliver had not yet begun to fill the car with petrol. He stared at her, this embodiment of an upside down society sitting in the roaring manifestation of an ivory tower. She looks beautiful, he thought...outwardly, at first glance, before she opens her mouth...

well, maybe not completely because look at the rings and the clothes. Eventually she looked across, perhaps tired of listening to the person on the other end of the phone, and her eyes caught Oliver's. Though physically lower than him he could feel her looking down his nose at him and he met her detached glance with a smile. The smile was not returned.

"Well, it's ridiculous, these people…they do nothing and want money handed to them for nothing. It's good that it's been cut, might force them to do something. Oh, and don't get me started about that, these people would march because they had nothing to march about. Get out and get another job, go and do something useful instead of sponging. God, Johnny junior came home a few days ago…maybe last week…they'd been doing politics and he came and asked 'What's socialism?' His dad told him: 'It's when people like me work to give all our money to people who do nothing. It's when we get women in dungarees and pullovers coming on tv all the time as experts and telling us how we should be caring more. It's like a form of brain cancer for ambition.' I don't think Johnny junior quite got it."

Oliver started to fill the car with petrol. Conscious that something was still there, the woman glanced across. Oliver flashed another smile which was met with a glower. He walked up to the shop to pay and glanced back at the car. Not his car, but the car in which the woman still sat. It blazed of bursting redness, bright and all consuming. But he also caught a flash of the woman in the car, almost cackling with her head back, glimpses of her white teeth and top, looking as though she was sitting on top of this monument. She didn't look as though she was going to fall anytime soon. She seemed completely in control.

"Bloody hell Olly, you didn't half take your time."

"Sorry, I struggled a bit with the petrol cap. My dexterity seems to have escaped me."

"Well, it's ok. You could have taken longer. All day if you wanted," said Euan. "We were spending our time watching that bird in the car opposite. Tasty or what? And look at the car, a bloody Ferrari! Mind you, she suits it, she looks really classy."

"Yep," chimed Ellis, "I was getting close to asking her if she might take me for a ride…a few minutes would be enough.."

"Jesus, look at her, a few seconds," said Aidan.

Oliver smiled, a smile of resignation, even disappointment, to himself. "Yeah, I saw her. And I heard her. Like you say, nice car."

Ellis turned the key. "Now why couldn't she be after us? We've got maniacs and monsters chasing us. Why can't we have a fabulous bird with breasts big enough to smother us to death chasing us?" He sighed. "Ok, boys, time to wave goodbye…."

It didn't take them very long to reach Leicester but it did take a while to find out where exactly they should be going. The car had no sat nav and those that the friends tried to use on their phones were unreliable as the connection was intermittent. Ellis had directions but they were vague rather than detailed and an hour or two was spent circumnavigating a similar area until they realised that they had taken a wrong turning.

When they reached the flat they appreciated they had not been given false information. This was not a very pleasant area and as the friends ventured out the car their eyes were everywhere. However the friend, Nathan, was very welcoming and spoke with a very strong southern English RP accent. The flat was small but clearly belonged to someone with wealth. All this incongruity made Oliver wonder how Nathan didn't get his head kicked in every day. It was a thought which Ellis felt comfortable enough to voice.

"Hey, this isn't where I live. I work here. If what I do can be called work, you know. But I'm here a lot." He spread his arms wide in front of him. "And these are my people. They are *my* people. They know me. I provide things to them. And I help solve any problems they might have. They're not going to hurt me! But I don't live here. It's convenient, you know?"

Ellis didn't really 'know' and neither did his friends but they nodded as if they did. Always a good idea to agree with anything anyone who's going to do you a favour might say. Oliver liked Nathan the moment he saw him. He had a twisted smile and an element of being over-the-top in almost everything he said or did. His floppy, foppish hair got in his eyes too often but he seemed to enjoy spending time sweeping it away from his face, which he did so in a majestic almost regal kind of way. If he was a drug dealer and drug-related handyman then he defied every stereotype and Oliver couldn't see this guy threatening, punching or physically engaging with anyone.

Nathan was clearly up for a chat and seemed to welcome the company. They must stay for a while – he had bought two or three cakes specially – and, look, Earl Grey. You can't turn down a cup of the world's best when you've been subjected to some Franco-garbage for a few days. Since his personality dominated the room and breezed effortlessly over them, they couldn't refuse.

They heard a noise, at first unclear, develop from next door. The walls were not particularly sound proof. Perhaps built by the same company that built the walls in the hotel where they had stayed. It sounded familiar –a guy shouting then maybe silence or, as you strained to hear, a girl's voice, softer, not raised.

"What's going on next door?" asked Ellis. "We've got half of France and a gang of mutant bastards after us, I'm sort of hoping that none of them have connections in that house next door to you."

"Ah," said Nathan, flicking his hair as he took his first sip of tea. He reacted to it as though he had taken a hit of heroin after a year's abstinence. "Jesus boys, is that not the best sensation? What beats an Earl Grey? Juice from the Gods. It should be on a prescription-only basis. Normal people shouldn't get to feel this way without it being illegal." He licked his lips. "Right, yes, next door. It's a sad tale. She's…the girl there, she's called Jill…well she was on benefits, she couldn't work. She had a kid and something happened, she got this terrible sciatica. No one knows if having the baby caused the sciatica – 'not medically possible', fellows, according to some doctor. But all she knows is this sciatica arrived at the same time as the baby. Bringing up a baby, good Lord, can you imagine the horrors of a pissing, shitting little thing…." He looked up, aware of his audience. "Have any of you got kids?" A few nods. "Well, yes, so you can imagine the horror of it all….a little screaming alien that won't talk your language, how awful…" He paused to drink his tea again and smiled, a similar sensation if not quite as intense a hit sparking through his body.

"So she had this kid, a boy….called Ethan…strange name…but she was in a lot of pain and the poor girl did such a fantastic job, is doing such a fantastic job, with the little one. But she couldn't work, she seems to be in constant pain, and she got benefits for it but about a month ago they took the benefits away. She had to be reassessed or something. Went to some centre or something, I don't know. But the long and the short of it was – they said she could stand up so she must be ok. So she lost her money. Terrible thing, terrible thing. She's the reason why people like you and me… though probably more you than me boys, I have to admit…she's the reason we pay our taxes. She's hardworking, does everything she believes it's right and proper to do. Sign of a decent society is the way we treat genuine folk like her, don't you think?"

It was a rhetorical question and he didn't pause for a response. "But it's worse than that. She's got this boyfriend. I don't know if he's the father of the sprog or not, I don't ask, but he's a horror, an absolute beast. There's more human dignity and compassion in a stone than in this chap. I heard him go mad at her for "failing" this test, said she should have spread it on thick, exaggerated, not stood up. Jill, you know, poor Jill, she did her best, as one should. I'm sure he took his anger out on her in some sort of physical form. And he goes about in these grand designer clothes…he's playing the system but he's not 'in the narcotics trade', so to speak. Maybe he's fiddling the system in incapacities, who knows. Or maybe he's knocking off shops. Anyway, he's a brute. She goes about in rags, pretty much rags. She's a lovely girl, it's such a shame. We're good friends…well, you know…"

He looked at the friends, sitting about munching cake with their eyes fixed on him. "I've helped her occasionally, financially, here and there, money for her, money to buy clothes for the little one." He smiled, a broad beaming smile. "He can be quite cute sometimes, actually. Anyway, I think that makes her feel some kind of…as if she owes me something and the poor girl only has one thing to give back. Which I have told her I would never take if it is offered in exchange for something. But if there is a free exchange, well, that's different. Sometimes the poor little thing wants to be held and I can hear her sobbing… "

He stood up and clicked the television on and immediately turned the sound completely down. "Oh, sorry, I like to watch the news, keep an eye on things, you know…. "

Oliver leaned forward. "The girl…Jill….doesn't she have family she can go to? Or go back to? She needs help."

"Yes, I know, I do what I can. But the family, her family, they sort of cast her aside when she got involved with the guy she had the baby with. As I said I don't know if that's this guy or another one. And then they were horrified when she got pregnant and it was a 'don't darken our door again you unwholesome bitch' sort of thing. They had money, her family, she didn't come from around here. But, you know, she thinks – 'well, I've made my bed, I have to lie in it', kind of thing…"

"But surely," said Oliver, "I mean, family, you know… they'd take her back….unconditional love and all that…"

"Well, my friend," said Nathan, "yeah, that's the way it should be. And the state should have supported her. And her boyfriend/father of the child should be there too and should be offering financial help. There are a lot of betrayals here. A lot of failures. Too many 'shoulds'. So that now, this responsible, adroit and well-intentioned girl is falling through the cracks. Because what…because she followed her belief, maybe misfounded, in a guy? And because she could stand up? If I wasn't benevolent towards her she would almost willingly have become a prostitute. She found it so hard to accept something for nothing she was willing to trade her body as a way of saying 'thank you'."

The shouting began to increase. Ellis looked at him. "Don't you interfere? When it gets like this? You clearly… feel something for her…"

"I'll knock on the wall sometimes. It's enough. The guy hates me but he knows who I am and that I….know people that might make his life difficult, let's say."

"Why don't you … I don 't know, get her away from it?" asked Oliver, puzzled.

"I can't say I haven't thought of it. But though my life is glorious it is also complex. And it may not look like it to you as we sit here drinking this beautiful drink and eating this quite marvellous cake, but it can be quite dangerous. Sometimes. I don't want, I can't have, baggage. But it's sad, of course it's sad. She's a beautiful girl you know…she was beautiful but now her face is white, she walks with a wince and limp when she walks and her eyes are dull and dark. When she smiles you see what she was and what she might be." He stood up. "She doesn't smile so often. But that can't be my fault. As I said, a lot of 'shoulds'. I've been about the only one who actually 'did'." And with an up till this point hidden ferocity he drew back his hand and hammered it with a force that defied belief into the wall. The flat, and the flat next door, shook momentarily. Immediately the shouting ceased and minutes later a door slammed as the guy exited. A small knock on the wall was returned. "That's her way of saying 'thank you'," said Nathan.

There was a small scratching at the door. Oliver cocked his ear towards it and immediately thought it might be a rat. "Do you hear that noise, that scraping?"

"Oh," said Nathan. "That'll be the dog. Fido."

"You have a dog? And it's roaming about outside? Does it take itself for a walk?" Ellis looked at him, confused.

"No, not my dog. Her dog. And his real name is something else….actually, it might be a she, I don't know…I call it 'Fido' because….that's what you call dogs, isn't it?"

Fido waddled in, as browbeaten and destroyed by life as his owner. He had a black coat but it was uneven, as though a toddler had been set loose on him with a pair of scissors. He was plump though hardly fat but looked as if the very thought of running would render him immobile. He held his head and his eyes downward, apologising for being there, almost apologising for being alive. He looked flea bitten though Nathan assured them he was clean. He struggled to the kitchen where Nathan had put out some food for him and ate slowly as if every mouthful was a struggle and then sank down at the edge of the sofa. Oliver looked at him with pity, this lifeless beast that had been abused, picked on, made ugly and no doubt kicked from pillar to post. The dog was only three years old but looked about twenty times that age, on his last legs literally, a victim simply because he fell through the same cracks as his owner. "She lets him come here," said Nathan, sensing the stares of the friends on the crippled, damaged beast as it lay helpless and hopeless. "I think she sends him sometimes because she knows I keep food for him. Otherwise maybe he wouldn't eat." He sighed. "You see a lot, working here, staying in a place like this. A lot of desperation. You learn a lot about survival." He shrugged his shoulders as though he could no longer find the words to express what he had seen, what he had felt and what he thought. "It's very tough. You know? Very tough. Flowers don't grow here, chaps. They're not allowed to."

He sank his tea in a massive gulp and gave a satisfied lick of his lips. "Well, anyway, boys, Ellis, whoever – any of you care to fill me in on why you might need something like a Taser?"

They decided that, since Ellis had been the one interested in the Taser, he should be the one who made the decision about which one to pick and what to do with it. None of the rest of them really wanted to be anywhere near it. "Aye, you go and pick it," said Oliver, "we'll stay and watch what's passing for news on the tv these days."

They turned the television up. The headline story related to police falsification of witness statements at a football-related tragedy over twenty years ago. There had been overcrowding at a football match as a result of police incompetence and witness statements had apparently been changed to give the impression that the spectators had been a drunken bunch of louts who had pretty much charged the police and forced entry to the ground. The official line had been that it was the fault of the supporters. But now it appeared that lie had been exposed and the supporters had been guilty of the heinous crime of wanting to see a football match.

Ali watched it with more than interest, more than horror. "I knew that Report was due," he said, "but I didn't realise it was going to be this explosive."

"Will you be writing about it?" asked Oliver.

"In some way, yes. Whether it's the effect on the footballers, or how football changed since then. Probably not the family stuff – it's a huge story, the news boys will do that. But….that's shocking. That'll go legal now, it has to. Look at the number, they're saying there over 1,000 statements were altered. That's unbelievable."

"You wouldn't have thought that, would you, in a country like ours?" said Aidan, almost hypnotised by the replaying of the terrible scenes of the original disaster on tv. "We don't think of the police in that way, do we? They're seen as…….I guess these bastions of law and order, aren't they?"

"Sure they are," said Oliver. "Guildford Four, Birmingham Six…"

"Yeah, well," said Aidan, "that was then. There was a war on. But this….this wasn't a war. This seems to be a nasty corrupt cover up. They seem to have simply fabricated stuff."

"You think that doesn't happen?" asked Euan. "You think the police don't fabricate things?" It was strongly put and Aidan was on the back foot.

"No….I suppose I don't."

"Look at the fucking tv Aidan," said Euan. "You can't trust them. Look!"

Oliver looked at the dog which had stirred itself very slightly at the sound of a raised voice. It had a frightened look in its eyes, an almost Pavlovian reaction to the sound of an increase in the volume of a male voice. Oliver thought on how strange that was, most dogs would have shown the protective side of their character in such a situation. But not this one. This dog has lost its trust in those who should have protected it a long time ago.

Oliver turned his head back towards the tv. The second story was about a widening of the enquiry into a famous tv celebrity who was now being accused of molesting and raping young girls over a period of what seemed to be about twenty to thirty years. From what was being reported it was one of those open secrets – oh, everyone knew what he was up to but nobody wanted to be the one who blew the whistle. He did a lot for charity. He was probably very nice to his mother too, thought Oliver. So all in all, well, it appeared to be the prevailing view was that nobody's perfect and we didn't want to say anything because, he was a big famous guy. Yet over the years it seemed there had been two to three hundred claims of rape or sexual assault. Children. Children who had gone to the

357

guy's dressing room, dreaming of meeting an idol, and had their entire being violated. Christ, thought Oliver, probably even their lives. How do you deal with, how do you cope with something like that, at that age? It's beyond the comprehension of anyone who hasn't experienced it.

"That's unbelievable," said Euan. "So many people, children. And undetected."

"It was a long time ago, by the sounds of it," said Aidan. "70s, 80s maybe. You'd like to think it wouldn't, it couldn't happen today."

"But it happened," said Oliver. He rested his head on his hand. Maybe that's the way things are. Were, are and will be. People in power get to do what they want. The others can eat cake if they can find it. Live on scraps, dainty little toffees thrown by way of advantage taken. He looked across at the dog again, its sad weeping eyes almost closed.

"What I don't understand," said Ali, "is how that culture of… silence…can exist for so long. From what I see, it's impossible to keep a secret about what has happened in a dressing room at a football match or what's been said between a caddie and a golfer. How do you keep a secret among that many people? For so long?"

"JFK," retorted Oliver. "Whatever went on there, we'll never know the truth. And it seemed to take the girls that were hanging about that golfer a bit of time to come out. Secrets can be kept alright. But this," he said, waving his hand at the television, "this is dark. These girls…they must have thought there was no chance of them being listened to if they went to the police. They accepted it. As if it was all they were worth." And he thought of the girl last night, lying on the bed and being beaten. "As if that's all she was worth."

The next item on the news related to a cyclist, a sparkling, magnificent and well decorated cyclist who had won innumerous tournaments and who appeared to have cheated his way to them by doping. The allegation, however, was that it represented doping on an as yet unprecedented scale, unseen in this or any other sport.

"Ah well Ali," said Euan, "it looks like you're going to have a busy time when you get back to work".

"Oh my God!" said Ali, drawing his hands to his face. "You know there were rumours. Always rumours about this and that, his performance was too good to be true. But he's never failed any test and you get to thinking 'Well, maybe the rumours are others being jealous and throwing rumours about to plant a bit of doubt, you know'….but this seems pretty clear, doesn't it?"

"The guy was like...an idol," said Euan. "This supreme athlete...."

Oliver sat, wondering what would happen when the pillars started to fall. Maybe they had already fallen. Corrupt sportsmen, corrupt police, evil and malevolent celebrities, money and power leading to corrupt privilege. Maybe there had been no pillars. Maybe people who spoke about the past as a golden halcyon age, about an age when you could leave your back door open, when your neighbour was your friend and whom you always addressed as "Mr" or "Mrs" whatever, about when you could be in the middle of town on a Saturday night and not worry about being stabbed, maybe these people saw the reflection of an ideal memory. What lay beneath never came to the surface. If celebrities abused people and it never made it to the police then maybe that was because it had been so widespread anyway, whether that was abuse of children or women or both. Maybe you never minded about leaving your back door open because you had nothing to steal. Maybe people lamented the loss of those days because they simply didn't understand the present, with its informal yet distant meshing of relationships, its rampant self-interest, its gloating commercialism. So maybe there had never been any pillars anyway. Take away God and you get spiritual freedom and no more serfdom but you also get spiritual anarchy. Maybe better with a false pillar than none at all. And God had supposedly died on or around 1912, as the lady kind of said. So these things came crashing down but they made the noise of invisible pillars, falling with the whiff of a feather, a silent blast met only with a rueful shake of the head and the defeatist acknowledgement of 'I knew there was something not right about that.' But beyond that, nothing. Life goes on. Oliver looked again at the dog, struggling to move itself into a different position to be a bit more comfortable. It goes on, but just. You have to do what Fido's doing, thought Oliver. Make yourself as comfortable as you can be, given the circumstances...

Jenny had been released from hospital when they were as certain as they could be that there was no damage and that the worst of her pain was over. She was given painkillers, told not to work for a week or two, depending upon how she felt and advised to take rest and walks that weren't too strenuous as often as she could. The police had advised her that they had reached a dead end. She knew this was because they felt she was withholding information. She was. That was fine. I've been

359

taught my lesson, she thought. Enough now, he's had his revenge.

Helen thought it would be a good idea, at least a nice idea, to visit Jenny. It was probably the right thing to do, she thought. And in truth it really wasn't such an unpleasant time as they exchanged pleasantries and sympathies. She told Jenny about Oliver being away and having a marathon journey home and Jenny told her about her headaches, her visitors, anything. Jenny was one of those people who talked about her friends, her family, people she knew as if you knew them too. She would come out with a name that you had never heard before and you were supposed to know right away who this person was. Helen had always thought it strange. You almost felt rude if you asked 'Sorry, who's that again?' The person was being spoken about in such familiar first name terms that it would have felt a bit like asking your sister what her name was. So Helen let Jenny warble and chatter because that's what she wanted to do and she was the one recuperating, after all. Helen nodded and smiled and appeared enthusiastic when she was supposed to. Helen could always do 'phoney' quite well, probably even before she had read *Catcher In The Rye*.

But she wasn't really listening. Not properly. Well, not properly until Jenny began to talk about her sister, Suzanne. Suzanne was a primary teacher at a school in Manchester.

"Oh God Helen, I was speaking with Suze a day or two ago, she came up to see me on Friday/Saturday. She was telling me about her kids, she teaches these really young primary school kids, P1 maybe P2. But they are young, you know?"

The 'You know' was a prompt that Helen recognised, something she knew she had to react to. "Oh yes, must be hard to control a class of children so young. Must be like crowd control."

"Well, yes, that too, yes. But she was telling me, she does this thing with them in class, she calls it something like 'Special Event' when the children can talk about something they've done that's…well, special, I guess. Maybe they went to a football match for the first time or went away for the weekend, you know the kind of thing. Anyway, there was this one child, a young boy, skinny wee thing, who never seemed to say very much. He'd never spoken at 'Special Event' time. That was ok, he was quite shy. But as she said he was a sullen, sad-looking little boy, always tired, he didn't smile very often and she wanted him to try to say something in front of the class. So she had a word and said 'Hey, tomorrow, I'd like you to say something.' He was hard to convince but when he agreed she knew he'd do it. She didn't care much if it was only that he'd gone to the supermarket with his mum – it was pretty obvious the family didn't have much money – as long as she got him saying something, try to build his confidence, you know?"

"Yes," said Helen, by now a little more attentive, a little more interested. She watched Jenny as she sipped her tea and ate her biscuits. She was bright eyed now and though there was still a bandage of sorts on her head she was her usual, normal self. Somehow that felt comforting. And Olly would soon be home, later today....

"Well the little one came in the next day and she asked him if he was going to speak and he said yes and she asked what it would be about and he said about his evening with daddy. 'Ok,' she said, 'great.' The little boy looked at the ground at first and sort of mumbled. It was hard to hear him. So Suze said, 'Hey, speak up a bit and look at me' as she was at the back. So he raised his voice so all could hear. And he told them all about what he and his daddy would do on some evenings. They would wait till it was dark and daddy would drive about in his car. Sometimes they would have a ladder with them, they usually did, and that was good because he – the boy – liked to climb up ladders. Suze said that when he spoke about climbing up a ladder it was about the one and only time she'd seen him smile. Anyway, he said they would drive till it was quiet and his daddy would put the ladder up against a window. Then the boy would clamber up the ladder and try to open the window. Sometimes there were windows open already and that made things easy. But if he couldn't open the window he would come back down and they would try somewhere else. Sometimes daddy knew that there wouldn't be anyone at home and sometimes he knew that the window was going to be left open. Those times were best and they were easiest.

The little boy then said that his job was to go inside and try to take anything that looked sparkly or golden and stick it in the plastic bag that his dad had given him. Sometimes it was easy, it was almost as if things had been left out for him. And, said the little boy, quite proud of himself, I am quite quick and I can be very quiet and be on my tip toes – and he mimicked walking on his tip toes – so nobody hears me. He said his daddy had said that if he got caught in any house that his dad would drive away without him so he had to be quick and quiet. But he said he usually did very well, he knew the places to look and his daddy was usually very happy with him.

The rest of the children seemed to find this hilarious and looked around to the teacher for approval as they whopped and hollered in their applause. Suze said she could only sit there, her face getting whiter and whiter. She said she put her head in her hands thinking 'What the hell do I do now?'

"What?" said Helen. "His father is making this kid go robbing in the middle of the night? That's....Jesus, that's unbelievable!"

"I know," said Jenny. "She was asking me what she should do – God, it's difficult, isn't it?"

Helen almost exploded. "No it isn't! She has to tell someone. Headmaster, police, someone. There are so many crimes there...."

"Yeah I know," said Jenny. "But what happens after? What happens to the kid? To the parent? Or parents?" This was black and white, thought Jenny, she's right......but then you shouldn't really have an affair with a student nor fail them for ending it.

"Well I'm sure the kid would get something better. That's evil. How can someone do that to a child? For the love of God, that's Terry's age." She said the last sentence more quietly and was more thoughtful. She wondered upon the little boy's delight at pleasing his dad and considered how impressionable his mind was. How his sense of right and wrong, of acceptable and unacceptable, of moral and immoral was being drip fed day by day. And how hard it might be to change that. It was a crime to use the child to commit a crime, sure, Helen thought, no court in the world would argue against that. But surely the greater crime was the poisoning and twisting of the child's mind. It was like taking a sapling and deliberately twisting it away from the light, bending it into a contorted form where it couldn't grow as it should. Perhaps even twisting it into a state where it turned back on itself. The malevolence in corrupting and filling this empty vessel horrified Helen. Was this the only case, the only place where this happened? Is this the only child that's been sent up a ladder? What kind of a place did we live in where people felt they could commit something as evil? And where those in responsibility struggled to know if they should report it or not.

She shook her head. "What's she going to do? Your sister? What's she going to do?"

Jenny was quiet, unusually quiet. "I don't know. I don't think she knows." She added, as an afterthought, "I don't think she's slept much since the story."

'Well,' thought Helen, 'that's ok then. She hasn't slept much. Poor her. So we'd sympathise or empathise with her for what she's gone through, poor thing having to listen to that story. But if she does nothing, or says nothing, she's as guilty of child abuse as the bastard who sent the kid up the ladder.' But she didn't say anything lest she offend Jenny.

Officer McLean was sitting at his desk when his superior came in and threw a folder at him. Not in an aggressive way but in a way that made it clear that what was landing on his desk was something that was now his responsibility and not his boss'.

"Here you go Chris, this'll get you off your backside."

"What is it?"

"A hit and run. Seems to be a tramp. Stepped out off the pavement at the wrong time. Hit by a car. He was probably drunk. But the car doesn't seem to have stopped. Doesn't seem to be a next of kin we can find. But it needs to be investigated. We need to at least make some attempt to find the guy driving the car. Or the woman. Whatever." He waved his hand dismissively. "Whatever. The details are all in there. Where it happened, etc. Go and talk to people, see if you can come up with anything. Don't waste too much time on it, though. The tramp died in hospital."

Officer McLean looked up but by this time his boss had picked up the phone. He opened the folder. There was minimal information – time of admission to hospital, time of death, location where the ambulance picked him up, a couple of statements from people who had seen the tramp but no one who had reported seeing the incident. He sighed. Great, just great. At least it would stop him sitting at his desk and thinking about where the next blackmail note might be coming from and what sort of false information he might pass to Helen.

The accident, assuming it was an accident, had taken place on a main road, a busy road. The tramp had sat outside the shop, begging as he usually did. It transpired that some of the staff in the shop knew him by sight. They should have actively moved him on but tended to be quite tolerant. He was a frail old man, hardly what you would term an aggressive beggar. He sat with his head down and his cup in front of him. He had always been unsteady on his feet. Whenever anyone had seen him walking it was with an unsteady gait, as though his legs were shaking with the pressure of carrying his slender frame. He wore a lot, there seemed to be layer upon layer, but underneath it all he was thin.

No one in the shop had seen the accident. Maybe someone outside had, the street was quite busy. Officer McLean knew that would mean putting out an appeal for witnesses. No one had seen or heard a driver leaving the scene with any haste. The most helpful was the store manager who had been up in his office on the 5th floor. When he looked out the window he saw the tramp lying on the street, double up, clutching his abdomen. He wasn't moving.

"Were there people there? Did anyone stop and tend to him?"

"No," said the manager. "Not that I saw. They gave him a wide berth. They walked around him. As if he was a pile of rubbish lying in the middle of the pavement. You don't stop to examine what's there, do you?"

Officer McLean winced at the image. "Well, it's true, isn't it? The guy could have been clutching a gun. Wouldn't be the first time that had happened – someone pretends to be injured but it's a ploy to get attention and you end up getting robbed."

"Did you phone for the ambulance?"

The manager looked down. "No I have to say….mea culpa and all that…I thought someone downstairs would have done it. I thought they would have seen it all."

"You didn't think to go downstairs? Have a look? See how the guy was?"

"Well, no. People downstairs would have, could have, done that. Officer, the guy was a beggar… I told my staff that, unless his behaviour was aggressive, they should let him beg. This is a decent shop, it attracts a decent clientele, they are rich people, you know? He was more likely to get money from these kind of people and we let him sit outside".

'That's debatable,' thought Officer McLean. "Ok," he said. "Do I have permission to speak with any of your staff? You'll appreciate, I'm sure, that I need to try and find out exactly what happened."

"Of course Officer, as you wish."

After a day or two of questioning Officer McLean began to put together a chain of events. No one really knew why or when the tramp had stood up and no one had seen him being hit by the car. However, given when the tramp was first seen on the ground, it was possible to put an approximate time on when this had happened. What was clear was that the tramp had lain on the ground for fifteen and a half minutes at least before someone had called an ambulance. The public had walked by him, over him, through him. Some of the shop staff had seen him but thought nothing of it, despite him never being seen before in a lying down position. The guy died. He had been left, with the world around him, to die. What was clear from the hospital records was that he had been alive, just, when he reached the hospital. When Officer McLean asked the doctor who had treated him if it would have made any difference to the tramp's life if he had arrived at hospital ten, fifteen minutes before he did, he said: 'Absolutely, yes.' He could, he should, have been saved.

It was only that no one had been interested enough in the life of a human being whose existence made them feel guilty. Guilty because he was the flip side of their dream, a dark and twisted nightmare where you didn't get the things you wanted or deserved. Guilty because somewhere in his ragged clothes and rugged face was a shadow of themselves, the part they tried to keep hidden from even themselves, the part that said that somehow we are all responsible. The part that said we are not above this, and it might not be his choice to be there, the part that said that when you pursue something and achieve that there must be others who don't achieve. And the fact that we partake means that we must face the consequence – there will be those who partake and don't achieve. There will be those who fail. They'll fail because they are too weak or because they were neglected or abused or spat on or they'll fail because not everyone can win. And how do we deal with those, those shadows of us? We forget they exist. They are a threat to us. The way people walked past this guy made it clear to Officer McLean how they manifestly made a threat of him – 'he may have had a gun.' No, he didn't, but he had the stare of death and perhaps those who walked by him had known that. And they had known that the stare of death of this neglected and abused soul, penniless and hopeless, holding a mirror up to their face, would have hurt much more than a bullet from a gun.

Officer McLean thought that, before closing this, he should at least have a look at the tramp. No one knew his name. He was never given a name by the hospital. Just 'the tramp'. Officer McLean had been in the army: he had fought in the odd war zone and seen some quite horrific things. He had seen the best and worst of humanity. But as a surgeon must very quickly become used to the sight of blood, he had very quickly become immune to bullets and blood and bombs and danger and the worst of man's inventions. As he looked upon the face of the tramp, however, he cried. He touched him, briefly, a dull lifeless form. 'At least,' he thought, 'no one can hurt you now. They won't ignore you anymore.'

After a while Ellis came through to join the others, a small Taser in his hand and a smile on his face.

"Well," said Nathan, "I'm going to enjoy another cup of that wonderful tea. I would ask you to join me but Ellis says you are in a hurry now so I wish you God speed, gentlemen. I'll get the Taser back sometime. And good luck!"

They thanked him for his help and hospitality. As Oliver made his way to the door he heard the noise of the little boy next door crying. "Ah," said Nathan, "feeding time for him I think. I'm not sure if she has food but I have some here I will take through."

Oliver looked back into the flat before he walked out the door and saw the dog again. Tired still, almost struggling to breathe. It stood up, unsteady on his legs and then tried to waddle to the door. Poor old thing, he thought. Everything seemed so difficult for it. As if life was something that happened elsewhere, to other people.

As if life was something that happened elsewhere, to other people.

CHAPTER 18

The Capo looked around him. Then he looked at his watch. It was half past midday. He shook his head.

"And you say this was unprovoked?" He glanced to the two dead bodies at his feet, their throats slit from side to side, their faces blackened, bruised and battered to beyond a state that he would have recognised.

"Absolutely." The man who spoke to him was small and stocky and looked as though he would, at one time, have been a rugby player. But he was a touch too chubby round the middle and the receding hair line told that the energies of youth had started to take their leave.

The Capo sighed. He had taken a call at nine o'clock his time that morning and been told that their good friends and partners, the Rizzalos, had been attacked in a vicious and unprovoked manner that had left two of their number dead. Four of them had been bundled into a car and driven to the nearby woods. Two had managed to escape. The Capo had got into his helicopter and was there as quickly as he could manage.

"How did they get you? At that time in the morning?"

"They know where we stay. Our houses are near each other. They came….maybe with guns, I don't know, I was away overnight….but they took two of our guys from each house. When I came back at eight the houses were empty. I phoned you when Frankie staggered back, beaten and in a hellish state, and said that they had killed two of our guys."

"Something like this is never unprovoked. Do you have an arrangement for distribution between your two groups that you ignored? Did you piss on their parade? This is business – you don't go and kill people in this way for nothing."

"Frankie's inside the house, we can talk with him. He said something about a woman, they were talking about us taking one of their women. It wasn't clear – and it's nonsense anyway. But we can ask him. Let's get back into the car."

The Capo pointed to the two dead bodies that lay at his feet. "You can't leave these guys here. Either put them in the boot or get someone to pick them up. Don't leave them here. They may get discovered by some member of the public. I don't think we want your police force poking their nose into this."

"Of course." The man made a call and they waited until a van came and bundled the corpses inside.

In the car The Capo was silent. The UK represented a significant market for what he offered but he could do without it. Financially, anyway, he could do without it. But these people – this gang – had been good to him. They were what you might call strategic partners. So if someone attacked them then they also attacked The Capo.

Frankie certainly was in a bit of a state. He could hardly open his eyes due to the huge swelling in his cheeks and his body was the colours of a dark twisted rainbow, all mixing together in a blur of dangerous blueish red. He should have been in the hospital.

"It's ok," said the stocky man to The Capo, "we can tend to him here. We know a doctor."

Frankie was lying down with various ice packs around and on him. The Capo knelt down and ruffled his hair. Frankie tried to smile.

"Can you tell us what happened? Why it happened? But if I'm to help you I need the truth. If this was provoked then I need to know. We're partners, we work together, we don't have secrets. Ok?"

Frankie nodded. Given the way he looked The Capo expected that Frankie would struggle to talk and that there would be a wait as syllable followed syllable. But he was clear and lucent and spoke at his normal pace if, at times, in obvious discomfort.

"Listen, Capo, I have no idea what happened. They came early this morning, pulled us from our beds with knives at our throats. They bundled us – four of us – into two cars and we drove to the woods. They didn't even bother to put hoods on us, I guess that made me scared. On the way there I had the awful thought – 'Christ, we're not coming back from this.' They said nothing in the car, nothing at all, just held these knives close to us. It wasn't long, it was a quick drive. Then we got out and they had each of us up against a tree. Maybe about six or seven of them. They were fuming, really angry about something. We tried to look at each other, we're all wondering what the hell this is about…"

"You said four of you?"

"Yes, four."

"Ok, you…two dead…where's the other guy?"

"Oh he's back in his house, he ran faster than I did, he's less injured. He's ok, you can see him of course if you want to…"

The Capo silenced him by putting his hand up. "Continue, please."

"We had no idea. We're trying to look at each other, each probably wondering if one of the others has gone solo, done something he shouldn't have, something that these bastards have taken great offence at. These guys, you see, sure, we're enemies. We're each trying to supply the same products to the same people but we have a sort of....well, unwritten agreement...no one wants a war, do they? They're there, we're there, and neither of us is going to go away. There is room for both of us. Things have been ok between us. There's always a spark, you know, a cross word, a fight between some of our guys and some of theirs....but it's lower level, Under Fives.."

"Under Fives?"

"Sorry, the name we give to our young members. Usually kids under sixteen... "

"Ok. And so? They must have told you some of what this was about, asked you questions..."

"They did. But what they asked made no sense. They wanted to know what we were doing in the Travelodge last night and what we had done to one of their girls, their women. They had knives to our throats but we're saying, listen pal you've made a mistake. As far as we know none of our guys were staying anywhere last night, they were at home and we know nothing about a woman. What woman? Which woman? And they started to get angry. One of them, I couldn't see him but I could hear him, the leader I think, said we clearly had guys in this hotel who had spent some or most of the evening with a girl who belonged to one of their guys. Then our guys, apparently, knocked at the door of one of their guys and started to threaten their guy. That's when they knew it was us, they said – because another guy appeared then there was another few in their room ready to appear. They realised it was some sort of ambush." He looked at The Capo. "I mean, it's rubbish, the lot of it. So of course we kept denying it and he said 'If you don't tell me the truth I'm going to slit each of your throats in turn'."

The Capo held his hand up. "Did he give you any names? Did he say how many of you he thought there were?"

"Oh, yeah, that's another thing. He said he didn't know how many of us there were exactly but he thought about five. And he heard a couple of names... Euan and Olly...Olly, Oliver maybe. We don't have anyone with these names in any part of our organisation! We shouted louder and he just slit Leonard's throat. Quick, flash....." He mimicked the action as best he could.

The stocky man saw the change in The Capo's expression. The eyes widened. The face changed colour, from a grey slate to a lifeless white. He held his hand up again to silence the man and turned to Davide.

"That's our guy. That's our fucking guy. And his friends." He turned to Frankie.

"About five of them you said?"

"Well that's what they said. Maybe their guys heard four or five voices, I don't know. Anyway, then he started on…"

"Stop!" said The Capo. It wasn't said with much force or volume but it brought Frankie to a sudden halt and caused the stocky man to turn his head immediately.

"Stop." He paced, very slowly. "Maybe we have misjudged this Oliver. Maybe he was in France to secure supply. With someone else." He turned to the stocky man. "My friend," he said, "there is a distinct possibility that the man and his friends who have been mistaken for your gang are actually part of another gang. Or group. A group who clearly knew who your enemies were and have probably posed as being part of your gang to try to drive a wedge between you. It's a tactic that is as old as the hills – don't fight your enemies, get them to fight each other and pick up the pieces when they are done. Then you are the last man standing. It's beginning to make sense. Because this stuff about a woman….you don't kill people in that way over a woman…"

Frankie tried to continue his story, which clearly included what he believed to be a heroic escape, but by then The Capo had stopped listening and started thinking. "Davide, get cctv from anywhere near that hotel, wherever it was. Find the car these guys were in. Get their registration number. Then let's find these guys and get this over with. It may mean that we are in Edinburgh by the end of today so cancel what I had planned this afternoon. And get the guys who are watching his wife to pay close attention. This has taken on another dimension." He looked around him. "I hate this rain infested country."

'Shit,' he thought to himself, 'how could I have been so wrong? Maybe Paul was right about this guy all along.'

"So what should we do…is there anything you can do to help us Capo?"

"Yes. Do nothing. I know you want revenge – an eye for an eye – and that is the way I work too. But you must, however difficult it may be, look at this with cold heart and distant eyes. These guys want you to take revenge. They want a war between the two of you. Don't give them it. Ask for a meeting, some sort of reconciliation. Let me sort out the nasty fly making trouble. Then you can have your status quo back." He ruffled Frankie's hair again and turned to Davide. With a nod of the head to each other they left the house together.

"Uh huh. Ok. Well, it's… something, it's something. And they are headed north? Maybe to Edinburgh? Well of course, of course, you don't know…but it's that road?"

Jacques clicked his phone off. "It was my friend. He says it might be something, it might be nothing. But in London yesterday morning, near the train station, there was some sort of incident. A car seemed to hit two guys on the pavement and sped off. It didn't seem to be an accident. The guy I was speaking to…he heard from a contact who had spoken with a guy in the hotel. His window looked right across the road. There were five guys in the car. No real descriptions but they stayed the night in a hotel last night and are headed north. We have a registration number. Black car. These could easily be our guys. It gives us something to look for. And we can get a monitor on them through every cctv camera. My friend says we are really not that far behind them, maybe a few hours."

"Why do you think that's them?" asked Natalie.

"We know there are people after them. Trying to capture them at the train station – it makes sense, doesn't it? And they escaped…"

"Ok, what's the registration number?" asked Natalie. "We can keep our eyes open for it."

When Jacques told her the first thing she did was text the number to Clotilde and write 'black car' after it.

The conversation between the friends had been engaging, vibrant, even funny at times. They were going home. With every minute they got closer and closer. The phone calls home became freer, the texts more frequent. All except Ali who found that in the main his texts went unanswered or were answered with curt responses. As though Lesley had something better to do. And he was with a group of people, friends he had known for years, who had stopped to get a Taser. Had you told me a week ago that I would even see a Taser, he thought… But then a great deal had changed in a week and Ali probably didn't know the proverbial half of it.

"Alright Ali?" Oliver had noticed his friend was quiet, even distant.

Ali was glancing out the window at nothing, more at the window itself than at what was outside.

"Oh, yeah. Was only thinking how mad this has been… "

"Well it's nearly over now," said Oliver, though it wasn't something he said with much conviction or truly believed himself.

"And we have a Taser…it seems crazy… I don't think I've ever hit anyone in my life and now I'm partly carrying this weapon that can maim. It's….a side of life I never thought I would see. I never wanted to see," he added hurriedly.

Again, Oliver felt the guilt stab at him. One simple impulsive defensive action, he thought, a thrust with a knife, had had such terrible repercussions. Even now, however, he couldn't say he regretted it. If that guy came at me again, he thought, I'd have to do the same thing again.

"I know," said Oliver quietly. "It's been absolutely hellish. And I'm sorry for it, for all of you, putting you through this. I truly regret what I've put you all through."

"Regrets, I've had a few," sang Ellis. The way he felt was probably the closest anyone got to feeling demob happy. He turned to Oliver. "What about the bird, Olly? Regret her yet?" Oliver looked down. He felt their eyes on him.

"Well," said Ellis, "my biggest regret is not going more on holiday with Olly before now. Fuck me, what an adventure! Never a dull moment, all action, women throwing themselves at you, every fucker you meet trying to kill you. Better than a Friday night in Glasgow! Euan, what's your biggest regret?"

Euan was silent and shifted a little uncomfortably. "What, of this trip?"

"No," said Ellis. "In life. Generally. Come on, we've still got a while to go. Let's play 'regrets'."

I can't tell them that, thought Euan. "Em…I don't know. Must be coming on this trip. No one's ever tried to kill me before. Had I stayed at home I don't think they would have. So it must be coming on this trip."

"Crap!" shouted Ellis. "That doesn't count. Come on, Boris, there must be something you regret. You know, a big pounding regret. Mine is…well, you know mine boys, you know mine…."

Euan looked around. He had done something years ago that he regretted very much. Something that no one knew. He had carried it and felt suffocated by it at times because he felt it made him a different person to the one the others saw. And if they knew what he had done they would see a very different person. If you do something once, something bad, something horrible, are you a bad person or a decent person who's made a mistake? It felt a bit like sleeping with your wife's sister for one night of the year: do you tell your wife to stop getting angry about it because, after all, you were loyal for the other 364 nights? After what had happened over the past week or so, now seemed the right time to share it with these people who were his best friends. Layer upon layer had been stripped from each of them for all to see. Cloaks had been pulled from faces, masks had been slowly taken off. He felt they were all bare in front of him. Except me. I still carry this thing.

The silence was intriguing to his friends. "Oh," said Ellis, "something's coming here. You're not going to tell us you've been Pope or something. Or turned down the chance to sleep with a superstar....or even better deliberately food poisoned a superstar in your restaurant..."

"No, no," said Euan, "nothing like that." He paused, not sure of where to start. "Ok, when I was at Uni – obviously a few years ago now – I played football for the Uni team as you probably know. It was quite a social thing too, as I guess most team sports are. We were of that ilk that 'the team that drinks together, wins together', you know the sort of thing. And we were a good team. We had some guys who could have gone on to become professional but they liked the bevvy a bit too much.

After a few socials you get to know people a bit better. Mostly people talk about the things that guys talk about – football, girls....that's probably about it, actually, thinking about it now. But there were four or five guys there....thinking back now, I can't remember if they knew each other before Uni or not....but there were these four or five guys and they were nice and everything, there was nothing wrong with them but they always made the odd comment that was a little...well, racist. It wasn't always overt, it wasn't always blatant, but I remember not being able to ignore it when they were talking about one lecturer who was black and they called him 'monkey' and 'nignog'. I was surprised, a bit shocked even and you pretend you don't hear, you sit farther across the table and hopefully manage to keep your distance. That apart though they were good guys – funny, good to be with, but at the back of your mind there was always that niggle that there was something about them you didn't know.

I remember one day we were playing a team that had a couple of black guys playing for them. Nothing much had happened in the first half and at half time I went to the toilet for a pee and two of them came through after me. They were talking to each other but included me because I was there.

"Just cripple the cunt!" the one said to the other, "black bastard has no right being on the same fucking pitch." He turned to me as he was peeing. "Euan, he's on your fucking side, anything's fair game against the fucker. Break the nigger's fucking leg."

"Steady guys," I said, about to go away, "it's a game of football."

"Fuck off!" said the other one. "What's your game? You a nigger lover?"

I shook my head and walked away. I had a word with the manager and he hauled them both off quite quickly into the second half. I think they knew I had said something and after that, I think…well, I think they tried to manufacture the situation that they did a few weeks later.

At the time we had gone top of the league. We were playing really well and it wasn't long before we had a break for Christmas. So we had a sort of Christmas night out. I'd kept away from a couple of their Saturday night binges after the conversation in the toilet but you can't stay away from a Christmas night out and anyway, the nights out were great. So we had a meal then after the meal I somehow ended up at their table, having a few drinks. I noticed afterwards how nice they were – they said nothing at all that could be considered racist. But I realised afterwards that they were always buying me drinks, saying how they couldn't keep up with me. I must have been having two to every one of theirs. But it felt good, you know – they didn't talk about anything bad and like I said they were most of the time good guys so you're thinking 'Ah, this is great, they've clearly said something in the heat of the moment, impulsive, they're not really like that, we can all say things we don't mean.' Fair enough…"

Euan paused. "But of course that's not where it finished. By the time we were getting ready to go I was quite drunk. Not so drunk that I couldn't remember anything or stand up but pleasantly, happily drunk. It was one of those times where you realised that you were more drunk than the people around you, though – and I remember looking at these guys at the time and thinking 'They're not drunk at all.' They said they wanted to go to a nightclub – neither I nor any of the others were interested – but coincidentally (though obviously there wasn't any coincidence) my flat was on the way to this club so they would walk back with me. It had all sounded so logical and so innocent. But I realised as

374

we were walking that we were taking a long way, there was a quicker, more direct way....I was having fun though, we were having a quiet post-match sing song the way you do, you know? I heard a couple of them talking in forceful whispers and I remember one saying, too loudly, 'One. On his own. We'll find one. We always do.'

Eventually they found what they were looking for. I had no idea what they had seen or what had happened but one of them grabbed my arm and we started running, sprinting. I immediately looked behind but there was no one, nothing there. We were in no danger at all. But the two running ahead of us had found and stopped a young black guy. They ran him down this alley, a dead end that he couldn't escape from. That sight, the sight of that guy will stay with me forever. By the time I arrived with the others the first two of them had got the guy on the ground and were battering him to death with their feet, jumping on him, kicking him, laying into him and screaming at him for being a 'fucking black bastard!'. They shoved me to the front and they stopped hitting him. The guy looked up. His face was this utter mess of blood. His nose was clearly broken, he was holding his head. He could hardly lift his body. God knows how many bones were broken. He could hardly find the energy to sob. And he was young. Maybe 16, maybe 15... " Euan paused, his voice beginning to shake.

"And they threw me to the front and said 'If you don't kick this cunt we'll make sure you're in a worse state than he is. Maybe,' one of them said, pulling out a knife, 'even worse.' I was thrown in front of this poor battered creature. I held up my hand. 'Boys, no, no. This isn't the way.' One of them got the knife to me and said 'Euan, I'd think nothing of killing you. A slit of the throat. You don't want to fucking mess with us. Now kick this piece of shit. One decent kick. You don't have to kill him, we'll do that. But I need to know you're on our side mate. You're not one of them.' I looked around them. I didn't feel quite so drunk anymore. Their faces were hard and fierce, brows tightly knitted, lips tight and tense. "Guys, no, you can't do this.' One made a sign and two of them went behind me. One held my arms whilst the other one got a knife near my throat. I tried to move and was almost screaming at them to stop. Then I saw this poor black guy almost look at up, almost inviting me to kick him. With what was almost a lunge he motioned his arm, pulling his arm towards himself."

"Look," said one of them "the cunt knows how worthless he is. He wants you to kick him. Good dog. Now boot the bastard!"

"They let me go and I drew my foot back. I connected with his stomach though I knew that anyone watching would have thought I kicked him harder than I did as I stopped my foot just in time. Not too early that they'd know it was false. They rejoiced and shouted and the black guy looked at me with this half smile, or the nearest he could manage to a smile. Two of them led me away and the others set to work on this guy again, jumping, punching, kicking with a ferocity that I hadn't seen. I shouted at them to stop, not to kill this guy and as I was led away one of them told me that they wouldn't kill him, they never did, but these folk needed to be taught a lesson. They needed to know their place. They weren't equals.

I never thought much about the guy that night, or on what I had done. I was too relieved at being alive. I think they would have killed me. Or maybe over the years it's something I have tried to convince myself of, I don't know. But the next day I realised what I had been part of. No stories on the news, nothing in the newspaper about this near-destruction of another human being…that was shocking to me, that something like this had not even made the news. It was horrific. And yet not so horrific that it was actually worth reporting. I wonder if the guy even went to the police. Probably not. Maybe thought he wouldn't be helped.

I felt terrible. The guys, these 'friends', well they had out of me what they wanted and didn't want to know me anymore. So I gave up the football, it was too distressing to even think of going back and facing them again. And of course I had to live with what I had done. I had kicked this poor defenceless battered guy. The kind of guy you would like to think of yourself as always standing up for. In the kind of situation where you think 'I would, in that situation, be strong enough to have the courage of my convictions.' But I wasn't. And I'm haunted by what might have happened had these guys taken it further. What if they'd wanted me to kill the guy? What if they'd given me the knife? Would I have had enough courage to have said no? I don't think so, I honestly don't think so. So you think – Christ, I'm a coward, I'm weak, I'm a racist, I'm a thug… "

At that point he struggled to maintain his equilibrium. His voice failed him in a series of chokes and gasps as he almost suffocated on the memory of a bleeding black guy inviting a kick onto and into himself. He didn't sob or cry, this was much more brutal, a catharsis that interrupted his breathing and made him sound as though he was, at times, drowning.

Oliver was the first to react. "Euan, mate, Euan, steady mate, steady, come on… there was nothing you could do…"

"Yeah," said Ali, "it's like the guard at the concentration camp, mate. If you don't kill you will be killed. It's a choice we can only make theoretically, hypothetically....when you are there and have to make it face to face in real life... it's different.."

"I know," said Euan, though the voice was unrecognisable, it sounded as though it came from someone else. Then, more clearly, "I know. But it doesn't stop these feelings. To save myself I might have killed that poor guy. What does that make me?"

"It makes you frightened. Frightened for your own life. Euan, you're not these guys. Doing what you did doesn't make you a racist. You don't go about battering ethnic minorities at the weekend, do you? We'd all have done the same in your situation Euan. All of us. As Ali said, it's easy to stand up and say 'Oh, I would hold on to my beliefs, I would have let them do their worst to me.' But in that situation, you had no choice." And again, with an emphasis on each word – "You had no choice."

Euan looked around his friends, four faces with empathy etched into every feature. "I realise it can't be done, it can't ever be done," he said, "but there are so many times I have wanted to go back, to try and find the guy, to try and say sorry. Then I think – the poor guy, he's probably been beaten up for his colour more times than I would want to imagine, it's maybe something that for him happened maybe like other beatings happened – so it would really be for me trying to appease my conscience. Maybe harder that I have to live with it, maybe that's the punishment."

"You can't punish yourself forever over it," said Ali. "You were forced to do something...."

"But that's the thing, isn't it?" said Euan. "I wasn't really forced. I knew what they were like. I didn't have to be there. I should have stayed clear of their company. I could have known something like that might happen..."

"Oh come on!" Ellis almost shouted. "There's a difference between guys shouting something in anger, passing racist comments and going and beating the shit out of someone. You can't have known Euan, you can't have known what they were really like...."

That's the thing, thought Oliver... that's just the whole thing about people saying things like that, things that you didn't know about them, or finding things out about them, that's just it....you don't know what they are really like at all...

Through a day or two of window cleaning and through paying quite a bit of attention, Anthony had managed to come up with a plan. It had helped that Helen had been agreeable. It had not helped that she didn't remember him, not even the slightest flicker in her translucent diamond –like eyes. He took it very slowly. He could see into the main bedroom, places he might hide. He could see into the sitting room, a kitchen leading off it to the back. Then round the back, looking all the time for a house alarm, a house alarm that didn't exist, nothing outside the house, no detectors inside. Great, nothing to disarm. He wasn't comfortable about the thought of an alarm. He understood such things but not to a level of expertise where he would remain calm if something started to go wrong. He would have cut something – a wire, all the wires he could see – but he knew that some systems started ringing when they were cut. So it was good that there wasn't one there. And, his heart skipped a beat, she was one of those idiots, one of those stupid clumsy people who left the key in the lock of the inside of the door. So all I need to do is either cut the glass or smash it in that bottom part, reach my hand through, turn the key and I am inside.

He watched as she took her child with her in the morning. He thought he knew, through his aural gymnastics the evening before, that she was going to see a friend who was in hospital, or who had recently got out of hospital. Her son would not be with her. She would take him to her parents. She would return to the house and her parents would bring her son back later that day. That seemed to be her agenda and he conservatively estimated that she might have two or three house in the house by herself before her parents brought her son back to her. 'This is my time,' he thought. He knew then that he had to get into the house via the back door that she would kindly leave almost open for him. It had to be quiet and quick for he knew there was a window that a neighbour across the way might see him from. Then he would hide. And how would he take her? With a gun? With a cloth over the mouth with something to knock her out? By persuasion? Perhaps not yet, perhaps she would need something more direct than persuasion. That would come. When she saw her new home, her new home that he had further filled with things she liked, with perfumes and creams and soaps that he had seen in the bedroom window, with even the same type of hankies that she kept by the bed, when she saw all these then she would simply fall into his arms. There had never been a love like this, no one would ever have loved her with this much force.

Whatever he did, he knew that he must get her into the car without raising suspicion. So if he put something over her mouth she would be unconscious. Much as the thought of carrying her touched and tingled him in places that thrilled him, he was bound to be seen. Carrying a woman into a car, with a registration number that was easy to spot, it wasn't a good idea. Because he was absolutely certain that he must never be caught. Of course he could do it in the dead of night but then he would have to wait... to wait for the return of the child, to stay hidden, where, in a wardrobe? Too difficult, too risky. And the child not being there, it was too good an opportunity to not take. The child was a problem, he always knew. He didn't want the child but he didn't want to kill it either and if he grabbed her when the child was there...well, everyone spots a screaming child, don't they? And the child was old enough to articulate what had happened. So now that the child was away, he had two to three hours surely – and that was enough, it had to be enough. It was as though it was knowingly being arranged for him, as if she almost kind of knew he would be waiting for her and was sending him a message.

Anthony was careful and he was quick. He used a sharp glass cutter to cut a hole no bigger than the size of his arm, reached inside and turned the key. He stepped into Helen's house and closed the door, locking it behind him. He drew in its smells, her smells, and sights, the sight and fragile presence of her everywhere. At first he stood in the kitchen, merely stood, transfixed, as though he could imagine himself being here, with her. As though this was home. Then he moved, through to the main room, her living room, which was open and left him nowhere to hide. Behind the sofa was not credible, she could have seen him as she came through the door into the room. He moved about slowly. There was another room downstairs, a study or maybe a dining room but to hide in there wasn't easy. Where? Under the table? Ok if you were a toddler, but otherwise....and a cupboard here and there but they were full, full of the rubbish that we stick into places like these, mess hidden from public and private view. If he really intended to hide in there he would have to put some of the rubbish out and where to put it? Even then he would have to crouch – and for how many hours would he need to stay like that? Maybe he could stay behind the front door......but there was a possibility of being seen by someone opening the door and anyway, a woman opening the door, being caught up in a fight, an altercation, something unusual, that can easily be seen.

No, he would have to go somewhere else. He trudged slowly

upstairs, shaking slightly at the thought of being inside her bedroom. There were four doors off the landing, a bathroom and three bedrooms. He looked about, one was clearly a spare room, one a room for the child and the other the main bedroom, Helen's bedroom. He almost danced into it, immediately sinking himself into the bed and burying his face in her pillow. It was one of the most beautiful sensations of his life. Taking his time, he looked at her clothes, her underwear, he opened every drawer to see what parts of her he could infuse. Little quaint, dainty socks. Sexy black stuff that made him struggle for breath as he rolled it out on the bed in front of him. Jerseys, warm polo necks that were warm and functional but he bet made her look gorgeous. And tops….low cut tops that would have shown the world what she had to offer. Trousers and skirts, all, he thought, tight and hugging, all part of that wonderful sway as she moved. Seeing what he saw made him appreciate again the full beauty of what lay beneath these garments. Mere fabric until she filled them, turning them into something she could use to beguile and hook.

He could have stayed there all day. He quickly looked into the other rooms. The child's room was untidy and his wardrobe was full. There was nowhere to hide. The spare room had a wardrobe but by the looks of the room no one went in there very often. It smelt unused. Not unpleasant, not musty, but it didn't have the linger of Helen's fragrance in it. So to hide in there….well, it might be ok but it would involve covering a bit of a distance to get to her. Not the best. But the wardrobe in her room was ideal. Ideal because there was space in it and all he had to do was move the shoes on the floor to be able to stay in a comfortable position. Also, it didn't shut properly and he could keek at her, know where she was if she was in the room, maybe even see her undress if she got changed. He decided that if she did get undressed that he would definitely let her do that first, put other clothes on, then take her. He couldn't let go the opportunity of watching her undress when she didn't know he was there. Anyway, it would probably be the only time from now on that that might happen – she was always going to know that he was watching her, wherever she was and whatever she did, from now on.

Anthony put himself into the wardrobe, leaving the door open. He reached for the gun that he had stuck down the front of his trousers, under his shirt. Just a precaution, of course, he could never hurt her. But it was a good way to force her to do something, anything, he wanted and he figured it would be a good idea to at least fire one shot somewhere to let her know he was serious. He took the gun out and twirled the barrel.

Instead of seeing six bullets in the barrel, however, he saw nothing. He felt a sense of panic consume him. 'They're in the car, they're still in the car….' With so many things to think about before he entered the house – glass cutter, gloves, put covers over the soles of his shoes to avoid any imprints – he had forgotten to put bullets in the gun.

He closed his eyes. He knew he had time. It was unlikely that she would be back for a while, maybe half an hour at the earliest. That wasn't the problem. The problem was remaining undetected. He was confident that he hadn't been seen up to this point. But to go back, would that be a chance too far, a risk not worth taking? 'No,' he thought, 'she has to know that I am serious'. Because what if he was nervous? What if the capture emboldened her and she fought? Without a gun there was no threat. But I have a gun. Does she need to know it has bullets? Yes… in case of…yes. He moved out of the wardrobe and stood almost in the middle of Helen's bedroom, debating with himself what the best thing to do was. It was this pause which sealed his fate.

Across the road, a mild curiosity of what seemed to be a small movement seen through a pair of binoculars had turned into something a bit more puzzling.

"There's a guy in there, look, look! He's standing I think, standing there. I don't think it's the husband, I think….let me focus up closer on him….I think that's the guy we've seen about the street over the last couple of days, I think that's the window cleaner. See for yourself, look."

The acquaintance looked through the binoculars. If this guy is trying to hide, he thought, he's not exactly doing it very well, standing in front of a big window in full view of everyone. "It's not the husband?" he asked his colleague, trying to use a combined thought process to determine who this guy could be.

"It can't be. He's the window cleaner. He's been about here for the last day or two. The husband's down in….well, fuck, who knows where he is but we know he's not here….at least he's not been here for the last day or two, has he? So who is this guy? Window cleaners don't get keys to clean inside the house, do they? And he's not cleaning the windows anyway." He paused. "What should we do with him?"

"We ask Davide." He quickly pushed the button on his phone and explained the situation. Davide held a hurried conversation with The Capo.

"Boys," said Davide. "Take him down. The Capo thinks he is with the husband, connected to him. The husband's network runs way beyond what we had originally thought. This guy is probably there to whisk her away, out of danger. We are sure he's working with the husband. Take him down. But discreetly. Not in public view if you can avoid it. Get his body out of the way quickly – wherever the wife is, she mustn't see the body. She mustn't know anything's wrong, she mustn't see anything unusual."

"He's in the house, Davide. How do we do that?"

Another hurried conversation with The Capo. "Find a way. You're both good at your job. You'll find a way." And at the other end the line clicked dead.

The two men held a quick conversation as Anthony stood debating the issue of bullets with himself. They decided that they had to go across to the house. They could shoot him from here and kill him without any problem. The guy was like a sitting duck. But that would have meant shooting him through the glass and that would have made a mess. They had seen the guy go round to the back of the house so they figured he had to have got in through the back door.

They made their way down from their place of observation and across the road at the same time as Anthony decided that he must have the bullets. As they began to venture round to the back of the house so Anthony had come down the stairs. As he made his way to the back door so did they, neither the men nor Anthony aware of the presence of the other. Anthony rested his gloved hand upon the back door, conscious that he would have to be quick, there was the potential to be seen as he stepped outside. He opened the door, lowered his head, then closed the door behind him. About three steps away the two men saw the window cleaner come out of the back door with his head bowed. Their guns were already drawn. Anthony had managed to turn his head to catch sight of two men as the first of the bullets from the silenced guns entered his body. It was the last thing he ever felt and his body was forced back with the strength of the bullets before it crumpled.

The two men had been forced to drag a carpet across with them and quickly put Anthony's body into the carpet. He was bleeding, blood seeping from a few places in his body. They quickly checked the patio – no blood. But there was blood on the grass – not much but enough – that they missed and they also had not thought about how he might have gained entry to the house and completely missed the hole that had been cut in the glass.

They had enough trouble carrying a big carpet without looking as though they were two guys carrying a dead body. They bundled the body into their van, called Davide to tell him that the job had been done to the desired level of satisfaction, and waited whilst The Capo told them where to take the body. Inside the van the blood began to ooze out of Anthony's increasingly lifeless form. If he had had time to have a last thought it would have been that, when people discovered his house, they realised that no one could have loved anyone the way he had loved Helen. No one could fail to realise what he had done, all for love...

When Helen came back she knew quite quickly that something had happened. She thought at first she had been robbed. There was a different smell in the house. In her bedroom her wardrobe door was open, her shoes had been moved, there was the shape of a body having been on the bed. That was odd. A burglar who not only, it seemed, hadn't stolen anything but who had decided to have a lie down in the process of not stealing anything. And of course she had that fear that whoever had been there was still there, hiding somewhere. She moved carefully and slowly till she had convinced herself that there was no one upstairs. Then downstairs with quick heartbeat and an unsteady step, she moved from the living room to the kitchen. Then she saw the back door, a very neat cut of glass taken out of it.

"Oh my God!" She was frightened to open the door. It was unlocked. But as she pushed it open a bit further, and a bit further again, she realised there was no one there. She looked about outside the door, on the patio, on the grass. There were marks on the grass, marks that told of someone having stood on it or having lain on it or something. She knew it hadn't been her. And there was….that was clearly blood, wasn't it? She felt her stomach turn. What on earth had been going on? The house had been broken into but nothing had been taken and there was no one there. There had been some kind of activity on the grass and there was blood.

She had to phone someone. This consumed her, drowned her. Since she thought Olly was the cause of this, somehow, at least in part, and since she really didn't know where he was, she decided to phone Officer McLean. At that moment, it felt as though he would protect her more than her never-quite-making-it-home husband.

Across the road the men could see none of this. They had seen her register surprise but of course that was the surprise she was bound to feel when the man she expected to be there, the man who was going to take her to a place of safety, wasn't there.

"Surely our job here is done now? I hate this place. We've been here forever. Can't we go home now? Can't our Capo get the guy now? He knows where he is, doesn't he? That guy is never going to make it back here."

"Oh, maybe he will, maybe he will. Anyway, from what Davide says, it looks as though The Capo's coming up here. Probably with a couple of other guys. We've to make sure our surveillance is good. To increase it. The guy is slippier than we thought. By the sounds of it there will about ten of us ready to pop this guy. It's going to be like a fucking shooting gallery."

"Well, as long as they throw us his wife. Oliver, whatever your name is – you're an utter bastard and I hate you for making me stay in this place and I look forward to putting the bullet in you myself… but Christ you knew how to spot a beautiful woman…."

CHAPTER 19

"She's called the police…but there's only one of them. Policemen normally come in twos, don't they?" He strained his eyes through the binoculars and saw a policeman looking around the living room. The woman ran her hands through her hair. "What the…….he's hugging her, look!"

His colleague took the binoculars and sure enough saw the policeman hugging this man Oliver's wife. "What the hell is he doing? That's not a comfort hug, these people know each other. I'd lay my money on them having an affair. Phone Davide, do we take this guy out?"

"A policeman? Not normally our scene. The police it's….well, problematic. Yeah, problematic." He paused on the word and let it swirl around his mouth.

The call was made, the situation was explained and the reply was clear and without equivocation. "Don't touch the fucker. But watch as much as you want. And observe everything."

"It doesn't look like much is going to happen to actually watch. I mean, they're not exactly taking their clothes off. God, she's pretty! Even as she is now, she looks like she's crying, what a shape. You know, statistically speaking, there's got to be one time at least we see her taking her clothes off. One time when she forgets to draw the curtains. You know?"

"I'd rather see her getting herself off. Could you stay here and watch that? We'd be running across the road, can you imagine?"

At that point Helen and Officer McLean walked through to the kitchen and out the back door. They could no longer by seen by two of the people observing them. Helen pointed to the grass, highlighted the blood, showed Officer McLean the cut in the glass. He made a call and the glass was replaced immediately.

He looked at the grass closely. "Maybe we'll get something from the blood. And of course we'll try the fingerprints thing. But I don't think we are going to find much."

"Why not?"

"It's too… clinical. I'm not sure, maybe that's not the right word. Not professional. Professionals wouldn't leave marks in the grass…."

"Or wouldn't cut themselves on the glass…"

"Hmmmm….yes….yes….though I'm not sure that the blood has actually come from someone cutting themselves."

"No?"

"No. Well, maybe, maybe. Maybe I should get Stephen involved, he's more logical than me, he sees an event and its consequence more clearly than I do….but still… look, the first we see of the blood is on the grass. Nothing on the glass. Nothing on the patio. Nothing anywhere else. It's possible, I suppose. But odd. Maybe I should call Stephen."

"Stephen Barclay?"

"Yeah. You know him?"

"He came here before. About the Jenny thing. I think he thought they mistook her for me. He thought I was hiding something…."

"Oh. Well, we'll see, maybe I'll call him. I should have waited for him before I came anyway. And he'd probably know right away that we were having an affair. Which I'd rather he didn't know." He said it in a very matter-of-fact type of way. "Can I see the bedroom?"

Helen had left it as she had found it. "It looks like someone was planning to hide in the wardrobe, doesn't it?"

"It does?" Helen sounded almost incredulous.

"Don't you think? Look, someone's pushed all these shoes out the way –Helen, how many pair of shoes do you own? – well, look, they've shoved them out the way. As if they were going to stand there." He shut the wardrobe door and noticed it didn't shut exactly as it should. There was a small gap, a very small gap. He went inside and realised that he could see through the gap. "It's almost as if someone was going to wait in here."

"But….the bed, look, they've been on the bed, you can see a shape, look?"

"Yeah, so I see. Helen, could you tell by opening the drawers what order things were in? I mean if we opened a drawer would you know that these socks were not on top of the drawer this morning? Would you know if the order had been changed?"

"I…what….would I what… what the hell are you suggesting? Are you saying someone has been here and gone through my stuff? Some sort of….sick guy…a pervert? Is that what you're saying?"

"I don't know. I'm trying to follow the evidence. You thought it was a burglar but look about you. Nothing taken. You're got a jewellery box over there which hadn't been touched. You've got twenty pound something lying over there which hasn't been touched. Whoever has been in here, I don't think it's a burglar. Or if it was a burglar, I'm not sure that what they wanted to steal was the sort of thing a burglar normally wants to steal."

"What does that mean?" She was almost shouting. "What the hell is that supposed to mean? What did they want to steal?"

"Well, weighing up what's here...and it's a long shot...but I think they were wanting to steal....you."

"What? Me? You mean kidnap me? Take me away? But who...why... "

Officer McLean held up his hand. "Helen, I don't know, I don't know. This looks a very unusual situation. Being dispassionate about it..."

"You know, maybe it was a burglar. Maybe he got disturbed. A noise outside, something. So he ran away."

"Just after he carved out a nice place to hide in the wardrobe you mean?"

"Maybe he was looking for a safe," said Helen, her voice brighter, suddenly lighter. "Yeah. Maybe he was looking for a safe. People have safes in their wardrobe. Anyway, what about the blood? What happened downstairs?"

"That's difficult. It doesn't make sense. I don't think the blood came from the glass...and of course, who would want to kidnap you, take you away?"

Well, thought Helen, the mind boggles at that, but if she read Olly correctly then potentially quite a few. "But," said Helen, "if it was someone who wanted to kidnap me, they wouldn't do it like this for God's sake. Hide in my wardrobe, that's nonsense. Professional people don't do that..."

But Officer Mclean wasn't really listening. He went to the spare room which overlooked the back garden and looked at the grass. "You know," he said more than himself to Helen, "if I was looking at this, only the grass and the marks, instinctively I'd have said that these are the marks of more than one person. There seems to be to be too many marks for one person. Odd. Very odd."

Helen heard the end of what he said. "You think there was more than one of them? One of them was lying on the bed and the other was in the wardrobe?" Standing behind him, she put her arms round his neck.

Officer McLean was thinking. Not listening...not listening properly anyway. If there was someone, if someone had been there, maybe they would come back. They may possibly do that quite quickly so a plan, an idea, began to develop. Just a thought…it couldn't do any harm….and they might find out what was going on here. But he would need to be unobserved…if things were as he thought Helen could be being watched, all the time. He shared it with her, as an idea….she couldn't see the harm, even if Olly did come back quickly. It was a bit of insurance.

He sighed. "They're not here now so we don't have that to worry about. We'll activate this thing when I go away. I'll wait to phone the forensics people. Maybe tomorrow will be too late for them….but maybe by then we won't have this….situation." Intuitively they had walked back through to the main bedroom. Officer McLean looked out of the window, cautious that he might be being watched. He drew the curtains.

"Why did you do that?" asked Helen, though by this time she was sitting on the bed.

Officer McLean took off his jacket. "Oh, you know… ," he smiled. "What do you think the chances are of your husband interrupting us in a different type of endeavour?"

"Small, I think. He's in the country but where….your guess is as good as mine…." She took her top off and began to unbutton her trousers. "We've more chance of being interrupted by my parents bringing Terrence back."

By this time Officer McLean was virtually down to his underwear. "Ah, well, then, we shall be quick," he said as he went to kiss her and thrust his hand into her knickers.

'Shouldn't be too difficult for you,' she thought as she again wondered why she was doing this.

Officer Chris McLean had a daughter. She was called Donna, she was sixteen, beautiful, very streetwise and what could be called very sexually active. She had also fallen in with what was always euphemistically called "the wrong crowd". She had fallen in with the wrong crowd for a number of reasons – possibly her father's long and unpredictable hours, possibly because he could never guarantee that he would be 'there for her', maybe because her mother was a little too tied up in being herself to pay her daughter too much attention. Or maybe it was because it was good to be with "the wrong crowd". They did things that were fun. They did things that gave you a kick. They did things that seemed to give a purpose to being alive that she didn't feel anywhere else. They had sex. They took drugs. They stole. Occasionally they fought. And some of them had connections, in some way, even if only a small way, to Important People.

Donna didn't enjoy school very much. Somewhere, she knew that it didn't matter if you enjoyed school or not – she knew you were probably not supposed to enjoy it – but you were supposed to take out of it the qualifications that would lay the base to what you wanted to do later. Get the qualifications to go to University. When they lectured her about school, it was always the bit about 'going to University' that her parents emphasised. Donna hated the idea of a University before she had even seen one. It was a place that other people felt she should aspire to be at. It was someone else's dream of her. It was their lives being imposed on her. Donna didn't want anyone's life being imposed on her, especially one that she didn't think she was good enough to aspire to. So, feeling a failure, it was quite easy to become a failure. She wasn't exactly gifted academically and she found it was very easy to fail examinations – much easier than it was to pass them. You simply had to do nothing. Passing involved cramming your head full of things that you would forget as soon as you had sat the exam and which would still be in the book anyway. There seemed no point to that.

And the teachers… well, she was usually quiet. She really didn't make a fuss. A bit like wallpaper. And since teachers seemed to have their hands full with crowd control and damage limitation, it was quite easy for background noise to pass along without being noticed. She didn't create trouble for them so they didn't hassle her. It was a good relationship. She wasn't very good – and she clearly wasn't getting better – but so what, she didn't throw physical or metaphorical stones so she passed through the system without raising eyebrows.

As she took the conscious decision to not work and so to fail so she also took the conscious decision to ingratiate herself with "the wrong crowd". She knew who they were. Everyone knew who they were. She smiled a bit more at a couple of the girls, a couple of the boys too, and they would start to talk to her. Like them, she didn't want to talk about how her parents didn't understand her nor about how the school system might be failing her. She wanted to talk about things, to do things, that indulged her sensations. If she'd had money, a foreign holiday might have done the trick – another culture, being another person… but she had no money and anyway it wasn't something that she could actually do. So they did other things. They would meet after school, at nights, meet in dark places and talk about dark things and dark deeds that they wanted to do. Boys and girls, with curiosity running wild and hormones running wilder, things would turn very quickly to the things that boys and girls want to see and want to do and the boys would have their competition at first – "Ok, how much for Donna's breasts – either a viewing or touching? How much?" Then to Donna's other areas, a dark fissured triangle that made the boys' eyes widen, then to fucking Donna. And she loved it. Oh, sure, the first time, maybe a bit sore but having some fifteen year old so excited that he trembled inside her after about a minute and a half was very thrilling. And of course, it wasn't only Donna, it was the other girls too. You got paid more if the others got to watch and Donna liked being watched because it paid more. Sometimes she would initiate an orgy, grabbing another of the boys, caressing the breasts of another of the girls whilst one of them hammered away inside her with silent angst.

Donna liked this because she was in control. She never felt humiliated or frightened. She understood quite quickly that she was pretty and she also had a confident, almost overarching, sexuality. She knew what she could do to raise a boy's – a man's – interest, in all senses of the word. And this was so much better than feeling stupid and a failure, it was a beautiful antidote to talk of University and exams. And as every conversation with her parents became a battleground so she dived deeper and deeper into her own world, full of dark corners, quick fucks and the interest of others. And money.

However, the interests and influences of "the wrong crowd" did not extend only as far as sexual activity. Some of the crowd knew others in another wrong crowd who could get hold of drugs – things to make you high. Things to make you feel that you never need have any concern about any conversation with your parents about anything ever again. Donna liked those drugs but she found them expensive. Certainly in the quantity she wanted to consume them, they became very expensive.

She avoided taking them before she went to school and this became more and more of a struggle. School got harder and harder to sit through. She felt controlled, a hand on her head propelling her through the day. Stand up and walk there. Sit down there. Be quiet. Now look attentive, you're being asked a question. The way Donna was developing, she was talking control of things. She was hating every minute of being within the control of someone else. So it was a struggle. And though she kept the drugs at home – some of them, she had other hiding places outside that were private – she tried to avoid taking them when she was at home. She knew she was different when she took them. Her mother and father would surely know. She knew they had an idea something was going on – she was out every night, she came back the times they saw her in a different state to the one she had left in, she was dishevelled, sometimes wide eyed, like she had been rolling around like a beast, with other beasts, for the last four hours. Which probably wasn't far wrong. There were conversations, lectures, shouting matches. There was talk of locking her in her room. Pointless, she'd have found a way out. She was becoming an addict. You lock an addict in a room and they'll break the window, dig a tunnel or set fire to the door. And they'll probably have a stash in the room anyway.

Then something happened that made life so much easier for her. Two things really. Firstly one of the people in her "wrong crowd" knew someone in another wrong crowd, a bigger wrong crowd and word would always get about when it was someone like Donna. A great lay, will do anything, good at it too….so she began to fall in with another wrong crowd, a higher class of wrong crowd which tended to specialise in what you might call a more organised form of sexual activity than schoolboys bidding a fiver or a tenner here and there. It was clear that this wrong crowd could introduce her to men, real men, not schoolboys. Men with money. They were fatter, perhaps slightly more unpleasant, they lasted longer inside her but to her a male organ was like a computer for almost everyone else – something you need to have to work and earn money. People paid more because she was so young. She didn't care. They paid more if she would do certain things. She didn't care. They paid more if she dressed up. She didn't care. The only thing she drew the line at was being physically hit.

She was earning a lot of money, more money than she might have imagined, but she quickly found ways of spending it. And since this was a more organised approach to selling her body, the man who was in charge of her always took a cut. But Donna didn't really care about that, she was still earning much more money than she could ever have imagined. Then, last night, the man who was in charge of her had told her that there was a rumour that the "Big Boss" was coming across. The Big Boss lived in France but there was a rumour, a whisper, that he might be headed across here and if so, he might want to 'see' Donna. Because he's the boss, he makes all this possible for us without interference from anyone, he gets what he wants for free. But if you make him happy, you might get a tip. Big tip. Interested? Willingly, said Donna.

The other thing that made Donna's life easier also brought her money but nothing on the scale to the work she undertook. No, the other thing brought her a bit of peace, a bit of power and so a bit of control. She happened, by coincidence, to be in a certain house on a certain night when the man suddenly heard his door open downstairs. "It can only be my wife, you must get out, get out, go to the back garden. Find a way out but get out without being seen." Donna didn't care about the rejection, he gave her more money to exit stage speedily. She initially hid in the garden then, being quite agile, realised she could quite easily climb over the fence. It was late, and dark, so as long as she was silent she could probably climb over the gardens until she found her way out. The gardens were not huge but big enough that someone who was smart enough could stay undetected.

Suddenly she was in one garden and she saw the back door open. She immediately cowered behind a bush, scared that she had been seen. But the woman who opened the door was only throwing something out. She heard the woman shout to someone inside and then heard a voice reply. The voice she recognised immediately as her father's voice. This in itself did not raise her curiosity too much – perhaps there had been a break-in, something, that would have involved her father being in that house at that time. She listened further, having no choice but to stay where she was. She tried to look at the woman – odd, she seemed to be wearing a dressing gown – and listened harder. The woman said "Ok, I'm coming back, just getting rid of the bottle." The woman closed the door and Donna ran up to the wall of the house, trying to hear or see something. But she surmised that the woman had gone upstairs. She found her way out of the garden, concluding quite correctly that there was too much nocturnal activity going on for anyone to be watching for trespassers in the garden, and made her way home, a warm glow inside her. On what she had heard alone she was convinced she had enough evidence.

She approached her father the next morning after her mother had left for work and she should have left for school. She seemed interested in him at first, asking about his work last night, about how much of a toil it must be working a night shift, then suddenly whilst chewing on her toast said:

"Though I guess things might be compensated for a little bit by fucking the blond in number 53…"

Had Officer McLean been holding a cup he would have dropped it. His reaction told her everything and she giggled, a small girlish pre-pubescent giggle and then clapped her hands together in the way a toddler might do.

"Ooh, daddy! Bad, bad boy!"

"Now," she said, casually eating her toast, "I'm guessing this is just a bit on the side. I'm guessing you don't want a divorce. I'm guessing that mum's salary is something you need to keep you and us in the style to which we've got used to over the years. Oh, you don't need to say anything, just nod."

He nodded. "Ah, I thought so! Well, daddy, I can be quiet. I know how to shut up. But things like that, turning the other way, they have a price, you know? Of course you know, you're a policeman!"

"Donna……what the….are you trying to blackmail me?"

"No, I'm not trying dad. I'm not trying. I'm succeeding. Because if you don't do what I want then I'll go straight to mum. And she'll go mental. You know what she's like. I've seen her go to work on you before, remember?"

Officer McLean put his head in his hands. "Donna, I'm so sorry for this, it's not what you think…."

"Daddy, I don't care. And don't cry for Christ's sake. Don't be pathetic. I'll only increase what I want."

He looked at her. "What do you want?"

"Well, I need some money… " She emphasised 'some' as though to make it clear that this was not her main demand. "Let's say £120 per month…" she held her hand up as her father's face brightened…"but most of all I want my life to be mine. So get off my back about going to University. In fact, get off my back. Let me do what I want. And get her off my back as well. Now, daddy, do you think you can do that? I hope so, because if not mummy's going to know all about you and the blond. Who's very pretty, by the way. From what I saw… "

"But Donna….your mother and I….we only want what's best for you. We know things you don't. Whatever you're doing, whatever you're up to…ok,ok, I'll get off your back…but you can't stop us wanting what's best for you. And as for your mother…how do you expect me to persuade her?"

"Well, you can use the same skills of persuasion as you used to get the blond to go to bed with you. You need to accept that you don't know best. I know best. For me. Right now." She paused. "It's your choice daddy. I'm giving you the choice. Other girls would be heartbroken by this and run to their mummies. I'm a bit more….let's say realistic. Maybe self-motivated. You find a way of doing this or…" And she made a noise like 'kaboom' and made an explosion gesture with her ten fingers.

Lesley had ended up spending the night with Tess. She hadn't wanted to

– and yet she had wanted to more than anything else. She felt it was a betrayal of herself and Ali – yet it felt like it was the most honest she had ever been with herself. She felt ashamed – yet tingled and danced when she remembered the sensations. She felt, as she had been instructed from birth, that we can only love one person – yet she felt love for both Tess and Ali. The love for Tess was new and sparkling and light and made her feel forever young: the love for Ali was like the wind beneath her, that allowed her to be able to feel the things she felt for Tess. As if Ali was a rock, the stability and the security giving her the strength that allowed her to develop her instinctive feel about who she was and what she was. I wouldn't have – couldn't have – done this without Ali being there in the first place.

But she couldn't exactly tell him that, could she? She looked at herself in the mirror in their hall, a full-blown full length thing that held no hiding place. She didn't look any different. Yet those trousers she now stood in had felt the caress of a woman on them and over them, that blouse had had buttons undone slowly by long delicate fingers. She looked at herself and undid her blouse. She tried to recreate Tess' touch and closed her eyes, lifting her blouse out of her trousers and taking it slowly off. She looked at herself again. She still looked no different. Instinctively she drew in her stomach, shut her eyes and slipped her hand under her trousers, under her underwear, gently sighing. She undid her trousers as deftly and confidently as Tess had done, slipped them down, stood out of them and slipped her hand under her underwear. She opened her eyes. She still looked the same. She reached behind and undid her bra, slipping it off, letting the back of her hand glide across her breasts, feeling Tess' hands, soft kisses, the feel of Tess' breasts against hers. Finally she took off her underwear and stood naked in front of the mirror, touching herself, gentle fingers moving slowly.

She tried to not recognise the body in front of her. She tried to think of herself as someone else now, a different body to the one that she had always had. But this had always been her body. This had always been her. She turned around and looked behind her, her hair over her shoulders and neck, the same hair style. Her hair style. But with female hands having run through it for the first time. Tess' fingers still there, inside her head. Her legs, getting too chunky at the top now, Tess's hands around them everywhere. Was there an inch of my body she didn't touch, thought Lesley? Because Lesley's feet had seemed as important as her breasts, her hair and face and neck had been kissed as much as her intimate parts, her fingers and hands had been caressed as much as anywhere else. As though Tess was taking everything, all of her, every part of her. It hadn't been a roll in a metaphorical haystack, two fumbling teenagers curious about what riches the other one might have held, it had been about taking and owning and claiming and possessing and being that other person. She had been one person before she went with Tess. Now she was another. 'If my body belongs to you,' thought Lesley, 'then it must also follow that my mind and all of me which let you take it belongs to you too.' But yet she looked no different. Tess's calm hands that had taken her felt so very different to Ali's grunts and gropes and fumbles – a cool champion against pure rough testosterone. The experience had been as wet is to dry, the joy so much a mutual and shared experience, the love so much made by a combination of both of them, that she should look different. She was a different person.

She almost cried at the thought of that. 'I'm a different person.' One that was unknown to Ali now. One that Ali could not begin to reach or bring back or appreciate or understand. She couldn't leave him, she couldn't ever leave him and she didn't want to. Ali had done nothing wrong. But yet how could she now share herself with him? She couldn't. He couldn't see her, all of her, ever again. Behind her smiles would be someone else, someone who told her that her smile was only at best three quarters there because there was a part of her now that he would neither have nor ever satisfy. A part of her was out of reach. Where he had been her friend and soul mate, he was now only a husband. Whereas she had felt she always been honest with him she now felt cautious, on her guard against saying anything lest she reveal herself. Less than honest. Less than trusting – not of him but of herself. Can you be less than trusting and still trust? Is it not like fidelity – absolute or non-existent? She tried to picture a stone wall, grey and featureless and without emotion. A wall that didn't feel, a façade which could have hidden anything, everything that you wanted people nowhere near, a wall with the same bland reflection. And she knew that was what she had to become. 'I can't let him in. I can't. It would break his heart. And it would break mine to break his.' After 36 years, Lesley knew she had to begin to construct another person.

"Davide, get the copter to take us up to Edinburgh. If he's not there yet, we'll wait for him. I might need a way of filling the afternoon. Get a

395

hotel suite. Get a girl or two….you know how I am when I'm in this way. As long as they don't disappoint. Young is good, younger the better."

"Yes boss. Em……"

"What is it? You look like you've got something to say. Either that or your teeth aren't working."

"Paul's been on the phone. He wants….he would like….an update… says he's desperate to get some of the action over here if you're close to catching the guy… wants to do something to the wife…you know what he's like, that temperament of his…"

"He's the last person I'm thinking about. He got us all into this mess. Though maybe he was right about the guy Oliver. No, tell him I'm not available. I'll get back to him sometime……sometime when I've exhausted everyone else on the list. Find a way to get this chopper up to some hotel room in Edinburgh as quickly as you can. And don't forget to order the girls. My medicine…" He lifted a hat from the seat of the helicopter, sank into it and placed the hat over his face. Davide smiled to himself. It was The Capo's retreat, his unequivocal way of telling the world "Do Not Disturb." Or, thought Davide, "Fuck Off Or I Will Have You Shot."

As they travelled north, nearer and nearer to Newcastle, Ellis had an idea. "Why don't we get the car spray painted? A grey or a blue or something?"

Oliver looked at him, a puzzled expression transforming his face. "You want to paint the car? Firstly, it's not our car to paint. Secondly, why? We don't exactly seem to have an army chasing us anymore."

"We can easily get it painted back, that's no problem…."

"Spray painting takes ages. We'd need to get it done, stay over somewhere till the bloody thing dried….probably we couldn't get it done anyway, it's afternoon… it's a daft idea…."

"No, no it isn't. Listen, we're up against a group of folk who tried to kill us at a train station. You think they don't know where we are, even if those guys didn't register the number plate? I've thought about it…short of changing car, which would be hard to do now unless any of you know anyone in Newcastle who would lend us a car, it's the only disguise we've got."

"Hire a car?" Euan hoisted it gingerly, as though he knew it wasn't an option.

"Nah, credit card," said Oliver. "We'd need to give a credit card. Best to try and not do anything that obvious."

"He's right, of course he's right," said Ellis. "So you see a spray paint is the only option, it's the only route open to us."

"But the time," said Ali, "the time... I want to get home. We're so close. We don't want to spend the night somewhere else. We're only two hours away."

"Only two hours", said Ellis, "but they might be the most dangerous two hours. And anyway, we don't need to stay over. We need it to be painted, that's all."

"I'm no Leonardo," said Aidan, "but even I know that paint has to dry. It's part of the deal with paint, isn't it? And anyway, won't it be an odd thing to do? Find a garage – and how do we do that, by the way? – and turn up and say 'Paint it mate but don't worry about letting it dry?' Or are you going to Taser the twat into painting it? Or should we find a big B&Q and get a tin of Dulux ourselves? I fancy primrose yellow...."

Ellis tried to make himself heard above the laughter. "No, listen, I've thought about it. I've got a friend in Edinburgh who's got his own garage. Nothing major, a two man business. But he has friends, contacts, people in the same line of business. I could phone him, he's not exactly going to grass us to anyone, and say we need a favour and does he know anyone in Newcastle who might help us. We don't need to wait for the damn thing to dry. What do we care if the paint is splodgy or untidy? The important thing is that, when it's seen going through a cctv monitor, it's not seen as black. That's what folk will look at. They'll see a black car then start to look at the registration number. So we'll be out of that filtering process..."

Oliver said: "what if we go through at night time? Won't all cars look black at night time, whatever their colour?"

"No," said Ellis. "That's the thing. You can still tell roughly what colour the car is."

Ali looked confused. "Can you?" he asked, to anyone who wanted to answer. "Are you sure?"

"Yeah," said Ellis, "haven't you seen these programmes on tv...car chases... you know, guys getting caught on cctv cameras...even in the dark you can see the colour of the car....well, roughly anyway."

"No," said Oliver. "I haven't watched these programmes. I guess I...well, I hadn't really appreciated this before but......I guess I have a life......"

"Me too....," added Aidan.

"Yeah ok, very good, very good. But I think we should phone him and see if it's possible. If not... then we will have to take our chances. And, up to this point, they haven't been great, have they?"

Ellis made the call. His friend made a call. His friend phoned back within five minutes. Unusual request and of course the car should be left overnight. But doable. Deliver the car. Go for a walk for an hour or two then come back. Reasonable fee involved.

The friends sat in a busy pub in an area that looked as though it was close to the city centre. They should have been hungry and should have eaten a decent meal but none of them felt particularly hungry – "peckish" was the closest anyone could get to hunger – and so they ordered three plates of chips and a salad concoction between them and picked at it as they sipped upon a beer. No one seemed in the mood to drink either and the food and the beer was almost nursed amidst brief, staccato interjections of talk that broke the silence. It wasn't that they were awkward with each other or fed up with each other. They were apprehensive, unsure – scared even. They all felt that, now, the nearer they got to home the nearer they came to some danger that they couldn't run from anymore. That home wasn't quite the sanctuary it had seemed a few days ago. That neither they, nor their families, were safe anymore. It was something that they didn't really want to think upon but which, paradoxically, they could do nothing but think upon. Not directly perhaps but in the form of a black pit in the stomach or a black cloud overhead or in the undisguisable flash of instinct that accompanied the thought of home. Danger. Danger.

There was enough going on in the pub anyway that their silence did not feel awkward. The television relayed sporting news and sporting events and was loud. The fruit machine, which seemed to be in constant use, was noisy and bright and flashed at any and every touch. There were various people, conversations, most of them on their own not particularly loud but put together they created a chatter that meant you had to raise your voice slightly if you wanted to speak. And there was a juke box, not often used it seemed, but when it was the music was a few decibels too loud. Odd, thought Euan. The place was almost designed, by its assault on the senses through varying sources of noise, to prevent conversation. The effort would give you a sore throat. Or a headache. Or both. He laughed to himself. That male thing, going down the pub...as if some sort of bonding took place there in a citadel of masculine openness. Au contraire... no bonding, only nods. Little conversation, only appreciation of something that had happened on the tv when a goal had been scored or disappointment when one had been conceded.

And anyway, the way the conversation not far away from them was beginning to develop, it would have drowned them out. At first it seemed as though that's all it was – a conversation. But as the voices became slightly louder, the seriousness and, at times what seemed like desperation, in the voices became clearer. Inevitably the friends' attention and gaze was drawn.

Oliver looked across first. They were more directly in his line of sight – unless he looked straight at his friends and didn't let his eyes take in their natural range of vision he could not have avoided seeing what was happening at the other table. Though the noise of voices at times made you feel as though there were about six people there, the reality was that there were only three. Two males and a female. The female had a desperate, almost haunted look about her. She was pale to begin with, long straight dark hair hanging about a white thin pasty unsmiling face. Her large brown eyes looked misplaced, as though they had been taken from someone else. She should have had blue or green eyes to light her up a bit. She looked dank, drab even. Yet somehow attractive, at times very attractive. Any animation seemed to breathe life into her features and when she started to talk, which she didn't seem to have the opportunity to do often, she become bustling and busy and engaging. She had long delicate white fingers which became the focal point of attention when she spoke. And when she did speak she seemed to spend most of her time using her hands to try and keep the two males apart.

Oliver looked at the males. Both wore t-shirts which emphasised biceps that Oliver thought could not be a naturally occurring phenomenon. Were these guys sportsmen? They were both of a similar "style" – gelled hair, handsome features, skin that told of some skincare regime. They seemed to be spending their time arguing with each other. They did the aggressive bit with their hands, their eyes, their gestures, their voices and their language. There was no physical manifestation at first. Oliver became intrigued as to the nature of the relationship between them. He watched with interest and strained to hear at the times when the voices did not naturally carry above the constant hubbub in the background.

The male with the shorter gelled hair, who looked slightly younger than the other one, began to point his finger in a threatening way at the other. "It wasn't your territory, mate. She wasn't yours to get involved with. You have to fucking accept that, you know? Now, you behaved in an improper way. I'm not going to make anything of that. Walk away and we'll forget everything. And me and her will go on as normal. And you fuck off into the sunset on your horse…"

The other guy, who had slightly longer hair which looked slightly wilder, sipped from his drink then banged it on the table. "She's nobody's property you dipshit bastard! I didn't know anything about you and her….though it would have made no difference to me at all. If we'd both wanted to do the good deed that's all that's matters, isn't it? The rest is… shite. So she may have been your girlfriend once but I don't think that's what she wants now. Is it?" And he stretched out a protective arm towards the girl who instinctively moved away from it. The other male thrust his arm out and she instinctively moved away from it too, shifting her chair back so that she was out of the reach of both of them. She put her head down and stretched her hands out to each of them, a gesture of separation, a bit like a referee trying to keep boxers apart.

Short Gel started again. "Listen mate I only agreed to this to keep her sweet. Personally I never want to see you again in my life. So, say, why don't you leave us both the fuck alone? Take some advice from a wise man and get to fuck. I don't want this to get….you know…."

Long Gel reached across the table. "You don't want it to get what….mate?" The 'mate' was heavily coated in sarcasm.

Short Gel replied – "I don't want to have to take this into my own hands. That's not what I came here for. But I want you to know that I'm prepared to dump you in the fucking river…"

Long Gel stood up. "Well maybe it's time we tried that out now… from where I'm standing I don't fancy your chances…"

The girl raised herself slowly. "Sit down," she said, deliberately and quietly. Her voice carried authority and Long Gel sat down. "This is what I wanted to avoid," she started, "this is exactly what I wanted to avoid. A cock fight. Any fight. I wanted us to talk this through like rational, normal human beings. Can you do that? Both of you? Can you?" She looked quickly and quizzically from one to the other.

Both nodded and briefly put their heads down. Short Gel spoke up. "Well it would help if you told us what you wanted. Who you wanted."

"I don't know what I want! I told you that. I told you that before we came here. I told you that. That's what I bloody said! That the only way all three of us come together like this is on the understanding that I don't know what I want and we all need to accept the outcome. I want both of you dammit! And I want neither of you. When you're like this I want to walk away from both of you." Both held their arms out and she drew back again. "God knows I'd accept it if you can't accept that. I told you that. I know how unreasonable this is, to both of you. So walk away, I deserve that. But if you're not walking away then we need to talk this through like human beings."

"I'd do anything for you, you know that," said Short Gel.

"Then start by shutting the fuck up," Long Gel retorted.

"But you must prefer one of us," said Short Gel, trying to catch her eyes as she held her head down. "And I'm better than this guy, you know I'm better than him. I'll take more care of you than he can. I'm stronger…."

Long Gel interrupted. "Then arm wrestle."

"What?"

"Arm wrestle. You and me. Let's agree it goes no further than that. No fighting. What do you say? Come on, you say you're stronger. And if you win I'll walk away. You'll never hear from me again." His eyes, clear and confident and full of the excitement of challenge, dominated those of his opponent. But Short Gel could not turn down such a blatant confrontation. The girl wanted to speak but he put his hand up to silence her.

"Ok," said Short Gel, "you're on."

"And you walk away if you lose? If you lose she's mine…"

The girl stood up. "I'm nobody's! I don't 'belong' to either of you!"

But the males were not listening. Short Gel was looking at his challenger, sizing up his arms. My arms are bigger than his, he thought….but Long Gel had seemed very confident and though he smiled outwardly Short Gel was apprehensive inside.

The friends watched on as the two males, their eyes fixed on each other, ignored whatever the female was saying and put their arms out ready to meet each other. They cleared the table, wiping away crumbs and liquids lest any exogenous factors influence an encounter that should be determined by inner force and desire. Their focus on each other's eyes became almost manic, like watching two heavyweights go into the middle of the ring at the beginning of the first round. By now the girl had given up. She looked as though she wanted to turn her back to them but she could not help to watch. Oliver looked on her and he thought she seemed annoyed as much as concerned, angry as much as frightened of the consequences. As though….well, as though the decision had now been taken out of her hands. Maybe she was angry because she was no longer in any kind of control.

"We clasp hands," said Long Gel. "We clasp hands then on the count of three we go…"

Short Gel nodded though it wasn't really a question. As they clasped hands they drilled their eyes into each other, both looking for a sign of weakness or submission. Whatever they found on their faces gave no hint of a reaction, both serious, both with, if anything, a thin smile of superiority on their face.

They counted three together and their faces changed, swiftly shifting from a calm veneer to a picture of brute physical effort. They shouted and grunted, manifestations of the force they put into what seemed inhuman effort. Their faces became quickly red, their heads quickly shook and shivered violently, yet their efforts yielded nothing. For about twenty seconds both hands, both arms, remained exactly where they were, the force of one being met by an equal effort of the other.

Entire bodies, strength that went from toes to fingers, became channelled into their respective right arms. They snarled at each other, two dogs barking and biting and growling and attacking each other, their faces and sounds a gnarled mess. Each fought the impulse to raise their elbow from the table, to put that extra pressure on the other, to win. But of course that would be cheating and it would be losing. Millimetres were gained as arms visibly strained. Sweat started to drip from both of them. Long Gel put his head down and took his eyes from Short Gel. The effect was significant but too brief, a minor gain quickly nullified by Short Gel shrieking and reclaiming lost ground.

By now all the friends were watching. 'They can't go on like this much longer,' thought Oliver. 'Something has to give. Something….' But in the dangerous red faces, the shaking bodies, the pressure as each hand pressed into the other with such force that the fingers would leave marks forever, nothing looked like giving. Yet this was impossible. To keep this going was impossible. Their shrieks became more rhythmical, in and out, sustaining and draining as they pushed every bit of energy they could find into each other.

Short Gel must have felt as though something might burst for he lifted his left hand from the table. His right hand stayed entwined in Long Gel's. Long Gel, fearing this may be a ploy to gain advantage, lifted his left hand too. Short Gel saw his opponent raise his left arm and quickly moved his closer. This was enough for Long Gel and he flashed his left hand at his opponent's face. Short Gel had caught what was happening as the arm came towards him and punched his arm at Long Gel. Both hands connected. The bond of the right hands was broken as both men fell to the ground.

As they stood up, ready to fight each other, they found a body between them. But it wasn't that of the female, who sat with her face in her hands, transfixed and numb. It was Oliver.

"Gentlemen….guys…not this way. Not here. Not outside. Not this way."

Both the men were breathless but were united in their condemnation of the man who stood between them.

"Who…….who….the hell… are you? Leave us….alone."

"Sit down please, guys. Please. Please sit down. Talk. Let's talk for a few minutes. Then if you still want to fight we will leave and you can batter each other till there's no blood left in your bodies."

The initial anger abating, the two males sat down with reluctance. Oliver sat between them. Oliver's friends looked at each other, unsure of where Olly had sprung from to get himself into that position. They were even more confused as to why he might have done it.

"Christ," said Ellis, "as if we weren't in enough trouble! That's just what we need, even more people with an excuse to give us a kicking."

"Got your Taser?" asked Ali.

"Strangely not," retorted Ellis. "I thought a pub, in the middle of a busy city centre at about six o'clock at night might be somewhere where we might not need a Taser. But then I forgot who I was with, didn't I? Bloody Olly, a one man United fucking Nations…"

"Guys, this is your business, it's not my business and of course I appreciate that. But yet you," and Oliver looked around to all three of them, deliberate in his inclusion of the girl, "have chosen to bring your private business into a public setting such as such. So it kind of is my business too, you know?"

Short Gel, still breathing heavily, looked at the girl. "You and him been playing about too, have you?"

The girl shook her head. Oliver looked at her. "No, this is the first time I have set eyes on any of you. Her included. No, I don't have a vested interest. I'm only someone sitting here, with my friends, trying to have something to eat in a quiet pub….which you've chosen to have a public argument and public duel in…"

"It wasn't exactly a duel," said Long Gel. "Just an arm wrestle."

"Hmmmm…," said Oliver, "as good as, though, wasn't it? That way of 'let's have a physical contest'. Same as a duel, same as a fight. Is that

403

the way that you see yourselves, guys? Vessels of strength? Couldn't your competition have been around writing her a poem? Drawing a picture? Telling a joke, seeing whose joke she laughed at loudest? Guessing what her favourite dress might be? What I'm saying is – why did you have to think of fighting each other, here, in a public place…"

"What the fuck? Who the fuck are you? Fuck off! And anyway, we didn't fight…."

"But you were about to. Had I not been standing between you, you would have. Would that have been a battle won? A war won? If either of you had won, what would you really have won?" He turned to the girl. "Is that what you would have wanted? To be with the one who was physically stronger than the other? I don't get how that becomes something you see as worthy of winning your hand."

He paused, as though all the despair of the last week, all the futility, all the hiding, the threat of violence, the actual violence, came at him all at once.

"We're not in the Middle Ages, are we? Christ, we're not back in ancient Greece. We've moved on, surely. We use our reason, our intelligence… Guys," and he made an inclusive gesture with his hands to include all three of them, "you made your business a public one when you had such a loud conversation next to us. And your situation seems a complex one and I think you…" and he pointed towards the girl, "seem to be in a very difficult way. And you," he pointed at both the males, "have to accept that and talk it through or walk away. By the sounds of it, she may love both of you or neither of you. Personally, if I was in the same situation as either of you," and he again pointed to the males, "I'd walk away. But of course it's not me that's in this, it's the three of you."

He paused again. Couldn't it all be talked out. This chasing, this running, this desperation. " You need to talk. Let each other know how you feel. Let her know how you feel. You're aggressive because you've been threatened by being rejected by another. But if you build anything on the basis of force, you're building on sand. It will come crashing down. You need to win her heart and her mind, not her fear. Aggression is…… God, it's the crutch we all lean on, it can be like an addiction and it can be comforting to justify actions through the strength of its impulse. But you have a mind too and you can reject that impulse. Even if she went with the one of you that might have won any fight, it wouldn't last. Not on that basis. That's the way animals behave, barbarians. Old ways, old ways……"

Need to talk....need to talk... "You know, real people, good people, real kings....aren't those who count how many they've killed. Real kings are those who think on how many lives might have been saved because of the wars they've managed to avoid through talking, through talking and reason and rational thought. This thing between you both, the three of you, would have... could still.......develop into a war. One of you beats the other one in a fight, one then waits for the other one, friends get involved." He looked at both of them and then at the girl. "There is no such thing as a war that you can win. It doesn't exist. No such thing. There are only degrees of losing. A war, a physical fight....it means we've lost. The power to talk, to reason, has broken down. We've lost. Who wins....whoever wins...it's hollow, it's meaningless. So, why don't the three of you sit and have a chat about it the way people do....or go back and do it in private......you might not resolve anything at first but if you talk, and don't swing at each other, you'll at least be on the way to resolving everything."

He hadn't really looked at them very much. Even his friends wondered if he was really talking to himself.

The three of them looked at Oliver. By this stage the girl was probably in love with him. The guys were unsure of whether to nod sagely or reject everything as being 'shite'. They sat motionless. The girl drew each of their right hands together, not to arm wrestle but to shake hands. They did so without enthusiasm but, at least, without hitting each other. "Ok," said Short Gel, still shaking the hand of Long Gel, "we talk..."

The pasty faced girl smiled at Olly. Ellis took a call at the same time.

"Who are you?" she asked, sweeping her hand to include Oliver's friends too. "What are you doing here?

"Ah," said Oliver, "that's a long story, you wouldn't believe the half of it. But, as a sweetener to you, we're about to pick up a car that was spray painted about an hour ago. We think some guys in the French mafia might be after us and we want to get back to Edinburgh before they threaten our families."

She laughed, a helpless feminine giggle. "Ok..."

"See, told you you wouldn't believe it.."

Olly looked at the two males. "Gentlemen... ," he said. They nodded at him, a quiet recognition, an acknowledgement that he had done something... something not bad at least....

As they walked out Ellis said: "the bird was tasty Olly, thought you might be in there..."

They laughed. And as they did so, Oliver realised that it was the first place he had left in the last ten days that he didn't feel he was creeping out of or waiting for someone to chase him or expecting to feel something thrown at him. He put his arms round his friends. Maybe only for that moment, the brief moment before they had to go back to the car, he was happy.

CHAPTER 20

As they started to approach the garage the noise in the sky turned into a low rumble. The grey had changed too from a mild benign grey to a dark foreboding grey, full of menace and heavy with the threat of a storm to come. The light gust of wind that had blown gently about them when they had gone into the pub was now billowing, whipping itself into them, swirling papers around and making white foam of the waves on the river. The air that swirled around them was warm: not hot but warm, and still the sort of temperature that would have been more appropriate in the south of France.

It was clear that the sky was going to do more than merely rain. It was going to leak and lash itself down, an aerial tsunami bursting and spewing its contents onto what lay below. It was no surprise, thought Oliver as he looked above him and paused briefly, letting the wind smother his body, it was no surprise that that they used to think of such weather as punishment sent from God. Or from The Gods. It was too dark, too dangerous, too upsetting to be normal. Even now it sent people scurrying with concern on their faces and skyward glances into a huddled form as they tried to make themselves smaller, invisible almost, in the face of what they knew was going to be unleashed upon them. How easy it must have been to rationalise it as a punishment for wrong doing. And how easy to find something that you had done that was wrong. After all, we all do things that are wrong. So we get together and think upon what we have done and vow to change it and the storm goes away. And we pray to God or a God that it isn't sent again. There was no weather man in Biblical times, no weather man in ancient Greece to say that perhaps this was a naturally occurring phenomenon. Yet still, as Oliver looked at the sky, he felt inside its darkness and its danger. Something has to give… ….the centre cannot hold……

The guy at the garage could not begin to understand why they would even conceive of taking a barely-painted car out into conditions that were going to practically destroy it.

"It's going to ruin it. Ruin it. You'll get lumps and ridges of paint. You'll probably get stuff stuck to it. And that's only with the wind. Goodness knows what damage the rain will do." As he finished the splattering started outside.

"Well," said Ellis, "then we'll have to get it painted again, won't we? As long as the damn thing still goes."

"Oh it goes. Of course it'll go. But it'll look like a dog's breakfast."

"We can live with that," said Ellis and took the keys. The friends smiled at the perplexed man who had just painted their car. He ran his hands through his hair and shook his head, smiling to himself as he counted the notes he had been handed.

"Oh," said Ellis, "and in case anyone asks……though I can't imagine anyone would of course….but please don't say you've done this thing for us." He paused. "We can trust you, can't we?"

"Guys," he said, looking at the friends, "when you see guys like you prepared to drive a newly painted car in conditions like this when you know it will ruin whatever has been done……you know not to ask too many questions. You have paid me well. You have my silence."

Ellis smiled. He turned the key and looked around all of his friends. "Right….now we only have a storm from hell to get through….should be easy for us, don't you think?"

'Storm from hell,' thought Oliver. That's exactly what this felt like. They were about two hours from home. Yet Oliver felt as far away from it as he had done when he was lying in Clotilde's bed – and somehow that had seemed safer than the situation he was in right now.

The storm began to let loose its force before they had left Newcastle. Ellis put the wipers onto full but still had to peer through the windscreen, looking for the gap after the wiper had pushed the torrent away and before another torrent came, to see where he was going. He navigated mostly by the taillights ahead of him for he knew that, being on the main road now, it wasn't necessary to look for any exits, branches etc. Follow the guy in front. The friends around him were mostly silent. It was one of those times when, however many years you had been driving, it was going to challenge you. You needed to concentrate and focus, and that needed silence. That and they were quietly concerned. Not with Ellis – all were secretly glad that it was not them that was driving – but with the strength and ferocity of the storm. The rain fell as a mass that was blown and battered around. It was almost impossible for them to see anything. How long could this continue before they would have to stop? All around them was dark, as if they were driving in the middle of fog. Headlights made little difference, it remained as though they were enveloped in a searing choking fog that both overpowered and blinded.

Ellis leaned forward. They began to move out of Newcastle, hoping that they would be travelling away from the storm. But all in front of them was black, as though the storm was determined that they should not escape it. And though it was nice to know they were moving nearer home, the taillights were not so frequent and it became harder to find someone to follow. Silence… an uneasy quiet…

A sign that they could not really see until they were almost upon it told them that they were very close to Berwick. Almost half way. Some lights in the middle of the road. They turned left to head north; on their right the thickening black sea that they could tell would be wild and whirling. And full of death. Oliver felt a desire, a perverse and twisted one, to open the window, a little, to listen to what was outside, to get some idea of the power of the force that was so close to them. The anger of nature, brutal and unforgiving…he felt his heart race a little quicker. Ellis steered the car along the road, new taillights to see, dashes of barely visible red on what was at least a dual carriageway. They moved closer to the sea till Oliver felt it must be almost below them. As he looked across there was a place on the other side of the road where you could stop, presumably to admire the view. Had you stopped there and got out, Oliver thought, you could surely not have survived. Even if you sat there in your car the sea would have drawn you into it, the force too strong to resist.

They began to move away. The sea was still there but more distant to their right, its dangers more remote. Though they began to move to a single carriageway, Euan, at least, relaxed. It's a storm, it'll pass…this too as everything else shall pass….the past ten days had felt like a storm… one wave after another crashing into them, one unseen danger after another ready to batter them….what sort of force had Olly let loose when he went with Clotilde to that dinner? What if he hadn't gone? Would he have come home and everything would have been the way everything normally was? But a chance invitation, a chance conversation with a drunk woman, a chance encounter with her husband, what if the table hadn't been set there, what if there had been no knives on the table… what were the chances… and what, from what Olly had said, a blatant opportunist like Clotilde who saw her chance and took it….chance… .chance… a series of random events that led to the fury that had been unleashed on them. What were the chances, ten days ago, of all that? Was it chance? Really? All of it… all….BANG!

"Jesus Christ, what the hell was that?"

Ellis felt the steering wheel pull violently to his left and the car slowed, as if it has gone into a pool of water. But the noise, which they all heard above the howls outside, told of something else. Ellis steered the car to a halt at the side of the road, part of it on the grass verge, and immediately put the hazard lights on to alert anyone who was behind them.

"It's a blowout," he said in a very matter of fact of fact voice. He looked round at his friends. "At least I think it's a blowout. I've never experienced one before."

"So....," said Aidan, "we now need to change a tyre I guess. In such beautiful conditions. What should we do, draw straws to see who changes this?"

"I don't think it really matters," said Ellis. "We can't change a tyre with someone sitting in the car anyway. We all need to go out." He looked at Oliver: "Olly, you didn't arrange all this, as the kind of final hurrah for us, did you?"

"Not quite," said Oliver. "No, not quite." He looked around at his friends. "I guess it's me that's changing this bloody thing, isn't it?"

"Well," said Euan, "unless Ellis can Taser the damn thing back to life, you certainly get my vote....though I think we're all better doing something than standing around. Come on guys, let's get this done and get back on our way... what's the betting there's no spare tyre...."

But there was a spare tyre and the requisite tools. Surviving the storm's brutality, however, was more of a problem. They struggled to open the door then, being slightly open, struggled to control the door before the wind broke it from its hinges. They inched out and were pummelled by water and wind, soaked within seconds. If you weren't right next to someone you couldn't hear them, no matter how loud they shouted. Their feet sank into pools of water lying on the surface, covering their shoes.

Ellis and Oliver set to work on the tyre, the others crouched and did what they could. But even crouching offered no escape from the wind and crouching on the arches of feet was precarious as first Aidan and then Ali were literally blown over. Euan looked around his friends, faces wet and contorted in this inferno that reduced them to helplessness. He saw the wind whip them away, almost roll them over, make the car wheel move, make the car shudder as it got underneath and tried to overturn it. Somewhere in the distance he thought he could near the sea, sporadic noises of crashing. It was too rhythmical, too structured, to be random things blowing into random things. It was repetitive and terrifying as force upon force, wave upon wave, crashed into the land and began to claim it back. He looked again at his friends, rats' tails for hair now and smiled inwardly. Are they ready to laugh or cry, he wondered?

Just at that moment, Euan was not the only one looking at his friends. Jacques had seen the car's hazard lights quite late and swerved, not quite enough to take him into the line of traffic coming the other way but enough to give him a start. Naturally enough, he watched the road and paid little attention to the car…except to think that, whatever was wrong with it, he wasn't getting out to help. Guy and Natalie, however, paid a little more attention to the car.

"That's it!" shrieked Natalie in what was a high-pitched yelp. "That's the car! Look, look, that's the car!"

"What?" said Jacques. "What? That car we passed? How do you know?"

"I saw the registration number. I saw it. I tell you, that's the car. That's it! Turn around, go and get them!"

Jacques looked at her and Guy. "What were they doing? These guys? Did you see? Why had they stopped?"

"I think…."said Natalie…. "I think they were changing a tyre."

By this time Jacques had driven onto a part of the road that had what looked to be some form of central reservation between his side and the other side. He looked across. Whatever it was, he couldn't simply turn around and go back. Not until there was a gap or a chance to turn right and who knows how long it might take for one to appear.

"Ok," he said, "ok…….well they must be going to Edinburgh….they must be going on this road…let us wait here and stop. Let them pass us. Then we can catch them. But if we turn back now…and who knows when we will be able to turn back…we may miss them….they may get far ahead of us again."

"Ok," said Guy. "Ok, we wait."

Given the conditions, it probably didn't take them long to change the wheel. But because they all felt danger very close to them, it felt like hours. Ellis and Oliver both took turns at tightening the wheel nuts as much as they could, both conscious that any compromise there could put them in even more danger. Rather than try to talk they nodded in silent agreement to each other.

Each of them dripped back into the car.

"Shit," said Euan, "we're going to make some mess of this thing... and stink it out.."

"Yes," said Aidan. "It would have been better if we could have taken all our clothes off before we went outside...then we'd have had something dry to put back on. Of course, knowing our luck, we'd have been caught by the police for cavorting around naked or attacked by some one-eyed monster or something... so maybe, on balance, all things considered, a wet car is probably the best of a series of fairly shit options...."

They took their shoes and socks off, Ellis apart, and tried to dry at least their feet on the floor of the car. It was not cold but, because they all felt it felt like they had taken a swim with their clothes on, they decided to blast the heating through the car. The convector couldn't work quickly enough to clear the steam from the windows so they each opened their windows, a little, enough to let some air in and out but enough also to hear the howling outside, enough for little splatterings of water to get inside.

The storm did not appear to be yielding. The sky in front of them, behind them, all around them was black, still an angry ferocious black that showed no sign of surrender. Still Ellis struggled to see through the windscreen, the condensation making things harder if anything. This storm is not done with us yet, thought Oliver. Ellis couldn't find anyone in front of him, no taillights to follow as the sheeted rain broke again and again on the windscreen and the hell of the storm smothered them. He slowed down, the others now feeling the car begin to pull and veer as it went through water which was lying on the road. As they started on another part of dual carriageway Oliver saw a car on his left....still with lights on, stopped....waiting. Instinctively he wondered if something was wrong... it could be an old guy, a puncture like us...

"Guys should we stop, that car...maybe someone old in there... should we help them?"

"No," said Aidan almost immediately. "We're soaked! And anyway, it's probably someone waiting till things get better."

The others nodded in silent consent, conscience compromised and inaction totally justified by the darkness that smothered them right now. "Ok," said Ellis, "ok." He looked in his mirror as they passed the car. "Ah!" he said, "that's a relief. That car is moving now. I think they were looking for someone to follow."

The following car quickly moved to behind them. It was closer than you might normally expect a car to be but, in these conditions, Ellis saw it as perfectly natural. He concluded that the other driver was nervous, was literally hanging on Ellis' taillights and didn't want to let him out of his sight. It made sense. And somehow it was quite comforting to know there was, at least, someone else there. Maybe the person in the car behind was alone, maybe that's what was going through their head too.

The car behind stayed behind until the section of dual carriageway came to an end. Then it seemed to want to overtake. It was the first time Ellis thought that something wasn't quite right here. If you want to be guided by someone, it's more of an issue on a single track road than on a dual carriageway. He saw the car behind move closer, begin to look as though it wanted to pull out to the right. He couldn't see anything of it except its lights. 'What the hell is he doing?' he thought. By now he was not alone. His friends had noticed the erratic movements of the car and had watched it pull in and out.

"Slow down," said Oliver, the suspicion in his voice clear to all of them. "Slow down, right down. Let him pass. Let him go. Maybe he is suddenly in a hurry. But I doubt it. When you slow down I think......he might try to block you...to stop you. Be ready for it, just in case...."

"What do you think?" said Ellis. "Who do you think it is?"

"I don't know," Oliver replied. "But that's what I'd do if I wanted to stop the people in front of me."

Ellis slowed down, almost to a halt. He moved the car into first gear. He put his arm out of the window to wave the car forward and he put on his hazard warning lights. The car behind seemed to move quickly to pass them. They all looked out the window but what they saw was nothing beyond a blur. Faces, yes, sure, but how many? Who knows. Male or female? Who knows. Ellis saw the car pass him and as it did so he stopped completely. He shifted the car into reverse. Sure enough the car swerved in front of them to try and block them. Ellis immediately reversed then hammered the car into first gear, pulling out almost violently and evading the car in front of them. As they passed it the faces were slightly clearer, a male in the front and a female in the back though none of them could see the driver.

"That girl, the girl," said Ali, "that girl, her face is familiar, I think we've seen her before."

"Jesus, Ali we've seen a lot of girls over the last few days. None of whom I'd like to see again. Who was it?"

By now Ellis was speeding further into the storm at a speed he felt to

413

be less than safe. The rain still made it impossible to see very far in front. His friends could tell by the way he was driving, by his quick erratic actions, that he was in a state of some panic. They glanced behind. The white headlights gleamed again and they knew it was a matter of time before the following car caught them.

The road swept round a corner, a corner that gave them brief covering from anyone following. There was an opening to the left, a small country road. Without saying a word Ellis pulled the car down the road, hoping he had enough space between them and the car behind to have fooled them. It was a gamble because suddenly they were on a narrow road, a twisty narrow road, with all the difficulties that brought.

Ellis began to take the car down the road, more quickly than he felt he should. A look up – white lights behind him.

"It might not be them," said Euan. "It might not be them." Maybe if he said it often enough, thought Oliver, like an incantation, it would keep them away. Oliver knew it was them. No other car had passed, no other car had gone past the turn off. Unless a car had overtaken them, then this was them.

The speed with which they made up the distance further confirmed that this was "them".

Ellis knew right away that it would be almost impossible for him to outrun them. It wasn't because of the size of the cars, their engines or horsepower, or even the weather. He knew that on a road like this it would be so much easier for the follower to navigate by the guy in front. Had they been on a motorway there may have been a chance to use any superior speed, if he had it, but here, on this bendy, twisty up and down road, he knew he had little chance. Ellis wasn't a rally driver, a stock car driver nor was he interested in fast cars in particular – he had no points on his licence, no convictions, never caught for speeding. If you had looked up "Safe Driver" in the dictionary it would probably have had his picture there.

He tried to consider what their pursuers might do. On this road, can they really do more than get close to us? Even if you could see all the road, was it possible to overtake? Wide enough? Straight enough? There seemed to be nothing straight about this road at all.

Oliver looked behind him. Headlights loomed nearer. They lit up the rain as it slashed down. Quite a bit of water now lying on the surface. He could see it and feel it as Ellis gripped the wheel, steering it through the forces that tried to drag the car down to a halt. Headlights getting closer. Their presence already forced Oliver to humanise and dehumanise them, seeing them as a pursuing mechanical monster. The monster came closer. Whoever was in the car had put on the full beam, flashing and blinding them, anger coming at them in intermittent blinks. The car pulled closer, closer and as they looked out the back Oliver thought that the person or persons behind must be able to physically see them by now.

Instinctively Ellis tried to outrun the car. He crossed a humpback bridge, a narrow bridge, and felt his wheels leave the ground as it lifted itself over. It returned to the ground with a thump that jolted them. Then a sharp turn that forced their back wheels out, a quick skid that he pulled and corrected. The car behind simply remained two to three yards behind them, unaffected. Ellis felt his control loosen as he revved the car, he felt the pulls from the lying water stronger and still he couldn't see, his vision blurred and indistinct. Except behind him, where the lights loomed large as moons. He shifted down a gear, trying anything to get his speed up. But the car moved closer and began to move out, as if it was trying to straddle them, one light on the back of their car, one light on the road ahead.

Suddenly the car moved out completely, as if to overtake. It was a movement that was both speedy and shocking. In a blink they were almost alongside Ellis, something Ellis thought could not happen, surely the road was not wide enough to take both cars. The car veered towards them and they felt it touch them, at first begin to gently, almost imperceptibly, push them into the side of the road. As they looked across now neither Oliver nor the others could see anyone. The passengers, if they had been there before, were hiding. Even the driver seemed as though his face was covered. It made the car more terrifying, less human…

Ellis felt himself being pushed across. The car began to get close to the grass at the side of the road. We are going too fast…… He slammed on the brakes. That would stop them being pushed but now the car would be in front of them. Neither he nor the others had time to think of what to do. The car in front of them screeched to a halt and three figures piled out, running at them with their arms extended. The three bodies surrounded the car, holding guns at it, at them, all hooded and covered, faces as yet unreachable, invisible.

Jacques had directed this. He had driven the car recklessly, a bit too recklessly maybe, but he had known what he was doing. He was the only one who had a gun. But he had said to the others to hold their hands out in front of them. Under such large coats no one would see that there was no gun there, not in this weather. He did, however, realise that they had a problem deciding what they would actually do with the guys in the car. Normally they would have ushered them outside but in these conditions a conversation would be impossible. Had they had more than one gun then they could have stuck two or three of them in the other car. But they didn't. So he came to the conclusion that they would have to put all of these guys in the back of the car and that he, Guy and Natalie would sit in the front. That's if it was necessary to talk to them at all. Maybe, perhaps, maybe, these guys had thrown the money in the boot. Maybe all that was needed was a quick search of the boot, then they could go without even talking to these guys.

Natalie stood at the boot and tried to open it. The boot flicked up. In the car the three in the back tried to swivel round, frightened and unsure. Two guys outside stood with arms extended, guns trained on them. Natalie scoured around, tossing bags out, rummaging about in the boot. Nothing. She wasn't going to go through anyone's luggage. She closed the boot and went back to Jacques, shaking her head.

Jacques knocked his gun at the window on the driver's side. He made a motion to roll down the window. Ellis rolled it down enough so he could hear what Jacques had to say.

"Listen to me," Jacques almost shouted, "two in front, get in back. Now! In back."

"But...", Ellis began, about to protest about the space.

Jacques' English was not great. He did not want to have a conversation that did not involve Natalie. He yelled back at Ellis, standing back and aiming his gun at him. "Get in back! Now! Do it!"

Ellis and Euan got out the car in haste and almost threw themselves in the back. It was not a big car: the three in the back had been squashed as it was. Ellis and Euan cowered on the edge of the seat. Oliver and Ali were squashed against their respective windows. Aidan, in the middle, was simply squashed. Collectively they still had no idea who was doing this. They were in the back of the car, together, for what seemed an interminable amount of time. Two figures outside stood at each window, arms extended, looking as if they were pointing guns at them.

"Who is it?" asked Ali.

"I don't know," said Ellis. "French accent, male....but I don't recognise it. Is there a girl there? Ali, you said you saw a girl, didn't you?"

"Yeah, I... "

Their confusion was answered soon enough. Firstly Jacques from the driver's side, then Natalie and Guy from the passenger side poured themselves into the car. Jacques kept the gun on the friends. They took their hoods off. At first the friends did not recognise the people in front of them. It was Ellis who saw Natalie, her beautiful sparkling face still there in his memory. Very different in the Nice sunshine...but her, her, definitely her.

Ellis was the first to speak. "Oh Christ," he said. "Of course, we stole your car. Listen we are so sorry for that. We thought at the time...we thought you were after us...so we panicked." He looked at Natalie. "Do you understand me? Do you understand what I'm saying? Can you tell your friends? We didn't mean to steal your car, of course we will give you the money for it. More, in fact. Three, four thousand euros? I'm sorry, we were frightened, we are not thieves. Do you understand?"

Natalie nodded and translated. Jacques began to speak to her in quick angry French. She held her hand up.

"It's not the car. You know it's not the car. It's the money...."

Ellis interrupted her. "I know. I know. We didn't pay you. I can give you that money for it."

Jacques shouted at him. "In the car! Money in the car! You monkey!"

Ellis looked from Natalie to Jacques, their urgent faces saying something that Ellis did not understand. He looked at his friends. "What? Money for the car? You want money for the car?" He looked quickly, quizzically, from Natalie to Jacques.

"No," said Natalie. "Well, perhaps....but that is not the big thing. The big thing is what was in the car."

Ellis looked at them again. "What was in the car? What do you mean, what was in the car?" His words were quick and he was confused. For the first time Jacques had doubts.

He thrust the gun at Ellis who recoiled, raising his hands in front of him, screaming neither words nor sounds, guttural primal pleads.

"Listen. You have the money. Give us all. Give us the money. Our money!" He waved the gun at Ellis.

Ellis looked to Natalie, shouting in desperation. "What fucking money? I'll give you money for the car, I'll give you twice what you wanted, we're sorry!"

Natalie turned to Jacques. They had a quick, loud and angry conversation in French. Guy intervened. Whatever he said involved pointing his hand towards the friends in the back. Jacques sank back and gave a nod of consent. Not a willing nod, something he made it clear he was doing under duress. He kept the gun trained on Ellis.

Natalie sighed. "Ok...ok." She ran her hands through her hair. She looked across the faces of the five men in front of her. They were frightened, confused. She took the gun from Jacques and held it at Ellis. She smiled at him, taking a little pleasure from the fear that rose from him.

"We want to know what you did with the 150,000 Euros that were in the car. Tell us."

She said it in a calm voice and had decided that their reaction would confirm to her whether they knew or did not know about the money. She looked across all five faces. Jaws dropped. Eyes widened.

"What the fuck..." said Ellis...."what the... you're saying there was money in that car? But that car wasn't worth that....that car wasn't worth....it wasn't valuable at all... "

"No," she said smiling, "it was in the car." She threw her emphasis on 'in'.

"There was no money in that car. None. We didn't see any. We didn't take any. There was nothing. Nothing. No money." Oliver said it blankly, matter of fact.

Natalie looked at him. He's the one, she thought, he's the one Clotilde is chasing. She looked at him, this way and that, knowingly. Was he worth chasing to another country? He looked like something that the cat had dragged in right now but there remained a handsomeness there, a rugged, mannish clarity about him. She wondered how Clotilde was with him...the leader or the led? She felt an immediate attraction and she smiled at him, a sweet innocent smile.

Jacques leaned forward. Like Natalie he had focused on their faces. Like Natalie he now had to admit that he thought it unlikely these guys had known anything about the money. He said something to Natalie.

She looked at the faces in front of her. "There was 150,000 Euros in the back of that car. Underneath the carpet in the back, the...." And she made a motion of lifting the back of a car up..

"The boot?" Ellis put in.

"Ok, yes, the boot. There was 150,000 Euros in there. What did you do with it?"

Above his head, for the first time, Oliver could hear the rain begin to lessen. The wind still howled but not in the same desperate way as before.

Ellis put his arms in front of him. "You must believe us. We did not know about that money. If that money was in the car then it is still there. It will still be there."

Jacques interjected. "Why buy the car?" And he almost barked at Natalie, who added, "and he wonders why your behaviour was so strange, you ran away with the car…."

Oliver sighed. "That was because of me. I was – am – in trouble. I made a mistake, I got into a fight with someone I shouldn't have and my life my threatened. I couldn't phone home, anything, in case my calls were discovered. These guys, my friends here, they came to get me, find me, bring me home. My wife – they – were worried. We thought – I thought – that maybe you people" …and he swung his arm round to include all three of them, "we thought you were maybe connected to the people trying to find me. We were worried. We fled. That's why we took your car." He looked at Natalie. "Do you understand?" Natalie understood. This tied with the little that Clotilde had told her. She translated for her father and boyfriend. Jacques put his head in his hands, Guy shook his head slowly, not in disbelief but at the confusion.

Jacques dropped his gun and reached across to talk to the five men in the back. "So where is the car? Where is it now?"

Ellis looked at his friends. "I think somewhere in Lyon. We left that car there after we got the other one."

Jacques slapped himself on the head and spoke to himself in French. "We knew the car was there, we knew it had been left there. I don't know if it will be there now….," said Natalie, "but we thought you had taken the money. We thought that was why you had changed car. We thought that was why you took our car in the first place, you knew we had not taken the money out of it. We thought you were…." she looked around at her father and boyfriend. They nodded. "We thought you were….mob, mafia…"

"Hah!" Ellis almost shouted, almost laughed back to her. "That's who we thought you were. We thought you might have been connected to whoever the fuck was after him," and he nodded towards Oliver.

Natalie looked at Oliver and smiled again. Not really knowing quite what to do Oliver smiled back, an uncertain, hesitant smile. "And" she said, "little guy…….who the fuck is after you?"

Oliver shrugged his shoulders. "I don't know exactly. As I said, I made a mistake, got into a fight with someone I shouldn't have…"

"Who, specifically, is after you?" Slowly, deliberately and with emphasis.

"I've just said, I don't really know. Oh, we have seen….hit men maybe, some strange girls……the list goes on," he said looking across at his friends who nodded in vigorous approval.

"There's a woman after you?"

"Maybe, who knows? We have lost count.." Where is she going with this, thought Oliver?

Natalie sank back and mouthed, deliberately and slowly, to Oliver only, "Clotilde". Oliver sprang up. He was about to speak but Ellis, not having seen this, had a few questions of his own.

"May I ask," he said, "and I know it's none of my business, none of our business, but why did you have 150,000 Euros? Why did you have 150,000 Euros in the boot of a car?"

Natalie looked at Guy who nodded. She had a quick conversation with Jacques who seemed noncommittal. He was like a balloon with its air let out, his disappointment at not getting his money almost touchable. He shrugged his shoulders.

"Ok," said Natalie. "I will try to explain this…event, these events. The money was from the mob, the mafia, crime people, whatever you call them in your country. It was for me, it was me who they paid off. I had been acting……I was an old woman in a play that my group was doing. After it finished, after the play finished, I didn't take my make up off or my clothes. Not on this night. Normally I do but on this night we finished late, there had been a stop to the electricity…it was late and I didn't want to miss the bus home. But, well, I did miss the bus. He…," she turned and pointed to Jacques, "he was away, he couldn't come for me in the car. I should have got a taxi but, you know, I thought, I will walk, it will be ok. Even late at night…."

She stopped and ran her hand across her forehead, trying to remember or to think of how to express herself in English. "I heard cars screeching ahead of me. It's not unusual where we are to have boys racing about. So nothing bad. But then I saw two cars had stopped. I heard shouting. I didn't want to know what was happening so I knew I could go a different way. I could take a road to the left and walk up there. Maybe a little longer, away from the main road, but quieter. I don't want to see, I don't want to know, what is happening. So I took the quieter road.

As I passed a little road on my right I saw something, something bad. I saw a man in a white coat, a long white coat and a hat, take out his gun and shoot a man on the ground. The man on the ground was pleading, asking for his life. But this man…his coat…everything I could see of him from where I was….this was an important man. He didn't speak. He hardly moved. He shot the man three times. I was in a doorway and I hid inside it. They did not see me. I stayed there. And this guy, this man, he walked….he didn't run, he walked away from what he had done. As if… the kind of thing that he did was normal, the kind of thing that you do every day. That is still so bad for me to think of now, that he was so calm about this. I stayed hidden till they left. They did not see me. They could not have seen me. But eventually I came out and walked home.

It was in the newspapers, a man being shot. No witnesses. But then someone said, someone in a flat near there, that they had seen an old woman walking about not long after, she was maybe the only witness. The police tried and tried to find this old woman. They searched and searched but of course they did not find her.

After three days, three days after there was the news that there was an old woman, I was at work – I'm a waitress – and a man said he needed to talk with me. He was very….em..good, em….charming, yes, charming… and I thought he was a man, trying to see if…well, you know… anyway, he waited for me and asked me if I knew the old woman the police were looking for. Of course I said no, I didn't, I didn't know what he was talking about. Then he made me sit down and said to me: 'this is very simple. I have 150,000 Euros which says the old lady must never talk. If they find the old lady she will die. That is not a threat. I am telling you what will happen. Take the 150,000 Euros and it will be yours as long as the old lady forgets how to talk.'

What could I do? I took the money and I forgot how to talk. But of course we are frightened, frightened that they want their money back, that they want to kill us anyway…."

"But why keep the money in the car?" asked Oliver.

"I didn't want to put it in to a bank. I always wanted to at least move it into the house. But we became….I don't know the word…we thought that all the time people might be watching us, trying to find the money. We thought they would take it back. So we thought – I thought – it was in a place that was safe. And then nothing happened for a while so I began to think that maybe it is safe to move it. And for a while I simply forgot it was there. I know, I know, it was stupid but I thought I had moved it. It was so much on my mind….our minds… sometimes you forget the important things. You see we didn't want to use it right away – we need it but we thought, maybe if we use it the notes will be discovered. Maybe the notes are not real notes, you know? If we wait, best to wait….

421

So when people like you came to buy the car....we were a little suspicious. It was only when the trouble between us happened and you took the car that we knew – well we thought we knew – that you had known the money was in the car and you had come to take it."

"Why sell the car?" asked Oliver. "We were told you were selling the car. Why sell it if the money was in it?"

"We intended to take the money out, of course, as I said," said Natalie. "And we felt that a car was easy for someone to find... a registration can be found anywhere. We thought we might be safer to buy another car. We had money to do that now. We had to sell the other one. And we wanted that done quite quickly. If we bought another one, maybe a good one that someone already used, we could pay with cash and they would not look out for the notes as much... if the notes were not proper notes. You see?"

"Who shot the man?" asked Ellis. "Do you know?"

"No, I don't know." She thought back, her thumbnail on the edge of her lips. "He was so well dressed...... so calm."

"Do you think that might be who's after us?"

Jacques leaned across to Natalie and had a quick conversation. "Maybe," she said. "We know – he knows – that someone is after you. People were asking questions. But we thought that maybe there had been confusion, maybe we got the wrong message. But someone is after you, yes. Someone big, maybe the same guy? You make bad friends, do the wrong thing to the wrong guy?"

Oliver looked at her. She was sparkling even though she was still drenched. "How do you know Clotilde?" he asked her. His friends looked at him with surprise.

"No, monsieur, I think I get to ask that one first. How do you..." and she pointed at him with a playful smile on her face, "....know Clotilde?"

"That's simple, I work with her. My job involves being, at times, in the south of France. She works with a supplier of ours....."

"But I think you know her a little better than as someone you would work with, no?"

Ellis started to laugh. "Yeah, well, you might say..."

"What do you know?" Oliver said to her, puzzled as to how this girl seemed to know so much about him.

"I know enough to know she is prepared to follow you. That she is someone with whom you are maybe even in love......or is in love with you... "

"She what? She's followed what? What do you mean?" Oliver shot bolt upright in his seat as though someone had passed an electrical current through his body. "You are fucking joking, tell me you are joking!"

Natalie laughed. "She told me she had things between you to resolve. She knew I was coming after you with Guy and Jacques. She said she would see you again, France or Edinburgh, it didn't matter where."

"Oh yes!" shouted Ellis. "As if it couldn't get better. There's a mad bitch of a stalker after us now! Well, after you, Olly. You're on your own with this one. Hey, maybe she's in Edinburgh already. Maybe her and Helen are sitting having tea and crumpet, talking about how good you are in bed….or how you'll soon be dead…."

His friends laughed. Oliver found the scenario less than amusing. Even Guy laughed and he couldn't have had a clue what was being said. Oliver looked again at Natalie. "So can you answer my question please? How do you know Clotilde?"

Jacques was fiddling with something. She reached across to Oliver quickly and whispered. "She is my lover." In a flash she was back where she was and said, "I know her, like you do, through work. We chatted, became friends…," she closed her eyes and let an imaginary thrill pass through her body. She shivered and smiled. "And that is really all there is to say. She spoke of you."

"Oh yeah," said Euan, "really? What did she say? There are no secrets between the five of us.."

She laughed, coquettish, hand over her mouth, smiling. "She said he is a lovely man. A good friend. Whom she now misses."

Outside the drumming on the roof of the car had stopped. The howl had dissipated, a little wind that could have passed for the gentle breeze of a summer night the only remnant of the fierce gale. The colour of the sky was shifting from dark to light.

Jacques spoke again with his girlfriend. "Ah!" she clapped her hands with enthusiasm and turned to the friends. "It seems the car is still in Lyon. The police have it but it is untouched. We can get it, we can get it maybe tomorrow or the next day. I hope still with the money."

"Well we don't have it. I promise you. But we must give you some money for it."

Natalie turned to Jacques who waved his hand. "No," she said. "We will get the car back. It's ok."

"But we had the use of it. And we left it in some God-forsaken hole.

Please, take at least 1,000 Euros," said Ellis, taking the 100 Euro notes out of his wallet. "I insist. Please. At least this. Please. Treat it as a gift if nothing else."

Natalie held up her hands and accepted the money.

"Thank....thank you," said Guy, smiling.

They all got out the car into what was now a restful sleepy summer night. Oliver was turning something over in his head.

"What if you had been found by the police?" he said to Natalie. "I mean if you hadn't been dressed as an old woman and been easier to find. Would you, could you, have identified the guy? Gone to trial?"

"From what I know," said Natalie, "I doubt that. I think I would have been killed somewhere. Even if I had said to the police that I wouldn't testify. I think if they had found me I would have been killed. These people are so powerful. I have my old lady costume to thank for that. My disguise. Sometimes it's good to pretend to be someone you're not, it can have some good fortune." She leant across to Oliver and whispered in his ear. "Not so unlike you, monsieur. I saw a photo of you and Clotilde. You looked more than happy."

Guy and Jacques stepped back into their car. Natalie turned around to look at Oliver before she opened the door. They were each thinking the same thing. But whereas Natalie welcomed and nurtured the thought Oliver tried to hide it away.

CHAPTER 21

Donna had been told it was "the big guy" who was coming across and she was lucky to have been chosen. It had been short notice but she couldn't pretend she wasn't even slightly thrilled. An important guy wants me….and maybe the tip….

She was told to be at a five-star hotel at a given time, told to ask for someone on the desk and she would be met. What should she wear? No problem there, she would be given clothes to change into – it really depended upon the mood of the guy at the time. She may have to wear a wig.

Donna looked around the hotel room as she stood there, waiting. Her contact was on the phone to some guy who seemed to be with the big guy himself. Beside her was a woman who opened a wardrobe to reveal a variety of clothes, different outfits. The room was beautiful. A huge bed, spacious, bathroom that was about the size of her house. Airily she looked above her, trying to convince the woman opposite her that this was nothing new to her. Inside she would admit to gasping a little. This was a long way from fifteen year olds fumbling at her breasts and her nervous giggles.

"Ok, ok, I get it, ok." The man put down the phone and had a quick conversation with the woman in whispers. Donna walked away from them, conscious that whatever they were trying to say, they did not want her to hear. She strayed into the bathroom, imaging being in that sunken bath for an hour or two, listening to music, losing yourself in its size…

"Right, my pretty….Donna… let's have a look at underwear first. Black or red is probably ok so let's see what we have." She opened a suitcase with underwear in it, mostly underwear and other things that looked like toys or instruments Donna had only heard spoken of. All the underwear seemed new, still in packages. Donna knew from the names on them that they were expensive.

The woman pulled out a black bra and thong. The bra was see-through in places, the thong thin and silky with a vague and indistinct pattern weaved across it. A little bow at the back, which seemed too delicate for what Donna believed she was about to do. It somehow seemed strange to be looking at such things in this place, in this situation, with all her clothes on.

The woman looked her up and down. 'A girl, still a girl…will she fill these….let's see.' She looked at Donna, she fingers moving towards her lips, a little more nervous now. 'Still very much a girl, too much a girl… still, not my job to question…'

She looked at Donna. "Come on dear, take your clothes off. Let's see if they fit." Donna held out her hands for the underwear. "No, dear, no. You take your clothes off here and we'll try them on."

"Oh… I thought I would take them into the bathroom and change there…"

"No," said the woman firmly. "Here." Donna looked tense though perhaps not as tense as she felt. She got to her underwear quite quickly then felt shamed by her white, bland, cheap matching bra and knickers. She stopped. "Keep going" said the woman firmly. She reached behind herself and undid her bra, tossing it to the floor. 'Relatively small,' thought the woman, 'but firm…delicate but firm….I think that should do.' She walked up to Donna and put her hands on Donna's breasts, closing her eyes as she gently massaged them.

"What the…"

"Be quiet!" the woman hissed at her. "You are here now. You must please this guy. If you don't please him it will be your fault but also, most likely, mine."

She massaged Donna's breasts in a mechanical soulless way at first. Closing her eyes again her fingertips softened. "Just relax dear, just relax." Donna closed her eyes too and tried to imagine it was not a woman's fingers that were tweaking her nipples, teasing them gently out. The woman looked down at Donna's breasts and smiled, clearly pleased with the result. "Good, good…."

The woman nodded her head towards Donna's knickers. Donna took them down then stood out of them, naked and vulnerable in front of this complete stranger. The woman stepped back. Hair, black hair…would he rather she were shaven? He never seemed to have a preference and if she shaved this girl now, for the first time in her life probably…no, no leave as is.

"Best try to enjoy this. At least, don't tense up. Now, stand with your legs slightly apart." Donna did as she was told. The woman closed her eyes and ran her hands on the inside of Donna's legs. Fine, no roughness, smooth, nice shape to them. "Turn around. Now bend over, legs slightly apart." The woman's hands glided on Donna's buttocks… shapely, sure – but the shape of a girl not a woman….well, he can't have both.

Donna felt the woman's hands caress her buttocks then move, both of them, to between her legs. Her fingers rubbed on her, gently and Donna heard a contented noise behind her. She was about to raise herself when the woman said "No, stay there." Donna gasped and yelped as she felt two firm fingers thrust inside her, into every orifice there was.

"Be quiet!" the woman reiterated. When she withdrew her fingers she simply said "Ok, get washed – quick shower, good wash down below and we'll see what you look like in these."

Donna tried on only two sets of underwear, the red one and the black one. They decided the black one might be best. With hold-up tights. Then the woman opened the wardrobe to reveal an array of dresses – sparkling, plain, elegant, any of them would have caught the eye at the best reception in town. Donna made a noise, something along the lines of "Wow!"

"Don't worry dear, they haven't all been bought specially for you. Black or red?" she looked across at the man.

"I think either will do."

"You've thought that before and I trusted you. From what you said, the tone, I think it is to be black."

When Donna had put the dress on and looked in the mirror she barely recognised herself. The woman had insisted on drying Donna's hair herself and she had turned it this way and that. She looked more grown up yet somehow the shape of her made her feel more like a girl. Which was exactly how the woman had wanted her to look.

"Shoes?" asked Donna. She had arrived in a pair of running shoes and she stifled a giggle as she looked across at them now.

"You don't need shoes. You're not going anywhere and in any case his room is the suite at the end of the corridor. Now, we await his call...."

"Em...who is he? This guy?"

"Don't ask. And especially don't ask him. Don't say anything to him unless you're asked a question. And do what he tells you. Whatever it is."

Donna nodded. "Is he British?"

The woman looked down. The man said "No, he's not British. But you need know no more than that. What you don't know and all that...."

"You're frightened of him," said Donna. "Should I be frightened of him?"

"Listen dear...if you do what he asks when he asks you to do it then you might be back here every time he's across in this country. You can be a very rich girl. This man can make you very rich. But... "

"But… ," said Donna.

"You have to do what he asks, that's all. That's not difficult, is it?"

"No. Is he…you know… quick?"

The woman laughed despite herself, holding her hand up to her mouth as if the laugh had escaped and she was trying to get it back. "I don't know. I've never…….but from what I've seen, it varies… "

"Ok," said Donna. She was sitting on the bed, lightly swinging her legs. 'She'll be fine,' thought the woman, 'she got through me. She doesn't know enough about the way things are to be frightened.'

They sat, waiting, three people becoming more and more comfortable with each other. Then the man got a call and he looked at Donna. "It's time," he said. "Out the door, turn right, the door facing you at the end of the corridor. Come back here. We will be here, whenever he is finished with you."

Donna stood up and flattened her dress. The woman came over and lightly touched her hair, her dress. She cupped her hands gently on Donna's face and said; "Good luck, my pretty."

When Donna returned she wasn't exactly skipping or dancing or walking on air but she felt like a sixteen year old who had experienced something wonderful for the first time. She knocked on the door and was let in, a huge, wide grin on her face. The woman noticed how wide Donna's grin was, how her happiness filled her whole face.

'What the hell,' thought the woman… She had half expected Donna to return with bruises, anal ruptures, even something stuck inside her. It had happened before, especially when he was in a bad mood. She even had a doctor on standby, just in case…

"You look… I mean, did it go well? Was he…is he….happy?"

"Well," smiled Donna, "he seemed happy. I am happy……I am very happy. He is a wonderful man, isn't he?"

'No, not really,' thought the woman, 'he's a murderous thug.' She shared a glance with the man. "If you say so dear." And she paused, curious to ask something she had never asked in this situation before. "What happened? You've been gone a while….maybe a couple of hours…."

"We spoke for a while….I sang to him….we made love….we talked…"

"You did what?" The woman almost exploded. Never, in all the time she had been involved with this man, had anyone ever referred to what he did sexually as making love. This guy fucked. At times like a brutal beast, at others like an evil bastard.

"We talked… "

"You made love?" she interrupted.

"Well, yeah, that's kind of why I thought I was here," and she glanced from the woman to the man for confirmation. The man nodded vigorously.

"Excuse me," said the woman. "You must excuse me. 'Making love' wasn't a phrase I had expected you to use."

"Oh, well, yes, he was very considerate…he made sure I…you know…got pleasure too…"

The woman sat down. Had the girl turned left instead of right and ended up with someone else?

"What did you talk about?"

"Oh, family… he was interested in my family…especially my dad who's a policeman …he said he didn't like policemen very much….I said I didn't like them very much either if they were all like my dad…he spoke about his dad…."

'He has a father?' thought the woman to herself. 'I thought he was brought up by a great white shark…'

"Anyway, he said he would like me to move to France…he said I relaxed him…"

"He said what?" The woman was now convinced the girl had turned left instead of right.

"He wanted me to move to France. Oh, he told me what he was like… he likes woman, he's going to take his pleasures where he finds them, and he's married…but I think I… I'm not sure, but I think I maybe gave his something he liked…by being me. Maybe just be being me. So he said, anyway, that he would like me to be there so he could, as he said it, 'be with me now and then, when he wanted'. He would make it worth my while, financially. Put me up somewhere nice, a big flat. South of France. Not bad," she said looking at her feet, "not bad for a girl with no qualifications." Saying it like that, the way she said it, she felt close to tears. As did the woman, who pinched her nose and rubbed at her eyes with undue force.

"What will you do?" asked the woman, softly.

"I think…yes, I think I'll probably go. He's quite persuasive you know."

'Sweet Jesus, my dear,' thought the woman, 'you don't know the half of it.'

"He said I could keep the underwear….all of it if I wanted…and this dress…if it's ok with you.."

The woman spread her hands in front of her. "Sure," she said. "Of course."

Donna changed back into her normal clothes but kept the underwear on. It made her feel much more than her sixteen years. In her hand she carried a leather bag full of underwear and a dress. In her pocket were notes that amounted to £2,500.

Clotilde had phoned Oliver's work. He had left something in France when he was there, she said. Some photographs of his son that he had brought across to show people but he had left them in the office and she was going to be in Edinburgh anyway, could she pop them in to his house…just want to check the address…yes, yes.

And so, with thunder and lightning flashing and roaring in the sky, and the rain beginning to sheet down, Clotilde found herself sitting in her car outside Oliver's house. It was quite obvious from the glimpses that she had inside that Oliver was not there. But his wife was. Clotilde was thrilled at the prospect of entering Oliver's world.

She rang the doorbell.

"Hi…you don't know me…I'm Anna…I work with your husband when he is in France, in the south of France. I heard through one of my colleagues that he was not well. I am in Edinburgh on business and I wanted to check if he was ok. Is he? Is he ok?"

Helen looked at the woman in front of her. Up and down…

"Come in," she said. Helen realised that she either had to tell the woman to go away or invite her in. It was too wet to have a conversation on the doorstep.

"How do you know our address Anna?" was the first thing Helen asked.

"Oh, we have it on file. Oliver asks us to send documents, contracts, to this address sometimes."

Helen ticked the box. It was true, Oliver sometimes wanted material delivered to his home address and she often had to sign for recorded delivery work related material. Helen looked at the smiling woman opposite her. Even with her hair – and her clothes – wet, she looked unmistakeably attractive, rich with the beauty that comes from being affluent and living in the south of France. Likewise Clotilde looked at

Helen, immediately seeing the attraction to someone like Oliver. Beautiful, lovely shape, she swayed as she walked, imagine her in a tight dress, emphasising everything about her…yes, Clotilde could see the attraction to someone like Oliver.

The least Helen could do was offer tea or coffee and Clotilde's eyes followed her as she moved. She imagined Oliver with this woman, what understandings they shared, little jokes, what playfulness…and she imagined Oliver's hands on her and hers on him and she wanted Helen. As she looked through Helen was in the kitchen, standing with her back to the living room, and Clotilde imagined her hands on her. How would she be if I went up and…

Helen turned and smiled at her. A weak almost pathetic and forced smile but nonetheless the first smile she had managed since inviting Anna into her house.

"Anna, what do you know? What do you know about my husband?" Helen eyed the woman opposite her with a little suspicion. As she dried out she became more beautiful.

"I heard from my colleagues he wasn't well…that he had trouble getting home. I tried the office but he wasn't there, they don't know where he is. I tried his mobile but..," she shrugged, "no answer. So I phoned my office and asked if they knew his address and phone number. No phone number but the address and so…… So, how is he?"

Helen looked at Anna. Anna gave her no reason in what she said, nor in the way she said it, to make her assume there was any more to this visit than met the eye. But yet it was odd…this quite beautiful French woman, turning up…though if she wasn't who she said she was then who was she? Someone having an affair with Oliver? Somebody who wished him harm? Would she really come to the house in that case? In this way… alone? Helen put her head in her hands. At times, these days, it felt as though she knew nothing, knew no one. She had analysed things to death and nothing, no further forward.

Helen sighed and said in a tired voice: "I don't know where he is. I think he is in the UK. He was the last time we spoke. Nearly home, I think he said. But he's not here," and she waved a hand around her. "He's not here. He got stuck in France, got into some sort of trouble he said, had to lie low…stay undetected….Christ," she said, more to herself, "it sounds like something out of a bloody spy film. He's not James Bond, what's happened is crazy. And they, all of them, seem to have been chased by…"

The woman opposite interrupted her. "I'm sorry, they? He's not alone?"

"No. My brother….we were alarmed, we hadn't heard from him at all for a few days….so my brother and some friends they went across, took a plane across to try and find him. And they did, they seemed to find him. I don't know where or why or how. But that was about a week ago. I think they have been chased……Christ, I don't know, it doesn't make any sense, none of it makes any sense. So I don't know where he is. He may be home in two minutes, two hours, two days, two years. Who knows? How do you know him anyway? Did you see him when he was in France? Do you know what happened? What the trouble was?"

Clotilde paused. Part of her wanted to. Part of her wanted to because she wanted to see this woman break down, then she could comfort her, touch her, think where that might lead… Part of her wanted to because then this woman would know how her husband had lived another life, even if only for a few days, in another bed. Part of her wanted to so that she could tell her that she had made love with her husband…and to describe things that no one could describe unless there had been intimacy. Part of her wanted to show her superiority over this woman who made her feel such jealousy.

But of course she didn't. "Yes, I saw him when he was in France. We fixed a contract for the next six months……he is a good negotiator, very good at his job…we, that is my company, we took him to a dinner on a Saturday night and that's where we lost him…"

Helen interrupted. "Then you were maybe the last people to see him…what happened?"

"Well of course we have no idea what happened. He disappeared. We did have a policeman come and talk to us a day or two after. But then we heard, a day or so ago, that he was unwell, or had been unwell, and was home…"

Helen interrupted again. "Did he do anything that night that was… odd? Was he nervous?" She paused. "You would you know?" she said more to herself, "you don't really know him, how would you know if he was behaving in an unusual way."

"Oh he seemed fine," said Clotilde, "he seemed fine." She chose her words carefully. "I know that of course I couldn't know him as you do but he seemed normal…happy…smiling, you know?"

'Not really,' thought Helen. Would she describe Olly as happy and smiling? He seemed to have been gone for so long that she could barely remember. Was that how he was with other people? She looked across at the woman... .or only with this woman?

"Is your husband with you, Anna?"

Clotilde recognised the question and wondered if she should dance. Why not? I'd quite like to make this woman feel at least uncomfortable... would still like to see her crumple.... "No, em, no, no, I'm not married actually. Never seem able to find the right man, you know? Well, you don't know, you have!"

And she laughed and Helen smiled, an uneasy smile. I don't know if I trust you, Anna.

"Does Olly ever speak of us? His son? Has he ever spoken to you of Terrence? And the baby?"

Clotilde smelt the trap. "Terrence, yes, all the time, he sent us photos by e-mail, you know. But I didn't know you had a baby! How old is the baby? When did you have it? Is it a boy or a girl?"

Helen held up her hand. "There isn't a baby. I had a thought that we might be talking about a different Oliver. But I think we are talking of the same man.."

"Oh," said Clotilde, "I see." She raised her cup to her lips and looked at Helen. Helen's head was down slightly, avoiding any gaze. This woman is unsure of me, she thought. She does not trust me. But maybe she does not know why she does not trust me. Good....

"He is a lovely man, your husband," she said. "We all look forward to his visits..."

Helen looked up. 'But perhaps you especially,' she thought...

"He must be ok. I am sure he will be." Clotilde saw Helen's head go down again, only a little, but she sensed vulnerability and decided to strike.

"It must have been such a worry for you, the past week...didn't he phone, hasn't he phoned?"

"Briefly, a couple of time. But he says he is worried about his line being tapped...his calls being traced. So he calls briefly." She laughed, an embarrassed laugh. "It sounds ridiculous, doesn't it? Calls being traced... ......ridiculous...."

"Ah. You must miss him so much. I'm so sorry. This must be terrible for you."

Helen's head was down, lower now, and Clotilde listened, listened closely for a little break, a little sob. "Are you ok?"

Helen nodded her head but didn't speak. Clotilde sniffed her chance and almost sprang across to Helen. She put her arm around her, gingerly at first, but the hand that pulled Helen into her was full of authority. In truth, Helen was hardly sobbing but she felt herself guided, with some assertion, into this woman and it felt comfortable and safe.

Clotilde breathed Helen in. She felt Helen's body against her, this shape every part of which Olly must have run his hands over. She held Helen. Her hands began to rub Helen's back, gently. Helen relaxed. She put her hand round Clotilde, at first lightly then she held as she was being held.

"Thank you," she whispered.

The phone rang and made them both jump. Clotilde closed her eyes tight in frustration. Helen walked to the phone in the kitchen. Clotilde could hear what she said but not easily, not with complete clarity.

"You're where……you're near, you're near," and then her speech quickened, "how near, soon tonight, where are you… ok, ok, I'm listening, I'm listening…….ok…… ok… but that doesn't make sense……why should we do that…….ok, ok, well, you're scaring me now……ok, and…," she shut the door and made it almost impossible for Clotilde to hear, "there is someone from your work here, someone from France, across here on business…Anna….ok, what does that mean? Ok, I will, I will…"

She put the phone down, trembling slightly. Everything full of danger. She breathed in and out deeply, trying to relax. When she went back into the living room she couldn't meet Clotilde's eyes. She said: "Anna, I'm sorry, I'm going to have to ask you to leave. I think my husband may be coming home soon and obviously, we would like to be alone….it has been a long time that we have been apart." With a meek smile she managed to look at Clotilde. "I'm sure you can understand?"

"Of course I do, of course," said Clotilde, standing up. "I am so glad he is well and everything is ok. He is near now?"

"From what he says, yes, he is near," said Helen. Again a weak, watery smile.

"Good." Clotilde gave her a firm hug, grasping Helen to her. "That is such good news," she said.

And with that she left. She left, but she didn't go. Clotilde had come too far to let it go as easily as that. So she got into her car, outside the house, and drove a street or two away. She vowed to wait a half hour or so and drive past the house to see if there was any sign of Oliver. Then she would make her presence known again.

Ambrose had been left in a state of rage by Helen's non-appearance at his planned meeting. He wondered what could have gone wrong. Helen had done what Oliver had suggested to her – phoned the agency and discovered that there was no such review taking place. Ambrose had not allowed for such a deviation. The plan had been meticulous. It had to work. He had spent hours planning it.

When he had realised that she wasn't coming it had put him into a state of fury that he hadn't experienced before. He killed that night, for the first time. He hadn't known he was going to kill, he hadn't intended to kill. He had intended to hit and to fuck, with all the rejection that his body could muster. But the girl…she was easy, a bit too easy, not very pretty, with a smile that always looked forced, never natural. He had charmed her and insisted on her place, a place where she lived alone. A quiet neighbourhood on the outskirts. At first it had been fine, he sensed she was a bit uncomfortable with the force that he thrust himself inside her. But then she wriggled and tried to move, saying "No, no, don't do that, that's sore." He felt the first release as his fist smashed into her, most likely breaking her nose. She tried to escape but he had grabbed her to him and instinctively thrust her hands around her throat. He had not intended to kill her but had not felt truly satisfied until he knew she had no more breath in her body. He was still inside her at the time.

He did panic when he realised what had happened. Had anyone seen him? Should he just leave? Was his DNA all over the place? Her house was at the end of the street. It was quite difficult for neighbours to see anyway, especially in the dark, even if they had been looking. So he moved her body into the boot of his car and drove for about two hours before he tossed the body into woodland off a back road where it would surely remain undiscovered for a while. He felt neither remorse nor guilt.

Anything he did feel came out as anger toward Helen. She had pushed him into this. Whatever was feeding him with these feelings could only be quenched by her. He had raped before and he was sure now that he would rape Helen. At least once. If she resisted……he wasn't sure himself where his own boundaries were anymore. He knew the back door of Helen's house was more or less hidden. Easier to hide in the garden without attracting the gaze of neighbours….there were fences, walls, though you might need a touch of luck with someone not looking out a certain window of a certain house at a certain time…

Ambrose had several ways of actually getting in. A few months ago, he and a friend had had a hypothetical conversation about getting into a house without a key, effectively about picking a lock. There were things you could do with androgynous keys that could bump anything. He had a glass cutter too. So he left his car, the car that had had a dead body in it for a few hours the night before, beside his flat and instead of going into his flat started to walk along the street and round the corner. His presence, in a big coat with big pockets, was noted. The coat, with enough room to hide anything he might need to use, drew no attention with the storm, though fading now, still coming down. But not going into his flat did draw attention. The man watching, however, registered it as 'a bit odd' but did nothing with the information.

Ambrose negotiated quite a complex way across gardens to get to Helen's. The sky was dark if not so threatening and it made seeing anything difficult. There was a real concern of tripping or slipping. But with the lights on in every house it made him harder to detect. So he made his way, cautiously and without being spotted, into Helen's garden. He knew she was – he knew someone was – in, as he had seen the light in the front. He saw the same light, less bright of course, from the back garden. He moved closer to the back door and slightly away from the patio window. The storm was dying now and it would be easy to see a human presence that was close to the window. And it was certainly less easy to hide than it would have been even half an hour ago. He crouched down. He breathed in, through his mouth, but as he did so an unexpected sheet of rain flew at him and caught the back of his throat. Instinctively he coughed. Not loudly. But it had been loud enough for those inside to hear.

When the friends reached their final destination, Oliver's home, they did not park in the street but a street or two away. Oliver, because he felt the house was being watched, had told Helen that someone would come for her, one of the friends but not him. They would go together out the back door, through the gardens and would meet each other in the car. Later he would go back to the house, she would go somewhere safe. Helen thought it odd but didn't question it. Oliver thought it odd too. But if he was going to have to face the people who were chasing him it was going to be at least partly on his terms. And, if it could at all be avoided, it was not going to involve his wife.

"I'll do it," said Aidan. "I'll go for Helen. What did you say we would do? Simply knock at the door?"

"No," said Olly, "Remember, I said whoever was coming for her would phone when they were a few seconds away so she would open the door and there would be no waiting. No waiting about for anyone."

"Yes, of course. Of course. Ok, so I'll take my phone. I'll get Helen. We'll go out the back door. Go out the garden and across your neighbour's to the left. We'll meet you on the street that runs parallel to the one your house is on." Aidan seemed to be looking at his phone and typing as he talked.

"Yes, that's… jeez Aidan, you don't need to write it down, do you? It's not that complex.."

"Oh," he said quickly, "no, no, putting the number in the phone so it's ready to go." He looked up at his friends and forced a smile. "Ok, I'm going…when we see each other again it will be with Helen." He clasped hands with each of them separately.

As he walked out of the car he sent a message from his phone. The rest of them were doing the same, all apparently perfectly naturally, Oliver to tell Helen that Aidan was coming for her, the others to spouses and partners. Five of them had sent messages at pretty much the same time. Sitting across the road, watching the house, the two men received a message telling them of the exact plans that Oliver had discussed with the others.

"Ok," said the one to the other, "tell him. I think, at last, the dog is returning to its kennel.."

They smiled knowingly at each other when they saw Aidan walk along the road. The storm had pretty much died though there was still rain. Aidan hadn't bothered with a jacket. He still wasn't dry from before. But he looked most odd, a man walking in the rain with no protection, and he was signposted as who he was and what he was doing as much as if he had had a neon sign above his head.

He neared the house and phoned. As he walked up the front garden the door opened and he walked in without breaking his stride. Helen wrapped herself around him and sobbed. She grabbed him, every bit of him, kissed every part of his cheeks, held his face between her hands and sobbed and laughed.

"You're safe! You're back! You're safe! You're all safe!"

Aidan couldn't help but smile but he didn't feel very safe. He had to take Helen through her own back garden and ensure she was not seen. Then she was to be hidden away somewhere. This did not feel like safety. But her joy was infectious and he found himself sharing in her tears. There was no time to recount stories, no time to talk of one-eyed men or huge dogs. This situation had to be resolved. Between Olly and whatever, whoever, had kicked this off. And Helen couldn't be a pawn in this so they had to go, to get out now. She would meet with Olly briefly and she could then take the car away, to his parents or her parents. The friends would return to the house. And wait.

Helen put on a coat as Aidan had advised her to cover her head. She turned out the lights in the living room and the kitchen and they made their way towards the back door. As they did so they heard a cough, not loud in itself but loud enough to let them know that someone was nearby. Not in the house but in the garden. Aidan put his fingers to his mouth and they both crouched down. He looked around the kitchen, searching for something that might be of use. No knives. He didn't want to open any drawers, certainly didn't want to put any lights on. The person outside should not know that they were aware of his presence. The only thing he could see were pots, pots and a frying pan. He picked up the frying pan, a big heavy stainless steel thing that could probably have stopped an elephant. He gripped it.

He motioned to Helen to crouch down with him, behind the cupboards. This meant that if anyone had come in the back door, he and Helen could not be seen right away. A few seconds – maybe minutes – later they heard a scratching at the lock of the door. The scratching got louder, as though someone was getting frustrated with what they were doing. It stopped. Aidan and Helen stayed hidden, stayed quiet. The scratching started again. Whatever the person had done had brought success and Helen clearly heard the distinctive 'click' of the lock as it went off and she could hear the distinctive moans and creaks of the door as it began to open.

Ambrose opened the door slowly. Where was she? She hadn't gone upstairs, he would have seen the light from that surely. Maybe she had gone out. That would be fine. He could wait, take his time, he knew how to wait, that would be good. Yeah, that's probably what's happened, she's gone out. He opened the door wider, cursing its whines. No one came. He stepped into the kitchen and closed the door behind him. He stopped to listen but heard nothing. At this point Aidan and Helen were hiding no more than a few feet away from him. In theory they could have heard each other breathing. Perhaps the wind helped.

Aidan, crouched down, could feel the discomfort in his legs. The man seemed to stay still, taking in the whole room, pausing. I can't sit like this much longer, Aidan thought. The man moved forward, one step. Aidan looked down and could see the front of a big black boot, dripping wet. A boot that looked like it was steel toe-capped. It was wide and threatening. The man must literally have been inches away from being able to look over the top of the washing board and the cupboards and see them. Aidan could not face looking up, scared of what may be looking up at him. 'Just another step or two,' he thought, 'just another step.'

By this time Ambrose was convinced that Helen had gone out. He had stopped and listened for what felt like minutes and all he could hear was the surrender of the wind outside. He took two steps forward and then had, literally, no idea what hit him. Aidan knew that he had to do whatever had to be done in one movement. To reach up with the pan and hit whoever it was. When he saw Ambrose take the steps he almost jumped and used both hands to smash the frying pan across the back of Ambrose's head. He hit him with the force that you would batter a tennis ball.

Ambrose blacked out almost instantly. He was a relatively big man but the force of the hit sent him sprawling across the floor and the front of his head banged against the wall. Helen covered her mouth with her hands. Aidan realised straight away that the man was unconscious at least, perhaps dead. He let him lie for a minute to be sure and scrambled for a knife before he leaned over the body. He turned the man over. Helen looked at his face.

"Do you recognise this guy?"

"No," said Helen. "No, I don't think so. Who is he? Is this the guy who you're in trouble with."

"No," said Aidan, firmly. "I don't think so. No, I don't know who this is." Aidan checked his pulse. "He's breathing…," and he put his hand on his own forehead, wondering what he could do with this guy. He was too big to move. Even if they moved him what would they do? Throw him in the garden?

"Helen, do you have any string? Rope? The only thing we can do is tie this guy up. And leave him here. Leave him here till we come back."

"Oh, Aidan… can't you phone Oliver and the rest and they can come here? Surely it is ok now?"

"No Helen, no. This doesn't feel right. This doesn't feel right at all. Let's stick to the plan. That's what Olly wants. This guy……..he's a fly in the ointment, he's nobody, maybe he's just a common thief." Aidan rifled through the man's pockets and discovered the instruments that would help him get in the house but beyond that, nothing. No wallet.

No picture. A key, probably for the man's own house and a car key... but no bag, not even a plastic bag. If you were a burglar, wouldn't you have brought a plastic bag, something, to take stuff away in? He didn't say anything to Helen.

She brought him string and strong black tape, no rope, but Aidan felt it would be strong enough and he set to work doing something he had never done before. Helen looked at the man as Aidan tied his legs, his feet, his arms, everything. He looked... nasty, evil... a cruel unforgettable face. Had she seen him before? Probably, he looked vaguely familiar, vaguely... what could he have wanted with her, with the house, if he wasn't connected with the men who were after Olly? Was he the guy that had been in the house, in the back garden, the man who Officer McLean thought might have been after her? Ready to take her? What had happened, really happened, over the last couple of weeks? Her world had move from being solid, a little dull, to almost imploding around her. I should never have got involved with McLean she thought. How could I have done that? To Olly....to Terrence....maybe if she was being threatened by someone unknown it was a contorted punishment. Maybe she deserved for her world to fall apart because that what she had initiated. 'I want Olly,' she thought as she wiped away tears. 'I want my Olly... '

By the time Aidan was finished, Ambrose was wound up with so much tape and string that he looked like a massive Christmas present.

"And you're going to leave him there?" asked Helen.

"Well," Aidan said, tightening the final pieces of string till further, "do you have any better ideas? We're coming back here in ten minutes. He should be ok for that time, no?"

Helen grimaced a little. "What now?"

"Now," he said, standing back from the body, tightening bits, then finally leaving it, "now... now...we go. Come on. Out the back door, across the garden...two gardens I think. Then down the street and round the corner where we see Olly. Come on, it'll only take a couple of minutes."

"Oh, ok, hold on." Helen ran upstairs and down. She held up running shoes. "Maybe better for clambering around gardens than high heels."

Aidan smiled. Yeah, that was Helen alright... always a lady... a pretty, shapely, solid symbol of femininity. She put her shoes on.

"Ok?" she said, looking at him with trusting inquisitive eyes.

Instinctively he smiled and hugged her. "This is going to be ok Helen. Trust me, whatever happens, this is going to be ok."

Helen was slightly puzzled......whatever happens....surely he meant 'whatever has happened'....this is the end of all this now, isn't it? No matter, no matter. He opened the door and she locked it, leaving an unknown man unconscious on her kitchen floor. She realised for the first time that she had never even thought of phoning an ambulance for him.

The grass was wet underneath but the rain had stopped. The sky was still dark, the storm taking longer to clear from Edinburgh than it had from further south. But it was clearly passing and there was going to be some daylight before the long summer's night eventually drew to a close. Perhaps not much, but some.

Aidan went in front and took Helen by the hand, leading her at first through her own garden. Even that felt surreptitious and full of subterfuge, as though she were stealing away from a crime scene. The fence between her and her neighbour's to the left was high but had supports on it and she managed to climb up it with relative ease. Not as speedily as Aidan who almost seemed to slide up it. There was a part of her neighbour's garden at the end that went down a slight incline and, with Aidan in front, they crouched down to remain undetected. The only way they could have been seen would have been by someone at a window upstairs.

The next fence was slightly harder, wooden spars about four to five feet tall. Aidan turned his body onto them and almost slithered over but Helen didn't find this quite so easy. She tried to put her foot on the fence and was conscious of the noise. She bent down, at the bottom of the incline, pausing a minute or so in case her crass attempt had been heard. Nothing. She looked at the fence this time. She was taller than it, tall enough so do something similar to Aidan...so she placed her hands on it, put pressure on them to lift her body up, and with shaking wrists she got herself into a state where she was almost lying on the fence. She put her feet over the other side and couldn't feel the ground where she expected it. But she felt Aidan's hands on her legs and his rough whisper – "it's ok, I've got you, let yourself go."

A bigger garden, easier to get out of. And once they got to the small wall that separated the house from the street, they were only one street away from Olly. Aidan sensed her enthusiasm and threw an arm round her waist. He dragged her back to him. "Wait," he whispered. "Quietly and slowly. We cannot get detected, we can't be seen. We can't afford for someone to call the police."

She nodded. It was a bigger garden but the incline had almost disappeared. The garden was flat, just grass, no bushes to hide behind. A big trampoline in the middle. A fence at the back. Instinctively Aidan went to the fence and moved slowly along it. Helen did the same. No signs of life in the house but that meant nothing, they couldn't see far enough into the house to see if there were lights at the front. Aidan inched along, looking up at the windows, across to his right. He could see the street where they were going, the small wall. He pulled Helen by the hand so they moved at the same speed. Closer, closer. Only ten yards or so away now. Aidan became conscious of the street, hoping there would be no one walking by as they stepped over a wall and out of someone else's garden. He stopped and listened. There was still some wind, making it hard to hear any footsteps. No clicks or quiet padding. Jesus, maybe it would have been easier fighting those mad bitches with the water cannons and the wolf. At least you could see what you were facing. On the other hand, he thought, as he moved closer, maybe not... Within a bound now, surely. Before he stepped over the wall he took a good look around him everywhere and was convinced he was alone. No one on the street. No one looking out of any windows. He quickly pulled Helen with him and she almost tripped her way onto the street.

She looked up at him, still holding his hand. "One street away," she said.

At that point a car appeared from what seemed like nowhere. It screeched to a halt in front of Helen and Aidan, careering onto the pavement to block their path. Three men piled out of the car. It was clear they were not going to seek for explanations or initiate a conversation. The one who went for Helen covered her mouth with a cloth in case she screamed. She wasn't drugged or harmed but she was silenced and was bundled into the car. The other two men held Aidan up against the hedge. One had a knife at his throat, the other a knife at his abdomen. Helen began to kick, to try to scream and make some noise. The man with his knife at Aidan's abdomen hastened across and helped bundle her into the car. Satisfied, he made a gruff and sudden noise to his colleague, whose knife was still trained on Aidan's throat. The man smiled at Aidan, a knowing smile and slapped his face, playfully twice. "I have to do something," he said to Aidan and punched him so that blood began to flow.

The car screeched away and Aidan flew back to his friends in the car, a street or two away. Amidst the bleeding nose, the cacophony of voices, the panic, amidst Olly's desperation and despair, amidst a hundred of questions without answers… in all that confusion and hell Oliver heard his phone ring. It took a few rings to hear it but it was ringing, definitely. Unknown number.

"Hello?"

"Is this the famous Oliver? Am I at last talking to Oliver? I think I have something of yours."

The voice was emotionless. French accent. Full of authority. Oliver had no doubt that he was at last talking to the man who had been pursuing him for what had seemed to be most of his life.

"Who am I talking to?" Oliver was calm, matter-of-fact.

"Are you Oliver?"

Ok, thought Oliver, you are in charge. You have my wife. You are in charge. "Yes, I am Oliver. Who are you?"

"Come to your house Oliver. We need to get this thing between us resolved. Resolved to my satisfaction. You have put obstacles in my way. I have been deceived by you. I have spent time on you. In case you need any persuasion, I have your wife here. She's very beautiful, isn't she? Just now anyway, for now she is. I'd hate to see an accident befall her that would leave her with something such as only one eye, for instance. People can be careless, can't they? A stray knife…a struggle….you know how it is Mr Oliver, don't you? We don't want that to happen to her."

"Who are you?"

"I know how nearby you are. So I will see you in a few minutes. Oh, and bring your friends too. The more people, the merrier we all shall be. We may discover things about them too. But hurry Mr Oliver. The desire to do something to your wife is getting stronger and stronger. Would you like me to describe the colour of her underwear to you?"

CHAPTER 22

Officer McLean was in hiding upstairs. As Helen was pulled back into her own house, and made to sit opposite this man in his white coat, she remembered McLean.

The man looked her up and down: "Take your jersey off and put your trousers at your knees for a few seconds. I will not harm you. I need your husband to come here and meet with me and I need him to know that I am serious in this. I therefore need to use you. Do you understand?"

Helen nodded and did as she was bid. By now there were a few people in her house. The three men who had been in the car. Someone else. This guy in the white coat. A guy who stood beside him and seemed to be his assistant, something. The guy in the white coat had clearly managed to speak to Olly then motioned to Helen to redress herself. Then they waited. The man in the white coat looked at her as he bit into strawberries. Helen had no idea where the strawberries had come from.

Upstairs, Officer McLean knew something was going on. He could tell that more people were due to arrive, the famous Olly at least, maybe his friends too. Though he did not, could not, have known it, he had been completely undetected. In that sense his quite elaborate plan had worked. It was something he had taken from a confession a few months ago, a guy who with an accomplice had gone back to rob a factory. The only significant difference was that they undertook their activity at night whereas McLean knew he was going to need some luck for it to be successful during the day.

McLean had appeared as a gas maintenance man with a friend who worked for a gas company. They had parked their vehicle mostly on the pavement with a small part of it on the road. This was important – a bus stopped outside Helen's house and they needed the bus to stop in the same place. Few people would question a gas van parked in a bus stop – it gave that impression of emergency. Those who were watching the house saw two men, in gas uniforms, go into the house and later, saw two men in gas uniforms drive away. There was nothing worth saying, nothing worthy of report – gas men had come, done whatever had needed to be done, and gone. At least that was how it seemed.

McLean knew that if the bus stopped, which it normally did, then he probably had about thirty seconds when he was hidden. That's if he was right in his assumption that Helen's house was being watched from across the road. In those thirty to forty seconds he moved quickly, out to the van, making sure he was seen. In the back, behind the seat, he had placed a foam dummy with a gas uniform on. As he pulled it into the seat he started the engine and left the dummy in the seat, back from it. He couldn't leave its hands on the wheel – if someone was watching with binoculars they would see the false hands right away. But an engine now running and a shape in the front seat…unless someone was looking from straight in front of the vehicle, and that was a chance he had to take, then it might be ok. He shifted and moved it, trying to make it visible without being noticeable. The bus was closing its doors… quickly… and he ran back into the house hoping he had not been seen.

A few minutes later, maybe not even that, his friend walked calmly to the driver's side of the van and gently slid the dummy across to the passenger side. He drove off, meeting only one odd look from a pedestrian coming the other way who had seen an unusual looking figure in the passenger side. McLean had succeeded. But now he had to stay undetected. Curtains were drawn upstairs, windows were closed and he stayed in the shadows, reading a book, doing Sudoku…he had made a convenient space in the wardrobe to settle into should it look like someone was coming. And he had a gun.

The friends walked towards the house and eventually reached the door. There had been little conversation between them. Ellis had rammed the Taser down the back of his trousers, covering its bulk with his loose shirt.

Oliver walked in first and immediately saw Helen sitting on the sofa, sobbing gently. When she saw him she stood up and he instinctively rushed towards her, embracing her briefly, revelling in her familiar smell, before they were gently but firmly pushed apart. This was not home. Not yet.

Oliver was pushed down, beside Helen. His friends stood against the wall as bid by a wave of The Capo's hand. There was nowhere for them to sit unless they sat on the floor. Oliver looked around him, at Helen beside him, and at these strangers in his house, standing around as if they owned the place. He looked at The Capo, who gave the appearance that he knew he owned the place. The Capo's eyes were on Oliver, looking at him, in him, around him as if an interrogation by the eye would tell him all he needed to know about this fly in the ointment. He barely looked at Oliver's friends though The Capo's acquaintances more than made up for this, ensuring that all the friends had their hands in front of them, visible at all times.

Davide held a quick hurried conversation with his boss. "Ok," said The Capo. "Housekeeping first. Who is the guy who is tied up in the kitchen? You – tell me," he stared at Helen with deathly unfeeling eyes.

"I….we……I don't know. He was, he looked like he was going to break in here and Aidan – the guy over there who came for me earlier – hit him on the head and knocked him out."

The Capo looked at her, unblinking. "A man was killed here yesterday. He also looked like he was trying to break in. Who was he?"

"A man… what…a man was killed? In this house? What?"

Helen seemed to him to be genuinely surprised, shocked. "Who killed him? Who was he?" she added.

"Never mind. Perhaps they are not important. The little flies that buzz around the honey, yes?" and he made a quick flying motion with his hand and thrust it towards Helen. "Such lovely honey too," he said, looking Helen up and down. It was provocative and Oliver recognised it, seeing The Capo's look towards him that said he could look at her any way he wished, he could do to her anything he wished. As threats went it was subtle, very subtle, but effective. Oliver looked down.

"Ok," said The Capo to one of his men. "Get that guy out of here. Put him in a car. Dump him at a hospital. Shoot him and dump him anywhere if he makes any trouble. But he does not concern us."

The Capo then stood up and walked the two or three steps until he reached Oliver. He put his hand down to clasp Oliver's jaw in a firm but not violent manner. He lifted Oliver's head till Oliver was forced to look at him. "You. I don't know whether to shake your hand or shoot you. Let us talk. You can help me come to a decision on this." He sat down again and looked at Oliver. "I'm listening," he said.

"What do you want me to say? What do you want me to talk about?"

The Capo held up his hand. "Whatever you do here, don't piss me off. I'd rape your wife and shoot her as she lay on the floor without blinking an eye. Don't play tennis with me. I want to know who you are, you slimy sonofabitch." Davide took out a gun. "Start talking."

"Yes, yes," said Oliver, holding his hands up. "Ok, yes. I think this is all, this has been, a huge misunderstanding. I think this has all been to do with an argument in Monte Carlo. Yes, I had a disagreement with a man I think is close to you. I thought he was going to attack me and…

.well, instinctively I picked up this knife to defend myself. He came towards me and I was back on a table. I pushed my hand forward, the hand that had the knife in it, it caught him in the eye….I'm sorry for it. Believe me I wished it had never happened. But that's what happened."

"My acquaintance…the man you blinded…he says something different. He says you had your hand up his wife's skirt. I believe him."

Oliver shook his head. "No I didn't. He's wrong. But even if I did….sir….isn't that between me and him? And his wife?"

"You know nothing of family, do you? You attack him, you attack me. Did you touch his wife?"

"No! Why would I touch his wife?"

"Why would anyone touch anyone else's wife?" He stood up and walked to Helen. He knelt in front of her. He ran his hands over her face, over her chest, over her legs. "Because they can." He sat down.

He looked at Oliver. "And the rest. Tell me about the rest."

"The rest? You mean our journey back?"

"Why start a war?"

Oliver looked at his friends. They gave him back the same glazed and confused expression that his face reflected to The Capo. "Sir," he said, "I am trying to understand and respond to your question. But I don't know what you mean. A war? What war?"

The Capo looked at him, tried again to look in him. The man opposite him did not behave as though he was anything more than he said he was. He did not look like a man who was connected to a gang in any way. His confusion looked genuine.

"Tell me about why you did what you did at the hotel."

"The hotel? What hotel? Which hotel?" Again Oliver shot a look at his friends. Shrugging of shoulders.

"Ok. Let me ask you a direct question. Are you trying to start a war between the Rizzalos and those others so you can pick up the pieces afterwards? And let me ask you another direct question. What enemies of mine are you working with when you are on these visits to the south of France?"

Oliver stood up. If he could have been outraged then he would have been outraged. If he could have laughed then he would have laughed. If he could have hit the guy for asking such insane questions then he would have hit him. He could do none of these and yet his incredulity demanded some release. So he simply stood up. From outside, that was all Clotilde saw – Oliver standing up. The view she had of a room with curtains almost drawn didn't permit her to see anything else and she made the assumption that it was Olly, only Olly….and maybe, probably, Helen was there too. Which was even better. She stopped the car.

The Capo waved Olly down and Davide trained his gun at the exact middle of Oliver's forehead. "Is this…," said Oliver, starting and stopping, his thought process too riddled with disbelief to allow him to make any sense…."Is this what you think? What's a Rizzalo? I have no idea what you mean. I honestly have no idea. And in France…Jesus… .sir… I go to buy metal for little war figures that my company manufactures. I work with people in my company and my suppliers." It was an impassioned defence, full of gestures and hand movements and high voice.

The Capo hated torture. He hated it because it was no way to find out the truth. He revelled in inflicting it upon those who deserved it because they needed to be hurt if they had hurt him but it was no way to attempt to try to find out the truth. People would admit to anything if you pushed hard enough and long enough in the right places. So he thought of doing things, anything, to this guy and doing things, lots of things, to his rather beautiful wife but he doubted that it would take him where he wanted to go. And the problem was that this guy sounded genuine. Most people, they know when the game is up. This guy is outnumbered. He knows I can kill him and his friends in a flash. Most people would admit it and hope for some form of sympathy, empathy, honour amongst thieves.

"What happened at the hotel? If you are who you say you are why did you start a war?" The Capo said it with resignation.

"What hotel? I..," he looked across at his friends, "we… don't know what you mean. We have stayed at a few places. Which hotel?"

"You stayed at a hotel by a service station last night…."

"That….there was noise next door to us….a girl was trying to get in to a door next to us…there was banging and shouting and they……it didn't seem very pleasant….but we had nothing to do with that. We ran away from it. We had to get away. They were ready to break our door down. They probably did. We got out through the window. We………why… what do you think it is that we did there? We were about to have the shit kicked out of us at the very least. Why do you think we caused something? Why would you think that?"

The Capo looked at him. Oliver looked back, innocent inquisitive eyes that darted over The Capo's face, looking for clarity. The Capo would have bet his life the guy was telling the truth. He shook his head. "Why would you get involved with these people? If not to aggravate them, to stir things up?"

"We didn't get involved!" Oliver shouted. "We wanted them to shut the fuck up! We wanted to sleep!"

"Try not to shout. That gun my friend is holding is sensitive to shouts."

Oliver leaned across and said gently. "You're in my house, sir. You're holding me prisoner, sir. You've threatened to rape and kill my wife, sir. And now, sir, you are accusing me of things which are unjust, incorrect... .simply insane. And you are surprised that I am shouting?"

At that point the doorbell went. The Capo shot a quick look at Davide and motioned him towards the door. It was difficult to appreciate who registered the biggest look of surprise as the door opened – Clotilde or Davide. Clotilde saw enough as the door opened to see that there was a house full of people which was surprising enough but seeing Davide's face made her all too aware of who else must be there. For his part, Davide didn't know quite who to expect but the speed with which he clasped his gun and motioned Clotilde inside made it clear that it was certainly not her.

Clotilde walked into the room and looked around her. Oliver's friends exchanged under-breath mutterings with each other. Oliver's heart almost jumped into his mouth. The Capo's smile widened.

"Ah! My dear! Sit down. Welcome to this little party. You were not invited, at least not by me anyway, but now you are here you are very welcome."

Clotilde looked around her for somewhere to sit. "Oh, my dear, you can squeeze yourself in on the other side of that man there. Oliver I think he is called. So you can be on one side of him and his wife can be on the other. Cosy! That'll do – for now anyway."

Helen looked puzzled at first but she wasn't blessed with naivety. It was clear that this Anna knew the man in the white coat but, with the glee that the man positioned her on the other side of Olly, quite clear that she knew Olly in perhaps a slightly different way than that of merely client/customer. Or maybe that's what this man thought. Having listened to what she had listened to for the past half hour, Helen didn't know what she thought anymore......even who Olly was.

Oliver tried to move his body away from Clotilde and towards Helen but the sofa was really only made for two and Clotilde slowly and deliberately edged in towards him, her leg touching his. The Capo watched the three of them position themselves. It was quite amusing to watch but it also began to cement his opinion of Oliver – he was not involved in anything beyond the blinding of Paul. The man opposite him was shifting with the guilt and discomfort that one would feel when one's lover and one's wife came together. It was something that reeked from him as soon as Clotilde stepped through the door. That was clearly his nature. There had been no such guilt or symptom of recognition at anything The Capo had thrown at him before. So maybe this guy was just what he said he was – someone in the wrong place at the wrong time who had defended himself in an all too vigorous manner. And yet he had taken up so much time, so much effort to find him… what could he really do to this guy? Kill him for taking up his time? Sleep with his wife? Let Paul loose on him, tell him where they stayed? He leaned up to Davide and asked him to remind him of the name of the woman who had just come in.

He looked across at the three uncomfortable bodies opposite him. "Clotilde. You have interrupted us. It was an interesting point in a very interesting story. But no matter. Let us hear what you have got to say. What brings you to this country?"

Helen looked across puzzled. Clotilde… no, Anna, surely……she got nothing back from the woman who sat there and looked, thought Helen, very comfortable, very much at home, in my house….

Clotilde looked at The Capo. "You must know why I am here." She hadn't quite sized up the situation – yes, of course, she understood why The Capo would want Olly but did he think Olly was harmless or an enemy…

"Don't play a game, Ms de Bresseau. Why are you here?"

"Him," she said and put her hand on Oliver's leg. Oliver tried to recoil but, in every sense possible, there was nowhere for him to go. "I wonder," she said, looking at The Capo, "how far you have got with him? You know, how much you have discovered?"

The Capo leant across to her. "It has been a bit like trying to do a crossword. But I think we are nearly there. Unless of course you have anything to add."

Before she could reply Helen lent across Oliver to look at her. "Who are you?" Then she glanced, quickly, from The Capo and, with burning eyes, to Oliver. "Who is she? Who is this woman?"

The Capo sat back and smiled. He didn't dislike torture enough to

450

not revel in this man trying to explain away a beautiful mistress to his beautiful wife. In France it would have been shrugged off but here… women tended to react differently so let's watch this little fish wriggle on the end of the line. He held up his hand to prevent Clotilde speaking and motioned with an open palm to Oliver. No words yet no doubt about who should explain this.

Oliver didn't turn to look at his wife. He looked straight ahead at the wall or focused his eyes on the carpet. "She's…Clotilde….is a woman who represents a company that we buy from. I've known her for quite a while. We have a good relationship." He straightened his back. "And that's all there is to it. I assume she must be across here on business herself, either to see us or another company. You would need to ask her why she came to the house. I have no idea."

Helen tried to look across at Clotilde. "Clotilde? You told me your name was Anna."

Clotilde looked at Helen, a long cold stare. "Tell me, when your husband comes inside you does his body shudder? Soft little shudders like a little earthquake? Does he gasp – a silent breathless gasp as he tries to hide the pleasure he's feeling? Or is that just with me?"

The Capo sat back, smiled and rubbed his hands. Olly looked ahead of him, trying to remain motionless. But his ear itched and his eyes twitched and his nose needed a scratch and his cheek was uncomfortable. His hands were everywhere. He couldn't look at Clotilde. She moved her leg closer onto, into, his. He tried to move away, towards Helen and she began to recoil.

Helen grabbed him, pulling him round to her. Her eyes searched his face and his downward look told her everything she needed to know. "Olly…Olly…" She was not desperate. She was angry. The force with which she almost spun him round to force him to look at her gave a good indication of the anger she was feeling. Her face was flashing, her eyes clear and dry and piercing.

"Explain. Explain now."

Oliver looked at her and looked away. "I don't think… there is so much to explain… so much that you don't know….but it's not what you feel, it's not what you think. It's not what you believe. I don't think this is the time. Or the place," and he motioned his hand around the room. "Let's not make this a public show, ok?"

"Au contraire," said The Capo. "You may be what you say you are Mr Oliver, you may be nothing more than a guy who defended himself. But you have taken too much of my time for me not to enjoy your misfortune, at the very least. So, please, explain to this beautiful woman why and how you have taken pleasure in fucking this other beautiful woman. And for how long. Please."

Clotilde picked up on it. It was only a slither, perhaps even the slightest glimmer, of an opportunity. But this man sitting opposite thought Olly was harmless. In all probability Olly might sort out his situation with Helen. And then I am back where I started, she thought. If she could sow a seed of doubt about Olly, maybe this man would take him back to France....question him further... make him meet other people who could verify or not that this man was innocent or guilty or connected or not connected...then maybe if he was in France and he was thrown away there, maybe then she would have a chance...

Oliver turned to his wife. "There is nothing in this. There is nothing in what he says. I stayed with this woman, in her house, for a few days. I was hiding. This woman....Clotilde....told me that I was only safe if I stayed hidden. I stayed with her, in her flat, for a few days. And that is it. That was it." He paused. "We do what we do to survive. When we need to survive, when all I could think about was you and Terrence, when I feared I may never see you again....we do what we have to do in order to survive." He had kept his eyes on her all the time he had spoken. But of course there were more questions than answers in what he said and Helen's face was frowned and puzzled and knotted and twisted to the point of complete incomprehension.

"What are you saying? Don't talk to me in riddles. What are you saying?"

The Capo joined in. "And would you say....sir....that this occasion was the first occasion that you stayed in Ms de Bresseau's flat?" He affected the tone of a policeman.

Oliver turned quickly to Clotilde and looked back to The Capo. "Yes," he said. "Yes of course. Absolutely. I had never seen the inside of Ms de Bresseau's flat before that Saturday night."

"Oh really," said The Capo, pretending to turn the pages of a notebook as a policeman might. "That's not the information we have, sir. No, no, our records show clear evidence of previous convictions of... .fuckings."

Oliver looked at Clotilde. Clotilde held her head down. When she looked up her eyes were moist. "I said it to protect you, Olly. To protect you. If you were with me....if I had said you were with me...on previous

452

visits that you had made… if I had said you were staying at my flat….that was believable…….it would be easy for people, people like him..," and she nodded her head towards The Capo, "….to believe that you had stayed there before. It was to protect you."

"What?" said Oliver, running hands through his hair. "To protect me? What the hell are you talking about? What do you mean? Protect me from what?"

"Oh Olly," she said, her eyes now wet with tears, her voice almost breaking. "I feel as though I've done this for a long time… I don't think I can protect you any further…"

The Capo was now curious. He liked Clotilde – she was attractive, very attractive, and someday he was sure he would enjoy her. But more than like, he trusted her and he didn't trust many women for he knew they made him vulnerable. This one, though… seemed genuine. He looked behind him at Davide who shrugged his shoulders…

Clotilde looked at Olly. "It is for the best now……that you speak with this man. Resolve the differences. Stop it going any further. Too many people, too much trouble….and Natalie will never feel safe again, as long as she walks the street….as long as you keep trying to get her into a court…"

At that moment it was the only name that Clotilde could think of. Amidst the generalities it was the only piece of hard evidence she could think of. That it was The Capo who was after Natalie she had only guessed at. That The Capo would even know the name Natalie she could only guess at. But something happened. The Capo reached behind to Davide and they held a quick and hurried conversation in French. The Capo turned back to see Clotilde sobbing.

Oliver looked at her, in too much disbelief to shake his head or feign anger. Where is she going with this? What is she trying to do?

The Capo looked at Oliver. "So perhaps you do have something to tell me."

"Natalie? Who the hell is Natalie? What is Natalie?" Oliver protested.

"The car….," said Euan, almost to himself, "we bought the car from Natalie… from a Natalie…"

The Capo looked across at him. "Blondie. Shut up." He turned to Oliver. "Continue."

"This woman…she's saying things that are not true… I don't know a Natalie…"

"You bought a car from one apparently…"

"Yes but we don't….I don't…know her. I'd never spoken to her before getting a car from her."

There was brief silence. Clotilde welcomed it for it represented The Capo thinking, pausing. She ventured: "this needs to get sorted out… once and for all… you people need to resolve your differences….talk them out, here……or France or anywhere…but sort them out."

Oliver could feel his anger rising. When she mentioned France, he could see what she was trying to do. "There are no differences!" he shouted.

The Capo motioned him to lower his voice with his hand. "Perhaps the beautiful Ms de Bressau is right. Perhaps it is best to have this conversation in France." He leaned across to Oliver. "If you are encouraging people to destroy me, to do things that hurt me and my people, then you know enough to know you are my enemy. You will only survive tonight because I will look for further evidence. But I think we will go back to France. Just you. Not your monkeys. Just you. And you will be my guest for a few days or however long it takes for me to find out. Then I will kill you or let you go."

"No!" shouted Oliver. "You can't be taken in by this! She's lying, she's completely lying," he almost spluttered.

"Why would she lie? For what reason would she lie?"

"Because she wants me….she wants me back in France…with her. Ask her. Go on, ask her!"

The Capo raised his eyebrows in a gentle inquisitive way towards Clotilde. She shook her head. "I did my best to protect you, Olly. To lie for you. Of course I took some pleasure from you. And I think you did too. Who would blame me for that? When gold comes into your home it is natural to touch it and savour it and keep it and caress it, to pretend it is yours, to hope it is yours, for only a little while. But I do not think of myself as unattractive. I think I am a beautiful woman. I think I am a great fuck. I would not say….that is….I would not go so far as to say that I could have any man I wanted but I know the way men are and I welcome their interest. Do you really think," she said as she looked around every man in the room, "do any of you really think that I would make up such fantasies to get this man, this one man who is very married with a beautiful child, back to France? He is beautiful and desirable and I will not deny to you that the time he spent with me was blissful and I wished it could continue. But I could say that about many men. So, I ask you again, do you really think I would make up stories for this one man?"

The Capo looked at her. He could feel a desire for her eating away at his logic but somewhere in there was a doubt. A nagging little doubt. She's quite like me, he thought. She's powerful and she knows it. She's right, she probably can have any man she wants. Except the man she can't have. And that would make her want him even more, as it would me in a similar situation. Whatever this Olly was guilty of, however much he may have made love with Clotilde, there was no doubt that he wanted to be here, with his wife. Not with Clotilde.

He sighed. The fundamentals here were that this man may be in a position to harm him, potentially even rock the foundations of his business. The Capo knew who Natalie was and knew that if she spoke he may not be able to stop the thing going to court. She was young, he knew, so he did not want her dead. He didn't kill young beautiful girls. But if this Olly was with his enemies, trying to drag her into court… maybe he was government, some branch of government…then maybe they both should die. Perhaps the best thing was to get them together, both of them, back in France…find out what they knew. Kill them both if needs be. Regrettable. But necessary….taking care of business…

He spoke quickly with Davide who nodded and raised his gun again to train it on Oliver's shoulder. Flesh wounds only, he had been told. The Capo stood up. "Ok, lover boy, you're coming with me. We're flying back to France tonight. We'll get this sorted out. Ms de Bressau, you can have a journey back with us if you like. Or drive. Your choice."

"I can't fly," said Oliver, at first to himself." He looked at The Capo. "I don't fly, I can't fly."

"That's the most of your worries? I'm taking you back to France, away from your home and, let's be blunt, possibly to your death, and your biggest concern is that you can't fly? What sort of a man are you? Anyway, don't worry about it – the state you'll be in, you'll need smelling salts to bring you round. You won't care where you are after my friends have played around with your head a little."

Olly stood up. "No!" he shouted. "This is wrong. She's wrong. I have nothing to do with this!"

It was loud enough for Officer McLean to feel that something was coming to an end. They had had their discussions. He had figured they were all in the same room. At least one of them had a gun, that was clear, but if he stood at the entrance to the living room he knew he would be able to see them all and that, unless someone came in the front door which it was almost impossible to do without him being aware of it, he could command them all.

He moved swiftly to the top of the stairs. No one there. He moved down, softly, gently, no squeaking floorboards, until he reached the bottom. The door to the living room was shut but it was obvious from what he could hear that people appeared to be standing up, beginning to move. Maybe under duress. He made to open the door. The action had to be definitive and swift. He had to stand back from it. He lifted his foot and swiftly kicked the door open. It stretched back on its hinges, leaving a man standing in the doorway with a gun in his hand.

"Sit down! Everyone. Down! On the floor if you have to. Down!" He looked to his right where three of The Capo's men were standing. "You guys, into the centre of the room. Sit down. Arms in front of you. That's right. Everybody's arms in front of them where I can see them." This left The Capo's men sitting directly in front of Ellis and the others. Officer McLean's immediate concern appeared to be for Helen and he looked at her and asked if she was ok. She nodded, her head down. Now Oliver found himself ravaged with similar sensations and emotions to those that had hit his wife a few minutes.

The Capo looked at him. "Who the fuck are you?" He looked at Davide. "Who the fuck is this guy?"

Officer McLean looked at the imposing man in the white coat. "Look at me. Yes, you – nice coat mate – yes you. Look at me. I'm asking the questions." The Capo looked at him, a long stare, neither threatening nor dangerous. There was something familiar about this man and he couldn't think of what it was. His mind struggled with the burden of memory and recognition.

Officer McLean looked at Oliver and let a wicked smile cross his lips. "At last. At last I am in the presence of......the unholy self-righteous..."

Oliver shook his head. "Who are you?" he asked. "And what are you doing in my house?"

"Oh, I think you know who I am. You and your lovely wife. Whatever else this is, whatever else is going on here, I'm telling you now that what you're doing is going to stop. It stops now."

Helen looked puzzled but Oliver was way beyond puzzled. He smiled at the insanity of it. "You....whoever you are..."

"My name is Officer McLean – but don't insult me by pretending that you don't already know that."

"How would I know that? I have never set eyes on you before in my bloody life! What is it that you think I'm doing?"

"Sent any nice letters from France, have you? Seen any decent videos recently? You know the type… where the good guys try to get the bad guys but the bad guys find ways of stopping the good guys and turning them into bad guys…"

Oliver looked around him. At Clotilde. At The Capo. At this lunatic with the gun. He felt like Josef K. I have no idea what these people are here for….what it is they think I have done. "Officer… I'm sorry, I can't help you. I do not understand what you are talking about. I do not know you. I have sent no letters from France. If I watch a video it is a harmless film, it's nothing…."

"That won't work. You people…," and he looked around as if addressing everyone in the room, "you don't see the effects of the stuff you supply. The children, just children."

"Wait!" Oliver almost shouted. "Do you think I have been supplying drugs? Is that what you think? Is that what you are accusing me of?"

Officer McLean waved his hand. "Did you plant the film? Are you blackmailing? And you," he said, pointing his head at Helen, "how long have been on this, trying to get information out of me?"

"Jesus Christ," whispered Helen, her head down.

"Officer," said Oliver, "I go to the south of France to buy metal. I work for a company that makes little war figures, that's what I do. That's why I go. I wish, with every last bone in my body, that I had never gone. I will never go there again. But that is what I do. That is what I do." He shot out each word with emphasis, slowly. "Do you understand? Do you? I know nothing of a film, or blackmailing…and why would you think my wife is trying to get information out of you? This stuff," he waved his hand at The Capo, "this stuff is much more to do with him…"

The Capo motioned to Davide and he exchanged words quickly with The Capo.

The Capo turned to look at him. "Officer McLean. You planted drugs in the home of an innocent man.."

Shocked, Officer McLean trained his gun on The Capo. "He wasn't innocent!"

"He was innocent. The drugs that he was found to be in possession of were not his. They were planted there by you and your colleagues in an attempt to take control of a situation that you could not control by legal means. You broke the law. And you got it wrong. He had given up dealing and an agreement had been reached. Part of that agreement guaranteed his protection. If you had stayed within the law, if you had done your job, if you had been good enough, you might have caught him. But you deserve what you have got. Be aware, Officer, that if you pursue this, you will be killed. Be aware, too, that I do not issue threats."

Officer McLean smiled. An awkward, nervous smile of defeat. The lower jaw line, the mouth – for one of the only times he could remember, The Capo was shocked.

"Officer McLean," he said. "It would be a shame for your life to end here because of this rather insignificant business. Especially when you have so much to live for. You have a wife….," The Capo was guessing at that bit, "….you have a lovely relationship with Oliver's wife..," and he paused as Helen, Oliver and Officer McLean's faces registered the anticipated emotions, "….and of course you have a beautiful daughter. Donna is quite wonderful, isn't she? Have you enjoyed her as I have?"

Officer McLean felt his sensations blur. His first thought was of rape and torture, kidnapping, a hostage taken to stop the attempt to take the drugs guy to court. He breathed heavily, inhaling and exhaling loudly, his gun on The Capo. "Where is she? What have you done?" His shout almost filled the street.

"Oh she's home I guess, out playing……whatever people her age do when they are not giving pleasure to old men like me. She looked…she is…beautiful. She tasted of cream on a warm summer day. And I tasted her everywhere. You know I asked her to come with me, back to France. I think she's going to jump at it. Would that please you? To know that your daughter is the whore of a man like me?"

The gun was right at The Capo's head. "You're lying. You're lying – you must be lying."

"No, I'm not lying. Would you like me to tell you about the shape of her breasts? How soft they are to touch? How large her nipples become when she is aroused? About the way her skin is slightly discoloured at the very top of her left thigh? About the colour of her pubic hair? Tell me what you want to know." He paused. "There is nothing of yours that I cannot take if I want to take it." He paused again. "Oh, and let me tell you, she knows how to make love to a man. I mean, really knows. She can make your dick dance." And he laughed and so Davide and the other three men laughed.

The Capo nodded his head at one of the three men on the floor. Before anyone could react the man had taken out a gun and shot at Officer McLean. The man knew that his task was not to kill McLean but to return order and control to where it should be. His shot was accurate and true, hitting McLean's shoulder and forcing him to drop his gun.

Amidst his screams, Davide reached down to pick the gun up.

The Capo shook his head. "This is the problem when people have illusions. Delusions. When they think they can control things that only people like me can control. You can trust me, you know," he said, looking at Oliver. "I am a better friend than an enemy. I am a loyal friend. A friend to be trusted. What you see is what you get. You are....I don't know what you are...but you seem to be a decent man. If you are involved with Natalie....and I will find that out...then you should turn her over to me and we can do things together. Whatever you want. Partners. Mutual interest."

Oliver looked at McLean, blood seeping from him, his cries dominating the room. "Shouldn't we get him to a hospital? Call an ambulance?"

"It's nothing more than a flesh wound. Pressure on it. He will be ok. If I wanted him dead he would be dead. It is you I am interested in. You should come back to France with me. Come on, let's go."

As he stood up his acquaintances stood up with him. Emboldened, Ellis felt he could possibly, if he was quick, get the three guys in front of him. Zap them each, individually, quickly. That would still leave the Big Guy and his henchman....maybe, in the confusion, Olly and the others could do something....maybe. But Oliver could not, must not, go back to France. If he went back there it was to his death.

Before he even gave himself time to properly think it through, Ellis had reached behind him, switched the instrument on and quickly thrust it into the man in front of him. 50.000 volts and the guy quivered like a jelly and began to topple. What happened next was quick, a series of events so speedy that they seemed like fast and fierce reactions to each other, a series of chemically infused dominos falling on top of each other. As the man in front of Ellis shook and began to fall, Oliver saw The Capo nod to one of the men still standing who whipped out a gun from his waist and turned quickly. As Ellis made to take the Taser from the falling man and apply it to another, the man who was neither falling nor reaching for a gun turned and with a force that was more bestial than human battered the Taser to the floor. The man with the gun who had turned around looked straight at Aidan, at the look of confusion on his face and fired his weapon three times into Aidan's body. Oliver rose up to rush across to his friend but two guns trained on him, from Davide and the man who had shot Aidan, coerced him down into his seat.

The Capo watched as his man picked up the Taser and looked at it,

459

buzzing it a bit, waving it at Ellis and vaguely threatening to use it on him. He took it across to The Capo who looked at Ellis then at Oliver. Oliver looked to Aidan but his friend was clearly dead and his dark blood began to flood the carpet. Helen gasped, struggling to breathe as the sobs came to her quicker than her body could process them. Clotilde looked around her but was clearly unaffected by the scene.

The Capo held up the Taser. "You guys, you're clearly big time, aren't you? A Taser? In your defence, it does tell me quite a bit about you… quite a lot about you."

Oliver felt his voice and everything inside begin to collapse. His words came out as guttural, primal noises. "You…killed…our…friend." In itself it was shocking. But what took Oliver to another place was that he knew it was deliberate. He knew that it was Aidan that they wanted to kill. Ellis had used the Taser but it wasn't a mistake, they hadn't killed the wrong guy. He had seen the gun raised at Aidan and he had seen the other guy disarm Ellis. It was a deliberate assassination.

"Yes," said The Capo. "I killed your friend. But he was my friend too. Not enough of my friend, it seems. How do you think we knew where you were? How do you think we got information about your movements? How do you think we knew you had stayed in rue Cassini? How do you think we got you to stay with Simone and Charlotte? Thing is though….he loved you, I'm sure. We never quite got anything that was bang up to date. He was always "we have just left and are going to go to.." not "we are here, come now". So he was, it seems, disloyal to me. Very disloyal. He knew how much I wanted you and he could have been a very rich man. Instead he is a poor dead one."

Oliver was crying, cries with such depth that they shook him physically. It was hard to ignore them. Instinctively Helen put her arm around him. Instinctively Clotilde wanted to. "But…he was…our friend. For years….I've known him… what you say, what you're suggesting…"

"Is unthinkable? Don't be the more deceived, Mr Oliver. Don't be naïve. He was a willing contact and a useful one. A man in his position, theatre… people in the theatre love their work but they don't get paid so much. There are always buttons to push. Maybe you'd be surprised. I thought you understood the way things worked. Where power rests and how it is disseminated. But maybe you don't. Maybe you're just another fucking Oswald…I'm just a pawn, I'm just a patsy….You remember what happened to that guy?"

Oliver looked at The Capo. "I came here tonight to do two things.

To kill your friend and to decide what to do with you. Your other friends..," he looked across at the three friends who stayed close to Aidan's body, "...they are decent people, they tried to help you and to save you. They can go. No harm will come to them from anyone in my organisation. You have my word. As for you...I could easily shoot you and have done with it. But someone like me, in my position, seeing all the things I do....some people deserve what they get. Your friend did. He tried to play both sides. But you....everything about you is a fucking riddle. You are in the south of France often, you communicate in business with people that can do me harm......you have slept with this woman on your right and yet I can almost believe you when you make it sound like she raped you and say that you do what you can to survive...that you know Natalie or have spoken to her you do not deny yet I am not convinced myself of Ms de Bressau's story. In my position, from my vantage point, I know people. I know what motivates them. I judge them quickly and I am never wrong. But I haven't got a fucking clue what to do with you."

He asked Davide for the gun and pointed it at Oliver. He reached inside his pocket and took out a coin. "So, let's go with heads or tails, shall we? You can call, or let one of these beautiful woman call if you wish. Tails and we talk, heads and you won't see the dawn tomorrow......."

CHAPTER 23

One of The Capo's men had taken Officer McLean and dumped him at a hospital. Another had taken Aidan away and would leave a message with his wife, telling her where to find him. Ali, Euan and Ellis had been told to get out. What was about to go on was something that they were to have no part of. They realised that whatever they had defeated together over the past few days, it was over. Whether it was fate or character or something else that had taken them to this point, they had lost. They were leaving Olly with a man who would probably kill him. And they could do nothing about it. They had seen their friend killed right in front of them. And they could do nothing about it. As helpless as flies at the hands of mischievous boys, they were left at the whims of The Capo.

They trooped home in resignation and defeat. They talked to partners and spouses but both the fear of what may happen to Olly and the horror of what had happened to Aidan meant that no catharsis could spew out their shock. So much had happened it was difficult for their minds to know what they should be disturbed by first. They tried to sleep but it never came.

In the morning Ali faced a grim-faced Lesley. She must have been shocked too, perhaps to her very being, by the things he had said. By him being hunted, by people wanting to kill him. They should walk. Go for a long walk. An underrated form of medicine. Understand each other again. Talk this through. Get away together, even if only for a few hours. Nothing but them and nature, nothing but their souls talking to each other. That would help. That would help them understand.

But then Lesley opened her mouth and she didn't talk about him and his experiences at all. She spoke about her and how she was feeling and Ali thought if this was happening to someone else, to anyone else then I could see where this was leading. But this wasn't happening to anyone else so he must have been wrong in what he was thinking. Because this couldn't be happening to him and Lesley. And yet he heard her speak and she finished it with – "and so I can't be here anymore. I can't stay here with you anymore." He had heard her but he had not listened. 'No,' he thought, 'she can't be saying that.'

His mind reacted, a reflexive jump. "Is there anyone else?" He didn't shout it or scream it. It was passionless. He barely heard himself say it.

Lesley held her head down. She blushed bright red. "No....well, no...no."

Ali was talking to himself. "I go away for a few days....to help a friend, to try to help a friend, he might be dead now....I think everything is fine before I go...it seems normal...and then I come back...though things maybe, maybe I thought things were... there was something not right when I spoke to her on the phone....but now I am here and she is going to go away and there isn't anyone else?" He looked up at Lesley. "There isn't anyone else? There must be. There must be."

Lesley leant out with a sign of exasperation. She grabbed his hand. "You wouldn't understand." She shook her head. "You would never understand."

"I can understand. I can understand. It happens to people......to other people...they get...bored, maybe...with each other and one strays, finds someone else, imagines a better life...I can understand." He looked around him. "But that happens to other people. Not to me. Not to me. This is my life. You are my life. There can't be someone else."

Lesley ran her hand through her hair. "Don't make this harder. Don't make us hurt each other."

Again Ali almost spoke to himself in quiet rational tones as if he was struggling to follow the logic of his own thought process. "But it's not possible. I go away...I nearly died...I go away trying to help my friend... .I do my best for you, for our family...we live, we live by God's rules... we are good people....I am a good person in this...in all endeavours I have been... always trying. So this can't be happening. No, it can't be." He looked up quickly at Lesley. "I know you, don't I? I know you. You are my wife and you vowed in front of God that you would be my wife forever. For better or worse. I remember that. Don't you? Don't you remember that?" Lesley looked at him. She had expected tears, a wave of sorrow but not this shell-shocked, haunted face. He had the look of a man whose brain was shutting down. Perhaps irrevocably.

He stood up, above her. "I know you, don't I? I do know you?"

She looked at him. "How can you," she whispered, "how can you when I know so little of myself?"

Suddenly he felt something inside himself. Inquisitive. Alert. "What does that mean?" he asked, his eyes probing her. "What does that mean?"

"Ali... Ali...if there is someone else....it's not what you think... it's......," she stopped, unable to say further. "It's not what you think."

463

"What? It's not what? I don't where I am any more, I don't know what I think......what I think is...," and he clearly struggled to spill the words out, "... you are leaving to go with someone else. So there is someone else. But it's not what I think. Either there is or isn't someone else." And again, the puzzled look. "So I don't know you? I don't know you anymore."

"Ali this is so difficult......"

He grabbed her with force. She felt his anger in the imprint of his fingers on her wrists. "Oh, believe me Lesley, this is difficult for me too."

She shook his hand from her. Perhaps his anger had emboldened her. He had hurt her. Perhaps that gave her justification in hurting him. "There is someone else." She looked at him, straight in the eye. "But that someone else is not a man."

Again the confusion. "A what... a...you're leaving me, you're going to leave our family...to be with a woman... a woman....you're what?"

"Yes. I'm going to leave to be with another woman. You don't know her," she added, almost as an afterthought.

Ali looked down. "How long? This isn't just.......it's not love, it's not only love, it's about.......sexuality...... about your...everything......your being....how long have you been....that way? Did you marry....did you marry me......for appearance?" He thought back to the sex they had had. It was ok, it was fine. Had she pretended all that time, these years?

"No of course not. This is recent, it's very recent..."

"It must be!"

"Listen Ali. You need reasons and I can't give you reasons. You want to know why and I can't tell you why. All I can tell you is something has happened to me that has changed me and I can't be what I was before. I can't go back to being that other person. I'm different now."

"So I never really knew you? I have never really known you? It's all been a...mask...you've been covering up yourself, your true self....like you've had to be....like you've been wearing a disguise when you were with me? Even when we were making love, when you were naked....especially when we were making love.... It's never been you?"

"Oh Ali....you can't say these things, you can't think like that. I did not know myself. I could never have known I would feel this way, that this would happen to me. Look at me. No, look at me, properly. How could you truly know me when I didn't know myself? Maybe I have always had sensations and feelings that I kept hidden even from myself. Maybe....if what you saw was what you think was a disguise then that disguise was keeping me from myself. Preventing me from seeing myself. A mechanism….a device…to hide away the truth….” She sighed. “Maybe that’s how it is for a lot of people. They get on with life and what they truly feel they keep hidden, don’t recognise, they change it into something else. They don’t want to say, or can’t say because it would upset things too much. But there comes a time when you can’t hide it, when you let your guard down and the façade slips and you can see the sunlight. Then the disguise goes… ”

Ali looked at her. She was another woman, a different woman to the one he had married. The one he had married reassured him. And the one he had married was one he comforted and protected. The one he had married was rooted in God with him. The one he had married had taken a vow. The woman in front of him looked different. The mask taken off, none of that meant anything to her. You could see it in her face. Her distant smile. Her look of pity. He was right. He hadn’t known her. He didn’t know her. And if he hadn’t known someone with whom he had shared every intimacy, how could he be sure that he knew anything anymore. For the first time in his life he doubted God’s existence.

Before The Capo had told Helen to go away, anywhere, he would have given her money to stay in a hotel if she wished, he knew a good one in the area….before that he had told her to be in a café at ten o’clock the next morning. Either her husband would come and meet her or The Capo himself would come to explain why he had had to kill her husband. Clotilde was sent away with the three men and The Capo remained alone in the house with Oliver and Davide.

Helen sat outside in bright sunshine. She lifted the spoon over the froth on the cup of stuff that sat on the table in front of her. She smoothed it this way and that, at times digging the spoon in then smoothing it again. White froth sitting on top. She hadn’t slept. She hadn’t eaten. And she couldn’t face this cup in front of her. Again she looked at her watch. It was after ten now, just after ten but still, definitively after ten. She tried to prepare herself for the man in the white coat walking down the street to see her. He wouldn’t be regretful or at all bothered by telling her he had killed her husband, she knew that. She wondered how she might be. Would she shake? Would she nod silently and cry? Or would she be numb? However much time she had had to think about this, and it felt like she had had at least a lifetime, your system couldn’t prepare you for the news that your husband, who you had clung to before you left a few hours ago, was now dead. Executed. Maybe he would tell her at least why. What did Olly do? What had he done? To be at the behest of this... powerful, terrifying, omniscient force....what had he done?

She looked up, directly into the sunlight. As Oliver came towards her his white shirt blinded her. Between it and the sun she couldn't see properly. Her head swirled and fell to the table. When she raised it Oliver's arm was round her and for the first time in two weeks they embraced together, alone. For a long while they sobbed into each other then held each other, taking the most wonderful joy in the recognition of the familiar.

"Where's Terrence?"

"Oh," said Helen, "he's with mum and dad. We'll get him after ... I'll get them to bring him. I didn't know....I didn't know quite what to do..." She touched his face as though it was something rich and strange. Oliver smiled at her and stroked her hair. He ran his fingers over her face. "We have so much...there is so much....so much to say.......and you are here.......Olly, Olly... I thought I would never see you again... ....never again...."

"Yes," he said. "There is so much. So much to tell you. So much has happened..."

"But last night," she interrupted. "How are you here? How did he let you go? Why?"

"I guess he believed me. We spoke for a long time. The threat was always there but somehow I always knew that he wasn't going to kill me. If he was going to kill me he would have done it before then. He must have...believed me."

"What did you talk about?"

"He was concerned with the girl called Natalie... "

"Who's she?"

"I don't truly know and that's what he believed. We – the five of us – bought a second hand car in Nice from a girl called Natalie and her brother and father. These guys... they chased us, they caught up with us last night...but it so happened they had money in that car they sold us, a lot of money. When they caught us they told us this......told us how the money was there and why it was there. Natalie had seen a shooting... .she'd been paid off by The Capo or his people. The Capo thought I was going to try to get Natalie to take this to court, to expose him. That would have made me his enemy..."

"But why would he think that? Why?"

"Clotilde. Clotilde dropped that hint yesterday night, don't you remember?"

"I don't remember very much about last night."

"She made him think I had something to do with Natalie… persuading her to go to court…"

"And did you? Do you?"

"Do I what?"

"Have anything to do with Natalie?"

"No! We bought a car from them. They nearly run us off the road after Berwick and told us their story, but we didn't steal their money, it's still in Lyon somewhere, and I don't have anything to do with Natalie going to damn court. Eventually The Capo believed that."

"And Clotilde?" Helen looked at him not with anger or sadness but with eyes that almost pleaded for the truth.

He watched Helen dip her spoon into her cappuccino and smooth the froth over. "Are you going to drink that?" She shook her head. He took it over and drank the entire mug in one gulp.

"I think Clotilde is a dangerous woman, maybe even slightly disturbed. After the incident on the Saturday night, when I was in Nice, she kept me in her flat for about three days. She told me I was in danger if I left. I was likely to be killed. No calls. No mobiles. No nothing. She terrified me with descriptions of the people that would be after me. To be fair she was right when she described The Capo and his men. We have seen how they are. You have seen how they are. So I stayed there for a few days, for three days….," and he looked away.

Gently Helen reached across and with her soft fingers touched his face back towards her. "Tell me. Tell me everything. So much has happened Olly…we need to know it, to know it all….before we can go on, we need to know it all."

"I was in her flat for three days. I can still describe it to you if you want…"

"Olly," said Helen with more assertion and control than she had felt about anything in the last ten days. "I want to know if you slept with her."

"If I say 'yes'," replied Oliver, slowly, "if I say yes then you will think it was consensual, mutual….that there was pleasure in it."

"Did you sleep with her?"

"Physically I was in the same bad so yes I slept with her….but that's not what you're asking, I know……yes I slept with her. It was the price of safety. She made it clear it was the price of safety. It wasn't something of pleasure...."

"No? She is a very beautiful woman." Helen didn't say it in a way that was spiteful or accusing. It was said almost in the abstract, as though she was talking about a painting or a sculpture.

"Yes I know she is."

"How many times did you... "

"I don't know Helen. I wouldn't know. I have tried to block it from my mind. With so much else of what has happened in the last few days."

Helen paused. "I am jealous of her. I am jealous of her because she is beautiful. And because she had you and could do what she wanted with you for three days. And she probably did. And because I bet you didn't struggle to get an erection."

Oliver shifted uncomfortably. "Can I ask you a question?"

She looked at him. "I don't want to sound... churlish......but you have not exactly been faithful, have you? The Capo told me that you and that policeman have been....well I suppose the right phrase is having an affair, isn't it?"

Helen thought she was prepared for this. Had he asked about it she would have denied it. But if that guy had told him...... that guy probably had people watching the house, he could have given Olly times and dates...she couldn't deny it. Her face crumpled and she held it in her hands.

"Olly I don't know why I did it. I don't know why. I don't love him. I don't love him, I never loved him. I can't think why."

"Try," said Oliver. "I need to know Helen. This needs...honesty... nothing hidden around corners...."

"It was silly, really silly. I don't know why. He flattered me. I felt wanted....I know it sounds pathetic, it sounds terrible, disgusting... it was flirting then it went too far and I never drew back, I should have let it go."

"But why Helen? If you don't know why then maybe it can happen again..."

"No! Never, never again. I was flattered, he made me feel special... I shouldn't have done it, I know, I have so much regret...That's the hardest thing, to try and give you an explanation. I can't. I don't know. I feel as though....as thought it was someone else, another me, that was having that affair. A different part of me."

Oliver was thoughtful. "Maybe it's me. Us. Maybe we need to be

468

with each other more. Spending more time together. Making us feel special. Us." He turned towards her again. "Did you ever think of leaving me? Leaving us?"

"No," she almost shouted. "No, I never ever thought of that…"

He interrupted her. "Clotilde wanted that, you know. She told me to take off with her. Go to Italy or Switzerland, get away from where we were in the south of France. Forget my other life. Just the two of us."

"It sounds………." Helen didn't really know how it sounded.

"And when it was presented like that…another life… you realise how much you value the one you have. You're right, Clotilde was a beautiful woman. But the life I have with you and Terrence is beauty. You don't always see it, sometimes the mundane gets in the way, but I realised then how much I loved what I had. And if you're the same…if you feel the same….then we can get through this… however difficult some things might be to understand." He was silent for a brief time. "Maybe it's a time, a phase, people go through when they are married, have children, things like temptation come calling…."

"I don't understand it myself. I don't understand it. He's nothing to me Olly, honestly. If you'd told me a few years ago I would have done this, this thing. I wouldn't have believed you."

Oliver was thoughtful. Not yet, not quite yet… "You know The Capo told me that he thinks you've had two….well, at least two… stalkers. People watching you, maybe even following you."

"What? Stalkers? What? Are you sure?"

"He eliminated any and every other possibility. No one in his organisation. No one known to him of any other organisation. But it turns out that he has had the house watched for quite a while, almost since I vanished off their radar. And his men saw another couple of men who were……well, watching the house. Strange men by all accounts. Both maybe dead now. One definitely dead because his men shot the guy. The other the guy that you and Aidan tied up. He showed me pictures of them both because he wanted to know who they were. He was convinced they must have been working for me or, as he put it, 'someone in my organisation.' Hah! Amazing how people can think such madness about you and your position, your power… I had never seen them before." He stopped and looked at her. She seemed confused, overwhelmed. "Have you been aware of anyone?"

"No.Not really. That false invitation apart… But, well, that's why McLean was upstairs. Someone had been in the house. In our bedroom.

McLean thought maybe… they were thinking of kidnapping me. That's why he was in the house. And another policeman…he thought that what happened to Jenny…they might have been actually looking for me and mistaken us. Mistaken Jenny for me….." She held his arm. "But these things don't make sense. Someone stalking me…"

"You're very beautiful, you know that… " he stroked her face and smiled. It wasn't a question, more a statement of fact. "Maybe these guys… maybe they were obsessional… something beautiful that we can't get any other way can drive us mad maybe. Takes us over, controls us…."

"That's crazy! You're not suggesting…."

Oliver held up his hand. "I'm not suggesting anything Helen. I'm trying to make sense of it. But think of Clotilde…as I said, a beautiful woman who did these crazy things to try and keep me with her. Something must have made her do that. Taken control of her, dominated her. Maybe she didn't even want that, even mean that to happen… it just happened." He took her hand and looked at her. "Well maybe that was the same with you. These guys….they wanted you…felt they needed you… that need dominated them and controlled them…."

"But…,." she put her head in her hands, "what you say is mad. There are other women…"

"Sure," he interrupted, "and there were other guys for Clotilde. But yet she wanted this one, this specific one, and the need or desire for this one drove her a little mad. She wouldn't be – and these guys wouldn't be – the first guys who had been taken out of control, almost literally been driven mad for love. All for love."

"But it's not real! I don't know them, I didn't know them. I didn't even know who they were. I've never been aware of them. It's mad…"

Oliver paused and ran his finger round the top of the coffee cup, little bits of froth still there. "Come, Helen, come…," and he smiled. "People fall in love with an image, don't they? The image of them with that person. Making them complete. Making them better. That's what Clotilde saw, I'm sure. The person she wanted to be was the one that she would be with me. Maybe it was the same with these guys. Whatever you represented to them… …maybe they fell in love with the need to have it. And when you need something….maybe it does take control of you and drive you slightly mad."

"There is no chance that guy is wrong?"

"What guy? The Capo?" Oliver shook his head. "Helen, if there's one thing that I'm very clear about it's that The Capo is not wrong. Omniscient presences don't make mistakes." He smiled, more to himself

470

than to Helen. Helen remained in another place, a dark world of dangerous corners and mazes where the familiar was blackened and no one recognised you.

Oliver looked at her. "Helen, I need to ask you something and I need you to be honest."

She nodded. She was probably prepared for anything now. Except what he asked her.

"We were married for about two years and then you....strayed, didn't you?"

He looked at her, unflinching. Whatever she said, or tried to say, with words he knew that it would be her eyes and her face that would talk to him. And he knew, absolutely and without any doubt, that he was correct.

She looked away immediately and gasped. "Helen. Helen...." He looked at her to beckon her back. "Look at me. Here, back here. This way. You strayed, didn't you?"

"I......I..." She struggled to speak. Revelation upon revelation. How did he know this? How did he know? Had The Capo told him? Not remotely conceivable surely. This was years ago. That man had only been aware of Olly in the past couple of weeks.

"How do you...," she still couldn't look at him, "what do you know?"

He held up his hands, softly and with a smile. "No, no. That's the thing. I need you to be honest. So what I know...what I don't know....maybe I need you to fill in the blanks and maybe I don't. I want you to be honest with me...."

"But even if that is the case Olly...that was... that was so long ago, it was a long long time ago...."

"Then no reason not to talk about it. Come on," he said, leaning across the table, "tell me." It wasn't a threatening gesture. Indeed it was quite the opposite, friendly, comforting...saying that 'whatever you tell me, I'll still be here. It's ok.'

"I was...," am I going to admit this, she thought, on top of what he knows about McLean, am I going to admit this.... "it was a long time ago Olly. He was... " She drew in a large breath. "Yes. Ok. Yes. I strayed. And of course it was a mistake and he meant...." She was about to say he meant nothing to me but he hadn't, Chicco had meant something to her. "It meant....it wasn't anything Olly."

"No?"

"No." But she was looking down at the table. Olly was aware of the beautiful sunshine making her hair sparkle. Beautiful and warm after last night's storm. She looked up at him. "How do you know? Did The Capo tell you?"

Now it was Oliver's turn to look confused. "The Capo? How would he know? Have you met him before? Did you know him when you knew this other guy?"

"No, no......but if he didn't tell you then who did? And how is it... how come you only know about this now? It was a long time ago....a long time ago....why now?"

"Who says I have only got to know about it now?"

She looked at him, her eyes moving all over his face. He was calm and relaxed, his eyes following her agitation.

"But that doesn't make any sense... you can't have known about it before now...."

"Why not?"

"You would have said...you would have said something before now...why wouldn't you say if you knew at the time?" She stopped and looked at him. "And why would you say now? If you hadn't said anything before, why would you say something now?"

"Well," he said, his finger tracing the froth again, "now is one of those times when it seems....we get everything into the open. When it all comes out. So it seemed a good time to ask you...."

"To ask me what?"

He looked at her. "Why?"

"Why what?"

"Why stray? Why the affair?"

"Are you telling me...," she looked at him and tried to pierce him with her eyes... "are you telling me, seriously, you haven't strayed?"

Oliver held up his hand. "Woah, Helen, woah, slow down. This is about you. Come on. It's ok. I'm here. I'm staying. I want to try to understand. And anyway," he looked at her, "no, I haven't."

"Not even...Lesley?"

Oliver laughed. "Ali's Lesley?"

"Yes."

"Are you joking?"

"No."

"Absolutely not, no. I know things about Lesley that Ali doesn't know. But I never slept with her. That's absurd!"

Did she believe him? Did she trust him? Truly...truly trust him? She sighed. "Ok...why....it was a long time ago... I was..."

472

"Flattered?"

She laughed, a nervous embarrassed laughed of one who has been caught stealing. "Yes. But also....we'd been married a year, maybe two... you want to know why?"

Oliver nodded. "I think we could all benefit from some unadulterated truth, don't you?"

"I think I was scared...terrified maybe...that that was it. Yours was the only body I would make love to for the rest of my life. I think I found that terrifying. You want me to be truthful. If you want me to be truthful then you must believe me. You must understand that those feelings... that feeling...had nothing to do with you. It was about me. About me being flattered and romanced and made love to... and feeling the eternity of being with a body I thought I knew everything about. That didn't mean I rejected you. I never fell out of love with you. It was about me. But I never thought that I would feel that way. If I ever thought I might have felt that you....were not enough....then I wouldn't have married. Not you, not anybody. Do you understand that? I think I need you to understand that... "

"Yes. Yes, I can understand that. Perhaps what he gave you at that time no man that was married to you could have given you..."

"Exactly..."

"Or maybe some men could....maybe I couldn't." He looked in her face for clarity. "So maybe it was just me?"

"No Olly no! I was the one in the wrong. Knowing what you know... .what I've done....you would be within your rights to walk away. Divorce me."

Oliver smiled. "Or kill these two other guys I guess." He held out his hand for hers and she took it.

"That might be a touch over dramatic," she said.

He shifted, uneasily. "Yeah. This other guy....the first guy...who was he?"

She quickly switched to being uncomfortable again. "Oh a guy at Uni...an exchange research student I think."

"What was his name?"

"Does it matter? You won't know him."

Oliver shrugged his shoulders. "No reason not to tell me then..."

She probably owed him it. The way she felt she owed him anything he asked for. If he'd wanted to make love to her across this table in this public space she probably owed him that. Christ, she thought. I'm exhausted in every way I can think of, and I'm sure he must be too, but I desperately want him to make love to me. She sighed. She felt like saying she wanted out of here and to be taken in any and every way he could conceive. She sighed. "Chicco….Enrico…that was his name."

"Italian?"

"Yes, yes, Italian."

"Do you ever… did you ever….keep in touch with him?"

She felt safer now. It had ended then. Absolutely and unequivocally. "No. Not at all. I haven't heard from him in these… I don't know…six or seven years…."

"So you don't know how he is now? Where he is now?"

"No. Olly, I told you. It was a long time ago. I haven't been in contact with him, I haven't sent an e-mail, seen anything on facebook, I have no idea about the guy. I don't want to know about him. I don't want to know where he is. It was a mistake and it was wrong. Leave it now, it's finished. It was a long time ago……is it something we can move on from?"

He looked at her. It was a very determined look. Assured. Confident. "Why now, Olly? Why bring this up now?"

"Well… you see….over the years I have kept a watch on Enrico… Chicco…I knew something was going on at the time and, let's face it, you really didn't do that much to keep things hidden…it was easy to find who he was. He was a very attractive guy, back then…."

"You what? You knew? Back then? You spied?" She was breathless, gasping in startled whispers.

"Not spied, no. Just… observed. It wasn't difficult… Anyway, I broadly followed him after he left here….you know the sort of thing… on-line.. I was intrigued I suppose. He was at university for a while and then he seemed to move. Then I lost him until by chance I saw him in Nice. What luck, eh? Just like that! And it was him alright. He looked different. Harder somehow. But it was him. I followed him for a few hours……the places he went, the shops he bought from, the restaurant he ate at….not places you would go to or eat at on a lecturer's salary… .he had clearly come into money….somehow…"

"You followed him? Why?"

"I was intrigued. I always wondered what I would do if I was face to face with him. And chance passed to me a large slice of luck there too because chance put me next to him at a dinner table in Nice……or maybe chance had nothing to do with it…."

"What? Olly, what the hell are you saying?"

"I wanted him to know how it felt. His wife was drunk. So I let her be all over me. I would have stuck my hand up her skirt and looked guilty about it ten times if I'd known he would definitely have seen it."

He turned to Helen quickly and his eyes flashed at her. He looked almost wild. "You know I never meant to only blind the bastard. I meant to kill him. I led him out the way, I knew he was following, to where it would be quiet. And as my left hand hammered the knife into his eye my right hand was grappling for the steak knife to ram in through his heart. But the way he fell I couldn't get to the knife. And the noise he made... that high pitched pathetic bloody yelp...he would attract others, I had no time. Someone might see me and know it wasn't self-defence."

She had watched him as he described this... attempted murder, she thought... and he was calm and thoughtful and his voice was firm but quiet. She would lay money on his blood pressure not having risen at all. He had known about this for years... he had... planned this. When she looked at him as he stopped talking he let his eyes follow his finger as it touched the froth.

"Look at me," she said. He raised his head. 'Do I know you anymore,' she thought, 'do I know you at all?' For a while they simply looked at each other, two people trying to find each other. "You would have killed him?" she almost whispered.

"I think I could have, yes. I loved you Helen. I love you still. He knew what he was doing. Love inspires such deep feelings that stay with you. I hated him and I wished him......harm. If not dead, then harm. Definitely harm."

She didn't know whether to feel flattered or appalled. She was trying to rationalise what he had done and it wasn't easy. To have someone feel that much for you that they would kill is a disturbingly beautiful thing... to hear him say such a thing is welcome but unwelcome too... it has taken me into the dark recesses of the unknown that I had thought I had left with Olly long ago, she thought. There is danger in not knowing. I thought I knew this man, my husband. The guy who sells little toys and plays little childish games with our son. I thought I knew him.

"Did you tell that guy...the guy in the white coat...does he have a name beyond The Capo?" Oliver shrugged his shoulders. "Did you tell him that you knew who the guy was? Or did he know?"

"No. I never told him. I maintained it was a freak accident. Your friend....Chicco...," he said it in a mock affectionate way, "he is now calling himself Paul. Maybe a false name, a deliberate one, who knows?

But he never knew me. We never met. Even if he was at the house when you were with him all he would have seen was a picture of me. He wouldn't have remembered that seven or eight years later. So there was no one else there who was going to contradict my story."

"You were lucky then."

"Lucky?"

"Well, yeah. That seems to be the only bit of information that that guy didn't know."

Oliver smiled. "I thought that too. I know something that this... God-like guy doesn't seem to know." He paused. "He did tell me one thing, though. He did say that Paul...Chicco....has a fierce temper...and he was desperate to get over here and, as he told me, 'rape the bastard's fucking wife'. He said it would take no small amount of his diplomacy to persuade Paul to let go."

Helen looked at him. "You think he'll come? You think he'll come over here?"

"Even if he does, Helen, The Capo would stop him. Or protect us."

She snorted. "I don't think so! When Enrico sees us....sees me...and knows who I am, The Capo will never believe that you haven't attacked him for revenge."

"Well, who knows....maybe it won't get that far. He did say Paul was a little too hot-headed. Such people have a habit of boiling until they eventually burst."

She reached across at him to hold his hand. They interlinked fingers in silence, weighted and enlightened by what had passed between them. She looked at him.

"So where are we now?" she asked. "Are you my blood-splattered hero or some....besmirched and dirty vagabond? Am I your beautiful prize... your little wife... or some....willing prostitute? Where are we Olly? Where do we go now?"

He smiled at her. "We go to bed, my beautiful Helen. We go to bed."

CHAPTER 24

The man who was hanging by his arms looked around him. His eyes darted quickly, impulsed by fear as they searched for any sign of escape. Instead he saw dark brown stains on a wall. They were about head height, dark enough and thick enough to tell of multiple horrors and many men who had gone before him. He looked underneath and saw a thick plastic blanket. He could see himself enveloped in it. He looked above him and saw a dirty white ceiling with many holes in it, signs of where men had hung like he did now.

But this man struggled with everything around him. He struggled with the knowledge that he was going to die. He struggled against the chains that held him. He struggled against the thick tape that covered his mouth. He tried to shout to the men below him, particularly to Davide. But for the men this was business as usual. And it was very usual for someone who had previously been an ally of The Capo to now be an enemy. This guy was no different. He had cut on his percentage, he had done the odd deal himself and excluded The Capo, he had told some lies…and he was becoming a liability, eaten up with his own sense of importance and his perceived injustices exaggerated by his own delusions of worth to The Capo and the organisation. The Capo had wondered whether he should speak with him or get rid of him. But it was so hard to educate people….you try to talk to them and then you've got this loose cannon with a grudge walking about the place, ready to do anything to get back at you. It really wasn't worth the effort. Best just to dispose of the situation, as easily as taking a stone out of your shoe and throwing it away. Why walk about with it in there when you're always going to feel uncomfortable?

Had Davide or anyone in the organisation been prepared to raise an argument in defence of the guy, he might even had listened. But Davide wasn't there to defend or argue, he carried out orders and facilitated requests.

When The Capo came in Paul was lowered down and positioned at the table opposite The Capo. His hands remained tied and the tape was kept over his mouth. His eye still had part of a bandage on it. He tried to gesticulate, shaking his head, pleading with the one eye that could be seen, for the tape on his mouth to be taken off. The Capo shook his head in return. "No, Paul. No. This time you listen. You were never very good at that."

The Capo stopped and took his coat off. He took his gun out of his pocket and laid it on the table. Paul's eyes widened at the sight of it and he began to shake his head, vigorously, in fear and defiance. Had you listened really closely you could have heard the distinctive repetition of "No! No!"

The Capo looked at him and shouted "Listen!" At this Paul was quiet. "You have cheated on me. You have done things behind my back. You have kept me out of what was rightfully mine. You have told lies. You have tried to get me involved in a situation by playing on my loyalty to you. You tried to get me to kill an innocent man. I told you when you first got involved with me, when I took you from your small salary and small world in a university, I told you then that you shouldn't cross me. I demand absolute loyalty. I also told you that I was a dangerous man, that you must know your place. You have gone against all of that. And now….you are impetuous, hot headed, your anger makes you lose focus and control….you get offended because some guy pisses you off at a dinner party and you want me to kill him, you want to go and rape his wife…." He paused. "If you were worth something, if you were…if you had been…truly loyal then I might have carried these things through. I might have turned a blind eye. But, frankly, you've shown that you're not worth it."

Paul was agitated again, desperate to speak, muffled noises. They were almost constant. "Be quiet!" The Capo came close to yelling at him. Davide looked at The Capo in an inquisitive way but The Capo shook his head.

"You know Paul…that guy who hit you… he was a decent man. A good man. I liked him. I tried hard to get him for you. Until I realised you were making a fool out of me. But I might have killed him. A good man. Oh," he said, almost as an afterthought, "and he did have… he has… a very beautiful wife."

The Capo reached into his coat pocket and pulled out his phone. He had taken a photograph of Helen with her trousers at her knees and her jersey off, in her bra, just in case it had to be sent to Oliver. Even though she was distraught, she still looked beautiful.

"Look, see, here she is."

Paul looked at the photo. With almost disinterest at first. Then he focused. And looked. And saw. The Capo was about to take his phone away and Paul almost screamed for it to be brought back. 'Fair enough,' thought The Capo, 'if I knew I was going to die then I think seeing a beautiful woman in her underwear is an image I would want to take to the grave.'

When he eventually took the photo away Paul's agitation became extreme. He banged his knees on the table. His eye widened till The Capo thought it was going to pop out of its socket. He desperately tried to get his hands from behind his back. He motioned in every way he could think of to get the tape off his mouth, to speak. With all these simultaneous motions he looked like a man having an epileptic fit. 'Just another man, begging for his life,' thought The Capo. He lifted his gun with resignation, looked at the beggar opposite him and simply said. "You deserve this. You absolutely deserve this." He fired three shots quickly. Paul and his actions and his words and his pleading stopped as his body was thrown back out of the chair and onto the floor.

The Capo looked at the picture of Helen again on his phone. 'Yeah,' he thought, 'she is nice, for sure. I can see why he got so… agitated.'

Before he had even stood up the body had been wrapped in plastic and carried away. He walked out to the car with Davide who opened the door for him then went round to the other side of the car and got in. "Ok," said The Capo, "what else?"

"Well, firstly, Natalie. You haven't said anything on that."

"There is no evidence, we don't have any, do we, that the girl has gone to the police?"

"No."

"Then leave her. I paid her off. She accepted. That's it."

"Ok. Clotilde?"

"Ah the beautiful Ms de Bresseau… Davide, do you really feel she is a threat to me? Has she done anything that would put her in that situation where we had to take action?"

"No. I don't think so."

"Me neither. She got a bit obsessional about a guy she couldn't have. We all get obsessional." He paused. "Maybe she could be useful to us. Maybe even do what Paul did. Let me think on that."

"The only thing is… there is some evidence, a bit sketchy but I can get it checked out… she knows Natalie."

"Knows her? As in they are friends?"

"More than friends."

The Capo smiled. He ran his hand over his mouth. "Well, well… two people, neither of whom are a threat to me, get together… so that's no threat to me. Natalie I don't remember, I don't have a clue what she looks like but I like the thought of them together. You might want to… you know, the usual surveillance… maybe I'll meet with both of them some time. Yes, I'm sure Ms de Bresseau would be of great use to someone like me."

"And your presence is still wanted in America…," The Capo waved his hand, "Francine still needs help with winning a government contract…"

The Capo interrupted. "Ok, I'll help her but she needs to help me. Put that to her and see how she reacts. She'll know exactly what you mean."

"And em…," Davide paused. The Capo looked across at him.

"Yes Davide?"

"There's a girl arrived… Donna… I think she wants to take you up on your offer."

The Capo's face broke into a broad smile. "The policeman's daughter. Ah, what a wonderful little thing. Let's go and see her. Put her up in a flat. Nice one. Maximum six months."

Davide looked at him. "And then?"

The Capo dismissed the question with a wave of the hand. He smiled at Davide. "Life is good, isn't it? We can do what we want, have what we want, have who we want, when we want…what we don't know isn't worth knowing… life is good, isn't it?"

Davide smiled with empathy because he had to though he wondered if Paul would have agreed.

Ellis had been chastised because he hadn't managed to get any presents for his daughters. His wife, too, he could tell was slightly irritated that he had been on such a holiday to this wondrous place and not even thought to bring back a blouse, jewellery, anything. And she thought his stories exaggerated. However, if anything, Ellis had underplayed the stories. He hadn't mentioned being drugged, he hadn't said anything about a fierce dog being let loose on them, nothing about water being fired at them and very little was said about jumping away for freedom through the window of a hotel by the side of the motorway. Ellis had said it had been a difficult time for them but he was sparse on the details. His wife did find it odd, however, when she saw the car he was driving, a car she didn't know, its paint messed and blotched and a Taser inside. She never asked anything.

When they went out for a meal, all together, it was the very picture of a contended and happy family. But as Ellis looked from his wife to his daughters, from their smiles which seemed genuine, he thought that they must look at him and see genuine smiles too. He thought on how much lay underneath and hidden, now seeing himself as an iceberg that they knew so little about. An almost compulsive desire for other women. A dead woman and a dead baby that were near his conscience. How little they know of me, he thought. And he realised, as he looked around them, probably for the first time, that this could not only be a one-way thing. He was forced to understand that he knew so little of them too.

Euan talked about it with Jennifer. About everything. At first, of course, she thought he was exaggerating. He was a normal guy. His friends were normal people. Even Olly, who had got them caught up in this madness. He was very normal... attractive, but normal. So she indulged him but she didn't really believe him, not at first. But when he found it impossible to sleep, when she would get up and see him sitting and staring into space, trying to rationalise things, then she began to believe him. And when he talked she would listen more, ask questions, get him to go into what he felt.

It worked, but only up to a point. There are some things that Euan either didn't want to communicate or couldn't communicate. It would be comforting to say that these things could only be shared with those who had gone through the experience with him but he knew that wasn't true either. What he felt, what he perceived, would never be the same as what Olly or Ellis or Ali had perceived. Like men in the trenches... some built events around them and it made them stronger, some were destroyed. Just because we have gone through the same thing, thought Euan, it doesn't mean that it has affected us the same way. It made it impossible to tell Jennifer, he couldn't find the words or expressions to describe how he felt to her. As though for all the development of language, it wasn't enough. He couldn't find anything to let her truly in. So his blank, featureless looks were not a window to his soul but instead acted as a door, stopping Jennifer from getting near. The thing is, he knew it. He knew it and he couldn't do anything about it. He couldn't find the words. Every time he tried he almost threw his hands up in exasperation. They weren't there, they didn't exist. He comforted himself with the thought that it was the failing of language, and not his own unwillingness, that made him unknowable.

Natalie and her family recovered the money from the car that had remained in a police compound in Lyon. She resumed her complex life, flitting between Jacques and Clotilde. Clotilde told her very little about what had happened in Edinburgh, only that she had seen Olly very much at home with his wife and had taken the decision to leave them alone. The guy was clearly happily married and you had to know when to let go. Natalie liked that story, it made her feel warm about Clotilde. It also took someone who was a rival for Clotilde's attention out of the picture.

Clotilde slowly came to accept that she was going to have let go of any image of Oliver that she had. It hurt. She wanted him more than she could find a way to express. But it was unlikely that he would ever be back in Nice and she could not imagine making the trip to Edinburgh again. She had a few pictures on her phone and some memories which she idealised. It needed to be closed now.

Life went on. She drifted through work. She saw Natalie. She existed. Then one day she walked into the office and there was a new presence there. A man she hadn't seen before. At first she saw him from behind, short black hair, tight shape... then he turned round... a flashing smile, a warm hand, confident but a little hesitant laugh showing a touch of discomfort. Nice. Then she could smell him. Very nice.

"This is Neville, Clotilde. He's coming over here instead of Oliver. I think... his company thought, you know, all those long train journeys, it's not fair on the guy... so they have decided to send someone else. Someone who's happy to fly. This is the new boy."

Neville smiled widely. "I told him, Clotilde, I hope it's ok, but I told him that you could maybe show him some of our beautiful city. So he gets to know his bearings. He's staying in a hotel, very central. Is that ok? I figured, well, you'd be working closely together anyway, best you do it."

Clotilde looked at him. "Oh, yes, absolutely."

As they made their way out of the office and started down the stairs, Clotilde pretended that she was struggling a little to walk down them in her high heels. It was a test. Neville looked around and immediately said, "Oh, I'm sorry... here Clotilde, please let me help." And he held out his arm for her to take.

"Thank you. Tell me, Neville, have you been to the south of France before?"

"Oh yes, it's such a lovely place. Such a beautiful place. So warm. It feels so safe, too. And the people, they are so…friendly, so genuine."

'Funny the perceptions people have,' thought Clotilde. "Yes," she said. They began to reach the bottom of the stairs and she tightened his arm into her side so that it would have been difficult for him to take his arm out. This meant that the back of his hand was pressing into her chest.

"Tell me a bit about you," she said. "Are you married?"

"No. I'm engaged though. We'll marry in two months."

She stopped. "Ah," she said. "Isn't that nice?" She smiled at him. She knew it wouldn't happen. The back of his hand was still gently pressed into her chest. His offer to help had been too quick, he wasn't at all for moving his hand and she could tell she had at least begun to hook him.

"Well," she said, touching his back gently as he went round to one side of the car, "let me show you some of our city. We can drive about a bit, stop where we want, eat in a beautiful restaurant, have a fabulous bottle of wine and start work tomorrow. What do you say?"

He sat down in the passenger seat beside her, his smile too broad and too genuine. "Sounds fantastic."

'And tonight,' she thought, 'you're going to have the best fuck you've ever had.' She returned his smile, a big flashing smile that captured him, full of sparkling white teeth and beautiful lips from a sexual goddess. He sat back – he would have lain back if he could – into the seat. 'Christ,' he thought, 'this is heaven. I wonder why Olly never told me about her…'

Of course they had all gone to Aidan's funeral. But it was only when his wife came round the next day to see Olly that they had anything approaching a conversation. Olly's overpowering feeling was one of guilt: had Aidan not trooped across dutifully to the south of France he probably would have been alive now. What was odd was that when Aidan's widow, Sarah, came to see him it seemed that her overriding feeling was of guilt too.

"Aidan was… he was complex, Olly, you have to understand that. Things happened to him that he couldn't control. And the world he moved in was… the world of the theatre… it was…"

Olly looked at her as she shook her head, distant. "You know he loved you Olly, don't you? He wouldn't have betrayed you, any of you, he wouldn't have done that. But his world was complicated. The choices he had to make… they were so pressurised, the pressures on him…I didn't know the half of it, I'm sure."

"Sarah," said Oliver. "Look at me. Look at me."

He walked over to where she was sitting and sat down in front of her. He looked into her eyes. He could have been no more than a foot away from her. "Listen. I have no idea what you are talking about. Ok?"

"But he would want you to know… he would have wanted you to know…how difficult.."

"Sarah. Listen to me. I have no idea what you are talking about."

Sarah started to cry, an almost silent weep of pity and loss. "He was a good man. I'm sure of that… he was a good man."

Oliver held her to him and whispered. "I know. We all know."

"He would never have wanted to… betray…" Her words come out in sobs.

"Sarah. Listen to me. I don't know…"

"I know Olly, I know." And they sat comforting each other over a man who was an enigma to them both yet whose loss they felt stripped them of a part of themselves.

Olly had crumpled when he first saw Terrence again. When he ran his hand over Terrence's mop of unkempt hair, when he breathed in the boy's smell, when he first heard his son's excited yelp of "Daddy!" Things he thought he would never ever hear or see or smell again. He held his son into him but his son squeezed him till Oliver almost burst, the untempered affection of youth almost killing him with its zest. At first Oliver laughed and smiled until his son said: "I missed you daddy." And he would have loved to have said "I missed you too," but the words couldn't get through his throat. He began to choke as delight and joy and relief all consumed him. He didn't so much cry as quiver. It wasn't only Terrence, it wasn't only seeing Terrence. Inside, he knew he was free. This wasn't a moment stolen. He wasn't going to be taken back somewhere. This hug with his beautiful son felt like the first moment of the start of the rest of his life. It was a perfect moment.

Helen stood back and watched them, smiling to herself. She watched Olly recover himself and ask his son hundreds, thousands, of questions and she watched his attentive answers. She watched them run into the garden and kick a ball and dive about and laugh and run about mad with their hands over their heads. It was bliss in that moment to see what she saw and feel what she felt.

These nights had seen them make love like they hadn't done since they were sixteen. It felt new yet reassuringly familiar. Helen's body became a picture of beauty that he always found something new in. And for her part he seemed to find new ways to take her to better places, physically and emotionally. And they talked… and talked… defences down, barriers removed. Even if it was only in these, and for these, brief few days, there was nothing to hide.

One Saturday morning they sat at breakfast, three of them doing a normal thing on a normal Saturday morning. Terence wasn't quite as interested in the conversation the adults were having and scuttled off to watch television or play in the garden.

"You know," said Helen, "I was thinking…maybe we should get away. Go somewhere. A short holiday. Now. Even if it's only for a few days. Just to get away."

"The three of us?"

"Three of us or two of us. If it was only two or three days Terrence could stay with my mum and dad. His cousins are here now anyway, he loves Davey and Jack. We could give him the choice. I would really like to be away with you, to kind of take time out, you know?"

"Yeah, I know."

"It feels like I'm getting to know you all over again. From the beginning. It's a very beautiful feeling. I want it to go on for ever. I don't want work to get in the way. Even if it's only for two or three days."

"Yes, it would be great." He recognised the feeling. What had been done in the past seemed as if it had been done by two other people. Now, they had made each other… new. And she was there. She wasn't going to go away. After all that had happened, all they had gone through over the past two weeks, every negative thing that they might have felt had been overpowered by everything that was positive between them. They loved each other – perhaps they had only come to an understanding of what that truly meant to them over the past few days. I'm not me without Helen, he thought. She's not the best of me, or the worst of me, or any part of me. For the first time, truly the first time, she's all of me. All that can be good or bad, all that is within me, she sees it all. And it felt wonderful and it made him feel as though he was the only one who could see the sun and feel how warm life was.

"Ok," she said, smiling at him and reaching for his hand. "Ok. So, where do we go? Where shall we go?"

He looked at her, returning her smile. "Well," he said, "I hear the south of France is beautiful at this time of year…"